Tom Victor

About the Author

The author of more than thirty books, RAY BRADBURY is one of the most celebrated fiction writers of our time. Among his best-known works are *Fahrenheit 451*, *The Martian Chronicles*, *The Illustrated Man*, *Dandelion Wine*, and *Something Wicked This Way Comes*. He has written for the theater and the cinema, including the screenplay for John Huston's classic film adaptation of *Moby-Dick*, and was nominated for an Academy Award. He adapted sixty-five of his stories for television's *Ray Bradbury Theater* and won an Emmy for his teleplay of *The Halloween Tree*. In 2000, Bradbury was honored by the National Book Foundation with a medal for Distinguished Contribution to American Letters. He is the recipient of the 2004 National Medal of Arts, which is presented to those who have made extraordinary contributions to the arts in the United States. Among his most recent works are the novels *Let's All Kill Constance*, *From the Dust Returned*—selected as one of the Best Books of the Year by the *Los Angeles Times*—and *One More for the Road*, a new story collection. Bradbury lives in Los Angeles, California.

BOOKS BY RAY BRADBURY

Ahmed and the Oblivion Machines

The Anthem Sprinters

A Chapbook for Burnt-Out Priests,
Rabbis, and Ministers

Dandelion Wine

Dark Carnival

Death Is a Lonely Business

Driving Blind

Fahrenheit 451

From the Dust Returned

The Golden Apples of the Sun

A Graveyard for Lunatics

Green Shadows, White Whale

The Halloween Tree

The Haunted Computer and
the Android Pope

I Sing the Body Electric!

The Illustrated Man

Let's All Kill Constance

Long After Midnight

The Machineries of Joy

The Martian Chronicles

A Medicine for Melancholy

The October Country

One More for the Road

Quicker Than the Eye

R Is for Rocket

S Is for Space

Something Wicked This Way Comes

The Stories of Ray Bradbury

Switch on the Night

They Have Not Seen the Stars

The Toynbee Convector

When Elephants Last in the
Dooryard Bloomed

Where Robot Mice and Robot Men
Run Round in Robot Towns

Witness and Celebrate

Yestermorrow

Zen in the Art of Writing

BRADBURY
STORIES

100 OF HIS MOST
CELEBRATED TALES

Perennial

An Imprint of HarperCollins*Publishers*

FIRST PERENNIAL EDITION PUBLISHED 2005.

Designed by Shubhani Sarkar

The Library of Congress has catalogued the hardcover edition as follows:

Bradbury, Ray
    [Short stories. Selections]
    Bradbury stories : 100 of his most celebrated tales / Ray Bradbury.
        p. cm.
    ISBN 0-06-054242-X
        1. Science fiction, American. 2. Fantasy fiction, American.
    I. Title.

PS3503.R167A6 2003
813'.54—dc21

2003042189

ISBN 0-06-054488-0 (pbk.)

08 09 ❖/RRD 10

WITH LOVE TO MY THREE SAMUELS:

Number One, in the past,
SAMUEL HINKSTON BRADBURY, my grandfather.

Number Two, in the present,
SAMUEL HANDLEMAN, my grandson.

Number Three, in the future,
SAM WELLER, who is writing my life.

✳

CONTENTS

INTRODUCTION

IT IS HARD FOR ME TO BELIEVE that in one lifetime I have written so many stories.

But on the other hand I often wonder what other writers do with their time.

Writing, for me, is akin to breathing. It is not something I plan or schedule; it's something I just *do*. All the stories collected in this book seized on me at the strangest hours, compelling me to head for my typewriter and put them down on paper before they went away.

A good example of this is "Banshee." When I was working for John Huston in Ireland on the screenplay of *Moby-Dick*, we spent many late evenings, sitting around the fire, drinking Irish whiskey, which I did not much care for, but only drank because he loved it. And sometimes Huston would pause in the middle of drinking and talking and close his eyes to listen to the wind wailing outside the house. Then his eyes would snap open and he would point a finger at me and cry that the banshees were out in the Irish weather and maybe I should go outdoors and see if it was true and bring them in.

He did this so often to scare me that it lodged in my mind and when I got home to America I finally wrote a story in response to his antics.

"The Toynbee Convector" was born because of my reaction to the bombardment of despair we so frequently find in our newspaper headlines and television reportage, and the feeling of imminent doom in a society that has triumphed over circumstances again and again, but fails to look back and realize where it has come from, and what it has achieved.

One day, overcome with this feeling, I had to do something about it and so created a character to speak my thoughts.

"The Laurel and Hardy Love Affair" comes from a lifetime of the affection I have for this wonderful team.

When I arrived in Ireland many years ago I opened the *Irish Times* and discovered therein a small ad, which read:

TODAY

ONE TIME ONLY!

A BENEFIT FOR THE IRISH ORPHANS

LAUREL & HARDY

IN PERSON!

I ran down to the theater and was fortunate enough to purchase the last available ticket, front row center! The curtain went up and those dear men performed the most wonderful scenes from their greatest films. I sat there in joy and amazement, with tears rolling down my cheeks.

When I got home I looked back on all this and remembered an occasion when a friend of mine took me to the stairs up which Laurel and Hardy had carried the piano box, only to be chased down the hill by it. My story had to follow.

"The Pedestrian" was a precursor to *Fahrenheit 451*. I had dinner with a friend fifty-five years ago and after dining we decided to take a walk along Wilshire Boulevard. Within minutes we were stopped by a police car. The policeman asked us what we were doing. I replied, "Putting one foot in front of the other," which was the wrong answer. The policeman looked at me suspiciously because, after all, the sidewalks were empty: nobody in the whole city of Los Angeles was using them as a walkway.

I went home, sorely irritated at being stopped for simply walking—a natural, human activity—and wrote a story about a pedestrian in the future who is arrested and executed for doing just that.

A few months later I took that pedestrian for a walk in the night, had him turn a corner and meet a young girl named Clarisse McClellan. Nine days later, *Fahrenheit 451* was born as a short novella called "The Firemen."

"The Garbage Collector" was inspired by my reaction to a newspaper item that appeared in the Los Angeles newspapers in early 1952, when the mayor announced that if an atomic bomb fell on Los Angeles, the resulting bodies would be picked up by garbage collectors. I was so inflamed by this remark that I sat down and wrote the story, fueled by my outrage.

"By the Numbers!" has its roots in reality. At one time, many years ago, I went, on occasional afternoons, to swim at the Ambassador Hotel pool with friends. The man in charge of that pool was a strict disciplinarian and used to stand his young son by the edge of the pool and give him all sorts of rigid instructions about life. Watching this ongoing lecture, day after day, I could not help but think that at some future time the son would react violently. Brooding at this seemingly unavoidable scenario, I sat down and wrote the story.

"Lafayette, Farewell" is based on a real and tragic tale told to me by a cinematographer who lived next door to Maggie and me for many years. Occasionally he came over to my house to visit with me and have a glass of wine. He told me how, way back in time, during the last months of World War I in 1918, he had been a member of the Lafayette Escadrille. As we talked, tears streamed down his face as he remembered shooting down German bi-planes; the faces of the doomed, handsome young men still haunted him after all those years. I could do nothing but offer my services as a storywriter to try to help him in the middle of his haunting.

At home, later that night, I wrote a letter to a friend of mine in Paris and said I had the most wonderful experience that afternoon of hearing the crowds of Mexico City over the telephone. As I wrote the letter to my friend it turned into a short story about an old man who listens to far places with long distance calls.

"The Sound of Summer Running" began with a bang. I was on a bus crossing Westwood Village when a young boy jumped on the bus, jammed his money in the box, ran down the aisle, and threw himself into a seat across from me. I looked at him with great admiration thinking, my god, if I had that much energy I could write a short story every day, three poems each night, and a novel by the end of the month. I looked down at his feet and saw there the reason for his vitality: a pair of wonderful bright new tennis shoes. And I suddenly remembered those special days of my growing up years—the beginning of every summer—when my father would take me down to the shoe store and buy me a new pair of tennis shoes, which gave me back the energy of the world. I could hardly wait to get home to sit down and write a story about a boy whose main desire is to own a pair of tennis shoes so he can run through summer.

"The Great Collision of Monday Last" was caused by my picking up a copy of the *Irish Times* in Dublin and reading the terrible fact that during the year 1953, 375 bike riders had been killed in Ireland. I thought, how amazing. We rarely read anything like that at home; it was always people dying in car accidents. Investigating further I discovered the reason. There were tens of thousands of bicycles all over Ireland; people going 40 or 50 miles an hour and colliding head on, so that when their heads struck, they sustained serious skull injuries. I thought: Nobody in the world knows this! Maybe I should write a short story about it. Which is what I did.

"The Drummer Boy of Shiloh" had its genesis in an obituary in the *Los Angeles Times* concerning a bit player in motion pictures named Olin Howland. I'd seen him in scores of films over the years and now I was reading his death notice, which mentioned the fact that his grandfather had been the drummer boy at Shiloh. Those words were so magical, so evocative, so sad, that I was shocked into going immediately to my typewriter and putting those words down. This short story followed within the next hour.

"Darling Adolf" was caused very simply. Crossing a Universal Studios lot one afternoon I encountered a movie extra dressed in a Nazi uniform and wearing a Hitler mustache. I wondered what might happen to him wandering around the studio or out in the street, what kind of reaction there might be to a person who resembles Hitler. The story was written that night.

I've never been in charge of my stories, they've always been in charge of me. As each new one has called to me, ordering me to give it voice and form and life, I've followed the advice I've shared with other writers over the years: Jump off the cliff and build your wings on the way down.

Over a period of more than sixty years I've jumped off many cliffs and struggled wildly on my typewriter to finish a story so as to make a soft landing. And, during the last few years I've looked back at the time when I was a teenager standing on a street corner, selling newspapers, and writing every day, not realizing how terrible my efforts were. Why did I do it, why did I keep jumping off those cliffs?

The answer is an immense cliché: Love.

I was so busy rushing headlong into the future, loving libraries and books and authors with all my heart and soul, was so consumed with becoming myself that I simply didn't notice that I was short, homely, and untalented. Perhaps, in some corner of my mind, I did know. But I persisted—the need to write, to create, coursed like blood through my body, and still does.

I always dreamed of someday going into a library and looking up and seeing a book of mine leaning against the shoulder of L. Frank Baum or Edgar Rice Burroughs, and down below my other heroes, Edgar Allan Poe, H. G. Wells, and Jules Verne. My wild love for them and their worlds, and for others like Somerset Maugham and John Steinbeck kept me so invigorated with passion that I could not see that I was the Hunchback of Notre Dame in their grand company.

But as the years passed I slipped my skins, one by one, and finally became a short story writer, an essayist, a poet, and a playwright. It took all those years to leave my other selves behind, but love was the thing that called me on.

Within this collection you will find representative tales from the many years of my long career. For all those years and for that great love that has kept me going, I am deeply grateful. My eyes fill with tears as I review the table of contents of this volume—all my dear, dear friends—the monsters and angels of my imagination.

Here they all are. A grand collection. I hope you will agree.

Ray Bradbury
DECEMBER 2002

THE WHOLE
TOWN'S SLEEPING

THE COURTHOUSE CLOCK CHIMED SEVEN TIMES. The echoes of the chimes faded.

Warm summer twilight here in upper Illinois country in this little town deep far away from everything, kept to itself by a river and a forest and a meadow and a lake. The sidewalks still scorched. The stores closing and the streets shadowed. And there were two moons; the clock moon with four faces in four night directions above the solemn black courthouse, and the real moon rising in vanilla whiteness from the dark east.

In the drugstore fans whispered in the high ceiling. In the rococo shade of porches, a few invisible people sat. Cigars glowed pink, on occasion. Screen doors whined their springs and slammed. On the purple bricks of the summer-night streets, Douglas Spaulding ran; dogs and boys followed after.

"Hi, Miss Lavinia!"

The boys loped away. Waving after them quietly, Lavinia Nebbs sat all alone with a tall cool lemonade in her white fingers, tapping it to her lips, sipping, waiting.

"Here I am, Lavinia."

She turned and there was Francine, all in snow white, at the bottom steps of the porch, in the smell of zinnias and hibiscus.

Lavinia Nebbs locked her front door and, leaving her lemonade glass half empty on the porch, said, "It's a fine night for the movie."

They walked down the street.

"Where you going, girls?" cried Miss Fern and Miss Roberta from their porch over the way.

Lavinia called back through the soft ocean of darkness: "To the Elite Theater to see CHARLIE CHAPLIN!"

"Won't catch us out on no night like this," wailed Miss Fern. "Not with the Lonely One strangling women. Lock ourselves up in our closet with a gun."

"Oh, bosh!" Lavinia heard the old women's door bang and lock, and she drifted on, feeling the warm breath of summer night shimmering off the oven-baked sidewalks. It was like walking on a hard crust of freshly warmed bread. The heat pulsed under your dress, along your legs, with a stealthy and not unpleasant sense of invasion.

"Lavinia, you don't believe all that about the Lonely One, do you?"

"Those women like to see their tongues dance."

"Just the same, Hattie McDollis was killed two months ago, Roberta Ferry the month before, and now Elizabeth Ramsell's disappeared. . . ."

"Hattie McDollis was a silly girl, walked off with a traveling man, I bet."

"But the others, all of them, strangled, their tongues sticking out their mouths, they say."

They stood upon the edge of the ravine that cut the town half in two. Behind them were the lit houses and music, ahead was deepness, moistness, fireflies and dark.

"Maybe we shouldn't go to the show tonight," said Francine. "The Lonely One might follow and kill us. I don't like that ravine. Look at it, will you!"

Lavinia looked and the ravine was a dynamo that never stopped running, night or day; there was a great moving hum, a bumbling and murmuring of creature, insect, or plant life. It smelled like a greenhouse, of secret vapors and ancient, washed shales and quicksands. And always the black dynamo humming, with sparkles like great electricity where fireflies moved on the air.

"It won't be *me* coming back through this old ravine tonight late, so darned late; it'll be you, Lavinia, you down the steps and over the bridge and maybe the Lonely One there."

"Bosh!" said Lavinia Nebbs.

"It'll be you alone on the path, listening to your shoes, not me. You all alone on the way back to your house. Lavinia, don't you get lonely living in that house?"

"Old maids love to live alone." Lavinia pointed at the hot shadowy path leading down into the dark. "Let's take the short cut."

"I'm afraid!"

"It's early. Lonely One won't be out till late." Lavinia took the other's arm and led her down and down the crooked path into the cricket warmth and frog sound and mosquito-delicate silence. They brushed through summer-scorched grass, burs prickling at their bare ankles.

"Let's run!" gasped Francine.

"No!"

They turned a curve in the path—and there it was.

In the singing deep night, in the shade of warm trees, as if she had laid herself out to enjoy the soft stars and the easy wind, her hands at either side of her like the oars of a delicate craft, lay Elizabeth Ramsell!

Francine screamed.

"Don't scream!" Lavinia put out her hands to hold onto Francine, who was whimpering and choking. "Don't! Don't!"

The woman lay as if she had floated there, her face moonlit, her eyes wide and like flint, her tongue sticking from her mouth.

"She's dead!" said Francine. "Oh, she's dead, dead! She's dead!"

Lavinia stood in the middle of a thousand warm shadows with the crickets screaming and the frogs loud.

"We'd better get the police," she said at last.

✳ Hold me, Lavinia, hold me, I'm cold, oh, I've never been so cold in all my life!"

Lavinia held Francine and the policemen were brushing through the crackling grass, flashlights ducked about, voices mingled, and the night grew toward eight-thirty.

"It's like December. I need a sweater," said Francine, eyes shut, against Lavinia.

The policeman said, "I guess you can go now, ladies. You might drop by the station tomorrow for a little more questioning."

Lavinia and Francine walked away from the police and the sheet over the delicate thing upon the ravine grass.

Lavinia felt her heart going loudly in her and she was cold, too, with a February cold; there were bits of sudden snow all over her flesh, and the moon washed her brittle fingers whiter, and she remembered doing all the talking while Francine just sobbed against her.

A voice called from far off, "You want an escort, ladies?"

"No, we'll make it," said Lavinia to nobody, and they walked on. They walked through the nuzzling, whispering ravine, the ravine of whispers and clicks, the little world of investigation growing small behind them with its lights and voices.

"I've never seen a dead person before," said Francine.

Lavinia examined her watch as if it was a thousand miles away on an arm and wrist grown impossibly distant. "It's only eight-thirty. We'll pick up Helen and get on to the show."

"The show!" Francine jerked.

"It's what we need. We've got to forget this. It's not good to remember. If we went home now we'd remember. We'll go to the show as if nothing happened."

"Lavinia, you don't *mean* it!"

"I never meant anything more in my life. We need to laugh now and forget."

"But Elizabeth's back there—your friend, my friend—"

"We can't help her; we can only help ourselves. Come on."

They started up the ravine side, on the stony path, in the dark. And suddenly there, barring their way, standing very still in one spot, not seeing them, but looking on down at the moving lights and the body and listening to the official voices, was Douglas Spaulding.

He stood there, white as a mushroom, with his hands at his sides, staring down into the ravine.

"Get home!" cried Francine.

He did not hear.

"You!" shrieked Francine. "Get home, get out of this place, you hear? Get home, get home, get *home!*"

Douglas jerked his head, stared at them as if they were not there. His mouth moved. He gave a bleating sound. Then, silently, he whirled about and ran. He ran silently up the distant hills into the warm darkness.

Francine sobbed and cried again and, doing this, walked on with Lavinia Nebbs.

✳ "There you are! I thought you ladies'd never come!" Helen Greer stood tapping her foot atop her porch steps. "You're only an hour late, that's all. What happened?"

"We—" started Francine.

Lavinia clutched her arm tight. "There was a commotion. Somebody found Elizabeth Ramsell in the ravine."

"Dead? Was she—dead?"

Lavinia nodded. Helen gasped and put her hand to her throat. "Who found her?"

Lavinia held Francine's wrist firmly. "We don't know."

The three young women stood in the summer night looking at each other. "I've got a notion to go in the house and lock the doors," said Helen at last.

But finally she went to get a sweater, for though it was still warm, she, too, complained of the sudden winter night. While she was gone Francine whispered frantically, "Why didn't you *tell* her?"

"Why upset her?" said Lavinia. "Tomorrow. Tomorrow's plenty of time."

The three women moved along the street under the black trees, past suddenly locked houses. How soon the news had spread outward from the ravine, from house to house, porch to porch, telephone to telephone. Now, passing, the three women felt eyes looking out at them from curtained windows as locks rattled into place. How strange the popsicle, the vanilla night, the night of close-packed ice cream, of mosquito-lotioned wrists, the night of running children suddenly veered from their games and put away behind glass, behind wood, the popsicles in melting puddles of lime and strawberry where they fell when the children were scooped indoors. Strange the hot rooms with the sweating people pressed tightly back into them behind the bronze knobs and knockers. Baseball bats and balls lay upon the unfootprinted lawns. A half-drawn, white-chalk game of hopscotch lay on the broiled, steamed sidewalk. It was as if someone had predicted freezing weather a moment ago.

"We're crazy being out on a night like this," said Helen.

"Lonely One won't kill three ladies," said Lavinia. "There's safety in numbers. And besides, it's too soon. The killings always come a month separated."

A shadow fell across their terrified faces. A figure loomed behind a tree. As if someone had struck an organ a terrible blow with his fist, the three women gave off a scream, in three different shrill notes.

"Got you!" roared a voice. The man plunged at them. He came into the light, laughing. He leaned against a tree, pointing at the ladies weakly, laughing again.

"Hey! I'm the Lonely One!" said Frank Dillon.

"Frank Dillon!"

"Frank!"

"Frank," said Lavinia, "if you ever do a childish thing like that again, may someone riddle you with bullets!"

"What a thing to do!"

Francine began to cry hysterically.

Frank Dillon stopped smiling. "Say, I'm sorry."

"Go away!" said Lavinia. "Haven't you heard about Elizabeth Ramsell—found dead in the ravine? You running around scaring women! Don't speak to us again!"

"Aw, now—"

They moved. He moved to follow.

"Stay right there, Mr. Lonely One, and scare yourself. Go take a look at Elizabeth Ramsell's face and see if it's funny. Good night!" Lavinia took the other two on along the street of trees and stars, Francine holding a kerchief to her face.

"Francine, it was only a joke." Helen turned to Lavinia. "Why's she crying so hard?"

"We'll tell you when we get downtown. We're going to the show no matter what! Enough's enough. Come on now, get your money ready, we're almost there!"

✳ The drugstore was a small pool of sluggish air which the great wooden fans stirred in tides of arnica and tonic and soda-smell out onto the brick streets.

"I need a nickel's worth of green peppermint chews," said Lavinia to the druggist. His face was set and pale, like all the faces they had seen on the half-empty streets. "For eating in the show," said Lavinia as the druggist weighed out a nickel's worth of the green candy with a silver shovel.

"You sure look pretty tonight, ladies. You looked cool this afternoon, Miss Lavinia, when you was in for a chocolate soda. So cool and nice that someone asked after you."

"Oh?"

"Man sitting at the counter—watched you walk out. Said to me, 'Say, who's that?' Why, that's Lavinia Nebbs, prettiest maiden lady in town, I said. 'She's beautiful,' he said. 'Where does she live?'" Here the druggist paused uncomfortably.

"You didn't!" said Francine. "You didn't give him her address, I hope? You didn't!"

"I guess I didn't think. I said, 'Oh, over on Park Street, you know, near the ravine.' A casual remark. But now, tonight, them finding the body, I heard a minute ago, I thought, My God, what've I done!" He handed over the package, much too full.

"You fool!" cried Francine, and tears were in her eyes.

"I'm sorry. Course, maybe it was nothing."

Lavinia stood with the three people looking at her, staring at her. She felt nothing. Except, perhaps, the slightest prickle of excitement in her throat. She held out her money automatically.

"There's no charge on those peppermints," said the druggist, turning to shuffle some papers.

"Well, I know what I'm going to do right now!" Helen stalked out of the drugshop. "I'm calling a taxi to take us all home. I'll be no part of a hunting party for you, Lavinia. That man was up to no good. Asking about you. You want to be dead in the ravine next?"

"It was just a man," said Lavinia, turning in a slow circle to look at the town.

"So is Frank Dillon a man, but maybe he's the Lonely One."

Francine hadn't come out with them, they noticed, and turning, they found her arriving. "I made him give me a description—the druggist. I made him tell what the man looked like. A stranger," she said, "in a dark suit. Sort of pale and thin."

"We're all overwrought," said Lavinia. "I simply won't take a taxi if you get one. If I'm the next victim, let me be the next. There's all too little excitement in life, especially for a maiden lady thirty-three years old, so don't you mind if I enjoy it. Anyway it's silly; I'm not beautiful."

"Oh, but you are, Lavinia; you're the loveliest lady in town, now that Elizabeth is—" Francine stopped. "You keep men off at a distance. If you'd only relax, you'd been married years ago!"

"Stop sniveling, Francine! Here's the theater box office, I'm paying forty-one cents to see Charlie Chaplin. If you two want a taxi, go on. I'll sit alone and go home alone."

"Lavinia, you're crazy; we can't let you do that—"

They entered the theater.

The first showing was over, intermission was on, and the dim auditorium was sparsely populated. The three ladies sat halfway down front, in the smell of ancient brass polish, and watched the manager step through the worn red velvet curtains to make an announcement.

"The police have asked us to close early tonight so everyone can be out at a decent hour. Therefore we are cutting our short subjects and running our feature again immediately. The show will be over at eleven. Everyone is advised to go straight home. Don't linger on the streets."

"That means us, Lavinia!" whispered Francine.

The lights went out. The screen leaped to life.

"Lavinia," whispered Helen.

"What?"

"As we came in, a man in a dark suit, across the street, crossed over. He just walked down the aisle and is sitting in the row behind us."

"Oh, Helen!"

"Right behind us?"

One by one the three women turned to look.

They saw a white face there, flickering with unholy light from the silver screen. It seemed to be all men's faces hovering there in the dark.

"I'm going to get the manager!" Helen was gone up the aisle. "Stop the film! Lights!"

"Helen, come back!" cried Lavinia, rising.

✳ They tapped their empty soda glasses down, each with a vanilla mustache on their upper lip, which they found with their tongues, laughing.

"You see how silly?" said Lavinia. "All that riot for nothing. How embarrassing."

"I'm sorry," said Helen faintly.

The clock said eleven-thirty now. They had come out of the dark theater, away from the fluttering rush of men and women hurrying everywhere, nowhere, on the street while laughing at Helen. Helen was trying to laugh at herself.

"Helen, when you ran up that aisle crying, 'Lights!' I thought I'd die! That poor man!"

"The theater manager's brother from Racine!"

"I apologized," said Helen, looking up at the great fan still whirling, whirling the warm late night air, stirring, restirring the smells of vanilla, raspberry, peppermint and Lysol.

"We shouldn't have stopped for these sodas. The police warned—"

"Oh, bosh the police," laughed Lavinia. "I'm not afraid of anything. The Lonely One is a million miles away now. He won't be back for weeks and the police'll get him then, just wait. Wasn't the film wonderful?"

"Closing up, ladies." The druggist switched off the lights in the cool white-tiled silence.

Outside, the streets were swept clean and empty of cars or trucks or people. Bright lights still burned in the small store windows where the warm wax dummies lifted pink wax hands fired with blue-white diamond rings, or flourished orange wax legs to reveal hosiery. The hot blue-glass eyes of the mannequins watched as the ladies drifted down the empty river bottom street, their images shimmering in the windows like blossoms seen under darkly moving waters.

"Do you suppose if we screamed they'd do anything?"

"Who?"

"The dummies, the window people."

"Oh, Francine."

"Well . . ."

There were a thousand people in the windows, stiff and silent, and three people on the street, the echoes following like gunshots from store fronts across the way when they tapped their heels on the baked pavement.

A red neon sign flickered dimly, buzzed like a dying insect, as they passed.

Baked and white, the long avenues lay ahead. Blowing and tall in a wind that touched only their leafy summits, the trees stood on either side of the three small women. Seen from the courthouse peak, they appeared like three thistles far away.

"First, we'll walk you home, Francine."

"No, I'll walk *you* home."

"Don't be silly. You live way out at Electric Park. If you walked me home you'd have to come back across the ravine alone, yourself. And if so much as a leaf fell on you, you'd drop dead."

Francine said, "I can stay the night at your house. You're the *pretty* one!"

And so they walked, they drifted like three prim clothes forms over a moonlit sea of lawn and concrete, Lavinia watching the black trees flit by each side of her, listening to the voices of her friends murmuring, trying to laugh; and the night seemed to quicken, they seemed to run while walking slowly, everything seemed fast and the color of hot snow.

"Let's sing," said Lavinia.

They sang, "Shine On, Shine On, Harvest Moon . . ."

They sang sweetly and quietly, arm in arm, not looking back. They felt the hot sidewalk cooling underfoot, moving, moving.

"Listen!" said Lavinia.

They listened to the summer night. The summer-night crickets and the far-off tone of the courthouse clock making it eleven forty-five.

"*Listen!*"

Lavinia listened. A porch swing creaked in the dark and there was Mr.

Terle, not saying anything to anybody, alone on his swing, having a last cigar. They saw the pink ash swinging gently to and fro.

Now the lights were going, going, gone. The little house lights and big house lights and yellow lights and green hurricane lights, the candles and oil lamps and porch lights, and everything felt locked up in brass and iron and steel, everything, thought Lavinia, is boxed and locked and wrapped and shaded. She imagined the people in their moonlit beds. And their breathing in the summer-night rooms, safe and together. And here we are, thought Lavinia, our footsteps on along the baked summer evening sidewalk. And above us the lonely street lights shining down, making a drunken shadow.

"Here's your house, Francine. Good night."

"Lavinia, Helen, stay here tonight. It's late, almost midnight now. You can sleep in the parlor. I'll make hot chocolate—it'll be such fun!" Francine was holding them both now, close to her.

"No, thanks," said Lavinia.

And Francine began to cry.

"Oh, not again, Francine," said Lavinia.

"I don't want you dead," sobbed Francine, the tears running straight down her cheeks. "You're so fine and nice, I want you alive. Please, oh, please!"

"Francine, I didn't know how much this has done to you. I promise I'll phone when I get home."

"Oh, will you?"

"And tell you I'm safe, yes. And tomorrow we'll have a picnic lunch at Electric Park. With ham sandwiches I'll make myself, how's that? You'll see, I'll live forever!"

"You'll phone, then?"

"I promised, didn't I?"

"Good night, good night!" Rushing upstairs, Francine whisked behind a door, which slammed to be snap-bolted tight on the instant.

"Now," said Lavinia to Helen, "I'll walk you home."

The courthouse clock struck the hour. The sounds blew across a town that was empty, emptier than it had ever been. Over empty streets and empty lots and empty lawns the sound faded.

"Nine, ten, eleven, twelve," counted Lavinia, with Helen on her arm.

"Don't you feel funny?" asked Helen.

"How do you mean?"

"When you think of us being out here on the sidewalks, under the trees, and all those people safe behind locked doors, lying in their beds. We're practically the only walking people out in the open in a thousand miles, I bet."

The sound of the deep warm dark ravine came near.

In a minute they stood before Helen's house, looking at each other for a long time. The wind blew the odor of cut grass between them. The moon was sinking in a sky that was beginning to cloud. "I don't suppose it's any use asking you to stay, Lavinia?"

"I'll be going on."

"Sometimes—"

"Sometimes what?"

"Sometimes I think people *want* to die. You've acted odd all evening."

"I'm just not afraid," said Lavinia. "And I'm curious, I suppose. And I'm using my head. Logically, the Lonely One can't be around. The police and all."

"The police are home with their covers up over their ears."

"Let's just say I'm enjoying myself, precariously, but safely. If there was any real chance of anything happening to me, I'd stay here with you, you can be sure of that."

"Maybe part of you doesn't want to live anymore."

"You and Francine. Honestly!"

"I feel so guilty. I'll be drinking some hot cocoa just as you reach the ravine bottom and walk on the bridge."

"Drink a cup for me. Good night."

Lavinia Nebbs walked alone down the midnight street, down the late summer-night silence. She saw houses with the dark windows and far away she heard a dog barking. In five minutes, she thought, I'll be safe at home. In five minutes I'll be phoning silly little Francine. I'll—"

She heard the man's voice.

A man's voice singing far away among the trees.

"Oh, give me a June night, the moonlight and you . . ."

She walked a little faster.

The voice sang, "In my arms . . . with all your charms . . ."

Down the street in the dim moonlight a man walked slowly and casually along.

I can run knock on one of these doors, thought Lavinia, if I must.

"Oh, give me a June night," sang the man, and he carried a long club in his hand. "The moonlight and you. Well, look who's *here*! What a time of night for you to be out, Miss Nebbs!"

"Officer Kennedy!"

And that's who it was, of course.

"I'd better see you home!"

"Thanks, I'll make it."

"But you live across the ravine. . . ."

Yes, she thought, but I won't walk through the ravine with any man, not even an officer. How do I know who the Lonely One is? "No," she said, "I'll hurry."

"I'll wait right here," he said. "If you need any help, give a yell. Voices carry good here. I'll come running."

"Thank you."

She went on, leaving him under a light, humming to himself, alone.

Here I am, she thought.

The ravine.

She stood on the edge of the one hundred and thirteen steps that went down the steep hill and then across the bridge seventy yards and up the hills leading to Park Street. And only one lantern to see by. Three minutes from now, she thought, I'll be putting my key in my house door. Nothing can happen in just one hundred eighty seconds.

She started down the long dark-green steps into the deep ravine.

"One, two, three, four, five, six, seven, eight, nine, ten steps," she counted in a whisper.

She felt she was running, but she was not running.

"Fifteen, sixteen, seventeen, eighteen, nineteen, twenty steps," she breathed.

"One fifth of the way!" she announced to herself.

The ravine was deep, black and black, black! And the world was gone behind, the world of safe people in bed, the locked doors, the town, the drugstore, the theater, the lights, everything was gone. Only the ravine existed and lived, black and huge, about her.

"Nothing's happened, has it? No one around, is there? Twenty-four, twenty-five steps. Remember that old ghost story you told each other when you were children?"

She listened to her shoes on the steps.

"The story about the dark man coming in your house and you upstairs in bed. And now he's at the first step coming up to your room. And now he's at the second step. And now he's at the third step and the fourth step and the fifth! Oh, how you used to laugh and scream at that story! And now the horrid dark man's at the twelfth step and now he's opening the door of your room and now he's standing by your bed. 'I GOT YOU!' "

She screamed. It was like nothing she'd ever heard, that scream. She had never screamed that loud in her life. She stopped, she froze, she clung to the wooden banister. Her heart exploded in her. The sound of the terrified beating filled the universe.

"There, *there!*" she screamed to herself. "At the bottom of the steps. A man, under the light! No, now he's gone! He was *waiting* there!"

She listened.

Silence.

The bridge was empty.

Nothing, she thought, holding her heart. Nothing. Fool! That story I told myself. How silly. What shall I do?

Her heartbeats faded.

Shall I call the officer—did he hear me scream?

She listened. Nothing. Nothing.

I'll go the rest of the way. That silly story.

She began again, counting the steps.

"Thirty-five, thirty-six, careful, don't fall. Oh, I am a fool. Thirty-seven steps, thirty-eight, nine and forty, and two makes forty-two—almost halfway."

She froze again.

Wait, she told herself.

She took a step. There was an echo.

She took another step.

Another echo. Another step, just a fraction of a moment later.

"Someone's following me," she whispered to the ravine, to the black crickets and dark-green hidden frogs and the black stream. "Someone's on the steps behind me. I don't dare turn around."

Another step, another echo.

"Every time I take a step, they take one."

A step and an echo.

Weakly she asked of the ravine, "Officer Kennedy, is that *you?*"

The crickets were still.

The crickets were *listening.* The night was listening to *her.* For a change, all of the far summer-night meadows and close summer-night trees were suspending motion; leaf, shrub, star, and meadow grass ceased their particular tremors and were listening to Lavinia Nebbs's heart. And perhaps a thousand miles away, across locomotive-lonely country, in an empty way station, a single traveler reading a dim newspaper under a solitary naked bulb, might raise up his head, listen, and think, What's that? and decide, Only a woodchuck, surely, beating on a hollow log. But it was Lavinia Nebbs, it was most surely the heart of Lavinia Nebbs.

Silence. A summer-night silence which lay for a thousand miles, which covered the earth like a white and shadowy sea.

Faster, faster! She went down the steps.

Run!

She heard music. In a mad way, in a silly way, she heard the great surge of music that pounded at her, and she realized as she ran, as she ran in panic and terror, that some part of her mind was dramatizing, borrowing from the turbulent musical score of some private drama, and the music was rushing and pushing her now, higher and higher, faster, faster, plummeting and scurrying, down, and down into the pit of the ravine.

Only a little way, she prayed. One hundred eight, nine, one hundred ten steps! The bottom! Now, run! Across the bridge!

She told her legs what to do, her arms, her body, her terror; she advised all parts of herself in this white and terrible moment, over the roaring creek waters, on the hollow, thudding, swaying almost alive, resilient bridge planks she ran, followed by the wild footsteps behind, behind, with the music following, too, the music shrieking and babbling.

He's following, don't turn, don't look, if you see him, you'll not be able to move, you'll be so frightened. Just run, run!

She ran across the bridge.

Oh, God, God, please, please let me get up the hill! Now up the path, now between the hills, oh God, it's dark, and everything so far away. If I screamed now it wouldn't help; I can't scream anyway. Here's the top of the path, here's the street, oh, God, please let me be safe, if I get home safe I'll never go out alone; I was a fool, let me admit it, I was a fool, I didn't know what terror was, but if you let me get home from this I'll never go without Helen or Francine again! Here's the street. Across the street!

She crossed the street and rushed up the sidewalk.

Oh God, the porch! My house! Oh God, please give me time to get inside and lock the door and I'll be safe!

And there—silly thing to notice—why did she notice, instantly, no time, no time—but there it was anyway, flashing by—there on the porch rail, the half-filled glass of lemonade she had abandoned a long time, a year, half an evening ago! The lemonade glass sitting calmly, imperturbably there on the rail . . . and . . .

She heard her clumsy feet on the porch and listened and felt her hands scrabbling and ripping at the lock with the key. She heard her heart. She heard her inner voice screaming.

The key fit.

Unlock the door, quick, quick!

The door opened.

Now, inside. Slam it!

She slammed the door.

"Now lock it, bar it, lock it!" she gasped wretchedly.

"Lock it, tight, *tight*!"

The door was locked and bolted tight.

The music stopped. She listened to her heart again and the sound of it diminishing into silence.

Home! Oh God, safe at home! Safe, safe and safe at home! She slumped against the door. Safe, safe. Listen. Not a sound. Safe, safe, oh thank God, safe at home. I'll never go out at night again. I'll stay home. I won't go over that ravine again ever. Safe, oh safe, safe home, so good, so good, safe! Safe inside, the door locked. Wait.

Look out the window.

She looked.

Why, there's no one there at all! Nobody. There was nobody following me at all. Nobody running after me. She got her breath and almost laughed at herself. It stands to *reason* If a man *had* been following me, he'd have *caught* me! I'm not a fast runner. . . . There's no one on the porch or in the yard. How silly of me. I wasn't running from anything. That ravine's as safe as anyplace. Just the same, it's nice to be home. Home's the really good warm place, the only place to be.

She put her hand out to the light switch and stopped.

"What?" she asked. "What, *what*?"

Behind her in the living room, someone cleared his throat.

THE ROCKET

MANY NIGHTS FIORELLO BODONI WOULD AWAKEN to hear the rockets sighing in the dark sky. He would tiptoe from bed, certain that his kind wife was dreaming, to let himself out into the night air. For a few moments he would be free of the smells of old food in the small house by the river. For a silent moment he would let his heart soar alone into space, following the rockets.

Now, this very night, he stood half naked in the darkness, watching the fire fountains murmuring in the air. The rockets on their long wild way to Mars and Saturn and Venus!

"Well, well, Bodoni."

Bodoni started.

On a milk crate, by the silent river, sat an old man who also watched the rockets through the midnight hush.

"Oh, it's you, Bramante!"

"Do you come out every night, Bodoni?"

"Only for the air."

"So? I prefer the rockets myself," said old Bramante. "I was a boy when they started. Eighty years ago, and I've never been on one yet."

"I will ride up in one someday," said Bodoni.

"Fool!" cried Bramante. "You'll never go. This is a rich man's world." He shook his gray head, remembering. "When I was young they wrote it in fiery letters: THE WORLD OF THE FUTURE! Science, Comfort, and New Things for All! Ha! Eighty years. The Future becomes Now! Do *we* fly rockets? No! We live in shacks like our ancestors before us."

"Perhaps my *sons*—" said Bodoni.

"No, nor *their* sons!" the old man shouted. "It's the rich who have dreams and rockets!"

Bodoni hesitated. "Old man, I've saved three thousand dollars. It took me six years to save it. For my business, to invest in machinery. But every night for a month now I've been awake. I hear the rockets. I think. And to-night I've made up my mind. One of us will fly to Mars!" His eyes were shining and dark.

"Idiot," snapped Bramante. "How will you choose? Who will go? If you go, your wife will hate you, for you will be just a bit nearer God, in space. When you tell your amazing trip to her, over the years, won't bitterness gnaw at her?"

"No, no!"

"Yes! And your children? Will their lives be filled with the memory of Papa, who flew to Mars while they stayed here? What a senseless task you will set your boys. They will think of the rocket all their lives. They will lie awake. They will be sick with wanting it. Just as you are sick now. They will want to die if they cannot go. Don't set that goal, I warn you. Let them be content with being poor. Turn their eyes down to their hands and to your junkyard, not up to the stars."

"But—"

"Suppose your wife went? How would you feel, knowing she had *seen* and you had not? She would become holy. You would think of throwing her in the river. No, Bodoni, buy a new wrecking machine, which you need, and pull your dreams apart with it, and smash them to pieces."

The old man subsided, gazing at the river in which, drowned, images of rockets burned down the sky.

"Good night," said Bodoni.

"Sleep well," said the other.

✳ When the toast jumped from its silver box, Bodoni almost screamed. The night had been sleepless. Among his nervous children, beside his mountainous wife, Bodoni had twisted and stared at nothing. Bramante was right. Better to invest the money. Why save it when only one of the family could ride the rocket, while the others remained to melt in frustration?

"Fiorello, eat your toast," said his wife, Maria.

"My throat is shriveled," said Bodoni.

The children rushed in, the three boys fighting over a toy rocket, the two girls carrying dolls which duplicated the inhabitants of Mars, Venus, and Neptune, green mannequins with three yellow eyes and twelve fingers.

"I saw the Venus rocket!" cried Paolo.

"It took off, *whoosh!*" hissed Antonello.

"Children!" shouted Bodoni, hands to his ears.

They stared at him. He seldom shouted.

Bodoni arose. "Listen, all of you," he said. "I have enough money to take one of us on the Mars rocket."

Everyone yelled.

"You understand?" he asked. "Only *one* of us. Who?"

"Me, me, me!" cried the children.

"You," said Maria.

"You," said Bodoni to her.

They all fell silent.

The children reconsidered. "Let Lorenzo go—he's oldest."

"Let Miriamne go—she's a girl!"

"Think what you would see," said Bodoni's wife to him. But her eyes were strange. Her voice shook. "The meteors, like fish. The universe. The Moon. Someone should go who could tell it well on returning. You have a way with words."

"Nonsense. So have you," he objected.

Everyone trembled.

"Here," said Bodoni unhappily. From a broom he broke straws of various lengths. "The short straw wins." He held out his tight fist. "Choose."

Solemnly each took his turn.

"Long straw."

"Long straw."

Another.

"Long straw."

The children finished. The room was quiet.

Two straws remained. Bodoni felt his heart ache in him. "Now," he whispered. "Maria."

She drew.

"The short straw," she said.

"Ah," sighed Lorenzo, half happy, half sad. "Mama goes to Mars."

Bodoni tried to smile. "Congratulations. I will buy your ticket today."

"Wait, Fiorello—"

"You can leave next week," he murmured.

She saw the sad eyes of her children upon her, with the smiles beneath their straight, large noses. She returned the straw slowly to her husband. "I cannot go to Mars."

"But why not?"

"I will be busy with another child."

"What!"

She would not look at him. "It wouldn't do for me to travel in my condition."

He took her elbow. "Is this the truth?"

"Draw again. Start over."

"Why didn't you tell me before?" he said incredulously.

"I didn't remember."

"Maria, Maria," he whispered, patting her face. He turned to the children. "Draw again."

Paolo immediately drew the short straw.

"I go to Mars!" He danced wildly. "Thank you, Father!"

The other children edged away. "That's swell, Paolo."

Paolo stopped smiling to examine his parents and his brothers and sisters. "I *can* go, can't I?" he asked uncertainly.

"Yes."

"And you'll *like* me when I come back?"

"Of course."

Paolo studied the precious broomstraw on his trembling hand and shook his head. He threw it away. "I forgot. School starts. I can't go. Draw again."

But no one would draw. A full sadness lay on them.

"None of us will go," said Lorenzo.

"That's best," said Maria.

"Bramante was right," said Bodoni.

✳ With his breakfast curdled within him, Fiorello Bodoni worked in his junkyard, ripping metal, melting it, pouring out usable ingots. His equipment flaked apart; competition had kept him on the insane edge of poverty for twenty years.

It was a very bad morning.

In the afternoon a man entered the junkyard and called up to Bodoni on his wrecking machine. "Hey, Bodoni, I got some metal for you!"

"What is it, Mr. Mathews?" asked Bodoni, listlessly.

"A rocket ship. What's wrong? Don't you want it?"

"Yes, yes!" He seized the man's arm, and stopped, bewildered.

"Of course," said Mathews, "it's only a mockup. *You* know. When they plan a rocket they build a full-scale model first, of aluminum. You might make a small profit boiling her down. Let you have her for two thousand—"

Bodoni dropped his hand. "I haven't the money."

"Sorry. Thought I'd help you. Last time we talked you said how every-one outbid you on junk. Thought I'd slip this to you on the q.t. Well—"

"I need new equipment. I saved money for that."

"I understand."

"If I bought your rocket, I wouldn't even be able to melt it down. My aluminum furnace broke down last week—"

"Sure."

"I couldn't possibly use the rocket if I bought it from you."

"I know."

Bodoni blinked and shut his eyes. He opened them and looked at Mr. Mathews. "But I am a great fool. I will take my money from the bank and give it to you."

"But if you can't melt the rocket down—"

"Deliver it," said Bodoni.

"All right, if you say so. Tonight?"

"Tonight," said Bodoni, "would be fine. Yes, I would like to have a rocket ship tonight."

✳ There was a moon. The rocket was white and big in the junkyard. It held the whiteness of the moon and the blueness of the stars. Bodoni looked at it and loved all of it. He wanted to pet it and lie against it, press-ing it with his cheek, telling it all the secret wants of his heart.

He stared up at it. "You are all mine," he said. "Even if you never move or spit fire, and just sit there and rust for fifty years, you are mine."

The rocket smelled of time and distance. It was like walking into a clock. It was finished with Swiss delicacy. One might wear it on one's watch fob. "I might even sleep here tonight," Bodoni whispered excitedly.

He sat in the pilot's seat.

He touched a lever.

He hummed in his shut mouth, his eyes closed.

The humming grew louder, louder, higher, higher, wilder, stranger, more exhilarating, trembling in him and leaning him forward and pulling him and the ship in a roaring silence and in a kind of metal screaming, while his fists flew over the controls, and his shut eyes quivered, and the sound grew and grew until it was a fire, a strength, a lifting and a pushing of power that threatened to tear him in half. He gasped. He hummed again and again, and did not stop, for it could not be stopped, it could only go on, his eyes tighter, his heart furious. "Taking off!" he screamed. *The jolting con-*

cussion! *The thunder!* "The Moon!" he cried, eyes blind, tight. "The meteors!" *The silent rush in volcanic light.* "*Mars.* Oh, yes! Mars! Mars!"

He fell back, exhausted and panting. His shaking hands came loose of the controls and his head tilted wildly. He sat for a long time, breathing out and in, his heart slowing.

Slowly, slowly, he opened his eyes.

The junkyard was still there.

He sat motionless. He looked at the heaped piles of metal for a minute, his eyes never leaving them. Then, leaping up, he kicked the levers. "Take off, blast you!"

The ship was silent.

"I'll show you!" he cried.

Out in the night air, stumbling, he started the fierce motor of his terrible wrecking machine and advanced upon the rocket. He maneuvered the massive weights into the moonlit sky. He readied his trembling hands to plunge the weights, to smash, to rip apart this insolently false dream, this silly thing for which he had paid his money, which would not move, which would not do his bidding. "I'll teach you!" he shouted.

But his hand stayed.

The silver rocket lay in the light of the Moon. And beyond the rocket stood the yellow lights of his home, a block away, burning warmly. He heard the family radio playing some distant music. He sat for half an hour considering the rocket and the house lights, and his eyes narrowed and grew wide. He stepped down from the wrecking machine and began to walk, and as he walked he began to laugh, and when he reached the back door of his house he took a deep breath and called, "Maria, Maria, start packing. We're going to Mars!"

✳ "Oh!"

"Ah!"

"I can't *believe* it!"

"You will, you will."

The children balanced in the windy yard, under the glowing rocket, not touching it yet. They started to cry.

Maria looked at her husband. "What have you done?" she said. "Taken our money for this? It will never fly."

"It will fly," he said, looking at it.

"Rocket ships cost millions. Have you millions?"

"It will fly," he repeated steadily. "Now, go to the house, all of you. I have phone calls to make, work to do. Tomorrow we leave! Tell no one, understand? It is a secret."

The children edged off from the rocket, stumbling. He saw their small, feverish faces in the house windows, far away.

Maria had not moved. "You have ruined us," she said. "Our money used for this—this thing. When it should have been spent on equipment."

"You will see," he said.

Without a word she turned away.

"God help me," he whispered, and started to work.

✳ Through the midnight hours trucks arrived, packages were delivered, and Bodoni, smiling, exhausted his bank account. With blowtorch and metal stripping he assaulted the rocket, added, took away, worked fiery magics and secret insults upon it. He bolted nine ancient automobile motors into the rocket's empty engine room. Then he welded the engine room shut, so none could see his hidden labor.

At dawn he entered the kitchen. "Maria," he said, "I'm ready for breakfast."

She would not speak to him.

At sunset he called to the children. "We're ready! Come on!" The house was silent.

"I've locked them in the closet," said Maria.

"What do you mean?" he demanded.

"You'll be killed in that rocket," she said. "What kind of rocket can you buy for two thousand dollars? A bad one!"

"Listen to me, Maria."

"It will blow up. Anyway, you are no pilot."

"Nevertheless, I can fly *this* ship. I have fixed it."

"You have gone mad," she said.

"Where is the key to the closet?"

"I have it here."

He put out his hand. "Give it to me."

She handed it to him. "You will kill them."

"No, no."

"Yes, you will. I *feel* it."

He stood before her. "You won't come along?"

"I'll stay here," she said.

"You will understand; you will see then," he said, and smiled. He unlocked the closet. "Come, children. Follow your father."

"Good-bye, good-bye, Mama!"

She stayed in the kitchen window, looking out at them, very straight and silent.

At the door of the rocket the father said, "Children, this is a swift rocket. We will be gone only a short while. You must come back to school, and I to my business." He took each of their hands in turn. "Listen. This rocket is very old and will fly only *one* more journey. It will not fly again. This will be the one trip of your life. Keep your eyes wide."

"Yes, Papa."

"Listen, keep your ears clean. Smell the smells of a rocket. *Feel. Remember.* So when you return you will talk of it all the rest of your lives."

"Yes, Papa."

The ship was quiet as a stopped clock. The airlock hissed shut behind them. He strapped them all, like tiny mummies, into rubber hammocks. "Ready? he called.

"Ready!" all replied.

"Blast-off!" He jerked ten switches. The rocket thundered and leaped. The children danced in their hammocks, screaming. "We're moving! We're off! Look!"

"Here comes the Moon!"

The moon dreamed by. Meteors broke into fireworks. Time flowed away in a serpentine of gas. The children shouted. Released from their hammocks, hours later, they peered from the ports. "There's Earth!" "There's Mars!"

The rocket dropped pink petals of fire while the hour dials spun; the child eyes dropped shut. At last they hung like drunken moths in their cocoon hammocks.

"Good," whispered Bodoni, alone.

He tiptoed from the control room to stand for a long moment, fearful, at the airlock door.

He pressed a button. The airlock door swung wide. He stepped out. Into space? Into the inky tides of meteor and gaseous torch? Into swift mileages and infinite dimensions?

No. Bodoni smiled.

All about the quivering rocket lay the junkyard.

Rusting, unchanged, there stood the padlocked junkyard gate, the little silent house by the river, the kitchen window lighted, and the river going down to the same sea. And in the center of the junkyard, manufacturing a magic dream, lay the quivering, purring rocket. Shaking and roaring, bouncing the netted children like flies in a web.

Maria stood in the kitchen window.

He waved to her and smiled.

He could not see if she waved or not. A small wave, perhaps. A small smile.

The sun was rising.

Bodoni withdrew hastily into the rocket. Silence. All still slept. He breathed easily. Tying himself into a hammock, he closed his eyes. To himself he prayed, Oh, let nothing happen to the illusion in the next six days. Let all of space come and go, and red Mars come up under our ship, and the moons of Mars, and let there be no flaws in the color film. Let there be three dimensions; let nothing go wrong with the hidden mirrors and screens that mold the fine illusion. Let time pass without crisis.

He awoke.

Red Mars floated near the rocket.

"Papa!" The children thrashed to be free.

Bodoni looked and saw red Mars and it was good and there was no flaw in it and he was very happy.

At sunset on the seventh day the rocket stopped shuddering.

"We are home," said Bodoni.

They walked across the junkyard from the open door of the rocket, their blood singing, their faces glowing. Perhaps they knew what he had done. Perhaps they guessed his wonderful magic trick. But if they knew, if they guessed, they never said. Now they only laughed and ran.

"I have ham and eggs for all of you," said Maria, at the kitchen door.

"Mama, Mama, you should have come, to see it, to see Mars, Mama, and meteors, and everything!"

"Yes," she said.

At bedtime the children gathered before Bodoni. "We want to thank you, Papa."

"It was nothing."

"We will remember it for always, Papa. We will never forget."

※ Very late in the night Bodoni opened his eyes. He sensed that his wife was lying beside him, watching him. She did not move for a very long time, and then suddenly she kissed his cheeks and his forehead. "What's this?" he cried.

"You're the best father in the world," she whispered.

"Why?"

"Now I see," she said. "I understand."

She lay back and closed her eyes, holding his hand. "Is it a very lovely journey?" she asked.

"Yes," he said.

"Perhaps," she said, "perhaps, some night, you might take me on just a little trip, do you think?"

"Just a little one, perhaps," he said.

"Thank you," she said. "Good night."

"Good night," said Fiorello Bodoni.

SEASON OF DISBELIEF

HOW IT BEGAN WITH THE CHILDREN, old Mrs. Bentley never knew. She often saw them, like moths and monkeys, at the grocer's, among the cabbages and hung bananas, and she smiled at them and they smiled back. Mrs. Bentley watched them making footprints in winter snow, filling their lungs with autumn smoke, shaking down blizzards of spring apple-blossoms, but felt no fear of them. As for herself, her house was in extreme good order, everything set to its station, the floors briskly swept, the foods neatly tinned, the hatpins thrust through cushions, and the drawers of her bedroom bureaus crisply filled with the paraphernalia of years.

Mrs. Bentley was a saver. She saved tickets, old theater programs, bits of lace, scarves, rail transfers; all the tags and tokens of existence.

"I've a stack of records," she often said. "Here's Caruso. That was in 1916, in New York; I was sixty and John was still alive. Here's June Moon, 1924, I think, right after John died."

That was the huge regret of her life, in a way. The one thing she had most enjoyed touching and listening to and looking at she hadn't saved. John was far out in the meadow country, dated and boxed and hidden under grasses, and nothing remained of him but his high silk hat and his cane and his good suit in the closet. So much of the rest of him had been devoured by moths.

But what she could keep she had kept. Her pink-flowered dresses crushed among moth balls in vast black trunks, and cut-glass dishes from her childhood—she had brought them all when she moved to this town five years ago. Her husband had owned rental property in a number of towns, and, like a yellow ivory chess piece, she had moved and sold one after another, until now she was here in a strange town, left with only the trunks and furniture, dark and ugly, crouched about her like the creatures of a primordial zoo.

The thing about the children happened in the middle of summer. Mrs. Bentley, coming out to water the ivy upon her front porch, saw two cool-colored sprawling girls and a small boy lying on her lawn, enjoying the immense prickling of the grass.

At the very moment Mrs. Bentley was smiling down upon them with her yellow mask face, around a corner like an elfin band came an ice-cream wagon. It jingled out icy melodies, as crisp and rimmed as crystal wine-glasses tapped by an expert, summoning all. The children sat up, turning their heads, like sunflowers after the sun.

Mrs. Bentley called, "Would you like some? Here!" The ice-cream wagon stopped and she exchanged money for pieces of the original Ice Age. The children thanked her with snow in their mouths, their eyes darting from her buttoned-up shoes to her white hair.

"Don't you want a bite?" said the boy.

"No, child. I'm old enough and cold enough; the hottest day won't thaw me," laughed Mrs. Bentley.

They carried the miniature glaciers up and sat, three in a row, on the shady porch glider.

"I'm Alice, she's Jane, and that's Tom Spaulding."

"How nice. And I'm Mrs. Bentley. They called me Helen."

They stared at her.

"Don't you believe they called me Helen?" said the old lady.

"I didn't know old ladies had first names," said Tom, blinking.

Mrs. Bentley laughed dryly.

"You never hear them used, he means," said Jane.

"My dear, when you are as old as I, they won't call you Jane, either. Old age is dreadfully formal. It's always 'Mrs.' Young People don't like to call you 'Helen.' It seems much too flip."

"How old *are* you?" asked Alice.

"I remember the pterodactyl." Mrs. Bentley smiled.

"No, but how old?"

"Seventy-two."

They gave their cold sweets an extra long suck, deliberating.

"That's *old*," said Tom.

"I don't feel any different now than when I was your age," said the old lady.

"Our age?"

"Yes. Once I was a pretty little girl just like you, Jane, and you, Alice."

They did not speak.

"What's the matter?"

"Nothing." Jane got up.

"Oh, you don't have to go so soon, I hope. You haven't finished eating. . . . Is something the matter?"

"My mother says it isn't nice to fib," said Jane.

"Of course it isn't. It's very bad," agreed Mrs. Bentley.

"And not to *listen* to fibs."

"Who was fibbing to you, Jane?"

Jane looked at her and then glanced nervously away. "You were."

"I?" Mrs. Bentley laughed and put her withered claw to her small bosom. "About what?"

"About your age. About being a little girl."

Mrs. Bentley stiffened. "But I *was*, many years ago, a little girl just like you."

"Come on, Alice, Tom."

"Just a moment," said Mrs. Bentley. "Don't you believe me?"

"I don't know," said Jane. "No."

"But how ridiculous! It's perfectly obvious. Everyone was young once!"

"Not you," whispered Jane, eyes down, almost to herself. Her empty ice stick had fallen in a vanilla puddle on the porch floor.

"But of course I was eight, nine, ten years old, like all of you."

The two girls gave a short, quickly-sealed-up laugh.

Mrs. Bentley's eyes glittered. "Well, I can't waste a morning arguing with ten-year-olds. Needless to say, I was ten myself once and just as silly."

The two girls laughed. Tom looked uneasy.

"You're joking with us," giggled Jane. "You weren't really ten ever, were you, Mrs. Bentley?"

"You run on home!" the woman cried suddenly, for she could not stand their eyes. "I won't have you laughing."

"And your name's not really Helen?"

"Of course it's Helen!"

"Good-bye," said the two girls, giggling away across the lawn under the seas of shade, Tom followed them slowly. "Thanks for the ice cream!"

"Once I played *hopscotch*!" Mrs. Bentley cried after them, but they were gone.

✳ Mrs. Bentley spent the rest of the day slamming teakettles about, loudly preparing a meager lunch, and from time to time going to the front door, hoping to catch those insolent fiends on their laughing excursions through the late day. But if they had appeared, what could she say to them, why should she worry about them?

"The idea!" said Mrs. Bentley to her dainty, rose-clustered teacup. "No one ever doubted I was a girl before. What a silly, horrible thing to do. I don't mind being old—not really—but I *do* resent having my childhood taken away from me."

She could see the children racing off under the cavernous trees with her youth in their frosty fingers, invisible as air.

After supper, for no reason at all, with a senseless certainty of motion, she watched her own hands, like a pair of ghostly gloves at a séance, gather together certain items in a perfumed kerchief. Then she went to her front porch and stood there stiffly for half an hour.

As suddenly as night birds the children flew by, and Mrs. Bentley's voice brought them to a fluttering rest.

"Yes, *Mrs.* Bentley?"

"Come up on this porch!" she commanded them, and the girls climbed the steps, Tom trailing after.

"Yes, Mrs. Bentley?" They thumped the "Mrs." like a bass piano chord, extra heavily, as if that were her first name.

"I've some treasures to show you." She opened the perfumed kerchief and peered into it as if she herself might be surprised. She drew forth a hair comb, very small and delicate, its rim twinkling with rhinestones.

"I wore this when I was nine," she said.

Jane turned it in her hand and said, "How nice."

"Let's see!" cried Alice.

"And here is a tiny ring I wore when I was eight," said Mrs. Bentley. "It doesn't fit my finger now. You look through it and see the Tower of Pisa ready to fall."

"Let's see it lean!" The girls passed it back and forth between them until Jane fitted it to her hand. "Why, it's just *my* size!" she exclaimed.

"And the comb fits *my* head!" gasped Alice.

Mrs. Bentley produced some jackstones. "Here," she said. "I once played with these."

She threw them. They made a constellation on the porch.

"And here!" In triumph she flashed her trump card, a postal picture of herself when she was seven years old, in a dress like a yellow butterfly, with her golden curls and blown blue-glass eyes and angelic pouting lips.

"Who's this little girl?" asked Jane.

"It's *me!*"

The two girls held onto it.

"But it doesn't look like you," said Jane simply. "Anybody could get a picture like this, somewhere."

They looked at her for a long moment.

"Any more pictures, Mrs. Bentley?" asked Alice. "Of you, later? You got a picture of you at fifteen, and one at twenty, and one at forty and fifty?"

The girls chortled.

"I don't have to show you anything!" said Mrs. Bentley.

"Then we don't have to believe you," replied Jane.

"But this picture proves I was young!"

"That's some other little girl, like us. You borrowed it."

"I was married!"

"Where's *Mr.* Bentley?"

"He's been gone a long time. If he were here, he'd tell you how young and pretty I was when I was twenty-two."

"But he's not here and he can't tell, so what does that prove?"

"I have a marriage certificate."

"You could have borrowed that, too. Only way I'll believe you were ever young"—Jane shut her eyes to emphasize how sure she was of herself—"is if you have someone say they saw you when you were ten."

"Thousands of people saw me but they're dead, you little fool—or ill, in other towns. I don't know a soul here, just moved here a few years ago, so no one saw me young."

"Well, there you *are!*" Jane blinked at her companions. "Nobody *saw* her!"

"Listen!" Mrs. Bentley seized the girl's wrist. "You must take these things on faith. Someday you'll be as old as I. People will say the same. 'Oh, no,' they'll say, 'those vultures were never hummingbirds, those owls were never orioles, those parrots were never bluebirds!' One day you'll be like me!"

"No, we won't!" said the girls. "Will we?" they asked one another.

"Wait and see!" said Mrs. Bentley.

And to herself she thought, Oh, God, children are children, old women are old women, and nothing in between. They can't imagine a change they can't see.

"Your mother," she said to Jane. "Haven't you noticed, over the years, the change?"

"No," said Jane. "She's always the same."

And that was true. You lived with people every day and they never altered a degree. It was only when people had been off on a long trip, for years, that they shocked you. And she felt like a woman who has been on a roaring black train for seventy-two years, landing at last upon the rail platform and everyone crying: "Helen Bentley, is that *you*?"

"I guess we better go home," said Jane. "Thanks for the ring. It just fits me."

"Thanks for the comb. It's fine."

"Thanks for the picture of the little girl."

"Come back—you can't have those!" Mrs. Bentley shouted as they raced down the steps. "They're *mine*!"

"Don't!" said Tom, following the girls. "Give them back!"

"No, she stole them! They belonged to some other little girl. She stole them. Thanks!" cried Alice.

So no matter how she called after them, the girls were gone, like moths through darkness.

"I'm sorry," said Tom, on the lawn, looking up at Mrs. Bentley. He went away.

They took my ring and my comb and my picture, thought Mrs. Bentley, trembling there on the steps. Oh, I'm empty, empty; it's part of my life.

✳ She lay awake for many hours into the night, among her trunks and trinkets. She glanced over at the neat stacks of materials and toys and opera plumes and said, aloud, "Does it really belong to me?"

Or was it the elaborate trick of an old lady convincing herself that she had a past? After all, once a time was over, it was done. You were always in the present. She may have been a girl once, but was not now. Her childhood was gone and nothing could fetch it back.

A night wind blew in the room. The white curtain fluttered against a dark cane, which had leaned against the wall near the other bric-a-brac for many years. The cane trembled and fell out into a patch of moonlight, with a soft thud. Its gold ferrule glittered. It was her husband's opera cane. It seemed as if he were pointing it at her, as he often had, using his soft, sad, reasonable voice when they, upon rare occasions, disagreed.

"Those children are right," he would have said. "They stole nothing from you, my dear. These things don't belong to you *here*, you *now*. They belonged to her, that other you, so long ago."

Oh, thought Mrs. Bentley. And then, as though an ancient phonograph record had been set hissing under a steel needle, she remembered a conversation she had once had with Mr. Bentley—Mr. Bentley, so prim, a pink carnation in his whisk-broomed lapel, saying, "My dear, you never will understand time, will you? You're always trying to be the things you were, instead of the person you are tonight. Why do you save those ticket stubs and theater programs? They'll only hurt you later. Throw them away, my dear."

But Mrs. Bentley had stubbornly kept them.

"It won't work," Mr. Bentley continued, sipping his tea. "No matter how hard you try to be what you once were you can only be what you are here and now. Time hypnotizes. When you're nine, you think you've always been nine years old and will always be. When you're thirty, it seems you've always been balanced there on that bright rim of middle life. And then when you turn seventy, you are always and forever seventy. You're in the present, you're trapped in a young now or an old now, but there is no other now to be seen."

It had been one of the few, but gentle, disputes of their quiet marriage. He had never approved of her bric-a-brackery. "Be what you are, bury what you are not," he had said. "Ticket stubs are trickery. Saving things is a magic trick, with mirrors."

If he were alive tonight, what would he say?

"You're saving cocoons." That's what he'd say. "Corsets, in a way, you can never fit again. So why save them? You can't really prove you were ever young. Pictures? No, they lie. You're not the picture."

"Affidavits?"

"No, my dear, you're not the dates, or the ink, or the paper. You're not these trunks of junk and dust. You're only you, here, now—the present you."

Mrs. Bentley nodded at the memory, breathing easier.

"Yes, I see. I see."

The gold-ferruled cane lay silently on the moonlit rug.

"In the morning," she said to it, "I will do something final about this, and settle down to being only me, and nobody else from any other year. Yes, that's what I'll do."

She slept. . . .

✻ The morning was bright and green, and there at her door, bumping softly on the screen, were the two girls. "Got any more to give us, Mrs. Bentley? More of the little girl's things?"

She led them down the hall to the library.

"Take this." She gave Jane the dress in which she had played the mandarin's daughter at fifteen. "And this, and this." A kaleidoscope, a magnifying glass. "Pick anything you want," said Mrs. Bentley. "Books, skates, dolls, everything—they're yours."

"Ours?"

"Only yours. And will you help me with a little work in the next hour? I'm building a big fire in my back yard. I'm emptying the trunks, throwing out this trash for the trashman. It doesn't belong to me. Nothing ever belongs to anybody."

"We'll help," they said.

Mrs. Bentley led the procession to the back yard, arms full, a box of matches in her hand.

So the rest of the summer you could see the two little girls and Tom like wrens on a wire, on Mrs. Bentley's front porch, waiting. And when the silvery chimes of the icicle man were heard, the front door opened, Mrs. Bentley floated out with her hand deep down the gullet of her silver-mouthed purse, and for half an hour you could see them there on the porch, the children and the old lady putting coldness into warmness, eating chocolate icicles, laughing. At last they were good friends.

"How old are you, Mrs. Bentley?"

"Seventy-two."

"How old were you fifty years ago?"

"Seventy-two."

"You weren't ever young, were you, and never wore ribbons or dresses like these?"

"No."

"Have you got a first name?"

"My name is Mrs. Bentley."

"And you've always lived in this one house?"

"Always."

"And never were pretty?"

"Never."

"Never in a million trillion years?" The two girls would bend toward the old lady, and wait in the pressed silence of four o'clock on a summer afternoon.

"Never," said Mrs. Bentley, "in a million trillion years."

AND THE ROCK CRIED OUT

THE RAW CARCASSES, HUNG IN THE SUNLIGHT, rushed at them, vibrated with heat and red color in the green jungle air, and were gone. The stench of rotting flesh gushed through the car windows, and Leonora Webb quickly pressed the button that whispered her door window up.

"Good Lord," she said, "those open-air butcher shops."

The smell was still in the car, a smell of war and horror.

"Did you see the flies?" she asked.

"When you buy any kind of meat in those markets," John Webb said, "you slap the beef with your hand. The flies lift from the meat so you can get a look at it."

He turned the car around a lush bend in the green rain-jungle road.

"Do you think they'll let us into Juatala when we get there?"

"I don't know."

"Watch out!"

He saw the bright things in the road too late, tried to swerve, but hit them. There was a terrible sighing from the right front tire, the car heaved about and sank to a stop. He opened his side of the car and stepped out. The jungle was hot and silent and the highway empty, very empty and quiet at noon.

He walked to the front of the car and bent, all the while checking his revolver in its underarm holster.

Leonora's window gleamed down. "Is the tire hurt much?"

"Ruined, utterly ruined!" He picked up the bright thing that had stabbed and slashed the tire.

"Pieces of a broken machete," he said, "placed in adobe holders pointing toward our car wheels. We're lucky it didn't get *all* our tires."

"But *why?*"

"You know as well as I." He nodded to the newspaper beside her, at the date, the headlines:

OCTOBER 4TH, 1963: UNITED STATES,
EUROPE SILENT!
THE RADIOS OF THE U.S.A. AND EUROPE ARE DEAD.

THERE IS A GREAT SILENCE. THE WAR HAS SPENT ITSELF.

It is believed that most of the population of the United States is dead. It is believed that most of Europe, Russia, and Siberia is equally decimated. The day of the white people of the earth is over and finished.

"It all came so fast," said Webb. "One week we're on another tour, a grand vacation from home. The next week—this."

They both looked away from the black headlines to the jungle.

The jungle looked back at them with a vastness, a breathing moss-and-leaf silence, with a billion diamond and emerald insect eyes.

"Be careful, Jack."

He pressed two buttons. An automatic lift under the front wheels hissed and hung the car in the air. He jammed a key nervously into the right wheel plate. The tire, frame and all, with a sucking pop, bounced from the wheel. It was a matter of seconds to lock the spare in place and roll the shattered tire back to the luggage compartment. He had his gun out while he did all this.

"Don't stand in the open, please, Jack."

"So it's starting already." He felt his hair burning hot on his skull. "News travels fast."

"For God's sake," said Leonora. "They can *hear* you!"

He stared at the jungle.

"I know you're in there!"

"Jack!"

He aimed at the silent jungle. "I see you!" He fired four, five times, quickly, wildly.

The jungle ate the bullets with hardly a quiver, a brief slit sound like torn silk where the bullets bored and vanished into a million acres of green leaves, trees, silence, and moist earth. The brief echo of the shots died. Only the car muttered its exhaust behind Webb. He walked around the car, got in, and shut the door and locked it.

He reloaded the gun, sitting in the front seat. Then they drove away from the place.

They drove steadily.

"Did you see anyone?"

"No. You?"

She shook her head.

"You're going too fast."

He slowed only in time. As they rounded a curve another clump of the bright flashing objects filled the right side of the road. He swerved to the left and passed.

"Sons-of-bitches!"

"They're not sons-of-bitches, they're just people who never had a car like this or anything at all."

Something ticked across the windowpane.

There was a streak of colorless liquid on the glass.

Leonora glanced up. "Is it going to rain?"

"No, an insect hit the pane."

Another tick.

"Are you sure that was an insect?"

Tick, tick, tick.

"Shut the window!" he said, speeding up.

Something fell in her lap.

She looked down at it. He reached over to touch the thing. "Quick!"

She pressed the button. The window snapped up.

Then she examined her lap again.

The tiny blowgun dart glistened there.

"Don't get any of the liquid on you," he said. "Wrap it in your handkerchief—we'll throw it away later."

He had the car up to sixty miles an hour.

"If we hit another road block, we're done."

"This is a local thing," he said. "We'll drive out of it."

The panes were ticking all the time. A shower of things blew at the window and fell away in their speed.

"Why," said Leonora Webb, "they don't even *know* us!"

"I only wish they did." He gripped the wheel. "It's hard to kill people you know. But not hard to kill strangers."

"I don't want to die," she said simply, sitting there.

He put his hand inside his coat. "If anything happens to me, my gun is here. Use it, for God's sake, and don't waste time."

She moved over close to him and they drove seventy-five miles an hour down a straight stretch in the jungle road, saying nothing.

※ With the windows up, the heat was oven-thick in the car.

"It's so silly," she said, at last. "Putting the knives in the road. Trying to hit us with the blowguns. How could they know that the next car along would be driven by white people?"

"Don't ask them to be that logical," he said. "A car is a car. It's big, it's rich. The money in one car would last them a lifetime. And anyway, if you road-block a car, chances are you'll get either an American tourist or a rich Spaniard, comparatively speaking, whose ancestors should have behaved better. And if you happen to road-block another Indian, hell, all you do is go out and help him change tires."

"What time is it?" she asked.

For the thousandth time he glanced at his empty wrist. Without expression or surprise, he fished in his coat pocket for the glistening gold watch with the silent sweep hand. A year ago he had seen a native stare at this watch and stare at it and stare at it with almost a hunger. Then the native had examined him, not scowling, not hating, not sad or happy; nothing except puzzled.

He had taken the watch off that day and never worn it since.

"Noon," he said.

Noon.

The border lay ahead. They saw it and both cried out at once. They pulled up, smiling, not knowing they smiled. . . .

John Webb leaned out the window, started gesturing to the guard at the border station, caught himself, and got out of his car. He walked ahead to the station where three young men, very short, in lumpy uniforms, stood talking. They did not look up at Webb, who stopped before them. They continued conversing in Spanish, ignoring him.

"I beg your pardon," said John Webb at last. "Can we pass over the border into Juatala?"

One of the men turned for a moment. "Sorry, *señor*."

The three men talked again.

"You don't understand," said Webb, touching the first man's elbow. "We've got to get through."

The man shook his head. "Passports are no longer good. Why should you want to leave our country, anyway?"

"It was announced on the radio. All Americans to leave the country, immediately."

"Ah, *sí, sí*." All three soldiers nodded and leered at each other with shining eyes.

"Or be fined or imprisoned, or both," said Webb.

"We could let you over the border, but Juatala would give you twenty-four hours to leave, also. If you don't believe me, listen!" The guard turned and called across the border, "Aye, there! Aye!"

In the hot sun, forty yards distant, a pacing man turned, his rifle in his arms.

"Aye there, Paco, you want these two people?"

"No, *gracias—gracias*, no," replied the man, smiling.

"You see?" said the guard, turning to John Webb.

All of the soldiers laughed together.

"I have money," said Webb.

The men stopped laughing.

The first guard stepped up to John Webb and his face was now not relaxed or easy; it was like brown stone.

"Yes," he said. "They always have money. I know. They come here and they think money will do everything. But what is money? It is only a promise, *señor*. This I know from books. And when somebody no longer likes your promise, what then?"

"I will give you anything you ask."

"Will you?" The guard turned to his friends. "He will give me *anything* I ask." To Webb: "It was a joke. *We* were always a joke to you, weren't we?"

"No."

"*Mañana*, you laughed at us; *mañana*, you laughed at our siestas and our *mañanas*, didn't you?"

"Not me. Someone else."

"Yes, you."

"I've never been to this particular station before."

"I know you, anyway. Run here, do this, do that. Oh, here's a peso, buy yourself a house. Run over there, do this, do that."

"It wasn't me."

"He looked like you, anyway."

They stood in the sun with their shadows dark under them, and the perspiration coloring their armpits. The soldier moved closer to John Webb. "I don't have to do anything for you anymore."

"You never had to before. I never asked it."

"You're trembling, *señor*."

"I'm all right. It's the sun."

"How much money have you got?" asked the guard.

"A thousand pesos to let us through, and a thousand for the other man over there."

The guard turned again. "Will a thousand pesos be enough?"

"No," said the other guard. "Tell him to report us!"

"Yes," said the guard, back to Webb again. "Report me. Get me fired. I was fired once, years ago, by you."

"It was someone else."

"Take my name. It is Carlos Rodriguez Ysotl. Go on now."

"I see."

"No, you don't see," said Carlos Rodriguez Ysotl. "Now give me two thousand pesos."

John Webb took out his wallet and handed over the money. Carlos Rodriguez Ysotl licked his thumb and counted the money slowly under the blue glazed sky of his country as noon deepened and sweat arose from hidden sources and people breathed and panted above their shadows.

"Two thousand pesos." He folded it and put it in his pocket quietly. "Now turn your car around and head for another border."

"Hold on now, damn it!"

The guard looked at him. "Turn your car."

They stood a long time that way, with the sun blazing on the rifle in the guard's hands, not speaking. And then John Webb turned and walked slowly, one hand to his face, back to the car and slid into the front seat.

"What're we going to do?" said Leonora.

"Rot. Or try to reach Porto Bello."

"But we need gas and our spare fixed. And going back over those high-ways . . . This time they might drop logs, and—"

"I know, I know." He rubbed his eyes and sat for a moment with his head in his hands. "We're alone, my God, we're alone. Remember how safe we used to feel? How safe? We registered in all the big towns with the American Consuls. Remember how the joke went? 'Everywhere you go you can hear the rustle of the eagle's wings!' Or was it the sound of paper money? I forget. Jesus, Jesus, the world got empty awfully quick. Who do I call on now?"

She waited a moment and then said, "I guess just me. That's not much."

He put his arm around her. "You've been swell. No hysterics, nothing."

"Tonight maybe I'll be screaming, when we're in bed, if we ever find a bed again. It's been a million miles since breakfast."

He kissed her, twice, on her dry mouth. Then he sat slowly back. "First thing is to try to find gas. If we can get that, we're ready to head for Porto Bello."

The three soldiers were talking and joking as they drove away.

After they had been driving a minute, he began to laugh quietly.

"What were you thinking?" asked his wife.

"I remember an old spiritual. It goes like this:

> " '*I went to the Rock to hide my face*
> *And the Rock cried out, "No Hiding Place,*
> *There's no Hiding Place down here."* ' "

"I remember that," she said.

"It's an appropriate song right now," he said. "I'd sing the whole thing for you if I could remember it all. And if I felt like singing."

He put his foot harder to the accelerator.

They stopped at a gas station and after a minute, when the attendant did not appear, John Webb honked the horn. Then, appalled, he snapped his hand away from the horn-ring, looking at it as if it were the hand of a leper.

"I shouldn't have done that."

The attendant appeared in the shadowy doorway of the gas station. Two other men appeared behind him.

The three men came out and walked around the car, looking at it, touching it, feeling it.

Their faces were like burned copper in the daylight. They touched the resilient tires, they sniffed the rich new smell of the metal and upholstery.

"*Señor*," said the gas attendant at last.

"We'd like to buy some gas, please."

"We are all out of gas, *señor*."

"But your tank reads full. I see the gas in the glass container up there."

"We are all out of gas," said the man.

"I'll give you ten pesos a gallon!"

"*Gracias*, no."

"We haven't enough gas to get anywhere from here." Webb checked the gauge. "Not even a quarter gallon left. We'd better leave the car here and go into town and see what we can do there."

"I'll watch the car for you, *señor*," said the station attendant. "If you leave the keys."

"We can't do that!" said Leonora. "Can we?"

"I don't see what choice we have. We can stall it on the road and leave it to anyone who comes along, or leave it with this man."

"That's better," said the man.

They climbed out of the car and stood looking at it.

"It was a beautiful car," said John Webb.

"Very beautiful," said the man, his hand out for the keys. "I will take good care of it, *señor*."

"But, Jack—"

She opened the back door and started to take out the luggage. Over her shoulder, he saw the bright travel stickers, the storm of color that had descended upon and covered the worn leather now after years of travel, after years of the best hotels in two dozen countries.

She tugged at the valises, perspiring, and he stopped her hands and they stood gasping there for a moment, in the open door of the car, looking at these fine rich suitcases, inside which were the beautiful tweeds and woolens and silks of their lives and living, the forty-dollar-an-ounce perfumes and the cool dark furs and the silvery golf shafts. Twenty years were packed into each of the cases; twenty years and four dozen parts they had played in Rio, in Paris, in Rome and Shanghai, but the part they played most frequently and best of all was the rich and buoyant, amazingly happy Webbs, the smiling people, the ones who could make that rarely balanced martini known as the Sahara.

"We can't carry it all into town," he said. "We'll come back for it later. Later."

"But . . ."

He silenced her by turning her away and starting her off down the road.

"But we can't leave it there, we can't leave all our luggage and we can't leave our car! Oh look here now, I'll roll up the windows and lock myself in the car, while you go for the gas, why not?" she said.

He stopped and glanced back at the three men standing by the car, which blazed in the yellow sun. Their eyes were shining and looking at the woman.

"There's your answer," he said. "Come on."

"But you just *don't* walk off and leave a four-thousand-dollar automobile!" she cried.

He moved her along, holding her elbow firmly and with quiet decision. "A car is to travel in. When it's not traveling, it's useless. Right now, we've got to travel; that's everything. The car isn't worth a dime without gas in it. A pair of good strong legs is worth a hundred cars, if you use the legs. We've just begun to toss things overboard. We'll keep dropping ballast until there's nothing left to heave but our hides."

He let her go. She was walking steadily now, and she fell into step with him. "It's so strange. So strange. I haven't walked like this in years." She watched the motion of her feet beneath her, she watched the road pass by, she watched the jungle moving to either side, she watched her husband striding quickly along, until she seemed hypnotized by the steady rhythm. "But I guess you can learn anything over again," she said, at last.

The sun moved in the sky and they moved for a long while on the hot road. When he was quite ready, the husband began to think aloud. "You know, in a way, I think it's good to be down to essentials. Now instead of worrying over a dozen damned things, it's just two items—you and me."

"Watch it, here comes a car—we'd better . . ."

They half turned, yelled, and jumped. They fell away from the highway and lay watching the automobile hurtle past at seventy miles an hour. Voices sang, men laughed, men shouted, waving. The car sped away into the dust and vanished around a curve, blaring its double horns again and again.

He helped her up and they stood in the quiet road.

"Did you see it?"

They watched the dust settle slowly.

"I hope they remember to change the oil and check the battery, at least. I hope they think to put water in the radiator," she said, and paused. "They were singing, weren't they?"

He nodded. They stood blinking at the great dust cloud filtering down like yellow pollen upon their heads and arms. He saw a few bright splashes flick from her eyelids when she blinked.

"Don't," he said. "After all, it was only a machine."

"I loved it."

"We're always loving everything too much."

Walking, they passed a shattered wine bottle which steamed freshly as they stepped over it.

＊ They were not far from the town, walking single file, the wife ahead, the husband following, looking at their feet as they walked, when a sound of tin and steam and bubbling water made them turn and look at the road behind them. An old man in a 1929 Ford drove along the road at a moderate speed. The car's fenders were gone, and the sun had flaked and burned the paint badly, but he rode in the seat with a great deal of quiet dignity, his face a thoughtful darkness under a dirty Panama hat, and when he saw the two people he drew the car up, steaming, the engine joggling under the hood, and opened the squealing door as he said, "This is no day for walking."

"Thank you," they said.

"It is nothing." The old man wore an ancient yellowed white summer suit, with a rather greasy tie knotted loosely at his wrinkled throat. He helped the lady into the rear seat with a gracious bow of his head. "Let us men sit up front," he suggested, and the husband sat up front and the car moved off in trembling vapors.

"Well. My name is Garcia."

There were introductions and noddings.

"Your car broke down? You are on your way for help?" said _Señor_ García.

"Yes."

"Then let me drive you and a mechanic back out," offered the old man.

They thanked him and kindly turned the offer aside and he made it once again, but upon finding that his interest and concern caused them embarrassment, he very politely turned to another subject.

He touched a small stack of folded newspapers on his lap.

"Do you read the papers? Of course, you do. But do you read them as I read them? I rather doubt that you have come upon my system. No, it was not exactly myself that came upon it; the system was forced upon me. But now I know what a clever thing it has turned out to be. I always get the newspapers a week late. All of us, those who are interested, get the papers a week late, from the Capital. And this circumstance makes for a man being a clear-thinking man. You are very careful with your thinking when you pick up a week-old paper."

The husband and wife asked him to continue.

"Well," said the old man, "I remember once, when I lived in the Capital for a month and bought the paper fresh each day, I went wild with love, anger, irritation, frustration; all of the passions boiled in me. I was young. I exploded at everything I saw. But then I saw what I was doing: I was believing what I read. Have you noticed? You believe a paper printed on the very day you buy it? This has happened but only an hour ago, you think! It must be true." He shook his head. "So I learned to stand back away and let the paper age and mellow. Back here, in Colonia, I saw the headlines diminish to nothing. The week-old paper—why, you can spit on it if you wish. It is like a woman you once loved, but you now see, a few days later, she is not quite what you thought. She has rather a plain face. She is no deeper than a cup of water."

He steered the car gently, his hands upon the wheel as upon the heads of his good children, with care and affection. "So here I am, returning to my home to read my weekly papers, to peek sideways at them, to toy with them." He spread one on his knee, glancing down to it on occasion as he drove. "How white this paper is, like the mind of a child that is an idiot, poor thing, all blank. You can put anything into an empty place like that. Here, do you see? This paper speaks and says that the light-skinned people of the world are dead. Now that is a very silly thing to say. At this very moment, there are probably millions upon millions of white men and women eating their noon meals or their suppers. The earth trembles, a town collapses, people run from the town, screaming, *All is lost!* In the next village, the population wonders what all of the shouting is about, since *they* have had a most splendid night's repose. Ah, ah, what a sly world it is. People do not see how sly it is. It is either night or day to them. Rumor flies. This very afternoon all of the little villages upon this highway, behind us and ahead of us, are in carnival. The white man is dead, the rumors say, and yet here I come into the town with two very lively ones. I hope you don't mind my speaking in this way? If I do not talk to you I would then be talking to this engine up in the front, which makes a great noise speaking back."

They were at the edge of town.

"Please," said John Webb, "it wouldn't be wise for you to be seen with us today. We'll get out here."

The old man stopped his car reluctantly and said, "You are most kind and thoughtful of me." He turned to look at the lovely wife.

"When I was a young man I was very full of wildness and ideas. I read all of the books from France by a man named Jules Verne. I see you know his name. But at night I many times thought I must be an inventor. That is all gone by; I never did what I thought I might do. But I remember clearly that one of the machines I wished to put together was a machine that would help every man, for an hour, to be like any other man. The machine was full of colors and smells and it had film in it, like a theater, and the machine was like a coffin. You lay in it. And you touched a button. And for an hour you could be one of those Eskimos in the cold wind up there, or you could be an Arab gentleman on a horse. Everything a New York man felt, you could feel. Everything a man from Sweden smelled, you could smell. Everything a man from China tasted, your tongue knew. The machine was like another man—do you see what I was after? And by touching many of the buttons, each time you got into my machine, you could be a white man or a yellow man or a Negrito. You could be a child or a woman, even, if you wished to be very funny."

The husband and wife climbed from the car.

"Did you ever try to invent that machine?"

"It was so very long ago. I had forgotten until today. And today I was thinking, we could make use of it, we are in need of it. What a shame I never tried to put it all together. Someday some other man will do it."

"Someday," said John Webb.

"It has been a pleasure talking with you," said the old man. "God go with you."

"*Adiós, Señor* Garcia," they said.

The car drove slowly away, steaming. They stood watching it go, for a full minute. Then, without speaking, the husband reached over and took his wife's hand.

✳ They entered the small town of Colonia on foot. They walked past the little shops—the butcher shop, the photographer's. People stopped and looked at them as they went by and did not stop looking at them as long as they were in sight. Every few seconds, as he walked, Webb put up his hand to touch the holster hidden under his coat, secretly, tentatively, like someone feeling for a tiny boil that is growing and growing every hour and every hour . . .

The patio of the Hotel Esposa was cool as a grotto under a blue waterfall. In it caged birds sang, and footsteps echoed like small rifle shots, clear and smooth.

"Remember? We stopped here years ago," said Webb, helping his wife up the steps. They stood in the cool grotto, glad of the blue shade.

"*Señor* Esposa," said John Webb, when a fat man came forward from the desk, squinting at them. "Do you remember me—John Webb? Five years ago—we played cards one night."

"Of course, of course." *Señor* Esposa bowed to the wife and shook hands briefly. There was an uncomfortable silence.

Webb cleared his throat. "We've had a bit of trouble, *señor*. Could we have a room for tonight only?"

"Your money is always good here."

"You mean you'll actually give us a room? We'll be glad to pay in advance. Lord, we need the rest. But, more than that, we need gas."

Leonora picked at her husband's arm. "Remember? We haven't a car anymore."

"Oh. Yes." He fell silent for a moment and then sighed. "Well. Never mind the gas. Is there a bus out of here for the Capital soon?"

"All will be attended to, in time," said the manager nervously. "This way."

As they were climbing the stairs they heard a noise. Looking out they saw their car riding around and around the plaza, eight times, loaded with men who were shouting and singing and hanging on to the front fenders, laughing. Children and dogs ran after the car.

"I would like to own a car like that," said *Señor* Esposa.

✳ He poured a little cool wine for the three of them, standing in the room on the third floor of the Esposa Hotel.

"To 'change,'" said *Señor* Esposa.

"I'll drink to that."

They drank. *Señor* Esposa licked his lips and wiped them on his coat sleeve. "We are always surprised and saddened to see the world change. It is insane, they have run out on us, you say. It is unbelievable. And now, well—you are safe for the night. Shower and have a good supper. I won't be able to keep you more than one night, to repay you for your kindness to me five years ago."

"And tomorrow?"

"Tomorrow? Do not take any bus to the Capital, please. There are riots in the streets there. A few people from the North have been killed. It is nothing. It will pass in a few days. But you must be careful until those few days pass and the blood cools. There are many wicked people taking advantage of this day, *señor*. For forty-eight hours anyway, under the guise of a great resurgence of nationalism, these people will try to gain power. Selfishness and patriotism, *señor*; today I cannot tell one from the other. So— you must hide. That is a problem. The town will know you are here in another few hours. This might be dangerous to my hotel. I cannot say."

"We understand. It's good of you to help *this* much."

"If you need anything, call me." *Señor* Esposa drank the rest of the wine in his glass. "Finish the bottle," he said.

✳ The fireworks began at nine that evening. First one skyrocket then another soared into the dark sky and burst out upon the winds, building architectures of flame. Each skyrocket, at the top of its ride, cracked open and let out a formation of streamers in red and white flame that made something like the dome of a beautiful cathedral.

Leonora and John Webb stood by the open window in their unlit room, watching and listening. As the hour latened, more people streamed into town from every road and path and began to roam, arm in arm, around the plaza, singing, barking like dogs, crowing like roosters, and then falling down on the tile sidewalks, sitting there, laughing, their heads thrown back, while the skyrockets burst explosive colors on the tilted faces. A brass band began to thump and wheeze.

"So here we are," said John Webb, "after a few hundred years of living high. So this is what's left of our white supremacy—you and I in a dark room in a hotel three hundred miles inside a celebrating country."

"You've got to see their side of it."

"Oh, I've seen it ever since I was that high. In a way, I'm glad they're happy. God knows they've waited long enough to be. But I wonder how long that happiness will last. Now that the scapegoat is gone, who will they blame for oppression, who will be as handy and as obvious and as guilty as you and I and the man who lived in this room before us?"

"I don't know."

"We were so convenient. The man who rented this room last month, he was convenient, he stood out. He made loud jokes about the natives' siestas. He refused to learn even a smattering of Spanish. Let them learn English, by God, and speak like men, he said. And he drank too much and whored too much with this country's women." He broke off and moved back from the window. He stared at the room.

The furniture, he thought. Where *he* put his dirty shoes upon the sofa, where *he* burned holes in the carpet with cigarettes; the wet spot on the wall near the bed, God knows what or how he did *that*. The chairs scarred and kicked. It wasn't his hotel or his room; it was borrowed, it meant nothing. So this son-of-a-bitch went around the country for the past one hundred years, a traveling commercial, a Chamber of Commerce, and now here *we* are, enough like him to be his brother and sister, and there *they* are down there on the night of the Butlers' Ball. They don't know, or if they know they won't think of it, that tomorrow they'll be just as poor, just as oppressed as ever, that the whole machine will only have shifted into another gear.

Now the band had stopped playing below; a man had leaped up, shouting, on the bandstand. There was a flash of machetes in the air and the brown gleam of half-naked bodies.

The man on the bandstand faced the hotel and looked up at the dark room where John and Leonora Webb now stood back out of the intermittent flares.

The man shouted.

"What does he say?" asked Leonora.

John Webb translated: " 'It is now a free world,' he says."

The man yelled.

John Webb translated again. "He says, 'We are *free*!'"

The man lifted himself on his toes and made a motion of breaking manacles. "He says, 'No one owns us, no one in all the world.' "

The crowd roared and the band began to play, and while it was playing, the man on the grandstand stood glaring up at the room window, with all of the hatred of the universe in his eyes.

＊ During the night there were fights and pummelings and voices lifted, arguments and shots fired. John Webb lay awake and heard the voice of *Señor* Esposa below, reasoning, talking quietly, firmly. And then the fading away of the tumult, the last rockets in the sky, the last breakings of bottles on the cobbles.

At five in the morning the air was warming into a new day. There was the softest of taps on the bedroom door.

"It is me, it is Esposa," said a voice.

John Webb hesitated, half-dressed, numbed on his feet from lack of sleep, then opened the door.

"What a night, what a night!" said *Señor* Esposa, coming in, shaking his head, laughing gently. "Did you hear that noise? Yes? They tried to come up here to your room. I prevented this."

"Thank you" said Leonora, still in bed, turned to the wall.

"They were all old friends. I made an agreement with them, anyway. They were drunk enough and happy enough so they agreed to wait. I am to make a proposition to you two." Suddenly he seemed embarrassed. He moved to the window. "Everyone is sleeping late. A few are up. A few men. See them there on the far side of the plaza?"

John Webb looked out at the plaza. He saw the brown men talking quietly there about the weather, the world, the sun, this town, and perhaps the wine.

"*Señor*, have you ever been hungry in your life?"

"For a day, once."

"Only for a day. Have you always had a house to live in and a car to drive?"

"Until yesterday."

"Were you ever without a job?"

"Never."

"Did all of your brothers and sisters live to be twenty-one years old?"

"All of them."

"Even I," said *Señor* Esposa, "even *I* hate you a little bit now. For *I* have been without a home. *I* have been hungry. *I* have three brothers and one sister buried in that graveyard on the hill beyond the town, all dead of tuberculosis before they were nine years old."

Señor Esposa glanced at the men in the plaza. "Now, I am no longer hungry or poor, I have a car, I am alive. But I am one in a thousand. What can *you* say to them out there today?"

"I'll try to think of something."

"Long ago I stopped trying. *Señor*, we have *always* been a minority, we white people. I am Spanish, but I was born here. They tolerate me."

"We have never let ourselves think about our being a minority," said Webb, "and now it's hard to get used to the fact."

"You have behaved beautifully."

"Is that a virtue?"

"In the bull ring, yes; in war, yes; in anything like this, most assuredly yes. You do not complain, you do not make excuses. You do not run and make a spectacle of yourself. I think you are both very brave."

The hotel manager sat down, slowly, helplessly.

"I've come to offer you the chance to settle down," he said.

"We wanted to move on, if possible."

The manager shrugged. "Your car is stolen, I can do nothing to get it back. You cannot leave town. Remain then and accept my offer of a position in my hotel."

"You don't think there is any way for us to travel?"

"It might be twenty days, señor, or twenty years. You cannot exist without money, food, lodging. Consider my hotel and the work I can give you."

The manager arose and walked unhappily to the door and stood by the chair, touching Webb's coat, which was draped over it.

"What's the job?" asked Webb.

"In the kitchen," said the manager, and looked away.

John Webb sat on the bed and said nothing. His wife did not move.

Señor Esposa said, "It is the best I can do. What more can you ask of me? Last night, those others down in the plaza wanted both of you. Did you see the machetes? I bargained with them. You were lucky. I told them you would be employed in my hotel for the next twenty years, that you were my employees and deserve my protection!"

"You said that!"

"Señor, señor, be thankful! Consider! Where will you go? The jungle? You will be dead in two hours from the snakes. Then can you walk five hundred miles to a capital which will not welcome you? No—you must face the reality." Señor Esposa opened the door. "I offer you an honest job and you will be paid the standard wages of two pesos a day, plus meals. Would you rather be with me, or out in the plaza at noon with our friends? Consider."

The door was shut. Señor Esposa was gone.

Webb stood looking at the door for a long while.

Then he walked to the chair and fumbled with the holster under the draped white shirt. The holster was empty. He held it in his hands and blinked at its emptiness and looked again at the door through which Señor Esposa had just passed. He went over and sat down on the bed beside his wife. He stretched out beside her and took her in his arms and kissed her, and they lay there, watching the room get brighter with the new day.

✳ At eleven o'clock in the morning, with the great doors on the windows of their room flung back, they began to dress. There were soap, towels, shaving equipment, even perfume in the bathroom, provided by Mr. Esposa.

John Webb shaved and dressed carefully.

At eleven-thirty he turned on the small radio near their bed. You could usually get New York or Cleveland or Houston on such a radio. But the air was silent. John Webb turned the radio off.

"There's nothing to go back to—nothing to go back for—nothing."

His wife sat on a chair near the door, looking at the wall.

"We could stay here and work," he said.

She stirred at last. "No. We couldn't do that, not really. Could we?"

"No, I guess not."

"There's no way we could do that. We're being consistent, anyway; spoiled, but consistent."

He thought a moment. "We could make for the jungle."

"I don't think we can move from the hotel without being seen. We don't want to try to escape and be caught. It would be far worse that way."

He nodded.

They both sat a moment.

"It might not be too bad, working here," he said.

"What would we be living for? Everyone's dead—your father, mine, your mother, mine, your brothers, mine, all our friends, everything gone, everything we understood."

He nodded.

"Or if we took the job, one day soon one of the men would touch me and you'd go after him, you know you would. Or someone would do something to you, and I'd do something."

He nodded again.

They sat for fifteen minutes, talking quietly. Then, at last, he picked up the telephone and ticked the cradle with his finger.

"*Bueno*," said a voice on the other end.

"*Señor Esposa?*"

"*Sí.*"

"*Señor Esposa*," he paused and licked his lips, "tell your friends we will be leaving the hotel at noon."

The phone did not immediately reply. Then with a sigh *Señor* Esposa said, "As you wish. You are sure—?"

The phone was silent for a full minute. Then it was picked up again and the manager said quietly, "My friends say they will be waiting for you on the far side of the plaza."

"We will meet them there," said John Webb.

"And *señor*—"

"Yes."

"Do not hate me, do not hate us."

"I don't hate anybody."

"It is a bad world, *señor*. None of us know how we got here or what we are doing. These men don't know what they are mad at, except they are mad. Forgive them and do not hate them."

"I don't hate them or you."

"Thank you, thank you." Perhaps the man on the far end of the telephone wire was crying. There was no way to tell. There were great lapses in his talking, in his breathing. After a while he said, "We don't know why we do anything. Men hit each other for no reason except they are unhappy. Remember that. I am your friend. I would help you if I could. But I cannot. It would be me against the town. Good-bye, *señor*." He hung up.

John Webb sat in the chair with his hand on the silent phone. It was a moment before he glanced up. It was a moment before his eyes focused on an object immediately before him. When he saw it clearly, he still did not move, but sat regarding it, until a look of immensely tired irony appeared on his mouth. "Look here," he said at last.

Leonora followed his motion, his pointing.

They both sat looking at his cigarette which, neglected on the rim of the table while he telephoned, had burned down so that now it had charred a black hole in the clean surface of the wood.

It was noon, with the sun directly over them, pinning their shadows under them as they started down the steps of the Hotel Esposa. Behind them, the birds fluted in their bamboo cages, and water ran in a little fountain bath. They were as neat as they could get, their faces and hands washed, their nails clean, their shoes polished.

Across the plaza two hundred yards away stood a small group of men, in the shade of a store-front overhang. Some of the men were natives from the jungle area, with machetes gleaming at their sides. They were all facing the plaza.

John Webb looked at them for a long while. That isn't everyone, he thought, that isn't the whole country. That's only the surface. That's only the thin skin over the flesh. It's not the body at all. Just the shell of an egg. Remember the crowds back home, the mobs, the riots? Always the same, there or here. A few mad faces up front, and the quiet ones far back, not taking part, letting things go, not wanting to be in it. The majority not moving. And so the few, the handful, take over and move for them.

His eyes did not blink. If we could break through that shell—God knows it's thin! he thought. If we could talk our way through that mob and get to the quiet people beyond. . . . Can I do it? Can I say the right things? Can I keep my voice down?

He fumbled in his pockets and brought out a rumpled cigarette package and some matches.

I can try, he thought. How would the old man in the Ford have done it? I'll try to do it his way. When we get across the plaza, I'll start talking, I'll whisper if necessary. And if we move slowly through the mob, we might just possibly find our way to the other people and we'll be on high ground and we'll be safe.

Leonora moved beside him. She was so fresh, so well groomed in spite of everything, so new in all this oldness, so startling, that his mind flinched and jerked. He found himself staring at her as if she'd betrayed him by her salt-whiteness, her wonderfully brushed hair and her cleanly manicured nails and her bright-red mouth.

Standing on the bottom step, Webb lit a cigarette, took two or three long drags on it, tossed it down, stepped on it, kicked the flattened butt into the street, and said, "Here we go."

They stepped down and started around the far side of the plaza, past the few shops that were still open. They walked quietly.

"Perhaps they'll be decent to us."

"We can hope so."

They passed a photographic shop.

"It's another day. Anything can happen. I believe that. No—I don't really believe it. I'm only talking. I've got to talk or I wouldn't be able to walk," she said.

They passed a candy shop.

"Keep talking, then."

"I'm afraid," she said. "This can't be happening to us! Are we the last ones in the world?"

"Maybe next to the last."

They approached an open air *carnecería*.

God! he thought. How the horizons narrowed, how they came in. A year ago there weren't four directions, there were a million for us. Yesterday they got down to four; we could go to Juatala, Porto Bello, San Juan Clementas, or Brioconbria. We were satisfied to have our car. Then when we couldn't get gas, we were satisfied to have our clothes, then when they took our clothes, we were satisfied to have a place to sleep. Each pleasure they took away left us with one other creature comfort to hold on to. Did you see how we let go of one thing and clutched another so quickly? I guess that's human. So they took away everything. There's nothing left. Except us. It all boils down to just you and me walking along here, and thinking too god-damn much for my own good. And what counts in the end is whether they can take you away from me or me away from you, Lee, and I don't think they can do that. They've got everything else and I don't blame them. But they can't really do anything else to us now. When you strip all the clothes away and the doodads, you have two human beings who were either happy or unhappy together, and we have no complaints.

"Walk slowly," said John Webb.

"I am."

"Not too slowly, to look reluctant. Not too fast, to look as if you want to get it over with. Don't give them the satisfaction, Lee, don't give them a damn bit."

"I won't."

They walked. "Don't even touch me," he said, quietly. "Don't even hold my hand."

"Oh, please!"

"No, not even that."

He moved away a few inches and kept walking steadily. His eyes were straight ahead and their pace was regular.

"I'm beginning to cry, Jack."

"Goddamn it!" he said, measuredly, between his teeth, not looking aside. "Stop it! Do you want me to run? Is that what you want—do you want me to take you and run into the jungle, and let them hunt us, is that what you want, goddamn it, do you want me to fall down in the street here and grovel and scream, shut up, let's do this right, don't give them *anything*!"

"All right," she said, hands tight, her head coming up. "I'm not crying now. I won't cry."

"Good, damn it, that's good."

And still, strangely, they were not past the *carnecería*. The vision of red horror was on their left as they paced steadily forward on the hot tile side-walk. The things that hung from hooks looked like brutalities and sins, like bad consciences, evil dreams, like gored flags and slaughtered promises.

The redness, oh, the hanging, evil-smelling wetness and redness, the hooked and hung-high carcasses, unfamiliar, unfamiliar.

As he passed the shop, something made John Webb strike out a hand. He slapped it smartly against a strung-up side of beef. A mantle of blue buzzing flies lifted angrily and swirled in a bright cone over the meat.

Leonora said, looking ahead, walking, "They're all strangers! I don't know any of them. I wish I knew even *one* of them. I wish even *one* of them knew me!"

They walked on past the *carnecería*. The side of beef, red and irritable-looking, swung in the hot sunlight after they passed.

The flies came down in a feeding cloak to cover the meat, once it had stopped swinging.

THE DRUMMER BOY OF SHILOH

In the April night, more than once, blossoms fell from the orchard trees and lit with rustling taps on the drumskin. At midnight a peach stone left miraculously on a branch through winter, flicked by a bird, fell swift and unseen, struck once, like panic, which jerked the boy upright. In silence he listened to his own heart ruffle away, away, at last gone from his ears and back in his chest again.

After that, he turned the drum on its side, where its great lunar face peered at him whenever he opened his eyes.

His face, alert or at rest, was solemn. It was indeed a solemn time and a solemn night for a boy just turned fourteen in the peach field near the Owl Creek not far from the church at Shiloh.

". . . thirty-one, thirty-two, thirty-three . . ."

Unable to see, he stopped counting.

Beyond the thirty-three familiar shadows, forty thousand men, exhausted by nervous expectation, unable to sleep for romantic dreams of battles yet unfought, lay crazily askew in their uniforms. A mile yet farther on, another army was strewn helter-skelter, turning slow, basting themselves with the thought of what they would do when the time came: a leap, a yell, a blind plunge their strategy, raw youth their protection and benediction.

Now and again the boy heard a vast wind come up, that gently stirred the air. But he knew what it was, the army here, the army there, whispering to itself in the dark. Some men talking to others, others murmuring to themselves, and all so quiet it was like a natural element arisen from south or north with the motion of the earth toward dawn.

What the men whispered the boy could only guess, and he guessed that it was: Me, I'm the one, I'm the one of all the rest won't die. I'll live through it. I'll go home. The band will play. And I'll be there to hear it.

Yes, thought the boy, that's all very well for them, they can give as good as they get!

For with the careless bones of the young men harvested by night and bindled around campfires were the similarly strewn steel bones of their rifles, with bayonets fixed like eternal lightning lost in the orchard grass.

Me, thought the boy, I got only a drum, two sticks to beat it, and no shield.

There wasn't a man-boy on this ground tonight did not have a shield he cast, riveted or carved himself on his way to his first attack, compounded of remote but nonetheless firm and fiery family devotion, flag-blown patriotism and cocksure immortality strengthened by the touchstone of very real gunpowder, ramrod, miniéball and flint. But without these last the boy felt his family move yet farther off away in the dark, as if one of those great prairie-burning trains had chanted them away never to return, leaving him with this drum which was worse than a toy in the game to be played tomorrow or some day much too soon.

The boy turned on his side. A moth brushed his face, but it was peach blossom. A peach blossom flicked him, but it was a moth. Nothing stayed put. Nothing had a name. Nothing was as it once was.

If he lay very still, when the dawn came up and the soldiers put on their bravery with their caps, perhaps they might go away, the war with them, and not notice him lying small here, no more than a toy himself.

✳ "Well, by God, now," said a voice.

The boy shut up his eyes, to hide inside himself, but it was too late. Someone, walking by in the night, stood over him.

"Well," said the voice quietly, "here's a soldier crying *before* the fight. Good. Get it over. Won't be time once it all starts."

And the voice was about to move on when the boy, startled, touched the drum at his elbow. The man above, hearing this, stopped. The boy could feel his eyes, sense him slowly bending near. A hand must have come down out of the night, for there was a little rat-tat as the fingernails brushed and the man's breath fanned his face.

"Why, it's the drummer boy, isn't it?"

The boy nodded, not knowing if his nod was seen. "Sir, is that *you*?" he said.

"I assume it is." The man's knees cracked as he bent still closer.

He smelled as all fathers should smell, of salt sweat, ginger tobacco, horse and boot leather, and the earth he walked upon. He had many eyes. No, not eyes, brass buttons that watched the boy.

He could only be, and was, the General.

"What's your name, boy?" he asked.

"Joby," whispered the boy, starting to sit up.

"All right, Joby, don't stir." A hand pressed his chest gently, and the boy relaxed. "How long you been with us, Joby?"

"Three weeks, sir."

"Run off from home or joined legitimately, boy?"

Silence.

"Damn-fool question," said the General. "Do you shave yet, boy? Even more of a damn-fool. There's your cheek, fell right off the tree overhead. And the others here not much older. Raw, raw, damn raw, the lot of you. You ready for tomorrow or the next day, Joby?"

"I think so, sir."

"You want to cry some more, go on ahead. I did the same last night."

"You, sir?"

"God's truth. Thinking of everything ahead. Both sides figuring the other side will just give up, and soon, and the war done in weeks, and us all home. Well, that's not how it's going to be. And maybe that's why I cried."

"Yes, sir," said Joby.

The General must have taken out a cigar now, for the dark was suddenly filled with the Indian smell of tobacco unlit as yet, but chewed as the man thought what next to say.

"It's going to be a crazy time," said the General. "Counting both sides, there's a hundred thousand men, give or take a few thousand out there tonight, not one as can spit a sparrow off a tree, or knows a horse clod from a miniéball. Stand up, bare the breast, ask to be a target, thank them and sit down, that's us, that's them. We should turn tail and train four months, they should do the same. But here we are, taken with spring fever and thinking it blood lust, taking our sulfur with cannons instead of with molasses as it should be, going to be a hero, going to live forever. And I can see all of them over there nodding agreement, save the other way around. It's wrong, boy, it's wrong as a head put on hind side front and a man marching backward through life. It will be a double massacre if one of their itchy generals decides to picnic his lads on our grass. More innocents will get shot out of pure Cherokee enthusiasm than ever got shot before. Owl Creek was full of boys splashing around in the noonday sun just a few hours ago. I fear it will be full of boys again, just floating, at sundown tomorrow, not caring where the tide takes them."

The General stopped and made a little pile of winter leaves and twigs in the darkness, as if he might at any moment strike fire to them to see his way through the coming days when the sun might not show its face because of what was happening here and just beyond.

The boy watched the hand stirring the leaves and opened his lips to say something, but did not say it. The General heard the boy's breath and spoke himself.

"Why am I telling you this? That's what you wanted to ask, eh? Well, when you got a bunch of wild horses on a loose rein somewhere, somehow you got to bring order, rein them in. These lads, fresh out of the milkshed, don't know what I know, and I can't tell them: men actually die, in war. So each is his own army. I got to make *one* army of them. And for that, boy, I need you."

"Me!" The boy's lips barely twitched.

"Now, boy," said the General quietly, "you are the heart of the army. Think of that. You're the heart of the army. Listen, now."

And, lying there, Joby listened.

And the General spoke on.

If he, Joby, beat slow tomorrow, the heart would beat slow in the men. They would lag by the wayside. They would drowse in the fields on their muskets. They would sleep forever, after that, in those same fields, their hearts slowed by a drummer boy and stopped by enemy lead.

But if he beat a sure, steady, ever faster rhythm, then, then their knees would come up in a long line down over that hill, one knee after the other, like a wave on the ocean shore! Had he seen the ocean ever? Seen the waves rolling in like a well-ordered cavalry charge to the sand? Well, that was it, that's what he wanted, that's what was needed! Joby was his right hand and his left. He gave the orders, but Joby set the pace!

So bring the right knee up and the right foot out and the left knee up and the left foot out. One following the other in good time, in brisk time. Move the blood up the body and make the head proud and the spine stiff and the jaw resolute. Focus the eye and set the teeth, flare the nostrils and tighten the hands, put steel armor all over the men, for blood moving fast in them does indeed make men feel as if they'd put on steel. He must keep at it, at it! Long and steady, steady and long! Then, even though shot or torn, those wounds got in hot blood—in blood he'd helped stir—would feel less pain. If their blood was cold, it would be more than slaughter, it would be murderous nightmare and pain best not told and no one to guess.

The General spoke and stopped, letting his breath slack off. Then, after a moment, he said, "So there you are, that's it. Will you do that, boy? Do you know now you're general of the army when the General's left behind?"

The boy nodded mutely.

"You'll run them through for me then, boy?"

"Yes, sir."

"Good. And, God willing, many nights from tonight, many years from now, when you're as old or far much older than me, when they ask you what you did in this awful time, you will tell them—one part humble and one part proud—'I was the drummer boy at the battle of Owl Creek,' or the Tennessee River, or maybe they'll just name it after the church there. 'I was the drummer boy at Shiloh.' Good grief, that has a beat and sound to it fitting for Mr. Longfellow. 'I was the drummer boy at Shiloh.' Who will ever hear those words and not know you, boy, or what you thought this night, or what you'll think tomorrow or the next day when we must get up on our legs and *move*?"

The General stood up. "Well, then. God bless you, boy. Good night."

"Good night, sir."

And, tobacco, brass, boot polish, salt sweat and leather, the man moved away through the grass.

Joby lay for a moment, staring but unable to see where the man had gone.

He swallowed. He wiped his eyes. He cleared his throat. He settled himself. Then, at last, very slowly and firmly, he turned the drum so that it faced up toward the sky.

He lay next to it, his arm around it, feeling the tremor, the touch, the muted thunder as, all the rest of the April night in the year 1862, near the Tennessee River, not far from the Owl Creek, very close to the church named Shiloh, the peach blossoms fell on the drum.

THE BEGGAR ON O'CONNELL BRIDGE

"A fool," I said. "That's what I am."

"Why?" asked my wife. "What for?"

I brooded by our third-floor hotel window. On the Dublin street below, a man passed, his face to the lamplight.

"Him," I muttered. "Two days ago . . ."

Two days ago, as I was walking along, someone had hissed at me from the hotel alley. "Sir, it's important! Sir!"

I turned into the shadow. This little man, in the direst tones, said, "I've a job in Belfast if I just had a pound for the train fare!"

I hesitated.

"A most important job!" he went on swiftly. "Pays well! I'll—I'll mail you back the loan! Just give me your name and hotel."

He knew me for a tourist. It was too late, his promise to pay had moved me. The pound note crackled in my hand, being worked free from several others.

The man's eye skimmed like a shadowing hawk.

"And if I had two pounds, why, I could eat on the way."

I uncrumpled two bills.

"And three pounds would bring the wife, not leave her here alone."

I unleafed a third.

"Ah, hell!" cried the man. "Five, just five poor pounds, would find us a hotel in that brutal city, and let me get to the job, for sure!"

What a dancing fighter he was, light on his toes, in and out, weaving, tapping with his hands, flicking with his eyes, smiling with his mouth, jabbing with his tongue.

"Lord thank you, bless you, sir!"

He ran, my five pounds with him.

I was half in the hotel before I realized that, for all his vows, he had not recorded my name.

"Gah!" I cried then.

"Gah!" I cried now, my wife behind me, at the window.

For there, passing below, was the very fellow who should have been in Belfast two nights ago.

"Oh, I know *him*," said my wife. "He stopped me this noon. Wanted train fare to Galway."

"Did you give it to him?"

"No," said my wife simply.

Then the worst thing happened. The demon far down on the sidewalk glanced up, saw us and damn if he didn't *wave*!

I had to stop myself from waving back. A sickly grin played on my lips.

"It's got so I hate to leave the hotel," I said.

"It's cold out, all right." My wife was putting on her coat.

"No," I said. "Not the cold. *Them*."

And we looked again from the window.

There was the cobbled Dublin street with the night wind blowing in a fine soot along one way to Trinity College, another to St. Stephen's Green. Across by the sweetshop two men stood mummified in the shadows. On the corner a single man, hands deep in his pockets, felt for his entombed bones, a muzzle of ice for a beard. Farther up, in a doorway, was a bundle of old newspapers that would stir like a pack of mice and wish you the time of evening if you walked by. Below, by the hotel entrance, stood a feverish hothouse rose of a woman with a mysterious bundle.

"Oh, the beggars," said my wife.

"No, not just 'oh, the beggars,'" I said, "but oh, the people in the streets, who somehow became beggars."

"It looks like a motion picture. All of them waiting down there in the dark for the hero to come out."

"The hero," I said. "That's me, damn it."

My wife peered at me. "You're not afraid of them?"

"Yes, no. Hell. It's that woman with the bundle who's worst. She's a force of nature, she is. Assaults you with her poverty. As for the others—

well, it's a big chess game for me now. We've been in Dublin what, eight weeks? Eight weeks I've sat up here with my typewriter, studying their off hours and on. When they take a coffee break I take one, run for the sweet-shop, the bookstore, the Olympia Theatre. If I time it right, there's no handout, no my wanting to trot them into the barbershop or the kitchen. I know every secret exit in the hotel."

"Lord," said my wife, "you sound driven."

"I am. But most of all by that beggar on O'Connell Bridge!"

"Which one?"

"Which one indeed. He's a wonder, a terror. I hate him, I love him. To see is to disbelieve him. Come on."

The elevator, which had haunted its untidy shaft for a hundred years, came wafting skyward, dragging its ungodly chains and dread intestines after. The door exhaled open. The lift groaned as if we had trod its stomach. In a great protestation of ennui, the ghost sank back toward earth, us in it.

On the way my wife said, "If you held your face right, the beggars wouldn't bother you."

"My face," I explained patiently, "is my face. It's from Apple Dumpling, Wisconsin, Sarsaparilla, Maine. 'Kind to Dogs' is writ on my brow for all to read. Let the street be empty, then let me step out and there's a strikers' march of freeloaders leaping out of manholes for miles around."

"If," my wife went on, "you could just learn to look over, around or through those people, stare them *down*." She mused. "Shall I show you how to handle them?"

"All right, show me! We're here!"

I flung the elevator door wide and we advanced through the Royal Hibernian Hotel lobby to squint out at the sooty night.

"Jesus come and get me," I murmured. "There they are, their heads up, their eyes on fire. They smell apple pie already."

"Meet me down by the bookstore in two minutes," said my wife. "Watch."

"Wait!" I cried.

But she was out the door, down the steps and on the sidewalk.

I watched, nose pressed to the glass pane.

The beggars on one corner, the other, across from, in front of, the hotel, *leaned* toward my wife. Their eyes glowed.

My wife looked calmly at them all for a long moment.

The beggars hesitated, creaking, I was sure, in their shoes. Then their bones settled. Their mouths collapsed. Their eyes snuffed out. Their heads sank down.

The wind blew.

With a tat-tat like a small drum, my wife's shoes went briskly away, fading.

From below, in the Buttery, I heard music and laughter. I'll run down, I thought, and slug in a quick one. Then, bravery resurgent . . .

Hell, I thought, and swung the door wide.

The effect was much as if someone had struck a great Mongolian bronze gong once.

I thought I heard a tremendous insuck of breath.

Then I heard shoe leather flinting the cobbles in sparks. The men came running, fireflies sprinkling the bricks under their hobnailed shoes. I saw hands waving. Mouths opened on smiles like old pianos.

Far down the street, at the bookshop, my wife waited, her back turned. But that third eye in the back of her head must have caught the scene: Columbus greeted by Indians, Saint Francis amidst his squirrel friends with a bag of nuts. For a terrific moment I felt like a pope on St. Peter's balcony with a tumult, or at the very least the Timultys, below.

I was not half down the steps when the woman charged up, thrusting the unwrapped bundle at me.

"Ah, see the poor child!" she wailed.

I stared at the baby.

The baby stared back.

God in heaven, did or did not the shrewd thing *wink* at me?

I've gone mad, I thought; the babe's eyes are shut. She's filled it with beer to keep it warm and on display.

My hands, my coins, blurred among them.

"Praise be!"

"The *child* thanks you, sir!"

"Ah, sure. There's only a few of us left!"

I broke through them and beyond, still running. Defeated, I could have scuffed slowly the rest of the way, my resolve so much putty in my mouth, but no, on I rushed, thinking, The baby *is* real, *isn't* it? Not a prop? No. I had heard it cry, often. Blast her, I thought, she pinches it when she sees Okeemogo, Iowa, coming. Cynic, I cried silently, and answered, No—coward.

My wife, without turning, saw my reflection in the bookshop window and nodded.

I stood getting my breath, brooding at my own image: the summer eyes, the ebullient and defenseless mouth.

"All right, say it." I sighed. "It's the way I hold my face."

"I love the way you hold your face." She took my arm. "I wish I could do it, too."

I looked back as one of the beggars strolled off in the blowing dark with my shillings.

" 'There's only a few of us left,' " I said aloud. "What did he mean, saying that?"

" 'There's only a few of us left.' " My wife stared into the shadows. "Is that what he said?"

"It's something to think about. A few of what? Left where?"

The street was empty now. It was starting to rain.

"Well," I said at last, "let me show you the even bigger mystery, the man who provokes me to strange wild rages, then calms me to delight. Solve him and you solve all the beggars that ever were."

"On O'Connell Bridge?" asked my wife.

"On O'Connell Bridge," I said.

And we walked on down in the gently misting rain.

Halfway to the bridge, as we were examining some fine Irish crystal in a window, a woman with a shawl over her head plucked at my elbow.

"Destroyed!" The woman sobbed. "My poor sister. Cancer, the doctor said, her dead in a month! And me with mouths to feed! Ah, God, if you had just a penny!"

I felt my wife's arm tighten to mine.

I looked at the woman, split as always, one half saying, "A penny is all she asks!," the other half doubting: "Clever woman, she knows that by her underasking you'll overpay!," and hating myself for the battle of halves.

I gasped. "You're . . ."

"I'm what, sir?"

Why, I thought, you're the woman who was just back by the hotel with the bundled baby!

"I'm sick!" She hid in shadow. "Sick with crying for the half dead!"

You've stashed the baby somewhere, I thought, and put on a green instead of a gray shawl and run the long way around to cut us off here.

"Cancer . . ." One bell in her tower, and she knew how to toll it. "Cancer . . ."

My wife cut across it. "Beg pardon, but aren't you the same woman we just met at our hotel?"

The woman and I were both shocked at this rank insubordination. It wasn't done!

The woman's face crumpled. I peered close. And yes, by God, it was a different face. I could not but admire her. She knew, sensed, had learned what actors know, sense, learn: that by thrusting, yelling, all fiery-lipped arrogance one moment, you are one character; and by sinking, giving way, crumpling the mouth and eyes, in pitiful collapse, you are another. The same woman, yes, but the same face and role? Quite obviously no.

She gave me a last blow beneath the belt. "Cancer."

I flinched.

It was a brief tussle then, a kind of disengagement from one woman and an engagement with the other. The wife lost my arm and the woman found my cash. As if she were on roller skates, she whisked around the corner, sobbing happily.

"Lord!" In awe, I watched her go. "She's studied Stanislavsky. In one book he says that squinting one eye and twitching one lip to the side will disguise you. I wonder if she has nerve enough to be at the hotel when we go back?"

"I wonder," said my wife, "when my husband will stop admiring and start criticizing such Abbey Theatre acting as that."

"But what if it were true? Everything she said? And she's lived with it so long she can't cry anymore, and so has to play-act in order to survive? What if?"

"It can't be true," said my wife slowly. "I just won't believe it."

But that single bell was still tolling somewhere in the chimney-smoking dark.

"Now," said my wife, "here's where we turn for O'Connell Bridge, isn't it?"

"It is."

That corner was probably empty in the falling rain for a long time after we were gone.

✳ There stood the graystone bridge bearing the great O'Connell's name, and there the River Liffey rolling cold gray waters under, and even from a block off I heard faint singing. My mind spun in a great leap back to December.

"Christmas," I murmured, "is the best time of all in Dublin."

For beggars, I meant, but left it unsaid.

For in the week before Christmas the Dublin streets teem with raven flocks of children herded by schoolmasters or nuns. They cluster in doorways, peer from theater lobbies, jostle in alleys, "God Rest You Merry, Gentlemen" on their lips, "It Came Upon a Midnight Clear" in their eyes, tambourines in hand, snowflakes shaping a collar of grace about their tender necks. It is singing everywhere and anywhere in Dublin on such nights, and there was no night my wife and I did not walk down along Grafton Street to hear "Away in a Manger" being sung to the queue outside the cinema or "Deck the Halls" in front of the Four Provinces pub. In all, we counted in Christ's season one night half a hundred bands of convent girls or public-school boys lacing the cold air and weaving great treadles of song up, down, over and across from end to end of Dublin. Like walking in snowfall, you could not walk among them and not be touched. The sweet beggars, I called them, who gave in turn for what you gave as you went your way.

Given such example, even the most dilapidated beggars of Dublin washed their hands, mended their torn smiles, borrowed banjos or bought a fiddle and killed a cat. They even gathered for four-part harmonies. How could they stay silent when half the world was singing and the other half, idled on the tuneful river, was paying dearly, gladly, for just another chorus?

So Christmas was best for all; the beggars *worked*—off key, it's true, but there they were, one time in the year, *busy*.

But Christmas was over, the licorice-suited children back in their aviaries, and the beggars of the town, shut and glad for the silence, returned to their workless ways. All save the beggars on O'Connell Bridge, who, all through the year, most of them, tried to give as good as they got.

"They have their self-respect," I said, walking my wife. "I'm glad this first man here strums a guitar, the next one a fiddle. And there, now, by God, in the very center of the bridge!"

"The man we're looking for?"

"That's him. Squeezing the concertina. It's all right to look. Or I *think* it is."

"What do you mean, you think it is? He's blind, isn't he?"

These raw words shocked me, as if my wife had said something indecent.

The rain fell gently, softly upon graystoned Dublin, graystoned riverbank, gray lava-flowing river.

"That's the trouble," I said at last. "I don't know."

And we both, in passing, looked at the man standing there in the very middle of O'Connell Bridge.

He was a man of no great height, a bandy statue swiped from some country garden perhaps, and his clothes, like the clothes of most in Ireland, too often laundered by the weather, and his hair too often grayed by the smoking air, and his cheeks sooted with beard, and a nest or two of witless hair in each cupped ear, and the blushing cheeks of a man who has stood too long in the cold and drunk too much in the pub so as to stand too long in the cold again. Dark glasses covered his eyes, and there was no telling what lay behind. I had begun to wonder, weeks back, if his sight prowled me along, damning my guilty speed, or if only his ears caught the passing of a harried conscience. There was that awful fear I might seize, in passing, the glasses from his nose. But I feared much more the abyss I might find, into which my senses, in one terrible roar, might tumble. Best not to know if civet's orb or interstellar space gaped behind the smoked panes.

But, even more, there was a special reason why I could not let the man be.

In the rain and wind and snow, for two solid months, I had seen him standing here with no cap or hat on his head.

He was the only man in all of Dublin I saw in the downpours and drizzles who stood by the hour alone with the drench mizzling his ears, threading his ash-red hair, plastering it over his skull, rivuleting his eyebrows, and purling over the coal-black insect lenses of the glasses on his rain-pearled nose.

Down through the greaves of his cheeks, the lines about his mouth, and off his chin, like a storm on a gargoyle's flint, the weather ran. His sharp chin shot the guzzle in a steady fauceting off in the air, down his tweed scarf and locomotive-colored coat.

"Why doesn't he wear a hat?" I said suddenly.

"Why," said my wife, "maybe he hasn't got one."

"He must have one," I said.

"Keep your voice down."

"He's got to have one," I said, quieter.

"Maybe he can't afford one."

"Nobody's that poor, even in Dublin. Everyone has a cap at least!"

"Well, maybe he has bills to pay, someone sick."

"But to stand out for weeks, months, in the rain, and not so much as flinch or turn his head, ignore the rain, it's beyond understanding." I shook my head. "I can only think it's a trick. That must be it. Like the others, this is his way of getting sympathy, of making you cold and miserable as himself as you go by, so you'll give him more."

"I bet you're sorry you said that already," said my wife.

"I am. I am." For even under my cap the rain was running off my nose. "Sweet God in heaven, what's the answer?"

"Why don't you ask him?"

"No." I was even more afraid of that.

Then the last thing happened, the thing that went with his standing bareheaded in the cold rain.

For a moment, while we had been talking at some distance, he had been silent. Now, as if the weather had freshened him to life, he gave his concertina a great mash. From the folding, unfolding snake box he squeezed a series of asthmatic notes which were no preparation for what followed.

He opened his mouth. He sang.

The sweet clear baritone voice which rang over O'Connell Bridge, steady and sure, was beautifully shaped and controlled, not a quiver, not a flaw, anywhere in it. The man just opened his mouth, which meant that all kinds of secret doors in his body gave way. He did not sing so much as let his soul free.

"Oh," said my wife, "how lovely."

"Lovely." I nodded.

We listened while he sang the full irony of Dublin's Fair City where it rains twelve inches a month the winter through, followed by the white-wine clarity of Kathleen Mavourneen, Macushlah, and all the other tired lads, lasses, lakes, hills, past glories, present miseries, but all somehow revived and moving about young and freshly painted in the light spring, suddenly-not-winter rain. If he breathed at all, it must have been through his ears, so smooth the line, so steady the putting forth of word following round belled word.

"Why," said my wife, "he could be on the stage."

"Maybe he was once."

"Oh, he's too good to be standing here."

"I've thought that often."

My wife fumbled with her purse. I looked from her to the singing man, the rain falling on his bare head, streaming through his shellacked hair, trembling on his ear lobes. My wife had her purse open.

And then, the strange perversity. Before my wife could move toward him, I took her elbow and led her down the other side of the bridge. She pulled back for a moment, giving me a look, then came along.

As we went away along the bank of the Liffey, he started a new song, one we had heard often in Ireland. Glancing back, I saw him, head proud, black glasses taking the pour, mouth open, and the fine voice clear:

> "I'll be glad when you're dead
> > in your grave, old man,
> Be glad when you're dead
> > in your grave, old man.
> Be glad when you're dead,
> Flowers over your head,
> And then I'll marry the journeyman. . . ."

It is only later, looking back, that you see that while you were doing all the other things in your life, working on an article concerning one part of Ireland in your rain-battered hotel, taking your wife to dinner, wandering in the museums, you also had an eye beyond to the street and those who served themselves who only stood to wait.

The beggars of Dublin, who bothers to wonder on them, look, see, know, understand? Yet the outer shell of the eye sees and the inner shell of the mind records, and yourself, caught between, ignores the rare service these two halves of a bright sense are up to.

So I did and did not concern myself with beggars. So I did run from them or walk to meet them, by turn. So I heard but did not hear, considered but did not consider:

"There's only a few of us left!"

One day I was sure the stone gargoyle man taking his daily shower on O'Connell Bridge while he sang Irish opera was *not* blind. And the next his head to me was a cup of darkness.

One afternoon I found myself lingering before a tweed shop near O'Connell Bridge, staring in, staring in at a stack of good thick burly caps. I did not need another cap, I had a life's supply collected in a suitcase, yet in I went to pay out money for a fine warm brown-colored cap which I turned round and round in my hands, in a strange trance.

"Sir," said the clerk. "That cap is a seven. I would guess your head, sir, at a seven and one half."

"This will fit me. This will fit me." I stuffed the cap into my pocket.

"Let me get you a sack, sir—"

"No!" Hot-cheeked, suddenly suspicious of what I was up to, I fled.

There was the bridge in the soft rain. All I need do now was walk over—

In the middle of the bridge, my singing man was not there.

In his place stood an old man and woman cranking a great piano-box hurdy-gurdy which racheted and coughed like a coffee grinder eating glass and stone, giving forth no melody but a grand and melancholy sort of iron indigestion.

I waited for the tune, if tune it was, to finish. I kneaded the new tweed cap in my sweaty fist while the hurdy-gurdy prickled, spanged and thumped.

"Be damned to ya!" the old man and old woman, furious with their job, seemed to say, their faces thunderous pale, their eyes red-hot in the rain. "Pay us! Listen! But we'll give you no tune! Make up your own!" their mute lips said.

And standing there on the spot where the beggar always sang without his cap, I thought, Why don't they take one fiftieth of the money they make each month and have the thing tuned? If I were cranking the box, I'd want a tune, at least for myself! If you were cranking the box, I answered. But you're not. And it's obvious they hate the begging job, who'd blame them, and want no part of giving back a familiar song as recompense.

How different from my capless friend.

My *friend*?

I blinked with surprise, then stepped forward and nodded.

"Beg pardon. The man with the concertina . . ."

The woman stopped cranking and glared at me.

"Ah?"

"The man with no cap in the rain."

"Ah, him!" snapped the woman.

"He's not here today?"

"Do you *see* him?" cried the woman.

She started cranking the infernal device.

I put a penny in the tin cup.

She peered at me as if I'd spit in the cup.

I put in another penny. She stopped.

"Do you know where he is?" I asked.

"Sick. In bed. The damn cold! We heard him go off, coughing."

"Do you know where he lives?"

"No!"

"Do you know his name?"

"Now, who would know that!"

I stood there, feeling directionless, thinking of the man somewhere off in the town, alone. I looked at the new cap foolishly.

The two old people were watching me uneasily.

I put a last shilling in the cup.

"He'll be all right," I said, not to them, but to someone, hopefully, myself.

The woman heaved the crank. The bucketing machine let loose a fall of glass and junk in its hideous interior.

"The tune," I said, numbly. "What is it?"

"You're deaf!" snapped the woman. "It's the national anthem! Do you mind removing your cap?"

I showed her the new cap in my hand.

She glared up. "Your cap, man, *your* cap!"

"Oh!" Flushing, I seized the old cap from my head.

Now I had a cap in each hand.

The woman cranked. The "music" played. The rain hit my brow, my eyelids, my mouth.

On the far side of the bridge I stopped for the hard, the slow decision: which cap to try on my drenched skull?

✳ During the next week I passed the bridge often, but there was always just the old couple there with their pandemonium device, or no one there at all.

On the last day of our visit, my wife started to pack the new tweed cap away with my others, in the suitcase.

"Thanks, no." I took it from her. "Let's keep it out, on the mantel, please. There."

That night the hotel manager brought a farewell bottle to our room. The talk was long and good, the hour grew late, there was a fire like an orange lion on the hearth, big and lively, and brandy in the glasses, and silence for a moment in the room, perhaps because quite suddenly we found silence falling in great soft flakes past our high windows.

The manager, glass in hand, watched the continual lace, then looked down at the midnight stones and at last said, under his breath, " 'There's only a few of us left.' "

I glanced at my wife, and she at me.

The manager caught us.

"Do you know him, then? Has he said it to you?"

"Yes. But what does the phrase mean?"

The manager watched all those figures down there standing in the shadows and sipped his drink.

"Once I thought he meant he fought in the Troubles and there's just a few of the I.R.A. left. But no. Or maybe he means in a richer world the begging population is melting away. But no to that also. So maybe, perhaps, he means there aren't many 'human beings' left who look, see what they look at, and understand well enough for one to ask and one to give. Everyone busy, running here, jumping there, there's no time to study one another. But I guess that's bilge and hogwash, slop and sentiment."

He half turned from the window.

"So you know There's Only a Few of Us Left, do you?"

My wife and I nodded.

"Then do you know the woman with the baby?"

"Yes," I said.

"And the one with the cancer?"

"Yes," said my wife.

"And the man who needs train fare to Cork?"

"Belfast," said I.

"Galway," said my wife.

The manager smiled sadly and turned back to the window.

"What about the couple with the piano that plays no tune?"

"Has it ever?" I asked.

"Not since I was a boy."

The manager's face was shadowed now.

"Do you know the beggar on O'Connell Bridge?"

"Which one?" I said.

But I knew which one, for I was looking at the cap there on the mantel.

"Did you see the paper today?" asked the manager.

"No."

"There's just the item, bottom half of page five, *Irish Times*. It seems he just got tired. And he threw his concertina over into the River Liffey. And he jumped after it."

He was back, then, yesterday! I thought. And I didn't pass by!

"The poor bastard." The manager laughed with a hollow exhalation.

"What a funny, horrid way to die. That damn silly concertina—I hate them, don't you?—wheezing on its way down, like a sick cat, and the man falling after. I laugh and I'm ashamed of laughing. Well. They didn't find the body. They're still looking."

"Oh, God!" I cried, getting up. "Oh, damn!"

The manager watched me carefully now, surprised at my concern. "You couldn't help it."

"I could! I never gave him a penny, not one, ever! Did you?"

"Come to think of it, no."

"But you're worse than I am!" I protested. "I've seen you around town, shoveling out pennies hand over fist. Why, why not to *him*?"

"I guess I thought he was overdoing it."

"Hell, yes!" I was at the window now, too, staring down through the falling snow. "I thought his bare head was a trick to make me feel sorry. Damn, after a while you think everything's a trick! I used to pass there winter nights with the rain thick and him there singing and he made me feel so cold I hated his guts. I wonder how many other people felt cold and hated him because he did that to them? So instead of getting money, he got nothing in his cup. I lumped him with the rest. But maybe he was one of the legitimate ones, the new poor just starting out this winter, not a beggar ever before, so you hock your clothes to feed a stomach and wind up a man in the rain without a hat."

The snow was falling fast now, erasing the lamps and the statues in the shadows of the lamps below.

"How do you tell the difference between them?" I asked. "How can you judge which is honest, which isn't?"

"The fact is," said the manager quietly, "you can't. There's no difference between them. Some have been at it longer than others, and have gone shrewd, forgotten how it all started a long time ago. On a Saturday they had food. On a Sunday they didn't. On a Monday they asked for credit. On a Tuesday they borrowed their first match. Thursday a cigarette. And a few Fridays later they found themselves, God knows how, in front of a place called the Royal Hibernian Hotel. They couldn't tell you what happened or why. One thing's sure though: they're hanging to the cliff by their finger-nails. Poor bastard, someone must've stomped on that man's hands on O'Connell Bridge and he just gave up the ghost and went over. So what does it prove? You cannot stare them down or look away from them. You cannot run and hide from them. You can only give to them all. If you start drawing lines, someone gets hurt. I'm sorry now I didn't give that blind singer a shilling each time I passed. Well. Well. Let us console ourselves, hope it wasn't money but something at home or in his past did him in. There's no way to find out. The paper lists no name."

Snow fell silently across our sight. Below, the dark shapes waited. It was hard to tell whether snow was making sheep of the wolves or sheep of the sheep, gently manteling their shoulders, their backs, their hats and shawls.

A moment later, going down in the haunted night elevator, I found the new tweed cap in my hand.

Coatless, in my shirtsleeves, I stepped out into the night.

I gave the cap to the first man who came. I never knew if it fit. What money I had in my pockets was soon gone.

Then, left alone, shivering, I happened to glance up. I stood, I froze, blinking up through the drift, the drift, the silent drift of blinding snow. I saw the high hotel windows, the lights, the shadows.

What's it like up there? I thought. *Are fires lit? Is it warm as breath? Who are all those people? Are they drinking? Are they happy?*

Do they even know I'm HERE?

THE FLYING MACHINE

IN THE YEAR A.D. 400, THE EMPEROR YUAN held his throne by the Great Wall of China, and the land was green with rain, readying itself toward the harvest, at peace, the people in his dominion neither too happy nor too sad.

Early on the morning of the first day of the first week of the second month of the new year, the Emperor Yuan was sipping tea and fanning himself against a warm breeze when a servant ran across the scarlet and blue garden tiles, calling, "Oh, Emperor, Emperor, a miracle!"

"Yes," said the Emperor, "the air *is* sweet this morning."

"No, no, a miracle!" said the servant, bowing quickly.

"And this tea is good in my mouth, surely that is a miracle."

"No, no, Your Excellency."

"Let me guess then—the sun has risen and a new day is upon us. Or the sea is blue. *That* now is the finest of all miracles."

"Excellency, a man is flying!"

"What?" The Emperor stopped his fan.

"I saw him in the air, a man flying with wings. I heard a voice call out of the sky, and when I looked up there he was, a dragon in the heavens with a man in its mouth, a dragon of paper and bamboo, colored like the sun and the grass."

"It is early," said the Emperor, "and you have just wakened from a dream."

"It is early, but I have seen what I have seen! Come, and you will see it too."

"Sit down with me here," said the Emperor. "Drink some tea. It must be a strange thing, if it is true, to see a man fly. You must have time to think of it, even as I must have time to prepare myself for the sight."

They drank tea.

"Please," said the servant at last, "or he will be gone."

The Emperor rose thoughtfully. "Now you may show me what you have seen."

They walked into a garden, across a meadow of grass, over a small bridge, through a grove of trees, and up a tiny hill.

"There!" said the servant.

The Emperor looked into the sky.

And in the sky, laughing so high that you could hardly hear him laugh, was a man; and the man was clothed in bright papers and reeds to make wings and a beautiful yellow tail, and he was soaring all about like the largest bird in a universe of birds, like a new dragon in a land of ancient dragons.

The man called down to them from high in the cool winds of morning, "I fly, I fly!"

The servant waved to him. "Yes, yes!"

The Emperor Yuan did not move. Instead he looked at the Great Wall of China now taking shape out of the farthest mist in the green hills, that splendid snake of stones which writhed with majesty across the entire land. That wonderful wall which had protected them for a timeless time from enemy hordes and preserved peace for years without number. He saw the town, nestled to itself by a river and a road and a hill, beginning to waken.

"Tell me," he said to his servant, "has anyone else seen this flying man?"

"I am the only one, Excellency," said the servant, smiling at the sky, waving.

The Emperor watched the heavens another minute and then said, "Call him down to me."

"Ho, come down, come down! The Emperor wishes to see you!" called the servant, hands cupped to his shouting mouth.

The Emperor glanced in all directions while the flying man soared down the morning wind. He saw a farmer, early in his fields, watching the sky, and he noted where the farmer stood.

The flying man alit with a rustle of paper and a creak of bamboo reeds. He came proudly to the Emperor, clumsy in his rig, at last bowing before the old man.

"What have you done?" demanded the Emperor.

"I have flown in the sky, Your Excellency," replied the man.

"What *have* you done?" said the Emperor again.

"I have just told you!" cried the flier.

"You have told me nothing at all." The Emperor reached out a thin hand to touch the pretty paper and the birdlike keel of the apparatus. It smelled cool, of the wind.

"Is it not beautiful, Excellency?"

"Yes, too beautiful."

"It is the only one in the world!" smiled the man. "And I am the inventor."

"The *only* one in the world?"

"I swear it!"

"Who else knows of this?"

"No one. Not even my wife, who would think me mad with the sun. She thought I was making a kite. I rose in the night and walked to the cliffs far away. And when the morning breezes blew and the sun rose, I gathered my courage, Excellency, and leaped from the cliff. I flew! But my wife does not know of it."

"Well for her, then," said the Emperor. "Come along."

They walked back to the great house. The sun was full in the sky now, and the smell of the grass was refreshing. The Emperor, the servant, and the flier paused within the huge garden.

The Emperor clapped his hands. "Ho, guards!"

The guards came running.

"Hold this man."

The guards seized the flier.

"Call the executioner," said the Emperor.

"What's this!" cried the flier, bewildered. "What have I done?" He began to weep, so that the beautiful paper apparatus rustled.

"Here is the man who has made a certain machine," said the Emperor, "and yet asks us what he has created. He does not know himself. It is only necessary that he create, without knowing why he has done so, or what this thing will do."

The executioner came running with a sharp silver ax. He stood with his naked, large-muscled arms ready, his face covered with a serene white mask.

"One moment," said the Emperor. He turned to a nearby table upon which sat a machine that he himself had created. The Emperor took a tiny golden key from his own neck. He fitted this key to the tiny, delicate machine and wound it up. Then he set the machine going.

The machine was a garden of metal and jewels. Set in motion, birds sang in tiny metal trees, wolves walked through miniature forests, and tiny people ran in and out of sun and shadow, fanning themselves with miniature fans, listening to the tiny emerald birds, and standing by impossibly small but tinkling fountains.

"Is it not beautiful?" said the Emperor. "If you asked me what I have done here, I could answer you well. I have made birds sing, I have made forests murmur, I have set people to walking in this woodland, enjoying the leaves and shadows and songs. That is what I have done."

"But, oh, Emperor!" pleaded the flier, on his knees, the tears pouring down his face. "I have done a similar thing! I have found beauty. I have flown on the morning wind. I have looked down on all the sleeping houses and gardens. I have smelled the sea and even *seen* it, beyond the hills, from my high place. And I have soared like a bird; oh, I cannot say how beautiful it is up there, in the sky, with the wind about me, the wind blowing me here like a feather, there like a fan, the way the sky smells in the morning! And how free one feels! *That* is beautiful, Emperor, that is beautiful too!"

"Yes," said the Emperor sadly, "I know it must be true. For I felt my heart move with you in the air and I wondered: What is it like? How does it feel? How do the distant pools look from so high? And how my houses and servants? Like ants? And how the distant towns not yet awake?"

"Then spare me!"

"But there are times," said the Emperor, more sadly still, "when one must lose a little beauty if one is to keep what little beauty one already has. I do not fear you, yourself, but I fear another man."

"What man?"

"Some other man who, seeing you, will build a thing of bright papers and bamboo like this. But the other man will have an evil face and an evil heart, and the beauty will be gone. It is this man I fear."

"Why? Why?"

"Who is to say that someday just such a man, in just such an apparatus of paper and reed, might not fly in the sky and drop huge stones upon the Great Wall of China?" said the Emperor.

No one moved or said a word.

"Off with his head," said the Emperor.

The executioner whirled his silver ax.

"Burn the kite and the inventor's body and bury their ashes together," said the Emperor.

The servants retreated to obey.

The Emperor turned to his hand-servant, who had seen the man flying. "Hold your tongue. It was all a dream, a most sorrowful and beautiful dream. And that farmer in the distant field who also saw, tell him it would pay him to consider it only a vision. If ever the word passes around, you and the farmer die within the hour."

"You are merciful, Emperor."

"No, not merciful," said the old man. Beyond the garden wall he saw the guards burning the beautiful machine of paper and reeds that smelled of the morning wind. He saw the dark smoke climb into the sky. "No, only very much bewildered and afraid." He saw the guards digging a tiny pit wherein to bury the ashes. "What is the life of one man against those of a million others? I must take solace from that thought."

He took the key from its chain about his neck and once more wound up the beautiful miniature garden. He stood looking out across the land at the Great Wall, the peaceful town, the green fields, the rivers and streams. He sighed. The tiny garden whirred its hidden and delicate machinery and set itself in motion; tiny people walked in forests, tiny foxes loped through sun-speckled glades in beautiful shining pelts, and among the tiny trees flew little bits of high song and bright blue and yellow color, flying, flying, flying in that small sky.

"Oh," said the Emperor, closing his eyes, "look at the birds, look at the birds!"

HEAVY-SET

THE WOMAN STEPPED TO THE KITCHEN WINDOW and looked out.

There in the twilight yard a man stood surrounded by barbells and dumbbells and dark iron weights of all kinds and slung jump ropes and elastic and coiled-spring exercisors. He wore a sweat suit and tennis shoes and said nothing to no one as he simply stood in the darkening world and did not know she watched.

This was her son, and everyone called him Heavy-Set.

Heavy-Set squeezed the little bunched, coiled springs in his big fists. They were lost in his fingers, like magic tricks; then they reappeared. He crushed them. They vanished. He let them go. They came back.

He did this for ten minutes, otherwise motionless.

Then he bent down and hoisted up the one-hundred-pound barbells, noiselessly, not breathing. He motioned it a number of times over his head, then abandoned it and went into the open garage among the various surf-boards he had cut out and glued together and sanded and painted and waxed, and there he punched a punching bag easily, swiftly, steadily, until his curly golden hair got moist. Then he stopped and filled his lungs until his chest measured fifty inches and stood eyes closed, seeing himself in an invisible mirror poised and tremendous, two hundred and twenty muscled pounds, tanned by the sun, salted by the sea wind and his own sweat.

He exhaled. He opened his eyes.

He walked into the house, into the kitchen and did not look at his mother, this woman, and opened the refrigerator and let the arctic cold steam him while he drank a quart of milk straight out of the carton, never putting it down, just gulping and swallowing. Then he sat down at the kitchen table to fondle and examine the Hallowe'en pumpkins.

He had gone out earlier in the day and bought the pumpkins and carved most of them and did a fine job: they were beauties and he was proud of them. Now, looking childlike in the kitchen, he started carving the last of them. You would never suspect he was thirty years old, he still moved so swiftly, so quietly, for a large action like hitting a wave with an uptilted and outthrust board, or here with the small action of a knife, giving sight to a Hallowe'en eye. The electric light bulb filled the summer wildness of his hair, but revealed no emotion, except this one intent purpose of carving, on his face. There was all muscle in him, and no fat, and that muscle waited behind every move of the knife.

His mother came and went on personal errands around the house and then came to stand and look at him and the pumpkins and smile. She was used to him. She heard him every night drubbing the punching bag outside, or squeezing the little metal springs in his hands or grunting as he lifted his world of weights and held it in balance on his strangely quiet shoulders. She was used to all these sounds even as she knew the ocean coming in on the shore beyond the cottage and laying itself out flat and shining on the sand. Even as she was used, by now, to hearing Heavy-Set each night on the phone saying he was tired to girls and said no, no he had to wax the car tonight or do his exercises to the eighteen-year-old boys who called.

She cleared her throat. "Was the dinner good tonight?"

"Sure," he said.

"I had to get special steak. I bought the asparagus fresh."

"It was good," he said.

"I'm glad you liked it, I always like to have you like it."

"Sure," he said, working.

"What time is the party?"

"Seven thirty." He finished the last of the smile on the pumpkin and sat back. "If they all show up, they might not show up, I bought two jugs of cider."

He got up and moved into his bedroom, quietly massive, his shoulders filling the door and beyond. In the room, in the half-dark, he made the strange pantomime of a man seriously and silently wrestling an invisible opponent as he got into his costume. He came to the door of the living room a minute later licking a gigantic peppermint-striped lollipop. He wore a pair of short black pants, a little boy's shirt with ruff collar, and a Buster Brown hat. He licked the lollipop and said, "I'm the mean little kid!" and the woman who had been watching him laughed. He walked with an exaggerated little child's walk, licking the huge lollipop, all around the room while she laughed at him and he said things and pretended to be leading a big dog on a rope. "You'll be the life of the party!" the woman cried, pink-faced and exhausted. He was laughing now, also.

The phone rang.

He toddled out to answer it in the bedroom. He talked for a long time and his mother heard him say Oh for gosh sakes several times and finally he came slowly and massively into the living room looking stubborn. "What's wrong?" she wanted to know. "Aw," he said, "half the guys aren't showing up at the party. They got other dates. That was Tommy calling. He's got a date with a girl from somewhere. Good grief." "There'll be enough," said his mother. "I don't know," he said. "There'll be enough for a party," she said. "You go on." "I ought to throw the pumpkins in the garbage," he said, scowling. "Well you just go on and have a good time," she said. "You haven't been out in weeks."

Silence.

He stood there twisting the huge lollipop as big as his head, turning it in his large muscular fingers. He looked as if at any moment now he would do what he did other nights. Some nights he pressed himself up and down on the ground with his arms and some nights he played a game of basket-ball with himself and scored himself, team against team, black against white, in the backyard. Some nights he stood around like this and then suddenly vanished and you saw him way out in the ocean swimming long and strong and quiet as a seal under the full moon or you could not see him those nights the moon was gone and only the stars lay over the water but you heard him there, on occasion, a faint splash as he went under and stayed under a long time and came up, or he went out some times with his surfboard as smooth as a girl's cheeks, sandpapered to a softness, and came riding in, huge and alone on a white and ghastly wave that creamed along the shore and touched the sands with the surfboard as he stepped off like a visitor from another world and stood for a long while holding the soft smooth surfboard in the moonlight, a quiet man and a vast tombstone-shaped thing held there with no writing on it. In all the nights like that in the past years, he had taken a girl out three times one week and she ate a lot and every time he saw her she said Let's eat and so one night he drove her up to a restaurant and opened the car door and helped her out and got back in and said There's the restaurant. So long. And drove off. And went back to swimming way out, alone. Much later, another time, a girl was half an hour late getting ready and he never spoke to her again.

Thinking all this, remembering all this, his mother looked at him now.

"Don't stand there," she said. "You make me nervous."

"Well," he said, resentfully.

"Go on!" she cried. But she didn't cry it strong enough. Even to herself her voice sounded faint. And she did not know if her voice was just naturally faint or if she made it that way.

She might as well have been talking about winter coming; everything she said had a lonely sound. And she heard the words again from her own mouth, with no force: "Go on!"

He went into the kitchen. "I guess there'll be enough guys there," he said. "Sure, there will," she said, smiling again. She always smiled again. Sometimes when she talked to him, night after night, she looked as if she were lifting weights, too. When he walked through the rooms she looked like she was doing the walking for him. And when he sat brooding, as he often did, she looked around for something to do which might be burn the toast or overfire the steak. She made a short barking faint and stifled laugh now, "Get out, have a good time." But the echoes of it moved around in the house as if it were already empty and cold and he should come back in the door. Her lips moved: "Fly away."

He snatched up the cider and the pumpkins and hurried them out to his car. It was a new car and had been new and unused for almost a year. He polished it and jiggered with the motor or lay underneath it for hours messing with all the junk underneath or just sat in the front seat glancing over the strength and health magazines, but rarely drove it. He put the cider and the cut pumpkins proudly in on the front seat, and by this time he was thinking of the possible good time tonight so he did a little child's stagger as if he might drop everything, and his mother laughed. He licked his lollipop again, jumped into the car, backed it out of the gravel drive, swerved it around down by the ocean, not looking out at this woman, and drove off along the shore road. She stood in the yard watching the car go away. Leonard, my son, she thought.

It was seven fifteen and very dark now; already the children were fluttering along the sidewalks in white ghost sheets and zinc-oxide masks, ringing bells, screaming, lumpy paper sacks banging their knees as they ran.

Leonard, she thought.

They didn't call him Leonard, they called him Heavy-Set and Sammy, which was short for Samson. They called him Butch and they called him Atlas and Hercules. At the beach you always saw the high-school boys around him feeling his biceps as if he was a new sports car, testing him, admiring him. He walked golden among them. Each year it was that way. And then the eighteen-year-old ones got to be nineteen and didn't come around so often, and then twenty and very rarely, and then twenty-one and never again, just gone, and suddenly there were new eighteen year olds to replace them, yes, always the new ones to stand where the others had stood in the sun, while the older ones went on somewhere to something and somebody.

Leonard, my good boy, she thought. We go to shows on Saturday nights. He works on the high power lines all day, up in the sky, alone, and sleeps alone in his room at night, and never reads a book or a paper or listens to a radio or plays a record, and this year he'll be thirty-one. And just where, in all the years, did the thing happen that put him up on that pole alone and working out alone every night? Certainly there had been enough women, here and there, now and then, through his life. Little scrubby ones, of course, fools, yes, by the look of them, but women, or girls, rather, and none worth glancing at a second time. Still, when a boy gets past thirty . . . ? She sighed. Why even as recent as last night the phone had rung. Heavy-Set had answered it, and she could fill in the unheard half of the conversation because she had heard thousands like it in a dozen years:

"Sammy, this is Christine." A woman's voice. "What you doing?"

His little golden eyelashes flickered and his brow furrowed, alert and wary. "Why?"

"Tom, Lu, and I are going to a show, want to come along?"

"It better be good!" he cried, indignantly.

She named it.

"That!" He snorted.

"It's a good film," she said.

"Not that one," he said. "Besides, I haven't shaved yet today."

"You can shave in five minutes."

"I need a bath, and it'd take a long time."

A long time, thought his mother, he was in the bathroom two hours today. He combs his hair two dozen times, musses it, combs it again, talking to himself.

"Okay for you." The woman's voice on the phone. "You going to the beach this week?"

"Saturday," he said, before he thought.

"See you there, then," she said.

"I meant Sunday," he said, quickly.

"I could change it to Sunday," she replied.

"If I can make it," he said, even more quickly. "Things go wrong with my car."

"Sure," she said. "Samson. So long."

And he had stood there for a long time, turning the silent phone in his hand.

Well, his mother thought, he's having a good time now. A good Hallowe'en party, with all the apples he took along, tied on strings, and the apples, untied, to bob for in a tub of water, and the boxes of candy, the sweet corn kernels that really taste like autumn. He's running around looking like the bad little boy, she thought, licking his lollipop, everyone shouting, blowing horns, laughing, dancing.

At eight, and again at eight thirty and nine she went to the screen door and looked out and could almost hear the party a long way off at the dark beach, the sounds of it blowing on the wind crisp and furious and wild, and wished she could be there at the little shack out over the waves on the pier, everyone whirling about in costumes, and all the pumpkins cut each a different way and a contest for the best homemade mask or makeup job, and too much popcorn to eat and—

She held to the screen door knob, her face pink and excited and suddenly realized the children had stopped coming to beg at the door. Hallowe'en, for the neighborhood kids anyway, was over.

She went to look out into the backyard.

The house and yard were too quiet. It was strange not hearing the basketball volley on the gravel or the steady bumble of the punching bag taking a beating. Or the little tweezing sound of the hand-squeezers.

What if, she thought, he found someone tonight, found someone down there, and just never came back, never came home. No telephone call. No letter, that was the way it could be. No word. Just go off away and never come back again. What if? What if?

No! she thought, there's no one, no one there, no one anywhere. There's just this place. This is the only place.

But her heart was beating fast and she had to sit down.

The wind blew softly from the shore.

She turned on the radio but could not hear it.

Now, she thought, they're not doing anything except playing blind man's buff, yes, that's it, blind tag, and after that they'll just be—

She gasped and jumped.

The windows had exploded with raw light.

The gravel spurted in a machine-gun spray as the car jolted in, braked, and stopped, motor gunning. The lights went off in the yard. But the motor still gunned up, idled, gunned up, idled.

She could see the dark figure in the front seat of the car, not moving, staring straight ahead.

"You—" she started to say, and opened the back screen door. She found a smile on her mouth. She stopped it. Her heart was slowing now. She made herself frown.

He shut off the motor. She waited. He climbed out of the car and threw the pumpkins in the garbage can and slammed the lid.

"What happened?" she asked. "Why are you home so early—?"

"Nothing." He brushed by her with the two gallons of cider intact. He set them on the kitchen sink.

"But it's not ten yet—"

"That's right." He went into the bedroom and sat down in the dark.

She waited five minutes. She always waited five minutes. He wanted her to come ask, he'd be mad if she didn't, so finally she went and looked into the dark bedroom.

"Tell me," she said.

"Oh, they all stood around," he said. "They just stood around like a bunch of fools and didn't do anything."

"What a shame."

"They just stood around like dumb fools."

"Oh, that's a shame."

"I tried to get them to do something, but they just stood around. Only eight of them showed up, eight out of twenty, eight, and me the only one in costume. I tell you. The only one. What a bunch of fools."

"After all your trouble, too."

"They had their girls and they just stood around with them and wouldn't do anything, no games, nothing. Some of them went off with the girls," he said, in the dark, seated, not looking at her. "They went off up the beach and didn't come back. Honest to gosh." He stood now, huge, and leaned against the wall, looking all disproportioned in the short trousers. He had forgotten the child's hat was on his head. He suddenly remembered it and took it off and threw it on the floor. "I tried to kid them. I played with a toy dog and did some other stuff but nobody did anything. I felt like a fool the only one there dressed like this, and them all different, and only eight out of twenty there, and most of them gone in half an hour. Vi was there. She tried to get me to walk up the beach, too. I was mad by then. I was really mad. I said no thanks. And here I am. You can have the lollipop. Where did I put it? Pour the cider down the sink, drink it, I don't care."

She had not moved so much as an inch in all the time he talked. She opened her mouth.

The telephone rang.

"If that's them, I'm not home."

"You'd better answer it," she said.

He grabbed the phone and whipped off the receiver.

"Sammy?" said a loud high clear voice. He was holding the receiver out on the air, glaring at it in the dark. "That you?" He grunted. "This is Bob." The eighteen-year-old voice rushed on. "Glad you're home. In a big rush, but—what about that game tomorrow?"

"What game?"

"What game? For cri-yi, you're kidding. Notre Dame and S.C.!"

"Oh, football."

"Don't say oh football like that, you talked it, you played it up, you said—"

"That's no game," he said, not looking at the telephone, the receiver, the woman, the wall, nothing.

"You mean you're not going? Heavy-Set, it won't be a *game* without you!"

"I got to water the lawn, polish the car—"

"You can do that Sunday!"

"Besides, I think my uncle's coming over to see me. So long."

He hung up and walked out past his mother into the yard. She heard the sounds of him out there as she got ready for bed.

He must have drubbed the punching bag until three in the morning. Three, she thought, wide awake, listening to the concussions. He's always stopped at twelve, before.

At three thirty he came into the house.

She heard him just standing outside her door.

He did nothing else except stand there in the dark, breathing.

She had a feeling he still had the little boy suit on. But she didn't want to know if this were true.

After a long while the door swung slowly open.

He came into her dark room and lay down on the bed, next to her, not touching her. She pretended to be asleep.

He lay face up and rigid.

She could not see him. But she felt the bed shake as if he were laughing. She could hear no sound coming from him, so she could not be sure.

And then she heard the squeaking sounds of the little steel springs being crushed and uncrushed, crushed and uncrushed in his fists.

She wanted to sit up and scream for him to throw those awful noisy things away. She wanted to slap them out of his fingers.

But then, she thought, what would he do with his hands? What could he put in them? What would he, yes, what would he do with his hands?

So she did the only thing she could do, she held her breath, shut her eyes, listened, and prayed, O God, let it go on, let him keep squeezing those things, let him keep squeezing those things, let him, let him, oh let, let him, let him keep squeezing . . . let . . . let . . .

It was like lying in bed with a great dark cricket.

And a long time before dawn.

THE FIRST NIGHT OF LENT

So you want to know all the whys and wherefores of the Irish? What shapes them to their Dooms and runs them on their way? you ask. Well, listen, then. For though I've known but a single Irishman in all my life, I knew him, without pause, for one hundred and forty-four consecutive nights. Stand close; perhaps in him you'll see that entire race which marches out of the rains but to vanish through the mists; hold on, here they come! Look out, there they go!

This Irishman, his name was Nick.

During the autumn of 1953, I began a screenplay in Dublin, and each afternoon a hired cab drove me thirty miles out from the River Liffey to the huge gray Georgian country house where my producer-director rode to hounds. There, we discussed my eight pages of daily script through the long fall, winter, and early spring evenings. Then, each midnight, ready to turn back to the Irish Sea and the Royal Hibernian Hotel, I'd wake the operator in the Kilcock village exchange and have her put me through to the warmest, if totally unheated, spot in town.

"Heber Finn's pub?" I'd shout, once connected. "Is Nick there? Could you send him along here, please?"

My mind's eye saw them, the local boys, lined up, peering over the barricade at that freckled mirror so like a frozen winter pond and themselves discovered all drowned and deep under that lovely ice. Amid all their jostlings and their now-here's-a-secret-in-a-stage-whisper commotion stood Nick, my village driver, his quietness abounding. I heard Heber Finn sing out from the phone. I heard Nick start up and reply:

"Just look at me, headin' for the door!"

Early on, I learned that "headin' for the door" was no nerve-shattering process that might affront dignity or destroy the fine filigree of any argument being woven with great and breathless beauty at Heber Finn's. It was, rather, a gradual disengagement, a leaning of the bulk so one's gravity was diplomatically shifted toward that far empty side of the public room where the door, shunned by all, stood neglected. Meantime, a dozen conversational warps and woofs must be ticked, tied, and labeled so next morn, with hoarse cries of recognition, patterns might be seized and the shuttle thrown with no pause for breath or thought.

Timing it, I figured the long part of Nick's midnight journey—the length of Heber Finn's—took half an hour. The short part—from Finn's to the house where I waited—took but five minutes.

So it was on the night before the first night of Lent. I called. I waited.

And at last, down through the night forest, thrashed the 1931 Chevrolet, peat-turf colored on top like Nick. Car and driver gasped, sighed, wheezed softly, easily, gently as they nudged into the courtyard and I groped down the front steps under a moonless but brightly starred sky.

I peered through the car window at unstirred dark; the dashboard had been dead these many years.

"Nick . . . ?"

"None other," he whispered secretly. "And ain't it a fine warm evenin'?"

The temperature was fifty. But, Nick'd been no nearer Rome than the Tipperary shore line; so weather was relative.

"A fine warm evening." I climbed up front and gave the squealing door its absolutely compulsory, rust-splintering slam. "Nick, how've you been since?"

"Ah." He let the car bulk and grind itself down the forest path. "I got me health. Ain't that all-and-everything with Lent comin' on tomorra?"

"Lent," I mused. "What will you give up for Lent, Nick?"

"I been turnin' it over." Nick sucked his cigarette suddenly; the pink, lined mask of his face blinked off the smoke. "And why not these terrible things ya see in me mouth? Dear as gold-fillin's, and a dread congestor of the lungs they be. Put it all down, add 'em up, and ya got a sick loss by the year's turnin', ya know. So ya'll not find these filthy creatures in me face again the whole time of Lent, and, who knows, after!"

"Bravo!" said I, a non-smoker.

"Bravo, says I to meself," wheezed Nick, one eye flinched with smoke.

"Good luck," I said.

"I'll need it," whispered Nick, "with the Sin's own habit to be broke."

And we moved with firm control, with thoughtful shift of weight, down and around a turfy hollow and through a mist and into Dublin at thirty-one easy miles an hour.

✳ Bear with me while I stress it: Nick was the most careful driver in all God's world, including any sane, small, quiet, butter-and-milk producing country you name.

Above all, Nick stands innocent and sainted when compared to those motorists who key that small switch marked paranoia each time they fuse themselves to their bucket seats in Los Angeles, Mexico City, or Paris. Also, to those blind men who, forsaking tin cups and canes, but still wearing their Hollywood dark-glasses, laugh insanely down the Via Veneto, shaking brake-drum lining like carnival serpentine out their race-car windows. Consider the Roman ruins; surely they are the wreckage strewn and left by those motor-biking otters who, all night beneath your hotel window, shriek down dark Roman alleys, Christians hell-bent for the Colosseum lion pits.

Nick, now. See his easy hands loving the wheel in a slow clocklike turning as soft and silent as winter constellations snow down the sky. Listen to his mist-breathing voice all night-quiet as he charms the road, his foot a tenderly benevolent pat on the whispering accelerator, never a mile under thirty, never two miles over. Nick, Nick, and his steady boat gentling a mild sweet lake where all Time slumbers. Look, compare. And bind such a man to you with summer grasses, gift him with silver, shake his hand warmly at each journey's end.

"Good night, Nick," I said at the hotel. "See you tomorrow."

"God willing," whispered Nick.

And he drove softly away.

✳ Let twenty-three hours of sleep, breakfast, lunch, supper, late night-cap pass. Let hours of writing bad script into fair script fade to peat mist and rain, and there I come again, another midnight, out of that Georgian mansion, its door throwing a warm hearth of color before me as I tread down the steps to feel Braille-wise in fog for the car I know hulks there; I hear its enlarged and asthmatic heart gasping in the blind air, and Nick coughing his "gold by the ounce is not more precious" cough.

"Ah, there you are, sir!" said Nick.

And I climbed in the sociable front seat and gave the door its slam. "Nick," I said, smiling.

And then the impossible happened. The car jerked as if shot from the blazing mouth of a cannon, roared, took off, bounced, skidded, then cast itself in full, stoning ricochet down the path among shattered bushes and writhing shadows. I snatched my knees as my head hit the car top four times.

Nick! I almost shouted. Nick!

Visions of Los Angeles, Mexico City, Paris, jumped through my mind. I gazed in frank dismay at the speedometer. Eighty, ninety, one hundred kilometers; we shot out a great blast of gravel behind and hit the main road, rocked over a bridge and slid down in the midnight streets of Kilcock. No sooner in than out of town at one hundred ten kilometers, I felt all Ireland's grass put down its ears when we, with a yell, jumped over a rise.

Nick! I thought, and turned, and there he sat, only one thing the same. On his lips a cigarette burned, blinding first one eye, then the other.

But the rest of Nick, behind the cigarette, was changed as if the Adversary himself had squeezed and molded and fired him with a dark hand. There he was, whirling the wheel round-about, over-around; here we frenzied under trestles, out of tunnels, here knocked crossroad signs spinning like weathercocks in whirlwinds.

Nick's face; the wisdom was drained from it, the eyes neither gentle nor philosophical, the mouth neither tolerant, nor at peace. It was a face washed raw, a scalded, peeled potato, a face more like a blinding searchlight raking its steady and meaningless glare ahead while his quick hands snaked and bit and bit the wheel again to lean us round curves and jump us off cliff after cliff of night.

It's not Nick, I thought, it's his brother. Or a dire thing's come in his life, some destroying affliction or blow, a family sorrow or sickness, yes, that's the answer.

And then Nick spoke, and his voice, it was changed too. Gone was the mellow peat bog, the moist sod, the warm fire in out of the cold rain, gone the gentle grass. Now the voice fairly cracked at me, a clarion, a trumpet, all iron and tin.

"Well, how ya been since!" Nick shouted. "How is it with ya!" he cried.

And the car, it too had suffered violence. It protested the change, yes, for it was an old and much-beaten thing that had done its time and now only wished to stroll along, like a crusty beggar toward sea and sky, careful of its breath and bones. But Nick would have none of that, and cadged the wreck on as if thundering toward Hell, there to warm his cold hands at some special blaze. Nick leaned, the car leaned; great livid gases blew out in fireworks from the exhaust. Nick's frame, my frame, the car's frame, all together, were wracked and shuddered and ticked wildly.

My sanity was saved from being torn clean off the bone by a simple act. My eyes, seeking the cause of our plaguing flight, ran over the man blazing here like a sheet of ignited vapor from the Abyss, and laid hands to the answering clue.

"Nick," I gasped, "it's the first night of Lent!"

"So?" Nick said, surprised.

"So," I said, "remembering your Lenten promise, why's that cigarette in your mouth?"

Nick did not know what I meant for a moment. Then he cast his eyes down, saw the jiggling smoke, and shrugged.

"Ah," he said, "I give up the *other*."

And suddenly it all came clear.

The other one hundred forty-odd nights, at the door of the old Georgian house I had accepted from my employer a fiery douse of scotch or bourbon or some-such drink "against the chill." Then, breathing summer wheat or barley or oats or whatever from my scorched and charcoaled mouth, I had walked out to a cab where sat a man who, during all the long evenings' wait for me to phone for his services, had *lived* in Heber Finn's pub.

Fool! I thought, how could you have forgotten this!

And there in Heber Finn's, during the long hours of lacy talk that was like planting and bringing to crop a garden among busy men, each contributing his seed or flower, and wielding the implements, their tongues, and the raised, foam-hived glasses, their own hands softly curled about the dear drinks, there Nick had taken into himself a mellowness.

And that mellowness had distilled itself down in a slow rain that damped his smoldering nerves and put the wilderness fires in every limb of him out. Those same showers laved his face to leave the tidal marks of wisdom, the lines of Plato and Aeschylus there. The harvest mellowness colored his cheeks, warmed his eyes soft, lowered his voice to a husking mist, and spread in his chest to slow his heart to a gentle jog trot. It rained out his arms to loosen his hard-mouthed hands on the shuddering wheel and sit him with grace and ease in his horse-hair saddle as he gentled us through the fogs that kept us and Dublin apart.

And with the malt on my own tongue, fluming up my sinus with burning vapors, I had never detected the scent of any spirits on my old friend here.

"Ah," said Nick again. "Yes; I give up the *other*."

The last bit of jigsaw fell in place.

Tonight, the first night of Lent.

Tonight, for the first time in all the nights I had driven with him, Nick was sober.

All those other one hundred and forty-odd nights, Nick hadn't been driving careful and easy just for my safety, no, but because of the gentle weight of mellowness sloping now on this side, now on that side of him as we took the long, scything curves.

Oh, who really knows the Irish, say I, and which half of them is which? Nick?—who is Nick?—and what in the world is he? Which Nick's the real Nick, the one that everyone knows?

I will not think on it!

There is only *one* Nick for me. The one that Ireland shaped herself with her weathers and waters, her seedings and harvestings, her brans and mashes, her brews, bottlings, and ladlings-out, her summer-grain-colored pubs astir and advance with the wind in the wheat and barley by night, you may hear the good whisper way out in forest, on bog, as you roll by. That's Nick to the teeth, eye, and heart, to his easygoing hands. If you ask what makes the Irish what they are, I'd point on down the road and tell where you turn to Heber Finn's.

The first night of Lent, and before you count nine, we're in Dublin! I'm out of the cab and it's puttering there at the curb and I lean in to put my money in the hands of my driver. Earnestly, pleadingly, warmly, with all the friendly urging in the world, I look into that fine man's raw, strange, torchlike face.

"Nick," I said.

"Sir!" he shouted.

"Do me a favor," I said.

"Anything!" he shouted.

"Take this extra money," I said, "and buy the biggest bottle of Irish moss you can find. And just before you pick me up tomorrow night, Nick, drink it down, drink it all. Will you do that, Nick? Will you promise me, cross your heart and hope to die, to do that?"

He thought on it, and the very thought damped down the ruinous blaze in his face.

"Ya make it terrible hard on me," he said.

I forced his fingers shut on the money. At last he put it in his pocket and faced silently ahead.

"Good night, Nick," I said. "See you tomorrow."

"God willing," said Nick.

And he drove away.

LAFAYETTE, FAREWELL

THERE WAS A TAP ON THE DOOR, the bell was not rung, so I knew who it was. The tapping used to happen once a week, but in the past few weeks it came every other day. I shut my eyes, said a prayer, and opened the door.

Bill Westerleigh was there, looking at me, tears streaming down his cheeks.

"Is this *my* house or *yours*?" he said.

It was an old joke now. Several times a year he wandered off, an eighty-nine-year-old man, to get lost within a few blocks. He had quit driving years ago because he had wound up thirty miles out of Los Angeles instead of at the center where we were. His best journey nowadays was from next door, where he lived with his wondrously warm and understanding wife, to here, where he tapped, entered, and wept. "Is this your house or *mine*?" he said, reversing the order.

"*Mi casa es su casa.*" I quoted the old Spanish saying.

"And thank God for that!"

I led the way to the sherry bottle and glasses in the parlor and poured two glasses while Bill settled in an easy chair across from me. He wiped his eyes and blew his nose on a handkerchief which he then folded neatly and put back in his breast pocket.

"Here's to you, buster." He waved his sherry glass. "The sky is full of 'em. I hope you come back. If not, we'll drop a black wreath where we think your crate fell."

I drank and was warmed by the drink and then looked a long while at Bill.

"The Escadrille been buzzing you again?" I asked.

"Every night, right after midnight. Every morning now. And, the last week, noons. I try not to come over. I tried for three days."

"I know. I missed you."

"Kind of you to say, son. You have a good heart. But I know I'm a pest, when I have my clear moments. Right now I'm clear and I drink your hospitable health."

He emptied his glass and I refilled it.

"You want to talk about it?"

"You sound just like a psychiatrist friend of mine. Not that I ever went to one, he was just a friend. Great thing about coming over here is it's free, and sherry to boot." He eyed his drink pensively. "It's a terrible thing to be haunted by ghosts."

"We all have them. That's where Shakespeare was so bright. He taught himself, taught us, taught psychiatrists. Don't do bad, he said, or your ghosts will get you. The old remembrance, the conscience which doth make cowards and scare midnight men, will rise up and cry, Hamlet, remember me, Macbeth, you're marked, Lady Macbeth, you, too! Richard the Third, beware, we walk the dawn camp at your shoulder and our shrouds are stiff with blood."

"God, you talk purty." Bill shook his head. "Nice living next door to a writer. When I need a dose of poetry, here you are."

"I tend to lecture. It bores my friends."

"Not me, dear buster, not me. But you're right. I mean, what we were talking about. Ghosts."

He put his sherry down and then held to the arms of his easy chair, as if it were the edges of a cockpit.

"I fly all the time now. It's nineteen eighteen more than it's nineteen eighty-seven. It's France more than it's the US of A. I'm up there with the old Lafayette. I'm on the ground near Paris with Rickenbacker. And there, just as the sun goes down, is the Red Baron. I've had quite a life, haven't I, Sam?"

It was his affectionate mode to call me by six or seven assorted names. I loved them all. I nodded.

"I'm going to do your story someday," I said. "It's not every writer whose neighbor was part of the Escadrille and flew and fought against von Richthofen."

"You couldn't write it, dear Ralph, you wouldn't know what to say."

"I might surprise you."

"You might, by God, you might. Did I ever show you the picture of myself and the whole Lafayette Escadrille team lined up by our junky biplane the summer of 'eighteen?"

"No," I lied, "let me see."

He pulled a small photo from his wallet and tossed it across to me. I had seen it a hundred times but it was a wonder and a delight.

"That's me, in the middle left, the short guy with the dumb smile next to Rickenbacker." Bill reached to point.

I looked at all the dead men, for most were long dead now, and there was Bill, twenty years old and lark-happy, and all the other young, young, oh, dear God, young men lined up, arms around each other, or one arm down holding helmet and goggles, and behind them a French 7-1 biplane, and beyond, the flat airfield somewhere near the Western Front. Sounds of flying came out of the damned picture. They always did, when I held it. And sounds of wind and birds. It was like a miniature TV screen. At any moment I expected the Lafayette Escadrille to burst into action, spin, run, and take off into that absolutely clear and endless sky. At that very moment in time, in the photo, the Red Baron still lived in the clouds; he would be there forever now and never land, which was right and good, for we wanted him to stay there always, that's how boys and men feel.

"God, I love showing you things." Bill broke the spell. "You're so damned appreciative. I wish I had had you around when I was making films at MGM."

That was the other part of William (Bill) Westerleigh. From fighting and photographing the Western Front half a mile up, he had moved on, when he got back to the States. From the Eastman labs in New York, he had drifted to some flimsy film studios in Chicago, where Gloria Swanson had once starred, to Hollywood and MGM. From MGM he had shipped to Africa to camera-shoot lions and the Watusi for *King Solomon's Mines*. Around the world's studios, there was no one he didn't know or who didn't know him. He had been principal cameraman on some two hundred films, and there were two bright gold Academy Oscars on his mantel next door.

"I'm sorry I grew up so long after you," I said. "Where's that photo of you and Rickenbacker alone? And the one signed by von Richthofen."

"You don't want to see *them*, buster."

"Like hell I don't!"

He unfolded his wallet and gently held out the picture of the two of them, himself and Captain Eddie, and the single snap of von Richthofen in full uniform, and signed in ink below.

"All gone," said Bill. "Most of 'em. Just one or two, and me left. And it won't be long"—he paused—"before there's not even me."

And suddenly again, the tears began to come out of his eyes and roll down and off his nose.

I refilled his glass.

He drank it and said:

"The thing is, I'm not afraid of *dying*. I'm just afraid of dying and going to *hell*!"

"You're not going there, Bill," I said.

"Yes, I am!" he cried out, almost indignantly, eyes blazing, tears streaming around his gulping mouth. "For what I did, what I can *never* be forgiven for!"

I waited a moment. "What was that, Bill?" I asked quietly.

"All those young boys I killed, all those young men I destroyed, all those beautiful people I murdered."

"You never did that, Bill," I said.

"Yes! I did! In the sky, dammit, in the air over France, over Germany, so long ago, but Jesus, there they are every night now, alive again, flying, waving, yelling, laughing like boys, until I fire my guns between the propellers and their wings catch fire and spin down. Sometimes they wave to me, *okay!* as they fall. Sometimes they curse. But, Jesus, every night, every morning now, the last month, they never leave. Oh, those beautiful boys, those lovely young men, those fine faces, the great shining and loving eyes, and down they go. And I did it. And I'll burn in hell for it!"

"You will not, I repeat *not*, burn in hell," I said.

"Give me another drink and shut up," said Bill. "What do *you* know about who burns and who doesn't? Are you Catholic? No. Are you Baptist? Baptists burn more slowly. There. Thanks."

I had filled his glass. He gave it a sip, the drink for his mouth meeting the stuff from his eyes.

"William." I sat back and filled my own glass. "No one burns in hell for war. War's that way."

"We'll *all* burn," said Bill.

"Bill, at this very moment, in Germany, there's a man your age, bothered with the same dreams, crying in his beer, remembering too much."

"As well they should! They'll burn, he'll burn too, remembering my friends, the lovely boys who got themselves screwed into the ground when their propellers chewed the way. Don't you see? *They* didn't know. *I* didn't know. No one told *them*, no one told *us*!"

"What?"

"What war *was*. Christ, we didn't know it would come after us, find us, so late in time. We thought it was all over; that we had a way to forget, put it off, bury it. Our officers didn't say. Maybe they just didn't know. None of us did. No one guessed that one day, in old age, the graves would bust wide, and all those lovely faces come up, and the whole war with 'em! How could we guess that? How could we know? But now the time's here, and the skies are full, and the ships just won't come down, unless they burn. And the young men won't stop waving at me at three in the morning unless I kill them all over again. Jesus Christ. It's so terrible. It's so sad. How do I save them? What do I do to go back and say, Christ, I'm sorry, it should never have happened, someone should have warned us when we were happy: war's not just dying, it's remembering and remembering *late* as well as soon. I wish them well. How do I say *that*, what's the next *move*?"

"There is no move," I said quietly. "Just sit here with a friend and have another drink. I can't think of anything to do. I wish I could. . . ."

Bill fiddled with his glass, turning it round and round.

"Let me tell you, then," he whispered. "Tonight, maybe tomorrow night's the last time you'll ever see me. Hear me out."

He leaned forward, gazing up at the high ceiling and then out the window where storm clouds were being gathered by wind.

"They've been landing in our backyards, the last few nights. You wouldn't have heard. Parachutes make sounds like kites, soft kind of whispers. The parachutes come down on our back lawns. Other nights, the bodies, without parachutes. The good nights are the quiet ones when you just hear the silk and the threads on the clouds. The bad ones are when you hear a hundred and eighty pounds of aviator hit the grass. Then you can't sleep. Last night, a dozen things hit the bushes near my bedroom window. I looked up in the clouds tonight and they were full of planes and smoke. Can you make them stop? Do you *believe* me?"

"That's the one thing; I *do* believe."

He sighed, a deep sigh that released his soul.

"Thank *God*! But what do I do *next*?"

"Have you," I asked, "tried talking to them? I mean," I said, "have you asked for their *forgiveness*?"

"Would they *listen*? Would they forgive? My God," he said. "Of course! Why not? Will you come *with* me? Your backyard. No trees for them to get strung up in. Christ, or on your porch. . . ."

"The porch, I think."

I opened the living room French doors and stepped out. It was a calm evening with only touches of wind motioning the trees and changing the clouds.

Bill was behind me, a bit unsteady on his feet, a hopeful grin, part panic, on his face.

I looked at the sky and the rising moon.

"Nothing out here," I said.

"Oh, Christ, yes, there is. Look," he said. "No, wait. Listen."

I stood turning white cold, wondering why I waited, and listened.

"Do we stand out in the middle of your garden, where they can see us? You don't have to if you don't want."

"Hell," I lied. "I'm not afraid." I lifted my glass. "To the Lafayette Escadrille?" I said.

"No, no!" cried Bill, alarmed. "Not tonight. They mustn't hear *that*. To *them*, Doug. *Them*." He motioned his glass at the sky where the clouds flew over in squadrons and the moon was a round, white, tombstone world.

"To von Richthofen, and the beautiful sad young men."

I repeated his words in a whisper.

And then we drank, lifting our empty glasses so the clouds and the moon and the silent sky could see.

"I'm ready," said Bill, "if they want to come get me now. Better to die out here than go in and hear them landing every night and every night in their parachutes and no sleep until dawn when the last silk folds in on itself and the bottle's empty. Stand right over there, son. That's it. Just half in the shadow. Now."

I moved back and we waited.

"What'll I say to them?" he asked.

"God, Bill," I said, "I don't know. They're not my friends."

"They weren't mine, either. More's the pity. I *thought* they were the enemy. Christ, isn't that a dumb stupid halfass word. The enemy! As if such a thing ever really happened in the world. Sure, maybe the bully that chased and beat you up in the schoolyard, or the guy who took your girl and laughed at you. But them, those beauties, up in the clouds on summer days or autumn afternoons? No, no!"

He moved farther out on the porch.

"All right," he whispered. "Here I am."

And he leaned way out, and opened his arms as if to embrace the night air.

"Come on! What you waiting for!"

He shut his eyes.

"Your turn," he cried. "My God, you *got* to hear, you got to come. You beautiful bastards, *here!*"

And he tilted his head back as if to welcome a dark rain.

"Are they coming?" he whispered aside, eyes clenched.

"No."

Bill lifted his old face into the air and stared upward, willing the clouds to shift and change and become something more than clouds.

"Damn it!" he cried, at last. "I killed you all. Forgive me or come kill me!" And a final angry burst. "Forgive me. I'm sorry!"

The force of his voice was enough to push me completely back into shadows. Maybe that did it. Maybe Bill, standing like a small statue in the middle of my garden, made the clouds shift and the wind blow south instead of north. We both heard, a long way off, an immense whisper.

"Yes!" cried Bill, and to me, aside, eyes shut, teeth clenched, "You *hear!?*"

We heard another sound, closer now, like great flowers or blossoms lifted off spring trees and run along the sky.

"There," whispered Bill.

The clouds seemed to form a lid and make a vast silken shape which dropped in serene silence upon the land. It made a shadow that crossed the town and hid the houses and at last reached our garden and shadowed the grass and put out the light of the moon and then hid Bill from my sight.

"Yes! They're coming," cried Bill. "Feel them? One, two, a dozen! Oh, God, yes."

And all around, in the dark, I thought I heard apples and plums and peaches falling from unseen trees, the sound of boots hitting my lawn, and the sound of pillows striking the grass like bodies, and the swarming of tapestries of white silk or smoke flung across the disturbed air.

"Bill!"

"No!" he yelled. "I'm okay! They're all around. Get back! *Yes!*"

There was a tumult in the garden. The hedges shivered with propeller wind. The grass lay down its nap. A tin watering can blew across the yard. Birds were flung from trees. Dogs all around the block yelped. A siren, from another war, sounded ten miles away. A storm had arrived, and was that thunder or field artillery?

And one last time, I heard Bill say, almost quietly, "I didn't know, oh, God, I didn't know what I was doing." And a final fading sound of "Please."

And the rain fell briefly to mix with the tears on his face.

And the rain stopped and the wind was still.

"Well." He wiped his eyes, and blew his nose on his big hankie, and looked at the hankie as if it were the map of France. "It's time to go. Do you think I'll get lost again?"

"If you do, come here."

"Sure." He moved across the lawn, his eyes clear. "How much do I owe you, Sigmund?"

"Only *this*," I said.

I gave him a hug. He walked out to the street. I followed to watch.

When he got to the corner, he seemed to be confused. He turned to his right, then his left. I waited and then called gently:

"To your *left*, Bill."

"God bless you, buster!" he said, and waved.

He turned and went into his house.

⁎ They found him a month later, wandering two miles from home. A month after that he was in the hospital, in France all the time now, and Rickenbacker in the bed to his right and von Richthofen in the cot to his left.

The day after his funeral the Oscar arrived, carried by his wife, to place on my mantel, with a single red rose beside it, and the picture of von Richthofen, and the other picture of the gang lined up in the summer of '18 and the wind blowing out of the picture and the buzz of planes. And the sound of young men laughing as if they might go on forever.

Sometimes I come down at three in the morning when I can't sleep and I stand looking at Bill and his friends. And sentimental sap that I am, I wave a glass of sherry at them.

"Farewell, Lafayette," I say. "Lafayette, farewell."

And they all laugh as if it were the grandest joke that they ever heard.

REMEMBER SASCHA?

REMEMBER? WHY, HOW COULD THEY FORGET? Although they knew him for only a little while, years later his name would arise and they would smile or even laugh and reach out to hold hands, remembering.

Sascha. What a tender, witty comrade, what a sly, hidden individual, what a child of talent; teller of tales, bon vivant, late-night companion, ever-present illumination on foggy noons.

Sascha!

He, whom they had never seen, to whom they spoke often at three A.M. in their small bedroom, away from friends who might roll their eyeballs under their lids, doubting their sanity, hearing *his* name.

Well, then, who and what was Sascha, and where did they meet or perhaps only dream him, and who were *they*?

Quickly: they were Maggie and Douglas Spaulding and they lived by the loud sea and the warm sand and the rickety bridges over the almost dead canals of Venice, California. Though lacking money in the bank or Goodwill furniture in their tiny two-room apartment, they were incredibly happy. He was a writer, and she worked to support him while he finished the great American novel.

Their routine was: she would arrive home each night from downtown

Los Angeles and he would have hamburgers waiting or they would walk down the beach to eat hot dogs, spend ten or twenty cents in the Penny Arcade, go home, make love, go to sleep, and repeat the whole wondrous routine the next night: hot dogs, Penny Arcade, love, sleep, work, etc. It was all glorious in that year of being very young and in love; therefore it would go on forever . . .

Until *he* appeared.

The nameless one. For then he had no name. He had threatened to arrive a few months after their marriage to destroy their economy and scare off the novel, but then he had melted away, leaving only his echo of a threat.

But now the true collision loomed.

One night over a ham omelet with a bottle of cheap red and the conversation loping quietly, leaning on the card table and promising each other grander and more ebullient futures, Maggie suddenly said, "I feel faint."

"What?" said Douglas Spaulding.

"I've felt funny all day. And I was sick, a little bit, this morning."

"Oh, my God." He rose and came around the card table and took her head in his hands and pressed her brow against his side, and looked down at the beautiful part in her hair, suddenly smiling.

"Well, now," he said, "don't tell me that Sascha is back?"

"Sascha! Who's *that*?"

"When he arrives, he'll *tell* us."

"Where did that name *come* from?"

"Don't know. It's been in my mind all year."

"Sascha?" She pressed his hands to her cheeks, laughing. "Sascha!"

"Call the doctor tomorrow," he said.

✳ "The doctor says Sascha has moved in for light housekeeping," she said over the phone the next day.

"Great!" He stopped. "I *guess.*" He considered their bank deposits. "No. *First* thoughts count. Great! When do we meet the Martian invader?"

"October. He's infinitesimal now, tiny, I can barely hear his voice. But now that he has a name, I hear it. He promises to grow, if we take care."

"The Fabulous Invalid! Shall I stock up on carrots, spinach, broccoli for *what* date?"

"Halloween."

"Impossible!"

"True!"

"People will claim we planned him and my vampire book to arrive that week, things that go bump and cry in the night."

"Oh, Sascha will surely do *that! Happy?*"

"Frightened, yes, but happy, Lord, yes. Come home, Mrs. Rabbit, and bring *him* along!"

✳ It must be explained that Maggie and Douglas Spaulding were best described as crazed romantics. Long before the interior christening of Sascha, they, loving Laurel and Hardy, had called each other Stan and Ollie. The machines, the dustbusters and can openers around the apartment, had names, as did various parts of their anatomy, revealed to no one.

So Sascha, as an entity, a presence growing toward friendship, was not unusual. And when he actually began to speak up, they were not surprised. The gentle demands of their marriage, with love as currency instead of cash, made it inevitable.

Someday, they said, if they owned a car, it too would be named.

They spoke on that and a dozen score of things late at night. When hyperventilating about life, they propped themselves up on their pillows as if the future might happen right *now*. They waited, anticipating, in séance, for the silent small offspring to speak his first words before dawn.

"I love our lives," said Maggie, lying there, "all the games. I hope it never stops. You're not like other men, who drink beer and talk poker. Dear God, I wonder, how many other marriages play like us?"

"No one, nowhere. Remember?"

"What?"

He lay back to trace his memory on the ceiling.

"The day we were married—"

"Yes!"

"Our friends driving and dropping us off here and we walked down to the drugstore by the pier and bought a tube of toothpaste and two tooth-brushes, big bucks, for our honeymoon . . . ? One red toothbrush, one green, to decorate our empty bathroom. And on the way back along the beach, holding hands, suddenly, behind us, two little girls and a boy fol-lowed us and sang:

> "*Happy marriage day to you,*
> *Happy marriage day to you.*

Happy marriage day, happy marriage day,
Happy marriage day to you . . ."

She sang it now, quietly. He chimed in, remembering how they had blushed with pleasure at the children's voices, but walked on, feeling ridiculous but happy and wonderful.

"How did they guess? Did we *look* married?"

"It wasn't our clothes! Our faces, don't you think? Smiles that made our jaws ache. We were exploding. They got the concussion."

"Those dear children. I can still hear their voices."

"And so here we are, seventeen months later." He put his arm around her and gazed at their future on the dark ceiling.

" 'And here *I* am," a voice murmured.

"Who?" Douglas said.

"Me," the voice whispered. "Sascha."

Douglas looked down at his wife's mouth, which had barely trembled.

"So, at last, you've decided to speak?" said Douglas.

"Yes," came the whisper.

"We wondered," said Douglas, "when we would hear from you." He squeezed his wife gently.

"It's time," the voice murmured. "So here I am."

"Welcome, Sascha," both said.

"Why didn't you talk sooner?" asked Douglas Spaulding.

"I wasn't sure that you *liked* me," the voice whispered.

"Why would you think *that?*"

"First I was, then I wasn't. Once I was only a name. Remember, last year, I was ready to come and stay. Scared you."

"We were broke," said Douglas quietly. "And nervous."

"What's so scary about life?" said Sascha. Maggie's lips twitched. "It's that *other* thing. *Not* being, ever. Not being wanted."

"On the contrary." Douglas Spaulding moved down on his pillow so he could watch his wife's profile, her eyes shut, but her mouth breathing softly. "We love you. But last year it was bad timing. Understand?"

"No," whispered Sascha. "I only understand you didn't want me. And now you *do.* I should leave."

"But you just *got* here!"

"Here I go, anyway."

"Don't, Sascha! Stay!"

"Good-bye." The small voice faded. "Oh, good-bye."

And then silence.

Maggie opened her eyes with quiet panic.

"Sascha's gone," she said.

"He *can't* be!"

The room was still.

"*Can't* be," he said. "It's only a game."

"More than a game. Oh, God, I feel cold. Hold me."

He moved to hug her.

"It's okay."

"No. I had the funniest feeling just now, as if he were real."

"He *is*. He's *not* gone."

"Unless we do something. Help me."

"Help?" He held her even tighter, then shut his eyes, and at last called: "Sascha?"

Silence.

"I know you're there. You can't hide."

His hand moved to where Sascha might be.

"Listen. Say something. Don't scare us, Sascha. We don't want to be scared or scare you. We need each other. We three against the world. Sascha?"

Silence.

"Well?" whispered Douglas.

Maggie breathed in and out.

They waited.

"Yes?"

There was a soft flutter, the merest exhalation on the night air.

"Yes."

"You're back!" both cried.

Another silence.

"Welcome?" asked Sascha.

"Welcome!" both said.

✳ And that night passed and the next day and the night and day after that, until there were many days, but especially midnights when he dared to declare himself, pipe opinions, grow stronger and firmer and longer in half-heard declarations, as they lay in anticipatory awareness, now she moving her lips, now he taking over, both open as warm, live ventriloquists' mouthpieces. The small voice shifted from one tongue to the other, with soft bouts of laughter at how ridiculous but loving it all seemed, never knowing what Sascha might say next, but letting him speak on until dawn and a smiling sleep.

"What's this about Halloween?" he asked, somewhere in the sixth month.

"Halloween?" both wondered.

"Isn't that a death holiday?" Sascha murmured.

"Well, yes . . ."

"I'm not sure I want to be born on a night like that."

"Well, what night *would* you like to be born on?"

Silence as Sascha floated a while.

"Guy Fawkes," he finally whispered.

"Guy Fawkes??!!"

"That's mainly fireworks, gunpowder plots, Houses of Parliament, yes? *Please to remember the fifth of November?*"

"Do you think you could wait until then?"

"I could try. I don't think I want to start out with skulls and bones. Gunpowder's more like it. I could write about that."

"Will you be a writer, then?"

"Get me a typewriter and a ream of paper."

"And keep us awake with the *typing*?"

"Pen, pencil, and pad, then?"

"Done!"

So it was agreed and the nights passed into weeks and the weeks leaned from summer into the first days of autumn and his voice grew stronger, as did the sound of his heart and the small commotions of his limbs. Sometimes as Maggie slept, his voice would stir her awake and she would reach up to touch her mouth, where the surprise of his dreaming came forth.

"There, there, Sascha. Rest now. Sleep."

"Sleep," he whispered drowsily, "sleep." And faded away.

✳ "Pork chops, please, for supper."

"No pickles with ice cream?" both said, almost at once.

"Pork chops," he said, and more days passed and more dawns arose and he said: "Hamburgers!"

"For *breakfast*?"

"With onions," he said.

October stood still for one day and then . . .

Halloween departed.

"Thanks," said Sascha, "for helping me past *that*. What's up ahead in five nights?"

"Guy Fawkes!"

"Ah, yes!" he cried.

And at one minute after midnight five days later, Maggie got up, wandered to the bathroom, and wandered back, stunned.

"Dear," she said, sitting on the edge of the bed.

Douglas Spaulding turned over, half awake. "Yes?"

"What day is it?" whispered Sascha.

"Guy Fawkes, at last. So?"

"I don't feel well," said Sascha. "Or, no, I feel fine. Full of pep. Ready to go. It's time to say good-bye. Or is it hello? What *do* I mean?"

"Spit it out."

"Are there neighbors who said, no matter when, they'd take us to the hospital?"

"Yes."

"Call the neighbors," said Sascha.

They called the neighbors.

At the hospital, Douglas kissed his wife's brow and listened.

"It's been nice," said Sascha.

"Only the best."

"We won't talk again. Good-bye," said Sascha.

"Good-bye," both said.

At dawn there was a small clear cry somewhere.

Not long after, Douglas entered his wife's hospital room. She looked at him and said, "Sascha's gone."

"I know," he said quietly.

"But he left word and someone else is here. Look."

He approached the bed as she pulled back a coverlet.

"Well, I'll be damned."

He looked down at a small pink face and eyes that for a brief moment flickered bright blue and then shut.

"Who's that?" he asked.

"Your daughter. Meet Alexandra."

"Hello, Alexandra," he said.

"And do you know what the nickname for Alexandra is?" she said.

"What?"

"Sascha," she said.

He touched the small cheek very gently.

"Hello, Sascha," he said.

JUNIOR

It was on the morning of October 1 that Albert Beam, aged eighty-two, woke to find an incredible thing had happened, if not in the night, miraculously at dawn.

He witnessed a warm and peculiar rise two-thirds of the way down the bed, under the covers. At first he thought he had drawn up one knee to ease a cramp, but then, blinking, he realized—

It was his old friend, Albert, Junior.

Or just Junior, as some frolicsome girl had dubbed it, how long, oh God . . . some sixty years ago!

And Junior was alive, well, and freshly alert.

Hallo, thought Albert Beam, Senior, to the scene, that's the first time he's waked before me since July 1970.

July 1970!

He stared. And the more he stared and mused, the more Junior blushed unseen; all resolute, a true beauty.

Well, thought Albert Beam, I'll just wait for him to go away.

He shut his eyes and waited, but nothing happened. Or rather, it *continued* to happen. Junior did not go away. He lingered, hopeful for some new life.

Hold on! thought Albert Beam. It *can't* be.

He sat bolt upright, his eyes popped wide, his breath like a fever in his mouth.

"Are you going to *stay*?" he cried down at his old and now bravely obedient friend.

Yes! he thought he heard a small voice say.

For as a young man, he and his trampoline companions had often enjoyed Charlie McCarthy talks with Junior, who was garrulous and piped up with outrageously witty things. Ventriloquism, amidst Phys. Ed. II, was one of Albert Beam's most engaging talents.

Which meant that Junior was talented, too.

Yes! the small voice seemed to whisper. *Yes!*

Albert Beam bolted from bed. He was halfway through his personal phonebook when he realized all the old numbers still drifted behind his left ear. He dialed three of them, furiously, voice cracking.

"Hello."

"Hello!"

"Hello!"

From this island of old age now he called across a cold sea toward a summer shore. There, three women answered. Still reasonably young, trapped between fifty and sixty, they gasped, crowed and hooted when Albert Beam stunned them with the news:

"Emily, you won't believe—"

"Cora, a *miracle!*"

"Elizabeth, Junior's back."

"Lazarus has returned!"

"Drop everything!"

"Hurry over!"

"Good-bye, good-bye, *good-bye!*"

He dropped the phone, suddenly fearful that after all the alarums and excursions, this Most Precious Member of the Hot-Dog Midnight Dancing-Under-the-Table Club might dismantle. He shuddered to think that Cape Canaveral's rockets would fall apart before the admiring crowd could arrive to gape in awe.

Such was not the case.

Junior, steadfast, stayed on, frightful in demeanor, a wonder to behold.

Albert Beam, ninety-five percent mummy, five percent jaunty peacock lad, raced about his mansion in his starkers, drinking coffee to give Junior courage and shock himself awake, and when he heard the various cars careen up the drive, threw on a hasty robe. With hair in wild disarray he rushed to let in three girls who were not girls, nor maids, and almost ladies.

But before he could throw the door wide, they were storming it with jackhammers, or so it seemed, their enthusiasm was so manic.

They burst through, almost heaving him to the floor, and waltzed him backward into the parlor.

One had once been a redhead, the next a blond, the third a brunette. Now, with various rinses and tints obscuring past colors false and real, each a bit more out of breath than the next, they laughed and giggled as they carried Albert Beam along through his house. And whether they were flushed with merriment or blushed at the thought of the antique miracle they were about to witness, who could say? They were scarcely dressed, themselves, having hurled themselves into dressing-gowns in order to race here and confront Lazarus triumphant in the tomb!

"Albert, is it *true*?"

"No *joke*?"

"You once pinched our legs, now are you *pulling* them?!"

"Chums!"

Albert Beam shook his head and smiled a great warm smile, sensing a similar smile on the hidden countenance of his Pet, his Pal, his Buddy, his Friend. Lazarus, impatient, jogged in place.

"No jokes. No lies. Ladies, sit!"

The women rushed to collapse in chairs and turn their rosy faces and July Fourth eyes full on the old moon rocket expert, waiting for countdown.

Albert Beam took hold of the edges of his now purposely elusive bathrobe, while his eyes moved tenderly from face to face.

"Emily, Cora, Elizabeth," he said, gently, "how special you were, are, and will *always* be."

"Albert, dear Albert, we're dying with curiosity!"

"A moment, please," he murmured. "I need to—*remember*."

And in the quiet moment, each gazed at the other, and suddenly saw the obvious; something never spoken of in their early afternoon lives, but which now loomed with the passing years.

The simple fact was that none of them had ever grown up.

They had used each other to stay in kindergarten, or at the most, fourth grade, forever.

Which meant endless champagne noon lunches, and prolonged late night foxtrot/waltzes that sank down in nibblings of ears and founderings in grass.

None had ever married, none had ever conceived of the notion of children, much less conceived them, so none had raised any family save the one gathered here, and they had not so much raised each other as prolonged an infancy and lingered an adolescence. They had responded only to the jolly or wild weathers of their souls and their genetic dispositions.

"Listen, dear, dear, ladies," whispered Albert Beam.

They continued to stare at each other's masks with a sort of fevered benevolence. For it had suddenly struck them that while they had been busy making each other happy they had made no one else unhappy!

It was something to sense that by some miracle they'd given each other only minor wounds and those long since healed, for here they were, forty years on, still friends in remembrance of three loves.

"Friends," thought Albert Beam aloud. "*That's* what we are. *Friends!*"

Because, many years ago, as each beauty departed his life on good terms, another had arrived on better. It was the exquisite precision with which he had clocked them through his existence that made them aware of their specialness as women unafraid and so never jealous.

They beamed at one another.

What a thoughtful and ingenious man, to have made them absolutely and completely happy before he sailed on to founder in old age.

"Come, Albert, my dear," said Cora.

"The matinée crowd's here," said Emily.

"Where's Hamlet?"

"Ready?" said Albert Beam. "Get set?"

He hesitated in the final moment, since it was to be his last annunciation or manifestation or whatever before he vanished into the halls of history.

With trembling fingers that tried to remember the difference between zippers and buttons, he took hold of the bathrobe curtains on the theater, as 'twere.

At which instant a most peculiar loud hum bumbled beneath his pressed lips.

The ladies popped their eyes and smartened up, leaning forward.

For it was that grand moment when the Warner Brothers logo vanished from the screen and the names and titles flashed forth in a fountain of brass and strings by Steiner or Korngold.

Was it a symphonic surge from *Dark Victory* or *The Adventures of Robin Hood* that trembled the old man's lips?

Was it the score from *Elizabeth and Essex, Now, Voyager* or *The Petrified Forest*?

Petrified forest!? Albert Beam's lips cracked with the joke of it. How fitting for him, for Junior!

The music rose high, higher, highest, and exploded from his mouth.

"Ta-*tah!*" sang Albert Beam.

He flung wide the curtain.

The ladies cried out in sweet alarms.

For there, starring in the last act of Revelations, was Albert Beam the Second.

Or perhaps, justifiably proud, Junior!

Unseen in years, he was an orchard of beauty and sweet Eden's Garden, all to himself.

Was he both Apple *and* Snake?

He *was*!

Scenes from *Krakatoa, the Explosion that Rocked the World* teemed through the ladies' sugar-plum minds. Lines like "Only God Can Make a Tree" leaped forth from old poems. Cora seemed to recall the score from *Last Days of Pompeii*, Elizabeth the music from *Rise and Fall of the Roman Empire*. Emily, suddenly shocked back into 1927, babbled the inane words to "Lucky Lindy . . . Spirit of St. Louis, high, stay aloft . . . we're *with* you . . . !"

The musical trio quieted into a sort of twilight-in-mid-morning-holy-hour, a time for veneration and loving regard. It almost seemed that a wondrous illumination sprang forth from the Source, the Shrine at which they gathered as motionless worshippers, praying that the moment would be prolonged by their silent alleluias.

And it was prolonged.

Albert Beam and Junior stood as one before the throng, a large smile on the old man's face, a smaller one on Junior's.

Time-travel shadowed the ladies' faces.

Each remembered Monte Carlo or Paris or Rome or splash-dancing the Plaza Hotel fount that night centuries ago with Scott and Zelda. Suns and moons rose and set in their eyes and there was no jealousy, only lives long lost but brought back and encircled in this moment.

"Well," everyone whispered, at last.

One by one, each of the three pal-friends stepped forward to kiss Albert Beam lightly on the cheek and smile up at him and then down at the Royal Son, that most Precious Member who deserved to be patted, but was not, in this moment, touched.

The three Grecian maids, the retired Furies, the ancient vest porch goddesses, stepped back a way to line up for a final view-halloo.

And the weeping began.

First Emily, then Cora, then Elizabeth, as all summoned back some midnight collision of young fools who somehow survived the crash.

Albert Beam stood amidst the rising salt sea, until the tears also ran free from his eyes.

And whether they were tears of somber remembrance for a past that was not a golden pavane, or celebratory wails for a present most salubrious and enchanting, none could say. They wept and stood about, not knowing what to do with their hands.

Until at last, like small children peering in mirrors to catch the strangeness and mystery of weeping, they ducked under to look at each other's sobs.

They saw each other's eyeglasses spattered with wet salt stars from the tips of their eyelashes.

"Oh, *hah!*"

And the whole damned popcorn machine exploded into wild laughter.

"Oh, *heee!*"

They turned in circles with the bends. They stomped their feet to get the barks and hoots of hilarity out. They became weak as children at four o'clock tea, that silly hour when anything said is the funniest crack in all the world and the bones collapse and you wander in dazed circles to fall and writhe in ecstasies of mirth on the floor.

Which is what now happened. The ladies let gravity yank them down to flag their hair on the parquetry, their last tears flung like bright comets from their eyes as they rolled and gasped, stranded on a morning beach.

"Gods! Oh! Ah!" The old man could not stand it. Their earthquake shook and broke him. He saw, in this final moment, that his pal, his dear and precious Junior, had at last in all the shouts and snorts and happy cries melted away like a snow memory and was now a ghost.

And Albert Beam grabbed his knees, sneezed out a great laugh of recognition at the general shape, size and ridiculousness of birthday-suit humans on an indecipherable earth, and fell.

He squirmed amidst the ladies, chuckling, flailing for air. They dared not look at each other for fear of merciless heart attacks from the seal barks and elephant trumpetings that echoed from their lips.

Waiting for their mirth to let go, they at last sat up to rearrange their hair, their smiles, their breathing and their glances.

"Dear me, oh, dear, dear," moaned the old man, with a last gasp of relief. "Wasn't that the best ever, the finest, the loveliest time we have ever had anytime, anywhere, in all the great years?"

All nodded "yes."

"But," said practical Emily, straightening her face, "drama's done. Tea's cold. Time to go."

And they gathered to lift the old tentbones of the ancient warrior, and he stood among his dear ones in a glorious warm silence as they clothed him in his robe and guided him to the front door.

"Why?" wondered the old man. "Why? Why did Junior return on *this* day?"

"Silly!" cried Emily. "It's your birthday!"

"Well, happy *me*! Yes, yes." He mused. "Well, do you imagine, maybe, next year, and the next, will I be gifted the *same*?"

"Well," said Cora.

"We—"

"Not in this lifetime," said Emily, tenderly.

"Good-bye, dear Albert, fine Junior," said each.

"Thanks for all of my life," said the old man.

He waved and they were gone, down the drive and off into the fine fair morning.

He waited for a long while and then addressed himself to his old pal, his good friend, his now sleeping forever companion.

"Come on, Fido, here, boy, time for our pre-lunch nap. And, who knows, with luck we may dream wild dreams until tea!"

And, my God, he thought he heard the small voice cry, *then won't we be famished!?*

"We *will*!"

And the old man, half-asleep on his feet, and Junior already dreaming, fell flat forward into a bed with three warm and laughing ghosts. . . .

And so slept.

THAT WOMAN ON THE LAWN

VERY LATE AT NIGHT HE HEARD the weeping on the lawn in front of his house. It was the sound of a woman crying. By its sound he knew it was not a girl or a mature woman, but the crying of someone eighteen or nineteen years old. It went on, then faded and stopped, and again started up, now moving this way or that on the late-summer wind.

He lay in bed listening to it until it made his eyes fill with tears. He turned over, shut his eyes, let the tears fall, but could not stop the sound. Why should a young woman be weeping long after midnight out there?

He sat up and the weeping stopped.

At the window, he looked down. The lawn was empty but covered with dew. There was a trail of footsteps across the lawn to the middle where someone had stood turning, and another trail going off toward the garden around the house.

The moon stood full in the sky and filled the lawn with its light, but there was no more sadness and only the footprints there.

He stepped back from the window, suddenly chilled, and went down to heat and drink a cup of chocolate.

He did not think of the weeping again until dusk the next day, and even then thought that it must be some woman from a house nearby, unhappy with life, perhaps locked out and in need of a place to let her sadness go.

Yet . . . ?

As the twilight deepened, coming home he found himself hurrying from the bus, at a steady pace which astonished him. Why, why all this?

Idiot, he thought. A woman unseen weeps under your window, and here at sunset the next day, you almost run.

Yes, he thought, but her *voice*!

Was it beautiful, then?

No. Only familiar.

Where had he heard such a voice before, wordless in crying?

Who could he ask, living in an empty house from which his parents had vanished long ago?

He turned in at his front lawn and stood still, his eyes shadowed.

What had he expected? That whoever she was would be waiting here? Was he that lonely that a single voice long after midnight roused all his senses?

No. Simply put: he must know who the crying woman was.

And he was certain she would return tonight as he slept.

He went to bed at eleven, and awoke at three, panicked that he had missed a miracle. Lightning had destroyed a nearby town or an earthquake had shaken half the world to dust, and he had slept through it!

Fool! he thought, and slung back the covers and moved to the window, to see that indeed he had overslept.

For there on the lawn were the delicate footprints.

And he hadn't even *heard* the weeping!

He would have gone out to kneel in the grass, but at that moment a police car motored slowly by, looking at nothing and the night.

How could he run to prowl, to probe, to touch the grass if that car came by again? What doing? Picking clover blossoms? Weeding dandelions? What, what?

His bones cracked with indecision. He would go down, he would not.

Already the memory of that terrible weeping faded the more he tried to make it clear. If he missed her one more night, the memory itself might be gone.

Behind him, in his room, the alarm clock rang.

Damn! he thought. What time *did* I set it for?

He shut off the alarm and sat on his bed, rocking gently, waiting, eyes shut, listening.

The wind shifted. The tree just outside the window whispered and stirred.

He opened his eyes and leaned forward. From far off, coming near, and now down below, the quiet sound of a woman weeping.

She had come back to his lawn and was not forever lost. Be very quiet, he thought.

And the sounds she made came up on the wind through the blowing curtains into his room.

Careful now. Careful but quick.

He moved to the window and looked down.

In the middle of the lawn she stood and wept, her hair long and dark on her shoulders, her face bright with tears.

And there was something in the way her hands trembled at her sides, the way her hair moved quietly in the wind, that shook him so that he almost fell.

He knew her and yet did *not*. He had seen her before, but had never seen.

Turn your head, he thought.

Almost as if hearing this, the young woman sank to her knees to half kneel on the grass, letting the wind comb her hair, head down and weeping so steadily and bitterly that he wanted to cry out: Oh, no! It kills my heart!

And as if she had heard, quite suddenly her head lifted, her weeping grew less as she looked up at the moon, so that he saw her face.

And it was indeed a face seen somewhere once, but *where*?

A tear fell. She blinked.

It was like the blinking of a camera and a picture taken.

"God save me!" he whispered. "No!"

He whirled and stumbled toward the closet to seize down an avalanche of boxes and albums. In the dark he scrabbled, then pulled on the closet light, tossed aside six albums until finally, dragging another forth and riffling pages, he gave a cry, stopped, and held a photo close, then turned and moved blindly to the window.

There he stared down at the lawn and then at the photograph, very old, very yellowed with age.

Yes, yes, the same! The image struck his eyes and then his heart. His whole body shook, made an immense pulsation, as he leaned at the album, leaned on the window frame, and almost shouted:

You! How dare you come back! How dare you be young! How dare you be *what*? A girl untouched, wandering late on my lawn!? You were *never* that young! Never! Damn, oh, damn your warm blood, damn your wild soul!

But this he did not shout or say.

For something in his eyes, like a beacon, must have flashed.

The crying of the young woman on the lawn stopped.

She looked up.

At which instant the album fell from his fingers, through the burst-wide screen, and down like a dark bird fluttering to strike the earth.

The young woman gave a muted cry, whirled, and ran.

"No, no!" he cried aloud. "I didn't *mean*—come back!"

He was down the stairs and out on the porch in a matter of seconds. The door slammed behind him like a gunshot. The explosion nailed him to the rail, half down to the lawn, where there was nothing to be seen but footprints. Either way, up the street lay empty sidewalks and shadows under trees. A radio played off in an upstairs window in a house behind trees. A car passed, murmuring, at a far intersection.

"Wait," he whispered. "Come back. I shouldn't have *said*—"

He stopped. He had said nothing, but only *thought* it. But his outrage, his jealousy?

She had felt that. She had somehow heard. And now . . . ?

She'll never come back, he thought. Oh God!

He sat on the porch steps for a while, quietly biting his knuckle.

At three in the morning, in bed, he thought he heard a sigh and soft footsteps in grass, and waited. The photo album lay closed on the floor. Even though it lay shut, he could see and know her face. And it was utterly impossible, utterly insane.

His last thought before sleep was: ghost.

The strangest ghost that ever walked.

The ghost of someone dead.

The ghost of someone who died very old.

But somehow come back not as her old self.

But a ghost that was somehow young.

Weren't ghosts always, when they returned, the same age as when they died?

No.

Not this one anyway.

"Why . . . ?" he whispered.

And dream took over the whisper.

✳ One night passed and then another and another, and there was nothing on the lawn but the light of a moon that changed its face from outright stare to half grimace.

He waited.

The first night a more than ordinarily casual cat crossed the yard at two A.M.

The second night a dog trotted by, wearing his tongue half out of his mouth like a loosely tied red cravat, smiling at trees.

The third night a spider spent from twelve-twenty-five until four A.M. building a baroque clockface on the air between lawn and trees, which a bird broke in passing at dawn.

He slept most of Sunday and awoke with a fever that was not an illness at dusk.

Late in the twilight of the fifth day, the color of the sky somehow promised her return, as did the way the wind leaned against the trees and the look of the moon when it finally rose to set the scene.

"All right," he said, half aloud. "*Now.*"

But at midnight, nothing.

"Come on," he whispered.

One o'clock, nothing.

You must, he thought.

No, you *will*.

He slept for ten minutes and woke suddenly at two-ten, knowing that when he went to the window—

She would be there.

She was.

At first, he didn't see her, and groaned, and then, in the shadow of the great oak far out on the edge of the lawn, he saw something move, and one foot came out, and she took a step and stood very still.

He held his breath, quieted his heart, told himself to turn, walk, and take each step down with precision, numbering them, fifteen, fourteen, thirteen, moving in darkness with no rush, six, five, four, and at last one. He opened the front screen door with only a whisper, and was on the porch without frightening what might be out beyond waiting for him.

Quietly, he moved down the porch steps to the edge of the lawn, like one who stands on the rim of a pond. Out in the center of that pond, the young woman stood, trapped like someone on thin ice that might at any moment break and drop her through.

She did not see him. And then . . .

She did a thing that was a signal. Tonight her hair was fixed in a knot at the back of her head. She lifted her white arms in a gesture and with one touch of her fingers, a touch of snow, loosened her hair.

It fell in a dark banner, to blow and repattern itself across her shoulders, which trembled with their shadows.

The wind stirred her hair in the night and moved it about her face and on her uplifted hands.

The shadows laid down by the moon under every tree leaned as if called by the motion.

The entire world shifted in its sleep.

The wind blew as the young woman waited.

But no footsteps sounded along the white sidewalks. No front doors opened far down the street. No windows were raised. No motion caused front porches to creak and shift.

He took another step out onto the small meadow of night.

"Who are you—?" she gasped, and stepped back.

"No, no," he said softly. "It's all right."

Another trembling had taken over her body. Where before it had been some hope, some anticipation, now it was fear. One hand stopped her hair from blowing; the other half shielded her face.

"I'll stand right here," he said. "Believe me."

She waited a long while, staring at him until her shoulders relaxed and the lines around her mouth vanished. Her whole body sensed the truth of his words.

"I don't understand," she said.

"I don't either."

"What are you doing here?"

"I don't know."

"What am *I* doing here?"

"You came to meet someone," he said.

"Did I?"

The town clock struck three in the morning far away. She listened to it, her face shadowed by the sound.

"But it's so late. People don't walk around late on front lawns!"

"They do if they *must*," he said.

"But why?"

"Maybe we can find out, if we talk."

"About what, *what*?!"

"About why you're here. If we talk long enough, we may know. I know why I'm here, of course. I heard you crying."

"Oh, I'm so ashamed."

"Don't be. Why are people ashamed of tears? I cry often. Then I start laughing. But the crying must come first. Go ahead."

"What a strange man you are."

Her hand fell away from her hair. Her other hand moved away so her face was illuminated by a small and growing curiosity.

"I thought I was the only one who knew about crying," she said.

"Everyone thinks that. It's one of those little secrets we keep from each other. Show me a serious man and I'll show you a man who has never wept. Show me a madman and I'll show you a man who dried his tears a long time ago. Go ahead."

"I think I'm done," she said.

"Any time, start over."

She burst out a tiny laugh. "Oh, you *are* strange. Who are you?"

"We'll come to that."

She peered across the lawn at his hands, his face, his mouth, and then at his eyes.

"Oh, I *know* you. But from *where*?!"

"That would spoil it. You wouldn't believe, anyway."

"I would!"

Now it was his turn to laugh quietly. "You're very young."

"No, nineteen! *Ancient!*"

"Girls, by the time they go from twelve to nineteen, are full of years, yes. I don't know; but it must be so. Now, please, why are you out here in the middle of the night?"

"I—" She shut her eyes to think in on it. "I'm waiting."

"Yes?"

"And I'm sad."

"It's the waiting that makes you sad, yes?"

"I think, no, yes, no."

"And you don't quite know what you're waiting for?"

"Oh, I wish I could be sure. All of me's waiting. I don't know, *all* of me. I don't understand. I'm impossible!"

"No, you're everyone that ever grew up too fast and wanted too much. I think girls, women, like you have slipped out at night since time began. If it wasn't here in Green Town, it was in Cairo or Alexandria or Rome or Paris in summer, anywhere there was a private place and late hours and no one to see, so they just rose up and out, as if someone had called their name—"

"I was called, yes! That's *it*! Someone *did* call my name! It's *true*. How did you know? Was it *you*!"

"No. But someone we both know. You'll know his name when you go back to bed tonight, wherever that is."

"Why, in that house, behind you," she said. "That's my house. I was born in it."

"Well"—he laughed—"so was I."

"You? How can that be? Are you sure?"

"Yes. Anyway, you heard someone calling. You had to come out—"

"I did. Many nights now. But, always, no one's here. They *must* be there, or why would I hear them?"

"One day there'll be someone to fit the voice."

"Oh, don't joke with me!"

"I'm not. Believe. There will be. That's what all those other women heard in other years and places, middle of summer, dead of winter, go out and risk cold, stand warm in snow banks, and listen and look for strange footprints on the midnight snow, and only an old dog trotting by, all smiles. Damn, damn."

"Oh, yes, damn, damn." And her smile showed for a moment, even as the moon came out of the clouds and went away. "Isn't it silly?"

"No. Men do the same. They take long walks when they're sixteen, seventeen. They don't stand on lawns, waiting, no. But, my God, how they *walk*! Miles and miles from midnight until dawn and come home exhausted and explode and die in bed."

"What a shame that those who stand and wait and those who walk all night can't—"

"Meet?"

"Yes; don't you think it's a shame?"

"They *do*, finally."

"Oh, no, I shall never meet anyone. I'm old and ugly and terrible and I don't know how many nights I've heard that voice making me come here and there's nothing and I just want to die."

"Oh, lovely young girl," he said gently. "Don't die. The cavalry is on its way. You will be saved."

There was such certainty in his voice that it made her glance up again, for she had been looking at her hands and her own soul in her hands.

"You *know*, don't you?" she asked.

"Yes."

"You truly *know*? You tell the *truth*?"

"Swear to God, swear by all that's living."

"Tell me more!"

"There's little more to tell."

"Tell me!"

"Everything will be all right with you. Some night soon, or some day, someone will call and they'll really be there when you come to find. The game will be over."

"Hide-and-seek, you mean? But it's gone on too long!"

"It's almost over, Marie."

"You know my name!"

He stopped, confused. He had not meant to speak it.

"How did you know, who are you?" she demanded.

"When you get back to sleep tonight, you'll know. If we say too much, you'll disappear, or I'll disappear. I'm not quite sure which of us is real or which is a ghost."

"Not me! Oh, surely not me. I can feel myself. I'm here. Why, look!" And she showed him the remainder of her tears brushed from her eyelids and held on her palms.

"Oh, that's real, all right. Well, then, dear young woman, *I* must be the visitor. I come to tell you it will all go right. Do you believe in special ghosts?"

"Are you *special*?"

"One of us is. Or maybe both. The ghost of young love or the ghost of the unborn."

"Is that what I am, you are?"

"Paradoxes aren't easy to explain."

"Then, depending on how you look at it, you're impossible, and so am I."

"If it makes it easier, just think I'm not really here. Do you believe in ghosts?"

"I think I do."

"It comes to me to imagine, then, that there are special ghosts in the world. Not ghosts of dead people. But ghosts of want and need, or I guess you might say desire."

"I don't understand."

"Well, have you ever lain in bed late afternoons, late nights and dreamed something so much, awake, you felt your soul jump out of your body as if something had yanked a long, pure white sheet straight out the window? You want something so much, your soul leaps out and follows, my God, fast?"

"Why . . . yes. Yes!"

"Boys do that, men do that. When I was twelve I read Burroughs' Mars novels. John Carter used to stand under the stars, hold up his arms to Mars, and ask to be taken. And Mars grabbed his soul, yanked him like an aching tooth across space, and landed him in dead Martian seas. That's boys, that's men."

"And girls, women?"

"*They* dream, yes. And their ghosts come out of their bodies. Living ghosts. Living wants. Living needs."

"And go to stand on lawns in the middle of winter nights?"

"That's about it."

"Am I a ghost, then?"

"Yes, the ghost of *wanting* so much it kills but doesn't kill you, shakes and almost breaks you."

"And you?"

"I must be the answer-ghost."

"The answer-ghost. What a funny name!"

"Yes. But you've *asked* and I know the *answer*."

"Tell me!"

"All right, the answer is this, young girl, young woman. The time of waiting is almost over. Your time of despair will soon be through. Very soon, now, a voice will call and when you come out, both of you, your ghost of want and your body with it, there will be a man to go with the voice that calls."

"Oh, please don't tell me that if it isn't true!" Her voice trembled. Tears flashed again in her eyes. She half raised her arms again in defense.

"I wouldn't dream to hurt you. I only came to tell."

The town clock struck again in the deep morning.

"It's late," she said.

"Very late. Get along, now."

"Is that all you're going to say?"

"You don't need to know any more."

The last echoes of the great clock faded.

"How strange," she murmured. "The ghost of a question, the ghost of an answer."

"What better ghosts can there be?"

"None that I ever heard of. We're twins."

"Far nearer than you think."

She took a step, looked down, and gasped with delight. "Look, oh, look. I *can* move!"

"Yes."

"What was it you said, boys walk all night, miles and miles?"

"Yes."

"I could go back in, but I can't sleep now. I must walk, too."

"Do that," he said gently.

"But where shall I *go*?"

"Why," he said, and he suddenly knew. He knew where to send her and was suddenly angry with himself for knowing, angry with her for asking. A burst of jealousy welled in him. He wanted to race down the street to a certain house where a certain young man lived in another year and break the window, burn the roof. And yet, oh, yet, if he *did* that!?

"Yes?" she said, for he had kept her waiting.

Now, he thought, you must tell her. There's no escape.

For if you don't tell her, angry fool, you yourself will never be born.

A wild laugh burst from his mouth, a laugh that accepted the entire night and time and all his crazed thinking.

"So you want to know where to go?" he said at last.

"Oh, yes!"

He nodded his head. "Up to that corner, four blocks to the right, one block to the left."

She repeated it quickly. "And the final number?!"

"Eleven Green Park."

"Oh, thank you, thank you!" She ran a few steps, then stopped, bewildered. Her hands were helpless at her throat. Her mouth trembled. "Silly. I hate to leave."

"Why?"

"Why, because . . . I'm afraid I'll never see *you* again!"

"You will. Three years from now."

"Are you sure?"

"I won't look quite the same. But it'll be me. And you'll know me forever."

"Oh, I'm glad for that. Your face *is* familiar. I somehow know you well."

She began to walk slowly, looking over at him as he stood near the porch of the house.

"Thanks," she said. "You've saved my life."

"And my own along with it."

The shadows of a tree fell across her face, touched her cheeks, moved in her eyes.

"Oh, Lord! Girls lie in bed nights listing the names for their future children. Silly. Joe. John. Christopher. Samuel. Stephen. And right now, Will." She touched the gentle rise of her stomach, then lifted her hand out halfway to point to him in the night. "Is your name Will?"

"Yes."

Tears absolutely burst from her eyes.

He wept with her.

"Oh, that's fine, fine," she said at last. "I can go now. I won't be out here on the lawn anymore. Thank God, thank you. Good night."

She went away into the shadows across the lawn and along the sidewalk down the street. At the far corner he saw her turn and wave and walk away.

"Good night," he said quietly.

I am not born yet, he thought, or she has been dead many years, which is it? which?

The moon sailed into clouds.

The motion touched him to step, walk, go up the porch stairs, wait, look out at the lawn, go inside, shut the door.

A wind shook the trees.

The moon came out again and looked upon a lawn where two sets of footprints, one going one way, one going another in the dew, slowly, slowly, as the night continued, vanished.

By the time the moon had gone down the sky there was only an empty lawn and no sign, and much dew.

The great town clock struck six in the morning. Fire showed in the east. A cock crowed.

FEBRUARY 1999: YLLA

THEY HAD A HOUSE OF CRYSTAL PILLARS on the planet Mars by the edge of an empty sea, and every morning you could see Mrs. K eating the golden fruits that grew from the crystal walls, or cleaning the house with handfuls of magnetic dust which, taking all dirt with it, blew away on the hot wind. Afternoons, when the fossil sea was warm and motionless, and the wine trees stood stiff in the yard, and the little distant Martian bone town was all enclosed, and no one drifted out their doors, you could see Mr. K himself in his room, reading from a metal book with raised hieroglyphs over which he brushed his hand, as one might play a harp. And from the book, as his fingers stroked, a voice sang, a soft ancient voice, which told tales of when the sea was red steam on the shore and ancient men had carried clouds of metal insects and electric spiders into battle.

Mr. and Mrs. K had lived by the dead sea for twenty years, and their ancestors had lived in the same house, which turned and followed the sun, flower-like, for ten centuries.

Mr. and Mrs. K were not old. They had the fair, brownish skin of the true Martian, the yellow coin eyes, the soft musical voices. Once they had liked painting pictures with chemical fire, swimming in the canals in the seasons when the wine trees filled them with green liquors, and talking into the dawn together by the blue phosphorous portraits in the speaking room.

They were not happy now.

This morning Mrs. K stood between the pillars, listening to the desert sands heat, melt into yellow wax, and seemingly run on the horizon.

Something was going to happen.

She waited.

She watched the blue sky of Mars as if it might at any moment grip in on itself, contract, and expel a shining miracle down upon the sand.

Nothing happened.

Tired of waiting, she walked through the misting pillars. A gentle rain sprang from the fluted pillar tops, cooling the scorched air, falling gently on her. On hot days it was like walking in a creek. The floors of the house glittered with cool streams. In the distance she heard her husband playing his book steadily, his fingers never tired of the old songs. Quietly she wished he might one day again spend as much time holding and touching her like a little harp as he did his incredible books.

But no. She shook her head, an imperceptible, forgiving shrug. Her eyelids closed softly down upon her golden eyes. Marriage made people old and familiar, while still young.

She lay back in a chair that moved to take her shape even as she moved. She closed her eyes tightly and nervously.

The dream occurred.

Her brown fingers trembled, came up, grasped at the air. A moment later she sat up, startled, gasping.

She glanced about swiftly, as if expecting someone there before her. She seemed disappointed; the space between the pillars was empty.

Her husband appeared in a triangular door. "Did you call?" he asked irritably.

"No!" she cried.

"I thought I heard you cry out."

"Did I? I was almost asleep and had a dream!"

"In the daytime? You don't often do that."

She sat as if struck in the face by the dream. "How strange, how very strange," she murmured. "The dream."

"Oh?" He evidently wished to return to his book.

"I dreamed about a man."

"A man?"

"A tall man, six feet one inch tall."

"How absurd; a giant, a misshapen giant."

"Somehow"—she tried the words—"he looked all right. In spite of being tall. And he had—oh, I know you'll think it silly—he had blue eyes!"

"Blue eyes! Gods!" cried Mr. K. "What'll you dream next? I suppose he had black hair?"

"How did you guess?" She was excited.

"I picked the most unlikely color," he replied coldly.

"Well, black it was!" she cried. "And he had a very white skin; oh, he was most unusual! He was dressed in a strange uniform and he came down out of the sky and spoke pleasantly to me." She smiled.

"Out of the sky; what nonsense!"

"He came in a metal thing that glittered in the sun," she remembered. She closed her eyes to shape it again. "I dreamed there was the sky and something sparkled like a coin thrown into the air, and suddenly it grew large and fell down softly to land, a long silver craft, round and alien. And a door opened in the side of the silver object and this tall man stepped out."

"If you worked harder you wouldn't have these silly dreams."

"I rather enjoyed it," she replied, lying back. "I never suspected myself of such an imagination. Black hair, blue eyes, and white skin! What a strange man, and yet—quite handsome."

"Wishful thinking."

"You're unkind. I didn't think him up on purpose; he just came in my mind while I drowsed. It wasn't like a dream. It was so unexpected and different. He looked at me and he said, 'I've come from the third planet in my ship. My name is Nathaniel York—'"

"A stupid name; it's no name at all," objected the husband.

"Of course it's stupid, because it's a dream," she explained softly. "And he said, 'This is the first trip across space. There are only two of us in our ship, myself and my friend Bert.'"

"*Another* stupid name."

"And he said, 'We're from a city on Earth; that's the name of our planet,'" continued Mrs. K. "That's what he said. 'Earth' was the name he spoke. And he used another language. Somehow I understood him. With my mind. Telepathy, I suppose."

Mr. K turned away. She stopped him with a word. "Yll?" she called quietly. "Do you ever wonder if—well, if there are people living on the third planet?"

"The third planet is incapable of supporting life," stated the husband patiently. "Our scientists have said there's far too much oxygen in their atmosphere."

"But wouldn't it be fascinating if there were people? And they traveled through space in some sort of ship?"

"Really, Ylla, you know how I hate this emotional wailing. Let's get on with our work."

✳ It was late in the day when she began singing the song as she moved among the whispering pillars of rain. She sang it over and over again.

"What's that song?" snapped her husband at last, walking in to sit at the fire table.

"I don't know." She looked up, surprised at herself. She put her hand to her mouth, unbelieving. The sun was setting. The house was closing itself in, like a giant flower, with the passing of light. A wind blew among the pillars; the fire table bubbled its fierce pool of silver lava. The wind stirred her russet hair, crooning softly in her ears. She stood silently looking out into the great sallow distances of sea bottom, as if recalling something, her yellow eyes soft and moist. " 'Drink to me only with thine eyes, and I will pledge with mine,' " she sang, softly, quietly, slowly. " 'Or leave a kiss within the cup, and I'll not ask for wine.' " She hummed now, moving her hands in the wind ever so lightly, her eyes shut. She finished the song.

It was very beautiful.

"Never heard that song before. Did you compose it?" he inquired, his eyes sharp.

"No. Yes. No, I don't know, really!" She hesitated wildly. "I don't even know what the words are; they're another language!"

"What language?"

She dropped portions of meat numbly into the simmering lava. "I don't know." She drew the meat forth a moment later, cooked, served on a plate for him. "It's just a crazy thing I made up, I guess. I don't know why."

He said nothing. He watched her drown meats in the hissing fire pool. The sun was gone. Slowly, slowly the night came in to fill the room, swallowing the pillars and both of them, like a dark wine poured to the ceiling. Only the silver lava's glow lit their faces.

She hummed the strange song again.

Instantly he leaped from his chair and stalked angrily from the room.

Later, in isolation, he finished supper.

When he arose he stretched, glanced at her, and suggested, yawning, "Let's take the flame birds to town tonight to see an entertainment."

"You don't mean it?" she said. "Are you feeling well?"

"What's so strange about that?"

"But we haven't gone for an entertainment in six months!"

"I think it's a good idea."

"Suddenly you're so solicitous," she said.

"Don't talk that way," he replied peevishly. "Do you or do you not want to go?"

She looked out at the pale desert. The twin white moons were rising. Cool water ran softly about her toes. She began to tremble just the least bit. She wanted very much to sit quietly here, soundless, not moving until this thing occurred, this thing expected all day, this thing that could not occur but might. A drift of song brushed through her mind.

"I——"

"Do you good," he urged. "Come along now."

"I'm tired," she said. "Some other night."

"Here's your scarf." He handed her a vial. "We haven't gone anywhere in months."

"Except you, twice a week to Xi City." She wouldn't look at him.

"Business," he said.

"Oh?" She whispered to herself.

From the vial a liquid poured, turned to blue mist, settled about her neck, quivering.

The flame birds waited, like a bed of coals, glowing on the cool smooth sands. The white canopy ballooned on the night wind, flapping softly, tied by a thousand green ribbons to the birds.

Ylla laid herself back in the canopy and, at a word from her husband, the birds leaped, burning, toward the dark sky. The ribbons tautened, the canopy lifted. The sand slid whining under; the blue hills drifted by, drifted by, leaving their home behind, the raining pillars, the caged flowers, the singing books, the whispering floor creeks. She did not look at her husband. She heard him crying out to the birds as they rose higher, like ten thousand hot sparkles, so many red-yellow fireworks in the heavens, tugging the canopy like a flower petal, burning through the wind.

She didn't watch the dead, ancient bone-chess cities slide under, or the old canals filled with emptiness and dreams. Past dry rivers and dry lakes they flew, like a shadow of the moon, like a torch burning.

She watched only the sky.

The husband spoke.

She watched the sky.

"Did you hear what I said?"

"What?"

He exhaled. "You might pay attention."

"I was thinking."

"I never thought you were a nature lover, but you're certainly interested in the sky tonight," he said.

"It's very beautiful."

"I was figuring," said the husband slowly. "I thought I'd call Hulle tonight. I'd like to talk to him about us spending some time, oh, only a week or so, in the Blue Mountains. It's just an idea—"

"The Blue Mountains!" She held to the canopy rim with one hand, turning swiftly toward him.

"Oh, it's just a suggestion."

"When do you want to go?" she asked, trembling.

"I thought we might leave tomorrow morning. You know, an early start and all that," he said very casually.

"But we never go this early in the year!"

"Just this once, I thought—" He smiled. "Do us good to get away. Some peace and quiet. You know. You haven't anything else planned? We'll go, won't we?"

She took a breath, waited, and then replied, "No."

"What?" His cry startled the birds. The canopy jerked.

"No," she said firmly. "It's settled. I won't go."

He looked at her. They did not speak after that. She turned away.

The birds flew on, ten thousand firebrands down the wind.

In the dawn the sun, through the crystal pillars, melted the fog that supported Ylla as she slept. All night she had hung above the floor, buoyed by the soft carpeting of mist that poured from the walls when she lay down to rest. All night she had slept on this silent river, like a boat upon a soundless tide. Now the fog burned away, the mist level lowered until she was deposited upon the shore of wakening.

She opened her eyes.

Her husband stood over her. He looked as if he had stood there for hours, watching. She did not know why, but she could not look him in the face.

"You've been dreaming again!" he said. "You spoke out and kept me awake. I *really* think you should see a doctor."

"I'll be all right."

"You talked a lot in your sleep!"

"Did I?" She started up.

Dawn was cold in the room. A gray light filled her as she lay there.

"What was your dream?"

She had to think a moment to remember. "The ship. It came from the sky again, landed, and the tall man stepped out and talked with me, telling me little jokes, laughing, and it was pleasant."

Mr. K touched a pillar. Founts of warm water leaped up, steaming; the chill vanished from the room. Mr. K's face was impassive.

"And then," she said, "this man, who said his strange name was Nathaniel York, told me I was beautiful and—and kissed me."

"Ha!" cried the husband, turning violently away, his jaw working.

"It's only a dream." She was amused.

"Keep your silly, feminine dreams to yourself!"

"You're acting like a child." She lapsed back upon the few remaining remnants of chemical mist. After a moment she laughed softly. "I thought of some more of the dream," she confessed.

"Well, what is it, what is it?" he shouted.

"Yll, you're so bad-tempered."

"Tell me!" he demanded. "You can't keep secrets from me!" His face was dark and rigid as he stood over her.

"I've never seen you this way," she replied, half shocked, half entertained. "All that happened was this Nathaniel York person told me—well, he told me that he'd take me away into his ship, into the sky with him, and take me back to his planet with him. It's really quite ridiculous."

"Ridiculous, is it!" he almost screamed. "You should have heard yourself, fawning on him, talking to him, singing with him, oh gods, all night; you should have heard yourself!"

"Yll!"

"When's he landing? Where's he coming down with his damned ship?"

"Yll, lower your voice."

"Voice be damned!" He bent stiffly over her. "And in this dream"—he seized her wrist—"didn't the ship land over in Green Valley, *didn't* it? Answer me!"

"Why, yes—"

"And it landed this afternoon, didn't it?" he kept at her.

"Yes, yes, I think so, yes, but only in a dream!"

"Well"—he flung her hand away stiffly—"it's good you're truthful! I heard every word you said in your sleep. You mentioned the valley and the time." Breathing hard, he walked between the pillars like a man blinded by a lightning bolt. Slowly his breath returned. She watched him as if he were quite insane. She arose finally and went to him. "Yll," she whispered.

"I'm all right."

"You're sick."

"No." He forced a tired smile. "Just childish. Forgive me, darling." He gave her a rough pat. "Too much work lately. I'm sorry. I think I'll lie down awhile—"

"You were so excited."

"I'm all right now. Fine." He exhaled. "Let's forget it. Say, I heard a joke about Uel yesterday, I meant to tell you. What do you say you fix breakfast, I'll tell the joke, and let's not talk about all this."

"It was only a dream."

"Of course." He kissed her cheek mechanically. "Only a dream."

* At noon the sun was high and hot and the hills shimmered in the light.

"Aren't you going to town?" asked Ylla.

"Town?" He raised his brows faintly.

"This is the day you always go." She adjusted a flower cage on its pedestal. The flowers stirred, opening their hungry yellow mouths.

He closed his book. "No. It's too hot, and it's late."

"Oh." She finished her task and moved toward the door. "Well, I'll be back soon."

"Wait a minute! Where are you going?"

She was in the door swiftly. "Over to Pao's. She invited me!"

"Today?"

"I haven't seen her in a long time. It's only a little way."

"Over in Green Valley, isn't it?"

"Yes, just a walk, not far, I thought I'd—" She hurried.

"I'm sorry, really sorry," he said, running to fetch her back, looking very concerned about his forgetfulness. "It slipped my mind. I invited Dr. Nlle out this afternoon."

"Dr. Nlle!" She edged toward the door.

He caught her elbow and drew her steadily in. "Yes."

"But Pao—"

"Pao can wait, Ylla. We must entertain Nlle."

"Just for a few minutes—"

"No, Ylla."

"No?"

He shook his head. "No. Besides, it's a terribly long walk to Pao's. All the way over through Green Valley and then past the big canal and down, isn't it? And it'll be very, very hot, and Dr. Nlle would be delighted to see you. Well?"

She did not answer. She wanted to break and run. She wanted to cry out. But she only sat in the chair, turning her fingers over slowly, staring at them expressionlessly, trapped.

"Ylla?" he murmured. "You will be here, won't you?"

"Yes," she said after a long time. "I'll be here."

"All afternoon?"

Her voice was dull. "All afternoon."

✳ Late in the day Dr. Nlle had not put in an appearance. Ylla's husband did not seem overly surprised. When it was quite late he murmured something, went to a closet, and drew forth an evil weapon, a long yellowish tube ending in a bellows and a trigger. He turned, and upon his face was a mask, hammered from silver metal, expressionless, the mask that he always wore when he wished to hide his feelings, the mask which curved and hollowed so exquisitely to his thin cheeks and chin and brow. The mask glinted, and he held the evil weapon in his hands, considering it. It hummed constantly, an insect hum. From it hordes of golden bees could be flung out with a high shriek. Golden, horrid bees that stung, poisoned, and fell lifeless, like seeds on the sand.

"Where are you going?" she asked.

"What?" He listened to the bellows, to the evil hum. "If Dr. Nlle is late, I'll be damned if I'll wait. I'm going out to hunt a bit. I'll be back. You be sure to stay right here now, won't you?" The silver mask glimmered.

"Yes."

"And tell Dr. Nlle I'll return. Just hunting."

The triangular door closed. His footsteps faded down the hill.

She watched him walking through the sunlight until he was gone. Then she resumed her tasks with the magnetic dusts and the new fruits to be plucked from the crystal walls. She worked with energy and dispatch, but on occasion a numbness took hold of her and she caught herself singing that odd and memorable song and looking out beyond the crystal pillars at the sky.

She held her breath and stood very still, waiting.

It was coming nearer.

At any moment it might happen.

It was like those days when you heard a thunderstorm coming and there was the waiting silence and then the faintest pressure of the atmosphere as the climate blew over the land in shifts and shadows and vapors. And the change pressed at your ears and you were suspended in the waiting time of the coming storm. You began to tremble. The sky was stained and colored; the clouds were thickened; the mountains took on an iron taint. The caged flowers blew with faint sighs of warning. You felt your hair stir softly. Somewhere in the house the voice-clock sang, "Time, time, time, time . . ." ever so gently, no more than water tapping on velvet.

And then the storm. The electric illumination, the engulfments of dark wash and sounding black fell down, shutting in, forever.

That's how it was now. A storm gathered, yet the sky was clear. Lightning was expected, yet there was no cloud.

Ylla moved through the breathless summer house. Lightning would strike from the sky any instant; there would be a thunderclap, a boll of smoke, a silence, footsteps on the path, a rap on the crystalline door, and her running to answer . . .

Crazy Ylla! she scoffed. Why think these wild things with your idle mind?

And then it happened.

There was a warmth as of a great fire passing in the air. A whirling, rushing sound. A gleam in the sky, of metal.

Ylla cried out.

Running through the pillars, she flung wide a door. She faced the hills. But by this time there was nothing.

She was about to race down the hill when she stopped herself. She was supposed to stay here, go nowhere. The doctor was coming to visit, and her husband would be angry if she ran off.

She waited in the door, breathing rapidly, her hand out.

She strained to see over toward Green Valley, but saw nothing.

Silly woman. She went inside. You and your imagination, she thought. That was nothing but a bird, a leaf, the wind, or a fish in the canal. Sit down. Rest.

She sat down.

A shot sounded.

Very clearly, sharply, the sound of the evil insect weapon.

Her body jerked with it.

It came from a long way off. One shot. The swift humming distant bees. One shot. And then a second shot, precise and cold, and far away.

Her body winced again and for some reason she started up, screaming, and screaming, and never wanting to stop screaming. She ran violently through the house and once more threw wide the door.

The echoes were dying away, away.

Gone.

She waited in the yard, her face pale, for five minutes.

Finally, with slow steps, her head down, she wandered about the pillared rooms, laying her hand to things, her lips quivering, until finally she sat alone in the darkening wine room, waiting. She began to wipe an amber glass with the hem of her scarf.

And then, from far off, the sound of footsteps crunching on the thin, small rocks.

She rose up to stand in the center of the quiet room. The glass fell from her fingers, smashing to bits.

The footsteps hesitated outside the door.

Should she speak? Should she cry out, "Come in, oh, come in"?

She went forward a few paces.

The footsteps walked up the ramp. A hand twisted the door latch.

She smiled at the door.

The door opened. She stopped smiling.

It was her husband. His silver mask glowed dully.

He entered the room and looked at her for only a moment. Then he snapped the weapon bellows open, cracked out two dead bees, heard them spat on the floor as they fell, stepped on them, and placed the empty bellows gun in the corner of the room as Ylla bent down and tried, over and over, with no success, to pick up the pieces of the shattered glass. "What were you doing?" she asked.

"Nothing," he said with his back turned. He removed the mask.

"But the gun—I heard you fire it. Twice."

"Just hunting. Once in a while you like to hunt. Did Dr. Nlle arrive?"

"No."

"Wait a minute." He snapped his fingers disgustedly. "Why, I remember now. He was supposed to visit us tomorrow afternoon. How stupid of me."

They sat down to eat. She looked at her food and did not move her hands. "What's wrong?" he asked, not looking up from dipping his meat in the bubbling lava.

"I don't know. I'm not hungry," she said.

"Why not?"

"I don't know; I'm just not."

The wind was rising across the sky; the sun was going down. The room was small and suddenly cold.

"I've been trying to remember," she said in the silent room, across from her cold, erect, golden-eyed husband.

"Remember what?" He sipped his wine.

"That song. That fine and beautiful song." She closed her eyes and hummed, but it was not the song. "I've forgotten it. And, somehow, I don't want to forget it. It's something I want always to remember." She moved her hands as if the rhythm might help her to remember all of it. Then she lay back in her chair. "I can't remember." She began to cry.

"Why are you crying?" he asked.

"I don't know, I don't know, but I can't help it. I'm sad and I don't know why, I cry and I don't know why, but I'm crying."

Her head was in her hands; her shoulders moved again and again.

"You'll be all right tomorrow," he said.

She did not look up at him; she looked only at the empty desert and the very bright stars coming out now on the black sky, and far away there was a sound of wind rising and canal waters stirring cold in the long canals. She shut her eyes, trembling.

"Yes," she said. "I'll be all right tomorrow."

BANSHEE

IT WAS ONE OF THOSE NIGHTS, crossing Ireland, motoring through the sleeping towns from Dublin, where you came upon mist and encountered fog that blew away in rain to become a blowing silence. All the country was still and cold and waiting. It was a night for strange encounters at empty crossroads with great filaments of ghost spiderweb and no spider in a hundred miles. Gates creaked far across meadows, where windows rattled with brittle moonlight.

It was, as they said, banshee weather. I sensed, I knew this as my taxi hummed through a final gate and I arrived at Courtown House, so far from Dublin that if that city died in the night, no one would know.

I paid my driver and watched the taxi turn to go back to the living city, leaving me alone with twenty pages of final screenplay in my pocket, and my film director employer waiting inside. I stood in the midnight silence, breathing in Ireland and breathing out the damp coal mines in my soul.

Then, I knocked.

The door flew wide almost instantly. John Hampton was there, shoving a glass of sherry into my hand and hauling me in.

"Good God, kid, you got me curious. Get that coat off. Give me the script. Finished it, eh? So you say. You got me curious. Glad you called from Dublin. The house is empty. Clara's in Paris with the kids. We'll have a good read, knock the hell out of your scenes, drink a bottle, be in bed by two and— what's that?"

The door still stood open. John took a step, tilted his head, closed his eyes, listened.

The wind rustled beyond in the meadows. It made a sound in the clouds like someone turning back the covers of a vast bed.

I listened.

There was the softest moan and sob from somewhere off in the dark fields.

Eyes still shut, John whispered, "You know what that is, kid?"

"What?"

"Tell you later. Jump."

With the door slammed, he turned about and, the grand lord of the empty manor, strode ahead of me in his hacking coat, drill slacks, polished half-boots, his hair, as always, windblown from swimming upstream or down with strange women in unfamiliar beds.

Planting himself on the library hearth, he gave me one of those beacon flashes of laugh, the teeth that beckoned like a lighthouse beam swift and gone, as he traded me a second sherry for the screenplay, which he had to seize from my hand.

"Let's see what my genius, my left ventricle, my right arm, has birthed. Sit. Drink. Watch."

He stood astride the hearthstones, warming his backside, leafing my manuscript pages, conscious of me drinking my sherry much too fast, shutting my eyes each time he let a page drop and flutter to the carpet. When he finished he let the last page sail, lit a small cigarillo and puffed it, staring at the ceiling, making me wait.

"You son of a bitch," he said at last, exhaling. "It's good. Damn you to hell, kid. It's good!"

My entire skeleton collapsed within me. I had not expected such a midriff blow of praise.

"It needs a little cutting, of course!"

My skeleton reassembled itself.

"Of course," I said.

He bent to gather the pages like a great loping chimpanzee and turned. I felt he wanted to hurl them into the fire. He watched the flames and gripped the pages.

"Someday, kid," he said quietly, "you must teach me to write."

He was relaxing now, accepting the inevitable, full of true admiration.

"Someday," I said, laughing, "you must teach me to direct."

"*The Beast* will be our film, son. Quite a team."

He arose and came to clink glasses with me.

"Quite a team we are!" He changed gears. "How are the wife and kids?"

"They're waiting for me in Sicily where it's warm."

"We'll get you to them, and sun, straight off! I—"

He froze dramatically, cocked his head, and listened.

"Hey, what goes on—" he whispered.

I turned and waited.

This time, outside the great old house, there was the merest thread of sound, like someone running a fingernail over the paint, or someone sliding down out of the dry reach of a tree. Then there was the softest exhalation of a moan, followed by something like a sob.

John leaned in a starkly dramatic pose, like a statue in a stage pantomime, his mouth wide, as if to allow sounds entry to the inner ear. His eyes now unlocked to become as huge as hen's eggs with pretended alarm.

"Shall I tell you what that sound is, kid? A banshee!"

"A what?" I cried.

"Banshee!" he intoned. "The ghosts of old women who haunt the roads an hour before someone dies. *That's* what that sound was!" He stepped to the window, raised the shade, and peered out. "Sh! Maybe it means—*us!*"

"Cut it out, John!" I laughed, quietly.

"No, kid, no." He fixed his gaze far into the darkness, savoring his melodrama. "I lived here ten years. Death's out there. The banshee always *knows!* Where were we?"

He broke the spell as simply as that, strode back to the hearth and blinked at my script as if it were a brand new puzzle.

"You ever figure, Doug, how much *The Beast* is like me? The hero plowing the seas, plowing women left and right, off round the world and no stops? Maybe that's why I'm doing it. You ever wonder how many women I've had? Hundreds! I—"

He stopped, for my lines on the page had shut him again. His face took fire as my words sank in.

"Brilliant!"

I waited, uncertainly.

"No, not that!" He threw my script aside to seize a copy of the London *Times* off the mantel. "*This!* A brilliant review of your new book of stories!"

"What?" I jumped.

"Easy, kid. I'll *read* this grand review to you! You'll love it. Terrific!"

My heart took water and sank. I could see another joke coming on or, worse, the truth disguised as a joke.

"Listen!"

John lifted the *Times* and read, like Ahab, from the holy text.

" 'Douglas Rogers's stories may well be the huge success of American literature—' " John stopped and gave me an innocent blink. "How you like it so far, kid?"

"Continue, John," I mourned. I slugged my sherry back. It was a toss of doom that slid down to meet a collapse of will.

" '—but here in London,' " John intoned, " 'we ask more from our tellers of tales. Attempting to emulate the ideas of Kipling, the style of Maugham, the wit of Waugh, Rogers drowns somewhere in mid-Atlantic. This is ramshackle stuff, mostly bad shades of superior scribes. Douglas Rogers, go home!' "

I leaped up and ran, but John with a lazy flip of his underhand, tossed the *Times* into the fire where it flapped like a dying bird and swiftly died in flame and roaring sparks.

Imbalanced, staring down, I was wild to grab that damned paper out, but finally glad the thing was lost.

John studied my face, happily. My face boiled, my teeth ground shut. My hand, stuck to the mantel, was a cold rock fist.

Tears burst from my eyes, since words could not burst from my aching mouth.

"What's wrong, kid?" John peered at me with true curiosity, like a monkey edging up to another sick beast in its cage. "You feeling poorly?"

"John, for Christ's sake!" I burst out. "Did you have to do *that!*"

I kicked at the fire, making the logs tumble and a great firefly wheel of sparks gush up the flue.

"Why, Doug, I didn't think—"

"Like hell you didn't!" I blazed, turning to glare at him with tear-splintered eyes. "What's *wrong* with you?"

"Hell, nothing, Doug. It was a fine review, great! I just added a few lines, to get your goat!"

"I'll never know now!" I cried. "Look!"

I gave the ashes a final, scattering kick.

"You can buy a copy in Dublin tomorrow, Doug. You'll see. They love you. God, I just didn't want you to get a big head, right. The joke's over. Isn't it enough, dear son, that you have just written the finest scenes you ever wrote in your life for your truly great screenplay?" John put his arm around my shoulder.

That was John: kick you in the tripes, then pour on the wild sweet honey by the larder ton.

"Know what your problem is, Doug?" He shoved yet another sherry in my trembling fingers. "Eh?"

"What?" I gasped, like a sniveling kid, revived and wanting to laugh again. "What?"

"The thing is, Doug—" John made his face radiant. His eyes fastened to mine like Svengali's. "You don't love me half as much as I love you!"

"Come on, John—"

"No, kid, I *mean* it. God, son, I'd kill for you. You're the greatest living writer in the world, and I love you, heart and soul. Because of that, I thought you could take a little leg-pull. I see that I was wrong—"

"No, John," I protested, hating myself, for now he was making *me* apologize. "It's all right."

"I'm sorry, kid, truly sorry—"

"Shut up!" I gasped a laugh. "I still love you. I—"

"That's a boy! Now—" John spun about, brisked his palms together, and shuffled and reshuffled the script pages like a cardsharp. "Let's spend an hour cutting this brilliant, superb scene of yours and—"

For the third time that night, the tone and color of his mood changed.

"Hist!" he cried. Eyes squinted, he swayed in the middle of the room, like a dead man underwater. "Doug, you hear?"

The wind trembled the house. A long fingernail scraped an attic pane. A mourning whisper of cloud washed the moon.

"Banshees." John nodded, head bent, waiting. He glanced up, abruptly. "Doug? Run out and *see*."

"Like hell I will."

"No, go on out," John urged. "This has been a night of misconceptions, kid. You doubt *me*, you doubt it. Get my overcoat, in the hall. Jump!"

He jerked the hall closet door wide and yanked out his great tweed overcoat which smelled of tobacco and fine whiskey. Clutching it in his two monkey hands, he beckoned it like a bullfighter's cape. "Huh, *toro*! Hah!"

"John," I sighed, wearily.

"Or are you a coward, Doug, are you yellow? You—"

For this, the fourth, time, we both heard a moan, a cry, a fading murmur beyond the wintry front door.

"It's waiting, kid!" said John, triumphantly. "Get out there. Run for the *team*!"

I was in the coat, anointed by tobacco scent and booze as John buttoned me up with royal dignity, grabbed my ears, kissed my brow.

"I'll be in the stands, kid, cheering you on. I'd go with you, but banshees are shy. Bless you, son, and if you don't come back—I loved you like a son!"

"Jesus," I exhaled, and flung the door wide.

But suddenly John leaped between me and the cold blowing moonlight.

"Don't go out there, kid. I've changed my mind! If you got killed—"

"John," I shook his hands away. "You *want* me out there. You've probably got Kelly, your stable girl, out there now, making noises for your big laugh—"

"Doug!" he cried in that mock-insult serious way he had, eyes wide, as he grasped my shoulders. "I swear to God!"

"John," I said, half-angry, half-amused, "so long."

I ran out the door to immediate regrets. He slammed and locked the portal. Was he laughing? Seconds later, I saw his silhouette at the library window, sherry glass in hand, peering out at this night theater of which he was both director and hilarious audience.

I spun with a quiet curse, hunched my shoulders in Caesar's cloak, ignored two dozen stab wounds given me by the wind, and stomped down along the gravel drive.

I'll give it a fast ten minutes, I thought, worry John, turn his joke inside out, stagger back in, shirt torn and bloody, with some fake tale of my own. Yes, by God, *that* was the trick—

I stopped.

For in a small grove of trees below, I thought I saw something like a large paper kite blossom and blow away among the hedges.

Clouds sailed over an almost full moon, and ran islands of dark to cover me.

Then there it was again, farther on, as if a whole cluster of flowers were suddenly torn free to snow away along the colorless path. At the same moment, there was the merest catch of a sob, the merest door-hinge of a moan.

I flinched, pulled back, then glanced up at the house.

There was John's face, of course, grinning like a pumpkin in the window, sipping sherry, toast-warm and at ease.

"Ohh," a voice wailed somewhere. ". . . God. . . ."

It was then that I saw the woman.

She stood leaning against a tree, dressed in a long, moon-colored dress over which she wore a hip-length heavy woollen shawl that had a life of its own, rippling and winging out and hovering with the weather.

She seemed not to see me or if she did, did not care; I could not frighten her, nothing in the world would ever frighten her again. Everything poured out of her steady and unflinching gaze toward the house, that window, the library, and the silhouette of the man in the window.

She had a face of snow, cut from that white cool marble that makes the finest Irish women; a long swan neck, a generous if quivering mouth, and eyes a soft and luminous green. So beautiful were those eyes, and her profile against the blown tree branches, that something in me turned, agonized, and died. I felt that killing wrench men feel when beauty passes and will not pass again. You want to cry out: Stay. I love you. But you do not speak. And the summer walks away in her flesh, never to return.

But now the beautiful woman, staring only at that window in the far house, spoke.

"Is he in there?" she said.

"What?" I heard myself say.

"Is that him?" she wondered. "The beast," she said, with quiet fury. "The monster. Himself."

"I don't—"

"The great animal," she went on, "that walks on two legs. He stays. All others go. He wipes his hands on flesh; girls are his napkins, women his midnight lunch. He keeps them stashed in cellar vintages and knows their years but not their names. Sweet Jesus, and is that *him*?"

I looked where she looked, at the shadow in the window, far off across the croquet lawn.

And I thought of my director in Paris, in Rome, in New York, in Hollywood, and the millraces of women I had seen John tread, feet printing their skins, a dark Christ on a warm sea. A picnic of women danced on tables, eager for applause and John, on his way out, saying, "Dear, lend me a fiver. That beggar by the door kills my heart—"

I watched this young woman, her dark hair stirred by the night wind, and asked:

"Who *should* he be?"

"Him," she said. "Him that lives there and loved me and now does not." She shut her eyes to let the tears fall.

"He doesn't live there anymore," I said.

"He does!" She whirled, as if she might strike or spit. "Why do you lie?"

"Listen." I looked at the new but somehow old snow in her face. "That was another time."

"No, there's only *now!*" She made as if to rush for the house. "And I love him still, so much I'd kill for it, and myself lost at the end!"

"What's his name?" I stood in her way. "His *name*?"

"Why, Will, of course. Willie. William."

She moved. I raised my arms and shook my head.

"There's only a Johnny there now. A John."

"You lie! I feel him there. His name's changed, but it's *him*. Look! Feel!"

She put her hands up to touch on the wind toward the house, and I turned and sensed with her and it was another year, it was a time between. The wind said so, as did the night and the glow in that great window where the shadow stayed.

"That's him!"

"A friend of mine," I said, gently.

"No friend of anyone, ever!"

I tried to look through her eyes and thought: my God, has it always been this way, forever some man in that house, forty, eighty, a hundred years ago! Not the same man, no, but all dark twins, and this lost girl on the road, with snow in her arms for love, and frost in her heart for comfort, and nothing to do but whisper and croon and mourn and sob until the sound of her weeping stilled at sunrise but to start again with the rising of the moon.

"That's my friend in there," I said, again.

"If that be true," she whispered fiercely, "then you are my enemy!"

I looked down the road where the wind blew dust through the grave-yard gates.

"Go back where you came from," I said.

She looked at the same road and the same dust, and her voice faded. "Is there to be no peace, then?" she mourned. "Must I walk here, year on year, and no comeuppance?"

"If the man in there," I said, "was really your Will, your William, what would you have me do?"

"Send him out to me," she said, quietly.

"What would you do with him?"

"Lie down with him," she murmured, "and ne'er get up again. He would be kept like a stone in a cold river."

"Ah," I said, and nodded.

"Will you ask him, then, to be sent?"

"No. For he's not yours. Much like. Near similar. And breakfasts on girls and wipes his mouth on their silks, one century called this, another that."

"And no love in him, ever?"

"He says the word like fishermen toss their nets in the sea," I said.

"Ah, Christ, and I'm caught!" And here she gave such a cry that the shadow came to the window in the great house across the lawn. "I'll stay here the rest of the night," she said. "Surely he will feel me here, his heart will melt, no matter what his name or how deviled his soul. What year is this? How long have I been waiting?"

"I won't tell you," I said. "The news would crack your heart."

She turned and truly looked at me. "Are you one of the good ones, then, the gentle men who never lie and never hurt and never have to hide? Sweet God, I wish I'd known you first!"

The wind rose, the sound of it rose in her throat. A clock struck some-where far across the country in the sleeping town.

"I must go in," I said. I took a breath. "Is there no way for me to give you rest?"

"No," she said, "for it was not you that cut the nerve."

"I see," I said.

"You don't. But you try. Much thanks for that. Get in. You'll catch your death."

"And you—?"

"Ha!" she cried. "I've long since caught mine. It will not catch again. Get!"

I gladly went. For I was full of the cold night and the white moon, old time, and her. The wind blew me up the grassy knoll. At the door, I turned. She was still there on the milky road, her shawl straight out on the weather, one hand upraised.

"Hurry," I thought I heard her whisper, "tell him he's needed!"

I rammed the door, slammed into the house, fell across the hall, my heart a bombardment, my image in the great hall mirror a shock of colorless lightning.

John was in the library drinking yet another sherry, and poured me some. "Someday," he said, "you'll learn to take anything I say with more than a grain of salt. Jesus, look at you! Ice cold. Drink that down. Here's another to go after it!"

I drank, he poured, I drank. "Was it all a joke, then?"

"What *else*?" John laughed, then stopped.

The croon was outside the house again, the merest fingernail of mourn, as the moon scraped down the roof.

"There's your banshee," I said, looking at my drink, unable to move.

"Sure, kid, sure, unh-huh," said John. "Drink your drink, Doug, and I'll read you that great review of your book from the London *Times* again."

"You burned it, John."

"Sure, kid, but I recall it all as if it were this morn. Drink up."

"John," I said, staring into the fire, looking at the hearth where the ashes of the burned paper blew in a great breath. "Does . . . did . . . that review really exist?"

"My God, of course, sure, yes. Actually. . . ." Here he paused and gave it great imaginative concern. "The *Times* knew my love for you, Doug, and asked me to review your book." John reached his long arm over to refill my glass. "I did it. Under an assumed name, of course, now ain't that swell of me? But I had to be fair, Doug, had to be fair. So I wrote what I truly felt were the good things, the not-so-good things in your book. Criticized it just the way I would when you hand in a lousy screenplay scene and I make you do it over. Now ain't that A-one double absolutely square of me? Eh?"

He leaned at me. He put his hand on my chin and lifted it and gazed long and sweetly into my eyes.

"You're not upset?"

"No," I said, but my voice broke.

"By God, now, if you aren't. Sorry. A joke, kid, only a joke." And here he gave me a friendly punch on the arm.

Slight as it was, it was a sledgehammer striking home.

"I wish you hadn't made it up, the joke, I wish the article was real," I said.

"So do I, kid. You look bad. I—"

The wind moved around the house. The windows stirred and whispered.

Quite suddenly I said, for no reason that I knew:

"The banshee. It's out there."

"That was a joke, Doug. You got to watch out for me."

"No," I said, looking at the window. "It's there."

John laughed. "You saw it, did you?"

"It's a young and lovely woman with a shawl on a cold night. A young woman with long black hair and great green eyes and a complexion like snow and a proud Phoenician prow of a nose. Sound like anyone you ever in your life knew, John?"

"Thousands." John laughed more quietly now, looking to see the weight of my joke. "Hell—"

"She's waiting for you," I said. "Down at the bottom of the drive."

John glanced, uncertainly, at the window.

"That was the sound we heard," I said. "She described you or someone like you. Called you Willy, Will, William. But I *knew* it was you."

John mused. "Young, you say, and beautiful, and out there right this moment . . . ?"

"The most beautiful woman I've ever seen."

"Not carrying a knife—?"

"Unarmed."

John exhaled. "Well, then, I think I should just go out there and have a chat with her, eh, don't you think?"

"She's waiting."

He moved toward the front door.

"Put on your coat, it's a cold night," I said.

He was putting on his coat when we heard the sound from outside, very clear this time. The wail and then the sob and then the wail.

"God," said John, his hand on the doorknob, not wanting to show the white feather in front of me. "She's *really* there."

He forced himself to turn the knob and open the door. The wind sighed in, bringing another faint wail with it.

John stood in the cold weather, peering down that long walk into the dark.

"Wait!" I cried, at the last moment.

John waited.

"There's one thing I haven't told you," I said. "She's out there, all right. And she's walking. But . . . she's dead."

"I'm not afraid," said John.

"No," I said, "but I am. You'll never come back. Much as I hate you right now, I can't let you go. Shut the door, John."

The sob again, and then the wail.

"Shut the door."

I reached over to knock his hand off the brass doorknob, but he held tight, cocked his head, looked at me and sighed.

"You're really good, kid. Almost as good as me. I'm putting you in my next film. You'll be a star."

Then he turned, stepped out into the cold night, and shut the door, quietly.

I waited until I heard his steps on the gravel path, then locked the door, and hurried through the house, putting out the lights. As I passed through the library, the wind mourned down the chimney and scattered the dark ashes of the London *Times* across the hearth.

I stood blinking at the ashes for a long moment, then shook myself, ran upstairs two at a time, banged open my tower room door, slammed it, undressed, and was in bed with the covers over my head when a town clock, far away, sounded one in the deep morning.

And my room was so high, so lost in the house and the sky, that no matter who or what tapped or knocked or banged at the door below, whispering and then begging and then screaming—

Who could possibly hear?

ONE FOR HIS LORDSHIP, AND
ONE FOR THE ROAD!

SOMEONE'S BORN, AND IT MAY TAKE the best part of a day for the news to ferment, percolate, or otherwise circumnavigate across the Irish meadows to the nearest town, and the nearest pub, which is Heeber Finn's.

But let someone die, and a whole symphonic band lifts in the fields and hills. The grand ta-ta slams across country to ricochet off the pub slates and shake the drinkers to calamitous cries for: more!

So it was this hot summer day. The pub was no sooner opened, aired, and mobbed than Finn, at the door, saw a dust flurry up the road.

"That's Doone," muttered Finn.

Doone was the local anthem sprinter, fast at getting out of cinemas ahead of the damned national tune, and swift at bringing news.

"And the news is bad," murmured Finn. "It's *that* fast he's running!"

"Ha!" cried Doone, as he leaped across the sill. "It's done, and he's dead!"

The mob at the bar turned.

Doone enjoyed his moment of triumph, making them wait.

"Ah, God, here's a drink. Maybe that'll make you talk!"

Finn shoved a glass in Doone's waiting paw. Doone wet his whistle and arranged the facts.

"Himself," he gasped, at last. "Lord Kilgotten. Dead. And not an hour past!"

"Ah, God," said one and all, quietly. "Bless the old man. A sweet nature. A dear chap."

For Lord Kilgotten had wandered their fields, pastures, barns, and this bar all the years of their lives. His departure was like the Normans rowing back to France or the damned Brits pulling out of Bombay.

"A fine man," said Finn, drinking to the memory, "even though he *did* spend two weeks a year in London."

"How old was he?" asked Brannigan. "Eighty-five? Eighty-eight? We thought we might have buried him long since."

"Men like that," said Doone, "God has to hit with an axe to scare them off the place. Paris, now, we thought that might have slain him, years past, but no. Drink, that should have drowned him, but he swam for the shore, no, no. It was that teeny bolt of lightning in the field's midst, an hour ago, and him under the tree picking strawberries with his nineteen-year-old secretary lady."

"Jesus," said Finn. "There's no strawberries this time of year. It was *her* hit him with a bolt of fever. Burned to a crisp!"

That fired off a twenty-one-gun salute of laughs that hushed itself down when they considered the subject and more townsfolk arrived to breathe the air and bless himself.

"I wonder," mused Heeber Finn, at last, in a voice that would make the Valhalla gods sit still at table, and not scratch, "I wonder. What's to become of all that wine? The wine, that is, which Lord Kilgotten has stashed in barrels and bins, by the quarts and the tons, by the scores and precious thousands in his cellars and attics, and, who knows, under his bed?"

"Aye," said everyone, stunned, suddenly remembering. "Aye. Sure. *What?*"

"It has been left, no doubt, to some damn Yank driftabout cousin or nephew, corrupted by Rome, driven mad by Paris, who'll jet in tomorrow, who'll seize and drink, grab and run, and Kilcock and us left beggared and buggered on the road behind!" said Doone, all in one breath.

"Aye." Their voices, like muffled dark velvet drums, marched toward the night. "Aye."

"There *are* no relatives!" said Finn. "No dumb Yank nephews or dimwit nieces falling out of gondolas in Venice, but swimming this way. I have made it my business to know."

Finn waited. It was his moment now. All stared. All leaned to hear his mighty proclamation.

"Why not, I been thinking, if Kilgotten, by God, left all ten thousand bottles of Burgundy and Bordeaux to the citizens of the loveliest town in Eire? To *us!*"

There was an antic uproar of comment on this, cut across when the front doorflaps burst wide and Finn's wife, who rarely visited the sty, stepped in, glared around and snapped.

"Funeral's in an hour!"

"An hour?" cried Finn. "Why, he's only just cold—"

"Noon's the time," said the wife, growing taller the more she looked at this dreadful tribe. "The doc and the priest have just come from the Place. Quick funerals was his lordship's will. 'Uncivilized,' said Father Kelly, 'and no hole dug.' 'But there *is!*' said the Doc. 'Hanrahan was supposed to die yesterday but took on a fit of mean and survived the night. I treated and treated him, but the man persists! Meanwhile, there's his hole, unfilled. Kilgotten can have it, dirt and headstone.' All's invited. Move your bums!"

The double-wing doors whiffled shut. The mystic woman was gone.

"A funeral!" cried Doone, prepared to sprint.

"No!" Finn beamed. "Get out. Pub's closed. A *wake!*"

✳ "Even Christ," gasped Doone, mopping the sweat from his brow, "wouldn't climb down off the cross to walk on a day like this."

"The heat," said Mulligan, "*is* intolerable."

Coats off, they trudged up the hill, past the Kilgotten gatehouse, to encounter the town priest, Father Padraic Kelly, doing the same. He had all but his collar off, and was beet faced in the bargain.

"It's hell's own day," he agreed, "*none* of us will keep!"

"Why all the rush?" said Finn, matching fiery stride for stride with the holy man. "I smell a rat. What's up?"

"Aye," said the priest. "There *was* a secret codicil in the will—"

"I *knew* it!" said Finn.

"What?" asked the crowd, fermenting close behind in the sun.

"It would have caused a riot if it got out," was all Father Kelly would say, his eyes on the graveyard gates. "You'll find out at the penultimate moment."

"Is that the moment before or the moment after the end, Father?" asked Doone, innocently.

"Ah, you're so dumb you're pitiful," sighed the priest. "Get your ass through that gate. Don't fall in the hole!"

Doone did just that. The others followed, their faces assuming a darker tone as they passed through. The sun, as if to observe this, moved behind a cloud, and a sweet breeze came up for some moment of relief.

"There's the hole." The priest nodded. "Line up on both sides of the path, for God's sake, and fix your ties, if you have some, and check your flies, above all. Let's run a nice show for Kilgotten, and here he *comes!*"

And here, indeed, came Lord Kilgotten, in a box carried on the planks of one of his farm wagons, a simple good soul to be sure, and behind that wagon, a procession of other vehicles, cars, trucks that stretched half down the hill in the now once more piercing light.

"What a procession!" cried Finn.

"I never seen the like!" cried Doone.

"Shut up," said the priest, politely.

"My God," said Finn. "Do you see the *coffin?*"

"We see, Finn, we *see!*" gasped all.

For the coffin, trundling by, was beautifully wrought, finely nailed together with silver and gold nails, but the special strange wood of it?

Plankings from wine-crates, staves from boxes that had sailed from France only to collide and sink in Lord Kilgotten's cellars!

A storm of exhalations swept the men from Finn's pub. They toppled on their heels. They seized each other's elbows.

"*You* know the words, Finn," whispered Doone. "Tell us the *names!*"

Finn eyed the coffin made of vintage shipping crates, and at last exhaled:

"Pull out my tongue and jump on it. Look! There's Château Lafite Roth-schild, nineteen seventy. Château-neuf du Pape, 'sixty-eight! Upside down, *that* label, Le Corton! Downside up: La Lagune! What style, my God, what class! I wouldn't so much mind being buried in burned-stamp-labeled wood like that, myself!"

"I wonder," mused Doone, "can he *read* the labels from *inside?*"

"Put a sock in it," muttered the priest. "Here comes the *rest!*"

If the body in the box was not enough to pull clouds over the sun, this second arrival caused an even greater ripple of uneasiness to oil the sweat-ing men.

"It was as if," Doone recalled, later, "someone had slipped, fallen in the grave, broken an ankle, and *spoiled* the whole afternoon!"

For the last part of the procession was a series of cars and trucks ramshackle-loaded with French vineyard crates, and finally a great old brewery wagon from early Guinness days, drawn by a team of proud white horses, draped in black, and sweating with the surprise they drew behind.

"I will be damned," said Finn. "Lord Kilgotten's brought his own wake *with* him!"

"Hurrah!" was the cry. "What a dear soul."

"He must've known the day would ignite a nun, or kindle a priest, and our tongues on our chests!"

"Gangway! Let it pass!"

The men stood aside as all the wagons, carrying strange labels from southern France and northern Italy, making tidal sounds of bulked liquids, lumbered into the churchyard.

"Someday," whispered Doone, "we must raise a statue to Kilgotten, a philosopher of friends!"

"Pull up your socks," said the priest. "It's too soon to tell. For here comes something *worse* than an undertaker!"

"What could be worse?"

With the last of the wine wagons drawn up about the grave, a single man strode up the road, hat on, coat buttoned, cuffs properly shot, shoes polished against all reason, mustache waxed and cool, unmelted, a prim case like a lady's purse tucked under his clenched arm, and about him an air of the ice house, a thing fresh born from a snowy vault, tongue like an icicle, stare like a frozen pond.

"Jesus," said Finn.

"It's a *lawyer*!" said Doone.

All stood aside.

The lawyer, for that is what it was, strode past like Moses as the Red Sea obeyed, or King Louis on a stroll, or the haughtiest tart on Piccadilly: choose *one*.

"It's Kilgotten's law," hissed Muldoon. "I seen him stalking Dublin like the Apocalypse. With a lie for a name: Clement! Half-ass Irish, full-ass Briton. The *worst*!"

"What can be worse than death?" someone whispered.

"We," murmured the priest, "shall soon see."

"Gentlemen!"

A voice called. The mob turned.

Lawyer Clement, at the rim of the grave, took the prim briefcase from under his arm, opened it, and drew forth a symboled and ribboned document, the beauty of which bugged the eye and rammed and sank the heart.

"Before the obsequies," he said. "Before Father Kelly orates, I have a message, this codicil in Lord Kilgotten's will, which I shall read aloud."

"I bet it's the eleventh Commandment," murmured the priest, eyes down.

"What would the eleventh Commandment *be*?" asked Doone, scowling.

"Why not: 'THOU SHALT SHUT UP AND LISTEN'" said the priest. "*Ssh*."

For the lawyer was reading from his ribboned document and his voice floated on the hot summer wind, like this:

"'And whereas my wines are the finest—'"

"They are *that!*" said Finn.

" '—and whereas the greatest labels from across the world fill my cellars, and whereas the people of this town, Kilcock, do not appreciate such things, but prefer the—er—hard stuff . . .' "

"Who *says?!*" cried Doone.

"Back in your ditch," warned the priest, *sotto voce.*

" 'I do hereby proclaim and pronounce,' " read the lawyer, with a great smarmy smirk of satisfaction, " 'that contrary to the old adage, a man can *indeed* take it with him. And I so order, write, and sign this codicil to my last will and testament in what might well be the final month of my life.' Signed, William, Lord Kilgotten. Last month, on the seventh."

The lawyer stopped, folded the paper and stood, eyes shut, waiting for the thunderclap that would follow the lightning bolt.

"Does that mean," asked Doone, wincing, "that the lord intends to—?"

Someone pulled a cork out of a bottle.

It was like a fusillade that shot all the men in their tracks.

It was only, of course, the good lawyer Clement, at the rim of the damned grave, corkscrewing and yanking open the plug from a bottle of La Vieille Ferme '73!

"Is this the *wake,* then?" Doone laughed, nervously.

"It is *not,*" mourned the priest.

With a smile of summer satisfaction, Clement, the lawyer, poured the wine, glug by glug, down into the grave, over the wine-carton box in which Lord Kilgotten's thirsty bones were hid.

"Hold on! He's gone mad! Grab the bottle! No!"

There was a vast explosion, like that from the crowd's throat that has just seen its soccer champion slain midfield!

"Wait! My God!"

"Quick. Run get the lord!"

"Dumb," muttered Finn. "His lordship's *in* that box, and his wine is *in* the grave!"

Stunned by this unbelievable calamity, the mob could only stare as the last of the first bottle cascaded down into the holy earth.

Clement handed the bottle to Doone, and uncorked a second.

"Now, wait just one moment!" cried the voice of the Day of Judgment.

And it was, of course, Father Kelly, who stepped forth, bringing his higher law with him.

"Do you mean to say," cried the priest, his cheeks blazing, his eyes

smoldering with bright sun, "you are going to dispense all that stuff in Kilgotten's pit?"

"That," said the lawyer, "is my intent."

He began to pour the second bottle. But the priest stiff-armed him, to
tilt the wine back.

"And do you mean for us to just stand and *watch* your blasphemy?!"

"At a wake, yes, that would be the polite thing to do." The lawyer moved
to pour again.

"Just hold it, right there!" The priest stared around, up, down, at his
friends from the pub, at Finn their spiritual leader, at the sky where God
hid, at the earth where Kilgotten lay playing Mum's the Word, and at last
at lawyer Clement and his damned, ribboned codicil. "Beware, man, you
are provoking civil strife!"

"Yah!" cried everyone, atilt on the air, fists at their sides, grinding and
ungrinding invisible rocks.

"What year is this wine?" Ignoring them, Clement calmly eyed the label
in his hands. "Le Corton. Nineteen-seventy. The best wine in the finest
year. Excellent." He stepped free of the priest and let the wine spill.

"*Do something!*" shouted Doone. "Have you no curse handy?"

"Priests do not curse," said Father Kelly. "But, Finn, Doone, Hannahan,
Burke. Jump! Knock heads."

The priest marched off and the men rushed after to knock their heads
in a bent-down ring and a great whisper with the father. In the midst of the
conference the priest stood up to see what Clement was doing. The lawyer
was on his third bottle.

"Quick!" cried Doone. "He'll waste the *lot!*"

A fourth cork popped, to another outcry from Finn's team, the Thirsty
Warriors, as they would later dub themselves.

"Finn!" the priest was heard to say, deep in the heads-together, "you're
a genius!"

"I am!" agreed Finn, and the huddle broke and the priest hustled back
to the grave.

"Would you mind, sir," he said, grabbing the bottle out of the lawyer's
grip, "reading one *last* time, that damned codicil?"

"Pleasure." And it was. The lawyer's smile flashed as he fluttered the
ribbons and snapped the will.

" '—that contrary to the old adage, a man can indeed take it with
him—' "

He finished and folded the paper, and tried another smile, which worked to his own satisfaction, at least. He reached for the bottle confiscated by the priest.

"Hold on." Father Kelly stepped back. He gave a look to the crowd who waited on each fine word. "Let me ask you a question, Mr. Lawyer, sir. Does it anywhere say there just *how* the wine is to get into the grave?"

"Into the grave is into the grave," said the lawyer.

"As long as it finally *gets* there, *that's* the important thing, do we agree?" asked the priest, with a strange smile.

"I can pour it over my shoulder, or toss it in the air," said the lawyer, "as long as it lights to either side or atop the coffin, when it comes down, all's well."

"Good!" exclaimed the priest. "Men! One squad here. One battalion over there. Line up! Doone!"

"Sir?"

"Spread the rations. Jump!"

"Sir!" Doone jumped.

To a great uproar of men bustling and lining up.

"I," said the lawyer, "am going to find the police!"

"Which is *me*," said a man at the far side of the mob, "Officer Bannion. Your complaint?"

Stunned, lawyer Clement could only blink and at last in a squashed voice, bleat: "I'm leaving."

"You'll not make it past the gate alive," said Doone, cheerily.

"I," said the lawyer, "am staying. But—"

"But?" inquired Father Kelly, as the corks were pulled and the corkscrew flashed brightly along the line.

"You go against the letter of the law!"

"No," explained the priest, calmly, "we but shift the punctuation, cross new t's, dot new i's."

"Tenshun!" cried Finn, for all was in readiness.

On both sides of the grave, the men waited, each with a full bottle of vintage Château Lafite Rothschild or Le Corton or Chianti.

"Do we drink it *all*?" asked Doone.

"Shut your gab," observed the priest. He eyed the sky. "Oh, Lord." The men bowed their heads and grabbed off their caps. "Lord, for what we are about to receive, make us truly thankful. And thank you, Lord, for the genius of Heeber Finn, who thought of this—"

"Aye," said all, gently.

"Twas nothin'," said Finn, blushing.

"And bless this wine, which may circumnavigate along the way, but finally wind up where it should be going. And if today and tonight won't do, and all the stuff not drunk, bless us as we return each night until the deed is done and the soul of the wine's at rest."

"Ah, you *do* speak dear," murmured Doone.

"Sh!" hissed all.

"And in the spirit of this time, Lord, should we not ask our good lawyer friend Clement, in the fullness of his heart, to join *with* us?"

Someone slipped a bottle of the best in the lawyer's hands. He seized it, lest it should break.

"And finally, Lord, bless the old Lord Kilgotten, whose years of saving-up now help us in this hour of putting-away. *Amen*."

"Amen," said all.

"Tenshun!" cried Finn.

The men stiffened and lifted their bottles.

"One for his lordship," said the priest.

"And," added Finn, "one for the road!"

There was a dear sound of drinking and, years later, Doone remembered, a glad sound of laughter from the box in the grave.

"It's all right," said the priest, in amaze.

"Yes." The lawyer nodded, having heard. "It's all right."

*

THE LAUREL AND HARDY
LOVE AFFAIR

HE CALLED HER STANLEY, SHE CALLED HIM OLLIE.

That was the beginning, that was the end, of what we will call the Laurel and Hardy love affair.

She was twenty-five, he was thirty-two when they met at one of those dumb cocktail parties where everyone wonders what they are doing there. But no one goes home, so everyone drinks too much and lies about how grand a late afternoon it all was.

They did not, as often happens, see each other across a crowded room, and if there was romantic music to background their collision, it couldn't be heard. For everyone was talking at one person and staring at someone else.

They were, in fact, ricocheting through a forest of people, but finding no shade trees. He was on his way for a needed drink, she was eluding a love-sick stranger, when they locked paths in the exact center of the fruit-less mob. They dodged left and right a few times, then laughed and he, on impulse, seized his tie and twiddled it at her, wiggling his fingers. Instantly, smiling, she lifted her hand to pull the top of her hair into a frowzy tassel, blinking and looking as if she had been struck on the head.

"Stan!" he cried, in recognition.

"Ollie!" she exclaimed. "Where have you *been*?"

"Why don't you do something to *help* me!" he exclaimed, making wide fat gestures.

They grabbed each other's arms, laughing again.

"I—" she said, and her face brightened even more. "I—I know the exact place, not two miles from here, where Laurel and Hardy, in nineteen thirty, carried that piano crate up and down one hundred and fifty steps!"

"Well," he cried, "let's get out of here!"

His car door slammed, his car engine roared.

Los Angeles raced by in late afternoon sunlight.

He braked the car where she told him to park. "Here!"

"I can't believe it," he murmured, not moving. He peered around at the sunset sky. Lights were coming on all across Los Angeles, down the hill. He nodded. "Are *those* the steps?"

"All one hundred and fifty of them." She climbed out of the open-topped car. "Come on, Ollie."

"Very well," he said, "Stan."

They walked over to the bottom of yet another hill and gazed up along the steep incline of concrete steps toward the sky. The faintest touch of wet-ness rimmed his eyes. She was quick to pretend not to notice, but she took his elbow. Her voice was wonderfully quiet:

"Go on up," she said. "Go on. Go."

She gave him a tender push.

He started up the steps, counting, and with each half-whispered count, his voice took on an extra decibel of joy. By the time he reached fifty-seven he was a boy playing a wondrous old-new game, and he was lost in time, and whether he was carrying the piano up the hill or whether it was chasing him down, he could not say.

"Hold it!" he heard her call, far away, "right there!"

He held still, swaying on step fifty-eight, smiling wildly, as if accompanied by proper ghosts, and turned.

"Okay," she called, "now come back down."

He started down, color in his cheeks and a peculiar suffering of happiness in his chest. He could hear the piano following now.

"Hold it right *there!*"

She had a camera in her hands. Seeing it, his right hand flew instinctively to his tie to flutter it on the evening air.

"Now, *me!*" she shouted, and raced up to hand him the camera. And he marched down and looked up and there she was, doing the thin shrug and the puzzled and hopeless face of Stan baffled by life but loving it all. He clicked the shutter, wanting to stay here forever.

She came slowly down the steps and peered into his face.

"Why," she said, "you're *crying.*"

She placed her thumbs under his eyes to press the tears away. She tasted the result. "Yep," she said. "*Real* tears."

He looked at her eyes, which were almost as wet as his.

"Another fine mess you've got us in," he said.

"Oh, Ollie," she said.

"Oh, Stan," he said.

He kissed her, gently.

And then he said:

"Are we going to know each other forever?"

"Forever," she said.

✳ And that was how the long love affair began.

They had real names, of course, but those don't matter, for Laurel and Hardy always seemed the best thing to call themselves.

For the simple fact was that she was fifteen pounds underweight and he was always trying to get her to add a few pounds. And he was twenty pounds overweight and she was always trying to get him to take off more than his shoes. But it never worked and was finally a joke, the best kind, which wound up being:

"You're Stan, no two ways about it, and I'm Ollie, let's face it. And, oh God, dear young woman, let's enjoy the mess, the wonderful mess, all the while we're in!"

It was, then, while it lasted, and it lasted some while, a French parfait, an American perfection, a wildness from which they would never recover to the end of their lives.

From that twilight hour on the piano stairs on, their days were long, heedless, and full of that amazing laughter that paces the beginning and the run-along rush of any great love affair. They only stopped laughing long enough to kiss and only stopped kissing long enough to laugh at how odd and miraculous it was to find themselves with no clothes to wear in the middle of a bed as vast as life and as beautiful as morning.

And sitting there in the middle of warm whiteness, he shut his eyes and shook his head and declared, pompously:

"I have *nothing* to say!"

"Yes, you do!" she cried. "*Say it!*"

And he said it and they fell off the edge of the earth.

✳ Their first year was pure myth and fable, which would grow outsize when remembered thirty years on. They went to see new films and old films, but mainly Stan and Ollie. They memorized all the best scenes and shouted them back and forth as they drove around midnight Los Angeles. He spoiled her by treating her childhood growing up in Hollywood as very special, and she spoiled him by pretending that his yesteryear on roller skates out front of the studios was not in the past but right now.

She proved it one night. On a whim she asked where he had roller-skated as a boy and collided with W. C. Fields. Where had he asked Fields for his autograph, and where was it that Fields signed the book, handed it back, and cried, "There you are, you little son-of-a-bitch!"

"Drive me there," she said.

And at ten o'clock that night they got out of the car in front of Paramount Studio and he pointed to the pavement near the gate and said, "He stood there," and she gathered him in her arms and kissed him and said, gently, "Now where was it you had your picture taken with Marlene Dietrich?"

He walked her fifty feet across the street from the studio. "In the late afternoon sun," he said, "Marlene stood here." And she kissed him again, longer this time, and the moon rising like an obvious magic trick, filling the street in front of the empty studio. She let her soul flow over into him like a tipped fountain, and he received it and gave it back and was glad.

"Now," she said, quietly, "where was it you saw Fred Astaire in nineteen thirty-five and Ronald Colman in nineteen thirty-seven and Jean Harlow in nineteen thirty-six?"

And he drove her to those three different places all around Hollywood until midnight and they stood and she kissed him as if it would never end.

And that was the first year. And during that year they went up and down those long piano steps at least once a month and had champagne picnics halfway up, and discovered an incredible thing:

"I think it's our mouths," he said. "Until I met you, I never knew I had a mouth. Yours is the most amazing in the world, and it makes me feel as if mine were amazing, too. Were you ever really kissed before I kissed you?"

"Never!"

"Nor was I. To have lived this long and not known mouths."

"Dear mouth," she said, "shut up and kiss."

But then at the end of the first year they discovered an even more incredible thing. He worked at an advertising agency and was nailed in one place. She worked at a travel agency and would soon be flying everywhere. Both were astonished they had never noticed before. But now that Vesuvius had erupted and the fiery dust was beginning to settle, they sat and looked at each other one night and she said, faintly:

"Good-bye . . ."

"What?" he asked.

"I can see good-bye coming," she said.

He looked at her face and it was not sad like Stan in the films, but just sad like herself.

"I feel like the ending of that Hemingway novel where two people ride along in the late day and say how it would be if they could go on forever but they know now they won't," she said.

"Stan," he said, "this is no Hemingway novel and this can't be the end of the world. You'll never leave me."

But it was a question, not a declaration and suddenly she moved and he blinked at her and said:

"What are you doing down there?"

"Nut," she said, "I'm kneeling on the floor and I'm asking for your hand. Marry me, Ollie. Come away with me to France. I've got a new job in Paris. No, don't say anything. Shut up. No one has to know I've got the money this year and will support you while you write the great American novel—"

"But—" he said.

"You've got your portable typewriter, a ream of paper, and me. Say it, Ollie, will you come? Hell, don't marry me, we'll live in sin, but fly with me, yes?"

"And watch us go to hell in a year and bury us forever?"

"Are you that afraid, Ollie? Don't you believe in me or you or anything? God, why are men such cowards, and why the hell do you have such thin skins and are afraid of a woman like a ladder to lean on. Listen, I've got things to do and you're coming with me. I can't leave you here, you'll fall down those damn stairs. But if I have to, I will. I want everything now, not tomorrow. That means you, Paris, and my job. Your novel will take time, but you'll do it. Now, do you do it here and feel sorry for yourself, or do we live in a cold-water walk-up flat in the Latin Quarter a long way off from here? This is my one and only offer, Ollie. I've never proposed before, I won't ever propose again, it's hard on my knees. Well?"

"Have we had this conversation before?" he said.

"A dozen times in the last year, but you never listened, you were hopeless."

"No, in love and helpless."

"You've got one minute to make up your mind. Sixty seconds." She was staring at her wristwatch.

"Get up off the floor," he said, embarrassed.

"If I do, it's out the door and gone," she said. "Forty-nine seconds to go, Ollie."

"Stan," he groaned.

"Thirty," she read her watch. "Twenty. I've got one knee off the floor. Ten. I'm beginning to get the other knee up. Five. One."

And she was standing on her feet.

"What brought this on?" he asked.

"Now," she said, "I am heading for the door. I don't know. Maybe I've thought about it more than I dared even notice. We are very special wondrous people, Ollie, and I don't think our like will ever come again in the world, at least not to us, or I'm lying to myself and I probably am. But I must go and you are free to come along, but can't face it or don't know it. And now—" she reached out. "My hand is on the door and—"

"And?" he said, quietly.

"I'm crying," she said.

He started to get up but she shook her head.

"No, don't. If you touch me I'll cave in, and to hell with that. I'm going. But once a year will be forbearance day, or forgiveness day or whatever in hell you want to call it. Once a year I'll show up at our flight of steps, no piano, same hour, same time as that night when we first went there and if you're there to meet me I'll kidnap you or you me, but don't bring along and show me your damn bank balance or give me any of your lip."

"Stan," he said.

"My God," she mourned.

"What?"

"This door is heavy. I can't move it." She wept. "There. It's moving. There." She wept more. "I'm gone."

The door shut.

"Stan!" He ran to the door and grabbed the knob. It was wet. He raised his fingers to his mouth and tasted the salt, then opened the door.

The hall was already empty. The air where she had passed was just coming back together. Thunder threatened when the two halves met. There was a promise of rain.

※ He went back to the steps on October 4 every year for three years, but she wasn't there. And then he forgot for two years but in the autumn of the sixth year, he remembered and went back in the late sunlight and walked up the stairs because he saw something halfway up and it was a bottle of good champagne with a ribbon and a note on it, delivered by someone, and the note read:

"Ollie, dear Ollie. Date remembered. But in Paris. Mouth's not the same, but happily married. Love. Stan."

And after that, every October he simply did not go to visit the stairs. The sound of that piano rushing down that hillside, he knew, would catch him and take him along to where he did not know.

And that was the end, or almost the end, of the Laurel and Hardy love affair.

There was, by amiable accident, a final meeting.

Traveling through France fifteen years later, he was walking on the Champs Elysées at twilight one afternoon with his wife and two daughters, when he saw this handsome woman coming the other way, escorted by a very sober-looking older man and a very handsome dark-haired boy of twelve, obviously her son.

As they passed, the same smile lit both their faces in the same instant.

He twiddled his necktie at her.

She tousled her hair at him.

They did not stop. They kept going. But he heard her call back along the Champs Elysées, the last words he would ever hear her say:

"Another fine mess you've got us in!" And then she added the old, the familiar name by which he had gone in the years of their love.

And she was gone and his daughters and wife looked at him and one daughter said, "Did that lady call you Ollie?"

"What lady?" he said.

"Dad," said the other daughter, leaning in to peer at his face. "You're crying."

"No."

"Yes, you are. *Isn't* he, Mom?"

"Your papa," said his wife, "as you well know, cries at telephone books."

"No," he said, "just one hundred and fifty steps and a piano. Remind me to show you girls, someday."

They walked on and he turned and looked back a final time. The woman with her husband and son turned at that very moment. Maybe he saw her mouth pantomime the words, So long, Ollie. Maybe he didn't. He felt his own mouth move, in silence: So long, Stan.

And they walked in opposite directions along the Champs Elysées in the late light of an October sun.

UNTERDERSEABOAT DOKTOR

THE INCREDIBLE EVENT OCCURRED DURING my third visit to Gustav Von Seyfertitz, my foreign psychoanalyst.

I should have guessed at the strange explosion before it came.

After all, my alienist, truly alien, had the coincidental name, Von Seyfertitz, of the tall, lean, aquiline, menacing, and therefore beautiful actor who played the high priest in the 1935 film *She*.

In *She*, the wondrous villain waved his skeleton fingers, hurled insults, summoned sulfured flames, destroyed slaves, and knocked the world into earthquakes.

After that, "At Liberty," he could be seen riding the Hollywood Boulevard trolley cars as calm as a mummy, as quiet as an unwired telephone pole.

Where was I? Ah, yes!

It was my *third* visit to my psychiatrist. He had called that day and cried, "Douglas, you stupid goddamn son of a bitch, it's time for beddy-bye!"

Beddy-bye was, of course, his couch of pain and humiliation where I lay writhing in agonies of assumed Jewish guilt and Northern Baptist stress as he from time to time muttered, "A fruitcake remark!" or "Dumb!" or "If you ever do *that* again, I'll kill you!"

As you can see, Gustav Von Seyfertitz was a most unusual *mine* specialist. Mine? Yes. Our problems are land mines in our heads. *Step* on them! Shock-troop therapy, he once called it, searching for words. "Blitzkrieg?" I offered.

"*Ja!*" He grinned his shark grin. "That's *it!*"

Again, this was my third visit to his strange, metallic-looking room with a most odd series of locks on a roundish door. Suddenly, as I was maundering and treading dark waters, I heard his spine stiffen behind me. He gasped a great death rattle, sucked air, and blew it out in a yell that curled and bleached my hair:

"Dive! Dive!"

I dove.

Thinking that the room might be struck by a titanic iceberg, I fell, to scuttle beneath the lion-claw-footed couch.

"Dive!" cried the old man.

"Dive?" I whispered, and looked up.

To see a submarine periscope, all polished brass, slide up to vanish in the ceiling.

Gustav Von Seyfertitz stood pretending not to notice me, the sweat-oiled leather couch, or the vanished brass machine. Very calmly, in the fashion of Conrad Veidt in *Casablanca*, or Erich Von Stroheim, the manservant in *Sunset Boulevard* . . . he . . .

. . . lit a cigarette and let two calligraphic dragon plumes of smoke write themselves (his initials?) on the air.

"You were saying?" he said.

"No." I stayed on the floor. "You were saying. Dive?"

"I did not say that," he purred.

"Beg pardon, you said, very clearly—Dive!"

"Not possible." He exhaled two more scrolled dragon plumes. "You hallucinate. Why do you stare at the ceiling?"

"Because," I said, "unless I am further hallucinating, buried in that valve lock up there is a nine-foot length of German Leica brass periscope!"

"This boy is incredible, listen to him," muttered Von Seyfertitz to his alter ego, which was always a third person in the room when he analyzed. When he was not busy exhaling his disgust with me, he tossed asides at himself. "How many martinis did you have at lunch?"

"Don't hand me that, Von Seyfertitz. I know the difference between a sex symbol and a periscope. That ceiling, one minute ago, swallowed a long brass pipe, yes!?"

Von Seyfertitz glanced at his large, one-pound-size Christmas watch, saw that I still had thirty minutes to go, sighed, threw his cigarette down, squashed it with a polished boot, then clicked his heels.

Have you ever heard the *whack* when a real pro like Jack Nicklaus hits a ball? *Bamm.* A hand grenade!

That was the sound my Germanic friend's boots made as he knocked them together in a salute.

Crrrack!

"Gustav Mannerheim Auschlitz Von Seyfertitz, Baron Woldstein, at your service!" He lowered his voice. "Unterderseaboat—"

I thought he might say "Doktor." But:

"Unterderseaboat *Captain*!"

I scrambled off the floor.

Another crrrack and—

The periscope slid calmly down out of the ceiling, the most beautiful Freudian cigar I had ever seen.

"No!" I gasped.

"Have I ever *lied* to you?"

"Many times!"

"But"—he shrugged—"little white ones."

He stepped to the periscope, slapped two handles in place, slammed one eye shut, and crammed the other angrily against the viewpiece, turning the periscope in a slow roundabout of the room, the couch, and me.

"Fire one," he ordered.

I almost heard the torpedo leave its tube.

"Fire *two!*" he said.

And a second soundless and invisible bomb motored on its way to infinity.

Struck midships, I sank to the couch.

"You, you!" I said mindlessly. "It!" I pointed at the brass machine. "This!" I touched the couch. "*Why?*"

"Sit down," said Von Seyfertitz.

"I am."

"*Lie* down."

"I'd rather not," I said uneasily.

Von Seyfertitz turned the periscope so its topmost eye, raked at an angle, glared at me. It had an uncanny resemblance, in its glassy coldness, to his own fierce hawk's gaze.

His voice, from behind the periscope, echoed.

"So you want to know, eh, how Gustav Von Seyfertitz, Baron Woldstein, suffered to leave the cold ocean depths, depart his dear North Sea ship, flee his destroyed and beaten fatherland, to become the Unterderseaboat *Doktor*—"

"Now that you mention—"

"I never mention! I declare. And my declarations are sea-battle commands."

"So I noticed . . ."

"Shut up. Sit back—"

"Not just now . . ." I said uneasily.

His heels knocked as he let his right hand spider to his top coat pocket and slip forth yet a fourth eye with which to fasten me: a bright, thin monocle which he screwed into his stare as if decupping a boiled egg. I winced. For now the monocle was part of his glare and regarded me with cold fire.

"Why the monocle?" I said.

"Idiot! It is to cover my *good* eye so that *neither* eye can *see* and my intuition is free to work!"

"Oh," I said.

And he began his monologue. And as he talked I realized his need had been pent up, capped, for years, so he talked on and on, forgetting me.

And it was during this monologue that a strange thing occurred. I rose slowly to my feet as the Herr Doktor Von Seyfertitz circled, his long, slim cigar printing smoke cumuli on the air, which he read like white Rorschach blots.

With each implantation of his foot, a word came out, and then another, in a sort of plodding grammar. Sometimes he stopped and stood poised with one leg raised and one word stopped in his mouth, to be turned on his tongue and examined. Then the shoe went down, the noun slid forth and the verb and object in good time.

Until at last, circling, I found myself in a chair, stunned, for I saw:

Herr Doktor Von Seyfertitz stretched on his couch, his long spider fingers laced on his chest.

"It has been no easy thing to come forth on land," he sibilated. "Some days I was the jellyfish, frozen. Others, the shore-strewn octopi, at *least* with tentacles, or the crayfish sucked back into my skull. But I have built my spine, year on year, and now I walk among the land men and survive."

He paused to take a trembling breath, then continued:

"I moved in stages from the depths to a houseboat, to a wharf bungalow, to a shore-tent and then back to a canal in a city and at last to New York, an island surrounded by water, eh? But where, where, in all this, I wondered, would a submarine commander find his place, his work, his mad love and activity?

"It was one afternoon in a building with the world's longest elevator that it struck me like a hand grenade in the ganglion. Going down, down, down, other people crushed around me, and the numbers descending and the floors whizzing by the glass windows, rushing by flicker-flash, flicker-flash, conscious, subconscious, id, ego-id, life, death, lust, kill, lust, dark, light, plummeting, falling, ninety, eighty, fifty, lower depths, high exhilaration, id, ego, id, until this shout blazed from my raw throat in a great all-accepting, panic-manic shriek:

" 'Dive! Dive!' "

"I remember," I said.

" 'Dive!' I screamed so loudly that my fellow passengers, in shock, peed merrily. Among stunned faces, I stepped out of the lift to find one-sixteenth of an inch of pee on the floor. 'Have a nice day!' I said, jubilant with self-discovery, then ran to self-employment, to hang a shingle and next my periscope, carried from the mutilated, divested, castrated unterderseaboat all these years. Too stupid to see in it my psychological future and my final downfall, my beautiful artifact, the brass genitalia of psychotic research, the Von Seyfertitz Mark Nine Periscope!"

"That's quite a story," I said.

"Damn right," snorted the alienist, eyes shut. "And more than half of it true. Did you listen? What have you learned?"

"That more submarine captains should become psychiatrists."

"So? I have often wondered: did Nemo really die when his submarine was destroyed? Or did he run off to become my great-grandfather and were his psychological bacteria passed along until I came into the world, thinking to command the ghostlike mechanisms that haunt the undertides, to wind up with the fifty-minute vaudeville routine in this sad, psychotic city?"

I got up and touched the fabulous brass symbol that hung like a scientific stalactite in mid-ceiling.

"May I look?"

"I wouldn't if I were you." He only half heard me, lying in the midst of his depression as in a dark cloud.

"It's only a periscope—"

"But a good cigar is a smoke."

I remembered Sigmund Freud's quote about cigars, laughed, and touched the periscope again.

"Don't!" he said.

"Well, you don't *actually* use this for anything, do you? It's just a remembrance of your past, from your last sub, yes?"

"You think that?" He sighed. "Look!"

I hesitated, then pasted one eye to the viewer, shut the other, and cried: "Oh, Jesus!"

"I warned you!" said Von Seyfertitz.

For *they* were there.

Enough nightmares to paper a thousand cinema screens. Enough phantoms to haunt ten thousand castle walls. Enough panics to shake forty cities into ruin.

My God, I thought, he could sell the film rights to this worldwide!

The first psychological kaleidoscope in history.

And in the instant another thought came: how much of that stuff in there is me? Or Von Seyfertitz? Or both? Are these strange shapes my maundering daymares, sneezed out in the past weeks? When I talked, eyes shut, did my mouth spray invisible founts of small beasts which, caught in the periscope chambers, grew outsize? Like the microscopic photos of those germs that hide in eyebrows and pores, magnified a million times to become elephants on *Scientific American* covers? Are these images from other lost souls trapped on that couch and caught in the submarine device, or leftovers from *my* eyelashes and psyche?

"It's worth millions!" I cried. "Do you *know* what this is!?"

"Collected spiders, Gila monsters, trips to the Moon without gossamer wings, iguanas, toads out of bad sisters' mouths, diamonds out of good fairies' ears, crippled shadow dancers from Bali, cut-string puppets from Geppetto's attic, little-boy statues that pee white wine, sexual trapeze performers' *allez-oop*, obscene finger-pantomimes, evil clown faces, gargoyles that talk when it rains and whisper when the wind rises, basement bins full of poisoned honey, dragonflies that sew up every fourteen-year-old's orifices to keep them neat until they rip the sutures, aged eighteen. Towers with mad witches, garrets with mummies for lumber—"

He ran out of steam.

"You get the general drift."

"Nuts," I said. "You're bored. I could get you a five-million-dollar deal with Amalgamated Fruitcakes Inc. and the Sigmund F. Dreamboats, split three ways!"

"You don't understand," said Von Seyfertitz. "I am keeping myself busy, busy, so I won't remember all the people I torpedoed, sank, drowned mid-Atlantic in 1944. I am not in the Amalgamated Fruitcake Cinema business. I only wish to keep myself occupied by paring fingernails, cleaning earwax, and erasing inkblots from odd beanbags like you. If I stop, I will fly apart. That periscope contains all and everything I have seen and known in the past forty years of observing pecans, cashews, and almonds. By staring at them I lose my own terrible life lost in the tides. If you won my periscope in some shoddy fly-by-night Hollywood strip poker, I would sink three times in my waterbed, never to be seen again. Have I *shown* you my waterbed? Three times as large as any pool. I do eighty laps asleep each night. Sometimes forty when I catnap noons. To answer your millionfold offer, no."

And suddenly he shivered all over. His hands clutched at his heart.

"My God!" he shouted.

Too late, he was realizing he had let me step into his mind and life. Now he was on his feet, between me and the periscope, staring at it and me, as if we were both terrors.

"You saw nothing in that! Nothing at all!"

"I did!"

"You lie! How could you *be* such a liar? Do you know what would happen if this got out, if you ran around making accusations—?

"My God," he raved on, "if the world knew, if someone said—" His words gummed shut in his mouth as if he were tasting the truth of what he said, as if he saw me for the first time and I was a gun fired full in his face. "I would be . . . laughed out of the city. Such a goddamn ridiculous . . . hey, wait a minute. You!"

It was as if he had slipped a devil mask over his face. His eyes grew wide. His mouth gaped.

I examined his face and saw murder. I sidled toward the door.

"You wouldn't *say* anything to anyone?" he said.

"No."

"How come you suddenly know *everything* about me?"

"You *told* me!"

"Yes," he admitted, dazed, looking around for a weapon. "Wait."

"If you don't mind," I said, "I'd rather not."

And I was out the door and down the hall, my knees jumping to knock my jaw.

"Come back!" cried Von Seyfertitz, behind me. "I must kill you!"

"I was afraid of that!"

I reached the elevator first and by a miracle it flung wide its doors when I banged the Down button. I jumped in.

"Say good-bye!" cried Von Seyfertitz, raising his fist as if it held a bomb.

"Good-bye!" I said. The doors slammed.

I did not see Von Seyfertitz again for a year.

Meanwhile, I dined out often, not without guilt, telling friends, and strangers on street corners, of my collision with a submarine commander become phrenologist (he who feels your skull to count the beans).

So with my giving one shake of the ripe fruit tree, nuts fell. Overnight they brimmed the Baron's lap to flood his bank account. His Grand Slam will be recalled at century's end: appearances on *Phil Donahue, Oprah Winfrey,* and *Geraldo* in one single cyclonic afternoon, with interchangeable hyperboles, positive-negative-positive every hour. There were Von Seyfertitz laser games and duplicates of his submarine periscope sold at the Museum of Modern Art and the Smithsonian. With the superinducement of a half-million dollars, he force-fed and easily sold a bad book. Duplicates of the animalcules, lurks, and curious critters trapped in his brass viewer arose in pop-up coloring books, paste-on tattoos, and inkpad rubber-stamp nightmares at Beasts-R-Us.

I had hoped that all this would cause him to forgive and forget. No.

One noon a year and a month later, my doorbell rang and there stood Gustav Von Seyfertitz, Baron Woldstein, tears streaming down his cheeks.

"How come I didn't kill you that day?" he mourned.

"You didn't catch me," I said.

"Oh, *ja*. That was it."

I looked into the old man's rain-washed, tear-ravened face and said, "Who died?"

"Me. Or is it *I*? Ah, to hell with it: *me*. You see before you," he grieved, "a creature who suffers from the Rumpelstiltskin Syndrome!"

"Rumpel—"

"—stiltskin! Two halves with a rip from chin to fly. Yank my forelock, go ahead! Watch me fall apart at the seam. Like zipping a psychotic zipper, I fall, two Herr Doktor Admirals for the sick price of one. And which is the Doktor who heals and which the sellout best-seller Admiral? It takes two mirrors to tell. Not to mention the smoke!"

He stopped and looked around, holding his head together with his hands.

"Can you see the crack? Am I splitting again to become this crazy sailor who desires richness and fame, being sieved through the hands of crazed ladies with ruptured libidos? Suffering catfish, I call them! But take their money, spit, and spend! You should *have* such a year. Don't laugh."

"I'm not laughing."

"Then cheer up while I finish. Can I lie down? Is that a couch? Too short. What do I do with my legs?"

"Sit sidesaddle."

Von Seyfertitz laid himself out with his legs draped over one side. "Hey, not bad. Sit behind. Don't look over my shoulder. Avert your gaze. Neither smirk nor pull long faces as I get out the crazy-glue and paste Rumpel back with Stiltskin, the name of my next book, God help me. Damn you to hell, you and your damned periscope!"

"Not mine. Yours. You wanted me to discover it that day. I suppose you had been whispering Dive, Dive, for years to patients, half asleep. But you couldn't resist the loudest scream ever: Dive! That was your captain speaking, wanting fame and money enough to chock a horse show."

"God," murmured Von Seyfertitz, "how I hate it when you're honest. Feeling better already. How much do I owe you?"

He arose.

"Now we go kill the monsters instead of you."

"Monsters?"

"At my office. If we can get in past the lunatics."

"You have lunatics outside as well as in, now?"

"Have I ever lied to you?"

"Often. But," I added, "little white ones."

"Come," he said.

❋ We got out of the elevator to be confronted by a long line of worshipers and supplicants. There must have been seventy people strung out between the elevator and the Baron's door, waiting with copies of books by Madame Blavatsky, Krishnamurti, and Shirley MacLaine under their arms. There was a roar like a suddenly opened furnace door when they saw the Baron. We beat it on the double and got inside his office before anyone could surge to follow.

"See what you have done to me!" Von Seyfertitz pointed.

The office walls were covered with expensive teak paneling. The desk was from Napoleon's age, an exquisite Empire piece worth at least fifty thousand dollars. The couch was the best soft leather I had ever seen, and the two pictures on the wall were originals—a Renoir and a Monet. My God, millions! I thought.

"Okay," I said. "The beasts, you said. You'll kill them, not me?"

The old man wiped his eyes with the back of one hand, then made a fist.

"Yes!" he cried, stepping up to the fine periscope, which reflected his face, madly distorted, in its elongated shape. "Like this. Thus and so!"

And before I could prevent, he gave the brass machine a terrific slap with his hand and then a blow and another blow and another, with both fists, cursing. Then he grabbed the periscope as if it were the neck of a spoiled child and throttled and shook it.

I cannot say what I heard in that instant. Perhaps real sounds, perhaps imagined temblors, like a glacier cracking in the spring, or icicles in midnight. Perhaps it was a sound like a great kite breaking its skeleton in the wind and collapsing in folds of tissue. Maybe I thought I heard a vast breath insucked, a cloud dissolving up inside itself. Or did I sense clock machineries spun so wildly they smoked off their foundations and fell like brass snowflakes?

I put my eye to the periscope.

I looked in upon—

Nothing.

It was just a brass tube with some crystal lenses and a view of an empty couch.

No more.

I seized the viewpiece and tried to screw it into some new focus on a far place and some dream bacteria that might fibrillate across an unimaginable horizon.

But the couch remained only a couch, and the wall beyond looked back at me with its great blank face.

Von Seyfertitz leaned forward and a tear ran off the tip of his nose to fall on one rusted fist.

"Are they dead?" he whispered.

"Gone."

"Good, they deserved to die. Now I can return to some kind of normal, sane world."

And with each word his voice fell deeper within his throat, his chest, his soul, until it, like the vaporous haunts within the peri-kaleidoscope, melted into silence.

He clenched his fists together in a fierce clasp of prayer, like one who beseeches God to deliver him from plagues. And whether he was once again praying for my death, eyes shut, or whether he simply wished me gone with the visions within the brass device, I could not say.

I only knew that my gossip had done a terrible and irrevocable thing. Me and my wild enthusiasm for a psychological future and the fame of this incredible captain from beneath Nemo's tidal seas.

"Gone," murmured Gustav Von Seyfertitz, Baron Woldstein, whispered for the last time. "Gone."

That was almost the end.

I went around a month later. The landlord reluctantly let me look over the premises, mostly because I hinted that I might be renting.

We stood in the middle of the empty room where I could see the dent marks where the couch had once stood.

I looked up at the ceiling. It was empty.

"What's wrong?" said the landlord. "Didn't they fix it so you can't see? Damn fool Baron made a damn big hole up into the office above. Rented that, too, but never used it for anything I knew of. There was just that big damn hole he left when he went away."

I sighed with relief.

"Nothing left upstairs?"

"Nothing."

I looked up at the perfectly blank ceiling.

"Nice job of repair," I said.

"Thank God," said the landlord.

What, I often wonder, ever happened to Gustav Von Seyfertitz? Did he move to Vienna, to take up residence, perhaps, in or near dear Sigmund's very own address? Does he live in Rio, aerating fellow Unterderseaboat Captains who can't sleep for seasickness, roiling on their waterbeds under the shadow of the Andes Cross? Or is he in South Pasadena, within striking distance of the fruit larder nut farms disguised as film studios?

I cannot guess.

All I know is that some nights in the year, oh, once or twice, in a deep sleep I hear this terrible shout, his cry,

"Dive! Dive! Dive!"

And wake to find myself, sweating, far under my bed.

ANOTHER FINE MESS

THE SOUNDS BEGAN IN THE MIDDLE of summer in the middle of the night.

Bella Winters sat up in bed about three A.M. and listened and then lay back down. Ten minutes later she heard the sounds again, out in the night, down the hill.

Bella Winters lived in a first-floor apartment on top of Vendome Heights, near Effie Street in Los Angeles, and had lived there now for only a few days, so it was all new to her, this old house on an old street with an old staircase, made of concrete, climbing steeply straight up from the lowlands below, one hundred and twenty steps, count them. And right now . . .

"Someone's on the steps," said Bella to herself.

"What?" said her husband, Sam, in his sleep.

"There are some men out on the steps," said Bella. "Talking, yelling, not fighting, but almost. I heard them last night, too, and the night before, but . . ."

"What?" Sam muttered.

"Shh, go to sleep. I'll look."

She got out of bed in the dark and went to the window, and yes, two men were indeed talking out there, grunting, groaning, now loud, now soft. And there was another noise, a kind of bumping, sliding, thumping, like a huge object being carted up the hill.

"No one could be moving in at this hour of the night, could they?" asked Bella of the darkness, the window, and herself.

"No," murmured Sam.

"It sounds like . . ."

"Like what?" asked Sam, fully awake now.

"Like two men moving—"

"Moving what, for God's sake?"

"Moving a piano. Up those steps."

"At three in the *morning*?"

"A piano and two men. Just listen."

The husband sat up, blinking, alert.

Far off, in the middle of the hill, there was a kind of harping strum, the noise a piano makes when suddenly thumped and its harp strings hum.

"There, did you *hear*?"

"Jesus, you're right. But why would anyone steal—"

"They're not stealing, they're delivering."

"A *piano*?"

"I didn't make the rules, Sam. Go out and ask. No, don't; I will."

And she wrapped herself in her robe and was out the door and on the sidewalk.

"Bella," Sam whispered fiercely behind the porch screen.

"Crazy."

"So what can happen at night to a woman fifty-five, fat, and ugly?" she wondered.

Sam did not answer.

She moved quietly to the rim of the hill. Somewhere down there she could hear the two men wrestling with a huge object. The piano on occasion gave a strumming hum and fell silent. Occasionally one of the men yelled or gave orders.

"The voices," said Bella. "I know them from somewhere," she whispered and moved in utter dark on stairs that were only a long pale ribbon going down, as a voice echoed:

"Here's *another* fine mess you've got us in."

Bella froze. Where have I heard that voice, she wondered, a million *times*!

"Hello," she called.

She moved, counting the steps, and stopped.

And there was no one there.

Suddenly she was very cold. There was nowhere for the strangers to have gone to. The hill was steep and a long way down and a long way up, and they had been burdened with an upright piano, *hadn't* they?

How come I know *upright*? she thought. I only *heard*. But—yes, *upright*! Not only that, but inside a box!

She turned slowly and as she went back up the steps, one by one, slowly, slowly, the voices began to sound again, below, as if, disturbed, they had waited for her to go away.

"What *are* you doing?" demanded one voice.

"I was just—" said the other.

"*Give* me that!" cried the first voice.

That *other* voice, thought Bella, I know that, too. And I know what's going to be said next!

"Now," said the echo far down the hill in the night, "just don't stand there, *help* me!"

"Yes!" Bella closed her eyes and swallowed hard and half fell to sit on the steps, getting her breath back as black-and-white pictures flashed in her head. Suddenly it was 1929 and she was very small, in a theater with dark and light pictures looming above the first row where she sat, transfixed, and then laughing, and then transfixed and laughing again.

She opened her eyes. The two voices were still down there, a faint wrestle and echo in the night, despairing and thumping each other with their hard derby hats.

Zelda, thought Bella Winters. I'll call Zelda. She knows everything. She'll tell me what this is. Zelda, yes!

Inside, she dialed Z and E and L and D and A before she saw what she had done and started over. The phone rang a long while until Zelda's voice, angry with sleep, spoke half-way across L.A.

"Zelda, this is Bella!"

"Sam just *died*?"

"No, no, I'm sorry—"

"*You're* sorry?"

"Zelda, I know you're going to think I'm crazy, but . . ."

"Go ahead, be crazy."

"Zelda, in the old days when they made films around L.A., they used lots of places, right? Like Venice, Ocean Park . . ."

"Chaplin did, Langdon did, Harold Lloyd, sure."

"Laurel and Hardy?"

"What?"

"Laurel and Hardy, did *they* use lots of locations?"

"Palms, they used Palms lots, Culver City Main Street, Effie Street."

"*Effie* Street!"

"Don't yell, Bella."

"Did you say *Effie* Street?"

"Sure, and God, it's three in the morning!"

"Right at the *top* of Effie Street!?"

"Hey, yeah, the stairs. Everyone knows them. That's where the music box chased Hardy downhill and ran over him."

"Sure, Zelda, *sure*! Oh, God, Zelda, if you could *see*, hear, what *I* hear!"

Zelda was suddenly wide awake on the line. "What's going *on*? You *serious*?"

"Oh, God, yes. On the steps just now, and last night and the night before maybe, I heard, I hear—two men hauling a—a piano up the hill."

"Someone's pulling your leg!"

"No, no, they're there. I go out and there's nothing. But the steps are haunted, Zelda! One voice says: 'Here's another fine mess you've got us in.' You got to *hear* that man's voice!"

"You're drunk and doing this because you know I'm a nut for them."

"No, no. Come, Zelda. Listen. Tell!"

Maybe half an hour later, Bella heard the old tin lizzie rattle up the alley behind the apartments. It was a car Zelda, in her joy at visiting silent-movie theaters, had bought to lug herself around in while she wrote about the past, always the past, and steaming into Cecil B. DeMille's old place or circling Harold Lloyd's nation-state, or cranking and banging around the Universal backlot, paying her respects to the Phantom's opera stage, or sitting on Ma and Pa Kettle's porch chewing a sandwich lunch. That was Zelda, who once wrote in a silent country in a silent time for *Silver Screen*.

Zelda lumbered across the front porch, a huge body with legs as big as the Bernini columns in front of St. Peter's in Rome, and a face like a harvest moon.

On that round face now was suspicion, cynicism, skepticism, in equal pie-parts. But when she saw Bella's pale stare she cried:

"Bella!"

"You *see* I'm *not* lying!" said Bella.

"I *see!*"

"Keep your voice down, Zelda. Oh, it's scary and strange, terrible and nice. So come on."

And the two women edged along the walk to the rim of the old hill near the old steps in old Hollywood, and suddenly as they moved they felt time take a half turn around them and it was another year, because nothing had changed, all the buildings were the way they were in 1928 and the hills beyond like they were in 1926 and the steps, just the way they were when the cement was poured in 1921.

"Listen, Zelda. *There!*"

And Zelda listened and at first there was only a creaking of wheels down in the dark, like crickets, and then a moan of wood and a hum of piano strings, and then one voice lamenting about this job, and the other voice claiming he had nothing to do with it, and then the thumps as two derby hats fell, and an exasperated voice announced:

"Here's *another* fine mess you've got us in."

Zelda, stunned, almost toppled off the hill. She held tight to Bella's arm as tears brimmed in her eyes.

"It's a trick. Someone's got a tape recorder or—"

"No, I checked. Nothing but the steps, Zelda, the steps!"

Tears rolled down Zelda's plump cheeks.

"Oh, God, that *is* his voice! I'm the expert, I'm the mad fanatic, Bella. That's Ollie. And that other voice, Stan! And you're *not* nuts after all!"

The voices below rose and fell and one cried: "Why don't you do something to *help* me?"

Zelda moaned. "Oh, God, it's so *beautiful.*"

"What does it mean?" asked Bella. "Why are they here? Are they really ghosts, and why would ghosts climb this hill every night, pushing that music box, night after night, tell me, Zelda, why?"

Zelda peered down the hill and shut her eyes for a moment to think. "Why do *any* ghosts go anywhere? Retribution? Revenge? No, not *those* two. Love maybe's the reason, lost loves or something. *Yes?*"

Bella let her heart pound once or twice and then said, "Maybe nobody *told* them."

"Told them *what?*"

"Or maybe they were told a lot but still didn't believe, because maybe in their old years things got bad, I mean they were sick, and sometimes when you're sick you forget."

"Forget *what?*"

"How much we loved them."

"They *knew!*"

"*Did* they? Sure, we told each other, but maybe not enough of us ever wrote or waved when they passed and just yelled '*Love!*' you think?"

"Hell, Bella, they're on TV every *night!*"

"Yeah, but that don't count. Has anyone, since they left us, come here to these steps and *said?* Maybe those voices down there, ghosts or whatever, have been here every night for years, pushing that music box, and nobody thought, or tried, to just whisper or yell all the love we had all the years. Why not?"

"Why not?" Zelda stared down into the long darkness where perhaps shadows moved and maybe a piano lurched clumsily among the shadows. "You're right."

"If I'm right," said Bella, "and you say so, there's only one thing to do—"

"You mean you and *me?*"

"Who else? Quiet. Come on."

They moved down a step. In the same instant lights came on around them, in a window here, another there. A screen door opened somewhere and angry words shot out into the night:

"Hey, what's going *on?*"

"Pipe down!"

"You know what *time* it is?"

"My God," Bella whispered, "everyone *else* hears now!"

"No, no." Zelda looked around wildly. "They'll spoil everything!"

"I'm calling the cops!" A window slammed.

"God," said Bella, "if the cops come—"

"What?"

"It'll be all wrong. If anyone's going to tell them to take it easy, pipe down, it's gotta be us. We *care, don't* we?"

"God, yes, but—"

"No buts. Grab on. Here we go."

The two voices murmured below and the piano tuned itself with hiccups of sound as they edged down another step and another, their mouths dry, hearts hammering, and the night so dark they could see only the faint streetlight at the stair bottom, the single street illumination so far away it was sad being there all by itself, waiting for shadows to move.

More windows slammed up, more screen doors opened. At any moment there would be an avalanche of protest, incredible outcries, perhaps shots fired, and all this gone forever.

Thinking this, the women trembled and held tight, as if to pummel each other to speak against the rage.

"Say something, Zelda, quick."

"*What?*"

"Anything! They'll get hurt if we don't—"

"*They?*"

"You know what I mean. Save them."

"Okay. Jesus!" Zelda froze, clamped her eyes shut to find the words, then opened her eyes and said, "Hello."

"Louder."

"Hello," Zelda called softly, then loudly.

Shapes rustled in the dark below. One of the voices rose while the other fell and the piano strummed its hidden harp strings.

"Don't be afraid," Zelda called.

"That's good. Go on."

"Don't be afraid," Zelda called, braver now. "Don't listen to those others yelling. We won't hurt you. It's just us. I'm Zelda, you wouldn't remember, and this here is Bella, and we've known you forever, or since we were kids, and we love you. It's late, but we thought you should know. We've loved you ever since you were in the desert or on that boat with ghosts or trying to sell Christmas trees door-to-door or in that traffic where you tore the head-lights off cars, and we still love you, right, Bella?"

The night below was darkness, waiting.

Zelda punched Bella's arm.

"Yes!" Bella cried, "what she *said*. We love you."

"We can't think of anything else to say."

"But it's enough, yes?" Bella leaned forward anxiously. "It's *enough?*"

A night wind stirred the leaves and grass around the stairs and the shadows below that had stopped moving with the music box suspended between them as they looked up and up at the two women, who suddenly began to cry. First tears fell from Bella's cheeks, and when Zelda sensed them, she let fall her own.

"So now," said Zelda, amazed that she could form words but managed to speak anyway, "we want you to know, you don't have to come back anymore. You don't have to climb the hill every night, waiting. For what we said just now is it, isn't it? I mean you wanted to hear it here on this hill, with those steps, and that piano, yes, that's the whole thing, it had to be that, didn't it? So now here we are and there you are and it's said. So rest, dear friends."

"Oh, there, Ollie," added Bella in a sad, sad whisper. "Oh, Stan, Stanley."

The piano, hidden in the dark, softly hummed its wires and creaked its ancient wood.

And then the most incredible thing happened. There was a series of shouts and then a huge banging crash as the music box, in the dark, rocketed down the hill, skittering on the steps, playing chords where it hit, swerving, rushing, and ahead of it, running, the two shapes pursued by the musical beast, yelling, tripping, shouting, warning the Fates, crying out to the gods, down and down, forty, sixty, eighty, one hundred steps.

And half down the steps, hearing, feeling, shouting, crying themselves, and now laughing and holding to each other, the two women alone in the night wildly clutching, grasping, trying to see, almost sure that they *did* see, the three things ricocheting off and away, the two shadows rushing, one fat, one thin, and the piano blundering after, discordant and mindless, until they reached the street, where, instantly, the one overhead street-lamp died as if struck, and the shadows floundered on, pursued by the musical beast.

And the two women, abandoned, looked down, exhausted with laughing until they wept and weeping until they laughed, until suddenly Zelda got a terrible look on her face as if shot.

"My God!" she shouted in panic, reaching out. "Wait. We didn't mean, we don't want—don't go *forever*! Sure, go, so the neighbors here sleep. But once a year, you *hear*? Once a year, one night a year from tonight, and every year after that, come back. It shouldn't bother anyone so much. But we got to tell you all over again, huh? Come back and bring the box with you, and we'll be here waiting, won't we, Bella?"

"Waiting, yes."

There was a long silence from the steps leading down into an old black-and-white, silent Los Angeles.

"You think they heard?"

They listened.

And from somewhere far off and down, there was the faintest explosion like the engine of an old jalopy knocking itself to life, and then the merest whisper of a lunatic music from a dark theater when they were very young. It faded.

After a long while they climbed back up the steps, dabbing at their eyes with wet Kleenex. Then they turned for a final time to stare down into the night.

"You know something?" said Zelda. "I think they *heard*."

THE DWARF

Aimee watched the sky, quietly.

Tonight was one of those motionless hot summer nights. The concrete pier empty, the strung red, white, yellow bulbs burning like insects in the air above the wooden emptiness. The managers of the various carnival pitches stood, like melting wax dummies, eyes staring blindly, not talking, all down the line.

Two customers had passed through an hour before. Those two lonely people were now in the roller coaster, screaming murderously as it plummeted down the blazing night, around one emptiness after another.

Aimee moved slowly across the strand, a few worn wooden hoopla rings sticking to her wet hands. She stopped behind the ticket booth that fronted the MIRROR MAZE. She saw herself grossly misrepresented in three rippled mirrors outside the Maze. A thousand tired replicas of herself dissolved in the corridor beyond, hot images among so much clear coolness.

She stepped inside the ticket booth and stood looking a long while at Ralph Banghart's thin neck. He clenched an unlit cigar between his long uneven yellow teeth as he laid out a battered game of solitaire on the ticket shelf.

When the roller coaster wailed and fell in its terrible avalanche again, she was reminded to speak.

"What kind of people go up in roller coasters?"

Ralph Banghart worked his cigar a full thirty seconds. "People wanna die. That rollie coaster's the handiest thing to dying there is." He sat listening to the faint sound of rifle shots from the shooting gallery. "This whole damn carny business's crazy. For instance, that dwarf. You seen him? Every night, pays his dime, runs in the Mirror Maze all the way back through to Screwy Louie's Room. You should see this little runt head back there. My God!"

"Oh, yes," said Aimee, remembering. "I always wonder what it's like to be a dwarf. I always feel sorry when I see him."

"I could play him like an accordion."

"Don't say that!"

"My Lord." Ralph patted her thigh with a free hand. "The way you carry on about guys you never even met." He shook his head and chuckled. "Him and his secret. Only he don't know I know, see? Boy howdy!"

"It's a hot night." She twitched the large wooden hoops nervously on her damp fingers.

"Don't change the subject. He'll be here, rain or shine."

Aimee shifted her weight.

Ralph seized her elbow. "Hey! You ain't mad? You wanna see that dwarf, don't you? Sh!" Ralph turned. "Here he comes now!"

The Dwarf's hand, hairy and dark, appeared all by itself reaching up into the booth window with a silver dime. An invisible person called, "One!" in a high, child's voice.

Involuntarily, Aimee bent forward.

The Dwarf looked up at her, resembling nothing more than a dark-eyed, dark-haired, ugly man who has been locked in a winepress, squeezed and wadded down and down, fold on fold, agony on agony, until a bleached, outraged mass is left, the face bloated shapelessly, a face you know must stare wide-eyed and awake at two and three and four o'clock in the morning, lying flat in bed, only the body asleep.

Ralph tore a yellow ticket in half. "One!"

The Dwarf, as if frightened by an approaching storm, pulled his black coat-lapels tightly about his throat and waddled swiftly. A moment later, ten thousand lost and wandering dwarfs wriggled between the mirror flats, like frantic dark beetles, and vanished.

"Quick!"

Ralph squeezed Aimee along a dark passage behind the mirrors. She felt him pat her all the way back through the tunnel to a thin partition with a peekhole.

"This is rich," he chuckled. "Go on—look."

Aimee hesitated, then put her face to the partition.

"You *see* him?" Ralph whispered.

Aimee felt her heart beating. A full minute passed.

There stood the Dwarf in the middle of the small blue room. His eyes were shut. He wasn't ready to open them yet. Now, now he opened his eyelids and looked at a large mirror set before him. And what he saw in the mirror made him smile. He winked, he pirouetted, he stood sidewise, he waved, he bowed, he did a little clumsy dance.

And the mirror repeated each motion with long, thin arms, with a tall, tall body, with a huge wink and an enormous repetition of the dance, ending in a gigantic bow!

"Every night the same thing," whispered Ralph in Aimee's ear. "Ain't that rich?"

Aimee turned her head and looked at Ralph steadily out of her motionless face, for a long time, and she said nothing. Then, as if she could not help herself, she moved her head slowly and very slowly back to stare once more through the opening. She held her breath. She felt her eyes begin to water.

Ralph nudged her, whispering.

"Hey, what's the little gink doin' *now*?"

✳ They were drinking coffee and not looking at each other in the ticket booth half an hour later, when the Dwarf came out of the mirrors. He took his hat off and started to approach the booth, when he saw Aimee and hurried away.

"He wanted something," said Aimee.

"Yeah." Ralph squashed out his cigarette, idly. "I know what, too. But he hasn't got the nerve to ask. One night in this squeaky little voice he says, 'I bet those mirrors are expensive.' Well, I played dumb. I said yeah they were. He sort of looked at me, waiting, and when I didn't say any more, he went home, but next night he said, 'I bet those mirrors cost fifty, a hundred bucks.' I bet they do, I said. I laid me out a hand of solitaire."

"Ralph," she said.

He glanced up. "Why you look at me that way?"

"Ralph," she said, "why don't you sell him one of your extra ones?"

"Look, Aimee, do I tell you how to run your hoop circus?"

"How much do those mirrors cost?"

"I can get 'em secondhand for thirty-five bucks."

"Why don't you tell him where he can buy one, then?"

"Aimee, you're not smart." He laid his hand on her knee. She moved her knee away. "Even if I told him where to go, you think he'd buy one? Not on your life. And why? He's self-conscious. Why, if he even knew I knew he was flirtin' around in front of that mirror in Screwy Louie's Room, he'd never come back. He plays like he's goin' through the Maze to get lost, like everybody else. Pretends like he don't care about that special room. Always waits for business to turn bad, late nights, so he has that room to himself. What he does for entertainment on nights when business is good, God knows. No, sir, he wouldn't dare go buy a mirror anywhere. He ain't got no friends, and even if he did he couldn't ask him to buy him a thing like that. Pride, by God, pride. Only reason he even mentioned it to me is I'm practically the only guy he knows. Besides, look at him—he ain't got enough to buy a mirror like those. He might be savin' up, but where in hell in the world today can a dwarf work? Dime a dozen, drug on the market, outside of circuses."

"I feel awful. I feel sad." Aimee sat staring at the empty boardwalk. "Where does he live?"

"Flytrap down on the waterfront. The Ganghes Arms. Why?"

"I'm madly in love with him, if you must know."

He grinned around his cigar. "Aimee," he said. "You and your very funny jokes."

✳ A warm night, a hot morning, and a blazing noon. The sea was a sheet of burning tinsel and glass.

Aimee came walking, in the locked-up carnival alleys out over the warm sea, keeping in the shade, half a dozen sun-bleached magazines under her arm. She opened a flaking door. The world of Giants far away, an ugly rumor beyond the garden wall. Poor mama, papa! They meant only the best for me. They kept me, like a porcelain vase, small and treasured, to themselves, in our ant world, our beehive rooms, our microscopic library, our land of beetle-sized doors and moth windows. Only now do I see the magnificent size of my parents' psychosis! They must have dreamed they would live forever, keeping me like a butterfly under glass. But first father died, and then fire ate up the little house, the wasp's nest, and every postage-stamp mirror and saltcellar closet within. Mama, too, gone! And myself alone, watching the fallen embers, tossed out into a world of Monsters and Titans, caught in a landslide of reality, rushed, rolled, and smashed to the bottom of the cliff!

"It took me a year to adjust. A job with a sideshow was unthinkable. There seemed no place for me in the world. And then, a month ago, the Persecutor came into my life, clapped a bonnet on my unsuspecting head, and cried to friends, 'I want you to meet the little woman!' "

Aimee stopped reading. Her eyes were unsteady and the magazine shook as she handed it to Ralph. "You finish it. The rest is a murder story. It's all right. But don't you see? That little man. That little man."

Ralph tossed the magazine aside and lit a cigarette lazily. "I like Westerns better."

'Ralph, you got to read it. He needs someone to tell him how good he is and keep him writing."

Ralph looked at her, his head to one side. "And guess who's going to do it? Well, well, ain't we just the Savior's right hand?"

"I won't listen!"

"Use your head, damn it! You go busting in on him he'll think you're handing him pity. He'll chase you screamin' outa his room."

She sat down, thinking about it slowly, trying to turn it over and see it from every side. "I don't know. Maybe you're right. Oh, it's not just pity, Ralph, honest. But maybe it'd look like it to him. I've got to be awful careful."

He shook her shoulder back and forth, pinching softly, with his fingers. "Hell, hell, lay off him, is all I ask; you'll get nothing but trouble for your dough. God, Aimee, I never *seen* you so hepped on anything. Look, you and me, let's make it a day, take a lunch, get us some gas, and just drive on down the coast as far as we can drive; swim, have supper, see a good show in some little town—to hell with the carnival, how about it? A damn nice day and no worries. I been savin' a coupla bucks."

"It's because I know he's different," she said, looking off into darkness. "It's because he's something we can never be—you and me and all the rest of us here on the pier. It's so funny, so funny. Life fixed him so he's good for nothing but carny shows, yet there he is on the land. And life made us so we wouldn't have to work in the carny shows, but here we are, anyway, way out here at sea on the pier. Sometimes it seems a million miles to shore. How come, Ralph, that we got the bodies, but he's got the brains and can think things we'll never even guess?"

"You haven't even been listening to me!" said Ralph.

She sat with him standing over her, his voice far away. Her eyes were half shut and her hands were in her lap, twitching.

"I don't like that shrewd look you're getting on," he said, finally.

She opened her purse slowly and took out a small roll of bills and started counting. "Thirty-five, forty dollars. There. I'm going to phone Billie Fine and have him send out one of those tall-type mirrors to Mr. Bigelow at the Ganghes Arms. Yes, I am!"

"What!"

"Think how wonderful for him, Ralph, having one in his own room any time he wants it. Can I use your phone?"

"Go ahead, *be* nutty."

Ralph turned quickly and walked off down the tunnel. A door slammed.

Aimee waited, then after a while put her hands to the phone and began to dial, with painful slowness. She paused between numbers, holding her breath, shutting her eyes, thinking how it might seem to be small in the world, and then one day someone sends a special mirror by. A mirror for your room where you can hide away with the big reflection of yourself, shining, and write stories and stories, never going out into the world unless you had to. How might it be then, alone, with the wonderful illusion all in one piece in the room. Would it make you happy or sad, would it help your writing or hurt it? She shook her head back and forth, back and forth. At least this way there would be no one to look down at you. Night after night, perhaps rising secretly at three in the cold morning, you could wink and dance around and smile and wave at yourself, so tall, so tall, so very fine and tall in the bright looking-glass.

A telephone voice said, "Billie Fine's."

"Oh, *Billie*!" she cried.

❋ Night came in over the pier. The ocean lay dark and loud under the planks. Ralph sat cold and waxen in his glass coffin, laying out the cards, his eyes fixed, his mouth stiff. At his elbow, a growing pyramid of burned cigarette butts grew larger. When Aimee walked along under the hot red and blue bulbs, smiling, waving, he did not stop setting the cards down slow and very slow. "Hi, Ralph!" she said.

"How's the love affair?" he asked, drinking from a dirty glass of iced water. "How's Charlie Boyer, or is it Cary Grant?"

"I just went and bought me a new hat," she said, smiling. "Gosh, I feel *good*! You know why? Billie Fine's sending a mirror out tomorrow! Can't you just see the nice little guy's face?"

"I'm not so hot at imagining."

"Oh, Lord, you'd think I was going to marry him or something."

"Why not? Carry him around in a suitcase. People say, Where's your husband? all you do is open your bag, yell, Here he is! Like a silver cornet. Take him outa his case any old hour, play a tune, stash him away. Keep a little sandbox for him on the back porch."

"I was feeling so good," she said.

"Benevolent is the word." Ralph did not look at her, his mouth tight. "Ben-eve-o-*lent*. I suppose this all comes from me watching him through that knothole, getting my kicks? That why you sent the mirror? People like you run around with tambourines, taking the joy out of my life."

"Remind me not to come to your place for drinks anymore. I'd rather go with no people at all than mean people."

Ralph exhaled a deep breath. "Aimee, Aimee. Don't you know you can't help that guy? He's bats. And this crazy thing of yours is like saying, Go ahead, *be* batty, I'll help you, pal."

"Once in a lifetime anyway, it's nice to make a mistake if you think it'll do somebody some good," she said.

"God deliver me from do-gooders, Aimee."

"Shut up, shut up!" she cried, and then said nothing more.

He let the silence lie awhile, and then got up, putting his finger-printed glass aside. "Mind the booth for me?"

"Sure. Why?"

She saw ten thousand cold white images of him stalking down the glassy corridors, between mirrors, his mouth straight and his fingers working themselves.

She sat in the booth for a full minute and then suddenly shivered. A small clock ticked in the booth and she turned the deck of cards over, one by one, waiting. She heard a hammer pounding and knocking and pounding again, far away inside the Maze; a silence, more waiting, and then ten thousand images folding and refolding and dissolving, Ralph striding, looking out at ten thousand images of her in the booth. She heard his quiet laughter as he came down the ramp.

"Well, what's put you in such a good mood?" she asked, suspiciously.

"Aimee," he said carelessly, "we shouldn't quarrel. You say tomorrow Billie's sending that mirror to Mr. Big's?"

"You're not going to try anything funny?"

"Me?" He moved her out of the booth and took over the cards, humming, his eyes bright. "Not me, oh no, not me." He did not look at her, but started quickly to slap out the cards. She stood behind him. Her right eye began to twitch a little. She folded and unfolded her arms. A minute ticked by. The only sound was the ocean under the night pier, Ralph breathing in the heat, the soft ruffle of the cards. The sky over the pier was hot and thick with clouds. Out at sea, faint glows of lightning were beginning to show.

"Ralph," she said at last.

"Relax, Aimee," he said.

"About that trip you wanted to take down the coast—"

"Tomorrow," he said. "Maybe next month. Maybe next year. Old Ralph Banghart's a patient guy. I'm not worried, Aimee. Look." He held up a hand. "I'm calm."

She waited for a roll of thunder at sea to fade away.

"I just don't want you mad, is all. I just don't want anything bad to happen, promise me."

The wind, now warm, now cool, blew along the pier. There was a smell of rain in the wind. The clock ticked. Aimee began to perspire heavily, watching the cards move and move. Distantly, you could hear targets being hit and the sound of the pistols at the shooting gallery.

And then, there he was.

Waddling along the lonely concourse, under the insect bulbs, his face twisted and dark, every movement an effort. From a long way down the pier he came, with Aimee watching. She wanted to say to him, This is your last night, the last time you'll have to embarrass yourself by coming here, the last time you'll have to put up with being watched by Ralph, even in secret. She wished she could cry out and laugh and say it right in front of Ralph. But she said nothing.

"Hello, hello!" shouted Ralph. "It's free, on the house, tonight! Special for old customers!"

The Dwarf looked up, startled, his little black eyes darting and swimming in confusion. His mouth formed the word thanks and he turned, one hand to his neck, pulling his tiny lapels tight up about his convulsing throat, the other hand clenching the silver dime secretly. Looking back, he gave a little nod, and then scores of dozens of compressed and tortured faces, burned a strange dark color by the lights, wandered in the glass corridors.

"Ralph," Aimee took his elbow. "What's going on?"

He grinned. "I'm being benevolent, Aimee, benevolent."

"Ralph," she said.

"Sh," he said. "*Listen.*"

They waited in the booth in the long warm silence.

Then, a long way off, muffled, there was a scream.

"Ralph!" said Aimee.

"Listen, listen!" he said.

There was another scream, and another and still another, and a threshing and a pounding and a breaking, a rushing around and through the Maze. There, there, wildly colliding and ricocheting, from mirror to mirror, shrieking hysterically and sobbing, tears on his face, mouth gasped open, came Mr. Bigelow. He fell out in the blazing night air, glanced about wildly, wailed, and ran off down the pier.

"Ralph, what happened?"

Ralph sat laughing and slapping at his thighs.

She slapped his face. "What'd you *do*?"

He didn't quite stop laughing. "Come on. I'll show you!"

And then she was in the Maze, rushed from white-hot mirror to mirror, seeing her lipstick all red fire a thousand times repeated on down a burning silver cavern where strange hysterical women much like herself followed a quick-moving, smiling man. "Come on!" he cried. And they broke free into a dust-smelling tiny room.

"Ralph!" she said.

They both stood on the threshold of the little room where the Dwarf had come every night for a year. They both stood where the Dwarf had stood each night, before opening his eyes to see the miraculous image in front of him.

Aimee shuffled slowly, one hand out, into the dim room.

The mirror had been changed.

This new mirror made even tall people little and dark and twisted smaller as you moved forward.

And Aimee stood before it thinking and thinking that if it made big people small, standing here, God, what would it do to a dwarf, a tiny dwarf, a dark dwarf, a startled and lonely dwarf?

She turned and almost fell. Ralph stood looking at her. "Ralph," she said. "God, why did you do it?"

"Aimee, come back!"

She ran out through the mirrors, crying. Staring with blurred eyes, it was hard to find the way, but she found it. She stood blinking at the empty pier, started to run one way, then another, then still another, then stopped.

Ralph came up behind her, talking, but it was like a voice heard behind a wall late at night, remote and foreign.

"Don't talk to me," she said.

Someone came running up the pier. It was Mr. Kelly from the shooting gallery. "Hey, any you see a little guy just now? Little stiff swiped a pistol from my place, loaded, run off before I'd get a hand on him! You help me find him?"

And Kelly was gone, sprinting, turning his head to search between all the canvas sheds, on away under the hot blue and red and yellow strung bulbs.

Aimee rocked back and forth and took a step.

"Aimee, where you going?"

She looked at Ralph as if they had just turned a corner, strangers passing, and bumped into each other. "I guess," she said, "I'm going to help search."

"You won't be able to do nothing."

"I got to try anyway. Oh God, Ralph, this is all my fault! I shouldn't have phoned Billie Fine! I shouldn't've ordered a mirror and got you so mad you did this! It's me should've gone to Mr. Big, not a crazy thing like I bought! I'm going to find him if it's the last thing I ever do in my life."

Swinging about slowly, her cheeks wet, she saw the quivery mirrors that stood in front of the Maze, Ralph's reflection was in one of them. She could not take her eyes away from the image; it held her in a cool and trembling fascination, with her mouth open.

"Aimee, what's wrong? What're you—"

He sensed where she was looking and twisted about to see what was going on. His eyes widened.

He scowled at the blazing mirror.

A horrid, ugly little man, two feet high, with a pale, squashed face under an ancient straw hat, scowled back at him. Ralph stood there glaring at himself, his hands at his sides.

Aimee walked slowly and then began to walk fast and then began to run. She ran down the empty pier and the wind blew warm and it blew large drops of hot rain out of the sky on her all the time she was running.

A WILD NIGHT IN GALWAY

WE WERE FAR OUT AT THE TIP OF IRELAND, in Galway, where the weather strikes from its bleak quarters in the Atlantic with sheets of rain and gusts of cold and still more sheets of rain. You go to bed sad and wake in the middle of the night thinking you heard someone cry, thinking you yourself were weeping, and feel your face and find it dry. Then you look at the window and turn over, sadder still, and fumble about for your dripping sleep and try to get it back on.

We were out, as I said, in Galway, which is gray stone with green beards on it, a rock town, and the sea coming in and the rain falling down; and we had been there a month solid working with our film director on a script which was, with immense irony, to be shot in the warm yellow sun of Mexico sometime in January. The pages of the script were full of fiery bulls and hot tropical flowers and burning eyes, and I typed it with chopped-off frozen fingers in my gray hotel room where the food was criminal's gruel and the weather a beast at the window.

On the thirty-first night, a knock at the door, at seven. The door opened, my film director stepped nervously in.

"Let's get the hell out and find some wild life in Ireland and forget this damn rain," he said, all in a rush.

"What rain?" I said, sucking my fingers to get the ice out. "The concussion here under the roof is so steady I'm shellshocked and have quite forgot the stuff's coming down!"

"Four weeks here and you're talking Irish," said the director.

"Hand me my clay pipe," I said. And we ran from the room.

"Where?" said I.

"Heber Finn's pub," said he.

And we blew along the stony street in the dark that rocked gently as a boat on the black flood because of the tilty-dancing streetlights above which made the shadows tear and fly, uneasy.

Then, sweating rain, faces pearled, we struck through the pub doors, and it was warm as a sheepfold because there were the townsmen pressed in a great compost heap at the bar and Heber Finn yelling jokes and foaming up drinks.

"Heber Finn," cried the director, "we're here for a wild night!"

"A wild night we'll make it," said Heber Finn, and in a moment a slug of poteen was burning lace patterns in our stomachs, to let new light in.

I exhaled fire. "That's a start," I said.

We had another and listened to the rollicking jests and the jokes that were less than half clean, or so we guessed, for the brogue made it difficult, and the whiskey poured on the brogue and thus combined made it double-difficult. But we knew when to laugh, because when a joke was finished the men hit their knees and then hit us. They'd give their limbs a great smack and then bang us on the arm or thump us in the chest.

As our breath exploded, we'd shape the explosion to hilarity and squeeze our eyes tight. Tears ran down our cheeks not from joy but from the exquisite torture of the drink scalding our throats. Thus pressed like shy flowers in a huge warm-moldy book, the director and I lingered on, waiting for some vast event.

At last my director's patience thinned. "Heber Finn," he called across the seethe, "it's been wild so far, all right, but we want it wilder, I mean, the biggest night Ireland ever saw!"

Whereupon Heber Finn whipped off his apron, shrugged his meat-cleaver shoulders into a tweed coat, jumped up in the air, slid down inside his raincoat, slung on his beardy cap, and thrust us at the door.

"Nail everything down till I get back," he advised his crew. "I'm taking these gents to the damnedest evening ever. Little do they know what waits for them out there."

He opened the door and pointed. The wind threw half a ton of ice water on him. Taking this as no more than an additional spur to rhetoric, Heber Finn, not wiping his face, added in a roar, "Out with you! On! Here we go!"

"Do you think we should?" I said, doubtful now that things seemed really on the move.

"What do you mean?" cried the director. "What do you want to do? Go freeze in your room? Rewrite that scene you did so lousily today?"

"No, no," I said, and slung on my own cap.

I was first outside thinking, I've a wife and three loud but lovely children, what am I doing here, eight thousand miles gone from them, on the dark side of God's remembrance? Do I *really* want to do this?

Then, like Ahab, I thought on my bed, a damp box with its pale cool winding-sheets and the window dripping next to it like a conscience: all night through. I groaned. I opened the door of Heber Finn's car, took my legs apart to get in, and we shot down the town like a ball in a bowling alley.

Heber Finn at the wheel talked fierce, half hilarity, half sobering King Lear.

"A wild night, is it? You'll have the grandest night ever," he said. "You'd never guess, would you, to walk through Ireland, so much could go on under the skin?"

"I knew there must be an outlet somewhere," I yelled.

The speedometer was up to fifty miles an hour. Stone walls raced by on the right, stone walls raced by on the left. It was raining the entire dark sky down on the entire dark land.

"Outlet indeed!" said Heber Finn. "If the Church knew, but it don't! Or then maybe it does, but figures—the poor craythurs—and lets us be!"

"Where, what—?"

"You'll see!" said Heber Finn.

The speedometer read sixty. My stomach was stone like the stone walls rushing left and right. Does the car have brakes? I wondered. Death on an Irish road, I thought, a wreck, and before anyone found us strewn we'd melt away in the pounding rain and be part of the turf by morn. What's death anyway? Better than hotel food.

"Can't we go a bit faster?" I asked.

"It's done," said Heber Finn, and made it seventy.

"That will do it, nicely," I said in a faint voice, wondering what lay ahead. Behind all the slate-stone weeping walls of Ireland, what happened? Beneath the rain-drenched sod, the flinty rock, at the numbed core of living, was there one small seed of fire which, fanned, might break volcanoes free and boil the rains to steam?

Was there then somewhere a Baghdad harem, nests awriggle and aslither with silk and tassel the absolutely perfect tint of women unadorned? Somewhere in this drizzling land were there hearth-fleshed peach-fuzz Renoir ladies bright as lamps you could hold your hands out to and warm your palms? We passed a church. No. We passed a convent. No. We passed a village slouched under its old men's thatch. No. Stone walls to left. Stone walls to right. No. Yet . . .

I glanced over at Heber Finn. We could have switched off our lights and driven by the steady piercing beams of his forward-directed eyes snatching at the dark, flicking away the rain.

Wife, I thought to myself, children, forgive me for what I do this night, terrible as it might be, for this is Ireland in the rain of an ungodly time and way out in Galway where the dead must go to die.

The brakes were hit. We slid a good ninety feet, my nose mashed on the windscreen. Heber Finn was out of the car.

"We're here." He sounded like a man drowning deep in the rain.

I looked left. Stone walls. I looked right. Stone walls.

"Where is it?" I shouted.

"Where, indeed." He pointed, mysteriously. "There."

I saw a hole in the wall, a tiny gate flung wide.

The director and I followed at a plunge. We saw other cars in the dark now, and many bikes. But not a light anywhere. A secret, I thought, oh, it *must* be wild to be *this* secret. What am I doing here? I yanked my cap lower. Rain crawled down my neck.

Through the hole in the wall we stumbled, Heber Finn clenching our elbows. "Here," he husked, "stand here. It'll be a moment. Swig on this to keep your blood high."

I felt a flask knock my fingers. I got the fire into my boilers and let the steam up the flues.

"It's a lovely rain," I said.

"The man's mad," said Heber Finn, and drank after the director, a shadow among shadows in the dark.

I squinted about. I had an impression of a midnight sea upon which men like little boats passed on the murmurous tides. Heads down, muttering, in twos and threes, a hundred men stirred out beyond.

It has an unholy air—Good God, what's it all about? I asked myself, incredibly curious now.

"Heber Finn—?" said the director.

"Wait," whispered Heber Finn. "This is *it*!"

What did I expect? Perhaps some scene like those old movies where innocent sailing ships suddenly flap down cabin walls and guns appear like magic to fire on the foe. Or a farmhouse falls apart like a cereal box, Long Tom rears up to blast a projectile five hundred miles to target Paris.

So here, maybe, I thought, the stones will spill away each from the others, the walls of that house will curtain back, rosy lights will flash forth, and from a monstrous cannon six, a dozen, ten dozen pink pearly women, not dwarf-Irish but willowy-French, will be shot out over the heads and down into the waving arms of the grateful multitude. Benison indeed! What's more—manna!

The lights came on. I blinked.

For I saw the entire unholy thing. There it was, laid out for me under the drizzling rain.

The lights came on. The men quickened, turned, gathered, us with them.

A mechanical rabbit popped out of a little box at the far end of the stony yard and ran. Eight dogs, let free from gates, yelping, ran after in a great circle. There was not one shout or murmur from the crowd of men. Their heads turned slowly, watching.

The rain rained down on the illuminated scene. The rain fell upon tweed caps and thin cloth coats. The rain dripped off thick eyebrows and thin noses. The rain beat on hunched shoulders. I stared. The rabbit ran. The dogs ran. At the finish, the rabbit popped into its electric hatch. The dogs collided into each other, barking. The lights went out.

In the dark, I turned to stare at the director as I knew he must be turning to stare at me.

I was thankful for the dark, the rain, so Heber Finn could not see our faces.

"Come on, now," he shouted, "place your bets!"

We were back in Galway, speeding, at ten o'clock. The rain was still raining, the wind was still blowing. The highway was a river working to erase the stone beneath as we drew up in a great tidal spray before my hotel.

"Well, now," said Heber Finn, not looking at us, but at the windscreen wiper beating, palpitating there. "Well."

The director and I had bet on five races and had lost between us two or three pounds. It worried Heber Finn.

"I won a great deal," he said, "and some of it I put down in your names. That last race, I swear to God, I bet and won for all of us. Let me pay you."

"No, Heber Finn, thanks," I said, my numb lips moving.

He took my hand and pressed two shillings into it. I didn't fight him. "That's better," he said.

Wringing out his cap in the hotel lobby my director looked at me and said, "It was a wild Irish night, wasn't it?"

"A wild night," I said. He left.

✳ I hated to go up to my room. So I sat for another hour in the reading lounge of the damp hotel and took the traveler's privilege, a glass and a bottle provided by the dazed hall porter.

I sat alone, listening to the rain and the rain on the cold hotel roof, thinking of Ahab's coffin-bed waiting for me up there under the drumbeat weather.

I thought of the only warm thing in the hotel, in the town, in all the land of Eire this night, the script in my typewriter this moment, with its sun of Mexico, its hot winds blowing from the Pacific, its mellow papayas, its yellow lemons, its fiery sand, and its women with dark charcoal-burning eyes.

And I thought of the darkness beyond the town, the light flashing on, the electric rabbit running, the dogs running, and the rabbit gone, and the light going out, and the rain falling down on the dank shoulders and the soaked caps, and trickling off the noses and seeping through the tweeds.

Going upstairs I glanced through a streaming window. There, riding by under a streetlight, was a man on a bicycle. He was terribly drunk, for the bike weaved back and forth across the road. He kept pumping on unsteadily, blearily. I watched him ride off into the raining dark.

Then I went on up to die in my room.

THE WIND

THE PHONE RANG AT FIVE-THIRTY that evening. It was December, and long since dark as Thompson picked up the phone.

"Hello."

"Hello, *Herb?*"

"Oh, it's you, Allin."

"Is your wife home, Herb?"

"Sure. Why?"

"Damn it."

Herb Thompson held the receiver quietly. "What's up? You sound funny."

"I wanted you to come over tonight."

"We're having company."

"I wanted you to spend the night. When's your wife going away?"

"That's next week," said Thompson. "She'll be in Ohio for about nine days. Her mother's sick. I'll come over then."

"I wish you could come over tonight."

"Wish I could. Company and all, my wife'd kill me."

"I wish you could come over."

"What's it? the wind again?"

"Oh, no. No."

"Is it the wind?" asked Thompson.

The voice on the phone hesitated. "Yeah. Yeah, it's the wind."

"It's a clear night, there's not much wind."

"There's enough. It comes in the window and blows the curtains a little bit. Just enough to tell me."

"Look, why don't you come and spend the night here?" said Herb Thompson looking around the lighted hall.

"Oh, no. It's too late for that. It might catch me on the way over. It's a damned long distance. I wouldn't dare, but thanks, anyway. It's thirty miles, but thanks."

"Take a sleeping-tablet."

"I've been standing in the door for the past hour, Herb. I can see it building up in the west. There are some clouds there and I saw one of them kind of rip apart. There's a wind coming, all right."

"Well, you just take a nice sleeping-tablet. And call me anytime you want to call. Later this evening if you want."

"Any time?" said the voice on the phone.

"Sure."

"I'll do that, but I wish you could come out. Yet I wouldn't want you hurt. You're my best friend and I wouldn't want that. Maybe it's best I face this thing alone. I'm sorry I bother you."

"Hell, what's a friend for? Tell you what you do, sit down and get some writing done this evening," said Herb. Thompson, shifting from one foot to the other in the hall. "You'll forget about the Himalayas and the Valley of the Winds and this preoccupation of yours with storms and hurricanes. Get another chapter done on your next travel book."

"I might do that. Maybe I will, I don't know. Maybe I will. I might do that. Thanks a lot for letting me bother you."

"Thanks, hell. Get off the line, now, you. My wife's calling me to dinner."

Herb Thompson hung up.

He went and sat down at the supper table and his wife sat across from him. "Was that Allin?" she asked. He nodded. "Him and his winds that blow up and winds that blow down and winds that blow hot and blow cold," she said, handing him his plate heaped with food.

"He did have a time in the Himalayas, during the war," said Herb Thompson.

"You don't believe what he said about that valley, do you?"

"It makes a good story."

"Climbing around, climbing up things. Why do men climb mountains and scare themselves?"

"It was snowing," said Herb Thompson.

"Was it?"

"And raining and hailing and blowing all at once, in that valley. Allin's told me a dozen times. He tells it well. He was up pretty high. Clouds, and all. The valley made a noise."

"I bet it did," she said.

"Like a lot of winds instead of just one. Winds from all over the world." He took a bite. "So says Allin."

"He shouldn't have gone there and looked, in the first place," she said. "You go poking around and first thing you know you get ideas. Winds start getting angry at you for intruding, and they follow you."

"Don't joke, he's my best friend," snapped Herb Thompson.

"It's all so silly!"

"Nevertheless he's been through a lot. That storm in Bombay, later, and the typhoon off New Guinea two months after that. And that time, in Cornwall."

"I have no sympathy for a man who continually runs into wind storms and hurricanes, and then gets a persecution complex because of it."

The phone rang just then.

"Don't answer it," she said.

"Maybe it's important."

"It's only Allin, again."

They sat there and the phone rang nine times and they didn't answer. Finally, it quieted. They finished dinner. Out in the kitchen, the window curtains gently moved in the small breeze from a slightly opened window.

The phone rang again.

"I can't let it ring," he said, and answered it. "Oh, hello, Allin."

"Herb! It's here! It got here!"

"You're too near the phone, back up a little."

"I stood in the open door and waited for it. I saw it coming down the highway, shaking all the trees, one by one, until it shook the trees just outside the house and it dived down toward the door and I slammed the door in its face!"

Thompson didn't say anything. He couldn't think of anything to say, his wife was watching him in the hall door.

"How interesting," he said, at last.

"It's all around the house, Herb. I can't get out now, I can't do anything. But I fooled it, I let it think it had me, and just as it came down to get me I slammed and locked the door! I was ready for it, I've been getting ready for weeks."

"Have you, now; tell me about it, Allin, old man." Herb Thompson played it jovially into the phone, while his wife looked on and his neck began to sweat.

"It began six weeks ago. . . ."

"Oh, yes? Well, well."

". . . I thought I had it licked. I thought it had given up following and trying to get me. But it was just waiting. Six weeks ago I heard the wind laughing and whispering around the corners of my house, out here. Just for an hour or so, not very long, not very loud. Then it went away."

Thompson nodded into the phone. "Glad to hear it, glad to hear it." His wife stared at him.

"It came back, the next night. It slammed the shutters and kicked sparks out of the chimney. It came back five nights in a row, a little stronger each time. When I opened the front door, it came in at me and tried to pull me out, but it wasn't strong enough. Tonight it is."

"Glad to hear you're feeling better," said Thompson.

"I'm not better, what's wrong with you? Is your wife listening to us?"

"Yes."

"Oh, I see. I know I sound like a fool."

"Not at all. Go on."

Thompson's wife went back into the kitchen. He relaxed. He sat down on a little chair near the phone. "Go on, Allin, get it out of you, you'll sleep better."

"It's all around the house now, like a great big vacuum machine nuzzling at all the gables. It's knocking the trees around."

"That's funny, there's no wind *here*. Allin."

"Of course not, it doesn't care about you, only about me."

"I guess that's one way to explain it."

"It's a killer, Herb, the biggest damnedest prehistoric killer that ever hunted prey. A big sniffling hound, trying to smell me out, find me. It pushes its big cold nose up to the house, taking air, and when it finds me in the parlor it drives its pressure there, and when I'm in the kitchen it goes there. It's trying to get in the windows, now, but I had them reinforced and I put new hinges on the doors, and bolts. It's a strong house. They built them strong in the old days. I've got all the lights in the house on, now. The house is all lighted up, bright. The wind followed me from room to room, looking through all the windows, when I switched them on. Oh!"

"What's wrong?"

"It just snatched off the front screen door!"

"I wish you'd come over here and spend the night, Allin."

"I can't! God, I can't leave the house. I can't do anything. I know this wind. Lord, it's big and it's clever. I tried to light a cigarette a moment ago, and a little draft sucked the match out. The wind likes to play games, it likes to taunt me, it's taking its time with me; it's got all night. And now! God, right now, one of my old travel books, on the library table, I wish you could see it. A little breeze from God knows what small hole in the house, the little breeze is—blowing the pages one by one. I wish you could see it. There's my introduction. Do you remember the introduction to my book on Tibet, Herb?"

"Yes."

"*This book is dedicated to those who lost the game of elements, written by one who has seen, but who has always escaped.*"

"Yes, I remember."

"The lights have gone out!"

The phone crackled.

"The power lines just went down. Are you there, Herb?"

"I still hear you."

"The wind doesn't like all that light in my house, it tore the power lines down. The telephone will probably go next. Oh, it's a real party, me and the wind, I tell you! Just a second."

"Allin?" A silence. Herb leaned against the mouthpiece. His wife glanced in from the kitchen. Herb Thompson waited. "Allin?"

"I'm back," said the voice on the phone. "There was a draft from the door and I shoved some wadding under it to keep it from blowing on my feet. I'm glad you didn't come out after all, Herb, I wouldn't want you in this mess. There! It just broke one of the living room windows and a regular gale is in the house, knocking pictures off the wall! Do you hear it?"

Herb Thompson listened. There was a wild sirening on the phone and a whistling and banging. Allin shouted over it. "Do you hear it?"

Herb Thompson swallowed dryly. "I hear it."

"It wants me alive, Herb. It doesn't dare knock the house down in one fell blow. That'd kill me. It wants me alive, so it can pull me apart, finger by finger. It wants what's inside me. My mind, my brain. It wants my life-power, my psychic force, my ego. It wants intellect."

"My wife's calling me, Allin. I have to go wipe the dishes."

"It's a big cloud of vapors, winds from all over the world. The same wind that ripped the Celebes a year ago, the same pampero that killed in Argentina, the typhoon that fed on Hawaii, the hurricane that knocked the coast of Africa early this year. It's part of all those storms I escaped. It followed me from the Himalayas because it didn't want me to know what I know about the Valley of the Winds where it gathers and plans its destruction. Something, a long time ago, gave it a start in the direction of life. I know its feeding grounds, I know where it is born and where parts of it expire. For that reason, it hates me; and my books that tell how to defeat it. It doesn't want me preaching anymore. It wants to incorporate me into its huge body, to give it knowledge. It wants me on its own side!"

"I have to hang up, Allin, my wife—"

"What?" A pause, the blowing of the wind in the phone, distantly. "What did you say?"

"Call me back in about an hour, Allin."

He hung up.

He went out to wipe the dishes. His wife looked at him and he looked at the dishes, rubbing them with a towel.

"What's it like out tonight?" he said.

"Nice. Not very chilly. Stars," she said. "Why?"

"Nothing."

The phone rang three times in the next hour. At eight o'clock the company arrived, Stoddard and his wife. They sat around until eight-thirty talking and then got out and set up the card table and began to play Gin.

Herb Thompson shuffled the cards over and over, with a clittering, shuttering effect and clapped them out, one at a time before the three other players. Talk went back and forth. He lit a cigar and made it into a fine gray ash at the tip, and adjusted his cards in his hand and on occasion lifted his head and listened. There was no sound outside the house. His wife saw him do this, and he cut it out immediately, and discarded a Jack of Clubs.

He puffed slowly on his cigar and they all talked quietly with occasional small eruptions of laughter, and the clock in the hall sweetly chimed nine o'clock.

"Here we all are," said Herb Thompson, taking his cigar out and looking at it reflectively. "And life is sure funny."

"Eh?" said Mr. Stoddard.

"Nothing, except here we are, living our lives, and some place else on earth a billion other people live their lives."

"That's a rather obvious statement."

"Life," he put his cigar back in his lips, "is a lonely thing. Even with married people. Sometimes when you're in a person's arms you feel a million miles away from them."

"I like *that*," said his wife.

"I didn't mean it that way," he explained, not with haste; because he felt no guilt, he took his time. "I mean we all believe what we believe and live our own little lives while other people live entirely different ones. I mean, we sit here in this room while a thousand people are dying. Some of cancer, some of pneumonia, some of tuberculosis. I imagine someone in the United States is dying right now in a wrecked car."

"This isn't very stimulating conversation," said his wife.

"I mean to say, we all live and don't think about how other people think or live their lives or die. We wait until death comes to us. What I mean is here we sit, on our self-assured butt-bones, while, thirty miles away, in a big old house, completely surrounded by night and God-knows-what, one of the finest guys who ever lived is—"

"Herb!"

He puffed and chewed on his cigar and stared blindly at his cards. "Sorry." He blinked rapidly and bit his cigar. "Is it my turn?"

"It's your turn."

The playing went around the table, with a flittering of cards, murmurs, conversation. Herb Thompson sank lower into his chair and began to look ill.

The phone rang. Thompson jumped and ran to it and jerked it off the hook.

"Herb! I've been calling and calling. What's it like at your house, Herb?"

"What do you mean, what's it like?"

"Has the company come?"

"Hell, yes, it has—"

"Are you talking and laughing and playing cards?"

"Christ, yes, but what has that got to do with—"

"Are you smoking your ten-cent cigar?"

"God damn it, yes, but . . ."

"Swell," said the voice on the phone. "That sure is swell. I wish I could be there. I wish I didn't know the things I know. I wish lots of things."

"Are you all right?"

"So far, so good. I'm locked in the kitchen now. Part of the front wall of the house blew in. But I planned my retreat. When the kitchen door gives, I'm heading for the cellar. If I'm lucky I may hold out there until morning. It'll have to tear the whole damned house down to get to me, and the cellar floor is pretty solid. I have a shovel and I may dig—deeper. . . ."

It sounded like a lot of other voices on the phone.

"What's *that*?" Herb Thompson demanded, cold, shivering.

"That?" asked the voice on the phone. "Those are the voices of twelve thousand killed by a typhoon, seven thousand killed by a hurricane, three thousand buried by a cyclone. Am I boring you? That's what the wind is. It's a lot of people dead. The wind killed them, took their minds to give itself intelligence. It took all their voices and made them into one voice. All those millions of people killed in the past ten thousand years, tortured and run from continent to continent on the backs and in the bellies of monsoons and whirlwinds. Oh Christ, what a poem you could write about it!"

The phone echoed and rang with voices and shouts and whinings.

"Come on back, Herb," called his wife from the card table.

"That's how the wind gets more intelligent each year, it adds to itself, body by body, life by life, death by death."

"We're waiting for you, Herb," called his wife.

"Damn it!" He turned, almost snarling. "Wait just a moment, won't you!" Back to the phone. "Allin, if you want me to come out there now, I will! I should have come earlier . . ."

"Wouldn't think of it. This is a grudge fight, wouldn't do to have you in it now. I'd better hang up. The kitchen door looks bad; I'll have to get in the cellar."

"Call me back, later?"

"Maybe, if I'm lucky. I don't think I'll make it. I slipped away and escaped so many times, but I think it has me now. I hope I haven't bothered you too much, Herb."

"You haven't bothered anyone, damn it. Call me back."

"I'll try. . . ."

Herb Thompson went back to the card game. His wife glared at him. "How's Allin, your friend?" she asked, "Is he sober?"

"He's never taken a drink in his life," said Thompson, sullenly, sitting down. "I should have gone out there hours ago."

"But he's called every night for six weeks and you've been out there at least ten nights to stay with him and nothing was wrong."

"He needs help. He might hurt himself."

"You were just out there, two nights ago, you can't always be running after him."

"First thing in the morning I'll move him into a sanatorium. Didn't want to. He seems so reasonable otherwise."

At ten-thirty coffee was served. Herb Thompson drank his slowly, looking at the phone. I wonder if he's in the cellar now, he thought.

Herb Thompson walked to the phone, called long-distance, gave the number.

"I'm sorry," said the operator. "The lines are down in that district. When the lines are repaired, we will put your call through."

"Then the telephone lines *are* down!" cried Thompson. He let the phone drop. Turning, he slammed open the closet door, pulled out his coat. "Oh Lord," he said. "Oh, Lord, Lord," he said, to his amazed guests and his wife with the coffee urn in her hand. "Herb!" she cried. "I've got to get out there!" he said, slipping into his coat.

There was a soft, faint stirring at the door.

Everybody in the room tensed and straightened up.

"Who could that be?" asked his wife.

The soft stirring was repeated, very quietly.

Thompson hurried down the hall where he stopped, alert.

Outside, faintly, he heard laughter.

"I'll be damned," said Thompson. He put his hand on the doorknob, pleasantly shocked and relieved. "I'd know that laugh anywhere. It's Allin. He came on over in his car, after all. Couldn't wait until morning to tell me his confounded stories." Thompson smiled weakly. "Probably brought some friends with him. Sounds like a lot of other . . ."

He opened the front door.

The porch was empty.

Thompson showed no surprise; his face grew amused and sly. He laughed. "Allin? None of your tricks now! Come on." He switched on the porch light and peered out and around. "Where are you, Allin? Come on, now."

A breeze blew into his face.

Thompson waited a moment, suddenly chilled to his marrow. He stepped out on the porch and looked uneasily, and very carefully, about.

A sudden wind caught and whipped his coat flaps, disheveled his hair. He thought he heard laughter again. The wind rounded the house and was a pressure everywhere at once, and then, storming for a full minute, passed on.

The wind died down, sad, mourning in the high trees, passing away; going back out to the sea, to the Celebes, to the Ivory Coast, to Sumatra and Cape Horn, to Cornwall and the Philippines. Fading, fading, fading.

Thompson stood there, cold. He went in and closed the door and leaned against it, and didn't move, eyes closed.

"What's wrong . . . ?" asked his wife.

NO NEWS, OR WHAT KILLED THE DOG?

IT WAS A DAY OF HOLOCAUSTS, cataclysms, tornadoes, earthquakes, blackouts, mass murders, eruptions, and miscellaneous dooms, at the peak of which the sun swallowed the earth and the stars vanished.

But to put it simply, the most respected member of the Bentley family up and died.

Dog was his name, and dog he was.

The Bentleys, arising late Saturday morning, found Dog stretched on the kitchen floor, his head toward Mecca, his paws neatly folded, his tail not a-thump but silent for the first time in twenty years.

Twenty years! My God, everyone thought, could it really have been that long? And now, without permission, Dog was cold and gone.

Susan, the younger daughter, woke everyone yelling:

"Something's wrong with Dog. Quick!"

Without bothering to don his bathrobe, Roger Bentley, in his underwear, hurried out to look at that quiet beast on the kitchen tiles. His wife, Ruth, followed, and then their son Skip, twelve. The rest of the family, married and flown, Rodney and Sal, would arrive later. Each in turn would say the same thing:

"No! Dog was *forever*."

Dog said nothing, but lay there like World War II, freshly finished, and a devastation.

Tears poured down Susan's cheeks, then down Ruth Bentley's, followed in good order by tears from Father and, at last, when it had sunk in, Skip.

Instinctively, they made a ring around Dog, kneeling to the floor to touch him, as if this might suddenly make him sit up, smile as he always did at his food, bark, and beat them to the door. But their touching did nothing but increase their tears.

But at last they rose, hugged each other, and went blindly in search of breakfast, in the midst of which Ruth Bentley said, stunned, "We can't just leave him *there*."

Roger Bentley picked Dog up, gently, and moved him out on the patio, in the shade, by the pool.

"What do we do next?"

"I don't know," said Roger Bentley. "This is the first death in the family in years and—" He stopped, snorted, and shook his head. "I mean—"

"You meant exactly what you said," said Ruth Bentley. "If Dog wasn't family, he was nothing. God, I loved him."

A fresh burst of tears ensued, during which Roger Bentley brought a blanket to put over Dog, but Susan stopped him.

"No, no. I want to see him. I won't be able to see him ever again. He's so beautiful. He's so—*old*."

They all carried their breakfasts out on the patio to sit around Dog, somehow feeling they couldn't ignore him by eating inside.

Roger Bentley telephoned his other children, whose response, after the first tears, was the same: they'd be right over. Wait.

When the other children arrived, first Rodney, twenty-one, and then the older daughter, Sal, twenty-four, a fresh storm of grief shook everyone and then they sat silently for a moment, watching Dog for a miracle.

"What are your plans?" asked Rodney at last.

"I know this is silly," said Roger Bentley after an embarrassed pause. "After all, he's only a dog—"

"*Only!?*" cried everyone instantly.

Roger had to back off. "Look, he deserves the Taj Mahal. What he'll get is the Orion Pet Cemetery over in Burbank."

"Pet Cemetery!?" cried everyone, but each in a different way.

"My God," said Rodney, "that's silly!"

"What's so *silly* about it?" Skip's face reddened and his lip trembled. "Dog, why, Dog was a pearl of . . . rare *price*."

"Yeah!" added Susan.

"Well, pardon me." Roger Bentley turned away to look at the pool, the bushes, the sky. "I suppose I could call those trash people who pick up dead bodies—"

"Trash people?" exclaimed Ruth Bentley.

"Dead bodies?" said Susan. "Dog isn't a *dead body!*"

"What is he, then?" asked Skip bleakly.

They all stared at Dog lying quietly there by the pool.

"He's," blurted Susan at last, "he's . . . he's my *love!*"

Before the crying could start again, Roger Bentley picked up the patio telephone, dialed the Pet Cemetery, talked, and put the phone down.

"Two hundred dollars," he informed everyone. "Not bad."

"For *Dog*?" said Skip. "Not enough!"

"Are you really serious about this?" asked Ruth Bentley.

"Yeah," said Roger. "I've made fun of those places all my life. But, now, seeing as how we'll never be able to visit Dog again—" He let a moment pass. "They'll come take Dog at noon. Services tomorrow."

"Services!" Snorting, Rodney stalked to the rim of the pool and waved his arms. "You won't get me to *that!*"

Everyone stared. Rodney turned at last and let his shoulders slump. "Hell, I'll be there."

"Dog would never forgive you if you didn't." Susan snuffed and wiped her nose.

But Roger Bentley had heard none of this. Staring at Dog, then his family, and up to the sky, he shut his eyes and exhaled a great whisper:

"Oh, my God!" he said, eyes shut. "Do you realize that this is the first terrible thing that's happened to our family? Have we ever been sick, gone to the hospital? Been in an accident?"

He waited.

"No," said everyone.

"Gosh," said Skip.

"Gosh, indeed! You sure as hell notice accidents, sickness, hospitals."

"Maybe," said Susan, and had to stop and wait because her voice broke. "Maybe Dog died just to *make* us notice how lucky we are."

"Lucky?!" Roger Bentley opened his eyes and turned. "Yes! You know what we *are*—"

"The science fiction generation," offered Rodney, lighting a cigarette casually.

"What?"

"You rave on about that, your school lectures, or during dinner. Can openers? Science fiction. Automobiles. Radio, TV, films. Everything! So science fiction!"

"Well, dammit, they are!" cried Roger Bentley and went to stare at Dog, as if the answers were there among the last departing fleas. "Hell, not so long ago there were no cars, can openers, TV. Someone had to dream them. Start of lecture. Someone had to build them. Mid-lecture. So science fiction dreams became finished science fact. Lecture *finis*!"

"*I bet!*" Rodney applauded politely.

Roger Bentley could only sink under the weight of his son's irony to stroke the dear dead beast.

"Sorry. Dog bit me. Can't help myself. Thousands of years, all we did is die. Now, that time's over. In sum: science fiction."

"Bull." Rodney laughed. "Stop reading that junk, Dad."

"Junk?" Roger touched Dog's muzzle. "Sure. But how about Lister, Pasteur, Salk? Hated death. Jumped to stop it. That's all science fiction was ever about. Hating the way things are, wanting to make things different. Junk?!"

"Ancient history, Pop."

"Ancient?" Roger Bentley fixed his son with a terrible eye. "Christ. When I was born in 1920, if you wanted to visit your family on Sundays you—"

"Went to the *graveyard*?" said Rodney.

"Yes. My brother and sister died when I was seven. Half of my family gone! Tell me, dear children, how many of *your* friends died while you were growing up. In grammar school? High school?"

He included the family in his gaze, and waited.

"None," said Rodney at last.

"None! You hear that? None! Christ. Six of my best friends died by the time I was ten! Wait! I just remembered!"

Roger Bentley hurried to rummage in a hall closet and brought out an old 78-rpm record into the sunlight, blowing off the dust. He squinted at the label:

"No News, Or What Killed The Dog?"

Everyone came to look at the ancient disc.

"Hey, how old *is* that?"

"Heard it a hundred times when I was a kid in the twenties," said Roger.

"No News, Or What Killed The Dog?" Sal glanced at her father's face.

"This gets played at Dog's funeral," he said.

"You're not *serious*?" said Ruth Bentley.

Just then the doorbell rang.

"That can't be the Pet Cemetery people come to take Dog—?"

"No!" cried Susan. "Not so *soon*!"

Instinctively, the family formed a wall between Dog and the doorbell sound, holding off eternity.

Then they cried, one more time.

✳ The strange and wonderful thing about the funeral was how many people came.

"I didn't know Dog had so many friends," Susan blubbered.

"He freeloaded all around town," said Rodney.

"Speak kindly of the dead."

"Well, he did, dammit. Otherwise why is Bill Johnson here, or Gert Skall, or Jim across the street?"

"Dog," said Roger Bentley, "I sure wish you could see this."

"He *does*." Susan's eyes welled over. "Wherever he is."

"Good old Sue," whispered Rodney, "who cries at telephone books—"

"Shut up!" cried Susan.

"Hush, both of you."

And Roger Bentley moved, eyes down, toward the front of the small funeral parlor where Dog was laid out, head on paws, in a box that was neither too rich nor too simple but just right.

Roger Bentley placed a steel needle down on the black record which turned on top of a flake-painted portable phonograph. The needle scratched and hissed. All the neighbors leaned forward.

"No funeral oration," said Roger quickly. "Just *this* . . ."

And a voice spoke on a day long ago and told a story about a man who returned from vacation to ask friends what had happened while he was gone.

It seemed that nothing whatsoever had happened.

Oh, just one thing. Everyone wondered what had killed the dog.

The dog? asked the vacationer. My *dog* died?

Yes, and maybe it was the burned horseflesh did it.

Burned *horseflesh*!? cried the vacationer.

Well, said his informant, when the barn burned, the horseflesh caught fire, so the dog ate the burned horseflesh, died.

The barn!? cried the vacationer. How did it catch fire?

Well, sparks from the house blew over, torched the barn, burned the horseflesh, dog ate them, died.

Sparks from the *house*!? shouted the vacationer. How—?

It was the curtains in the house, caught fire.

Curtains? Burned!?

From the candles around the coffin.

Coffin!?

Your aunt's funeral coffin, candles there caught the curtains, house burned, sparks from the house flew over, burned down the barn, dog ate the burned horseflesh—

In sum: no news, or what killed the dog!

The record hissed and stopped.

In the silence, there was a little quiet laughter, even though the record had been about dogs and people dying.

"*Now*, do we get the lecture?" said Rodney.

"No, a sermon."

Roger Bentley put his hands on the pulpit to stare for long moments at notes he hadn't made.

"I don't know if we're here for Dog or ourselves. Both, I suppose. We're the nothing-ever-happened-to-us people. Today is a first. Not that I want a rush of doom or disease. God forbid. Death, come slowly, please."

He turned the phonograph record round and round in his hands, trying to read the words under the grooves.

"No news. Except the aunt's funeral candles catch the curtains, sparks fly, and the dog goes west. In *our* lives, just the opposite. No news for years. Good livers, healthy hearts, good times. So—what's it all *about*?"

Roger Bentley glanced at Rodney, who was checking his wristwatch.

"Someday we must die, also." Roger Bentley hurried on. "Hard to believe. We're spoiled. But Susan was right. Dog died to tell us this, gently, and we must believe. And at the same time celebrate. What? The fact that we're the start of an amazing, dumbfounding history of survival that will only get better as the centuries pass. You may argue that the next war will take us all. Maybe.

"I can only say I think you will grow to be old, *very* old people. Ninety years from now, most people will have cured hearts, stopped cancers, and jumped life cycles. A lot of sadness will have gone out of the world, thank God. Will this be easy to do? No. Will we do it? Yes. Not in all countries, right off. But, finally, in most.

"As I said yesterday, fifty years ago, if you wanted to visit your aunts, uncles, grandparents, brothers, sisters, the graveyard was it. Death was *all* the talk. You *had* to talk it. Time's up, Rodney?"

Rodney signaled his father he had one last minute.

Roger Bentley wound it down:

"Sure, kids still die. But not millions. Old folks? Wind up in Sun City instead of Marble Orchard."

The father surveyed his family, bright-eyed, in the pews.

"God, look at you! Then look back. A thousand centuries of absolute terror, absolute grief. How parents stayed sane to raise their kids when half of them died, damned if I know. Yet with broken hearts, they did. While millions died of flu or the Plague.

"So here we are in a new time that we can't see because we stand in the eye of the hurricane, where everything's calm.

"I'll shut up now, with a last word for Dog. Because we loved him, we've done this almost silly thing, this service, but now suddenly we're not ashamed or sorry we bought him a plot or had me speak. We may never come visit him, who can say? But he has a place. Dog, old boy, bless you. Now, everyone, blow your nose."

Everyone blew his nose.

"Dad," said Rodney suddenly, "could—we hear the record again?"

Everyone looked at Rodney, surprised.

"Just," said Roger Bentley, "what I was going to suggest."

He put the needle on the record. It hissed.

About a minute in, when the sparks from the house flew over to burn the barn and torch the horseflesh and kill the dog, there was a sound at the back doorway to the small parlor.

Everyone turned.

A strange man stood in the door holding a small wicker basket from which came familiar, small yapping sounds.

And even as the flames from the candles around the coffin caught the curtains and the last sparks blew on the wind . . .

The whole family, drawn out into the sunlight, gathered around the stranger with the wicker basket, waiting for Father to arrive to throw back the coverlet on the small carrier so they could all dip their hands in.

That moment, as Susan said later, was like reading the telephone book one more time.

A LITTLE JOURNEY

THERE WERE TWO IMPORTANT THINGS—one, that she was very old; two, that Mr. Thirkell was taking her to God. For hadn't he patted her hand and said: "Mrs. Bellowes, we'll take off into space in my rocket, and go to find Him together"?

And that was how it was going to be. Oh, this wasn't like any other group Mrs. Bellowes had ever joined. In her fervor to light a path for her delicate, tottering feet, she had struck matches down dark alleys, and found her way to Hindu mystics who floated their flickering, starry eyelashes over crystal balls. She had walked on the meadow paths with ascetic Indian philosophers imported by daughters-in-spirit of Madame Blavatsky. She had made pilgrimages to California's stucco jungles to hunt the astrological seer in his natural habitat. She had even consented to signing away the rights to one of her homes in order to be taken into the shouting order of a temple of amazing evangelists who had promised her golden smoke, crystal fire, and the great soft hand of God coming to bear her home.

None of these people had ever shaken Mrs. Bellowes' faith, even when she saw them sirened away in a black wagon in the night, or discovered their pictures, bleak and unromantic, in the morning tabloids. The world had roughed them up and locked them away because they knew too much, that was all.

And then, two weeks ago, she had seen Mr. Thirkell's advertisement in New York City:

COME TO MARS!
STAY AT THE THIRKELL RESTORIUM FOR ONE WEEK. AND THEN,
ON INTO SPACE ON THE GREATEST ADVENTURE LIFE CAN OFFER!
SEND FOR FREE PAMPHLET: "NEARER MY GOD TO THEE."
EXCURSION RATES. ROUND TRIP SLIGHTLY LOWER.

"Round trip," Mrs. Bellowes had thought. "But who would come back after seeing *Him*?"

And so she had bought a ticket and flown off to Mars and spent seven mild days at Mr. Thirkell's Restorium, the building with the sign on it which flashed: THIRKELL'S ROCKET TO HEAVEN! She had spent the week bathing in limpid waters and erasing the care from her tiny bones, and now she was fidgeting, ready to be loaded into Mr. Thirkell's own special private rocket, like a bullet, to be fired on out into space beyond Jupiter and Saturn and Pluto. And thus—who could deny it?—you would be getting nearer and nearer to the Lord. How wonderful! Couldn't you just *feel* Him drawing near? Couldn't you just sense His breath, His scrutiny, His Presence?

"Here I am," said Mrs. Bellowes, "an ancient rickety elevator, ready to go up the shaft. God need only press the button."

Now, on the seventh day, as she minced up the steps of the Restorium, a number of small doubts assailed her.

"For one thing," she said aloud to no one, "it isn't quite the land of milk and honey here on Mars that they said it would be. My room is like a cell, the swimming pool is really quite inadequate, and, besides, how many widows who look like mushrooms or skeletons want to swim? And, finally, the whole Restorium smells of boiled cabbage and tennis shoes!"

She opened the front door and let it slam, somewhat irritably.

She was amazed at the other women in the auditorium. It was like wandering in a carnival mirror-maze, coming again and again upon yourself—the same floury face, the same chicken hands, and jingling bracelets. One after another of the images of herself floated before her. She put out her hand, but it wasn't a mirror; it was another lady shaking her fingers and saying:

"We're waiting for Mr. Thirkell. *Sh!*"

"Ah," whispered everyone.

The velvet curtains parted.

Mr. Thirkell appeared, fantastically serene, his Egyptian eyes upon everyone. But there was something, nevertheless, in his appearance which made one expect him to call "Hi!" while fuzzy dogs jumped over his legs, through his hooped arms, and over his back. Then, dogs and all, he should dance with a dazzling piano-keyboard smile off into the wings.

Mrs. Bellowes, with a secret part of her mind which she constantly had to grip tightly, expected to hear a cheap Chinese gong sound when Mr. Thirkell entered. His large liquid dark eyes were so improbable that one of the old ladies had facetiously claimed she saw a mosquito cloud hovering over them as they did around summer rain barrels. And Mrs. Bellowes sometimes caught the scent of the theatrical mothball and the smell of calliope steam on his sharply pressed suit.

But with the same savage rationalization that had greeted all other disappointments in her rickety life, she bit at the suspicion and whispered, "This time it's *real*. This time it'll work. Haven't we got a *rocket*?"

Mr. Thirkell bowed. He smiled a sudden Comedy Mask smile. The old ladies looked in at his epiglottis and sensed chaos there.

Before he even began to speak, Mrs. Bellowes saw him picking up each of his words, oiling it, making sure it ran smooth on its rails. Her heart squeezed in like a tiny fist, and she gritted her porcelain teeth.

"Friends," said Mr. Thirkell, and you could hear the frost snap in the hearts of the entire assemblage.

"No!" said Mrs. Bellowes ahead of time. She could hear the bad news rushing at her, and herself tied to the track while the immense black wheels threatened and the whistle screamed, helpless.

"There will be a slight delay," said Mr. Thirkell.

In the next instant, Mr. Thirkell might have cried, or been tempted to cry, "Ladies, be seated!" in minstrel-fashion, for the ladies had come up at him from their chairs, protesting and trembling.

"Not a very long delay." Mr. Thirkell put up his hands to pat the air.

"How long?"

"Only a week."

"A week!"

"Yes. You can stay here at the Restorium for seven more days, can't you? A little delay won't matter, will it, in the end? You've waited a lifetime. Only a few more days."

At twenty dollars a day, thought Mrs. Bellowes, coldly.

"What's the trouble?" a woman cried.

"A legal difficulty," said Mr. Thirkell.

"We've a rocket, haven't we?"

"Well, ye-ess."

"But I've been here a whole month, waiting," said one old lady. "Delays, delays!"

"That's right," said everyone.

"Ladies, ladies," murmured Mr. Thirkell, smiling serenely.

"We want to see the rocket!" It was Mrs. Bellowes forging ahead, alone, brandishing her fist like a toy hammer.

Mr. Thirkell looked into the old ladies' eyes, a missionary among albino cannibals.

"Well, now," he said.

"Yes, now!" cried Mrs. Bellowes.

"I'm afraid—" he began.

"So am I!" she said. "That's why we want to see the ship!"

"No, no, now, Mrs.—" He snapped his fingers for her name.

"Bellowes!" she cried. She was a small container, but now all the seething pressures that had been built up over long years came steaming through the delicate vents of her body. Her cheeks became incandescent. With a wail that was like a melancholy factory whistle, Mrs. Bellowes ran forward and hung to him, almost by her teeth, like a summer-maddened Spitz. She would not and never could let go until he died, and the other women followed, jumping and yapping like a pound let loose on its trainer, the same one who had petted them and to whom they had squirmed and whined joyfully an hour before, now milling about him, creasing his sleeves and frightening the Egyptian serenity from his gaze.

"This way!" cried Mrs. Bellowes, feeling like Madame Lafarge. "Through the back! We've waited long enough to see the ship. Every day he's put us off, every day we've waited, now let's see."

"No, no, ladies!" cried Mr. Thirkell, leaping about.

They burst through the back of the stage and out a door, like a flood, bearing the poor man with them into a shed, and then out, quite suddenly, into an abandoned gymnasium.

"There it is!" said someone. "The rocket."

And then a silence fell that was terrible to entertain.

There was the rocket.

Mrs. Bellowes looked at it and her hands sagged away from Mr. Thirkell's collar.

The rocket was something like a battered copper pot. There were a thousand bulges and rents and rusty pipes and dirty vents on and in it. The ports were clouded over with dust, resembling the eyes of a blind hog.

Everyone wailed a little sighing wail.

"Is that the rocket ship *Glory Be to the Highest?*" cried Mrs. Bellowes, appalled.

Mr. Thirkell nodded and looked at his feet.

"For which we paid out our one thousand dollars apiece and came all the way to Mars to get on board with you and go off to find Him?" asked Mrs. Bellowes.

"Why, that isn't worth a sack of dried peas," said Mrs. Bellowes.

"It's nothing but junk!"

Junk, whispered everyone, getting hysterical.

"Don't let him get away!"

Mr. Thirkell tried to break and run, but a thousand possum traps closed on him from every side. He withered.

Everybody walked around in circles like blind mice. There was a confusion and a weeping that lasted for five minutes as they went over and touched the Rocket, the Dented Kettle, the Rusty Container for God's Children.

"Well," said Mrs. Bellowes. She stepped up into the askew doorway of the rocket and faced everyone. "It looks as if a terrible thing has been done to us," she said. "I haven't any money to go back home to Earth and I've too much pride to go to the Government and tell them a common man like this has fooled us out of our life's savings. I don't know how you feel about it, all of you, but the reason all of us came is because I'm eighty-five, and you're eighty-nine, and you're seventy-eight, and all of us are nudging on toward a hundred, and there's nothing on Earth for us, and it doesn't appear there's anything on Mars either. We all expected not to breathe much more air or crochet many more doilies or we'd never have come here. So what I have to propose is a simple thing—to take a chance."

She reached out and touched the rusted hulk of the rocket.

"This is *our* rocket. We paid *for* our trip. And we're going to *take* our trip!"

Everyone rustled and stood on tiptoes and opened an astonished mouth.

Mr. Thirkell began to cry. He did it quite easily and very effectively.

"We're going to get in this ship," said Mrs. Bellowes, ignoring him. "And we're going to take off to where we were going."

Mr. Thirkell stopped crying long enough to say, "But it was all a fake. I don't know anything about space. He's not out there, anyway. I lied. I don't know where He is, and I couldn't find Him if I wanted to. And you were fools to ever take my word on it."

"Yes," said Mrs. Bellowes, "we were fools. I'll go along on that. But you can't blame us, for we're old, and it was a lovely, good and fine idea, one of the loveliest ideas in the world. Oh, we didn't really fool ourselves that we could get nearer to Him physically. It was the gentle, mad dream of old people, the kind of thing you hold onto for a few minutes a day, even though you know it's not true. So, all of you who want to go, you follow me in the ship."

"But you can't go!" said Mr. Thirkell. "You haven't got a navigator. And that ship's a ruin!"

"You," said Mrs. Bellowes, "will be the navigator."

She stepped into the ship, and after a moment, the other old ladies pressed forward. Mr. Thirkell, windmilling his arms frantically, was nevertheless pressed through the port, and in a minute the door slammed shut. Mr. Thirkell was strapped into the navigator's seat, with everyone talking at once and holding him down. The special helmets were issued to be fitted over every gray or white head to supply extra oxygen in case of a leakage in the ship's hull, and at long last the hour had come and Mrs. Bellowes stood behind Mr. Thirkell and said, "We're ready, sir."

He said nothing. He pleaded with them silently, using his great, dark, wet eyes, but Mrs. Bellowes shook her head and pointed to the control.

"Takeoff," agreed Mr. Thirkell morosely, and pulled a switch.

Everybody fell. The rocket went up from the planet Mars in a great fiery glide, with the noise of an entire kitchen thrown down an elevator shaft, with a sound of pots and pans and kettles and fires boiling and stews bubbling, with a smell of burned incense and rubber and sulfur, with a color of yellow fire, and a ribbon of red stretching below them, and all the old women singing and holding to each other, and Mrs. Bellowes crawling upright in the sighing, straining, trembling ship.

"Head for space, Mr. Thirkell."

"It can't last," said Mr. Thirkell, sadly. "This ship can't last. It will—"

It did.

The rocket exploded.

Mrs. Bellowes felt herself lifted and thrown about dizzily, like a doll. She heard the great screamings and saw the flashes of bodies sailing by her in fragments of metal and powdery light.

"Help, help!" cried Mr. Thirkell, far away, on a small radio beam.

The ship disintegrated into a million parts, and the old ladies, all one hundred of them, were flung straight on ahead with the same velocity as the ship.

As for Mr. Thirkell, for some reason of trajectory, perhaps, he had been blown out the other side of the ship. Mrs. Bellowes saw him falling separate and away from them, screaming, screaming.

There goes Mr. Thirkell, thought Mrs. Bellowes.

And she knew where he was going. He was going to be burned and roasted and broiled good, but very good.

Mr. Thirkell was falling down, into the Sun.

And here we are, thought Mrs. Bellowes. *Here we are, going on out, and out, and out.*

There was hardly a sense of motion at all, but she knew that she was traveling at fifty thousand miles an hour and would continue to travel at that speed for an eternity, until. . . .

She saw the other women swinging all about her in their own trajectories, a few minutes of oxygen left to each of them in their helmets, and each was looking up to where they were going.

Of course, thought Mrs. Bellowes. *Out into space. Out and out, and the darkness like a great church, and the stars like candles, and in spite of everything, Mr. Thirkell, the rocket, and the dishonesty, we are going toward the Lord.*

And there, yes, there, as she fell on and on, coming toward her, she could almost discern the outline now, coming toward her was His mighty golden hand, reaching down to hold her and comfort her like a frightened sparrow.

"I'm Mrs. Amelia Bellowes," she said quietly, in her best company voice. "I'm from the planet Earth."

ANY FRIEND OF
NICHOLAS NICKLEBY'S IS
A FRIEND OF MINE

Imagine a summer that would never end.

Nineteen twenty-nine.

Imagine a boy who would never grow up.

Me.

Imagine a barber who was never young.

Mr. Wyneski.

Imagine a dog that would live forever.

Mine.

Imagine a small town, the kind that isn't lived in anymore.

Ready? Begin . . .

Green Town, Illinois . . . Late June.

Dog barking outside a one-chair barbershop.

Inside, Mr. Wyneski, circling his victim, a customer snoozing in the steambath drowse of noon.

Inside, me, Ralph Spaulding, a boy of some twelve years, standing still as an iron Civil War statue, listening to the hot wind, feeling all that hot summer dust out there, a bakery world where nobody could be bad or good, boys just lay gummed to dogs, dogs used boys for pillows under trees that lazed with leaves which whispered in despair: Nothing Will Ever Happen Again.

The only motion anywhere was the cool water dripping from the huge coffin-sized ice block in the hardware store window.

The only cool person in miles was Miss Frostbite, the traveling magician's assistant, tucked into that lady-shaped long cavity hollowed in the ice block displayed for three days now without, they said, her breathing, eating, or talking. That last, I thought, must have been terrible hard on a woman.

Nothing moved in the street but the barbershop striped pole which turned slowly to show its red, white, and then red again, slid up out of nowhere to vanish nowhere, a motion between two mysteries.

"... hey ..."

I pricked my ears.

"... something's coming ..."

"Only the noon train, Ralph." Mr. Wyneski snicked his jackdaw scissors, peering in his customer's ear. "Only the train that comes at noon."

"No ..." I gasped, eyes shut, leaning. "Something's *really* coming ..."

I heard the far whistle wail, lonesome, sad, enough to pull your soul out of your body.

"*You* feel it, don't you, Dog?"

Dog barked.

Mr. Wyneski sniffed. "What can a dog feel?"

"Big things. Important things. Circumstantial coincidences. Collisions you can't escape. Dog says. I say. *We* say."

"That makes *four* of you. Some team." Mr. Wyneski turned from the summer-dead man in the white porcelain chair. "Now, Ralph, my problem is hair. Sweep."

I swept a ton of hair. "Gosh, you'd think this stuff just grew up out of the floor."

Mr. Wyneski watched my broom. "Right! I didn't cut all that. Darn stuff just grows, I swear, lying there. Leave it a week, come back, and you need hip boots to trod a path." He pointed with his scissors. "Look. You ever *see* so many shades, hues, and tints of forelocks and chin fuzz? There's Mr. Tompkins's receding hairline. There's Charlie Smith's topknot. And here, here's all that's left of Mr. Harry Joe Flynn."

I stared at Mr. Wyneski as if he had just read from Revelation. "Gosh, Mr. Wyneski, I guess you know everything in the world!"

"Just about."

"I—I'm going to grow up and be—a barber!"

Mr. Wyneski, to hide his pleasure, got busy.

"Then watch this hedgehog, Ralph, peel an eye. Elbows thus, wrists so! Make the scissors *talk*! Customers appreciate. Sound *twice* as busy as you are. Snickety-snick, boy, snickety-snick. Learned this from the French! Oh, yes, the French! They *do* prowl about the chair light on their toes, and the sharp scissors whispering and nibbling, Ralph, nibbling and whispering, you *hear*!"

"Boy!" I said, at his elbow, right in with the whispers and nibbles, then stopped: for the wind blew a wail way off in summer country, so sad, so strange.

"There it is again. The train. And something *on* the train . . ."

"Noon train don't stop here."

"But I got this feeling—"

"The hair's going to grab me, Ralph . . ."

I swept hair.

After a long while I said, "I'm thinking of changing my name."

Mr. Wyneski sighed. The summer-dead customer stayed dead.

"What's *wrong* with you today, boy?"

"It's not me. It's the name is out of hand. Just listen. Ralph." I grrred it. "Rrrralph."

"Ain't exactly harp music . . ."

"Sounds like a mad dog." I caught myself.

"No offense, Dog."

Mr. Wyneski glanced down. "He seems pretty calm about the whole subject."

"Ralph's dumb. Gonna change my name by tonight."

Mr. Wyneski mused. "Julius for Caesar? Alexander for the Great?"

"Don't care what. Help me, huh, Mr. Wyneski? Find me a *name* . . ."

Dog sat up. I dropped the broom.

For way down in the hot cinder railroad yards a train furnaced itself in, all pomp, all fire-blast shout and tidal churn, summer in its iron belly bigger than the summer outside.

"Here it comes!"

"There it goes," said Mr. Wyneski.

"No, there it *doesn't* go!"

It was Mr. Wyneski's turn to almost drop his scissors.

"Goshen. Darn noon train's putting on the brakes!"

We heard the train stop.

"How many people getting off the train, Dog?"

Dog barked once.

Mr. Wyneski shifted uneasily. "U.S. Mail bags—"

"No . . . *a man!* Walking light. Not much luggage. Heading for our house. A new boarder at Grandma's, I bet. And he'll take the empty room right next to you, Mr. Wyneski! Right, Dog?"

Dog barked.

"That dog talks too much," said Mr. Wyneski.

"I just *gotta* go see, Mr. Wyneski. Please?"

The far footsteps faded in the hot and silent streets.

Mr. Wyneski shivered.

"A goose just stepped on my grave."

Then he added, almost sadly:

"Get along, Ralph."

"Name ain't Ralph."

"Whatchamacallit . . . run see . . . come tell the worst."

"Oh, thanks, Mr. Wyneski, thanks!"

I ran. Dog ran. Up a street, along an alley, around back, we ducked in the ferns by my grandma's house. "Down, boy," I whispered. "Here the Big Event comes, whatever it is!"

And down the street and up the walk and up the steps at a brisk jaunt came this man who swung a cane and carried a carpetbag and had long brown-gray hair and silken mustaches and a goatee, politeness all about him like a flock of birds.

On the porch near the old rusty chain swing, among the potted geraniums, he surveyed Green Town.

Far away, maybe, he heard the insect hum from the barbershop, where Mr. Wyneski, who would soon be his enemy, told fortunes by the lumpy heads under his hands as he buzzed the electric clippers. Far away, maybe, he could hear the empty library where the golden dust slid down the raw sunlight and way in back someone scratched and tapped and scratched forever with pen and ink, a quiet woman like a great lonely mouse burrowed away. And she was to be part of this new man's life, too, but right now . . .

The stranger removed his tall moss-green hat, mopped his brow, and not looking at anything but the hot blind sky said:

"Hello, boy. Hello, Dog."

Dog and I rose up among the ferns.

"Heck. How'd you know where we were hiding?"

The stranger peered into his hat for the answer. "In another incarnation, I was a boy. Time before that, if memory serves, I was a more than usually happy dog. But . . . !" His cane rapped the cardboard sign BOARD AND ROOM thumbtacked on the porch rail. "Does the sign say true, boy?"

"Best rooms on the block."

"Beds?"

"Mattresses so deep you sink down and drown the third time, happy."

"Boarders at table?"

"Talk just enough, not too much."

"Food?"

"Hot biscuits every morning, peach pie noon, shortcake every supper!"

The stranger inhaled, exhaled those savors.

"I'll sign my soul away!"

"I beg your pardon?!" Grandma was suddenly at the screen door, scowling out.

"A manner of speaking, ma'am." The stranger turned. "Not meant to sound un-Christian."

And he was inside, him talking, Grandma talking, him writing and flourishing the pen on the registry book, and me and Dog inside, breathless, watching, spelling:

"C.H."

"Read upside down, do you, boy?" said the stranger, merrily, giving pause with the inky pen.

"Yes, sir!"

On he wrote. On I spelled:

"A.R.L.E.S. Charles!"

"Right."

Grandma peered at the calligraphy. "Oh, what a fine hand."

"Thank you, ma'am." On the pen scurried. And on I chanted. "D.I.C.K.E.N.S."

I faltered and stopped. The pen stopped. The stranger tilted his head and closed one eye, watchful of me.

"Yes?" He dared me, "What, *what*?"

"Dickens!" I cried.

"Good!"

"Charles Dickens, Grandma!"

"I can read, Ralph. A *nice* name . . ."

"Nice?" I said, agape. "It's *great*! But . . . I thought you were—"

"Dead?" The stranger laughed. "No. Alive, in fine fettle, and glad to meet a recognizer, fan, and fellow reader here!"

And we were up the stairs, Grandma bringing fresh towels and pillowcases and me carrying the carpetbag, gasping, and us meeting Grandpa, a great ship of a man, sailing down the other way.

"Grandpa," I said, watching his face for shock. "I want you to meet . . . Mr. Charles Dickens!"

Grandpa stopped for a long breath, looked at the new boarder from top to bottom, then reached out, took hold of the man's hand, shook it firmly, and said:

"Any friend of Nicholas Nickleby's is a friend of mine!"

Mr. Dickens fell back from the effusion, recovered, bowed, said, "Thank you, sir," and went on up the stairs, while Grandpa winked, pinched my cheek, and left me standing there, stunned.

In the tower cupola room, with windows bright, open, and running with cool creeks of wind in all directions, Mr. Dickens drew off his horse-carriage coat and nodded at the carpetbag.

"Anywhere will do, Pip. Oh, you don't mind I call you Pip, eh?"

"Pip?!" My cheeks burned, my face glowed with astonishing happiness. "Oh, boy. Oh, no, sir. Pip's *fine*!"

Grandma cut between us. "Here are your clean linens, Mr. . . . ?"

"Dickens, ma'am." Our boarder patted his pockets, each in turn. "Dear me, Pip, I seem to be fresh out of pads and pencils. Might it be possible—"

He saw one of my hands steal up to find something behind my ear. "I'll be darned," I said, "a yellow Ticonderoga Number 2!" My other hand slipped to my back pants pocket. "And hey, an Iron-Face Indian Ring-Back Notepad Number 12!"

"Extraordinary!"

"Extraordinary!"

Mr. Dickens wheeled about, surveying the world from each and every window, speaking now north, now north by east, now east, now south:

"I've traveled two long weeks with an idea. Bastille Day. Do you know it?"

"The French Fourth of July?"

"Remarkable boy! By Bastille Day this book must be in full flood. Will you help me breach the tide gates of the Revolution, Pip?"

"With *these*?" I looked at the pad and pencil in my hands.

"Lick the pencil tip, boy!"

I licked.

"Top of the page: the title. Title." Mr. Dickens mused, head down, rubbing his chin whiskers. "Pip, what's a rare fine title for a novel that happens half in London, half in Paris?"

"A—" I ventured.

"Yes?"

"*A Tale*," I went on.

"Yes?!"

"*A Tale of . . . Two Cities*?!"

"Madame!" Grandma looked up as he spoke. "This boy is a genius!"

"I read about this day in the Bible," said Grandma. "Everything Ends by noon."

"Put it down, Pip." Mr. Dickens tapped my pad. "Quick. *A Tale of Two Cities*. Then, mid-page. Book the First. 'Recalled to Life.' Chapter 1. 'The Period.'"

I scribbled. Grandma worked. Mr. Dickens squinted at the sky and at last intoned:

"It was the best of times, it was the worst of times, it was the age of wisdom, it was the age of foolishness, it was the epoch of belief, it was the epoch of incredulity, it was the season of Light, it was the season of Darkness, it was the spring of hope, it was the winter—"

"My," said Grandma, "you speak *fine*."

"Madame." The author nodded, then, eyes shut, snapped his fingers to remember, on the air. "Where was I, Pip?"

"It was the winter," I said, "of *despair*."

✳ Very late in the afternoon I heard Grandma calling someone named Ralph, Ralph, down below. I didn't know who that was. I was writing hard.

A minute later, Grandpa called, "Pip!"

I jumped. "Yes, sir!"

"Dinnertime, Pip," said Grandpa, up the stairwell.

I sat down at the table, hair wet, hands damp. I looked over at Grandpa. "How did you know . . . Pip?"

"Heard the name fall out the window an hour ago."

"Pip?" said Mr. Wyneski, just come in, sitting down.

"Boy," I said. "I been everywhere this afternoon. The Dover Coach on the Dover Road. Paris! Traveled so much I got writer's cramp! I—"

"Pip?" said Mr. Wyneski, again.

Grandpa came warm and easy to my rescue.

"When I was twelve, changed my name—on several occasions." He counted the tines on his fork. "Dick. That was Dead-Eye Dick. And . . . John. That was for Long John Silver. Then: Hyde. That was for the other half of Jekyll—"

"I never had any other name except Bernard Samuel Wyneski," said Mr. Wyneski, his eyes still fixed to me.

"None?" cried Grandpa, startled.

"None."

"Have you proof of childhood, then, sir?" asked Grandpa. "Or are you a natural phenomenon, like a ship becalmed at sea?"

"Eh?" said Mr. Wyneski.

Grandpa gave up and handed him his full plate.

"Fall to, Bernard Samuel, fall to."

Mr. Wyneski let his plate lie. "Dover Coach . . . ?"

"With Mr. Dickens, of course," supplied Grandpa. "Bernard Samuel, we have a new boarder, a novelist, who is starting a new book and has chosen Pip there, Ralph, to work as his secretary—"

"Worked all afternoon," I said. "Made a quarter!"

I slapped my hand to my mouth. A swift dark cloud had come over Mr. Wyneski's face.

"A novelist? Named Dickens? Surely you don't believe—"

"I believe what a man tells me until he tells me otherwise, then I believe that. Pass the butter," said Grandpa.

The butter was passed in silence.

". . . hell's fires . . ." Mr. Wyneski muttered.

I slunk low in my chair.

Grandpa, slicing the chicken, heaping the plates, said, "A man with a good demeanor has entered our house. He says his name is Dickens. For all I know that is his name. He implies he is writing a book. I pass his door, look in, and, yes, he is indeed writing. Should I run tell him not to? It is obvious he needs to set the book down—"

"*A Tale of Two Cities!*" I said.

"*A Tale!*" cried Mr. Wyneski, outraged, "*of Two*—"

"Hush," said Grandma.

For down the stairs and now at the door of the dining room there was the man with the long hair and the fine goatee and mustaches, nodding, smiling, peering in at us doubtful and saying, "Friends . . . ?"

"Mr. Dickens," I said, trying to save the day. "I want you to meet Mr. Wyneski, the greatest barber in the world—"

The two men looked at each other for a long moment.

"Mr. Dickens," said Grandpa. "Will you lend us your talent, sir, for grace?"

"An honor, sir."

We bowed our heads. Mr. Wyneski did not.

Mr. Dickens looked at him gently.

Muttering, the barber glanced at the floor.

Mr. Dickens prayed:

"O Lord of the bounteous table, O Lord who furnishes forth an infinite harvest for your most respectful servants gathered here in loving humiliation, O Lord who garnishes our feast with the bright radish and the resplendent chicken, who sets before us the wine of the summer season, lemonade, and maketh us humble before simple potato pleasures, the lowborn onion and, in the finale, so my nostrils tell me, the bread of vast experiments and fine success, the highborn strawberry shortcake, most beautifully smothered and amiably drowned in fruit from your own warm garden patch, for these, and this good company, much thanks. Amen."

"Amen," said everyone but Mr. Wyneski.

We waited.

"Amen, I guess," he said.

✳ O what a summer that was!

None like it before in Green Town history.

I never got up so early so happy ever in my life! Out of bed at five minutes to, in Paris by one minute after . . . six in the morning the English Channel boat from Calais, the White Cliffs, sky a blizzard of seagulls, Dover, then the London Coach and London Bridge by noon! Lunch and lemonade out under the trees with Mr. Dickens, Dog licking our cheeks to cool us, then back to Paris and tea at four and . . .

"Bring up the cannon, Pip!"

"Yes, sir!"

"Mob the Bastille!"

"Yes, sir!"

And the guns were fired and the mobs ran and there I was, Mr. C. Dickens A-I First Class Green Town, Illinois, secretary, my eyes bugging, my ears popping, my chest busting with joy, for I dreamed of being a writer some day, too, and here I was unraveling a tale with the very finest best.

"Madame Defarge, oh how she sat and knitted, knitted, sat—"

I looked up to find Grandma knitting in the window.

"Sidney Carton, what and who was he? A man of sensibility, a reading man of gentle thought and capable action . . ."

Grandpa strolled by mowing the grass.

Drums sounded beyond the hills with guns; a summer storm cracked and dropped unseen walls . . .

Mr. Wyneski?

Somehow I neglected his shop, somehow I forgot the mysterious barber pole that came up from nothing and spiraled away to nothing, and the fabulous hair that grew on his white tile floor . . .

So Mr. Wyneski then had to come home every night to find that writer with all the long hair in need of cutting, standing there at the same table thanking the Lord for this, that, and t'other, and Mr. Wyneski not thankful. For there I sat staring at Mr. Dickens like *he* was God until one night:

"Shall we say grace?" said Grandma.

"Mr. Wyneski is out brooding in the yard," said Grandpa.

"Brooding?" I glanced guiltily from the window.

Grandpa tilted his chair back so he could see.

"Brooding's the word. Saw him kick the rose bush, kick the green ferns by the porch, decide against kicking the apple tree. God made it too firm. There, he just jumped on a dandelion. Oh, oh. Here he comes, Moses crossing a Black Sea of bile."

The door slammed. Mr. Wyneski stood at the head of the table.

"I'll say grace tonight!"

He glared at Mr. Dickens.

"Why, I mean," said Grandma. "Yes. Please."

Mr. Wyneski shut his eyes tight and began his prayer of destruction:

"O Lord, who delivered me a fine June and a less fine July, help me to get through August somehow.

"O Lord, deliver me from mobs and riots in the streets of London and Paris which drum through my room night and morn, chief members of said riot being one boy who walks in his sleep, a man with a strange name and a Dog who barks after the ragtag and bobtail.

"Give me strength to resist the cries of Fraud, Thief, Fool, and Bunk Artists which rise in my mouth.

"Help me not to run shouting all the way to the Police Chief to yell that in all probability the man who shares our simple bread has a true name of Red Joe Pyke from Wilkesboro, wanted for counterfeiting life, or Bull Hammer from Hornbill, Arkansas, much desired for mean spitefulness and penny-pilfering in Oskaloosa.

"Lord, deliver the innocent boys of this world from the fell clutch of those who would tomfool their credibility.

"And Lord, help me to say, quietly, and with all deference to the lady present, that if one Charles Dickens is not on the noon train tomorrow bound for Potters Grave, Lands End, or Kankakee, I shall like Delilah, with malice, shear the black lamb and fry his mutton-chop whiskers for twilight dinners and late midnight snacks.

"I ask, Lord, not mercy for the mean, but simple justice for the malignant.

"All those agreed, say 'Amen.' "

He sat down and stabbed a potato.

There was a long moment with everyone frozen.

And then Mr. Dickens, eyes shut said, moaning:

"Ohhhhhhhhhh . . . !"

It was a moan, a cry, a despair so long and deep it sounded like the train way off in the country the day this man had arrived.

"Mr. Dickens," I said.

But I was too late.

He was on his feet, blind, wheeling, touching the furniture, holding to the wall, clutching at the doorframe, blundering into the hall, groping up the stairs.

"Ohhhhh . . ."

It was the long cry of a man gone over a cliff into Eternity.

It seemed we sat waiting to hear him hit bottom.

Far off in the hills in the upper part of the house, his door banged shut.

My soul turned over and died.

"Charlie," I said. "Oh, Charlie."

＊ Late that night, Dog howled.

And the reason he howled was that sound, that similar, muffled cry from up in the tower cupola room.

"Holy Cow," I said. "Call the plumber. Everything's down the drain."

Mr. Wyneski strode by on the sidewalk, walking nowhere, off and gone.

"That's his fourth time around the block." Grandpa struck a match and lit his pipe.

"Mr. Wyneski!" I called.

No answer. The footsteps went away.

"Boy oh boy, I feel like I lost a war," I said.

"No, Ralph, beg pardon, Pip," said Grandpa, sitting down on the step with me. "You just changed generals in midstream is all. And now one of the generals is so unhappy he's turned mean."

"Mr. Wyneski? I—I almost hate him!"

Grandpa puffed gently on his pipe. "I don't think he even knows why he is so unhappy and mean. He has had a tooth pulled during the night by a mysterious dentist and now his tongue is aching around the empty place where the tooth was."

"We're not in church, Grandpa."

"Cut the Parables, huh? In simple words, Ralph, you used to sweep the hair off that man's shop floor. And he's a man with no wife, no family, just a job. A man with no family needs someone somewhere in the world, whether he knows it or not."

"I," I said. "I'll wash the barbershop windows tomorrow. I-I'll oil the red-and-white striped pole so it spins like crazy."

"I know you will, son."

A train went by in the night.

Dog howled.

Mr. Dickens answered in a strange cry from his room.

I went to bed and heard the town clock strike one and then two and at last three.

Then it was I heard the soft crying. I went out in the hall to listen by our boarder's door.

"Mr. Dickens?"

The soft sound stopped.

The door was unlocked. I dared open it.

"Mr. Dickens?"

And there he lay in the moonlight, tears streaming from his eyes, eyes wide open staring at the ceiling, motionless.

"Mr. Dickens?"

"Nobody by that name here," said he. His head moved side to side. "Nobody by that name in this room in this bed in this world."

"You," I said. "You're Charlie Dickens."

"You ought to know better," was the mourned reply. "Long after midnight, moving on toward morning."

"All I know is," I said, "I seen you writing every day. I heard you talking every night."

"Right, right."

"And you finish one book and start another, and write a fine calligraphy sort of hand."

"I do that." A nod. "Oh yes, by the demon possessions, I do."

"So!" I circled the bed. "What call you got to feel sorry for yourself, a world-famous author?"

"You know and I know, I'm Mr. Nobody from Nowhere, on my way to Eternity with a dead flashlight and no candles."

"Hells bells," I said. I started for the door. I was mad because he wasn't holding up his end. He was ruining a grand summer. "Good night!" I rattled the doorknob.

"Wait!"

It was such a terrible soft cry of need and almost pain, I dropped my hand, but I didn't turn.

"Pip," said the old man in the bed.

"Yeah?" I said, grouching.

"Let's both be quiet. Sit down."

I slowly sat on the spindly wooden chair by the night table.

"Talk to me, Pip."

"Holy Cow, at three—"

"—in the morning, yes. Oh, it's a fierce awful time of night. A long way back to sunset, and ten thousand miles on to dawn. We have need of friends then. *Friend*, Pip? Ask me things."

"Like what?"

"I think you know."

I brooded a moment and sighed. "Okay, okay. Who *are* you?"

He was very quiet for a moment lying there in his bed and then traced the words on the ceiling with a long invisible tip of his nose and said, "I'm a man who could never fit his dream."

"What?"

"I mean, Pip, I never became what I wanted to be."

I was quiet now, too, "What'd you *want* to be?"

"A writer."

"Did you *try*?"

"Try!" he cried, and almost gagged on a strange wild laugh. "Try," he said, controlling himself. "Why Lord of Mercy, son, you never saw so much spit, ink, and sweat fly. I wrote my way through an ink factory, broke and busted a paper company, ruined and dilapidated six dozen typewriters, devoured and scribbled to the bone ten thousand Ticonderoga Soft Lead pencils."

"Wow!"

"You may well say Wow."

"What did you write?"

"What *didn't* I write. The poem. The essay. The play *tragique*. The farce. The short story. The novel. A thousand words a day, boy, every day for thirty years, no day passed I did not scriven and assault the page. Millions of words passed from my fingers onto paper and it was all bad."

"It couldn't have been!"

"It *was*. Not mediocre, not passing fair. Just plain outright mudbath bad. Friends knew it, editors knew it, teachers knew it, publishers knew it, and one strange fine day about four in the afternoon, when I was fifty, *I* knew it."

"But you can't write thirty years without—"

"Stumbling upon excellence? Striking a chord? Gaze long, gaze hard, Pip, look upon a man of peculiar talent, outstanding ability, the only man in history who put down five million words without slapping to life one small base of a story that might rear up on its frail legs and cry Eureka! we've done it!"

"You never sold *one* story?!"

"Not a two-line joke. Not a throwaway newspaper sonnet. Not a want ad or obit. Not a home-bottled autumn pickle recipe. Isn't that rare? To be so outstandingly dull, so ridiculously inept, that nothing ever brought a chuckle, caused a tear, raised a temper, or discharged a blow. And do you know what I did on the day I discovered I would never be a writer? I killed myself."

"Killed?!"

"Did away with, destroyed. How? I packed me up and took me away on a long train ride and sat on the back smoking-car platform a long time in the night and then one by one let the confetti of my manuscripts fly like panicked birds away down the tracks. I scattered a novel across Nebraska, my Homeric legends over North, my love sonnets through South Dakota. I abandoned my familiar essays in the men's room at the Harvey House in Clear Springs, Idaho. The late summer wheatfields knew my prose. Grand fertilizer, it probably jumped up bumper crops of corn long after I passed. I rode two trunks of my soul on that long summer's journey, celebrating my badly served self. And one by one, slow at first, and then faster, faster, over I chucked them, story after story, out, out of my arms out of my head, out of my life, and down they went, sunk drowning night rivers of prairie dust, in lost continents of sand and lonely rock. And the train wallowed around a curve in a great wail of darkness and release, and I opened my fingers and let the last stillborn darlings fall. . . .

"When I reached the far terminus of the line, the trunks were empty. I had drunk much, eaten little, wept on occasion in my private room, but had heaved away my anchors, dead-weights, and dreams, and came to the sliding soft-chuffing end of my journey, praise God, in a kind of noble peace and certainty. I felt reborn. I said to myself, why, what's this, what's this? I'm—I'm a new man."

He saw it all on the ceiling, and I saw it, too, like a movie run up the wall in the moonlit night.

"I-I'm a new man I said, and when I got off the train at the end of that long summer of disposal and sudden rebirth, I looked in a fly-specked, rain-freckled gum-machine mirror at a lost depot in Peachgum, Missouri, and my beard grown long in two months of travel and my hair gone wild with wind that combed it this way sane, that way mad, and I peered and stood back and exclaimed softly, 'Why, Charlie Dickens, is that you?!'"

The man in the bed laughed softly.

"Why, Charlie," said I, "Mr. Dickens, there you are!" And the reflection in the mirror cried out, "Dammit, sir, who else *would* it be!? Stand back. I'm off to a great lecture!"

"Did you really say that, Mr. Dickens?"

"God's pillars and temples of truth, Pip. And I got out of his way! And I strode through a strange town and I knew who I was at last and grew fevers thinking on what I might do in my lifetime now reborn and all that grand fine work ahead! For, Pip, this thing *must* have been growing. All those years of writing and snuffing up defeat, my old subconscious must have been whispering, 'Just you wait. Things will be black midnight bad but then in the nick of time, *I'll* save you!'

"And maybe the thing that saved me was the thing ruined me in the first place: respect for my elders; the grand moguls and tall muckymucks in the lush literary highlands and me in the dry river bottom with my canoe.

"For, oh God, Pip, how I devoured Tolstoy, drank Dostoevsky, feasted on De Maupassant, had wine and chicken picnics with Flaubert and Molière. I gazed at gods too high. I read too *much*! So, when my work vanished, theirs stayed. Suddenly I found I could *not* forget their books, Pip!"

"Couldn't?"

"I mean I could not forget any letter of any word of any sentence or any paragraph of any book ever passed under these hungry omnivorous eyes!"

"Photographic memory!"

"Bull's-eye! All of Dickens, Hardy, Austen, Poe, Hawthorne, trapped in this old box Brownie waiting to be printed off my tongue, all those years, never knew, Pip, never guessed, I had hid it all away. Ask me to speak in tongues. Kipling is one. Thackeray another. Weigh flesh, I'm Shylock. Snuff out the light, I'm Othello. All, all, Pip, all!"

"And then? And so?"

"Why then and so, Pip, I looked another time in that fly-specked mirror and said, 'Mr. Dickens, all this being true, *when* do you write your first book?'

"'Now!' I cried. And bought fresh paper and ink and have been delirious and joyful, lunatic and happy frantic ever since, writing all the books of my own dear self, me, I, Charles Dickens, one by one.

"I have traveled the continental vastness of the United States of North America and settled me in to write and act, act and write, lecturing here, pondering there, half in and then half out of my mania, known and unknown, lingering here to finish *Copperfield*, loitering there for *Dombey and Son*, turning up for tea with Marley's Ghost on some pale Christmas noon. Sometimes I lie whole snowbound winters in little whistle stops and no one there guessing that Charlie Dickens bides hibernation there, then pop forth like the ottermole of spring and so move on. Sometimes I stay whole summers in one town before I'm driven off. Oh, yes, driven. For such as your Mr. Wyneski cannot forgive the fantastic, Pip, no matter how particularly practical that fantastic be.

"For he has no humor, boy.

"He does not see that we all do what we must to survive, survive.

"Some laugh, some cry, some bang the world with fists, some run, but it all sums up the same: they *make do*.

"The world swarms with people, each one drowning, but each swimming a different stroke to the far shore.

"And Mr. Wyneski? He makes do with scissors and understands not my inky pen and littered papers on which I would flypaper-catch my borrowed English soul."

Mr. Dickens put his feet out of bed and reached for his carpetbag.

"So I must pick up and go."

I grabbed the bag first.

"No! You can't leave! You haven't finished the book!"

"Pip, dear boy, you haven't been listening—"

"The world's waiting! You can't just quit in the middle of *Two Cities*!"

He took the bag quietly from me.

"Pip, Pip . . ."

"You *can't*, Charlie!"

He looked into my face and it must have been so white hot he flinched away.

"I'm waiting," I cried. "They're waiting!"

"They . . . ?"

"The mob at the Bastille. Paris! London. The Dover sea. The guillotine!"

I ran to throw all the windows even wider as if the night wind and the moonlight might bring in sounds and shadows to crawl on the rug and sneak in his eyes, and the curtains blew out in phantom gestures and I swore I heard, Charlie heard, the crowds, the coach wheels, the great slicing downfall of the cutting blades and the cabbage heads falling and battle songs and all that on the wind . . .

"Oh, Pip, Pip . . ."

Tears welled from his eyes.

I had my pencil out and my pad.

"Well?" I said.

"Where were we, this afternoon, Pip?"

"Madame Defarge, knitting."

He let the carpetbag fall. He sat on the edge of the bed and his hands began to tumble, weave, knit, motion, tie and untie, and he looked and saw his hands and spoke and I wrote and he spoke again, stronger, and stronger, all through the rest of the night . . .

"Madame Defarge . . . yes . . . well. Take this, Pip. She—"

✳ "Morning, Mr. Dickens!"

I flung myself into the dining room chair. Mr. Dickens was already half through his stack of pancakes.

I took one bite and then saw the even greater stack of pages lying on the table between us.

"Mr. Dickens?" I said. "*The Tale of Two Cities*. It's . . . finished?"

"Done." Mr. Dickens ate, eyes down. "Got up at six. Been working steady. Done. Finished. Through."

"Wow!" I said.

A train whistle blew. Charlie sat up, then rose suddenly, to leave the rest of his breakfast and hurry out in the hall. I heard the front door slam and tore out on the porch to see Mr. Dickens half down the walk, carrying his carpetbag.

He was walking so fast I had to run to circle round and round him as he headed for the rail depot.

"Mr. Dickens, the book's finished, yeah, but not *published* yet!"

"You be my executor, Pip."

He fled. I pursued, gasping.

"What about David Copperfield?! Little Dorrit?!"

"Friends of yours, Pip?"

"Yours, Mr. Dickens, Charlie, oh, gosh, if you don't write them, they'll never *live*."

"They'll get on somehow." He vanished around a corner. I jumped after.

"Charlie, wait. I'll give you—a new title! *Pickwick Papers*, sure, *Pickwick Papers!*"

The train was pulling into the station.

Charlie ran fast.

"And after that, *Bleak House*, Charlie, and *Hard Times* and *Great*—Mr. Dickens, listen—*Expectations!* Oh, my gosh!"

For he was far ahead now and I could only yell after him:

"Oh, blast, go on! get off! get away! You know what I'm going to do!? You don't deserve reading! You don't! So right now, and from here on, see if I even *bother* to finish reading *Tale of Two Cities!* Not me! Not this one! No!"

The bell was tolling in the station. The steam was rising. But, Mr. Dickens had slowed. He stood in the middle of the sidewalk. I came up to stare at his back.

"Pip," he said softly. "You mean what you just said?"

"You!" I cried. "You're nothing but—" I searched in my mind and seized a thought: "—a blot of mustard, some undigested bit of raw potato—!"

" 'Bah, Humbug, Pip?' "

"Humbug! I don't give a blast *what* happens to Sidney Carton!"

"Why, it's a far, far better thing I do than I have ever done, Pip. You must read it."

"Why!?"

He turned to look at me with great sad eyes.

"Because I wrote it for you."

It took all my strength to half-yell back: "So—?"

"So," said Mr. Dickens, "I have just missed my train. Forty minutes till the next one—"

"Then you got time," I said.

"Time for what?"

"To meet someone. Meet them, Charlie, and I promise I'll finish reading your book. In there. In *there*, Charlie."

He pulled back.

"That place? The library?!"

"Ten minutes, Mr. Dickens, give me ten minutes, just ten, Charlie. Please."

"Ten?"

And at last, like a blind man, he let me lead him up the library steps and half-fearful, sidle in.

✳ The library was like a stone quarry where no rain had fallen in ten thousand years.

Way off in that direction: silence.

Way off in that direction: hush.

It was the time between things finished and things begun. Nobody died here. Nobody was born. The library, and all its books, just *were*.

We waited, Mr. Dickens and I, on the edge of the silence.

Mr. Dickens trembled. And I suddenly remembered I had never seen him here all summer. He was afraid I might take him near the fiction shelves and see all his books, written, done, finished, printed, stamped, bound, borrowed, read, repaired, and shelved.

But I wouldn't be that dumb. Even so, he took my elbow and whispered:

"Pip, what are we doing here? Let's go. There's . . ."

"Listen!" I hissed.

And a long way off in the stacks somewhere, there was a sound like a moth turning over in its sleep.

"Bless me," Mr. Dickens's eyes widened. "I *know* that sound."

"Sure!"

"It's the sound," he said, holding his breath, then nodding, "of someone writing."

"Yes, sir."

"Writing with a pen. And . . . and writing . . ."

"What?"

"Poetry," gasped Mr. Dickens. "That's it. Someone off there in a room, how many fathoms deep, Pip, I swear, writing a poem. There! Eh? Flourish, flourish, scratch, flourish on, on, on, that's not figures, Pip, not numerals, not dusty-dry facts, you feel it *sweep*, feel it *scurry*? A poem, by God, yes, sir, no doubt, a poem!"

✳ "Ma'am," I called.

The moth-sound ceased.

"Don't stop her!" hissed Mr. Dickens. "Middle of inspiration. Let her go!"

The moth-scratch started again.

Flourish, flourish, scratch, on, on, stop. Flourish, flourish. I bobbed my head. I moved my lips, as did Mr. Dickens, both of us suspended, held, leaned forward on the cool marble air listening to the vaults and stacks and echoes in the subterrane.

Flourish, flourish, scratch, on, on.

Silence.

"There." Mr. Dickens nudged me.

"Ma'am!" I called ever so urgently soft.

And something rustled in the corridors.

And there stood the librarian, a lady between years, not young, not old; between colors, not dark, not pale; between heights, not short, not tall, but rather frail, a woman you often heard talking to herself off in the dark dust-stacks with a whisper like turned pages, a woman who glided as if on hidden wheels.

She came carrying her soft lamp of face, lighting her way with her glance.

Her lips were moving, she was busy with words in the vast room behind her clouded gaze.

Charlie read her lips eagerly. He nodded. He waited for her to halt and bring us to focus, which she did, suddenly. She gasped and laughed at herself.

"Oh, Ralph, it's you and—" A look of recognition warmed her face. "Why, you're Ralph's friend. Mr. Dickens, isn't it?"

Charlie stared at her with a quiet and almost alarming devotion.

"Mr. Dickens," I said. "I want you to meet—"

"'Because I could not stop for Death—'" Charlie, eyes shut, quoted from memory.

The librarian blinked swiftly and her brow like a lamp turned high, took white color.

"Miss Emily," he said.

"Her name is—" I said.

"Miss Emily." He put out his hand to touch hers.

"Pleased," she said. "But how did you—?"

"Know your name? Why, bless me, ma'am, I heard you scratching way off in there, runalong rush, only poets do that!"

"It's nothing."

"Head high, chin up," he said, gently. "It's something. 'Because I could not stop for death' is a fine A-1 first-class poem."

"My own poems are so poor," she said, nervously. "I copy hers out to learn."

"Copy who?" I blurted.

"Excellent way to learn."

"Is it, *really*?" She looked close at Charlie. "You're not . . . ?"

"Joking? No, not with Emily Dickinson, ma'am!"

"Emily Dickinson?" I said.

"That means much coming from you, Mr. Dickens," she flushed. "I have read all your books."

"All?" He backed off.

"All," she added hastily, "that you have published so far, sir."

"Just finished a new one." I put in, "Sockdolager! *A Tale of Two Cities*."

"And you, ma'am?" he asked, kindly.

She opened her small hands as if to let a bird go.

"Me? Why, I haven't even sent a poem to our town newspaper."

"You must!" he cried, with true passion and meaning. "Tomorrow. No, today!"

"But," her voice faded. "I have no one to read them to, first."

"Why," said Charlie quietly. "You have Pip here, and, accept my card, C. Dickens, Esquire. Who will, if allowed, stop by on occasion, to see if all's well in this Arcadian silo of books."

She took his card. "I couldn't—"

"Tut! You must. For I shall offer only warm sliced white bread. Your words must be the marmalade and summer honey jam. I shall read long and plain. You: short and rapturous of life and tempted by that odd delicious Death you often lean upon. Enough." He pointed. "There. At the far end of the corridor, her lamp lit ready to guide your hand . . . the Muse awaits. Keep and feed her well. Good-bye."

"Good-bye?" she asked. "Doesn't that mean 'God be with you'?"

"So I have heard, dear lady, so I have heard."

And suddenly we were back out in the sunlight, Mr. Dickens almost stumbling over his carpetbag waiting there.

In the middle of the lawn, Mr. Dickens stood very still and said, "The sky is blue, boy."

"Yes, sir."

"The grass is green."

"Sure." Then I stopped and really looked around. "I mean, heck, *yeah*!"

"And the wind . . . smell that sweet wind?"

We both smelled it. He said:

"And in this world are remarkable boys with vast imaginations who know the secrets of salvation . . ."

He patted my shoulder. Head down, I didn't know what to do. And then I was saved by a whistle:

"Hey, the next train! Here it *comes!*"

We waited.

After a long while, Mr. Dickens said:

"There it *goes* . . . and let's go home, boy."

"Home!" I cried, joyfully, and then stopped. "But what about . . . Mr. Wyneski?"

"O, after all this, I have such confidence in you, Pip. Every afternoon while I'm having tea and resting my wits, you must trot down to the barbershop and—"

"Sweep hair!"

"Brave lad. It's little enough. A loan of friendship from the Bank of England to the First National Bank of Green Town, Illinois. And now, Pip . . . pencil!"

I tried behind one ear, found gum; tried the other ear and found: "Pencil!"

"Paper?"

"Paper!"

We strode along under the soft green summer trees.

"Title, Pip—"

He reached up with his cane to write a mystery on the sky. I squinted at the invisible penmanship.

"*The*—"

He blocked out a second word on the air.

"*Old,*" I translated.

A third.

"C.U." I spelled. "R.I. . . . *Curiosity!*"

"How's that for a title, Pip?"

I hesitated. "It . . . doesn't seem, well, quite *finished,* sir."

"What a Christian you are. There!"

He flourished a final word on the sun.

"S.H.O. . . . *Shop! The Old Curiosity Shop.*"

"Take a novel, Pip!"

"Yes, sir," I cried. "Chapter One!"

✳ A blizzard of snow blew through the trees.

"What's that?" I asked, and answered:

Why, summer gone. The calendar pages, all the hours and days, like in the movies, the way they just blow off over the hills. Charlie and I working together, finished, through. Many days at the library, over! Many nights reading aloud with Miss Emily done! Trains come and gone. Moons waxed and waned. New trains arriving and new lives teetering on the brink, and Miss Emily suddenly standing right there, and Charlie here with all their suitcases and handing me a paper sack.

"What's this?"

"Rice, Pip, plain ordinary white rice, for the fertility ritual. Throw it at us, boy. Drive us happily away. Hear those bells, Pip? Here goes Mr. and Mrs. Charlie Dickens! Throw, boy, throw! Throw!"

I threw and ran, ran and threw, and them on the back train platform waving out of sight and me yelling good-bye, Happy marriage, Charlie! Happy times! Come back! Happy . . . Happy . . .

And by then I guess I was crying, and Dog chewing my shoes, jealous, glad to have me alone again, and Mr. Wyneski waiting at the barbershop to hand me my broom and make me his son once more.

And autumn came and lingered and at last a letter arrived from the married and traveling couple.

I kept the letter sealed all day and at dusk, while Grandpa was raking leaves by the front porch I went out to sit and watch and hold the letter and wait for him to look up and at last he did and I opened the letter and read it out loud in the October twilight:

"Dear Pip," I read, and had to stop for a moment seeing my old special name again, my eyes were so full.

"Dear Pip. We are in Aurora tonight and Felicity tomorrow and Elgin the night after that. Charlie has six months of lectures lined up and looking forward. Charlie and I are both working steadily and are most happy . . . very happy . . . need I say?

"He calls me Emily.

"Pip, I don't think you know who she was, but there was a lady poet once, and I hope you'll get her books out of the library someday.

"Well, Charlie looks at me and says: 'This is my Emily' and I almost believe. No, I do believe."

I stopped and swallowed hard and read on:

"We are crazy, Pip.

"People have said it. We know it. Yet we go on. But being crazy together is fine.

"It was being crazy alone I couldn't stand any longer.

"Charlie sends his regards and wants you to know he has indeed started a fine new book, perhaps his best yet . . . one you suggested the title for, *Bleak House*.

"So we write and move, move and write, Pip. And some year soon we may come back on the train which stops for water at your town. And if you're there and call our names as we know ourselves now, we shall step off the train. But perhaps meanwhile you will get too old. And if when the train stops, Pip, you're not there, we shall understand, and let the train move us on to another and another town.

"Signed, Emily Dickinson.

"P.S. Charlie says your grandfather is a dead ringer for Plato, but not to tell him.

"P.P.S. Charlie is my darling."

"Charlie is my darling," repeated Grandpa, sitting down and taking the letter to read it again. "Well, well . . ." he sighed. "Well, well . . ."

We sat there a long while, looking at the burning soft October sky and the new stars. A mile off, a dog barked. Miles off, on the horizon line, a train moved along, whistled, and tolled its bell, once, twice, three times, gone.

"You know," I said. "I don't think they're crazy."

"Neither do I, Pip," said Grandpa, lighting his pipe and blowing out the match. "Neither do I."

THE GARBAGE COLLECTOR

THIS IS HOW HIS WORK WAS: He got up at five in the cold dark morning and washed his face with warm water if the heater was working and cold water if the heater was not working. He shaved carefully, talking out to his wife in the kitchen, who was fixing ham and eggs or pancakes or whatever it was that morning. By six o'clock he was driving on his way to work alone, and parking his car in the big yard where all the other men parked their cars as the sun was coming up. The colors of the sky that time of morning were orange and blue and violet and sometimes very red and sometimes yellow or a clear color like water on white rock. Some mornings he could see his breath on the air and some mornings he could not. But as the sun was still rising he knocked his fist on the side of the green truck, and his driver, smiling and saying hello, would climb in the other side of the truck and they would drive out into the great city and go down all the streets until they came to the place where they started work. Sometimes, on the way, they stopped for black coffee and then went on, the warmness in them. And they began the work which meant that he jumped off in front of each house and picked up the garbage cans and brought them back and took off their lids and knocked them against the bin edge, which made the orange peels and cantaloupe rinds and coffee grounds fall out and thump down and begin to fill the empty truck. There were always steak bones and the heads of fish and pieces of green onion and stale celery. If the garbage was new it wasn't so bad, but if it was very old it was bad. He was not sure if he liked the job or not, but it was a job and he did it well, talking about it a lot at some times and sometimes not thinking of it in any way at all. Some days the job was wonderful, for you were out early and the air was cool and fresh until you had worked too long and the sun got hot and the garbage steamed early. But mostly it was a job significant enough to keep him busy and calm and looking at the houses and cut lawns he passed by and seeing how everybody lived. And once or twice a month he was surprised to find that he loved the job and that it was the finest job in the world.

It went on just that way for many years. And then suddenly the job changed for him. It changed in a single day. Later he often wondered how a job could change so much in such a few short hours.

He walked into the apartment and did not see his wife or hear her voice, but she was there, and he walked to a chair and let her stand away from him, watching him as he touched the chair and sat down in it without saying a word. He sat there for a long time.

"What's wrong?" At last her voice came through to him. She must have said it three or four times.

"Wrong?" He looked at this woman and yes, it was his wife all right, it was someone he knew, and this was their apartment with the tall ceilings and the worn carpeting.

"Something happened at work today," he said.

She waited for him.

"On my garbage truck, something happened." His tongue moved dryly on his lips and his eyes shut over his seeing until there was all blackness and no light of any sort and it was like standing alone in a room when you got out of bed in the middle of a dark night. "I think I'm going to quit my job. Try to understand."

"Understand!" she cried.

"It can't be helped. This is all the strangest damned thing that ever happened to me in my life." He opened his eyes and sat there, his hands feeling cold when he rubbed his thumb and forefingers together. "The thing that happened was strange."

"Well, don't just *sit* there!"

He took part of a newspaper from the pocket of his leather jacket. "This is today's paper," he said. "December 10, 1951. Los Angeles *Times*. Civil Defense Bulletin. It says they're buying radios for our garbage trucks."

"Well, what's so bad about a little music?"

"No music. You don't understand. No music."

He opened his rough hand and drew with one clean fingernail, slowly, trying to put everything there where he could see it and she could see it. "In this article the mayor says they'll put sending and receiving apparatus on every garbage truck in town." He squinted at his hand. "After the atom bombs hit our city, those radios will talk to us. And then our garbage trucks will go pick up the bodies."

"Well, that seems practical. When—"

"The garbage trucks," he said, "go out and pick up all the bodies."

"You can't just leave bodies around, can you? You've got to take them and—" His wife shut her mouth very slowly. She blinked, one time only, and she did this very slowly also. He watched that one slow blink of her eyes. Then, with a turn of her body, as if someone else had turned it for her, she walked to a chair, paused, thought how to do it, and sat down, very straight and stiff. She said nothing.

He listened to his wristwatch ticking, but with only a small part of his attention.

At last she laughed. "They were joking!"

He shook his head. He felt his head moving from left to right and from right to left, as slowly as everything else had happened. "No. They put a receiver on my truck today. They said, at the alert, if you're working, dump your garbage anywhere. When we radio you, get *in* there and haul out the dead."

Some water in the kitchen boiled over loudly. She let it boil for five seconds and then held the arm of the chair with one hand and got up and found the door and went out. The boiling sound stopped. She stood in the door and then walked back to where he still sat, not moving, his head in one position only.

"It's all blueprinted out. They have squads, sergeants, captains, corporals, everything," he said. "We even know where to bring the bodies."

"So you've been thinking about it all day," she said.

"All day since this morning. I thought: Maybe now I don't want to be a garbage collector anymore. It used to be Tom and me had fun with a kind of game. You got to do that. Garbage is bad. But if you work at it you can make a game. Tom and me did that. We watched people's garbage. We saw what kind they had. Steak bones in rich houses, lettuce and orange peel in poor ones. Sure it's silly, but a guy's got to make his work as good as he can and worthwhile or why in hell do it? And you're your own boss, in a way, on a truck. You get out early in the morning and it's an outdoor job, anyway; you see the sun come up and you see the town get up, and that's not bad at all. But now, today, all of a sudden it's not the kind of job for me anymore."

His wife started to talk swiftly. She named a lot of things and she talked about a lot more, but before she got very far he cut gently across her talking. "I know, I know, the kids and school, our car, I know," he said. "And bills and money and credit. But what about that farm Dad left us? Why can't we move there, away from cities? I know a little about farming. We could stock up, hole in, have enough to live on for months if anything happened."

She said nothing.

"Sure, all of our friends are here in town," he went on reasonably. "And movies and shows and the kids' friends, and . . ."

She took a deep breath. "Can't we think it over a few more days?"

"I don't know. I'm afraid of that. I'm afraid if I think it over, about my truck and my new work, I'll get used to it. And, oh Christ, it just doesn't seem right a man, a human being, should ever let himself get used to any idea like that."

She shook her head slowly, looking at the windows, the gray walls, the dark pictures on the walls. She tightened her hands. She started to open her mouth.

"I'll think tonight," he said. "I'll stay up a while. By morning I'll know what to do."

"Be careful with the children. It wouldn't be good, their knowing all this."

"I'll be careful."

"Let's not talk anymore, then. I'll finish dinner!" She jumped up and put her hands to her face and then looked at her hands and at the sunlight in the windows. "Why, the kids'll be home any minute."

"I'm not very hungry."

"You got to eat, you just got to keep on going." She hurried off, leaving him alone in the middle of a room where not a breeze stirred the curtains, and only the gray ceiling hung over him with a lonely bulb unlit in it, like an old moon in a sky. He was quiet. He massaged his face with both hands. He got up and stood alone in the dining room door and walked forward and felt himself sit down and remain seated in a dining room chair. He saw his hands spread on the white tablecloth, open and empty.

"All afternoon," he said, "I've thought."

She moved through the kitchen, rattling silverware, crashing pans against the silence that was everywhere.

"Wondering," he said, "if you put the bodies in the trucks lengthwise or endwise, with the heads on the right, or the *feet* on the right. Men and women together, or separated? Children in one truck, or mixed with men and women? Dogs in special trucks, or just let them lay? Wondering how *many* bodies one garbage truck can hold. And wondering if you stack them on top of each other and finally knowing you must just have to. I can't figure it. I can't work it out. I try, but there's no guessing, no guessing at all how many you could stack in one single truck."

He sat thinking of how it was late in the day at his work, with the truck full and the canvas pulled over the great bulk of garbage so the bulk shaped the canvas in an uneven mound. And how it was if you suddenly pulled the canvas back and looked in. And for a few seconds you saw the white things like macaroni or noodles, only the white things were alive and boiling up, millions of them. And when the white things felt the hot sun on them they simmered down and burrowed and were gone in the lettuce and the old ground beef and the coffee grounds and the heads of white fish. After ten seconds of sunlight the white things that looked like noodles or macaroni were gone and the great bulk of garbage silent and not moving, and you drew the canvas over the bulk and looked at how the canvas folded unevenly over the hidden collection, and underneath you knew it was dark again, and things beginning to move as they must always move when things get dark again.

He was still sitting there in the empty room when the front door of the apartment burst wide. His son and daughter rushed in, laughing, and saw him sitting there, and stopped.

Their mother ran to the kitchen door, held to the edge of it quickly, and stared at her family. They saw her face and they heard her voice:

"Sit down, children, sit down!" She lifted one hand and pushed it toward them. "You're just in time."

THE VISITOR

Saul Williams awoke to the still morning. He looked wearily out of his tent and thought about how far away Earth was. Millions of miles, he thought. But then what could you do about it? Your lungs were full of the "blood rust." You coughed all the time.

Saul arose this particular morning at seven o'clock. He was a tall man, lean, thinned by his illness. It was a quiet morning on Mars, with the dead sea bottom-flat and silent—no wind on it. The sun was clear and cool in the empty sky. He washed his face and ate breakfast.

After that he wanted very much to be back on Earth. During the day he tried every way that it was possible to be in New York City. Sometimes, if he sat right and held his hands a certain way, he did it. He could almost smell New York. Most of the time, though, it was impossible.

Later in the morning Saul tried to die. He lay on the sand and told his heart to stop. It continued beating. He imagined himself leaping from a cliff or cutting his wrists, but laughed to himself—he knew he lacked the nerve for either act.

Maybe if I squeeze tight and think about it enough, I'll just sleep and never wake, he thought. He tried it. An hour later he awoke with a mouth full of blood. He got up and spat it out and felt very sorry for himself. This blood rust—it filled your mouth and your nose; it ran from your ears, your fingernails; and it took a year to kill you. The only cure was shoving you in a rocket and shooting you out to exile on Mars. There was no known cure on

Earth, and remaining there would contaminate and kill others. So here he was, bleeding all the time, and lonely.

Saul's eyes narrowed. In the distance, by an ancient city ruin, he saw another man lying on a filthy blanket.

When Saul walked up, the man on the blanket stirred weakly.

"Hello, Saul," he said.

"Another morning," said Saul. "Christ, I'm lonely!"

"It is an affliction of the rusted ones," said the man on the blanket, not moving, very pale and as if he might vanish if you touched him.

"I wish to God," said Saul, looking down at the man, "that you could at least talk. Why is it that intellectuals never get the blood rust and come up here?"

"It is a conspiracy against you, Saul," said the man, shutting his eyes, too weary to keep them open. "Once I had the strength to be an intellectual. Now, it's a job to think."

"If only we could talk," said Saul Williams.

The other man merely shrugged indifferently.

"Come tomorrow. Perhaps I'll have enough strength to talk about Aristotle then. I'll try. Really I will." The man sank down under the worn tree. He opened one eye. "Remember, once we did talk on Aristotle, six months ago, on that good day I had."

"I remember," said Saul, not listening. He looked at the dead sea. "I wish I were as sick as you, then maybe I wouldn't worry about being an intellectual. Then maybe I'd get some peace."

"You'll get just as bad as I am now in about six months," said the dying man. "Then you won't care about anything but sleep and more sleep. Sleep will be like a woman to you. You'll always go back to her, because she's fresh and good and faithful and she always treats you kindly and the same. You only wake up so you can think about going back to sleep. It's a nice thought." The man's voice was a bare whisper. Now it stopped and a light breathing took over.

Saul walked off.

Along the shores of the dead sea, like so many emptied bottles flung up by some long-gone wave, were the huddled bodies of sleeping men. Saul could see them all down the curve of the empty sea. One, two, three—all of them sleeping alone, most of them worse off than he, each with his little cache of food, each grown into himself, because social converse was weakening and sleep was good.

At first there had been a few nights around mutual campfires. And they had all talked about Earth. That was the only thing they talked about. Earth and the way the waters ran in town creeks and what homemade strawberry pie tasted like and how New York looked in the early morning coming over on the Jersey ferry in the salt wind.

I want Earth, thought Saul. I want it so bad it hurts. I want something I can never have again. And they all want it and it hurts them not to have it. More than food or a woman or anything, I just want Earth. This sickness puts women away forever; they're not things to be wanted. But Earth, yes. That's a thing for the mind and not the weak body.

The bright metal flashed on the sky.

Saul looked up.

The bright metal flashed again.

A minute later the rocket landed on the sea bottom. A valve opened, a man stepped out, carrying his luggage with him. Two other men, in protective germicide suits, accompanied him, bringing out vast cases of food, setting up a tent for him.

Another minute and the rocket returned to the sky. The exile stood alone.

Saul began to run. He hadn't run in weeks, and it was very tiring, but he ran and yelled.

"Hello, hello!"

The young man looked Saul up and down when he arrived.

"Hello. So this is Mars. My name's Leonard Mark."

"I'm Saul Williams."

They shook hands. Leonard Mark was very young—only eighteen; very blond, pink-faced, blue-eyed and fresh in spite of his illness.

"How are things in New York?" said Saul.

"Like this," said Leonard Mark. And he looked at Saul.

New York grew up out of the desert, made of stone and filled with March winds. Neons exploded in electric color. Yellow taxis glided in a still night. Bridges rose and tugs chanted in the midnight harbors. Curtains rose on spangled musicals.

Saul put his hands to his head, violently.

"Hold on, hold on!" he cried. "What's happening to me? What's wrong with me? I'm going crazy!"

Leaves sprouted from trees in Central Park, green and new. On the pathway Saul strolled along, smelling the air.

"Stop it, stop it, you fool!" Saul shouted at himself. He pressed his forehead with his hands. "This can't be!"

"It is," said Leonard Mark.

The New York towers faded. Mars returned. Saul stood on the empty sea bottom, staring limply at the young newcomer.

"You," he said, putting his hand out to Leonard Mark. "You did it. You did it with your mind."

"Yes," said Leonard Mark.

Silently they stood facing each other. Finally, trembling, Saul seized the other exile's hand and wrung it again and again, saying, "Oh, but I'm glad you're here. You can't know how glad I am!"

⁂ They drank their rich brown coffee from the tin cups.

It was high noon. They had been talking all through the warm morning time.

"And this ability of yours?" said Saul over his cup, looking steadily at the young Leonard Mark.

"It's just something I was born with," said Mark, looking into his drink. "My mother was in the blowup of London back in '57. I was born ten months later. I don't know what you'd call my ability. Telepathy and thought transference, I suppose. I used to have an act, I traveled all around the world. Leonard Mark, the mental marvel, they said on the billboards. I was pretty well off. Most people thought I was a charlatan. You know what people think of theatrical folks. Only I knew I was really genuine, but I didn't let anybody know. It was safer not to let it get around too much. Oh, a few of my close friends knew about my *real* ability. I had a lot of talents that will come in handy now that I'm here on Mars."

"You sure scared the hell out of me," said Saul, his cup rigid in his hand. "When New York came right up out of the ground that way, I thought I was insane."

"It's a form of hypnotism which affects all of the sensual organs at once—eyes, ears, nose, mouth, skin—all of them. What would you like to be doing now most of all?"

Saul put down his cup. He tried to hold his hands very steady. He wet his lips. "I'd like to be in a little creek I used to swim in in Mellin Town, Illinois, when I was a kid. I'd like to be stark-naked and swimming."

"Well," said Leonard Mark and moved his head ever so little.

Saul fell back on the sand, his eyes shut.

Leonard Mark sat watching him.

Saul lay on the sand. From time to time his hands moved, twitched excitedly. His mouth spasmed open; sounds issued from his tightening and relaxing throat.

Saul began to make slow movements of his arms, out and back, out and back, gasping with his head to one side, his arms going and coming slowly on the warm air, stirring the yellow sand under him, his body turning slowly over.

Leonard Mark quietly finished his coffee. While he drank he kept his eyes on the moving, whispering Saul lying there on the dead sea bottom.

"All right," said Leonard Mark.

Saul sat up, rubbing his face.

After a moment he told Leonard Mark, "I saw the creek. I ran along the bank and I took off my clothes," he said breathlessly, his smile incredulous. "And I *dived in* and swam around!"

"I'm pleased," said Leonard Mark.

"Here!" Saul reached into his pocket and drew forth his last bar of chocolate. "This is for you."

"What's this?" Leonard Mark looked at the gift. "Chocolate? Nonsense, I'm not doing this for pay. I'm doing it because it makes you happy. Put that thing back in your pocket before I turn it into a rattlesnake and it bites you."

"Thank you, thank you!" Saul put it away. "You don't know how good that water was." He fetched the coffeepot. "More?"

Pouring the coffee, Saul shut his eyes a moment.

I've got Socrates here, he thought; Socrates and Plato, and Nietzsche and Schopenhauer. This man, by his talk, is a genius. By his talent, he's incredible! Think of the long, easy days and the cool nights of talk we'll have. It won't be a bad year at all. Not half.

He spilled the coffee.

"What's wrong?"

"Nothing." Saul himself was confused, startled.

We'll be in Greece, he thought. In Athens. We'll be in Rome, if we want, when we study the Roman writers. We'll stand in the Parthenon and the Acropolis. It won't be just talk, but it'll be a place to be, besides. This man can do it. He has the power to do it. When we talk the plays of Racine, he can make a stage and players and all of it for me. By Christ, this is better than life ever was! How much better to be sick and here than well on Earth without these abilities! How many people have ever seen a Greek drama played in a Greek amphitheater in the year 31 B.C.?

And if I ask, quietly and earnestly, will this man take on the aspect of Schopenhauer and Darwin and Bergson and all the other thoughtful men of the ages . . . ? Yes, why not? To sit and talk with Nietzsche in person, with Plato himself . . . !

There was only one thing wrong. Saul felt himself swaying.

The other men. The other sick ones along the bottom of this dead sea.

In the distance men were moving, walking toward them. They had seen the rocket flash, land, dislodge a passenger. Now they were coming, slowly, painfully, to greet the new arrival.

Saul was cold. "Look," he said. "Mark, I think we'd better head for the mountains."

"Why?"

"See those men coming? Some of them are insane."

"Really?"

"Yes."

"Isolation and all make them that way?"

"Yes, that's it. We'd better get going."

"They don't look very dangerous. They move slowly."

"You'd be surprised."

Mark looked at Saul. "You're trembling. Why's that?"

"There's no time to talk," said Saul, getting up swiftly. "Come on. Don't you realize what'll happen once they discover your talent? They'll fight over you. They'll kill each other—kill you—for the right to own you."

"Oh, but I don't belong to anybody," said Leonard Mark. He looked at Saul. "No. Not even you."

Saul jerked his head. "I didn't even think of that."

"Didn't you now?" Mark laughed.

"We haven't time to argue," answered Saul, eyes blinking, cheeks blazing. "Come on!"

"I don't want to. I'm going to sit right here until those men show up. You're a little too possessive. My life's my own."

Saul felt an ugliness in himself. His face began to twist. "You *heard* what I said."

"How very quickly you changed from a friend to an enemy," observed Mark.

Saul hit at him. It was a neat quick blow, coming down.

Mark ducked aside, laughing. "No, you don't!"

They were in the center of Times Square. Cars roared, hooting, upon them. Buildings plunged up, hot, into the blue air.

"It's a lie!" cried Saul, staggering under the visual impact. "For God's sake, don't, Mark! The men are coming. You'll be killed!"

Mark sat there on the pavement, laughing at his joke. "Let them come. I can fool them all!"

New York distracted Saul. It was meant to distract—meant to keep his attention with its unholy beauty, after so many months away from it. Instead of attacking Mark he could only stand, drinking in the alien but familiar scene.

He shut his eyes. "No." And fell forward, dragging Mark with him. Horns screamed in his ears. Brakes hissed and caught violently. He smashed at Mark's chin.

Silence.

Mark lay on the sea bottom.

Taking the unconscious man in his arms, Saul began to run, heavily.

New York was gone. There was only the wide soundlessness of the dead sea. The men were closing in around him. He headed for the hills with his precious cargo, with New York and green country and fresh springs and old friends held in his arms. He fell once and struggled up. He did not stop running.

✳ Night filled the cave. The wind wandered in and out, tugging at the small fire, scattering ashes.

Mark opened his eyes. He was tied with ropes and leaning against the dry wall of the cave, facing the fire.

Saul put another stick on the fire, glancing now and again with a cat-like nervousness at the cave entrance.

"You're a fool."

Saul started.

"Yes," said Mark, "you're a fool. They'll find us. If they have to hunt for six months they'll find us. They saw New York, at a distance, like a mirage. And us in the center of it. It's too much to think they won't be curious and follow our trail."

"I'll move on with you then," said Saul, staring into the fire.

"And they'll come after."

"Shut up!"

Mark smiled. "Is that the way to speak to your wife?"

"You heard me!"

"Oh, a fine marriage this is—your greed and my mental ability. What do you want to see now? Shall I show you a few more of your childhood scenes?"

Saul felt the sweat coming out on his brow. He didn't know if the man was joking or not. "Yes," he said.

"All right," said Mark, "watch!"

Flame gushed out of the rocks. Sulfur choked him. Pits of brimstone exploded, concussions rocked the cave. Heaving up, Saul coughed and blundered, burned, withered by hell!

Hell went away. The cave returned.

Mark was laughing.

Saul stood over him. "You," he said coldly, bending down.

"What else do you expect?" cried Mark. "To be tied up, toted off, made the intellectual bride of a man insane with loneliness—do you think I enjoy this?"

"I'll untie you if you promise not to run away."

"I couldn't promise that. I'm a free agent. I don't belong to anybody."

Saul got down on his knees. "But you've *got* to belong, do you hear? You've *got* to belong. I can't let you go away!"

"My dear fellow, the more you say things like that, the more remote I am. If you'd had any sense and done things intelligently, we'd have been friends. I'd have been glad to do you these little hypnotic favors. After all, they're no trouble for me to conjure up. Fun, really. But you've botched it. You wanted me all to yourself. You were afraid the others would take me away from you. Oh, how mistaken you were. I have enough power to keep them all happy. You could have shared me, like a community kitchen. I'd have felt quite like a god among children, being kind, doing favors, in return for which you might bring me little gifts, special tidbits of food."

"I'm sorry, I'm sorry!" Saul cried. "But I know those men too well."

"Are you any different? Hardly! Go out and see if they're coming. I thought I heard a noise."

Saul ran. In the cave entrance he cupped his hands, peering down into the night-filled gully. Dim shapes stirred. Was it only the wind blowing the roving clumps of weeds? He began to tremble a fine, aching tremble.

"I don't see anything." He came back into an empty cave.

He stared at the fireplace. "Mark!"

Mark was gone.

There was nothing but the cave, filled with boulders, stones, pebbles, the lonely fire flickering, the wind sighing. And Saul standing there, incredulous and numb.

"Mark! Mark! Come back!"

The man had worked free of his bonds, slowly, carefully, and using the ruse of imagining he heard other men approaching, had gone—where?

The cave was deep, but ended in a blank wall. And Mark could not have slipped past him into the night. How then?

Saul stepped around the fire. He drew his knife and approached a large boulder that stood against the cave wall. Smiling, he pressed the knife against the boulder. Smiling, he tapped the knife there. Then he drew his knife back to plunge it into the boulder.

"Stop!" shouted Mark.

The boulder vanished. Mark was there.

Saul suspended his knife. The fire played on his cheeks. His eyes were quite insane.

"It didn't work," he whispered. He reached down and put his hands on Mark's throat and closed his fingers. Mark said nothing, but moved uneasily in the grip, his eyes ironic, telling things to Saul that Saul knew.

If you kill me, the eyes said, where will all your dreams be? If you kill me, where will all the streams and brook trout be? Kill me, kill Plato, kill Aristotle, kill Einstein; yes, kill all of us! Go ahead, strangle me. I dare you.

Saul's fingers released the throat.

Shadows moved into the cave mouth.

Both men turned their heads.

The other men were there. Five of them, haggard with travel, panting, waiting in the outer rim of light.

"Good evening," called Mark, laughing. "Come in, come in, gentlemen!"

＊ By dawn the arguments and ferocities still continued. Mark sat among the glaring men, rubbing his wrists, newly released from his bonds. He created a mahogany-paneled conference hall and a marble table at which they all sat, ridiculously bearded, evil-smelling, sweating and greedy men, eyes bent upon their treasure.

"The way to settle it," said Mark at last, "is for each of you to have certain hours of certain days for appointments with me. I'll treat you all equally. I'll be city property, free to come and go. That's fair enough. As for Saul here, he's on probation. When he's proved he can be a civil person once more, I'll give him a treatment or two. Until that time, I'll have nothing more to do with him."

The other exiles grinned at Saul.

"I'm sorry," Saul said. "I didn't know what I was doing. I'm all right now."

"We'll see," said Mark. "Let's give ourselves a month, shall we?"

The other men grinned at Saul.

Saul said nothing. He sat staring at the floor of the cave.

"Let's see now," said Mark. "On Mondays it's your day, Smith."

Smith nodded.

"On Tuesdays I'll take Peter there, for an hour or so."

Peter nodded.

"On Wednesdays I'll finish up with Johnson, Holtzman, and Jim, here."

The last three men looked at each other.

"The rest of the week I'm to be left strictly alone, do you hear?" Mark told them. "A little should be better than nothing. If you don't obey, I won't perform at all."

"Maybe we'll *make* you perform," said Johnson. He caught the other men's eye. "Look, we're five against his one. We can make him do anything we want. If we cooperate, we've got a great thing here."

"Don't be idiots," Mark warned the other men.

"Let me talk," said Johnson. "He's telling us what he'll do. Why don't we tell *him*! Are we bigger than him, or not? And him threatening not to perform! Well, just let me get a sliver of wood under his toenails and maybe burn his fingers a bit with a steel file, and we'll see if he performs! Why shouldn't we have performances, I want to know, every night in the week?"

"Don't listen to him!" said Mark. "He's crazy. He can't be depended on. You know what he'll do, don't you? He'll get you all off guard, one by one, and kill you; yes, kill all of you, so that when he's done, he'll be alone—just him and me! That's his sort."

The listening men blinked. First at Mark, then at Johnson.

"For that matter," observed Mark, "none of you can trust the others. This is a fool's conference. The minute your back is turned one of the other men will murder you. I dare say, at the week's end, you'll all be dead or dying."

A cold wind blew into the mahogany room. It began to dissolve and became a cave once more. Mark was tired of his joke. The marble table splashed and rained and evaporated.

The men gazed suspiciously at each other with little bright animal eyes. What was spoken was true. They saw each other in the days to come, surprising one another, killing—until that last lucky one remained to enjoy the intellectual treasure that walked among them.

Saul watched them and felt alone and disquieted. Once you have made a mistake, how hard to admit your wrongness, to go back, start fresh. They were *all* wrong. They had been lost a long time. Now they were worse than lost.

"And to make matters very bad," said Mark at last, "one of you has a gun. All the rest of you have only knives. But one of you, I know, has a gun."

Everybody jumped up. "Search!" said Mark. "Find the one with the gun or you're all dead!"

That did it. The men plunged wildly about, not knowing whom to search first. Their hands grappled, they cried out, and Mark watched them in contempt.

Johnson fell back, feeling in his jacket. "All right," he said. "We might as well have it over now! Here, you, Smith."

And he shot Smith through the chest. Smith fell. The other men yelled. They broke apart. Johnson aimed and fired twice more.

"Stop!" cried Mark.

New York soared up around them, out of rock and cave and sky. Sun glinted on high towers. The elevated thundered; tugs blew in the harbor. The green lady stared across the bay, a torch in her hand.

"Look, you fools!" said Mark. Central Park broke out constellations of spring blossoms. The wind blew fresh-cut lawn smells over them in a wave.

And in the center of New York, bewildered, the men stumbled. Johnson fired his gun three times more. Saul ran forward. He crashed against Johnson, bore him down, wrenched the gun away. It fired again.

The men stopped milling.

They stood. Saul lay across Johnson. They ceased struggling.

There was a terrible silence. The men stood watching. New York sank down into the sea. With a hissing, bubbling, sighing; with a cry of ruined metal and old time, the great structures leaned, warped, flowed, collapsed.

Mark stood among the buildings. Then, like a building, a neat red hole drilled into his chest, wordless, he fell.

Saul lay staring at the men, at the body.

He got up, the gun in his hand.

Johnson did not move—was afraid to move.

They all shut their eyes and opened them again, thinking that by so doing they might reanimate the man who lay before them.

The cave was cold.

Saul stood up and looked, remotely, at the gun in his hand. He took it and threw it far out over the valley and did not watch it fall.

They looked down at the body as if they could not believe it. Saul bent down and took hold of the limp hand. "Leonard!" he said softly. "Leonard?" He shook the hand. "Leonard!"

Leonard Mark did not move. His eyes were shut; his chest had ceased going up and down. He was getting cold.

Saul got up. "We've killed him," he said, not looking at the men. His mouth was filling with a raw liquor now. "The only one we didn't want to kill, we killed." He put his shaking hand to his eyes. The other men stood waiting.

"Get a spade," said Saul. "Bury him." He turned away. "I'll have nothing to do with you."

Somebody walked off to find a spade.

✳ Saul was so weak he couldn't move. His legs were grown into the earth, with roots feeding deep of loneliness and fear and the cold of the night. The fire had almost died out and now there was only the double moonlight riding over the blue mountains.

There was the sound of someone digging in the earth with a spade.

"We don't need him anyhow," said somebody, much too loudly.

The sound of digging went on. Saul walked off slowly and let himself slide down the side of a dark tree until he reached and was sitting blankly on the sand, his hands blindly in his lap.

Sleep, he thought. We'll all go to sleep now. We have that much, anyway. Go to sleep and try to dream of New York and all the rest.

He closed his eyes wearily, the blood gathering in his nose and his mouth and in his quivering eyes.

"How did he do it?" he asked in a tired voice. His head fell forward on his chest. "How did he bring New York up here and make us walk around in it? Let's try. It shouldn't be too hard. Think! Think of New York," he whispered, falling down into sleep. "New York and Central Park and then Illinois in the spring, apple blossoms and green grass."

It didn't work. It wasn't the same. New York was gone and nothing he could do would bring it back. He would rise every morning and walk on the dead sea looking for it, and walk forever around Mars, looking for it, and never find it. And finally lie, too tired to walk, trying to find New York in his head, but not finding it.

The last thing he heard before he slept was the spade rising and falling and digging a hole into which, with a tremendous crash of metal and golden mist and odor and color and sound, New York collapsed, fell, and was buried.

He cried all night in his sleep.

THE MAN

CAPTAIN HART STOOD IN THE DOOR of the rocket. "Why don't they come?" he said.

"Who knows?" said Martin, his lieutenant. "Do I know, Captain?"

"What kind of a place is this, anyway?" The captain lighted a cigar. He tossed the match out into the glittering meadow. The grass started to burn.

Martin moved to stamp it out with his boot.

"No," ordered Captain Hart, "let it burn. Maybe they'll come see what's happening then, the ignorant fools."

Martin shrugged and withdrew his foot from the spreading fire.

Captain Hart examined his watch. "An hour ago we landed here, and does the welcoming committee rush out with a brass band to shake our hands? No indeed! Here we ride millions of miles through space and the fine citizens of some silly town on some unknown planet ignore us!" He snorted, tapping his watch. "Well, I'll just give them five more minutes, and then—"

"And then what?" asked Martin, ever so politely, watching the captain's jowls shake.

"We'll fly over their damned city again and scare hell out of them." His voice grew quieter. "Do you think, Martin, maybe they didn't see us land?"

"They saw us. They looked up as we flew over."

"Then why aren't they running across the field? Are they hiding? Are they yellow?"

Martin shook his head. "No. Take these binoculars, sir. See for yourself. Everybody's walking around. They're not frightened. They—well, they just don't seem to care."

Captain Hart placed the binoculars to his tired eyes. Martin looked up and had time to observe the lines and the grooves of irritation, tiredness, nervousness there. Hart looked a million years old; he never slept, he ate little, and drove himself on, on. Now his mouth moved, aged and drear, but sharp, under the held binoculars.

"Really, Martin, I don't know why we bother. We build rockets, we go to all the trouble of crossing space, searching for them, and this is what we get. Neglect. Look at those idiots wander about in there. Don't they realize how big this is? The first space flight to touch their provincial land. How many times does that happen? Are they that blasé?"

Martin didn't know.

Captain Hart gave him back the binoculars wearily. "Why do we do it, Martin? This space travel, I mean. Always on the go. Always searching. Our insides always tight, never any rest."

"Maybe we're looking for peace and quiet. Certainly there's none on Earth," said Martin.

"No, there's not, is there?" Captain Hart was thoughtful, the fire damped down. "Not since Darwin, eh? Not since everything went by the board, everything we used to believe in, eh? Divine power and all that. And so you think maybe that's why we're going out to the stars, eh, Martin? Looking for our lost souls, is that it? Trying to get away from our evil planet to a good one?"

"Perhaps, sir. Certainly we're looking for something."

Captain Hart cleared his throat and tightened back into sharpness. "Well, right now we're looking for the mayor of that city there. Run in, tell them who we are, the first rocket expedition to Planet Forty-three in Star System Three. Captain Hart sends his salutations and desires to meet the mayor. On the double!"

"Yes, sir." Martin walked slowly across the meadow.

"Hurry!" snapped the captain.

"Yes, sir!" Martin trotted away. Then he walked again, smiling to himself.

The captain had smoked two cigars before Martin returned.

Martin stopped and looked up into the door of the rocket, swaying, seemingly unable to focus his eyes or think.

"Well?" snapped Hart. "What happened? Are they coming to welcome us?"

"No." Martin had to lean dizzily against the ship.

"Why not?"

"It's not important," said Martin. "Give me a cigarette, please, Captain." His fingers groped blindly at the rising pack, for he was looking at the golden city and blinking. He lighted one and smoked quietly for a long time.

"Say something!" cried the captain. "Aren't they interested in our rocket?"

Martin said, "What? Oh. The rocket?" He inspected his cigarette. "No, they're not interested. Seems we came at an inopportune time."

"Inopportune time!"

Martin was patient. "Captain, listen. Something big happened yesterday in that city. It's so big, so important that we're second-rate—second fiddle. I've got to sit down." He lost his balance and sat heavily, gasping for air.

The captain chewed his cigar angrily. "What happened?"

Martin lifted his head, smoke from the burning cigarette in his fingers, blowing in the wind. "Sir, yesterday, in that city, a remarkable man appeared—good, intelligent, compassionate, and infinitely wise!"

The captain glared at his lieutenant. "What's that to do with us?"

"It's hard to explain. But he was a man for whom they'd waited a long time—a million years maybe. And yesterday he walked into their city. That's why today, sir, our rocket landing means nothing."

The captain sat down violently. "Who was it? Not Ashley? He didn't arrive in his rocket before us and steal my glory, did he?" He seized Martin's arm. His face was pale and dismayed.

"Not Ashley, sir."

"Then it was Burton! I knew it. Burton stole in ahead of us and ruined my landing! You can't trust anyone anymore."

"Not Burton, either, sir," said Martin quietly.

The captain was incredulous. "There were only three rockets. We were in the lead. This man who got here ahead of us? What was his name!"

"He didn't have a name. He doesn't need one. It would be different on every planet, sir."

The captain stared at his lieutenant with hard, cynical eyes.

"Well, what did he do that was so wonderful that nobody even looks at our ship?"

"For one thing," said Martin steadily, "he healed the sick and comforted the poor. He fought hypocrisy and dirty politics and sat among the people, talking, through the day."

"Is that so wonderful?"

"Yes, Captain."

"I don't get this." The captain confronted Martin, peered into his face and eyes. "You been drinking, eh?" He was suspicious. He backed away. "I don't understand."

Martin looked at the city. "Captain, if you don't understand, there's no way of telling you."

The captain followed his gaze. The city was quiet and beautiful and a great peace lay over it. The captain stepped forward, taking his cigar from his lips. He squinted first at Martin, then at the golden spires of the buildings.

"You don't mean—you *can't* mean—That man you're talking about couldn't be—"

Martin nodded. "That's what I mean, sir."

The captain stood silently, not moving. He drew himself up.

"I don't believe it," he said at last.

At high noon Captain Hart walked briskly into the city, accompanied by Lieutenant Martin and an assistant who was carrying some electrical equipment. Every once in a while the captain laughed loudly, put his hands on his hips and shook his head.

The mayor of the town confronted him. Martin set up a tripod, screwed a box onto it, and switched on the batteries.

"Are you the mayor?" The captain jabbed a finger out.

"I am," said the mayor.

The delicate apparatus stood between them, controlled and adjusted by Martin and the assistant. Instantaneous translations from any language were made by the box. The words sounded crisply on the mild air of the city.

"About this occurrence yesterday," said the captain. "It occurred?"

"It did."

"You have witnesses?"

"We have."

"May we talk to them?"

"Talk to any of us," said the mayor. "We are all witnesses."

In an aside to Martin the captain said, "Mass hallucination." To the mayor, "What did this man—this stranger—look like?"

"That would be hard to say," said the mayor, smiling a little.

"Why would it?"

"Opinions might differ slightly."

"I'd like your opinion, sir, anyway," said the captain. "Record this," he snapped to Martin over his shoulder. The lieutenant pressed the button of a hand recorder.

"Well," said the mayor of the city, "he was a very gentle and kind man. He was of a great and knowing intelligence."

"Yes—yes, I know, I know." The captain waved his fingers. "Generalizations. I want something specific. What did he look like?"

"I don't believe that is important," replied the mayor.

"It's very important," said the captain sternly. "I want a description of this fellow. If I can't get it from you, I'll get it from others." To Martin, "I'm sure it must have been Burton, pulling one of his practical jokes."

Martin would not look him in the face. Martin was coldly silent.

The captain snapped his fingers. "There was something or other—a healing?"

"Many healings," said the mayor.

"May I see one?"

"You may," said the mayor. "My son." He nodded at a small boy who stepped forward. "He was afflicted with a withered arm. Now, look upon it."

At this the captain laughed tolerantly. "Yes, yes. This isn't even circumstantial evidence, you know. I didn't see the boy's withered arm. I see only his arm whole and well. That's no proof. What proof have you that the boy's arm was withered yesterday and today is well?"

"My word is my proof," said the mayor simply.

"My dear man!" cried the captain. "You don't expect me to go on hearsay, do you? Oh, no!"

"I'm sorry," said the mayor, looking upon the captain with what appeared to be curiosity and pity.

"Do you have any pictures of the boy before today?" asked the captain.

After a moment a large oil portrait was carried forth, showing the son with a withered arm.

"My dear fellow!" The captain waved it away. "Anybody can paint a picture. Paintings lie. I want a photograph of the boy."

There was no photograph. Photography was not a known art in their society.

"Well," sighed the captain, face twitching, "let me talk to a few other citizens. We're getting nowhere." He pointed at a woman. "You." She hesitated. "Yes, you; come here," ordered the captain. "Tell me about this *wonderful* man you saw yesterday."

The woman looked steadily at the captain. "He walked among us and was very fine and good."

"What color were his eyes?"

"The color of the sun, the color of the sea, the color of a flower, the color of the mountains, the color of the night."

"That'll do." The captain threw up his hands. "See, Martin? Absolutely nothing. Some charlatan wanders through whispering sweet nothings in their ears and—"

"Please, stop it," said Martin.

The captain stepped back. "What?"

"You heard what I said," said Martin. "I like these people. I believe what they say. You're entitled to your opinion, but keep it to yourself, sir."

"You can't talk to me this way," shouted the captain.

"I've had enough of your high-handedness," replied Martin. "Leave these people alone. They've got something good and decent, and you come and foul up the nest and sneer at it. Well, I've talked to them too. I've gone through the city and seen their faces, and they've got something you'll never have— a little simple faith, and they'll move mountains with it. You, you're boiled because someone stole your act, got here ahead and made you unimportant."

"I'll give you five seconds to finish," remarked the captain. "I understand. You've been under a strain, Martin. Months of traveling in space, nostalgia, loneliness. And now, with this thing happening, I sympathize, Martin. I overlook your petty insubordination."

"I don't overlook your petty tyranny," replied Martin. "I'm stepping out. I'm staying here."

"You can't do that!"

"Can't I? Try and stop me. This is what I came looking for. I didn't know it, but this is it. This is for me. Take your filth somewhere else and foul up other nests with your doubt and your—scientific method!" He looked swiftly about. "These people have had an experience, and you can't seem to get it through your head that it's really happened and we were lucky enough to almost arrive in time to be in on it.

"People on Earth have talked about this man for twenty centuries after he walked through the old world. We've all wanted to see him and hear him, and never had the chance. And now, today, we just missed seeing him by a few hours."

Captain Hart looked at Martin's cheeks. "You're crying like a baby. Stop it."

"I don't care."

"Well, I do. In front of these natives we're to keep up a front. You're overwrought. As I said, I forgive you."

"I don't want your forgiveness."

"You idiot. Can't you see this is one of Burton's tricks, to fool these people, to bilk them, to establish his oil and mineral concerns under a religious guise! You fool, Martin. You absolute fool! You should know Earthmen by now. They'll do anything—blaspheme, lie, cheat, steal, kill, to get their ends. Anything is fine if it works; the true pragmatist, that's Burton. You know him!"

The captain scoffed heavily. "Come off it, Martin, admit it, this is the sort of scaly thing Burton might carry off, polish up these citizens and pluck them when they're ripe."

"No," said Martin, thinking of it.

The captain put his hands up. "That's Burton. That's him. That's his dirt, that's his criminal way. I have to admire the old dragon. Flaming in here in a blaze and a halo and a soft word and a loving touch, with a medicated salve here and a healing ray there. That's Burton all right!"

"No." Martin's voice was dazed. He covered his eyes. "No, I won't believe it."

"You don't want to believe." Captain Hart kept at it. "Admit it now. Admit it. It's just the thing Burton would do. Stop daydreaming, Martin. Wake up! It's morning. This is a real world and we're real, dirty people—Burton the dirtiest of us all!"

Martin turned away.

"There, there, Martin," said Hart, mechanically patting the man's back. "I understand. Quite a shock for you. I know. A rotten shame, and all that. That Burton is a rascal. You go take it easy. Let me handle this."

Martin walked off slowly toward the rocket.

Captain Hart watched him go. Then, taking a deep breath, he turned to the woman he had been questioning. "Well. Tell me some more about this man. As you were saying, madam?"

✳ Later the officers of the rocket ship ate supper on card tables outside. The captain correlated his data to a silent Martin who sat red-eyed and brooding over his meal.

"Interviewed three dozen people, all of them full of the same milk and hogwash," said the captain. "It's Burton's work all right, I'm positive. He'll be spilling back in here tomorrow or next week to consolidate his miracles and beat us out in our contracts. I think I'll stick on and spoil it for him."

Martin glanced up sullenly. "I'll kill him," he said.

"Now, now, Martin! There, there, boy."

"I'll kill him—so help me, I will."

"We'll put an anchor on his wagon. You have to admit he's clever. Unethical but clever."

"He's dirty."

"You must promise not to do anything violent." Captain Hart checked his figures. "According to this, there were thirty miracles of healing performed, a blind man restored to vision, a leper cured. Oh, Burton's efficient, give him that."

A gong sounded. A moment later a man ran up. "Captain, sir. A report! Burton's ship is coming down. Also the Ashley ship, sir!"

"See!" Captain Hart beat the table. "Here come the jackals to the harvest! They can't wait to feed. Wait till I confront them. I'll make them cut me in on this feast—I will!"

Martin looked sick. He stared at the captain.

"Business, my dear boy, business," said the captain.

Everybody looked up. Two rockets swung down out of the sky.

When the rockets landed they almost crashed.

"What's wrong with those fools?" cried the captain, jumping up. The men ran across the meadowlands to the steaming ships. The captain arrived. The airlock door popped open on Burton's ship.

A man fell out into their arms.

"What's wrong?" cried Hart.

The man lay on the ground. They bent over him and he was burned, badly burned. His body was covered with wounds and scars and tissue that was inflamed and smoking. He looked up out of puffed eyes and his thick tongue moved in his split lips.

"What happened?" demanded the captain, kneeling down, shaking the man's arm.

"Sir, sir," whispered the dying man. "Forty-eight hours ago, back in Space Sector Seventy-nine DFS, off Planet One in this system, our ship, and Ashley's ship, ran into a cosmic storm, sir." Liquid ran gray from the man's nostrils. Blood trickled from his mouth. "Wiped out. All crew. Burton dead. Ashley died an hour ago. Only three survivals."

"Listen to me!" shouted Hart, bending over the bleeding man. "You didn't come to this planet before this very hour?"

Silence.

"Answer me!" cried Hart.

The dying man said, "No. Storm. Burton dead two days ago. This first landing on any world in six months."

"Are you sure?" shouted Hart, shaking violently, gripping the man in his hands. "Are you sure?"

"Sure, sure," mouthed the dying man.

"Burton died two days ago? You're positive?"

"Yes, yes," whispered the man. His head fell forward. The man was dead.

The captain knelt beside the silent body. The captain's face twitched, the muscles jerking involuntarily. The other members of the crew stood back of him looking down. Martin waited. The captain asked to be helped to his feet, finally, and this was done. They stood looking at the city. "That means—"

"That means?" said Martin.

"We're the only ones who've been here," whispered Captain Hart. "And that man—"

"What about that man, Captain?" asked Martin.

The captain's face twitched senselessly. He looked very old indeed, and gray. His eyes were glazed. He moved forward in the dry grass.

"Come along, Martin. Come along. Hold me up; for my sake, hold me. I'm afraid I'll fall. And hurry. We can't waste time—"

They moved, stumbling, toward the city, in the long dry grass, in the blowing wind.

✳ Several hours later they were sitting in the mayor's auditorium. A thousand people had come and talked and gone. The captain had remained seated, his face haggard, listening, listening. There was so much light in the faces of those who came and testified and talked he could not bear to see them. And all the while his hands traveled, on his knees, together; on his belt, jerking and quivering.

When it was over, Captain Hart turned to the mayor and with strange eyes said:

"But you must know where he went?"

"He didn't say where he was going," replied the mayor.

"To one of the other nearby worlds?" demanded the captain.

"I don't know."

"You must know."

"Do you see him?" asked the mayor, indicating the crowd.

The captain looked. "No."

"Then he is probably gone," said the mayor.

"Probably, probably!" cried the captain weakly. "I've made a horrible mistake, and I want to see him now. Why, it just came to me, this is a most unusual thing in history. To be in on something like this. Why, the chances are one in billions we'd arrived at one certain planet among millions of planets the day after *he* came! You must know where he's gone!"

"Each finds him in his own way," replied the mayor gently.

"You're hiding him." The captain's face grew slowly ugly. Some of the old hardness returned in stages. He began to stand up.

"No," said the mayor.

"You know where he is then?" The captain's fingers twitched at the leather holster on his right side.

"I couldn't tell you where he is, exactly," said the mayor.

"I advise you to start talking," and the captain took out a small steel gun.

"There's no way," said the mayor, "to tell you anything."

"Liar!"

An expression of pity came into the mayor's face as he looked at Hart.

"You're very tired," he said. "You've traveled a long way and you belong to a tired people who've been without faith a long time, and you want to believe so much now that you're interfering with yourself. You'll only make it harder if you kill. You'll never find him that way."

"Where'd he go? He told you; you know. Come on, tell me!" The captain waved the gun.

The mayor shook his head.

"Tell me! Tell me!"

The gun cracked once, twice. The mayor fell, his arm wounded.

Martin leaped forward. "Captain!"

The gun flashed at Martin. "Don't interfere."

On the floor, holding his wounded arm, the mayor looked up. "Put down your gun. You're hurting yourself. You've never believed, and now that you think you believe, you hurt people because of it."

"I don't need you," said Hart, standing over him. "If I missed him by one day here, I'll go on to another world. And another and another. I'll miss him by half a day on the next planet, maybe, and a quarter of a day on the third planet, and two hours on the next, and an hour on the next, and half an hour on the next, and a minute on the next. But after that, one day I'll catch up with him! Do you hear that?" He was shouting now, leaning wearily over the man on the floor. He staggered with exhaustion. "Come along, Martin." He let the gun hang in his hand.

"No," said Martin. "I'm staying here."

"You're a fool. Stay if you like. But I'm going on, with the others, as far as I can go."

The mayor looked up at Martin. "I'll be all right. Leave me. Others will tend my wounds."

"I'll be back," said Martin. "I'll walk as far as the rocket."

They walked with vicious speed through the city. One could see with what effort the captain struggled to show all the old iron, to keep himself going. When he reached the rocket he slapped the side of it with a trembling hand. He holstered his gun. He looked at Martin.

"Well, Martin?"

Martin looked at him. "Well, Captain?"

The captain's eyes were on the sky. "Sure you won't—come with—with me, eh?"

"No, sir."

"It'll be a great adventure, by God. I know I'll find him."

"You are set on it now, aren't you, sir?" asked Martin.

The captain's face quivered and his eyes closed. "Yes."

"There's one thing I'd like to know."

"What?"

"Sir, when you find him—*if* you find him," asked Martin, "what will you ask of him?"

"Why—" The captain faltered, opening his eyes. His hands clenched and unclenched. He puzzled a moment and then broke into a strange smile. "Why, I'll ask him for a little—peace and quiet." He touched the rocket. "It's been a long time, a long, long time since—since I relaxed."

"Did you ever just try, Captain?"

"I don't understand," said Hart.

"Never mind. So long, Captain."

"Good-bye, Mr. Martin."

The crew stood by the port. Out of their number only three were going on with Hart. Seven others were remaining behind, they said, with Martin.

Captain Hart surveyed them and uttered his verdict: "Fools!"

He, last of all, climbed into the airlock, gave a brisk salute, laughed sharply. The door slammed.

The rocket lifted into the sky on a pillar of fire.

Martin watched it go far away and vanish.

At the meadow's edge the mayor, supported by several men, beckoned.

"He's gone," said Martin, walking up.

"Yes, poor man, he's gone," said the mayor. "And he'll go on, planet after planet, seeking and seeking, and always and always he will be an hour late, or a half hour late, or ten minutes late, or a minute late. And finally he will miss out by only a few seconds. And when he has visited three hundred worlds and is seventy or eighty years old he will miss out by only a fraction of a second, and then a smaller fraction of a second. And he will go on and on, thinking to find that very thing which he left behind here, on this planet, in this city—"

Martin looked steadily at the mayor.

The mayor put out his hand. "Was there ever any doubt of it?" He beckoned to the others and turned. "Come along now. We mustn't keep him waiting."

They walked into the city.

HENRY THE NINTH

"THERE HE IS!"

The two men leaned. The helicopter tilted with their lean. The coastline whipped by below.

"No. Just a bit of rock and some moss—"

The pilot lifted his head, which signaled the lift of the helicopter to swivel and rush away. The white cliffs of Dover vanished. They broke over green meadows and so wove back and forth, a giant dragonfly excursioning the stuffs of winter that sleeted their blades.

"Wait! There! Drop!"

The machine fell down; the grass came up. The second man, grunting, pushed the bubble-eye aside and, as if he needed oiling, carefully let himself to the earth. He ran. Losing his breath instantly he slowed to cry bleakly against the wind:

"Harry!"

His yell caused a ragged shape on the rise ahead to stumble up and run.

"I've done nothing!"

"It's not the law, Harry! It's me! Sam Welles!"

The old man who fled before him slowed, then stopped, rigid, on the edge of the cliff above the sea, holding to his long beard with two gloved hands.

Samuel Welles, gasping, trudged up behind, but did not touch, for fear of putting him to flight.

"Harry, you damn fool. It's been weeks. I was afraid I might not find you."

"And I was afraid you *would*."

Harry, whose eyes had been tight shut, now opened them to look tremblingly down at his beard, his gloves, and over at his friend Samuel. Here they were, two old men, very gray, very cold, on a rise of raw stone on a December day. They had known each other so long, so many years, they had passed each other's expressions back and forth between their faces. Their mouths and eyes, therefore, were similar. They might have been ancient brothers. The only difference showed in the man who had unhinged himself from the helicopter. Under his dark clothes you could spy an incongruous Hawaiian-colored sport shirt. Harry tried not to stare at it.

Right now, anyway, both their eyes were wet.

"Harry, I came to warn you."

"No need. Why do you think I've been hiding. This is the final day?"

"The final, yes."

They stood and thought on it.

Christmas tomorrow. And now this Christmas Eve afternoon the last boats leaving. And England, a stone in a sea of mist and water, would be a marble monument to herself left written on by rain and buried in fog. After today, only the gulls would own the island. And a billion monarch butterflies in June rising up like celebrations tossed on parades to the sea.

Harry, his eyes fixed to the tidal shore, spoke:

"By sunset, will every damn stupid idiot fool clear off the Isle?"

"That's about the shape of it."

"And a dread shape it is. And you, Samuel, have you come to kidnap me?"

"Persuade is more like it."

"Persuade? Great God, Sam, don't you know me after fifty years? Couldn't you guess I would want to be the last man in all Britain, no, that hasn't the proper sound, *Great Britain*?"

Last man in Great Britain, thought Harry, Lord, listen. It tolls. It is the great bell of London heard through all the mizzles down through time to this strange day and hour when the last, the very last save one, leave this racial mound, this burial touch of green set in a sea of cold light. The last. The last.

"Samuel, listen. My grave is dug. I'd hate to leave it behind."

"Who'll put you *in* it?"

"Me, when the time's right."

"And who's to cover over?"

"Why, there's dust to cover dust, Sam. The wind will see to it. Ah, God!" Not wishing it, the words exploded from his mouth. He was amazed to see tears flung out on the air from his blinking eyes. "What are we doing here? Why all the good-byes? Why are the last boats in the Channel and the last jets gone? Where did people go, Sam? What happened, what *happened!*"

"Why," said Samuel Welles quietly, "it's simple, Harry. The weather here is bad. Always *has* been. No one dared speak of it, for nothing could be done. But now, England is finished. The future belongs—"

Their eyes moved jointly south.

"To the damn Canary Islands?"

"Samoa."

"To the Brazilian shores?"

"Don't forget California, Harry."

Both laughed, gently.

"California. All the jokes. That funny place. And yet, aren't there a million English from Sacramento to Los Angeles this noon?"

"And another million in Florida."

"Two million Down Under, the past four years alone."

They nodded at the sums.

"Well, Samuel, man says one thing. The sun says another. So man goes by what his skin tells his blood. And the blood at last says: South. It has been saying it for two thousand years. But we pretended not to hear. A man with his first sunburn is a man in the midst of a new love affair, know it or not. Finally, he lies out under some great foreign sky and says to the blinding light: Teach me, oh God, gently, teach."

Samuel Welles shook his head with awe. "Keep talking like that and I won't *have* to kidnap you!"

"No, the sun may have taught you, Samuel, but cannot quite teach me. I wish it could. The truth is, 'twill be no fun here alone. Can't I argue you, Sam, to stay on, the old team, you and me, like when we were boys, eh?" He buffed the other's elbow roughly, dearly.

"God, you make me feel I'm deserting King and Country."

"Don't. You desert nothing, for no one's here. Who would have dreamed, when we were kids in 1980, the day would come when a promise of always summer would leak John Bull to the four corners of beyond?"

"I've been cold all my life, Harry. Too many years putting on too many sweaters and not enough coal in the scuttle. Too many years when the sky did not show so much as a crack of blue on the first day of June nor a smell of hay in July nor a dry day and winter begun August 1st, year on year. I can't take it anymore, Harry, I can't."

"Nor need you. Our race has suffered itself well. You have earned, all of you, you deserve, this long retirement in Jamaica, Port-au-Prince, and Pasadena. Give me that hand. Shake hard again! It's a great moment in history. You and me, *we're* living it!"

"So we are, by God."

"Now look here, Sam, when you've gone and settled in Sicily, Sidney, or Navel Orange, California, tell this 'moment' to the news. They might write you in a column. And history books? Well, shouldn't there be half a page for you and me, the last gone and the last stayed behind? Sam, Sam, you're breaking the bones, but shake away, hold tight, this is our last tussle."

They stood off, panting, wet-eyed.

"Harry, now, will you walk me as far as the copter?"

"No. I fear the damn contraption. The thought of the sun on his dark day might leap me in and fly me off with you."

"And what harm in that?"

"Harm! Why, Samuel, I must guard our coast from invasion. The Normans, the Vikings, the Saxons. In the coming years I'll walk the entire isle, stand guard from Dover north on round the reefs and back through Folkestone, here again."

"Will Hitler invade, chum?"

"He and his iron ghosts just might."

"And how will you fight him, Harry?"

"Do you think I walk alone? No. Along the way, I may find Caesar on the shore. He loved it so he left a road or two. Those roads I'll take, and borrow just those ghosts of choice invaders to repel less choice. It's up to me, yes, to commit or uncommit ghosts, choose or not choose out of the whole damn history of the land?"

"It is. It is."

The last man wheeled to the north and then to the west and then to the south.

"And when I've seen all's well from castle here to lighthouse there, and listened to battles of gunfires in the plunge off Firth, and bagpiped round Scotland with a sour mean pipe, in each New Year's week, Sam, I'll scull back down-Thames and there each December 31st to the end of my life, the night watchman of London, meaning me, yes, me, will make his clock rounds and say out the bells of the old rhymed churches. Oranges and lemons say the bells of St. Clemens. Bow bells. St. Marguerite's. Paul's. I shall dance rope-ends for you, Sam, and hope the cold wind blown south to the warm wind wherever you are stirs some small gray hairs in your sunburned ears."

"I'll be listening, Harry."

"Listen more! I'll sit in the houses of Lords and Commons and debate, losing one hour but to win the next. And say that never before in history did so many owe so much to so few and hear the sirens again from old remembered records and things broadcast before we both were born.

"And a few seconds before January 1st I shall climb and lodge with mice in Big Ben as it strikes the changing of the year.

"And somewhere along the line, no doubt, I shall sit on the Stone of Scone."

"You wouldn't!"

"Wouldn't I? Or the place where it was, anyway, before they mailed it south to Summer's Bay. And hand me some sort of sceptre, a frozen snake perhaps stunned by snow from some December garden. And fit a kind of paste-up crown upon my head. And name me friend to Richard, Henry, out-cast kin of Elizabeths I and II. Alone in Westminster's desert with Kipling mum and history underfoot, very old, perhaps mad, mightn't I, ruler and ruled, elect myself king of the misty isles?"

"You might, and who would blame you?"

Samuel Welles bearhugged him again, then broke and half ran for his waiting machine. Halfway he turned to call back:

"Good God. I just thought. Your name is Harry. What a *fine* name for a king!"

"Not bad."

"Forgive me for leaving?!"

"The sun forgives all, Samuel. Go where it wants you."

"But will England forgive?"

"England is where her people are. I stay with old bones. You go with her sweet flesh, Sam, her fair sunburned skin and blooded body, get!"

"Good-bye."

"God be with you, too, oh you and that bright yellow sport shirt!"

And the wind snatched between and though both yelled more neither heard, waved, and Samuel hauled himself into that machine which swarmed the air and floated off like a vast white summer flower.

And the last man left behind in great gasps and sobs cried out to himself:

Harry! Do you hate change? Against progress? You do see, don't you, the reasons for all this? That ships and jets and planes and a promise of weather piped all the folk away? I see, he said, I see. How could they resist when at long last forever August lay just across the sill?

Yes, yes! He wept and ground his teeth and leaned up from the cliff rim to shake his fists at the vanishing craft in the sky.

"Traitors! Come back!"

You can't leave old England, can't leave Pip and Humbug, Iron Duke and Trafalgar, the Horse Guard in the rain, London burning, buzz bombs and sirens, the new babe held high on the palace balcony, Churchill's funeral cortege still in the street, man, *still* in the street! and Caesar not gone to his Senate, and strange happenings this night at Stonehenge! Leave all this, this, *this*!?

Upon his knees, at the cliff's edge, the last and final king of England, Harry Smith wept alone.

The helicopter was gone now, called toward august isles where summer sang its sweetness in the birds.

The old man turned to see the countryside and thought, why this is how it was one hundred thousand years ago. A great silence and a great wilderness and now, quite late, the empty shell towns and King Henry, Old Harry, the Ninth.

He rummaged half blindly about in the grass and found his lost book bag and chocolate bits in a sack and hoisted his Bible, and Shakespeare and much-thumbed Johnson and much-tongued Dickens and Dryden and Pope, and stood out on the road that led all round England.

Tomorrow: Christmas. He wished the world well. Its people had gifted themselves already with sun, all over the globe. Sweden lay empty. Norway had flown. None lived any longer in God's cold climes. All basked upon the continental hearths of His best lands in fair winds under mild skies. No more fights just to survive. Men, reborn like Christ on such as tomorrow, in southern places, were truly returned to an eternal and fresh-grown manger.

Tonight, in some church, he would ask forgiveness for calling them traitors.

"One last thing, Harry. Blue."

"Blue?" he asked himself.

"Somewhere down the road find some blue chalk. Didn't English men once color themselves with such?"

"Blue men, yes, from head to foot!"

"Our ends are in our beginnings, eh?"

He pulled his cap tight. The wind was cold. He tasted the first snowflakes that fell to brush his lips.

"O remarkable boy!" he said, leaning from an imaginary window on a golden Christmas morn, an old man reborn and gasping for joy, "Delightful boy, there, is the great bird, the turkey, still hung in the poulterer's window down the way?"

"It's hanging there now," said the boy.

"Go buy it! Come back with the man and I'll give you a shilling. Come back in less than five minutes and I'll give you a crown!"

And the boy went to fetch.

And buttoning his coat, carrying his books, Old Harry Ebenezer Scrooge Julius Caesar Pickwick Pip and half a thousand others marched off along the road in winter weather. The road was long and beautiful. The waves were gunfire on the coast. The wind was bagpipes in the north.

Ten minutes later, when he had gone singing beyond a hill, by the look of it, all the lands of England seemed ready for a people who someday soon in history might arrive . . .

THE MESSIAH

"WE ALL HAVE THAT SPECIAL DREAM when we are young," said Bishop Kelly.

The others at the table murmured, nodded.

"There is no Christian boy," the Bishop continued, "who does not some night wonder: am I Him? Is this the Second Coming at long last, and am I It? What, what, oh, what, dear God, if I *were* Jesus? How grand!"

The Priests, the Ministers, and the one lonely Rabbi laughed gently, remembering things from their own childhoods, their own wild dreams, and being great fools.

"I suppose," said the young priest, Father Niven, "that Jewish boys imagine themselves Moses?"

"No, no, my dear friend," said Rabbi Nittler. "The Messiah! The *Messiah*!"

More quiet laughter, from all.

"Of course," said Father Niven out of his fresh pink-and-cream face, "how stupid of me. Christ *wasn't* the Messiah, was he? And your people are still waiting for Him to arrive. Strange. Oh, the ambiguities."

"And nothing more ambiguous than this." Bishop Kelly rose to escort them all out onto a terrace which had a view of the Martian hills, the ancient Martian towns, the old highways, the rivers of dust, and Earth, sixty million miles away, shining with a clear light in this alien sky.

"Did we ever in our wildest dreams," said the Reverend Smith, "imagine that one day each of us would have a Baptist Church, a St. Mary's Chapel, a Mount Sinai Synagogue here, here on Mars?"

The answer was no, no, softly, from them all.

Their quiet was interrupted by another voice which moved among them. Father Niven, as they stood at the balustrade, had tuned his transistor radio to check the hour. News was being broadcast from the small new American-Martian wilderness colony below. They listened:

"—rumored near the town. This is the first Martian reported in our community this year. Citizens are urged to respect any such visitor. If—"

Father Niven shut the news off.

"Our elusive congregation," sighed the Reverend Smith. "I must confess, I came to Mars not only to work with Christians, but hoping to invite *one* Martian to Sunday supper, to learn of his theologies, *his* needs."

"We are still too new to them," said Father Lipscomb. "In another year or so I think they will understand we're not buffalo hunters in search of pelts. Still, it *is* hard to keep one's curiosity in hand. After all, our *Mariner* photographs indicated no life whatsoever here. Yet life there is, very mysterious and half-resembling the human."

"Half, Your Eminence?" The Rabbi mused over his coffee. "I feel they are even more human than ourselves. They have *let* us come in. They have hidden in the hills, coming among us only on occasion, we guess, disguised as Earthmen—"

"Do you really believe they have telepathic powers, then, and hypnotic abilities which allow them to walk in our towns, fooling us with masks and visions, and none of us the wiser?"

"I do so believe."

"Then this," said the Bishop, handing around brandies and crème-de-menthes, "is a true evening of frustrations. Martians who will not reveal themselves so as to be Saved by Us the Enlightened—"

Many smiles at this.

"—and Second Comings of Christ delayed for several thousand years. How long must we wait, O Lord?"

"As for myself," said young Father Niven, "I never wished to *be* Christ, the Second Coming. I just always wanted, with all my heart, to *meet* Him. Ever since I was eight I have thought on that. It might well be the first reason I became a priest."

"To have the inside track just in case He ever *did* arrive again?" suggested the Rabbi, kindly.

The young Priest grinned and nodded. The others felt the urge to reach and touch him, for he had touched some vague small sweet nerve in each. They felt immensely gentle.

"With your permission, Rabbi, gentlemen," said Bishop Kelly, raising his glass. "To the First Coming of the Messiah, or the Second Coming of Christ. May they be more than some ancient, some foolish dreams."

They drank and were quiet.

The Bishop blew his nose and wiped his eyes.

* The rest of the evening was like many another for the Priests, the Reverends, and the Rabbi. They fell to playing cards and arguing St. Thomas Aquinas, but failed under the onslaught of Rabbi Nittler's educated logic. They named him Jesuit, drank nightcaps, and listened to the late radio news:

"—it is feared this Martian may feel trapped in our community. Anyone meeting him should turn away, so as to let the Martian pass. Curiosity seems his motive. No cause for alarm. That concludes our—"

While heading for the door, the Priests, Ministers, and Rabbi discussed translations they had made into various tongues from Old and New Testaments. It was then that young Father Niven surprised them:

"Did you know I was once asked to write a screenplay on the Gospels? They needed an *ending* for their film!"

"Surely," protested the Bishop, "there's only *one* ending to Christ's life?"

"But, Your Holiness, the Four Gospels tell it with four variations. I compared. I grew excited. Why? Because I rediscovered something I had almost forgotten. The Last Supper isn't really the Last Supper!"

"Dear me, what is it then?"

"Why, Your Holiness, the first of several, sir. The first of several! After the Crucifixion and Burial of Christ, did not Simon-called-Peter, with the Disciples, fish the Sea of Galilee?"

"They did."

"And their nets were filled with a miracle of fish?"

"They were."

"And seeing on the shore of Galilee a pale light, did they not land and approach what seemed a bed of white-hot coals on which fresh-caught fish were baking?"

"Yes, ah, yes," said the Reverend Smith.

"And there beyond the glow of the soft charcoal fire, did they not sense a Spirit Presence and call out to it?"

"They did."

"Getting no answer, did not Simon-called-Peter whisper again, 'Who is there?' And the unrecognized Ghost upon the shore of Galilee put out its hand into the firelight, and in the palm of that hand, did they not see the mark where the nail had gone in, the stigmata that would never heal?

"They would have fled, but the Ghost spoke and said, 'Take of these fish and feed thy brethren.' And Simon-called-Peter took the fish that baked upon the white-hot coals and fed the Disciples. And Christ's frail Ghost then said, 'Take of my word and tell it among the nations of all the world and preach therein forgiveness of sin.'

"And then Christ left them. And, in my screenplay, I had Him walk along the shore of Galilee toward the horizon. And when anyone walks toward the horizon, he seems to ascend, yes? For all land rises at a distance. And He walked on along the shore until He was just a small mote, far away. And then they could see Him no more.

"And as the sun rose upon the ancient world, all His thousand footprints that lay along the shore blew away in the dawn winds and were as nothing.

"And the Disciples left the ashes of that bed of coals to scatter in sparks, and with the taste of Real and Final and True Last Supper upon their mouths, went away. And in my screenplay, I had my CAMERA drift high above to watch the Disciples move some north, some south, some to the east, to tell the world what Needed to Be Told about One Man. And their footprints, circling in all directions, like the spokes of an immense wheel, blew away out of the sand in the winds of morn. And it was a new day. THE END."

The young Priest stood in the center of his friends, cheeks fired with color, eyes shut. Suddenly he opened his eyes, as if remembering where he was:

"Sorry."

"For what?" cried the Bishop, brushing his eyelids with the back of his hand, blinking rapidly. "For making me weep twice in one night? What, self-conscious in the presence of your own love for Christ? Why, you have given the Word back to me, me! who has known the Word for what seems a thousand years! You have freshened my soul, oh good young man with the heart of a boy. The eating of fish on Galilee's shore is the True Last Supper. Bravo. You deserve to meet Him. The Second Coming, it's only fair, must be for you!"

"I am unworthy!" said Father Niven.

"So are we all! But if a trade of souls were possible, I'd loan mine out on this instant to borrow yours fresh from the laundry. Another toast, gentlemen? To Father Niven! And then, good night, it's late, good night."

The toast was drunk and all departed; the Rabbi and the Ministers down the hill to their holy places, leaving the Priests to stand a last moment at their door looking out at Mars, this strange world, and a cold wind blowing.

✳ Midnight came and then one and two, and at three in the cold deep morning of Mars, Father Niven stirred. Candles flickered in soft whispers. Leaves fluttered against his window.

Suddenly he sat up in bed, half-startled by a dream of mob-cries and pursuits. He listened.

Far away, below, he heard the shutting of an outside door.

Throwing on a robe, Father Niven went down the dim rectory stairs and through the church where a dozen candles here or there kept their own pools of light.

He made the rounds of all the doors, thinking: Silly, why lock churches? What is there to steal? But still he prowled the sleeping night . . .

. . . and found the front door of the church unlocked, and softly being pushed in by the wind.

Shivering, he shut the door.

Soft running footsteps.

He spun about.

The church lay empty. The candle flames leaned now this way, now that in their shrines. There was only the ancient smell of wax and incense burning, stuffs left over from all the market-places of time and history; other suns, and other noons.

In the midst of glancing at the crucifix above the main altar, he froze.

There was a sound of a single drop of water falling in the night.

Slowly he turned to look at the baptistery in the back of the church.

There were no candles there, yet—

A pale light shone from that small recess where stood the baptismal font.

"Bishop Kelly?" he called, softly.

Walking slowly up the aisle, he grew very cold, and stopped because—

Another drop of water had fallen, hit, dissolved away.

It was like a faucet dripping somewhere. But there were no faucets. Only the baptismal font itself, into which, drop by drop, a slow liquid was falling, with three heartbeats between each sound.

At some secret level, Father Niven's heart told itself something and raced, then slowed and almost stopped. He broke into a wild perspiration. He found himself unable to move, but move he must, one foot after the other, until he reached the arched doorway of the baptistery.

There was indeed a pale light within the darkness of the small place.

No, not a light. A shape. A figure.

The figure stood behind and beyond the baptismal font. The sound of falling water had stopped.

His tongue locked in his mouth, his eyes flexed wide in a kind of madness, Father Niven felt himself struck blind. Then vision returned, and he dared cry out:

"Who!"

A single word, which echoed back from all around the church, which made candle flames flutter in reverberation, which stirred the dust of incense, which frightened his own heart with its swift return in saying: Who!

The only light within the baptistery came from the pale garments of the figure that stood there facing him. And this light was enough to show him an incredible thing.

As Father Niven watched, the figure moved. It put a pale hand out upon the baptistery air.

The hand hung there as if not wanting to, a separate thing from the Ghost beyond, as if it were seized and pulled forward, resisting, by Father Niven's dreadful and fascinated stare to reveal what lay in the center of its open white palm.

There was fixed a jagged hole, a cincture from which, slowly, one by one, blood was dripping, falling away down and slowly down, into the baptismal font.

The drops of blood struck the holy water, colored it, and dissolved in slow ripples.

The hand remained for a stunned moment there before the Priest's now-blind, now-seeing eyes.

As if struck a terrible blow, the Priest collapsed to his knees with an outgasped cry, half of despair, half of revelation, one hand over his eyes, the other fending off the vision.

"No, no, no, no, no, no, no, it *can't!*"

It was as if some dreadful physician of dentistry had come upon him without narcotic and with one seizure entire-extracted his soul, bloodied raw, out of his body. He felt himself prized, his life yanked forth, and the roots, O God, were . . . *deep!*

"No, no, no, no!"

But, yes.

Between the lacings of his fingers, he looked again.

And the Man was there.

And the dreadful bleeding palm quivered dripping upon the baptistery air.

"Enough!"

The palm pulled back, vanished. The Ghost stood waiting.

And the face of the Spirit was good and familiar. Those strange beautiful deep and incisive eyes were as he knew they always must be. There was the gentleness of the mouth, and the paleness framed by the flowing locks of hair and beard. The Man was robed in the simplicity of garments worn upon the shores and in the wilderness near Galilee.

The Priest, by a great effort of will, prevented his tears from spilling over, stopped up his agony of surprise, doubt, shock, these clumsy things which rioted within and threatened to break forth. He trembled.

And then saw that the Figure, the Spirit, the Man, the Ghost, Whatever, was trembling, too.

No, thought the Priest, He can't be! Afraid? Afraid of . . . *me?*

And now the Spirit shook itself with an immense agony not unlike his own, like a mirror image of his own concussion, gaped wide its mouth, shut up its own eyes, and mourned:

"Oh, please, let me go."

At this the young Priest opened his eyes wider and gasped. He thought: But you're free. No one keeps you here!

And in that instant: "Yes!" cried the Vision. "*You* keep me! Please! Avert your gaze! The more you look the more I become *this!* I am *not* what I seem!"

But, thought the Priest, I did not speak! My lips did not move! How does this Ghost know my mind?

"I know all you think," said the Vision, trembling, pale, pulling back in baptistery gloom. "Every sentence, every word. I did not mean to come. I ventured into town. Suddenly I was many things to many people. I ran. They followed. I escaped here. The door was open. I entered. And then and then—oh, and then was trapped."

No, thought the Priest.

"Yes," mourned the Ghost. "By you."

Slowly now, groaning under an even more terrible weight of revelation, the Priest grasped the edge of the font and pulled himself, swaying, to his feet. At last he dared force the question out:

"You are not . . . what you seem?"

"I am not," said the other. "Forgive me."

I, thought the Priest, shall go mad.

"Do not," said the Ghost, "or I shall go down to madness with you."

"I can't give you up, oh, dear God, now that you're here, after all these years, all my dreams, don't you see, it's asking too *much*. Two thousand years, a whole race of people have waited for your return! And I, I am the one who meets you, sees you—"

"You meet only your own dream. You see only your own need. Behind all this—" the figure touched its own robes and breast, "I am another thing."

"What must I *do*!" the Priest burst out, looking now at the heavens, now at the Ghost which shuddered at his cry. *"What?"*

"Avert your gaze. In that moment I will be out the door and gone."

"Just—just like that?"

"Please," said the Man.

The Priest drew a series of breaths, shivering.

"Oh, if this moment could last for just an hour."

"Would you kill me?"

"No!"

"If you keep me, force me into this shape some little while longer, my death will be on your hands."

The Priest bit his knuckles, and felt a convulsion of sorrow rack his bones.

"You—you are a Martian, then?"

"No more. No less."

"And I have done this to you with my thoughts?"

"You did not mean. When you came downstairs, your old dream seized and made me over. My palms still bleed from the wounds you gave out of your secret mind."

The Priest shook his head, dazed.

"Just a moment more . . . wait . . ."

He gazed steadily, hungrily, at the darkness where the Ghost stood out of the light. That face was beautiful. And, oh, those hands were loving and beyond all description.

The Priest nodded, a sadness in him now as if he had within the hour come back from the true Calvary. And the hour was gone. And the coals strewn dying on the sand near Galilee.

"If—if I let you go—"

"You must, oh you must!"

"If I let you go, will you promise—"

"What?"

"Will you promise to come back?"

"Come back?" cried the figure in the darkness.

"Once a year, that's all I ask, come back once a year, here to this place, this font, at the same time of night—"

"Come back . . . ?"

"Promise! Oh, I must know this moment again. You don't know how important it is! Promise, or I won't let you go!"

"I—"

"Say it! Swear it!"

"I promise," said the pale Ghost in the dark. "I swear."

"Thank you, oh thanks."

"On what day a year from now must I return?"

The tears had begun to roll down the young Priest's face now. He could hardly remember what he wanted to say and when he said it he could hardly hear:

"Easter, oh, God, yes, Easter, a year from now!"

"Please, don't weep," said the figure. "I will come. Easter, you say? I know your calendar. Yes. Now—" The pale wounded hand moved in the air, softly pleading. "May I go?"

The Priest ground his teeth to keep the cries of woe from exploding forth. "Bless me, and go."

"Like this?" said the voice.

And the hand came out to touch him ever so quietly.

"Quick!" cried the Priest, eyes shut, clenching his fists hard against his ribs to prevent his reaching out to seize. "Go before I keep you forever. Run. Run!"

The pale hand touched him a last time upon his brow. There was a soft run of naked feet.

A door opened upon stars; the door slammed.

There was a long moment when the echo of the slam made its way through the church, to every altar, into every alcove and up like a blind flight of some single bird seeking and finding release in the apse. The church stopped trembling at last, and the Priest laid his hands on himself as if to tell himself how to behave, how to breathe again; be still, be calm, stand tall. . . .

Finally, he stumbled to the door and held to it, wanting to throw it wide, look out at the road which must be empty now, with perhaps a figure in white, far fleeing. He did not open the door.

He went about the church, glad for things to do, finishing out the ritual of locking up. It was a long way around to all the doors. It was a long way to next Easter.

He paused at the font and saw the clear water with no trace of red. He dipped his hand and cooled his brow and temples and cheeks and eyelids.

Then he went slowly up the aisle and laid himself out before the altar and let himself burst forth and really weep. He heard the sound of his sadness go up and come back in agonies from the tower where the bell hung silent.

And he wept for many reasons.

For himself.

For the Man who had been here a moment ago.

For the long time until the rock was rolled back and the tomb found empty again.

Until Simon-called-Peter once more saw the Ghost upon the Martian shore, and himself Simon-Peter.

And most of all he wept because, oh, because, because . . . never in his life could he speak of this night to anyone. . . .

BANG! YOU'RE DEAD!

JOHNNY CHOIR CAME LIKE THE SPRING LAMBS over the green Italian hills, gamboling at the game of war. He leaped a line of bullets as if it were the hedge fronting his Iowa home. He ducked and dodged; a pedestrian in war traffic. Most of all, he laughed and was indefatigable as some khaki kangaroo, forever hopping.

Bullets, mortar shells and shrapnel were only rumors in the air to Johnny. They were not true.

He moved with long-legged strides near San Vittore, froze, pointed his gun, fingered the trigger, cried, "Bang! I gotcha!" and watched a German fall with a red orchid pinned to one lapel. Then Johnny jigged again, to escape the answering machine gun blast.

An artillery shell approached. Johnny twisted, crying, "Missed!"

It did. It missed, *like always*.

Private Smith followed in Johnny's wake. Only Smith traveled on his thin-muscled stomach, face sweaty and juju'd with Italian mud. Smith crawled, ran, fell, got up again, and never let those enemy bullets near him. Frequently he yelled angrily at Johnny:

"Lie down, you dumb egg! They'll gut you!"

But Johnny danced on to the metal music of bullets like new, bright hummingbirds on the air. While Smith crawled earthworm-wise taking each kilometer, Johnny catapulted toward the enemy, giggling. Tall as the sky, loud as a bazooka gun! Smith broke out a ration of cold sweat just watching the kid.

Germans screamed and ran away from Johnny. When they saw his limbs flourished in a kind of classical St. Vitus—while bullets whistled under his earlobes, between his knees and betwixt thumb and forefinger—German morale disintegrated. They fled wildly!

Laughing heartily, Johnny Choir sat down, pulled out a chocolate ration and teethed on it, while Smith came inching up. Johnny glimpsed the crawling figure's exposed rump, and inquired, "Smith?"

The anonymous rump went down, a familiar thin face came up. "Yeah." Firing had ceased in the area. They were alone and safe. Smith wiped dirt from his chin. "Honest to God, I get the weemies watching you. You gallop around like a kid in the rain. Only it's the wrong kind of rain."

"I'll duck," said Johnny, munching.

He had a big handsome face with blue child eyes captured in innocent wonder in it, and small pink child lips. His shorn hair resembled the blond stubble of a clothes brush. Now immersed deeply in the enjoyment of candy, he had forgotten war.

"I duck," he explained again.

A thousand times Smith'd heard that excuse. It was *too* simple an explanation. God had a hand in this somewhere, Smith was certain. Johnny had probably been dunked in holy water. Bullets detoured around him, not daring to touch. Yeah. That was it. Smith laughed musingly.

"What happens if you forget to duck, Johnny?"

Johnny replied "I play dead."

"YOU—" said Smith, blinking, staring, "—you play dead. Uh-huh." He exhaled slowly. "Yeah. Sure. Okay."

Johnny threw away the candy wrapper. "I been thinking. It's almost my turn to play dead, isn't it? Everybody's done it, except me. It's only fair I take my turn. Everybody's been so decent about it, I think I'll play dead today."

Smith found that his hands were shaking. His appetite was gone, too. "Now what do you want to talk that way for?" he argued.

"I'm tired," said Johnny simply.

"Take a nap, then. You're the damnedest one for snoozing. Take a nap."

Johnny considered that with a pout. Then he arranged himself on the grass in the shape of a fried shrimp. "All right, Private Smith. If you say so."

Smith consulted his watch. "You got twenty minutes. Snooze fast. We'll be moving up as soon as the captain shows. And we don't want him finding you asleep."

But Johnny was already deep in soft dreams. Smith looked at him with wonder and envy. God, what a guy. Sleeping in the middle of hell. Smith had to stay, watching over him. It wouldn't do to have some stray German sniping Johnny while he couldn't duck. Strangest damn thing he ever knew . . .

A soldier ran heavily up, panting. "Hi, Smith!"

Smith recognized the soldier, uneasily. "Oh, it's you, Melter . . ."

"Somebody wounded?" Melter was big, too, but off-center with his fat and too high and hoarse with his voice. "Oh, it's Johnny Choir. Dead?"

"Taking a nap."

Melter gaped. "A nap? For cripes sake, that infant! That moron!"

Smith said, quietly, "Moron, hell. He just brushed the Heinies off this rise with one hand. I saw them throw a thousand rounds at Johnny, a thousand rounds, mind you, and Johnny slipped through it like a knife through warm ribs."

Melter's pink face looked worried. "What makes him tick, anyway?"

Smith shrugged. "As far as I can figure, he thinks this is all a game. He never grew up. He's got a big body with a kid's mind in it. He doesn't take war serious. He thinks we're all playing at this."

Melter swore. "Don't I wish we were." He eyed Johnny jealously. "I've watched him before, running like a fool, and he's still alive. Him and that shimmy of his, and yelling, 'Missed me!' like a kid, and yelling, 'Gotcha' when he shot a Heinie. How do you explain that?"

Johnny turned in his sleep, and his lips fumbled with words. A couple came out, soft, easy. "Mom! Hey, Mom! You there? Mom? You there, Mom?"

Smith reached over to take Johnny's hand. Johnny squeezed it in his sleep, saying with a little smile, "Oh, Mom."

"So now," said Smith, "after all this, I'm a mother."

They stayed there, the three of them, for all of three minutes, silent. Melter finally cleared his throat, nervously. "Some—somebody ought to tell Johnny about the facts of life. Death is real, and war is real, and bullets can knock out your guts. Let's tell him when he wakes up."

Smith laid Johnny's hand aside. He pointed at Melter, and his face got paler and harder with each word. "Look now, don't come around here with your philosophy! What's bad for you ain't bad for him! Let him dream his dreams, if he wants. I been with him since boot-camp, watching over him like a brother. I know. There's only one thing that keeps him in one piece, and that's thinking the things he thinks, believing that war is fun and we're all kids! And if you so much as flip your lip, I'll drop you in the Gagliano River with anchors on."

"Okay, okay, don't get tough. I only thought—"

Smith stood up. "You thought. You thought! Why, damn you, I can see the stinking look on your face! You'd like to see Johnny dead. You're yellow jealous, that's what! Well, now look—" He made a sweep of his arm furiously. "—you keep away! From now on, you romp on the other side of any hill we're on! I don't want you running off at the mouth! Now, get the hell out of here!"

Melter's fat face was red as Italian *vino*. He held his gun hard. His fingers itched the butt end of it. "It ain't fair," he replied tightly, hoarsely. "It ain't fair to us that he gets by. It ain't fair he lives while we die. What you expect, me to love him? Ha! When I gotta die, he lives, so I should kiss him? I don't work that way!"

Melter strode off, his back stiff and working funny, his neck like a ramrod, his fingers tight fists, his strides short and jolting.

Smith watched him. There I go with my big mouth, he thought. I should have stroked him nice. Now, maybe he tells the captain, and the captain turns Johnny over to the psychiatric ward for observation. Then maybe they trundle him back to the States and I lose my best friend. God, Smith, you lummox! Why ain't you got lock-jaw?

Johnny was waking up, rubbing eyes with big farmer-boy knuckles, tongue exploring the outer reaches of his chin for stray particles of ration chocolate.

They went over another hill together, Johnny Choir and Private Smith.

Johnny dancing in his special way, always ahead. Smith wisely but not happily bringing up the rear; afraid where Johnny was never afraid, careful where Johnny always splurged, groaning while Johnny was laughing into enemy fire. . . .

✳ "Johnny!"

It was inevitable. As Smith felt the machine-gun bullet enter his right side, just above the hip, felt pain hammer, pound, wallop through him under tremendous striking impact, felt blood running in pulses through suddenly slippery, numb fingers, smelled his own blood like some nightmare chemical, he knew it was inevitable.

He yelled again.

"Johnny!"

Johnny stopped. He came running back, grinning. He put away his grin when he saw Smith lying there giving a blood transfusion to the body of the Earth.

"Hey, Private Smith, what's this about?" he asked.

"I'm—I'm playing wounded," said Smith on one elbow, not looking up, sucking in air, blowing it out. "You—go on ahead, Johnny, and don't mind me."

Johnny looked like a kid told to stand in the corner.

"Hey. That's not fair. You should've told me, and I could play wounded, too. I'll get too far ahead and you won't be able to catch up."

Smith forced a sick smile, weak and pale, and the blood pumped. "You were always too far ahead of me anyway, Johnny. Even if I ran in circles around you, I could never catch up."

That was too subtle for Johnny, who gave forth with a confused scowl. "I thought you were my pal, Smith?"

"Sure. Sure I am, Johnny. I am." Smith coughed. "Sure. But, you see, I just sudden-like found out I was tired. It came on me quick, you see. No time to tell you. So I'm playing wounded."

Johnny brightened, crouching down. "I'll play wounded, too."

"Like hell you will!" Smith tried to rise, but pain clenched him in a hot, tight fist, and he couldn't speak for half a minute. Then: "Look now—you keep your nose out of this. You get the hell on to Rome!"

Johnny said, "You don't want me to play—wounded?"

"No, dammit!" cried Smith, and things got darker, darker.

Johnny said nothing, just stood there, tall and quiet and not understanding, and lost. Here was the man who had been his best friend since the first day in the army, since leaving New York harbor; his best friend all up through Africa, the Sicilian hills and Italy, now lying here and telling him to go on—alone.

In the webbed dark of his mind, Smith felt it, too. Keen and sharp like a new kind of razor slicing him down the middle. Wounded, and Johnny going on alone.

Who would tell Johnny to keep away from bodies, it was against the rules? Who would assure him, as Smith'd done, to keep intact that incredible fantasy of Johnny's beliefs; who would assure him that those wounds were fake, that this blood was only something like catsup carried by soldiers when they wanted time out? Who would censor Johnny's outbursts like that time in Tunis when Johnny asked his commanding officer?

"When do I get my bottle of catsup, sir?"

"Catsup. Catsup?"

"Yes, sir, for when I want to be wounded, sir?"

Who would storm in and explain to the commanding officer, "You see, sir, Johnny means, does he carry his blood plasma with him from the Red Cross, sir? In case he needs a transfusion, sir."

"Uh. Oh, is *that* what he means? No. The medical unit carries that. They'll give it to you when the necessity arises."

Who will extricate Johnny from situations like that? Or the time Johnny asked a senior officer, "If I play dead, sir, how long do I stay dead before I'm allowed to get up, sir?"

Who will tell the officer that Johnny is only joking, sir, only joking, ha ha, and not an infant in overgrown skin. Who? thought Smith.

✳ Someone hurried up in the dimness of pain and the sounds of conflict. By the sound of the big clumsy feet, Smith knew it was Melter.

Melter's voice came from the gathering dark.

"Oh, it's you, Johnny. Who's that at your feet? Well—" Melter laughed. Johnny laughed, too, to be compatible. Oh, Johnny, how can you laugh? If you only knew, son. "Well, well, if it ain't Smith. Dead?"

Johnny said, eagerly. "No, only playing wounded."

"Playing?" said Melter. Smith couldn't see the man, but he heard the subtle sound of Melter's tongue touching that word. "Playing, eh? Playing wounded. So. Hmm."

Smith got his eyes open, but he couldn't speak, he could only blink, watching Melter.

Melter spat on the ground. "Can you talk, Smith? No? Good." Melter looked in four directions, nodding, satisfied. He took Johnny by the shoulder. "Come here, Johnny, I'd like to ask a few questions."

"Sure, Private Melter."

Melter patted Johnny's arm, and his eyes shone hot and funny. "I hear you're the lad who knows how to duck bullets?"

"Sure. Best ducker in the army. Smith's pretty good, too. A little slower, maybe, but I'm teaching him."

Melter said, "Think you can teach me, Johnny?"

Johnny said, "You already learned, haven't you?"

"Have I?" Melter wondered. "Well, yeah, I guess I have—a little. Sure. But not like you, Johnny. You got the technique down good. What—what's the secret?"

Johnny considered a moment, and Smith tried to say something, tried to shout or scream or even wriggle, and he didn't have the strength. He heard Johnny say, far away.

"I don't know. You know how it is when you're a kid and play cops and robbers. The other guy is selfish. He never wants to lie down when you say 'Bang, gotcha!' The whole secret is in saying, 'Bang, I gotcha!' first. Then they've got to lie down."

"Oh." Melter looked at him as if he were crazy. "Say that again, will you?"

Johnny said it again, and Smith had to laugh inside his hell of pain. Melter thought he was being kidded. Johnny said it again.

"Don't hand me that!" snarled Melter, impatiently. "There's a good deal more to it than that! You go running and jumping around like a bull moose and nobody even touches you!"

"I duck," said Johnny.

Smith laughed some more. Old jokes are the best jokes.

Then Smith's stomach caught and held pain.

Melter's face was all deep-cut lines and suspicion and hate.

"Okay, smart guy, if you're so good—suppose you walk off a hundred feet and let me take potshots at you?"

Johnny smiled. "Sure. Why not?"

He walked off and left Melter standing there. He walked off a hundred paces and stood there tall and blond and so damn young and clean as butter. Smith wiggled his fingers, screaming inside. "Johnny, don't do it,

Johnny! For Crissake, God, knock Melter down with the butt-end of a lightning bolt!"

* They were in a kind of depression between hills, a small place where you could do things and not be seen too well by anyone. Melter stood against the trunk of an olive tree so as to shield his action, just in case, and casually lifted his gun.

Melter loved his gun with his fingers, carefully adjusting it to his eyes, finding Johnny in the sights, caressing the trigger, pulling back slowly.

Where in hell IS everybody! wondered Smith. AH!

Melter fired.

"Missed me!" came Johnny's good-humored shout.

Johnny stood intact. Melter swore. Melter aimed again, even slower this time. He found Johnny's heart with the sight and Smith screamed some more, but none of it got out of his mouth. Melter licked his lips and—fired!

"Missed again!" observed Johnny.

Melter fired four times more, quicker, faster, angered and potent and furious, color gorging his neck, rage in his eyes, hands fumbling—and with each report that knocked the warm afternoon air, Johnny skipped rope or ducked doors or sidestepped elbows or kicked a football or did a ballet dance, and Melter's gun fumed empty.

Melter rammed more bullets in it, his face now blanched white, his knees sagging.

Johnny came running up.

Melter whispered, fearfully. "How in God's name did you do it?"

"Like I told you."

A long pause. "Do you think I could learn."

"Anybody can learn, if they want."

"Teach me. Teach me, Johnny. I don't want to die, I don't want to die. I hate this whole damn war. Teach me, Johnny. Teach me, and I'll be your friend."

Johnny shrugged. "Do just like I told you, that's all."

Melter said, slowly. "Now, you are joking again."

"No, I'm not."

"Yes, I think you are joking again," said Melter in a pale, thick anger. He shifted his gun to the ground, considering new tactics and decided about it. "Well, listen here, smart boy, for your information, I will tell you something." He jerked one hand. "Those men you passed in the field, they weren't playing, no, they were really, actually, finally dead! Dead, yes, dead, you hear! Dead! Not playing, not kidding, not joking, but dead, dead, cold dead!" He beat it at Johnny like fists. He beat the air with it and turned the day into winter cold. "Dead!"

Smith winced inside. Johnny, don't listen to him! Don't let him hurt you, Johnny! Go on believing the world is a good place. Go on living intact and unafraid! Don't let fear in, Johnny. You'll crumble with it!

Johnny said to Melter, "What're you talking about?"

"Death!" bellowed Melter wildly. "That's what I'm talking about! Death. You can die, and Smith can die, and I can die from bullets. Gangrene, rot, death! You've been fooling yourself. Grow up, you fool, before it's too late! Grow up!"

Johnny stood there a long time, and then he began to sway, his fists in big farmer-knotted pendulums. "No. You're lying," he said stubbornly.

"Bullets can kill, this is war!"

"You're lying to me," said Johnny.

"You can die, so can Smith. Smith's dying now. Smell his blood! What do you think that stench is from the fox-holes, wild grapes for the winepresses of war? Yes, death and bones!"

Johnny looked around with unsteady eyes. "No, I won't believe it." He bit his lips and closed his eyes. "I won't. You're mean, you're bad, you're—"

"You can die, Johnny, die!"

Johnny began to cry, then. Like a babe in some barren wilderness, and Smith wrenched his shoulder trying to get up. Johnny cried and it was a new and small sound in the wide world.

Melter pushed Johnny staggeringly toward the front lines. "Go on. Get out there and die, Johnny. Get out there and get your heart pinned on a stone wall like a dripping medal!"

Don't go, Johnny, Smith's shouting got lost in the red, pain cavern of his interior, lost and useless and mute. Don't go, kid. Stay here, don't listen to this guy! Stick around, Johnny-lad!

Johnny stumbled away, sobbing, toward the blunt staccato of machine guns, toward the whine of artillery shells. His gun was held in one long limp arm, its butt dragging pebbles in a dry rattling stone laughter.

Melter looked after him in a hysterical kind of triumph.

Then Melter hefted his weapon and walked east over another hill, out of view.

Smith lay there, his thoughts getting sicker and dimmer, and Johnny walked on and on. If only there were some way to cry out. Johnny, look out!

An artillery shell came over and burst. Johnny fell down on the ground without a sound and lay there, not making a movement of his once-miraculous limbs.

Johnny!

Have you stopped believing? Johnny, get up! Are you dead now? Johnny?

And then darkness mercifully gathered Smith in and swallowed him down.

✳ Scalpels rose and fell like small keen guillotines, cutting away death and decay, beheading misery, eliminating metal pain. The bullet, plucked from Smith's wound, was cast away, small, dark, clattering into a metal pan. The doctors pantomimed over and around him in a series of blurred frenzies. Smith breathed easily.

Across the dim interior of the tent Johnny's body lay on another operating table, doctors curious over him in a sterile tableau.

"Johnny?" and this time Smith had a voice.

"Easy does it," a doctor cautioned. The lips under the white mask moved. "that a friend of yours—over there?"

"Yeah. How is he?"

"Not so good. Head injury. Fifty-fifty chance."

They concluded with Smith, stitches, swabbings, bandages and all. Smith watched the wound vanish under white gauze, then he looked at the assembled crowd of medics. "Let me help with him, will you?"

"Well, now, after all, soldier—"

"I know the guy. I know the guy. I know him. He's funny. If it means keeping him alive, how's about it?"

The scowl formed over the surgical mask, and Smith's heart beat slow. The doctor blinked. "I can't chance it. What can you possibly do to help me?"

"Wheel me over. I tell you I can help. I'm his bosom-pal. I can't let him conk out now. Hell, no!"

The doctors conferred.

They transferred Smith to a portable stretcher and two orderlies delivered him across the tent where the surgeons were engaged with Johnny's shaved, naked skull. Johnny looked asleep and dreaming a nightmare. His face twisted, worried, frightening, wondering, disappointed and dismayed. One of the surgeons sighed.

Smith touched one surgical elbow. "Don't give up, Doc. Oh, God, don't give up." To Johnny: "Johnny-lad. Listen. Listen to me. Forget everything

Melter said. Forget everything he said—you hear me? He was full of crap up to here!"

Johnny's face still was irritated, changing like disturbed water. Smith gathered his breath and continued.

"Johnny, you gotta go on playing, like always. Go on ducking, like in the old days. You always knew how, Johnny. It was part of you. It didn't take learning or teaching, it was natural. And you let Melter put ideas in your head. Ideas that may be okay for people like Melter and me and others, but don't jibe for you."

One surgeon made an impatient gesture with a rubber-gloved hand.

Smith asked him, "Is his head hurt bad, Doc?"

"Pressure on the skull, on the brain. May cause temporary loss of memory."

"Will he remember being wounded?"

"It's hard to say. Probably not."

Smith had to be held down. "Good! Good! Look," he whispered quickly, confidentially to Johnny's head. "Johnny, just think about being a kid, and how it was then, and don't think about what happened today. Think about running in ravines and through creeks and skipping pebbles on water, and ducking b-b guns, and laughing, Johnny!"

Inside, Johnny thought about it.

✳ A mosquito hummed somewhere, hummed and circled for an endless time. Somewhere guns rumbled.

Someone finally told Smith, "Respiration improved."

Someone else said, "Heart action picking up."

Smith kept talking, part of him that wasn't pain, that was only hope and anxiety in his larynx, and fear-fever in his brain. The war thunder came closer, closer, but it was only the blood hurled through his head by his heart. Half an hour passed by. Johnny listened like a kid in school to an over-patient teacher. Listened and smoothed out the pain, erased the dismay in his expression, and regained the old certainty and youth and sureness and calm acceptance of belief.

The surgeon stripped off his tight rubber gloves.

"He'll pull through."

Smith felt like singing. "Thanks, Doc. Thanks."

The Doc said, "You from Unit 45, you and Choir and a guy named Melter?"

"Yeah. What about Melter?"

"Funniest darn thing. Ran head on into a burst of German machine-gun fire. Ran down a hill screaming something about being a kid again." The doc scratched his jaw. "We picked up his body with fifty bullets in it."

Smith swallowed, lying back to sweat. Ice-cold, shivering sweat.

"That's Melter for you. He just didn't know how. He grew up, too fast, like all of us. He didn't know how to stay young, like Johnny. That's why it didn't work. I—I gotta give him credit for trying, though, the nut. But there's only one Johnny Choir."

"You," diagnosed the surgeon, "are delirious. Better take a sedative."

Smith shook his head. "What about home? Are we going, Johnny and I, with our wounds?"

The surgeon formed a smile under the mask. "Home to America, the two of you."

"Now, you're delirious!" Smith let out a careful whoop of glee. He twisted to get a good look at Johnny sleeping so peacefully and easily and dreaming, and he said, "You hear that, Johnny? We're going home! You and me! Home!"

And Johnny replied, softly, "Mom? Oh, Mom."

Smith held Johnny's hand. "Okay," he said to the surgeons. "So now I'm a mother. Pass the cigars!"

DARLING ADOLF

THEY WERE WAITING FOR HIM to come out. He was sitting inside the little Bavarian café with a view of the mountains, drinking beer, and he had been in there since noon and it was now two-thirty, a long lunch, and much beer, and they could see by the way he held his head and laughed and lifted one more stein with the suds fluffing in the spring breeze that he was in a grand humor now, and at the table with him the two other men were doing their best to keep up, but had fallen long behind.

On occasion their voices drifted on the wind, and then the small crowd waiting out in the parking lot leaned to hear. What was he saying? and now what?

"He just said the shooting was going well."

"What, where?!"

"Fool. The film, the film is shooting well."

"Is that the director sitting with him?"

"Yes. And the other unhappy one is the producer."

"He doesn't look like a producer."

"No wonder! He's had his nose changed."

"And him, doesn't he look *real*?"

"To the hair and the teeth."

And again everyone leaned to look in at the three men, at the man who didn't look like a producer, at the sheepish director who kept glancing out at the crowd and slouching down with his head between his shoulders, shutting his eyes, and the man between them, the man in the uniform with the swastika on his arm, and the fine military cap put on the table beside the almost-untouched food, for he was talking, no, making a speech.

"That's the Führer, all right!"

"God in heaven, it's as if no time had passed. I don't believe this is 1973. Suddenly it's 1934 again, when first I saw him."

"Where?"

"The Nuremberg Rally, the stadium, that was the autumn, yes, and I was thirteen and part of the Youth and one hundred thousand soldiers and young men in that big place that late afternoon before the torches were lit. So many bands, so many flags, so much heartbeat, yes, I tell you, I could hear one hundred thousand hearts banging away, we were all so in love, he had come down out of the clouds. The gods had sent him, we knew, and the time of waiting was over, from here on we could *act*, there was nothing he couldn't *help* us to do."

"I wonder how that actor in there feels, playing him?"

"Sh, he hears you. Look, he waves. Wave back."

"Shut up," said someone else. "They're talking again. I want to hear—"

The crowd shut up. The men and women leaned into the soft spring wind. The voices drifted from the café table.

Beer was being poured by a maiden waitress with flushed cheeks and eyes as bright as fire.

"More beer!" said the man with the toothbrush mustache and the hair combed forward on the left side of his brow.

"No, thanks," said the director.

"No, no," said the producer.

"More beer! It's a splendid day," said Adolf. "A toast to the film, to us, to me. Drink!"

The other two men put their hands on their glasses of beer.

"To the film," said the producer.

"To darling Adolf." The director's voice was flat.

The man in the uniform stiffened.

"I do not look upon myself—" he hesitated, "upon *him* as darling."

"He was darling, all right, and you're a doll." The director gulped his drink. "Does anyone mind if I get drunk?"

"To be drunk is not permitted," said Der Führer.

"Where does it say that in the script?"

The producer kicked the director under the table.

"How many more weeks' work do you figure we have?" asked the producer, with great politeness.

"I figure we should finish the film," said the director, taking huge swigs, "around about the death of Hindenburg, or the *Hindenburg* gasbag going down in flames at Lakehurst, New Jersey, whichever comes first."

Adolf Hitler bent to his plate and began to eat rapidly, snapping at his meat and potatoes in silence.

The producer sighed heavily. The director, nudged by this, calmed the waters. "Another three weeks should see the masterwork in the can, and us sailing home on the *Titanic*, there to collide with the Jewish critics and go down bravely singing 'Deutschland Uber Alles.' "

Suddenly all three were voracious and snapping and biting and chewing their food, and the spring breeze blew softly, and the crowd waited outside.

At last, Der Führer stopped, had another sip of beer, and lay back in his chair, touching his mustache with his little finger.

"Nothing can provoke me on a day like this. The rushes last night were so beautiful. The casting for this film, ah! I find Göring to be incredible. Goebbels? Perfection!" Sunlight dazzled out of Der Führer's face. "So. So, I was thinking just last night, here I am in Bavaria, me, a pure Aryan—"

Both men flinched slightly, and waited.

"—making a film," Hitler went on, laughing softly, "with a Jew from New York and a Jew from Hollywood. So amusing."

"I am not amused," said the director, lightly.

The producer shot him a glance which said: the film is not finished yet. Careful.

"And I was thinking, wouldn't it be fun . . ." Here Der Führer stopped to take a big drink, ". . . to have another . . . ah . . . Nuremberg Rally?"

"You mean for the *film*, of course?"

The director stared at Hitler. Hitler examined the texture of the suds in his beer.

"My God," said the producer, "do you know how much it would cost to reproduce the Nuremberg Rally? How much did it cost Hitler for the original, Marc?"

He blinked at his director, who said, "A bundle. But he had a lot of free extras, of course."

"Of course! The Army, the Hitler Youth."

"Yes, yes," said Hitler. "But think of the publicity, all over the world? Let us go to Nuremberg, eh, and film my plane, eh, and me coming down out of the clouds? I heard those people out there, just now: Nuremberg and plane and torches. *They* remember. *I* remember. I held a torch in that stadium. My God, it was beautiful. And now, now I am exactly the age Hitler was when he was at his prime."

"He was never at his prime," said the director. "Unless you mean hung-meat."

Hitler put down his glass. His cheeks grew very red. Then he forced a smile to widen his lips and change the color of his face. "That is a joke, of course."

"A joke," said the producer, playing ventriloquist to his friend.

"I was thinking," Hitler went on, his eyes on the clouds again, seeing it all, back in another year. "If we shot it next month, with the weather good. Think of all the tourists who would come to watch the filming!"

"Yeah. Bormann might even come back from Argentina."

The producer shot his director another glare.

Hitler cleared his throat and forced the words out: "As for expense, if you took one small ad, *one* mind you! in the Nuremberg papers one week before, why, you would have an army of people there as extras at fifty cents a day, no, a quarter, no, *free!*"

Der Führer emptied his stein, ordered another. The waitress dashed off to refill. Hitler studied his two friends.

"You know," said the director, sitting up, his own eyes taking a kind of vicious fire, his teeth showing as he leaned forward, "there is a kind of idiot grace to you, a kind of murderous wit, a sort of half-ass style. Every once in a while you come dripping up with some sensational slime that gleams and stinks in the sun, buster. Archie, *listen* to him. Der Führer just had a great bowel movement. Drag in the astrologers! Slit the pigeons and filch their guts. Read me the casting sheets."

The director leaped to his feet and began to pace.

"That *one* ad in the paper, and all the trunks in Nuremberg get flung wide! Old uniforms come out to cover fat bellies! Old armbands come out to fit flabby arms! Old military caps with skull-eagles on them fly out to fit on fat-heads!"

"I will not sit here—" cried Hitler.

He started to get up but the producer was tugging his arm and the director had a knife at his heart: his forefinger, stabbing hard.

"Sit."

The director's face hovered two inches from Hitler's nose. Hitler slowly sank back, his cheeks perspiring.

"God, you *are* a genius," said the director. "Jesus, your people *would* show up. Not the young, no, but the old. All the Hitler Youth, your age now, those senile bags of tripe yelling '*Sieg Heil,*' saluting, lighting torches at sunset, marching around the stadium crying themselves blind."

The director swerved to his producer.

"I tell you, Arch, this Hitler here has bilge for brains but this time he's on target! If we don't shove the Nuremberg Rally *up* this film, I quit. I mean it. I will simply walk out and let Adolf here take over and direct the damned thing himself! Speech over."

He sat down.

Both the producer and Der Führer appeared to be in a state of shock.

"Order me another goddamn beer," snapped the director.

Hitler gasped in a huge breath, tossed down his knife and fork, and shoved back his chair.

"I do not break bread with such as you!"

"Why, you bootlicking lapdog son of a bitch," said the director. "I'll hold the mug and you'll do the licking. Here." The director grabbed the beer and shoved it under Der Führer's nose. The crowd, out beyond, gasped and almost surged. Hitler's eyes rolled, for the director had seized him by the front of his tunic and was yanking him forward.

"Lick! Drink the German filth! Drink, you scum!"

"Boys, boys," said the producer.

"Boys, crud! You know what this swill-hole, this chamberpot Nazi, has been thinking, sitting here, Archibald, and drinking your beer? Today Europe, tomorrow the world!"

"No, no, Marc!"

"No, no," said Hitler, staring down at the fist which clenched the material of his uniform. "The buttons, the buttons—"

"Are loose on your tunic and inside your head, worm. Arch, look at him pour! Look at the grease roll off his forehead, look at his stinking armpits. He's a sea of sweat because I've read his mind! Tomorrow the world! Get this film set up, him cast in the lead. Bring him down out of the clouds, a month from now. Brass bands. Torchlight. Bring back Leni Riefenstahl to show us how she shot the Rally in '34. Hitler's lady-director friend. Fifty cameras she used, fifty she used, by God, to get all the German crumbs lined up and vomiting lies, and Hitler in his creaking leather and Göring awash in his blubber, and Goebbels doing his wounded-monkey walk, the three superfags of history aswank in the stadium at dusk, make it all happen again, with this bastard up front, and do you know what's going through his little graveyard mind behind his bloater eyes at this very moment?"

"Marc, Marc," whispered the producer, eyes shut, grinding his teeth. "Sit down. Everyone sees."

"Let them see! Wake up, you! Don't you shut your eyes on me, too! I've shut my eyes on you for days, filth. Now I want some attention. Here."

He sloshed beer on Hitler's face, which caused his eyes to snap wide and his eyes to roll yet again, as apoplexy burned his cheeks.

The crowd, out beyond, hissed in their breath.

The director, hearing, leered at them.

"Boy, is this funny. They don't know whether to come in or not, don't know if you're real or not, and neither do I. Tomorrow, you bilgy bastard, you really dream of becoming Der Führer."

He bathed the man's face with more beer.

The producer had turned away in his chair now and was frantically dabbing at some imaginary breadcrumbs on his tie. "Marc, for God's sake—"

"No, no, seriously, Archibald. This guy thinks because he puts on a ten-cent uniform and plays Hitler for four weeks at good pay that if we actually put together the Rally, why Christ, History would turn back, oh turn back, Time, Time in thy flight, make me a stupid Jew-baking Nazi again for tonight. Can you see it, Arch, this lice walking up to the microphones and shouting, and the crowd shouting back, and him *really* trying to take over, as if Roosevelt still lived and Churchill wasn't six feet deep, and it was all to be lost or won again, but mainly won, because *this* time they wouldn't stop at the Channel but just cross on over, give or take a million German boys dead, and stomp England and stomp America, isn't *that* what's going on inside your little Aryan skull, Adolf? *Isn't it!*"

Hitler gagged and hissed. His tongue stuck out. At last he jerked free and exploded:

"Yes! Yes, goddamn you! Damn and bake and burn you! You dare to lay hands on Der Führer! The Rally! Yes! It must be in the film! We must make it again! The plane! The landing! The long drive through streets. The blond girls. The lovely blond boys. The stadium. Leni Riefenstahl! And from all the trunks, in all the attics, a black plague of armbands winging on the dusk, flying to assault, battering to take the victory. Yes, yes, I, Der Führer, I will stand at that Rally and dictate terms! I—I—"

He was on his feet now.

The crowd, out beyond in the parking lot, shouted.

Hitler turned and gave them a salute.

The director took careful aim and shot a blow of his fist to the German's nose.

After that the crowd arrived, shrieking, yelling, pushing, shoving, falling.

* They drove to the hospital at four the next afternoon.

Slumped, the old producer sighed, his hands over his eyes. "Why, why, why are we going to the hospital? To visit that—monster?"

The director nodded.

The old man groaned. "Crazy world. Mad people. I never saw such biting, kicking, biting. That mob almost killed you."

The director licked his swollen lips and touched his half-shut left eye with a probing finger. "I'm okay. The important thing is I hit Adolf, oh, how I hit him. And now—" He stared calmly ahead, "I think I am going to the hospital to finish the job."

"Finish, *finish*?" The old man stared at him.

"Finish." The director wheeled the car slowly around a corner. "Remember the twenties, Arch, when Hitler got shot at in the street and not hit, or beaten in the streets, and nobody socked him away forever, or he left a beer hall ten minutes before a bomb went off, or was in that officers' hut in 1944 and the briefcase bomb exploded and *that* didn't get him. Always the charmed life. Always he got out from under the rock. Well, Archie, no more charms, no more escapes. I'm walking in that hospital to make sure that when that half-ass extra comes out and there's a mob of krauts to greet him, he's walking wounded, a permanent soprano. Don't try to stop me, Arch."

"Who's stopping? Belt him one for me."

They stopped in front of the hospital just in time to see one of the studio production assistants run down the steps, his hair wild, his eyes wilder, shouting.

"Christ," said the director. "Bet you forty to one, our luck's run out again. Bet you that guy running toward us says—"

"Kidnaped! Gone!" the man cried. "Adolf's been taken away!"

"Son of a bitch."

They circled the empty hospital bed; they *touched* it.

A nurse stood in one corner wringing her hands. The production assistant babbled.

"Three men it was, three men, three men."

"Shut up." The director was snowblind from simply looking at the white sheets. "Did they force him or did he go along quietly?"

"I don't know, I can't say, yes, he was making speeches, making speeches as they took him out."

"Making speeches?" cried the old producer, slapping his bald pate. "Christ, with the restaurant suing us for broken tables, and Hitler maybe suing us for—"

"Hold on." The director stepped over and fixed the production assistant with a steady gaze. "*Three* men, you say?"

"Three, yes, three, three, three, oh, three men."

A small forty-watt lightbulb flashed on in the director's head.

"Did, ah, did one man have a square face, a good jaw, bushy eyebrows?"

"Why . . . yes!"

"Was one man short and skinny like a chimpanzee?"

"Yes!"

"Was one man big, I mean, slobby fat?"

"How did you *know*?"

The producer blinked at both of them. "What goes on? What—"

"Stupid attracts stupid. Animal cunning calls to laughing jackass cunning. Come on, Arch!"

"Where?" The old man stared at the empty bed as if Adolf might materialize there any moment now.

"The back of my car, quick!"

From the back of the car, on the street, the director pulled a German cinema directory. He leafed through the character actors. "Here."

The old man looked. A forty-watt bulb went on in his head.

The director riffled more pages. "And here. And, finally, here."

They stood now in the cold wind outside the hospital and let the breeze turn the pages as they read the captions under the photographs.

"Goebbels," whispered the old man.

"An actor named Rudy Steihl."

"Göring."

"A hambone named Grofe."

"Hess."

"Fritz Dingle."

The old man shut the book and cried to the echoes.

"Son of a bitch!"

"Louder and funnier, Arch. Funnier and louder."

"You mean right now out there somewhere in the city three dumbkopf out-of-work actors have Adolf in hiding, held maybe for ransom? and do we *pay* it?"

"Do we want to finish the film, Arch?"

"God, I don't know, so much money already, time, and—" The old man shivered and rolled his eyes. "What if—I mean—what if they don't *want* ransom?"

The director nodded and grinned. "You mean, what if this is the true start of the Fourth Reich?"

"All the peanut brittle in Germany might put itself in sacks and show up if they knew that—"

"Steihl, Grofe, and Dingle, which is to say, Goebbels, Göring, and Hess, were back in the saddle with dumbass Adolf?"

"Crazy, awful, mad! It couldn't happen!"

"Nobody was ever going to clog the Suez Canal. Nobody was ever going to land on the Moon. Nobody."

"What do we do? This waiting is horrible. Think of something, Marc, think, think!"

"I'm thinking."

"And—"

This time a hundred-watt bulb flashed on in the director's face. He sucked air and let out a great braying laugh.

"I'm going to help them organize and speak up, Arch! I'm a genius. Shake my hand!"

He seized the old man's hand and pumped it, crying with hilarity, tears running down his cheeks.

"You, Marc, on their side, helping form the Fourth Reich!?"

The old man backed away.

"Don't hit me, help me. Think, Arch, think. What was it Darling Adolf said at lunch, and damn the expense! What, what?"

The old man took a breath, held it, exploded it out, with a final light blazing in his face.

"Nuremberg?" he asked.

"Nuremberg! What month is this, Arch?"

"October!"

"October! October, forty years ago, October, the big, big Nuremberg Rally. And this coming Friday, Arch, an Anniversary Rally. We shove an ad in the international edition of *Variety*: RALLY AT NUREMBERG. TORCHES. BANDS. FLAGS. Christ, he won't be able to stay away. He'd shoot his kidnapers to be there and play the greatest role in his life!"

"Marc, we can't afford—"

"Five hundred and forty-eight bucks? For the ad plus the torches plus a full military band on a phonograph record? Hell, Arch, hand me that phone."

The old man pulled a telephone out of the front seat of his limousine.

"Son of a bitch," he whispered.

"Yeah." The director grinned, and ticked the phone. "Son of a bitch."

❋ The sun was going down beyond the rim of Nuremberg Stadium. The sky was bloodied all across the western horizon. In another half-hour it would be completely dark and you wouldn't be able to see the small platform down in the center of the arena, or the few dark flags with the swastikas put up on temporary poles here or there making a path from one side of the stadium to the other. There was a sound of a crowd gathering, but the place was empty. There was a faint drum of band music but there was no band.

Sitting in the front row on the eastern side of the stadium, the director waited, his hands on the controls of a sound unit. He had been waiting for two hours and was getting tired and feeling foolish. He could hear the old man saying:

"Let's go home. Idiotic. He won't come."

And himself saying, "He will. He must," but not believing it.

He had the records waiting on his lap. Now and again he tested one, quietly, on the turntable, and then the crowd noises came from lilyhorns stuck up at both ends of the arena, murmuring, or the band played, not loudly, no, that would be later, but very softly. Then he waited again.

The sun sank lower. Blood ran crimson in the clouds. The director tried not to notice. He hated nature's blatant ironies.

The old man stirred feebly at last and looked around.

"So this was the place. It was really it, back in 1934."

"This was it. Yeah."

"I remember the films. Yes, yes. Hitler stood—what? Over there?"

"That was it."

"And all the kids and men down there and the girls there, and fifty cameras."

"Fifty, count 'em, fifty. Jesus, I would have liked to have been here with the torches and flags and people and cameras."

"Marc, Marc, you don't *mean* it?"

"Yes, Arch, sure! So I could have run up to Darling Adolf and done what I did to that pig-swine half-ass actor. Hit him in the nose, then hit him in the teeth, then hit him in the *blinis!* You got it, Leni? Action! *Swot!* Camera! *Bam!* Here's one for Izzie. Here's one for Ike. Cameras running, Leni? Okay. *Zot!* Print!"

They stood looking down into the empty stadium where the wind prowled a few newspapers like ghosts on the vast concrete floor.

Then, suddenly, they gasped.

Far up at the very top of the stadium a small figure had appeared.

The director quickened, half rose, then forced himself to sit back down.

The small figure, against the last light of the day, seemed to be having difficulty walking. It leaned to one side, and held one arm up against its side, like a wounded bird.

The figure hesitated, waited.

"Come on," whispered the director.

The figure turned and was about to flee.

"Adolf, no!" hissed the director.

Instinctively, he snapped one of his hands to the sound-effects tape deck, his other hand to the music.

The military band began to play softly.

The "crowd" began to murmur and stir.

Adolf, far above, froze.

The music played higher. The director touched a control knob. The crowd mumbled louder.

Adolf turned back to squint down into the half-seen stadium. Now he must be seeing the flags. And now the few torches. And now the waiting platform with the microphones, two *dozen* of them! *one* of them real.

The band came up in full brass.

Adolf took one step forward.

The crowd roared.

Christ, thought the director, looking at his hands, which were now suddenly hard fists and now again just fingers leaping on the controls, all to themselves. Christ, what do I do with him when I get him down here? What, *what*?

And then, just as insanely, the thought came. Crud. You're a director. And that's *him*. And this *is* Nuremberg.

So . . . ?

Adolf took a second step down. Slowly his hand came up in a stiff salute.

The crowd went wild.

Adolf never stopped after that. He limped, he tried to march with pomp, but the fact was he limped down the hundreds of steps until he reached the floor of the stadium. There he straightened his cap, brushed his tunic, resaluted the roaring emptiness, and came gimping across two hundred yards of empty ground toward the waiting platform.

The crowd kept up its tumult. The band responded with a vast heartbeat of brass and drum.

Darling Adolf passed within twenty feet of the lower stands where the director sat fiddling with the tape-deck dials. The director crouched down. But there was no need. Summoned by the *"Sieg Heils"* and the fanfare of trumpets and brass, Der Führer was drawn inevitably toward that dais where destiny awaited him. He was walking taller now and though his uniform was rumpled and the swastika emblem torn, and his mustache motheaten and his hair wild, it was the old Leader all right, it was him.

The old producer sat up straight and watched. He whispered. He pointed.

Far above, at the top of the stadium, three more men had stepped into view.

My God, thought the director, that's the team. The men who grabbed Adolf.

A man with bushy eyebrows, a fat man, and a man like a wounded chimpanzee.

Jesus. The director blinked. Goebbels. Göring. Hess. Three actors at liberty. Three half-ass kidnapers staring down at . . .

Adolf Hitler climbing up on the small podium by the fake microphones and the real one under the blowing torches which bloomed and blossomed and guttered and smoked on the cold October wind under the sprig of lily-horns which lifted in four directions.

Adolf lifted his chin. That did it. The crowd went absolutely mad. Which is to say, the director's hand, sensing the hunger, went mad, twitched the volume high so the air was riven and torn and shattered again and again and again with *Sieg Heil, Sieg Heil, Sieg Heil!*

Above, high on the stadium rim, the three watching figures lifted their arms in salute to their Führer.

Adolf lowered his chin. The sounds of the crowd faded. Only the torch flames whispered.

Adolf made his speech.

He must have yelled and chanted and brayed and sputtered and whispered hoarsely and wrung his hands and beat the podium with his fist and plunged his fist at the sky and shut his eyes and shrieked like a disemboweled trumpet for ten minutes, twenty minutes, half an hour as the sun vanished beyond the earth and the three other men up on the stadium rim watched and listened and the producer and the director waited and watched. He shouted things about the whole world and he yelled things about Germany and he shrieked things about himself and he dammed this and blamed that and praised yet a third, until at last he began to repeat, and repeat the same words over and over as if he had reached the end of a record inside himself and the needle was fastened to a circle track which hissed and hiccuped, hiccuped and hissed, and then faded away at last into a silence where you could only hear his heavy breathing, which broke at last into a sob and he stood with his head bent while the others now could not look at him but looked only at their shoes or the sky or the way the wind blew dust across the field. The flags fluttered. The single torch bent and lifted and twisted itself again and talked under its breath.

At last, Adolf raised his head to finish his speech.

"Now I must speak of them."

He nodded up to the top of the stadium where the three men stood against the sky.

"They are nuts. I am nuts, too. But at least I know I am nuts. I told them: crazy, you are crazy. Mad, you are mad. And now, my own craziness, my own madness, well, it has run itself down. I am tired.

"So now, what? I give the world back to you. I had it for a small while here today. But now you must keep it and keep it better than I would. To each of you I give the world, but you must promise, each of you to keep your own part and work with it. So there. Take it."

He made a motion with his free hand to the empty seats, as if all the world were in his fingers and at last he were letting it go.

The crowd murmured, stirred, but said nothing loud.

The flags softly tongued the air. The flames squatted on themselves and smoked.

Adolf pressed his fingers onto his eyeballs as if suddenly seized with a blinding headache. Without looking over at the director or the producer, he said, quietly:

"Time to go?"

The director nodded.

Adolf limped off the podium and came to stand below where the old man and the younger director sat.

"Go ahead, if you want, again, hit me."

The director sat and looked at him. At last he shook his head.

"Do we finish the film?" asked Adolf.

The director looked at the producer. The old man shrugged and could find nothing to say.

"Ah, well," said the actor. "Anyway, the madness is over, the fever has dropped. I have *made* my speech at Nuremberg. God, look at those idiots up there. Idiots!" he called suddenly at the stands. Then back to the director, "Can you think? They wanted to hold me for ransom. I told them what fools they were. Now I'll go tell them again. I had to get away from them. I couldn't stand their stupid talk. I had to come here and be my own fool in my own way for the last time. Well . . ."

He limped off across the empty field, calling back quietly:

"I'll be in your car outside, waiting. If you want, I am yours for the final scenes. If not, no, and that ends it."

The director and the producer waited until Adolf had climbed to the top of the stadium. They could hear his voice drift down, cursing those other three, the man with the bushy eyebrows, the fat man, and the ugly chimpanzee, calling them many things, waving his hands. The three backed off and went away, gone.

Adolf stood alone high in the cold October air.

The director gave him a final lift of the sound volume. The crowd, obedient, banged out a last *"Sieg Heil."*

Adolf lifted his free hand, not into a salute, but some sort of old, easy, half-collapsed mid-Atlantic wave. Then he was gone, too.

The sunlight went with him. The sky was no longer blood-colored. The wind blew dust and want ads from a German paper across the stadium floor.

"Son of a bitch," muttered the old man. "Let's get out of here."

They left the torches to burn and the flags to blow, but shut off the sound equipment.

"Wish I'd brought a record of 'Yankee Doodle' to march us out of here," said the director.

"Who needs records. We'll whistle. Why not?"

"Why not!"

He held the old man's elbow going up the stairs in the dusk, but it was only halfway up, they had the guts to try to whistle.

And then it was suddenly so funny they couldn't finish the tune.

THE BEAUTIFUL SHAVE

He came into town riding fast and firing his guns at the blue sky. He shot a chicken in the dust and kicked it around, using his horse as a mauler, and then, reloading and yelling, his three-week beard red and irritable in the sunlight, he rode on to the Saloon where he tethered his horse and carried his guns, still hot, into the bar where he glared at his own sunburned image in the mirror and yelled for a glass and a bottle.

The bartender slid them over the edge of the bar and went away.

The men along the bar moved down to the free lunch at the far end, and conversation withered.

"What in hell's wrong with everyone?!" cried Mr. James Malone. "Talk, laugh, everyone. Go on, now, or I'll shoot your damn eyebrows off!"

Everyone began to talk and laugh.

"That's better," said James Malone, drinking his drinks one upon another.

He rammed the wing doors of the Saloon wide and in the resulting wind stomped out like an elephant into the afternoon street where other men were riding up from the mines or the mountains and tying their horses to the worn hitching poles.

The barber shop was directly across the street.

Before crossing to it, he rechecked his bright blue pistols and snuffed at them with his red nose, saying Ah! at the scent of gunpowder. Then he saw a tin can in the talcumy dust and shot it three times ahead of him as he strode laughing, and the horses all along the street jumped nervously and flickered their ears. Reloading again, he kicked the barber shop door wide and confronted a full house. The four barber chairs were full of lathered customers, waiting with magazines in their hands, and the mirrors behind them repeated the comfort and the creamy lather and the pantomime of efficient barbers.

Along the wall on a bench sat six other men waiting to be cleansed of the mountain and the desert.

"Have a seat," said one of the barbers, glancing up.

"I sure will," said Mr. James Malone, and pointed his pistol at the first chair. "Get out of there, mister, or I'll sew you right back into the upholstery."

The man's eyes were startled, then angry, then apprehensive in turn above his creamy mask, but after a long hesitation, he levered himself up with difficulty, swiped the white stuff off his chin with the apron, flung the apron to the floor, and walked over to shove in and sit with the other waiting men.

James Malone snorted at this, laughed, jounced into the black leather chair, and cocked his two pistols.

"I *never* have to wait," he said to no one and everyone at once. His gaze wandered over their heads and touched on the ceiling. "If you live right, you don't have to wait for anything. You ought to know that by now!"

The men looked at the floor. The barber cleared his throat and put an apron over Jamie Malone. The pistols stuck up, making white tents underneath. There was a sharp click as he knocked the pistols together, just to let everyone know they were there, and pointed.

"Give me the works," he said to the barber, not looking at him. "A shave first, I feel itchy and mean, then a haircut. You men there, starting on the right, tell jokes. Make 'em good jokes. I want entertainment while I'm being shorn. Ain't been entertained in months. You, there, mister, you start."

The man who had been evicted from his comfortable chair unfroze himself slowly and rolled his eyes at the other men and talked as if someone had hit him in the mouth.

"I knew a gent once who . . ." he said, and word by word, white-faced, he launched himself into a tale. "That gent, he . . ."

To the barber, James Malone now said, "Listen, you, I want a shave, I want a beautiful shave. But I got a fine-skinned face and it's a pretty face with the beard off, and I been in the mountains for a long time and I had no luck with gold-panning, so I'm feeling mean. I just want to warn you of one little thing. If you so much as nick my face once with your straight razor, I'll kill you. You hear that? I mean I'll kill you. If you so much as bring one little speck of blood to the surface, I'll plug you clean through the heart. You hear?"

The barber nodded quietly. The barber shop was silent. Nobody was telling jokes or laughing.

"Not one drop of blood, not one little cut, mind you," repeated Mr. James Malone, "or you'll be dead on the floor a second later."

"I'm a married man," said the barber.

"I don't give a damn if you're a Mormon with six wives and fifty-seven children. You're dead if you scratch me once."

"I happen to have two children," said the barber. "A fine little girl and a boy."

"Don't hand me any of that," said Malone, settling back, closing his eyes. "Start."

The barber began to get the hot towels ready. He put them on James Malone's face, and under them the man cursed and yelled and waved his pistols under the white apron. When the hot towels came off and the hot lather was put on his beard, James Malone still chewed on his profanity and threats, and the men waiting sat white-faced and stiff with the pistols pointing at them. The other barbers had almost stopped moving and stood like statues by their customers in the chairs, and the barber shop was cold for a summer day.

"What's wrong with the stories?" snapped James Malone. "All right, then sing. You four there, sing something like 'My Darling Clementine.' Start it up. You heard me."

The barber was stropping his razor slowly with a trembling hand. "Mr. Malone," he said.

"Shut up and get to work." Malone tilted his head back, grimacing.

The barber stropped his razor some more and looked at the men seated all around the shop. He cleared his throat and said, "Did all of you gentlemen hear what Mr. Malone said to me?"

Everyone nodded mutely.

"You heard him threaten to kill me," said the barber, "if I so much as drew a drop of blood to his skin?"

The men nodded again.

"And you'd swear to it in a court of law, if necessary?" asked the barber.

The men nodded for the last time.

"Cut the malarkey," said Mr. James Malone. "Get to work."

"That's all I wanted to be sure of," said the barber, letting the leather strop fall and clatter against the chair. He raised the razor in the light and it gleamed and glittered with cold metal there.

He tilted Mr. James Malone's head back and put the razor against the hairy throat.

"We'll start here," he said. "We'll start *here*."

COLONEL STONESTEEL'S GENUINE HOME-MADE TRULY EGYPTIAN MUMMY

THAT WAS THE AUTUMN THEY FOUND the genuine Egyptian mummy out past Loon Lake.

How the mummy got there, and how long it had been there, no one knew. But there it was, all wrapped up in its creosote rags, looking a bit spoiled by time, and just waiting to be found.

The day before, it was just another autumn day with the trees blazing and letting down their burned-looking leaves and a sharp smell of pepper in the air when Charlie Flagstaff, aged twelve, stepped out and stood in the middle of a pretty empty street, hoping for something big and special and exciting to happen.

"Okay," said Charlie to the sky, the horizon, the whole world. "I'm waiting. Come on!"

Nothing happened. So Charlie kicked the leaves ahead of him across
town until he came to the tallest house on the greatest street, the house
where everyone in Green Town came with troubles. Charlie scowled and
fidgeted. He had troubles, all right, but just couldn't lay his hand on
their shape or size. So he shut his eyes and just yelled at the big house
windows:

"Colonel Stonesteel!"

The front door flashed open, as if the old man had been waiting there,
like Charlie, for something incredible to happen.

"Charlie," called Colonel Stonesteel, "you're old enough to rap. What is
there about boys makes them shout around houses? Try again."

The door shut.

Charlie sighed, walked up, knocked softly.

"Charlie Flagstaff, is that you?" The door opened again, the colonel
squinted out and down. "I thought I told you to *yell* around the house!"

"Heck," sighed Charlie, in despair.

"Look at that weather. Hell's bells!" The colonel strode forth to hone his
fine hatchet nose on the cool wind. "Don't you love autumn, boy? Fine, fine
day! Right?"

He turned to look down into the boy's pale face.

"Why, son, you look as if your last friend left and your dog died. What's
wrong? School starts next week?"

"Yep."

"Halloween not coming fast enough?"

"Still six weeks off. Might as well be a year. You ever notice, colonel. . . ." The boy heaved an even greater sigh, staring out at the autumn
town. "Not much ever happens around here?"

"Why, it's Labor Day tomorrow, big parade, seven cars, the mayor,
maybe fireworks—er." The colonel came to a dead stop, not impressed with
his grocery list. "How old are you, Charlie?"

"Thirteen, almost."

"Things do tend to run down, come thirteen." The colonel rolled his
eyes inward on the rickety data inside his skull. "Come to a dead halt when
you're fourteen. Might as well die, sixteen. End of the world, seventeen.
Things only start up again, come twenty or beyond. Meanwhile, Charlie,
what do we do to survive until noon this very morn before Labor Day?"

"If anyone knows, it's you, colonel," said Charlie.

"Charlie," said the old man, flinching from the boy's clear stare, "I can move politicians big as prize hogs, shake the Town Hall skeletons, make locomotives run backward uphill. But small boys on long autumn weekends, glue in their head, and a bad case of Desperate Empties? Well. . . ."

Colonel Stonesteel eyed the clouds, gauged the future.

"Charlie," he said, at last. "I am moved by your condition, touched by your lying there on the railroad tracks waiting for a train that will never come. How's this? I'll bet you six Baby Ruth candy bars against your mowing my lawn, that Green Town, Upper Illinois, population five thousand sixty-two people, one thousand dogs, will be changed forever, changed for the best, by God, some time in the next miraculous twenty-four hours. That sound good? A bet?"

"Gosh!" Charlie, riven, seized the old man's hand and pumped it. "A bet! Colonel Stonesteel, I knew you could do it!"

"It ain't done yet, son. But look there. The town's the Red Sea. I order it to *part*. Gangway!"

✳ The colonel marched, Charlie ran, into the house.

"Here we are, Charles, the junkyard or the graveyard. Which?"

The colonel sniffed at one door leading down to raw basement earth, another leading up to dry timber attic.

"Well—"

The attic ached with a sudden flood of wind, like an old man dying in his sleep. The colonel yanked the door wide on autumn whispers, high storms trapped and shivering in the beams.

"Hear that, Charlie? What's it say?"

"Well—"

A gust of wind blew the colonel up the dark stairs like so much flimsy chaff.

"Time, mostly, it says, and oldness and memory, lots of things. Dust, and maybe pain. Listen to those beams! Let the wind shift the timber skeleton on a fine fall day, and you truly got time-talk. Burnings and ashes, Bombay snuffs, tomb-yard flowers gone to ghost—"

"Boy, colonel," gasped Charlie, climbing, "you oughta write for *Top Notch Story Magazine*!"

"Did once! Got rejected. Here we are!"

And there indeed they were, in a place with no calendar, no months, no days, no year, but only vast spider shadows and glints of light from collapsed chandeliers lying about like great tears in the dust.

"Boy!" cried Charlie, scared, and glad of it.

"Chuck!" said the colonel. "You ready for me to birth you a real, live, half-dead sockdolager, on-the-spot mystery?"

"Ready!"

The colonel swept charts, maps, agate marbles, glass eyes, cobwebs and sneezes of dust off a table, then rolled up his sleeves.

"Great thing about midwifing mysteries is, you don't have to boil water or wash up. Hand me that papyrus scroll over there, boy, that darning needle just beyond, that old diploma on the shelf, that wad of cannonball cotton on the floor. Jump!"

"I'm jumping." Charlie ran and fetched, fetched and ran.

Bundles of dry twigs, clutches of pussy willow and cattails flew. The colonel's sixteen hands were wild in the air, holding sixteen bright needles, flakes of leather, rustling of meadow grass, flickers of owl feather, glares of bright yellow fox-eye. The colonel hummed and snorted as his miraculous eight sets of arms and hands swooped and prowled, stitched and danced.

"There!" he cried, and pointed with a chop of his nose. "Half-done. Shaping up. Peel an eye, boy. What's it commence to start to resemble?"

Charlie circled the table, eyes stretched so wide it gaped his mouth. "Why—why—" he gasped.

"Yes?"

"It looks like—"

"Yes, yes?"

"A mummy! *Can't* be!"

"Is! Bull's-eye on, boy! *Is!*"

The colonel leaned down on the long-strewn object. Wrists deep in his creation, he listened to its reeds and thistles and dry flowers whisper.

"Now, you may well ask, why would anyone *build* a mummy in the first place? You, you inspired this, Charlie. You put me up to it. Go look out the attic window there."

Charlie spat on the dusty window, wiped a clear viewing spot, peered out.

"Well," said the colonel. "What do you see? Anything happening out there in the town, boy? Any murders being transacted?"

"Heck, no—"

"Anyone falling off church steeples or being run down by a maniac lawnmower?"

"Nope."

"Any *Monitors* or *Merrimacs* sailing up the lake, dirigibles falling on the Masonic Temple and squashing six thousand Masons at a time?"

"Heck, colonel, there's only five thousand people *in* Green Town!"

"Spy, boy. Look. Stare. Report!"

Charlie stared out at a very flat town.

"No dirigibles. No squashed Masonic Temples."

"Right!" The colonel ran over to join Charlie, surveying the territory. He pointed with his hand, he pointed with his nose. "In all Green Town, in all your life, not one murder, one orphanage fire, one mad fiend carving his name on librarian ladies' wooden legs! Face it, boy, Green Town, Upper Illinois, is the most common mean ordinary plain old bore of a town in the eternal history of the Roman, German, Russian, English, American empires! If Napoleon had been born here, he would've committed hara-kiri by the age of nine. Boredom. If Julius Caesar had been raised here, he'd have got himself in the Roman Forum, aged ten, and shoved in his own dagger—"

"Boredom," said Charlie.

"Kee-rect! Keep staring out that window while I work, son." Colonel Stonesteel went back to flailing and shoving and pushing a strange growing shape around on the creaking table. "Boredom by the pound and ton. Boredom by the doomsday yard and the funeral mile. Lawns, homes, fur on the dogs, hair on the people, suits in the dusty store windows, all cut from the same cloth. . . ."

"Boredom," said Charlie, on cue.

"And what do you do when you're bored, son?"

"Er—break a window in a haunted house?"

"Good grief, we got no haunted houses in Green Town, boy!"

"Used to be. Old Higley place. Torn down."

"See my *point*? Now what *else* do we do so's not to be bored?"

"Hold a massacre?"

"No massacres here in dogs' years. Lord, even our police chief's honest! Mayor—not corrupt! Madness. Whole town faced with stark staring ennuis and lulls! Last chance, Charlie, what do we *do*!"

"Build a mummy?" Charlie smiled.

"Bulldogs in the belfry! Watch my dust!"

The old man, cackling, grabbed bits of stuffed owl and bent lizard tail and old nicotine bandages left over from a skiing fall that had busted his ankle and broken a romance in 1895, and some patches from a 1922 Kissel Kar inner tube, and some burned-out sparklers from the last peaceful summer of 1913, and all of it weaving, shuttling together under his brittle insect-jumping fingers.

"*Voilà!* There, Charlie! Finished!"

"Oh, colonel." The boy stared and gasped. "Can I make him a crown?"

"Make him a crown, boy. Make him a crown."

✳ The sun was going down when the colonel and Charlie and their Egyptian friend came down the dusky backstairs of the old man's house, two of them walking iron-heavy, the third floating light as toasted cornflakes on the autumn air.

"Colonel," wondered Charlie. "What we going to do with this mummy, now we *got* him? It ain't as if he could talk much, or walk around—"

"No need, boy. Let folks talk, let folks run. Look there!"

They cracked the door and peered out at a town smothered in peace and ruined with nothing-to-do.

"Ain't enough, is it, son, you've recovered from your almost fatal seizure of Desperate Empties. Whole town out there is up to their earlobes in watchsprings, no hands on the clocks, afraid to get up every morning and find it's always and forever Sunday! Who'll offer salvation, boy?"

"Amon Bubastis Rameses Ra the Third, just arrived on the four o'clock limited?"

"God love you, boy, yes. What we got here is a giant seed. Seed's no good unless you do *what* with it?"

"Why," said Charlie, one eye shut. "Plant it?"

"Plant! Then watch it grow! Then what? Harvest time. Harvest! Come on, boy. Er—bring your friend."

The colonel crept out into the first nightfall.

The mummy came soon after, helped by Charlie.

✳ Labor Day at high noon, Osiris Bubastis Rameses Amon-Ra-Tut arrived from the Land of the Dead.

An autumn wind stirred the land and flapped doors wide not with the sound of the usual Labor Day Parade, seven tour cars, a fife-and-drum corps, and the mayor, but a mob that grew as it flowed the streets and fell in a tide to inundate the lawn out front of Colonel Stonesteel's house. The colonel and Charlie were sitting on the front porch, had been sitting there for some hours waiting for the conniption fits to arrive, the storming of the Bastille to occur. Now with dogs going mad and biting boys' ankles and boys dancing around the fringes of the mob, the colonel gazed down upon the Creation (his and Charlie's) and gave his secret smile.

"Well, Charlie . . . do I win my bet?"

"You sure do, colonel!"

"Come on."

Phones rang all across town and lunches burned on stoves, as the colonel strode forth to give the parade his papal blessings.

At the center of the mob was a horse-drawn wagon. On top of the wagon, his eyes wild with discovery, was Tom Tuppen, owner of a half-dead farm just beyond town. Tom was babbling, and the crowd was babbling, because in the back of the wagon was the special harvest delivered out of four thousand lost years of time.

"Well, flood the Nile and plant the Delta," gasped the colonel, eyes wide, staring. "Is or is not that a genuine old Egyptian mummy lying there in its original papyrus and coal-tar wrappings?"

"Sure is!" cried Charlie.

"Sure is!" yelled everyone.

"I was plowing the field this morning," said Tom Tuppen. "Plowing, just plowing! and—bang! Plow turned this right up, right *before* me! Like to had a stroke! Think! The Egyptians must've marched through Illinois three thousand years ago and no one knew! Revelations, I call it! Outa the way, kids! I'm taking this find to the post office lobby. Set it up on display! Giddap, now, git!"

The horse, the wagon, the mummy, the crowd, moved away, leaving the colonel behind, his eyes still pretend-wide, his mouth open.

"Hot dog," whispered the colonel, "we did it, Charles. This uproar, babble, talk and hysterical gossip will last for a thousand days or till Armageddon, whichever comes first!"

"Yes *sir*, colonel!"

"Michelangelo couldn't've done better. Boy David's a castaway-lost-and-forgotten wonder compared to our Egyptian surprise and—"

The colonel stopped as the mayor rushed by.

"Colonel, Charlie, howdy! Just phoned Chicago. News folks here tomorrow breakfast! Museum folks by lunch! Glory Hallelujah for the Green Town Chamber of Commerce!"

The mayor ran off after the mob.

An autumn cloud crossed the colonel's face and settled around his mouth.

"End of Act One, Charlie. Start thinking fast. Act Two coming up. We *do* want this commotion to last forever, don't we?"

"Yes, sir—"

"Crack your brain, boy. What does Uncle Wiggily say?"

"Uncle Wiggily says—ah—go *back* two hops?"

"Give the boy an A-plus, a gold star, and a brownie! The Lord giveth and the Lord taketh away, eh?"

Charlie looked into the old man's face and saw visitations of plagues there. "Yes, sir."

The colonel watched the mob milling around the post office two blocks away. The fife-and-drum corps arrived and played some tune vaguely inclined toward the Egyptian.

"Sundown, Charlie," whispered the colonel, eyes shut. "We make our final move."

✻ What a day it was! Years later people said: That was a day! The mayor went home and got dressed up and came back and made three speeches and held two parades, one going up Main Street toward the end of the trolley line, the other coming back, and Osiris Bubastis Rameses Amon-Ra-Tut at the center of both, smiling now to the right as gravity shifted his flimsy weight, and now to the left as they rounded a corner. The fife-and-drum corps, now heavily implemented by accumulated brass, had spent an hour drinking beer and learning the triumphal march from *Aïda* and this they played so many times that mothers took their screaming babies into the house, and men retired to bars to soothe their nerves. There was talk of a third parade and a fourth speech, but sunset took the town unawares, and everyone, including Charlie, went home to a dinner mostly talk and short on eats.

By eight o'clock, Charlie and the colonel were driving along the leafy streets in the fine darkness, taking the air in the old man's 1924 Moon, a car that took up trembling where the colonel left off.

"Where we going, colonel?"

"Well," mused the colonel, steering at ten philosophical miles per hour, nice and easy, "everyone, including your folks, is out at Grossett's Meadow right now, right? Final Labor Day speeches. Someone'll light the gasbag mayor and he'll go up about forty feet, kee-rect? Fire department'll be setting off the big skyrockets. Which means the post office, plus the mummy, plus the police chief sitting there with him, will be empty and vulnerable. Then, the miracle will happen, Charlie. It *has* to. Ask me why."

"Why?"

"Glad you asked. Well, boy, folks from Chicago'll be jumping off the train steps tomorrow hot and fresh as pancakes, with their pointy noses and glass eyes and microscopes. Those museum snoopers, plus the Associated Press, will rummage our Egyptian Pharaoh seven ways from Christmas and blow their fuse boxes. That being so, Charles—"

"We're on our way to mess around."

"You put it indelicately, boy, but truth is at the core. Look at it this way, child, life is a magic show, or *should* be if people didn't go to sleep on each other. Always leave folks with a bit of mystery, son. Now, before people get used to our ancient friend, before he wears out the wrong bath towel, like any smart weekend guest he should grab the next scheduled camel west. There!"

The post office stood silent, with one light shining in the foyer. Through the great window, they could see the sheriff seated alongside the mummy-on-display, neither of them talking, abandoned by the mobs that had gone for suppers and fireworks.

"Charlie." The colonel brought forth a brown bag in which a mysterious liquid gurgled. "Give me thirty-five minutes to mellow the sheriff down. Then you creep in, listen, follow my cues, and work the miracle. Here goes nothing!"

And the colonel stole away.

Beyond town, the mayor sat down and the fireworks went up.

Charlie stood on top of the Moon and watched them for half an hour. Then, figuring the mellowing time was over, dogtrotted across the street and moused himself into the post office to stand in the shadows.

"Well, now," the colonel was saying, seated between the Egyptian Pharaoh and the sheriff, "why don't you just finish that bottle, sir?"

"It's finished," said the sheriff, and obeyed.

The colonel leaned forward in the half-light and peered at the gold amulet on the mummy's breast.

"You believe them old sayings?"

"What old sayings?" asked the sheriff.

"If you read them hieroglyphics out loud, the mummy comes alive and walks."

"Horse radish," said the sheriff.

"Just look at all those fancy Egyptian symbols!" the colonel pursued.

"Someone stole my glasses. You read that stuff to me," said the sheriff. "Make the fool mummy walk."

Charlie took this as a signal to move, himself, and sidled around through the shadows, closer to the Egyptian king.

"Here goes." The colonel bent even closer to the Pharaoh's amulet, meanwhile slipping the sheriff's glasses out of his cupped hand into his side pocket. "First symbol on here is a hawk. Second one's a jackal. That third's an owl. Fourth's a yellow fox-eye—"

"Continue," said the sheriff.

The colonel did so, and his voice rose and fell, and the sheriff's head nodded, and all the Egyptian pictures and words flowed and touched around the mummy until at last the colonel gave a great gasp.

"Good grief, sheriff, look!"

The sheriff blinked both eyes wide.

"The mummy," said the colonel. "It's going for a walk!"

"Can't be!" cried the sheriff. "Can't be!"

"Is," said a voice, somewhere, maybe the Pharaoh under his breath.

And the mummy lifted up, suspended, and drifted toward the door.

"Why," cried the sheriff, tears in his eyes.

"I think he might just—*fly!*"

"I'd better follow and bring him back," said the colonel.

"Do that!" said the sheriff.

The mummy was gone. The colonel ran. The door slammed.

"Oh, dear." The sheriff lifted and shook the bottle. "Empty."

✳ They steamed to a halt out front of Charlie's house.

"Your folks ever go up in your attic, boy?"

"Too small. They poke me up to rummage."

"Good. Hoist our ancient Egyptian friend out of the back seat there, don't weigh much, twenty pounds at the most, you carried him fine, Charlie. Oh, that was a sight. You running out of the post office, making the mummy walk. You shoulda seen the sheriff's face!"

"I hope he don't get in trouble because of this."

"Oh, he'll bump his head and make up a fine story. Can't very well admit he saw the mummy go for a walk, can he? He'll think of something, organize a posse, you'll see. But right now, son, get our ancient friend here up, hide him good, visit him weekly. Feed him night talk. Then, thirty, forty years from now—"

"What?" asked Charlie.

"In a bad year so brimmed up with boredom it drips out your ears, when the town's long forgotten this first arrival and departure, on a morning, I say, when you lie in bed and don't want to get up, don't even want to twitch your ears or blink, you're so damned bored. . . . Well, on *that* morning, Charlie, you just climb up in your rummage-sale attic and shake this mummy out of bed, toss him in a cornfield and watch new hellfire mobs break loose. Life starts over that hour, that day, for you, the town, every-one. Now grab, git, and hide, boy!"

"I hate for the night to be over," said Charlie, very quietly. "Can't we go around a few blocks and finish off some lemonade on your porch? And have *him* come, too."

"Lemonade it is." Colonel Stonesteel banged his heel on the car-floor. The car exploded into life. "For the lost king and the Pharaoh's son!"

✳ It was late on Labor Day evening, and the two of them sat on the colo-nel's front porch again, rocking up a fair breeze, lemonades in hand, ice in mouth, sucking the sweet savor of the night's incredible adventures.

"Boy," said Charlie. "I can just see tomorrow's *Clarion* headlines: PRICE-LESS MUMMY KIDNAPPED. RAMESES-TUT VANISHES. GREAT FIND GONE. REWARD OFFERED. SHERIFF NONPLUSSED. BLACKMAIL EXPECTED."

"Talk on, boy. You *do* have a way with words."

"Learned from you, colonel. Now it's your turn."

"What do you want me to say, boy?"

"About the mummy. What he really is. What he's truly made of. Where he came from. What's he *mean* . . . ?"

"Why, boy, you were there, you helped, you *saw*—"

Charles looked at the old man steadily.

"No." A long breath. "Tell me, colonel."

The old man rose to stand in the shadows between the two rocking chairs. He reached out to touch their ancient harvest-tobacco dried-up-Nile-River-bottom old-time masterpiece, which leaned against the porch slattings.

The last Labor Day fireworks were dying in the sky. Their light died in the lapis lazuli eyes of the mummy, which watched Colonel Stonesteel, even as did the boy, waiting.

"You want to know who he *truly* was, once upon a time?"

The colonel gathered a handful of dust in his lungs and softly let it forth.

"He was everyone, no one, someone." A quiet pause. "You. Me."

"Go on," whispered Charlie.

Continue, said the mummy's eyes.

"He was, he is," murmured the colonel, "a bundle of old Sunday comic pages stashed in the attic to spontaneously combust from all those forgotten notions and stuffs. He's a stand of papyrus left in an autumn field long before Moses, a papier-mâché tumbleweed blown out of time, this way long-gone dusk, that way at come-again dawn . . . maybe a nightmare scrap of nicotine/dogtail flag up a pole at high noon, promising something, everything . . . a chart-map of Siam, Blue River Nile source, hot desert dust-devil, all the confetti of lost trolley transfers, dried-up yellow cross-country road maps petering off in sand dunes, journey aborted, wild jaunts yet to night-dream and commence. His body? . . . Mmmm . . . made of . . . all the crushed flowers from brand new weddings, dreadful old funerals, ticker-tapes unraveled from gone-off-forever parades to Far Rockaway, punched tickets for sleepless Egyptian Pharaoh midnight trains. Written promises, worthless stocks, crumpled deeds. Circus posters—see there? Part of his paper-wrapped ribcage? Posters torn off seedbarns in North Storm, Ohio, shuttled south toward Fulfillment, Texas, or Promised Land, Calif-orn-I-aye! Commencement proclamations, wedding notices, birth announcements . . . all things that were once need, hope, first nickel in the pocket, framed dollar on the café wall. Wallpaper scorched by the burning look, the blueprint etched there by the hot eyes of boys, girls, failed old men, time-orphaned women, saying: Tomorrow! Yes! *It* will happen! Tomorrow! Everything that died so many nights and was born again, glory human spirit, so many rare new daybreaks! All the dumb strange shadows you ever thought, boy, or I ever inked out inside my head at three A.M. All, crushed, stashed, and now shaped into one form under our hands and here in our gaze. That, that is what old King Pharaoh Seventh Dynasty Holy Dust Himself *is*."

"Wow," whispered Charlie.

The colonel sat back down to travel again in his rocker, eyes shut, smiling.

"Colonel." Charlie gazed off into the future. "What if, even in my old age, I don't ever *need* my own particular mummy?"

"Eh?"

"What if I have a life chock-full of things, never bored, find out what I want to do, do it, make every day count, every night swell, sleep tight, wake up yelling, laugh lots, grow old still running fast, what then, colonel?"

"Why then, boy, you'll be one of God's luckiest people!"

"For you see, colonel," Charlie looked at him with pure round, unblinking eyes, "I made up my mind. I'm going to be the greatest writer that ever lived."

The colonel braked his rocker and searched the innocent fire in that small face.

"Lord, I see it. Yes. You will! Well then, Charles, when you are very old, you must find some lad, not as lucky as you, to give Osiris-Ra to. Your life may be full, but others, lost on the road, will need our Egyptian friend. Agreed? Agreed."

The last fireworks were gone, the last fire balloons were sailing out among the gentle stars. Cars and people were driving or walking home, some fathers or mothers carrying their tired and already sleeping children. As the quiet parade passed Colonel Stonesteel's porch, some folks glanced in and waved at the old man and the boy and the tall dim-shadowed servant who stood between. The night was over forever. Charlie said:

"Say some more, colonel."

"No. I'm shut. Listen to what he has to say now. Let him tell your future, Charlie. Let him start you on stories. Ready . . . ?"

A wind came up and blew in the dry papyrus and sifted the ancient wrappings and trembled the curious hands and softly twitched the lips of their old/new four-thousand-year night-time visitor, whispering.

"What's he saying, Charles?"

Charlie shut his eyes, waited, listened, nodded, let a single tear slide down his cheek, and at last said:

"Everything. Just everything. Everything I always wanted to hear."

I SEE YOU NEVER

THE SOFT KNOCK CAME AT THE KITCHEN DOOR, and when Mrs. O'Brian opened it, there on the back porch were her best tenant, Mr. Ramirez, and two police officers, one on each side of him. Mr. Ramirez just stood there, walled in and small.

"Why, Mr. Ramirez!" said Mrs. O'Brian.

Mr. Ramirez was overcome. He did not seem to have words to explain.

He had arrived at Mrs. O'Brian's rooming house more than two years earlier and had lived there ever since. He had come by bus from Mexico City to San Diego and had then gone up to Los Angeles. There he had found the clean little room, with glossy blue linoleum, and pictures and calendars on the flowered walls, and Mrs. O'Brian as the strict but kindly landlady. During the war he had worked at the airplane factory and made parts for the planes that flew off somewhere, and even now, after the war, he still held his job. From the first he had made big money. He saved some of it, and he got drunk only once a week—a privilege that, to Mrs. O'Brian's way of thinking, every good workingman deserved, unquestioned and unreprimanded.

Inside Mrs. O'Brian's kitchen, pies were baking in the oven. Soon the pies would come out with complexions like Mr. Ramirez'—brown and shiny and crisp, with slits in them for the air almost like the slits of Mr. Ramirez' dark eyes. The kitchen smelled good. The policemen leaned forward, lured by the odor.

Mr. Ramirez gazed at his feet as if they had carried him into all this trouble.

"What happened, Mr. Ramirez?" asked Mrs. O'Brian.

Behind Mrs. O'Brian, as he lifted his eyes, Mr. Ramirez saw the long table laid with clean white linen and set with a platter, cool, shining glasses, a water pitcher with ice cubes floating inside it, a bowl of fresh potato salad and one of bananas and oranges, cubed and sugared. At this table sat Mrs. O'Brian's children—her three grown sons, eating and conversing, and her two younger daughters, who were staring at the policemen as they ate.

"I have been here thirty months," said Mr. Ramirez quietly, looking at Mrs. O'Brian's plump hands.

"That's six months too long," said one policeman. "He only had a temporary visa. We've just got around to looking for him."

Soon after Mr. Ramirez had arrived he bought a radio for his little room; evenings, he turned it up very loud and enjoyed it. And he had bought a wristwatch and enjoyed that too. And on many nights he had walked silent streets and seen the bright clothes in the windows and bought some of them, and he had seen the jewels and bought some of them for his few lady friends. And he had gone to picture shows five nights a week for a while. Then, also, he had ridden the streetcars—all night some nights—smelling the electricity, his dark eyes moving over the advertisements, feeling the wheels rumble under him, watching the little sleeping houses and big hotels slip by. Besides that, he had gone to large restaurants, where he had eaten many-course dinners, and to the opera and the theater. And he had bought a car, which later, when he forgot to pay for it, the dealer had driven off angrily from in front of the rooming house.

"So here I am," said Mr. Ramirez now, "to tell you I must give up my room, Mrs. O'Brian. I come to get my baggage and clothes and go with these men."

"Back to Mexico?"

"Yes. To Lagos. That is a little town north of Mexico City."

"I'm sorry, Mr. Ramirez."

"I'm packed," said Mr. Ramirez hoarsely, blinking his dark eyes rapidly and moving his hands helplessly before him. The policemen did not touch him. There was no necessity for that.

"Here is the key, Mrs. O'Brian," Mr. Ramirez said. "I have my bag already."

Mrs. O'Brian, for the first time, noticed a suitcase standing behind him on the porch.

Mr. Ramirez looked in again at the huge kitchen, at the bright silver cutlery and the young people eating and the shining waxed floor. He turned and looked for a long moment at the apartment house next door, rising up three stories, high and beautiful. He looked at the balconies and fire escapes and backporch stairs, at the lines of laundry snapping in the wind.

"You've been a good tenant," said Mrs. O'Brian.

"Thank you, thank you, Mrs. O'Brian," he said softly. He closed his eyes.

Mrs. O'Brian stood holding the door half open. One of her sons, behind her, said that her dinner was getting cold, but she shook her head at him and turned back to Mr. Ramirez. She remembered a visit she had once made to some Mexican border towns—the hot days, the endless crickets leaping and falling or lying dead and brittle like the small cigars in the shop windows, and the canals taking river water out to the farms, the dirt roads, the scorched scape. She remembered the silent towns, the warm beer, the hot, thick foods each day. She remembered the slow, dragging horses and the parched jack rabbits on the road. She remembered the iron mountains and the dusty valleys and the ocean beaches that spread hundreds of miles with no sound but the waves—no cars, no buildings, nothing.

"I'm sure sorry, Mr. Ramirez," she said.

"I don't want to go back, Mrs. O'Brian," he said weakly. "I like it here, I want to stay here. I've worked, I've got money. I look all right, don't I? And I don't want to go back!"

"I'm sorry, Mr. Ramirez," she said. "I wish there was something I could do."

"Mrs. O'Brian!" he cried suddenly, tears rolling out from under his eyelids. He reached out his hand and took her hand fervently, shaking it, wringing it, holding to it. "Mrs. O'Brian, I see you never, I see you never!"

The policemen smiled at this, but Mr. Ramirez did not notice it, and they stopped smiling very soon.

"Good-bye, Mrs. O'Brian. You have been good to me. Oh, good-bye, Mrs. O'Brian. I see you never!"

The policemen waited for Mr. Ramirez to turn, pick up his suitcase, and walk away. Then they followed him, tipping their caps to Mrs. O'Brian. She watched them go down the porch steps. Then she shut the door quietly and went slowly back to her chair at the table. She pulled the chair out and sat down. She picked up the shining knife and fork and started once more upon her steak.

"Hurry up, Mom," said one of the sons. "It'll be cold."

Mrs. O'Brian took one bite and chewed on it for a long, slow time; then she stared at the closed door. She laid down her knife and fork.

"What's wrong, Ma?" asked her son.

"I just realized," said Mrs. O'Brian—she put her hand to her face—"I'll never see Mr. Ramirez again."

THE EXILES

T HEIR EYES WERE FIRE AND THE BREATH flamed out the witches' mouths as they bent to probe the caldron with greasy stick and bony finger.

> *"When shall we three meet again*
> *In thunder, lightning, or in rain?"*

They danced drunkenly on the shore of an empty sea, fouling the air with their three tongues, and burning it with their cats' eyes malevolently aglitter:

> *"Round about the cauldron go,*
> *In the poison'd entrails throw. . . .*
> *Double, double, toil and trouble,*
> *Fire burn, and cauldron bubble!"*

They paused and cast a glance about. "Where's the crystal? Where's the needles?"

"Here!"

"Good!"

"Is the yellow wax thickened?"

"Yes!"

"Pour it in the iron mold!"

"Is the wax figure done?" They shaped it like molasses adrip on their green hands.

"Shove the needle through the heart!"

"The crystal, the crystal, fetch it from the tarot bag. Dust it off, have a look!"

They bent to the crystal, their faces white.

> *"See, see, see . . ."*

✳ A rocket ship moved through space from the planet Earth to the planet Mars. On the rocket ship men were dying.

The captain raised his head, tiredly. "We'll have to use the morphine."

"But, Captain—"

"You see yourself this man's condition." The captain lifted the wool blanket and the man restrained beneath the wet sheet moved and groaned. The air was full of sulfurous thunder.

"I saw it—I saw it." The man opened his eyes and stared at the port where there were only black spaces, reeling stars, Earth far removed, and the planet Mars rising large and red. "I saw it—a bat, a huge thing, a bat with a man's face, spread over the front port. Fluttering and fluttering, fluttering and fluttering."

"Pulse?" asked the captain.

The orderly measured it. "One hundred and thirty."

"He can't go on with that. Use the morphine. Come along, Smith."

They moved away. Suddenly the floor plates were laced with bone and white skulls that screamed. The captain did not dare look down, and over the screaming he said, "Is this where Perse is?" turning in at a hatch.

A white-smocked surgeon stepped away from a body. "I just don't understand it."

"How did Perse die?"

"We don't know, Captain. It wasn't his heart, his brain, or shock. He just—died."

The captain felt the doctor's wrist, which changed to a hissing snake and bit him. The captain did not flinch. "Take care of yourself. You've a pulse too."

The doctor nodded. "Perse complained of pains—needles, he said—in his wrists and legs. Said he felt like wax, melting. He fell. I helped him up. He cried like a child. Said he had a silver needle in his heart. He died. Here he is. We can repeat the autopsy for you. Everything's physically normal."

"That's impossible! He died of *something*?"

The captain walked to a port. He smelled of menthol and iodine and green soap on his polished and manicured hands. His white teeth were dentrified, and his ears scoured to a pinkness, as were his cheeks. His uniform was the color of new salt, and his boots were black mirrors shining below him. His crisp crew-cut hair smelled of sharp alcohol. Even his breath was sharp and new and clean. There was no spot to him. He was a fresh instrument, honed and ready, still hot from the surgeon's oven.

The men with him were from the same mold. One expected huge brass keys spiraling slowly from their backs. They were expensive, talented, well-oiled toys, obedient and quick.

The captain watched the planet Mars grow very large in space.

"We'll be landing in an hour on that damned place, Smith, did you see any bats, or have other nightmares?"

"Yes, sir. The month before our rocket took off from New York, sir. White rats biting my neck, drinking my blood. I didn't tell. I was afraid you wouldn't let me come on this trip."

"Never mind," sighed the captain. "I had dreams too. In all of my fifty years I never had a dream until that week before we took off from Earth. And then every night I dreamed I was a white wolf. Caught on a snowy hill. Shot with a silver bullet. Buried with a stake in my heart." He moved his head toward Mars. "Do you think, Smith, *they* know we're coming?"

"We don't know if there *are* Martian people, sir."

"Don't we? They began frightening us off eight weeks ago, before we started. They've killed Perse and Reynolds now. Yesterday they made Grenville go blind. How? I don't know. Bats, needles, dreams, men dying for no reason. I'd call it witchcraft in another day. But this is the year 2120, Smith. We're rational men. This all can't be happening. But it is! Whoever they are, with their needles and their bats, they'll try to finish us all." He swung about. "Smith, fetch those books from my file. I want them when we land."

Two hundred books were piled on the rocket desk.

"Thank you, Smith. Have you glanced at them? Think I'm insane? Perhaps. It's a crazy hunch. At that last moment I ordered these books from the Historical Museum. Because of my dreams. Twenty nights I was stabbed, butchered, a screaming bat pinned to a surgical mat, a thing rotting underground in a black box; bad, wicked dreams. Our whole crew dreamed of witch-things and were-things, vampires and phantoms, things they *couldn't* know anything about. Why? Because books on such ghastly subjects were destroyed a century ago. By law. Forbidden for anyone to own the grisly volumes. These books you see here are the *last* copies, kept for historical purposes in the locked museum vaults."

Smith bent to read the dusty titles:

"*Tales of Mystery and Imagination*, by Edgar Allan Poe. *Dracula*, by Bram Stoker. *Frankenstein*, by Mary Shelley. *The Turn of the Screw*, by Henry James.

The Legend of Sleepy Hollow, by Washington Irving. *Rappaccini's Daughter*, by Nathaniel Hawthorne. *An Occurrence at Owl Creek Bridge*, by Ambrose Bierce. *Alice in Wonderland*, by Lewis Carroll. *The Willows*, by Algernon Blackwood. *The Wizard of Oz*, by L. Frank Baum. *The Weird Shadow Over Innsmouth*, by H. P. Lovecraft. And more! Books by Walter de la Mare, Wakefield, Harvey, Wells, Asquith, Huxley—all forbidden authors. All burned in the same year that Halloween was outlawed and Christmas was banned! But, sir, what good are these to us on the rocket?"

"I don't know," sighed the captain, "yet."

✳ The three hags lifted the crystal where the captain's image flickered, his tiny voice tinkling out of the glass:

"I don't know," sighed the captain, "yet."

The three witches glared redly into one another's faces.

"We haven't much time," said one.

"Better warn *Them* in the City."

"They'll want to know about the books. It doesn't look good. That fool of a captain!"

"In an hour they'll land their rocket."

The three hags shuddered and blinked up at the Emerald City by the edge of the dry Martian sea. In its highest window a small man held a blood-red drape aside. He watched the wastelands where the three witches fed their caldron and shaped the waxes. Farther along, ten thousand other blue fires and laurel incenses, black tobacco smokes and fir weeds, cinnamons and bone dusts rose soft as moths through the Martian night. The man counted the angry, magical fires. Then, as the three witches stared, he turned. The crimson drape, released, fell, causing the distant portal to wink, like a yellow eye.

✳ Mr. Edgar Allan Poe stood in the tower window, a faint vapor of spirits upon his breath. "Hecate's friends are busy tonight," he said, seeing the witches, far below.

A voice behind him said, "I saw Will Shakespeare at the shore, earlier, whipping them on. All along the sea Shakespeare's army alone, tonight, numbers thousands: the three witches, Oberon, Hamlet's father, Puck—all, all of them—thousands! Good lord, a regular sea of people."

"Good William." Poe turned. He let the crimson drape fall shut. He stood for a moment to observe the raw stone room, the black-timbered table, the candle flame, the other man, Mr. Ambrose Bierce, sitting very idly there, lighting matches and watching them burn down, whistling under his breath, now and then laughing to himself.

"We'll have to tell Mr. Dickens now," said Mr. Poe. "We've put it off too long. It's a matter of hours. Will you go down to his home with me, Bierce?"

Bierce glanced up merrily. "I've just been thinking—what'll happen to us?"

"If we can't kill the rocket men off, frighten them away, then we'll have to leave, of course. We'll go on to Jupiter, and when they come to Jupiter, we'll go on to Saturn, and when they come to Saturn, we'll go to Uranus, or Neptune, and then on out to Pluto—"

"Where then?"

Mr. Poe's face was weary; there were fire coals remaining, fading, in his eyes, and a sad wildness in the way he talked, and a uselessness of his hands and the way his hair fell lankly over his amazing white brow. He was like a satan of some lost dark cause, a general arrived from a derelict invasion. His silky, soft, black mustache was worn away by his musing lips. He was so small his brow seemed to float, vast and phosphorescent, by itself, in the dark room.

"We have the advantages of superior forms of travel," he said. "We can always hope for one of their atomic wars, dissolution, the dark ages come again. The return of superstition. We could go back then to Earth, all of us, in one night." Mr. Poe's black eyes brooded under his round and luminant brow. He gazed at the ceiling. "So they're coming to ruin *this* world too? They won't leave *anything* undefiled, will they?"

"Does a wolf pack stop until it's killed its prey and eaten the guts? It should be quite a war. I shall sit on the sidelines and be the scorekeeper. So many Earthmen boiled in oil, so many Mss. Found in Bottles burned, so many Earthmen stabbed with needles, so many Red Deaths put to flight by a batter of hypodermic syringes—ha!"

Poe swayed angrily, faintly drunk with wine. "What did we do? Be with us, Bierce, in the name of God! Did we have a fair trial before a company of literary critics? No! Our books were plucked up by neat, sterile, surgeon's pliers, and flung into vats, to boil, to be killed of all their mortuary germs. Damn them all!"

"I find our situation amusing," said Bierce.

They were interrupted by a hysterical shout from the tower stair.

"Mr. Poe! Mr. Bierce!"

"Yes, yes, we're coming!" Poe and Bierce descended to find a man gasping against the stone passage wall.

"Have you heard the news?" he cried immediately, clawing at them like a man about to fall over a cliff. "In an hour they'll land! They're bringing books with them—*old* books, the witches said! What're you doing in the tower at a time like this? Why aren't you acting?"

Poe said: "We're doing everything we can, Blackwood. You're new to all this. Come along, we're going to Mr. Charles Dickens' place—"

"—to contemplate our doom, our black doom," said Bierce, with a wink.

✳ They moved down the echoing throats of the castle, level after dim green level, down into mustiness and decay and spiders and dreamlike webbing. "Don't worry," said Poe, his brow like a huge white lamp before them, descending, sinking. "All along the dead sea tonight I've called the others. Your friends and mine, Blackwood—Bierce. They're all there. The animals and the old women and the tall men with the sharp white teeth. The traps are waiting; the pits, yes, and the pendulums. The Red Death." Here he laughed quietly. "Yes, even the Red Death. I never thought—no, I never thought the time would come when a thing like the Red Death would actually *be*. But *they* asked for it, and they shall have it!"

"But are we strong enough?" wondered Blackwood.

"How strong is strong? They won't be prepared for us, at least. They haven't the imagination. Those clean young rocket men with their antiseptic bloomers and fish-bowl helmets, with their new religion. About their necks, on gold chains, scalpels. Upon their heads, a diadem of microscopes. In their holy fingers, steaming incense urns which in reality are only germicidal ovens for steaming out superstition. The names of Poe, Bierce, Hawthorne, Blackwood—blasphemy to their clean lips."

Outside the castle they advanced through a watery space, a tarn that was not a tarn, which misted before them like the stuff of nightmares. The air filled with wing sounds and a whirring, a motion of winds and blacknesses. Voices changed, figures swayed at campfires. Mr. Poe watched the needles knitting, knitting, knitting, in the firelight; knitting pain and misery, knitting wickedness into wax marionettes, clay puppets. The caldron smells of wild garlic and cayenne and saffron hissed up to fill the night with evil pungency.

"Get on with it!" said Poe. "I'll be back!"

All down the empty seashore black figures spindled and waned, grew up and blew into black smoke on the sky. Bells rang in mountain towers and licorice ravens spilled out with the bronze sounds and spun away to ashes.

✳ Over a lonely moor and into a small valley Poe and Bierce hurried, and found themselves quite suddenly on a cobbled street, in cold, bleak, biting weather, with people stomping up and down stony courtyards to warm their feet; foggy withal, and candles flaring in the windows of offices and shops where hung the Yuletide turkeys. At a distance some boys, all bundled up, snorting their pale breaths on the wintry air, were trilling, "God Rest Ye Merry, Gentlemen," while the immense tones of a great clock continuously sounded midnight. Children dashed by from the baker's with dinners all asteam in their grubby fists, on trays and under silver bowls.

At a sign which read SCROOGE, MARLEY AND DICKENS Poe gave the Marley-faced knocker a rap, and from within, as the door popped open a few inches, a sudden gust of music almost swept them into a dance. And there, beyond the shoulder of the man who was sticking a trim goatee and mustaches at them, was Mr. Fezziwig clapping his hands, and Mrs. Fezziwig, one vast substantial smile, dancing and colliding with other merrymakers, while the fiddle chirped and laughter ran about a table like chandelier crystals given a sudden push of wind. The large table was heaped with brawn and turkey and holly and geese; with mince pies, suckling pigs, wreaths of sausages, oranges and apples; and there was Bob Cratchit and Little Dorrit and Tiny Tim and Mr. Fagin himself, and a man who looked as if he might be an undigested bit of beef, a blot of mustard, a crumb of cheese, a fragment of an underdone potato—who else but Mr. Marley, chains and all, while the wine poured and the brown turkeys did their excellent best to steam!

"What do you want?" demanded Mr. Charles Dickens.

"We've come to plead with you again, Charles; we need your help," said Poe.

"Help? Do you think I would help you fight against those good men coming in the rocket? I don't belong here, anyway. My books were burned by mistake. I'm no supernaturalist, no writer of horrors and terrors like you, Poe; you, Bierce, or the others. I'll have nothing to do with you terrible people!"

"You are a persuasive talker," reasoned Poe. "You could go to meet the rocket men, lull them, lull their suspicions and then—then we would take care of them."

Mr. Dickens eyed the folds of the black cape which hid Poe's hands. From it, smiling, Poe drew forth a black cat. "For *one* of our visitors."

"And for the others?"

Poe smiled again, well pleased. "The Premature Burial?"

"You are a grim man, Mr. Poe."

"I am a frightened and an angry man. I am a god, Mr. Dickens, even as you are a god, even as we all are gods, and our inventions—our people, if you wish—have not only been threatened, but banished and burned, torn up and censored, ruined and done away with. The worlds we created are falling into ruin. Even gods must fight!"

"So?" Mr. Dickens tilted his head, impatient to return to the party, the music, the food. "Perhaps you can explain why we are here? How did we come here?"

"War begets war. Destruction begets destruction. On Earth, a century ago, in the year 2020 they outlawed our books. Oh, what a horrible thing—to destroy our literary creations that way! It summoned us out of—what? Death? The Beyond? I don't like abstract things. I don't know. I only know that our worlds and our creations called us and we tried to save them, and the only saving thing we could do was wait out the century here on Mars, hoping Earth might overweight itself with these scientists and their doubtings; but now they're coming to clean us out of here, us and our dark things, and all the alchemists, witches, vampires, and were-things that, one by one, retreated across space as science made inroads through every country on Earth and finally left no alternative at all but exodus. You must help us. You have a good speaking manner. We need you."

"I repeat, I am not of you, I don't approve of you and the others," cried Dickens angrily. "I was no player with witches and vampires and midnight things."

"What of *A Christmas Carol*?"

"Ridiculous! *One* story. Oh, I wrote a few others about ghosts, perhaps, but what of that? My basic works had none of that nonsense!"

"Mistaken or not, they grouped you with us. They destroyed your books—your worlds too. You must hate them, Mr. Dickens!"

"I admit they are stupid and rude, but that is all. Good day!"

"Let Mr. Marley come, at least!"

"*No!*"

The door slammed. As Poe turned away, down the street, skimming over the frosty ground, the coachman playing a lively air on a bugle, came a great coach, out of which, cherry-red, laughing and singing, piled the Pick-wickians, banging on the door, shouting Merry Christmas good and loud, when the door was opened by the fat boy.

＊ Mr. Poe hurried along the midnight shore of the dry sea. By fires and smoke he hesitated, to shout orders, to check the bubbling caldrons, the poisons and the chalked pentagrams. "Good!" he said, and ran on. "Fine!" he shouted, and ran again. People joined him and ran with him. Here were Mr. Coppard and Mr. Machen running with him now. And there were hating serpents and angry demons and fiery bronze dragons and spitting vipers and trembling witches like the barbs and nettles and thorns and all the vile flotsam and jetsam of the retreating sea of imagination, left on the melancholy shore, whining and frothing and spitting.

Mr. Machen stopped. He sat like a child on the cold sand. He began to sob. They tried to soothe him, but he would not listen. "I just thought," he said. "What happens to us on the day when the *last* copies of our books are destroyed?"

The air whirled.

"Don't speak of it!"

"We must," wailed Mr. Machen. "Now, now, as the rocket comes down, you, Mr. Poe; you, Coppard; you, Bierce—all of you grow faint. Like wood smoke. Blowing away. Your faces melt—"

"Death! *Real* death for all of us."

"We exist only through Earth's sufferance. If a final edict tonight destroyed our last few works we'd be like lights put out."

Coppard brooded gently. "I wonder who I am. In what Earth mind to-night do I exist? In some African hut? Some hermit, reading my tales? Is he the lonely candle in the wind of time and science? The flickering orb sustaining me here in rebellious exile? Is it him? Or some boy in a dis-carded attic, finding me, only just in time! Oh, last night I felt ill, ill, ill to the marrows of me, for there is a body of the soul as well as a body of the body, and this soul body ached in all of its glowing parts, and last night I felt myself a candle, guttering. When suddenly I sprang up, given new light! As some child, sneezing with dust, in some yellow garret on Earth once more found a worn, time-specked copy of me! And so I'm given a short respite!"

A door banged wide in a little hut by the shore. A thin short man, with flesh hanging from him in folds, stepped out and, paying no attention to the others, sat down and stared into his clenched fists.

"There's the one I'm sorry for," whispered Blackwood. "Look at him, dying away. He was once more real than we, who were men. They took him, a skeleton thought, and clothed him in centuries of pink flesh and snow beard and red velvet suit and black boot; made him reindeers, tinsel, holly. And after centuries of manufacturing him they drowned him in a vat of Lysol, you might say."

The men were silent.

"What must it be on Earth?" wondered Poe. "Without Christmas? No hot chestnuts, no tree, no ornaments or drums or candles—nothing; nothing but the snow and wind and the lonely, factual people. . . ."

They all looked at the thin little old man with the scraggly beard and faded red velvet suit.

"Have you heard his story?"

"I can imagine it. The glitter-eyed psychiatrist, the clever sociologist, the resentful, froth-mouthed educationalist, the antiseptic parents—"

"A regrettable situation," said Bierce, smiling, "for the Yuletide merchants who, toward the last there, as I recall, were beginning to put up holly and sing Noel the day before Halloween. With any luck at all this year they might have started on Labor Day!"

Bierce did not continue. He fell forward with a sigh. As he lay upon the ground he had time to say only, "How interesting." And then, as they all watched, horrified, his body burned into blue dust and charred bone, the ashes of which fled through the air in black tatters.

"Bierce, Bierce!"

"Gone!"

"His last book gone. Someone on Earth just now burned it."

"God rest him. Nothing of him left now. For what are we but books, and when those are gone, nothing's to be seen."

A rushing sound filled the sky.

They cried out, terrified, and looked up. In the sky, dazzling it with sizzling fire clouds, was the rocket! Around the men on the seashore lanterns bobbed; there was a squealing and a bubbling and an odor of cooked spells. Candle-eyed pumpkins lifted into the cold clear air. Thin fingers clenched into fists and a witch screamed from her withered mouth:

> "Ship, ship, break, fall!
> Ship, ship, burn all!

Crack, flake, shake, melt!
Mummy dust, cat pelt!"

"Time to go," murmured Blackwood. "On to Jupiter, on to Saturn or Pluto."

"Run away?" shouted Poe in the wind. "Never!"

"I'm a tired old man!"

Poe gazed into the old man's face and believed him. He climbed atop a huge boulder and faced the ten thousand gray shadows and green lights and yellow eyes on the hissing wind.

"The powders!" he shouted.

A thick hot smell of bitter almond, civet, cumin, wormseed and orris!

The rocket came down—steadily down, with the shriek of a damned spirit! Poe raged at it! He flung his fists up and the orchestra of heat and smell and hatred answered in symphony! Like stripped tree fragments, bats flew upward! Burning hearts, flung like missiles, burst in bloody fireworks on the singed air. Down, down, relentlessly down, like a pendulum the rocket came. And Poe howled, furiously, and shrank back with every sweep and sweep of the rocket cutting and ravening the air! All the dead sea seemed a pit in which, trapped, they waited the sinking of the dread machinery, the glistening ax; they were people under the avalanche!

"The snakes!" screamed Poe.

And luminous serpentines of undulant green hurtled toward the rocket. But it came down, a sweep, a fire, a motion, and it lay panting out exhaustions of red plumage on the sand, a mile away.

"At it!" shrieked Poe. "The plan's changed! Only one chance! Run! At it! At it! Drown them with our bodies! Kill them!"

And as if he had commanded a violent sea to change its course, to suck itself free from primeval beds, the whirls and savage gouts of fire spread and ran like wind and rain and stark lightning over the sea sands, down empty river deltas, shadowing and screaming, whistling and whining, sputtering and coalescing toward the rocket which, extinguished, lay like a clean metal torch in the farthest hollow. As if a great charred caldron of sparkling lava had been overturned, the boiling people and snapping animals churned down the dry fathoms.

"Kill them!" screamed Poe, running.

✳ The rocket men leaped out of their ship, guns ready. They stalked about, sniffing the air like hounds. They saw nothing. They relaxed.

The captain stepped forth last. He gave sharp commands. Wood was gathered, kindled, and a fire leaped up in an instant. The captain beckoned his men into a half circle about him.

"A new world," he said, forcing himself to speak deliberately, though he glanced nervously, now and again, over his shoulder at the empty sea. "The old world left behind. A new start. What more symbolic than that we here dedicate ourselves all the more firmly to science and progress." He nodded crisply to his lieutenant. "The books."

Firelight limned the faded gilt titles: *The Willows, The Outsider, Behold, The Dreamer, Dr. Jekyll and Mr. Hyde, The Land of Oz, Pellucidar, The Land That Time Forgot, A Midsummer Night's Dream,* and the monstrous names of Machen and Edgar Allan Poe, and Cabell and Dunsany and Blackwood and Lewis Carroll; the names, the old names, the evil names.

"A new world. With a gesture, we burn the last of the old."

The captain ripped pages from the books. Leaf by seared leaf, he fed them into the fire.

A scream!

Leaping back, the men stared beyond the firelight at the edges of the encroaching and uninhabited sea.

Another scream! A high and wailing thing, like the death of a dragon and the thrashing of a bronzed whale left gasping when the waters of a leviathan's sea drain down the shingles and evaporate.

It was the sound of air rushing in to fill a vacuum, where, a moment before, there had been *something!*

The captain neatly disposed of the last book by putting it into the fire.

The air stopped quivering.

Silence!

The rocket men leaned and listened.

"Captain, did you hear it?"

"No."

"Like a wave, sir. On the sea bottom! I thought I saw something. Over there. A black wave. Big. Running at us."

"You were mistaken."

"There, sir!"

"What?"

"See it? There! The city! Way over! That green city near the lake! It's splitting in half. It's falling!"

The men squinted and shuffled forward.

Smith stood trembling among them. He put his hand to his head as if to find a thought there. "I remember. Yes, now I do. A long time back. When I was a child. A book I read. A story. Oz, I think it was. Yes, Oz, *The Emerald City of Oz . . .*"

"Oz? Never heard of it."

"Yes, Oz, that's what it was. I saw it just now, like in the story. I saw it fall."

"Smith!"

"Yes, sir?"

"Report for psychoanalysis tomorrow."

"Yes, sir!" A brisk salute.

"Be careful."

Then men tiptoed, guns alert, beyond the ship's aseptic light to gaze at the long sea and the low hills.

"Why," whispered Smith, disappointed, "there's no one here at all, is there? No one here at all."

The wind blew sand over his shoes, whining.

AT MIDNIGHT,
IN THE MONTH OF JUNE

HE HAD BEEN WAITING A LONG, LONG TIME in the summer night, as the darkness pressed warmer to the earth and the stars turned slowly over the sky. He sat in total darkness, his hands lying easily on the arms of the Morris chair. He heard the town clock strike nine and ten and eleven, and then at last twelve. The breeze from an open back window flowed through the midnight house in an unlit stream, that touched him like a dark rock where he sat silently watching the front door—silently watching.

At midnight, in the month of June. . . .

The cool night poem by Mr. Edgar Allan Poe slid over his mind like the waters of a shadowed creek.

The lady sleeps! Oh, may her sleep,
Which is enduring, so be deep!

He moved down the black shapeless halls of the house, stepped out of the back window, feeling the town locked away in bed, in dream, in night. He saw the shining snake of garden hose coiled resiliently in the grass. He turned on the water. Standing alone, watering the flower bed, he imagined himself a conductor leading an orchestra that only night-strolling dogs might hear, passing on their way to nowhere with strange white smiles. Very carefully he planted both feet and his tall weight into the mud beneath the window, making deep, well-outlined prints. He stepped inside again and walked, leaving mud, down the absolutely unseen hall, his hands seeing for him.

Through the front porch window he made out the faint outline of a lemonade glass, one-third full, sitting on the porch rail where *she* had left it. He trembled quietly.

Now, he could feel her coming home. He could feel her moving across town, far away, in the summer night. He shut his eyes and put his mind out to find her; and felt her moving along in the dark; he knew just where she stepped down from a curb and crossed a street, and up on a kerb and tack-tacking, tack-tacking along under the June elms and the last of the lilacs, with a friend. Walking the empty desert of night, he *was* she. He felt a purse in his hands. He felt long hair prickle his neck, and his mouth turn greasy with lipstick. Sitting still, he was walking, walking, walking on home after midnight.

"Good night!"

He heard but did not hear the voices, and she was coming nearer, and now she was only a mile away and now only a matter of a thousand yards, and now she was sinking, like a beautiful white lantern on an invisible wire, down into the cricket- and frog- and water-sounding ravine. And he knew the texture of the wooden ravine stairs as if, a boy, he was rushing down them, feeling the rough grain and the dust and the leftover heat of the day. . . .

He put his hands out on the air, open. The thumbs of his hands touched, and then the fingers, so that his hands made a circle, enclosing emptiness, there before him. Then, very slowly, he squeezed his hands tighter and tighter together, his mouth open, his eyes shut.

He stopped squeezing and put his hands, trembling, back on the arms of the chair. He kept his eyes shut.

Long ago, he had climbed, one night, to the top of the courthouse tower fire escape, and looked out at the silver town, at the town of the moon, and the town of summer. And he had seen all the dark houses with two things in them, people and sleep, the two elements joined in bed and all their tiredness and terror breathed upon the still air, siphoned back quietly, and breathed out again, until that element was purified, the problems and hatreds and horrors of the previous day exorcized long before morning and done away with forever.

He had been enchanted with the hour, and the town, and he had felt very powerful, like the magic man with the marionettes who strung destinies across a stage on spider threads. On the very top of the courthouse tower he could see the least flicker of leaf turning in the moonlight five miles away; the last light, like a pink pumpkin eye, wink out. The town did not escape his eye—it could do nothing without his knowing its every tremble and gesture.

And so it was tonight. He felt himself a tower with the clock in it pounding slow and announcing hours in a great bronze tone, and gazing upon a town where a woman, hurried or slowed by fitful gusts and breezes now of terror and now of self-confidence, took the chalk white midnight sidewalks home, fording solid avenues of tar and stone, drifting among fresh cut lawns, and now running, running down the steps, through the ravine, up, up the hill, up the hill!

He heard her footsteps before he really heard them. He heard her gasping before there was a gasping. He fixed his gaze to the lemonade glass outside, on the banister. Then the real sound, the real running, the gasping, echoed wildly outside. He sat up. The footsteps raced across the street, the pavement, in a panic. There was a babble, a clumsy stumble up the porch steps, a key ratcheting the door, a voice yelling in a whisper, praying to itself. "Oh, God, dear God!" Whisper! Whisper! And the woman crashing in the door, slamming it, bolting it, talking, whispering, talking to herself in the dark room.

He felt, rather than saw, her hand move toward the light switch.

He cleared his throat.

She stood against the door in the dark. If moonlight could have struck in upon her, she would have shimmered like a small pool of water on a windy night. He felt the fine sapphire jewels come out upon her face, and her face all glittering with brine.

"Lavinia," he whispered.

Her arms were raised across the door like a crucifix. He heard her mouth open and her lungs push a warmness upon the air. She was a beautiful dim white moth; with the sharp needle point of terror he had her pinned against the wooden door. He could walk all around the specimen, if he wished, and look at her, look at her.

"Lavinia," he whispered.

He heard her heartbeating. She did not move.

"It's me," he whispered.

"Who?" she said, so faint it was a small pulse-beat in her throat.

"I won't tell you," he whispered. He stood perfectly straight in the center of the room. God, but he felt *tall*! Tall and dark and very beautiful to himself, and the way his hands were out before him was as if he might play a piano at any moment, a lovely melody, a waltzing tune. The hands were wet, they felt as if he had dipped them into a bed of mint and cool menthol.

"If I told you who I am, you might not be afraid," he whispered. "I want you to be afraid. Are you afraid?"

She said nothing. She breathed out and in, out and in, a small bellows which, pumped steadily, blew upon her fear and kept it going, kept it alight.

"Why did you go to the show tonight?" he whispered. "*Why* did you go to the show?"

No answer.

He took a step forward, heard her breath take itself, like a sword hissing in its sheath.

"Why did you come back through the ravine, alone?" he whispered. "You *did* come back alone, didn't you? Did you think you'd meet me in the middle of the bridge? Why did you go to the show tonight? Why did you come back through the ravine, alone?"

"I—" she gasped.

"You," he whispered.

"No—" she cried, in a whisper.

"Lavinia," he said. He took another step.

"Please," she said.

"Open the door. Get out. And run," he whispered.

She did not move.

"Lavinia, open the door."

She began to whimper in her throat.

"Run," he said.

In moving he felt something touch his knee. He pushed, something tilted in space and fell over, a table, a basket, and a half-dozen unseen balls of yarn tumbled like cats in the dark, rolling softly. In the one moonlit space on the floor beneath the window, like a metal sign pointing, lay the sewing shears. They were winter ice in his hand. He held them out to her suddenly, through the still air.

"Here," he whispered.

He touched them to her hand. She snatched her hand back.

"Here," he urged.

"Take this," he said, after a pause.

He opened her fingers that were already dead and cold to the touch, and stiff and strange to manage, and he pressed the scissors into them. "Now," he said.

He looked out at the moonlit sky for a long moment, and when he glanced back it was some time before he could see her in the dark.

"I waited," he said. "But that's the way it's always been. I waited for the others, too. But they all came looking for me, finally. It was that easy. Five lovely ladies in the last two years. I waited for them in the ravine, in the country, by the lake, everywhere I waited, and they came out to find me, and found me. It was always nice, the next day, reading the newspapers. And you went looking tonight, I know, or you wouldn't have come back alone through the ravine. Did you scare yourself there, and run? Did you think I was down there waiting for you? You should have *heard* yourself running up the walk! Through the door! And *locking* it! You thought you were safe inside, home at last, safe, safe, safe, didn't you?"

She held the scissors in one dead hand, and she began to cry. He saw the merest gleam, like water upon the wall of a dim cave. He heard the sounds she made.

"No," he whispered. "You have the scissors. Don't cry."

She cried. She did not move at all. She stood there, shivering, her head back against the door, beginning to slide down the length of the door toward the floor.

"Don't cry," he whispered.

"I don't like to hear you cry," he said. "I can't stand to hear that."

He held his hands out and moved them through the air until one of them touched her cheek. He felt the wetness of that cheek, he felt her warm breath touch his palm like a summer moth. Then he said only one more thing:

"Lavinia," he said, gently. "Lavinia."

✳ How clearly he remembered the old nights in the old times, in the times when he was a boy and them all running and running, and hiding and hiding, and playing hide-and-seek. In the first spring nights and in the warm summer nights and in the late summer evenings and in those first sharp autumn nights when doors were shutting early and porches were empty except for blowing leaves. The game of hide-and-seek went on as long as there was sun to see by, or the rising snow-crusted moon. Their feet upon the green lawns were like the scattered throwing of soft peaches and crab apples, and the counting of the Seeker with his arms cradling his buried head, chanting to the night: five, ten, fifteen, twenty, twenty-five, thirty, thirty-five, forty, forty-five, fifty. . . . And the sound of thrown apples fading, the children all safely closeted in tree or bush shade, under the latticed porches with the clever dogs minding not to wag their tails and give their secret away. And the counting done: eighty-five, ninety, ninety-five, a hundred!

Ready or not, here I come!

And the Seeker running out through the town wilderness to find the Hiders, and the Hiders keeping their secret laughter in their mouths, like precious June strawberries, with the help of clasped hands. And the Seeker seeking after the smallest heartbeat in the high elm tree or the glint of a dog's eye in a bush, or a small water sound of laughter that could not help burst out as the Seeker ran right on by and did not see the shadow within the shadow. . . .

He moved into the bathroom of the quiet house, thinking all this, enjoying the clear rush, the tumultuous gushing of memories like a waterfalling of the mind over a steep precipice, falling and falling toward the bottom of his head.

God, how secret and tall they had felt, hidden away. God, how the shadows mothered and kept them, sheathed in their own triumph. Glowing with perspiration how they crouched like idols and thought they might hide *forever*! While the silly Seeker went pelting by on his way to failure and inevitable frustration.

Sometimes the Seeker stopped right *at* your tree and peered up at you crouched there in your invisible warm wings, in your great colorless windowpane bat wings, and said, "I *see* you there!" But you said nothing. "You're *up* there all right." But you said nothing. "Come on *down*!" But not a word, only a victorious Cheshire smile. And doubt coming over the Seeker below. "It is *you*, isn't it?" The backing off and away. "Aw, I *know* you're up there!" No answer. Only the tree sitting in the night and shaking quietly, leaf upon leaf. And the Seeker, afraid of the dark within darkness, loping away to seek easier game, something to be named and certain of. "All right for you!"

He washed his hands in the bathroom, and thought, Why am I washing my hands? And then the grains of time sucked back up the flue of the hour-glass again and it was another year . . .

He remembered that sometimes when he played hide-and-seek they did not find him at all; he would not let them find him. He said not a word, he stayed so long in the apple tree that he was a white-fleshed apple; he lingered so long in the chestnut tree that he had the hardness and the brown brightness of the autumn nut. And God, how powerful to be undiscovered, how immense it made you, until your arms were branching, growing out in all directions, pulled by the stars and the tidal moon until your secretness enclosed the town and mothered it with your compassion and tolerance. You could do anything in the shadows, anything. If you chose to do it, you could do it. How powerful to sit above the sidewalk and see people pass under, never aware you were there and watching, and might put out an arm to brush their noses with the five-legged spider of your hand and brush their thinking minds with terror.

He finished washing his hands and wiped them on a towel.

But there was always an end to the game. When the Seeker had found all the other Hiders and these Hiders in turn were Seekers and they were all spreading out, calling your name, looking for you, how much more powerful and important *that* made you.

"Hey, hey! Where *are* you! Come in, the game's *over*!"

But you not moving or coming in. Even when they all collected under your tree and saw, or thought they saw you there at the very top, and called up at you. "Oh, come down! Stop fooling! Hey! We see you. We know you're there!"

Not answering even then—not until the final, the fatal thing happened. Far off, a block away, a silver whistle screaming, and the voice of your mother calling your name, and the whistle again. "Nine o'clock!" her voice wailed. "Nine o'clock! Home!"

But you waited until all the children were gone. Then, very carefully unfolding yourself and your warmth and secretness, and keeping out of the lantern light at corners, you ran home alone, alone in darkness and shadow, hardly breathing, keeping the sound of your heart quiet and in yourself, so if people heard anything at all they might think it was only the wind blowing a dry leaf by in the night. And your mother standing there, with the screen door wide . . .

He finished wiping his hands on the towel. He stood a moment thinking of how it had been the last two years here in town. The old game going on, by himself, playing it alone, the children gone, grown into settled middle age, but now, as before, himself the final and last and only Hider, and the whole town seeking and seeing nothing and going on home to lock their doors.

But tonight, out of a time long past, and on many nights now, he had heard that old sound, the sound of the silver whistle, blowing and blowing. It was certainly not a night bird singing, for he knew each sound so well. But the whistle kept calling and calling and a voice said, *Home* and *Nine o'clock*, even though it was now long after midnight. He listened. There was the silver whistle. Even though his mother had died many years ago, after having put his father in an early grave with her temper and her tongue. "Do this, do that, do this, do that, do this, do that, do this, do that . . ." A phonograph record, broken, playing the same cracked turn again, again, again, her voice, her cadence, around, around, around, around, repeat, repeat, repeat.

And the clear silver whistle blowing and the game of hide-and-seek over. No more of walking in the town and standing behind trees and bushes and smiling a smile that burned through the thickest foliage. An automatic thing was happening. His feet were walking and his hands were doing and he knew everything that must be done now.

His hands did not belong to him.

He tore a button off his coat and let it drop into the deep dark well of the room. It never seemed to hit bottom. It floated down. He waited.

It seemed never to stop rolling. Finally, it stopped.

His hands did not belong to him.

He took his pipe and flung that into the depths of the room. Without waiting for it to strike emptiness, he walked quietly back through the kitchen and peered outside the open, blowing, white-curtained window at the footprints he had made there. He was the Seeker, seeking now, instead of the Hider hiding. He was the quiet searcher finding and sifting and putting away clues, and those footprints were now as alien to him as something from a prehistoric age. They had been made a million years ago by some other man on some other business; they were no part of him at all. He marveled at their precision and deepness and form in the moonlight. He put his hand down almost to touch them, like a great and beautiful archaeological discovery! Then he was gone, back through the rooms, ripping a piece of material from his trousers turn-up and blowing it off his open palm like a moth.

His hands were not his hands anymore, or his body his body.

He opened the front door and went out and sat for a moment on the porch rail. He picked up the lemonade glass and drank what was left, made warm by an evening's waiting, and pressed his fingers tight to the glass, tight, tight, very tight. Then he put the glass down on the railing.

The silver whistle!

Yes, he thought. Coming, coming.

The silver whistle!

Yes, he thought. Nine o'clock. Home, home. Nine o'clock. Studies and milk and graham crackers and white cool bed, home, home; nine o'clock and the silver whistle.

He was off the porch in an instant, running softly, lightly, with hardly a breath or a heartbeat, as one barefooted runs, as one all leaf and green June grass and night can run, all shadow, forever running, away from the silent house and across the street, and down into the ravine . . .

✳ He pushed the door wide and stepped into the Owl Diner, this long railroad car that, removed from its track, had been put to a solitary unmoving destiny in the center of town. The place was empty. At the far end of the counter, the counterman glanced up as the door shut and the customer walked along the line of empty swivel seats. The counterman took the toothpick from his mouth.

"Tom Dillon, you old so-and-so! What *you* doing up this time of night, Tom?"

Tom Dillon ordered without the menu. While the food was being prepared, he dropped a nickel in the wall phone, got his number, and spoke quietly for a time. He hung up, came back, and sat, listening. Sixty seconds later, both he and the counterman heard the police siren wail by at fifty miles an hour. "Well—hell!" said the counterman. "Go get 'em, boys!"

He set out a tall glass of milk and a plate of six fresh graham crackers.

Tom Dillon sat there for a long while, looking secretly down at his ripped trousers turn-up and muddied shoes. The light in the diner was raw and bright, and he felt as if he were on a stage. He held the tall cool glass of milk in his hand, sipping it, eyes shut, chewing the good texture of the graham crackers, feeling it all through his mouth, coating his tongue.

"Would or would you not," he asked, quietly, "call this a hearty meal?"

"I'd call that very hearty indeed," said the counterman, smiling.

Tom Dillon chewed another graham cracker with great concentration, feeling all of it in his mouth. It's just a matter of time, he thought, waiting.

"More milk?"

"Yes," said Tom.

And he watched with steady interest, with the purest and most alert concentration in all of his life, as the white carton tilted and gleamed, and the snowy milk poured out, cool and quiet, like the sound of a running spring at night, and filled the glass up all the way, to the very brim, to the very brim, and over . . .

THE WITCH DOOR

IT WAS A POUNDING ON A DOOR, a furious, frantic, insistent pounding, born of hysteria and fear and a great desire to be heard, to be freed, to be let loose, to escape. It was a wrenching at hidden paneling, it was a hollow knocking, a rapping, a testing, a clawing! It was a scratching at hollow boards, a ripping at bedded nails; it was a muffled closet shouting and demanding, far away, and a call to be noticed, followed by a silence.

The silence was the most empty and terrible of all.

Robert and Martha Webb sat up in bed.

"Did you hear it?"

"Yes, again."

"Downstairs."

Now whoever it was who had pounded and rapped and made his fingers raw, drawn blood with his fever and quest to be free, had drawn into silence, listening himself to see if his terror and drumming had summoned any help.

The winter night lay through the house with a falling-snow silence,

silence snowing into every room, drifting over tables and floors, and banking up the stairwell.

Then the pounding started again. And then:

A sound of soft crying.

"Downstairs."

"Someone in the house."

"Lotte, do you think? The front door's unlocked."

"She'd have knocked. Can't be Lotte."

"She's the only one it *could* be. She *phoned*."

They both glanced at the phone. If you lifted the receiver, you heard a winter stillness. The phones were dead. They had died days ago with the riots in the nearest towns and cities. Now, in the receiver, you heard only your own heartbeat. "Can you put me up?" Lotte had cried from six hundred miles away. "Just overnight?"

But before they could answer her, the phone had filled itself with long miles of silence.

"Lotte *is* coming. She sounded hysterical. That *might* be her," said Martha Webb.

"No," said Robert. "I heard that crying other nights, too. Dear God."

They lay in the cold room in this farmhouse back in the Massachusetts wilderness, back from the main roads, away from the towns, near a bleak river and a black forest. It was the frozen middle of December. The white smell of snow cut the air.

They arose. With an oil lamp lit, they sat on the edge of the bed as if dangling their legs over a precipice.

"There's no one downstairs, there *can't* be."

"Whoever it is sounds frightened."

"We're *all* frightened, damn it. That's why we came out here, to be away from cities, riots, all that damned foolishness. No more wiretaps, arrests, taxes, neurotics. Now when we find it at last, people call and upset us. And tonight *this*, Christ!" He glanced at his wife. "You afraid?"

"I don't know. I don't believe in ghosts. This *is* 1999; I'm sane. Or like to *think* I am. Where's your gun?"

"We won't need it. Don't ask me why, but we won't."

They picked up their oil lamps. In another month the small power plant would be finished in the white barns behind the house and there'd be power to spare, but now they haunted the farm, coming and going with dim lamps or candles.

They stood at the stairwell, both thirty-three, both immensely practical.

The crying, the sadness, and the plea came from below in the winter rooms.

"She sounds so damned sad," said Robert. "God, I'm sorry for her, but don't even know who it *is*. Come on."

They went downstairs.

As if hearing their footsteps, the crying grew louder. There was a dull thudding against a hidden panel somewhere.

"The *Witch* Door!" said Martha Webb at last.

"Can't be."

"*Is*."

They stood in the long hall looking at that place under the stairs, where the panels trembled faintly. But now the cries faded, as if the crier was exhausted, or something had diverted her, or perhaps their voices had startled her and she was listening for them to speak again. Now the winter-night house was silent and the man and wife waited with the oil lamps quietly fuming in their hands.

Robert Webb stepped to the Witch Door and touched it, probing for the hidden button, the secret spring. "There can't be anyone in there," he said. "My God, we've *been* here six months, and that's just a cubby. Isn't that what the Realtor said when he sold the place? No one could hide in there and us not know it. We—"

"Listen!"

They listened.

Nothing.

"She's gone, it's gone, whatever it was, hell, that door hasn't been opened in our lifetime. Everyone's forgotten where the spring is that unlocks it. I don't think there *is* a door, only a loose panel, and rats' nests, that's all. The walls, scratching. Why not?" He turned to look at his wife, who was staring at the hidden place.

"Silly," she said. "Good Lord, rats don't cry. That was a voice, asking to be saved. Lotte, I thought. But now I know it wasn't she, but someone else in as much trouble."

Martha Webb reached out and trembled her fingertips along the beveled edge of ancient maple. "*Can't* we open it?"

"With a crowbar and hammer, tomorrow."

"Oh, Robert!"

"Don't 'Oh, Robert' me. I'm tired."

"You *can't* leave her in there to—"

"She's quiet now. Christ, I'm exhausted. I'll come down at the crack of dawn and knock the damned thing apart, okay?"

"All right," she said, and tears came to her eyes.

"Women," said Robert Webb. "Oh, my God, you and Lotte, Lotte and you. If she *is* coming here, *if* she makes it, I'll have a houseful of lunatics!"

"Lotte's *fine!*"

"Sure, but she should keep her mouth shut. It doesn't pay now to say you're Socialist, Democrat, Libertarian, Pro-Life Abortionist, Sinn Fein Fascist, Commie, any damn thing. The towns are bombed out. People are looking for scapegoats and Lotte has to shoot from the hip, get herself smeared and now, hell, on the run."

"They'll jail her if they catch her. Or kill her, yes, kill her. We're lucky to be here with our own food. Thank God we planned ahead, we saw it coming, the starvation, the massacres. We helped ourselves. Now we help Lotte if she makes it through."

Without answering, he turned to the stairs. "I'm dead on my feet. I'm tired of saving anyone. Even Lotte. But hell, if she comes through the front door, she's saved."

They went up the stairs taking the lamps, advancing in an ever-moving aura of trembling white glow. The house was as silent as snow falling. "God," he whispered. "Damn, I don't *like* women crying like that."

It sounded like the whole world crying, he thought. The whole world dying and needing help and lonely, but what can you *do*? Live in a farm like this? Far off the main highway where people don't pass, away from all the stupidity and death? What can you *do*?

They left one of the lamps lit and drew the covers over their bodies and lay, listening to the wind hit the house and creak the beams and parquetry.

A moment later there was a cry from downstairs, a splintering crash, the sound of a door flung wide, a bursting out of air, footsteps rapping all the rooms, a sobbing, almost an exultation, then the front door banged open, the winter wind blowing wildly in, footsteps across the front porch and gone.

"There!" cried Martha. "*Yes!*"

With the lamp they were down the stairs swiftly. Wind smothered their faces as they turned now toward the Witch Door, opened wide, still on its hinges, then toward the front door where they cast their light out upon a snowing winter darkness and saw nothing but white and hills, no moon, and in the lamplight the soft drift and moth-flicker of snowflakes falling from the sky to the mattressed yard.

"Gone," she whispered.

"Who?"

"We'll never know, unless she comes back."

"She won't. Look."

They moved the lamplight toward the white earth and the tiny footprints going off, across the softness, toward the dark forest.

"It *was* a woman, then. But . . . *why?*"

"God knows. Why anything, now in this crazy world?"

They stood looking at the footprints a long while until, shivering, they moved back through the hall to the open Witch Door. They poked the lamp into this hollow under the stairs.

"Lord, it's just a cell, hardly a closet, and look . . ."

Inside stood a small rocking chair, a braided rug, a used candle in a copper holder, and an old, worn Bible. The place smelled of must and moss and dead flowers.

"Is this where they used to hide people?"

"Yes. A long time back they hid people called witches. Trials, witch trials. They hanged or burned some."

"Yes, yes," they both murmured, staring into the incredibly small cell.

"And the witches hid here while the hunters searched the house and gave up and left?"

"Yes, oh, my God, yes," he whispered.

"Rob . . ."

"Yes?"

She bent forward. Her face was pale and she could not look away from the small, worn rocking chair and the faded Bible.

"Rob. How old? This house, how old?"

"Maybe three hundred years."

"*That* old?"

"Why?"

"Crazy. Stupid . . ."

"Crazy?"

"Houses, old like this. All the *years.* And more years and more after that. God, *feel!* If you put your hand in, yes? Would you feel it change, silly, and what if I sat in that rocking chair and shut the door, *what?* That woman . . . how long was she *in* there? How'd she get there? From way, way back. Wouldn't it be *strange?*"

"Bull!"

"But *if* you wanted to run away badly enough, wished for it, prayed for it, and people ran after you, and someone hid you in a place like this, a witch behind a door, and heard the searchers run through the house, closer and closer, wouldn't you *want* to get away? Anywhere? To another place? Why not another time? And then, in a house like this, a house so old nobody knows, if you *wanted* and *asked* for it enough, couldn't you run to another year! Maybe"—she paused—"here . . . ?"

"No, no," he muttered. "*Really* stupid!"

But still, some quiet motion within the closeted space caused both, at almost the same instant, to hold their hands out on the air, curious, like people testing invisible waters. The air seemed to move one way and then another, now warm, now cold, with a pulsation of light and a sudden turning toward dark. All this they thought but could not say. There was weather here, now a quick touch of summer and then a winter cold, which could not be, of course, but there it was. Passing along their fingertips, but unseen by their eyes, a stream of shadows and sun ran as invisible as time itself, clear as crystal, but clouded by a shifting dark. Both felt if they thrust their hands deep, they might be drawn in to drown in a mighty storm of seasons within an incredibly small space. All this, too, they thought or almost felt but could not say.

They seized their frozen but sunburned hands back, to stare down and hold them against the panic in their breasts.

"Damn," whispered Robert Webb. "Oh, damn!"

He backed off and went to open the front door again and look at the snowing night where the footprints had almost vanished.

"No," he said. "No, no."

Just then the yellow flash of headlights on the road braked in front of the house.

"Lotte!" cried Martha Webb. "It *must* be! Lotte!"

The car lights went out. They ran to meet the running woman half up the front yard.

"Lotte!"

The woman, wild-eyed, hair windblown, threw herself at them.

"Martha, Bob! God, I thought I'd *never* find you! Lost! I'm being followed, let's get inside. Oh, I didn't mean to get you up in the middle of the night, it's good to *see* you! Jesus! Hide the car! Here are the keys!"

Robert Webb ran to drive the car behind the house. When he came back around he saw that the heavy snowfall was already covering the tracks.

Then the three of them were inside the house, talking, holding onto each other. Robert Webb kept glancing at the front door.

"I can't thank you," cried Lotte, huddled in a chair. "You're at risk! I won't stay long, a few hours until it's safe. Then . . ."

"Stay as long as you want."

"No. They'll *follow*! In the cities, the fires, the murders, everyone starving, I stole gas. Do you have *more*? Enough to get me to Phil Merdith's in Greenborough? I—"

"Lotte," said Robert Webb.

"Yes?" Lotte stopped, breathless.

"Did you see anyone on your way up here? A woman? Running on the road?"

"What? I drove so fast! A *woman*? Yes! I almost hit her. Then she was gone! Why?"

"Well . . ."

"She's not *dangerous*?"

"No, no."

"It *is* all right, my *being* here?"

"Yes, fine, fine. Sit back. We'll fix some coffee—"

"Wait! I'll check!" And before they could stop her, Lotte ran to the front door, opened it a crack, and peered out. They stood with her and saw distant headlights flourished over a low hill and gone into a valley. "They're coming," whispered Lotte. "They might search here. God, where can I hide?"

Martha and Robert glanced at each other.

No, no, thought Robert Webb. God, no! Preposterous, unimaginable, fantastic, so damned coincidental the mind raves at it, crows, hoots, guffaws! No, none of *this*! Get off, circumstance! Get away with your goings and comings on not neat, or too neat, schedules. Come back, Lotte, in ten years, five years, maybe a year, a month, a week, and ask to hide. Even tomorrow show up! But don't come with coincidence in each hand like idiot children and ask, only half an hour after one terror, one miracle, to test our disbelief! I'm not, after all, Charles Dickens, to blink and let this pass.

"What's wrong?" said Lotte.

"I—" said Robert.

"No place to hide me?"

"Yes," he said. "We've a place."

"Well?"

"Here." He turned slowly away, stunned.

They walked down the hall to the half-open paneling.

"This?" Lotte said. "Secret? Did you—?"

"No, it's been here since the house was built long ago."

Lotte touched and moved the door on its hinges. "Does it work? Will they know where to look and *find* it?"

"No. It's beautifully made. Shut, you can't tell it's there."

Outside in the winter night, cars rushed, their beams flashing up the road, across the house windows.

Lotte peered into the Witch Door as one peers down a deep, lonely well.

A filtering of dust moved about her. The small rocking chair trembled.

Moving in silently, Lotte touched the half-burned candle.

"Why, it's still *warm!*"

Martha and Robert said nothing. They held to the Witch Door, smelling the odor of warm tallow.

Lotte stood rigidly in the little space, bowing her head beneath the beamed ceiling.

A horn blew in the snowing night. Lotte took a deep breath and said, "Shut the door."

They shut the Witch Door. There was no way to tell that a door was there.

They blew out the lamp and stood in the cold, dark house, waiting.

The cars rushed down the road, their noise loud, and their yellow headlights bright in the falling snow. The wind stirred the footprints in the yard, one pair going out, another coming in, and the tracks of Lotte's car fast vanishing, and at last gone.

"Thank God," whispered Martha.

The cars, honking, whipped around the last bend and down the hill and stopped, waiting, looking in at the dark house. Then, at last, they started up away into the snow and the hills.

Soon their lights were gone and their sound gone with them.

"We were lucky," said Robert Webb.

"But *she's* not."

"She?"

"That woman, whoever she was, ran out of here. *They'll* find her. Some-body'll find her."

"Christ, that's right."

"And she has no ID, no proof of herself. And she doesn't know what's *happened* to her. And when she tells them who she is and where she *came* from!"

"Yes, yes."

"God help her."

They looked into the snowing night but saw nothing. Everything was still. "You can't escape," she said. "No matter what you do, no one can escape."

They moved away from the window and down the hall to the Witch Door and touched it.

"Lotte," they called.

The Witch Door did not tremble or move.

"Lotte, you can come out now."

There was no answer; not a breath or a whisper.

Robert tapped the door. "Hey in there."

"Lotte!"

He knocked at the paneling, his mouth agitated.

"Lotte!"

"Open it!"

"I'm trying, damn it!"

"Lotte, we'll get you out, wait! Everything's all *right!*"

He beat with both fists, cursing. Then he said, "Watch out!" took a step back, raised his leg, kicked once, twice, three times; vicious kicks at the paneling that crunched holes and crumbled wood into kindling. He reached in and yanked the entire paneling free. "Lotte!"

They leaned together into the small place under the stairs.

The candle flickered on the small table. The Bible was gone. The small rocking chair moved quietly back and forth, in little arcs, and then stood still.

"Lotte!"

They stared at the empty room. The candle flickered.

"Lotte," they said.

"You don't believe . . ."

"I don't know. Old houses are *old* . . . old . . ."

"You think Lotte . . . she . . . ?"

"I don't know, I don't know."

"Then she's safe at least, safe! Thank God!"

"Safe? Where's she *gone*? You really *think* that? A woman in new clothes, red lipstick, high heels, short skirt, perfume, plucked brows, diamond rings, silk stockings, safe? Safe!" he said, staring deep into the open frame of the Witch Door.

"Yes, safe. Why not?"

He drew a deep breath.

"A woman of that description, lost in a town called Salem in the year 1680?"

He reached over and shut the Witch Door.

They sat waiting by it for the rest of the long, cold night.

THE WATCHERS

IN THIS ROOM THE SOUND of the tapping of the typewriter keys is like knuckles on wood, and my perspiration falls down upon the keys that are being punched unceasingly by my trembling fingers. And over and above the sound of my writing comes the ironical melody of a mosquito circling over my bent head, and a number of flies buzzing and colliding with the wire screen. And around the naked filament-skeleton of the yellow bulb in the ceiling a bit of torn white paper that is a moth, flutters. An ant crawls up the wall; I watch it—I laugh with a steady, unceasing bitterness. How ironical the shining flies and the red ants and the armored crickets. How mistaken we three were: Susan and I and William Tinsley.

Whoever you are, wherever you are, if you do happen upon this, do not ever again crush the ants upon the sidewalk, do not smash the bumblebee that thunders by your window, do not annihilate the cricket upon your hearth!

That's where Tinsley made his colossal error. You remember William Tinsley, certainly? The man who threw away a million dollars on fly-sprays and insecticides and ant pastes?

There was never a spot for a fly or a mosquito in Tinsley's office. Not a white wall or green desk or any immaculate surface where a fly might land before Tinsley destroyed it with an instantaneous stroke of his magnificent flyswatter. I shall never forget that instrument of death. Tinsley, a monarch, ruled his industry with that flyswatter as a scepter.

I was Tinsley's secretary and right-hand man in his kitchenware industry; sometimes I advised him on his many investments.

Tinsley carried the flyswatter to work with him under his arm in July, 1944. By the week's end, if I happened to be in one of the filing alcoves out of sight when Tinsley arrived, I could always tell of his arrival when I heard the swicking, whistling passage of the flyswatter through the air as Tinsley killed his morning quota.

As the days passed, I noted Tinsley's preoccupied alertness. He'd dictate to me, but his eyes would be searching the north-southeast-west walls, the rug, the bookcases, even my clothing. Once I laughed and made some comment about Tinsley and Clyde Beatty being fearless animal trainers, and Tinsley froze and turned his back on me. I shut up. People have a right, I thought, to be as damned eccentric as they please.

"Hello, Steve." Tinsley waved his flyswatter one morning as I poised my pencil over my pad. "Before we start, would you mind cleaning away the corpses."

Spread in a rumpled trail over the thick sienna rug were the fallen conquered, the flies; silent, mashed, dewinged. I threw them one by one in the waste-bin, muttering.

"To S. H. Little, Philadelphia. Dear Little: Will invest money in your insect spray. Five thousand dollars—"

"Five thousand?" I complained. I stopped writing.

Tinsley ignored me. "Five thousand dollars. Advise immediate production as soon as war conditions permit. Sincerely." Tinsley twisted his flyswatter. "You think I'm crazy," he said.

"Is that a P.S., or are you talking to me?" I asked.

The phone rang and it was the Termite Control Company, to whom Tinsley told me to write a thousand-dollar check for having termite-proofed his house. Tinsley patted his metal chair. "One thing I like about my offices— all iron, cement, solid; not a chance for termites."

He leaped from his chair, the swatter shone swiftly in the air.

"Damn it, Steve, has THAT been here all this time!"

Something buzzed in a small arc somewhere, into silence. The four walls moved in around us in that silence, it seemed, the blank ceiling stared over us and Tinsley's breath arched through his nostrils. I couldn't see the infernal insect anywhere. Tinsley exploded. "Help me find it! Damn you, help me!"

"Now, hold on—" I retorted.

Somebody rapped on the door.

"Stay out!" Tinsley's yell was high, afraid. "Get away from the door, and stay away!" He flung himself headlong, bolted the door with a frantic gesture and lay against it, wildly searching the room. "Quickly now, Steve, systematically! Don't sit there!"

Desk, chairs, chandelier, walls. Like an insane animal, Tinsley searched, found the buzzing, struck at it. A bit of insensate glitter fell to the floor where he crushed it with his foot in a queerly triumphant sort of action.

He started to dress me down, but I wouldn't have it. "Look here," I came back at him. "I'm a secretary and right-hand stooge, not a spotter for high-flying insects. I haven't got eyes in the back of my head!"

"Either have they!" cried Tinsley. "So you know what They do?"

"They? Who in hell are They?"

He shut up. He went to his desk and sat down, wearily, and finally said, "Never mind. Forget it. Don't talk about this to anyone."

I softened up. "Bill, you should go see a psychiatrist about—"

Tinsley laughed bitterly. "And the psychiatrist would tell his wife, and she'd tell others, and then They'd find out. They're everywhere, They are. I don't want to be stopped with my campaign."

"If you mean the one hundred thousand bucks you've sunk in your insect sprays and ant pastes in the last four weeks," I said. "Someone should stop you. You'll break yourself, me, and the stockholders. Honest to God, Tinsley—"

"Shut up!" he said. "You don't understand."

I guess I didn't, then. I went back to my office and all day long I heard that damned flyswatter hissing in the air.

✳ I had supper with Susan Miller that evening. I told her about Tinsley and she lent a sympathetically professional ear. Then she tapped her cigarette and lit it and said, "Steve, I may be a psychiatrist, but I wouldn't have a tinker's chance in hell, unless Tinsley came to see me. I couldn't help him unless he wanted help." She patted my arm. "I'll look him over for you, if you insist, though, for old time's sake. But half the fight's lost if the patient won't cooperate."

"You've got to help me, Susan," I said. "He'll be stark raving in another month. I think he has delusions of persecution—"

We drove to Tinsley's house.

The first date worked out well. We laughed, we danced we dined late at the Brown Derby, and Tinsley didn't suspect for a moment that the slender, soft-voiced woman he held in his arms to a waltz was a psychiatrist picking his reactions apart. From the table, I watched them, together, and I shielded a small laugh with my hand, and heard Susan laughing at one of his jokes.

We drove along the road in a pleasant, relaxed silence, the silence that follows on the heels of a good, happy evening. The perfume of Susan was in the car, the radio played dimly, and the car wheels whirled with a slight whisper over the highway.

I looked at Susan and she at me, her brows going up to indicate that she'd found nothing so far this evening to show that Tinsley was in any way unbalanced. I shrugged.

At that very instant, a moth flew in the window, fluttering, flickering its velvety white wings upon the imprisoning glass.

Tinsley screamed, wrenched the car involuntarily, struck out a gloved hand at the moth, gabbling, his face pale. The tires wobbled. Susan seized the steering wheel firmly and held the car on the road until we slowed to a stop.

As we pulled up, Tinsley crushed the moth between tightened fingers and watched the odorous powder of it sift down upon Susan's arm. We sat there, the three of us, breathing rapidly.

Susan looked at me, and this time there was comprehension in her eyes. I nodded.

Tinsley looked straight ahead, then. In a dream he said, "Ninety-nine percent of all life in the world is insect life—"

He rolled up the windows without another word, and drove us home.

Susan phoned me an hour later. "Steve, he's built a terrific complex for himself. I'm having lunch with him tomorrow. He likes me, I might find out what we want to know. By the way, Steve, does he own any pets?"

Tinsley had never owned a cat or dog. He detested animals.

"I might have expected that," said Susan. "Well, good-night, Steve, see you tomorrow."

The flies were breeding thick and golden and buzzing like a million intricately fine electric machines in the pouring direct light of summer noon. In vortexes they whirled and curtained and fell upon refuse to inject their eggs, to mate, to flutter, to whirl again, as I watched them, and in their whirling my mind intermixed. I wondered why Tinsley should fear them so, should dread and kill them, and as I walked the streets, all about me, cutting arcs and spaces from the sky, omnipresent flies hummed and sizzled and beat their lucid wings. I counted darning needles, mud-daubers and hornets, yellow bees and brown ants. The world was suddenly much

more alive to me than ever before, because Tinsley's apprehensive awareness had set me aware.

✳ Before I knew my actions, brushing a small red ant from my coat that
had fallen from a lilac bush as I passed, I turned in at a familiar white
house and knew it to be Lawyer Remington's who had been Tinsley's family
representative for forty years, even before Tinsley was born. Remington
was only a business acquaintance to me but there I was, touching his gate
and ringing his bell and in a few minutes looking at him over a sparkling
good glass of his sherry.

"I remember," said Remington, remembering. "Poor Tinsley. He was
only seventeen when it happened."

I leaned forward intently. "It happened?" The ant raced in wild frenzies upon the golden stubble on my fingers' backs, becoming entangled in
the bramble of my wrist, turning back, hopelessly clenching its mandibles.
I watched the ant. "Some unfortunate accident?"

Lawyer Remington nodded grimly and the memory lay raw and naked
in his old brown eyes. He spread the memory out on the table and pinned it
down so I could look at it with a few accurate words:

"Tinsley's father took him hunting up in the Lake Arrowhead region in
the autumn of the young lad's seventeenth year. Beautiful country, a lovely
clear cold autumn day: I remember it because I was hunting not seventy
miles from there on that selfsame afternoon. Game was plentiful. You
could hear the sound of guns passing over and back across the lakes
through the scent of pine trees. Tinsley's father leaned his gun against a
bush to lace his shoe, when a flurry of quail arose, some of them, in their
fright, straight at Tinsley senior and his son."

Remington looked into his glass to see what he was telling. "A quail
knocked the gun down, it fired off, and the charge struck the elder. Tinsley
full in the face!"

"Good God!"

In my mind I saw the elder Tinsley stagger, grasp at his red mask of face,
drop his hands now gloved with scarlet fabric, and fall, even as the young
boy, struck numb and ashen, swayed and could not believe what he saw.

I drank my sherry hastily, and Remington continued:

"But that wasn't the least horrible of details. One might think it sufficient. But what followed later was something indescribable to the lad. He
ran five miles for help, leaving his father behind, dead, but refusing to

believe him dead. Screaming, panting, ripping his clothes from his body, young Tinsley made it to a road and back with a doctor and two other men in something like six hours. The sun was just going down when they hurried back through the pine forest to where the father lay." Remington paused and shook his head from side to side, eyes closed. "The entire body, the arms, the legs, and the shattered contour of what was once a strong, handsome face, was clustered over and covered with scuttling, twitching insects, bugs, ants of every and all descriptions, drawn by the sweet odor of blood. It was impossible to see one square inch of the elder Tinsley's body!"

✳ Mentally, I created the pine trees, and the three men towering over the small boy who stood before a body upon which a tide of small, attentively hungry creatures ebbed and flowed, subsided and returned. Somewhere, a woodpecker knocked, a squirrel scampered, and the quail beat their small wings. And the three men held onto the small boy's arms and turned him away from the sight. . . .

Some of the boy's agony and terror must have escaped my lips, for when my mind returned to the library, I found Remington staring at me, and my sherry glass broken in half causing a bleeding cut which I did not feel.

"So that's why Tinsley has this fear of insects and animals," I breathed, several minutes later, settling back, my heart pounding. "And it's grown like a yeast over the years, to obsess him."

Remington expressed an interest in Tinsley's problem, but I allayed him and inquired, "What was his father's profession?"

"I thought you knew!" cried Remington in faint surprise. "Why the elder Tinsley was a very famous naturalist. Very famous indeed. Ironic, in a way, isn't it, that he should be killed by the very creatures which he studied, eh?"

"Yes." I rose up and shook Remington's hand. "Thanks, Lawyer. You have helped me very much. I must get going now."

"Good-bye."

I stood in the open air before Remington's house and the ant still scrambled over my hand, wildly. I began to understand and sympathize deeply with Tinsley for the first time. I went to pick up Susan in my car.

Susan pushed the veil of her hat back from her eyes and looked off into the distance and said, "What you've told me pretty well puts the finger on Tinsley, all right. He's been brooding." She waved a hand. "Look around. See how easy it would be to believe that insects are really the horrors he makes them out to be. There's a Monarch butterfly pacing us." She flicked a fingernail. "Is it listening to our every word? Tinsley the elder was a naturalist. What happened? He interfered, busybodied where he wasn't wanted, so They, They who control the animals and insects, killed him. Night and day for the last ten years that thought has been on Tinsley's mind, and everywhere he looked he saw the numerous life of the world and the suspicions began to take shape, form and substance!"

"I can't say I blame him," I said. "If my father had been killed in a like fashion—"

"He refuses to talk when there's an insect in the room, isn't that it, Steve?"

"Yes, he's afraid they'll discover that he knows about them."

"You can see how silly that is, yourself, can't you. He couldn't possibly keep it a secret, granting that butterflies and ants and houseflies are evil, for you and I have talked about it, and others, too. But he persists in his delusion that as long as he himself says no word in Their presence . . . well, he's still alive, isn't he? They haven't destroyed him, have They? And if They were evil and feared his knowledge, wouldn't They have destroyed him long since?"

"Maybe They're playing with him?" I wondered. "You know it is strange. The elder Tinsley was on the verge of some great discovery when he was killed. It sort of fits a pattern:"

"I'd better get you out of this hot sun," laughed Susan, swerving the car into a shady lane.

✳ The next Sunday morning, Bill Tinsley and Susan and I attended church and sat in the middle of the soft music and the vast muteness and quiet color. During the service, Bill began to laugh to himself until I shoved him in the ribs and asked him what was wrong.

"Look at the Reverend up there," replied Tinsley, fascinated. "There's a fly on his bald spot. A fly in church. They go everywhere, I tell you. Let the minister talk, it won't do a bit of good. Oh, gentle, Lord."

After the service we drove for a picnic lunch in the country under a warm blue sky. A few times, Susan tried to get Bill on the subject of his fear, but Bill only pointed at the train of ants swarming across the picnic linen and shook his head, angrily. Later, he apologized and with a certain tenseness, asked us to come up to his house that evening, he couldn't go on much longer by himself, he was running low on funds, the business was liable to go on the rocks, and he needed us. Susan and I held onto his hands and understood. In a matter of forty minutes we were inside the locked study of his house, cocktails in our midst, with Tinsley pacing anxiously back and forth, dandling his familiar flyswatter, searching the room and killing two flies before he made his speech.

He tapped the wall. "Metal. No maggots, ticks, woodbeetles, termites. Metal chairs, metal everything. We're alone; aren't we?"

I looked around: "I think so."

"Good." Bill drew in a breath and exhaled. "Have you ever wondered about God and the Devil and the Universe, Susan, Steve? Have you ever realized how cruel the world is? How we try to get ahead, but are hit over the head every time we succeed a fraction?" I nodded silently, and Tinsley went on. "You sometimes wonder where God is, or where the Forces of Evil are. You wonder how these forces get around, if they are invisible angels. Well, the solution is simple and clever and scientific. We are being watched constantly. Is there ever a minute in our lives that passes without a fly buzzing in our room with us, or an ant crossing our path, or a flea on a dog, or a cat itself, or a beetle or moth rushing through the dark, or a mosquito skirting around a netting?"

Susan said nothing, but looked at Tinsley easily and without making him self-conscious. Tinsley sipped his drink.

"Small winged things we pay no heed to, that follow us every day of our lives, that listen to our prayers and our hopes and our desires and fears, that listen to us and then tell what there is to be told to Him or Her or It, or whatever Force sends them out into the world."

"Oh, come now," I said impulsively.

To my surprise, Susan hushed me. "Let him finish," she said. Then she looked at Tinsley. "Go on."

Tinsley said, "It sounds silly, but I've gone about this in a fairly scientific manner. First, I've never been able to figure out a reason for so many insects, for their varied profusion. They seem to be nothing but irritants to we mortals, at the very least. Well, a very simple explanation is as follows: the government of Them is a small body, it may be one person alone, and It or They can't be everywhere. Flies can be. So can ants and other insects. And since we mortals cannot tell one ant from another, all identity is impossible and one fly is as good as another, their set-up is perfect. There are so many of them and there have been so many for years, that we pay no attention to them. Like Hawthorne's 'Scarlet Letter,' they are right before our eyes and familiarity has blinded us to them."

"I don't believe any of that," I said directly.

"Let me finish!" cried Tinsley, hurriedly. "Before you judge. There is a Force, and it must have a contractual system, a communicative set-up, so that life can be twisted and adjusted according to each individual. Think of it, billions of insects, checking, correlating and reporting on their special subjects, controlling humanity!"

"Look here!" I burst out. "You've grown worse ever since that accident back when you were a kid! You've let it feed on your mind! You can't go on fooling yourself!" I got up.

"Steve!" Susan rose, too, her cheeks reddening. "You won't help with talk like that! Sit down." She pressed against my chest. Then she turned rapidly to Tinsley. "Bill, if what you say should be true, if all of your plans, your insect-proofing your house, your silence in the presence of Their small winged creatures your campaign, your ant pastes and pitifully small insect sprays, should really mean something, why are you still alive?"

"Why?" shouted Tinsley. "Because I've worked alone."

"But if there is a They, Bill, They have known of you for a month now, because Steve and I have told them, haven't we Steve and yet you live. Isn't that proof that you must be wrong."

"You told them? You fool!" Tinsley's eyes showed white and furious. "No, you didn't, I made Steve promise!"

"Listen to me." Susan's voice shook him, as she might shake a small boy by the scruff of his neck. "Listen, before you scream. Will you agree to an experiment?"

"What kind of experiment?"

"From new on, all of your plans will be aboveboard, in the open. If nothing happens to you, in the next eight weeks, then you'll have to agree that your fears are baseless."

"But they'll kill me!"

"Listen! Steve and I will stake our lives on it, Bill. If you die, Steve and I'll die with you. I value my life greatly, Bill, and Steve values his. We don't believe in your horrors, and we want to get you out of this."

Tinsley hung his head and looked at the floor. "I don't know. I don't know."

"Eight weeks, Bill. You can go on the rest of your life, if you wish, manufacturing insecticides, but for God's sake don't have a nervous breakdown over it. The very fact of your living should be some sort of proof that They bear you no ill-will, and have left you intact?"

✳ Tinsley had to admit to that. But he was reluctant to give in. He murmured almost to himself. "This is the beginning of the campaign. It might take a thousand years, but in the end we can liberate ourselves."

"You can be liberated in eight weeks, Bill, don't you see? If we can prove that insects are blameless? For the next eight weeks, carry on your campaign, advertise it in weekly magazines and papers, thrust it to the hilt, tell everyone, so that if you should die, the world will be left behind. Then, when the eight weeks are up, you'll be liberated and free, and won't that feel good to you, Bill, after all these years?"

Something happened then that startled us. Buzzing over our heads, a fly came by. It had been in the room with us all the time, and yet I had sworn that, earlier, I had seen none. Tinsley began to shiver. I didn't know what I was doing, I seemed to react mechanically to some inner drive. I grabbed at the air and caught the tight buzzing in a cupped hand. Then I crushed it hard, staring at Bill and Susan. Their faces were chalky.

"I got it," I said crazily. "I got the damned thing, and I don't know why."

I opened my hand. The fly dropped to the floor. I stepped on it as I had seen Bill often step on them, and my body was cold for no reason. Susan stared at me as if she'd lost her last friend.

"What am I saying?" I cried. "I don't believe a damn word of all this filth!"

It was dark outside the thick-glassed window. Tinsley managed to light a cigarette and then, because all three of us were in a strange state of nerves, offered to let us have rooms in the house for the night. Susan said she would stay if: "You promise to give the eight-week trial a chance."

"You'd risk your life on it?" Bill couldn't make Susan out.

Susan nodded gravely. "We'll be joking about it next year."

Bill said, "All right. The eight-week trial it is."

My room, upstairs, had a fine view of the spreading country hills. Susan stayed in the room next to mine, and Bill slept across the hall. Lying in bed I heard the crickets chirping outside my window, and I could barely bear the sound.

I closed the window.

Later in the night I got no sleep so I began imagining that a mosquito was soaring freely about in the dark of my room. Finally, I robed myself and fumbled down to the kitchen, not actually hungry, but wanting something to do to stop my nervousness. I found Susan bending over the refrigerator trays, selecting food.

We looked at one another. We handed plates of stuff to the table and sat stiffly down. The world was unreal to us. Somehow, being around Tinsley made the universe insecure and misty underfoot. Susan, for all her training and mind-culture, was still a woman, and deep under, women are superstitious.

To top it all, we were about to plunge our knives into the half-shattered carcass of a chicken when a fly landed upon it.

We sat looking at the fly for five minutes. The fly walked around on the chicken, flew up, circled, and came back to promenade a drumstick.

We put the chicken back in the icebox, joking very quietly about it, talked uneasily for awhile, and returned upstairs, where we shut our doors and felt alone. I climbed into bed and began having bad dreams before I shut my eyes. My wrist-watch set up an abominable loud clicking in the blackness, and it had clicked several thousand times when I heard the scream.

✳ I don't mind hearing a woman scream occasionally, but a man's scream is so strange, and is heard so rarely, that when it finally comes, it turns your blood into an arctic torrent. The screaming seemed to be borne all through the house and it seemed I heard some frantic words babbled that sounded like, "Now I know why They let me live!"

I pulled the door wide in time to see Tinsley running down the hall, his clothing drenched and soaked, his body wet from head to foot. He turned when he saw me, and cried out. "Stay away from me, oh, God, Steve, don't touch me, or it'll happen to you, too! I was wrong! I was wrong, yes, but near the truth, too, so very near!"

Before I could prevent him, he had descended the stairs and slammed the door below. Susan suddenly stood beside me. "He's gone mad for certain this time, Steve, we've got to stop him."

A noise from the bathroom drew my attention. Peering in, I turned off the shower which was steaming hot, drumming insistently, scaldingly, on the yellow tiles.

Bill's car thundered into life, a jerking of gears, and the car careened down the road at an insane speed.

"We've got to follow him," insisted Susan. "He'll kill himself! He's trying to run away from something. Where's your car?"

We ran to my car through a cold wind, under very cold stars, climbed in, warmed the motor, and were off, bewildered and breathless. "Which way?" I shouted.

"He went east, I'm certain."

"East it is, then." I poked up the speed and muttered, "Oh, Bill, you idiot, you fool. Slow down. Come back. Wait for me, you nut." I felt Susan's arm creep through my elbow and hold tight. She whispered, "Faster!" and I said, "We're going sixty now, and there are some bad turns coming!"

The night had gotten into us; the talk of insects, the wind, the roaring of the tires over hard concrete, the beating of our frightened hearts. "There!" Susan pointed. I saw a gash of light cutting through the hills a mile away. "More speed, Steve!"

More speed. Aching foot pressing out the miles, motor thundering, stars wheeling crazily overhead, lights cutting the dark away into dismembered sections. And in my mind I saw Tinsley again, in the hall, drenched to the skin. He had been standing under the hot, scalding shower! Why? Why?

"Bill, stop, you idiot! Stop driving! Where are you going, what are you running away from, Bill?"

We were catching up with him now. We drew closer, yard by yard, bit by bit, around curves where gravity yanked at us and tried to smash us against huge granite bulwarks of earth, over hills and down into night-filled valleys, over streams and bridges, around curves again.

"He's only about six hundred yards ahead, now," said Susan.

"We'll get him," I twisted the wheel. "So help me God, we'll get to him!"

Then, quite unexpectedly, it happened.

* Tinsley's car slowed down. It slowed and crept along the road. We were on a straight length of concrete that continued for a mile in a firm line, no curves or hills. His car slowed to a crawling, puttering pace. By the time we pulled up in back of him, Tinsley's roadster was going three miles an hour, just poking along at a pace like a man walking, its lights glaring.

"Steve—" Susan's fingernails cut my wrist, tight, hard. "Something's—wrong."

I knew it. I honked the horn. Silence. I honked again and it was a lonely, blatant sound in the darkness and the emptiness. I parked the car. Tinsley's car moved on like a metal snail ahead of us, its exhaust whispering to the night. I opened the door and slid out. "Stay here," I warned Susan. In the reflected glare her face was like snow and her lips were trembling.

I ran to the car, calling: "Bill, Bill—!"

Tinsley didn't answer. He couldn't.

He just lay there behind the wheel, quietly, and the car moved ahead, slowly, so very slowly.

I got sick to my stomach. I reached in and braked the car and cut the ignition, not looking at him, my mind working in a slow kind of new and frightened horror.

I looked once more at Bill where he slumped with his head back.

It didn't do any good to kill flies, kill moths, kill termites, kill mosquitoes. The Evil ones were too clever for that.

Kill all the insects you find, destroy the dogs and the cats and the birds, the weasels and the chipmunks, and the termites, and all animals and insects in the world, it can be done, eventually by man, killing, killing, killing, and after you are finished, after that job is done you still have—microbes.

Bacteria. Microbes. Yes. Unicellular and bi-cellular and multi-cellular microscopic life!

Millions of them, billions of them on every pore, on every inch of flesh of your body. On your lips when you speak, inside your ears when you listen, on your skin when you feel, on your tongue when you taste, in your eyes when you see! You can't wash them off, you can't destroy all of them in the world! It would be an impossible task, impossible! You discovered that, didn't you, Bill. I stared at him. We almost convinced you, didn't we, Bill, that insects were not guilty, were not Watchers. We were right about that part of it. We convinced you and you got to thinking tonight, and you hit upon the real crux of the situation. Bacteria. That's why the shower was running at home just now! But you can't kill bacteria fast enough. They multiply and multiply, instantly!

I looked at Bill, slumped there. "The flyswatter, you thought the flyswatter was enough. That's a—laugh."

Bill, is that you lying there with your body changed by leprosy and gangrene and tuberculosis and malaria and bubonic all at once? Where is the skin of your face, Bill, and the flesh of your bones, your fingers lying clenched to the steering wheel. Oh, God, Tinsley, the color and the smell of you—the rotting fetid combination of disease you are!

Microbes. Messengers. Millions of them. Billions of them.

God can't be everywhere at once. Maybe He invented flies, insects to watch his peoples.

But the Evil Ones were brilliant, too. They invented bacteria!

Bill, you look so *different* . . .

You'll not tell your secret to the world now. I returned to Susan, looked in at her, not able to speak. I could only point for her to go home, without me. I had a job to do, to drive Bill's car into the ditch and set fire to him and it. Susan drove away, not looking back.

✳ And now, tonight, a week later, I am typing this out for what it is worth, here and now, in the summer evening, with flies buzzing about my room. Now I realize why Bill Tinsley lived so long. While his efforts were directed against insects, ants, birds, animals, who were representatives of the Good Forces, the Evil Forces let him go ahead. Tinsley, unaware, was working for the Evil Ones. But when he comprehended that bacteria were the real enemy, and were more numerous and invisibly insidious, then the Evil Ones demolished him.

In my mind, I still remember the picture of the Elder Tinsley's death when he was shot as a result of the quail flying against his gun. On the face of it, it doesn't seem to fit into the picture. Why would the quail, representative of Good, kill the Elder Tinsley? The answer to this comes clear now. Quail, too, have disease, and disease disrupts their neutral set-up, and disease, on that day long ago, caused the birds to strike down Tinsley's weapon, killing him, and thus, subtly, animals and insects.

And another thought in my mind is the picture of the Elder Tinsley as he lay covered with ants in a red, quivering blanket. And I wonder if perhaps they were not giving solace to him in his dying and decay, talking in some silent mandibled tongue none of us can hear until we die. Or perhaps they are all.

The game of chess continues. Good against Evil, I hope. And I am losing.

Tonight I sit here writing and waiting, and my skin itches and softens, and Susan is on the other side of town, unaware, safe from this knowledge which I must set on paper even if it kills me. I listen to the flies, as if to detect some good message in their uneven whirring, but I hear nothing.

Even as I write, the skin of my fingers loosens and changes color and my face feels partially dry and flaking, partially wet, slippery and released from its anchorage of softening bone, my eyes water with a kind of leprosy and my skin darkens with something akin to bubonic, my stomach gripes me with sickening gastric wrenches, my tongue tastes bitter and acid, my teeth loosen in my mouth, my ears ring, and in a few minutes the structure of my fingers, the muscles, the small thin, fine bones will be enmeshed, entangled, so much fallen gelatin spread over and down between the black lettered keys of this typewriter, the flesh of me will slide like a decayed, diseased cloak from my skeleton, but I must write on and on and on until etaoin shrdlucmfwyp . . . cmfwaaaaa ddddddddddddddddddddd . . .

2004–05:
THE NAMING OF NAMES

THEY CAME TO THE STRANGE BLUE LANDS and put their names upon the lands. Here was Hinkston Creek and Lustig Corners and Black River and Driscoll Forest and Peregrine Mountain and Wilder Town, all the names of people and the things that the people did. Here was the place where Martians killed the first Earth Men, and it was Red Town and had to do with blood. And here where the second expedition was destroyed, and it was named Second Try, and each of the other places where the rocket men had set down their fiery caldrons to burn the land, the names were left like cinders, and of course there was a Spender Hill and a Nathaniel York Town. . . .

The old Martian names were names of water and air and hills. They were the names of snows that emptied south in stone canals to fill the empty seas. And the names of sealed and buried sorcerers and towers and obelisks. And the rockets struck at the names like hammers, breaking away the marble into shale, shattering the crockery milestones that named the old towns, in the rubble of which great pylons were plunged with new names: IRON TOWN, STEEL, TOWN, ALUMINUM, CITY, ELECTRIC VILLAGE, CORN TOWN, GRAIN VILLA, DETROIT II, all the mechanical names and the metal names from Earth.

And after the towns were built and named, the graveyards were built and named, too: Green Hill, Moss Town, Boot Hill, Bide 'a Wee; and the first dead went into their graves. . . .

But after everything was pinned down and neat and in its place, when everything was safe and certain, when the towns were well enough fixed and the loneliness was at a minimum, then the sophisticates came in from Earth. They came on parties and vacations, on little shopping trips for trinkets and photographs and the "atmosphere"; they came to study and apply sociological laws; they came with stars and badges and rules and regulations, bringing some of the red tape that had crawled across Earth like an alien weed, and letting it grow on Mars wherever it could take root. They began to plan people's lives and libraries; they began to instruct and push about the very people who had come to Mars to get away from being instructed and ruled and pushed about.

And it was inevitable that some of these people pushed back. . . .

HOPSCOTCH

VINIA WOKE TO THE SOUND of a rabbit running down and across an endless moonlit field; but it was only the soft, quick beating of her heart. She lay on the bed for a moment, getting her breath. Now the sound of the running faded and was gone at a great distance. At last she sat up and looked down from her second-story bedroom window and there below, on the long sidewalk, in the faint moonlight before dawn, was the hopscotch.

Late yesterday, some child had chalked it out, immense and endlessly augmented, square upon square, line after line, numeral following numeral. You could not see the end of it. Down the street it built its crazy pattern, 3, 4, 5, on up to 10, then 30, 50, 90, on away to turn far corners. Never in all the children's world a hopscotch like this! You could jump forever toward the horizon.

Now in the very early, very quiet morning, her eyes traveled and jumped, paused and hopped, along that presumptuous ladder of chalk-scratches and she heard herself whisper:

"Sixteen."

But she did not run on from there.

The next square waited, she knew, with the scribbled blue-chalk 17, but her mind flung out its arms and balanced, teetering, poised with her numb foot planted across the 1 and the 6, and could go no farther.

Trembling, she lay back down.

The room was like the bottom of a cool well all night and she lay in it like a white stone in a well, enjoying it, floating in the dark yet clear element of half dreams and half wakening. She felt the breath move in small jets from her nostrils and she felt the immense sweep of her eyelids shutting and opening again and again. And at last she felt the fever brought into her room by the presence of the sun beyond the hills.

Morning, she thought. It might be a special day. After all, it's my birthday. Anything might happen. And I hope it does.

The air moved the white curtains like a summer breath.

"Vinia . . . ?"

A voice was calling. But it couldn't be a voice. Yet—Vinia raised herself—there it was again.

"Vinia . . . ?"

She slipped from bed and ran to the window of her high second-story window.

There on the fresh lawn below, calling up to her in the early hour, stood James Conway, no older than she, seventeen, very seriously smiling, waving his hand now as her head appeared.

"Jim, what're you doing here?" she said, and thought, Does he know *what* day this is?

"I've been up an hour already," he replied. "I'm going for a walk, starting early, all day. Want to come along?"

"Oh, but I couldn't . . . my folks won't be back till late tonight, I'm alone, I'm supposed to stay . . ."

She saw the green hills beyond the town and the roads leading out into summer, leading out into August and rivers and places beyond this town and this house and this room and this particular moment.

"I can't go . . ." she said faintly.

"I can't hear you!" he protested mildly, smiling up at her under a shielding hand.

"Why did you ask me to walk with you, and not someone else?"

He considered this for a moment. "I don't know," he admitted. He thought it over again, and gave her his most pleasant and agreeable look. "Because, that's all, just because."

"I'll be down," she said.

"Hey!" he said.

But the window was empty.

✳ They stood in the center of the perfect, jeweled lawn, over which one set of prints, hers, had run, leaving marks, and another, his, had walked in great slow strides to meet them. The town was silent as a stopped clock. All the shades were still down.

"My gosh," said Vinia, "it's early. It's crazy-early. I've never been up this early and out this early in years. Listen to everyone sleeping."

They listened to the trees and the whiteness of the houses in this early whispering hour, the hour when mice went back to sleep and flowers began untightening their bright fists.

"Which way do we go?"

"Pick a direction."

Vinia closed her eyes, whirled, and pointed blindly.

"Which way am I pointing?"

"North."

She opened her eyes. "Let's go north out of town, then. I don't suppose we should."

"Why?"

And they walked out of town as the sun rose above the hills and the grass burned greener on the lawns.

✳ There was a smell of hot chalk highway, of dust and sky and waters flowing in a creek the color of grapes. The sun was a new lemon. The forest lay ahead with shadows stirring like a million birds under each tree, each bird a leaf-darkness, trembling. At noon, Vinia and James Conway had crossed vast meadows that sounded brisk and starched underfoot. The day had grown warm, as an iced glass of tea grows warm, the frost burning off, left in the sun.

They picked a handful of grapes from a wild barbed-wire vine. Holding them up to the sun, you could see the clear grape thoughts suspended in the dark amber fluid, the little hot seeds of contemplation stored from many afternoons of solitude and plant philosophy. The grapes tasted of fresh, clear water and something that they had saved from the morning dews and the evening rains. They were the warmed-over flesh of April ready now, in August, to pass on their simple gain to any passing stranger. And the lesson was this; sit in the sun, head down, within a prickly vine, in flickery light or open light, and the world will come to you. The sky will come in its time, bringing rain, and the earth will rise through you, from beneath, and make you rich and make you full.

"Have a grape," said James Conway. "Have *two*."

They munched their wet, full mouths.

They sat on the edge of a brook and took off their shoes and let the water cut their feet off to the ankles with an exquisite cold razor.

My feet are gone! thought Vinia. But when she looked, there they were, underwater, living comfortably apart from her, completely acclimated to an amphibious existence.

They ate egg sandwiches Jim had brought with him in a paper sack.

"Vinia," said Jim, looking at his sandwich before he bit it. "Would you mind if I kissed you?"

"I don't know," she said, after a moment. "I hadn't thought."

"Will you think it over?" he asked.

"Did we come on this picnic just so you could kiss me?" she asked suddenly.

"Oh, don't get me wrong! It's been a swell day! I don't want to spoil it. But if you should decide, later, that it's all right for me to kiss you, would you tell me?"

"I'll tell you," she said, starting on her second sandwich, "if I ever decide."

✳ The rain came as a cool surprise.

It smelled of soda water and limes and oranges and the cleanest, freshest river in the world, made of snow-water, falling from the high, parched sky.

First there had been a motion, as of veils, in the sky. The clouds had enveloped each other softly. A faint breeze had lifted Vinia's hair, sighing and evaporating the moisture from her upper lip, and then, as she and Jim began to run, the raindrops fell down all about without touching them and then at last began to touch them, coolly, as they leaped green-moss logs and darted among vast trees into the deepest, muskiest cavern of the forest. The forest sprang up in wet murmurs overhead, every leaf ringing and painted fresh with water.

"This way!" cried Jim.

And they reached a hollow tree so vast that they could squeeze in and be warmly cozy from the rain. They stood together, arms about each other, the first coldness from the rain making them shiver, raindrops on their noses and cheeks, laughing. "Hey!" He gave her brow a lick. "Drinking water!"

"Jim!"

They listened to the rain, the soft envelopment of the world in the velvet clearness of falling water, the whispers in deep grass, evoking odors of old, wet wood and leaves that had lain a hundred years, moldering and sweet.

Then they heard another sound. Above and inside the hollow warm darkness of the tree was a constant humming, like someone in a kitchen, far away, baking and crusting pies contentedly, dipping in sweet sugars and snowing in baking powders, someone in a warm, dim, summer-rainy kitchen making a vast supply of food, happy at it, humming between lips over it.

"Bees, Jim, up there! Bees!"

"Shh!"

Up the channel of moist, warm hollow they saw little yellow flickers. Now the last bees, wettened, were hurrying home from whatever pasture or meadow or field they had covered, dipping by Vinia and Jim, vanishing up the warm flue of summer into hollow dark.

"They won't bother us. Just stand still."

Jim tightened his arms; Vinia tightened hers. She could smell his breath with the wild tart grapes still on it. And the harder the rain drummed on the tree, the tighter they held, laughing, at last quietly letting their laughter drain away into the sound of the bees home from the far fields. And for a moment, Vinia thought that she and Jim might be caught by a sudden drop of great masses of honey from above, sealing them into this tree forever, enchanted, in amber, to be seen by anyone in the next thousand years who strolled by, while the weather of all ages rained and thundered and turned green outside the tree.

It was so warm, so safe, so protected here, the world did not exist, there was raining silence, in the sunless, forested day.

"Vinia," whispered Jim, after a while. "May I now?"

His face was very large, near her, larger than any face she had ever seen.

"Yes," she said.

He kissed her.

The rain poured hard on the tree for a full minute while everything was cold outside and everything was tree-warmth and hidden away inside.

It was a very sweet kiss. It was very friendly and comfortably warm and it tasted like apricots and fresh apples and as water tastes when you rise at night and walk into a dark, warm summer kitchen and drink from a cool tin cup. She had never imagined that a kiss could be so sweet and immensely tender and careful of her. He held her not as he had held her a moment before, hard, to protect her from the green rain weather, but he held her now as if she were a porcelain clock, very carefully and with consideration. His eyes were closed and the lashes were glistening dark; she saw this in the instant she opened her eyes and closed them again.

The rain stopped.

It was a moment before the new silence shocked them into an awareness of the climate beyond their world. Now there was nothing but the suspension of water in all the intricate branches of the forest. Clouds moved away to show the blue sky in great quilted patches.

They looked out at the change with some dismay. They waited for the rain to come back, to keep them, by necessity, in this hollow tree for another minute or an hour. But the sun appeared, shining through upon everything, making the scene quite commonplace again.

They stepped from the hollow tree slowly and stood with their hands out, balancing, finding their way, it seemed, in these woods where the water was drying fast on every limb and leaf.

"I think we'd better start walking," said Vinia. "That way."

They walked off into the summer afternoon.

＊ They crossed the town limits at sunset and walked hand in hand in the last glowing of the summer day. They had talked very little the rest of the afternoon, and now as they turned down one street after another, they looked at the passing sidewalk under their feet.

"Vinia," he said at last. "Do you think this is the beginning of something?"

"Oh, gosh, Jim, I don't know."

"Do you think maybe we're in love?"

"Oh, I don't know that either!"

They passed down into the ravine and over the bridge and up the other side to her street.

"Do you think we'll ever be married?"

"It's too early to tell, isn't it?" she said.

"I guess you're right." He bit his lip. "Will we go walking again soon?"

"I don't know. I don't know. Let's wait and see, Jim."

The house was dark, her parents not home yet. They stood on her porch and she shook his hand gravely.

"Thanks, Jim, for a really fine day," she said.

"You're welcome," he said.

They stood there.

Then he turned and walked down the steps and across the dark lawn. At the far edge of lawn he stopped in the shadows and said, "Good night."

He was almost out of sight, running, when she, in turn, said good night.

✳ In the middle of the night, a sound wakened her.

She half sat up in bed, trying to hear it again. The folks were home, everything was locked and secure, but it hadn't been them. No, this was a special sound. And lying there, looking out at the summer night that had, not long ago, been a summer day, she heard the sound again, and it was a sound of hollowing warmth and moist bark and empty, tunneled tree, the rain outside but comfortable dryness and secretness inside, and it was the sound of bees come home from distant fields, moving upward in the flue of summer into wonderful darkness.

And this sound, she realized, putting her hand up in the summer-night room to touch it, was coming from her drowsy, half-smiling mouth.

Which made her sit bolt upright, and very quietly move downstairs, out through the door, onto the porch, and across the wet-grass lawn to the sidewalk, where the crazed hopscotch chalked itself way off into the future.

Her bare feet hit the first numbers, leaving moist prints up to 10 and 12, thumping, until she stopped at 16, staring down at 17, hesitating, swaying. Then she gritted her teeth, made fists, reared back, and . . .

Jumped right in the middle of the square 17.

She stood there for a long moment, eyes shut, seeing how it felt.

Then she ran upstairs and lay out on the bed and touched her mouth to see if a summer afternoon was breathing out of it, and listening for that drowsy hum, the golden sound, and it was there.

And it was this sound, eventually, which sang her to sleep.

THE ILLUSTRATED MAN

"Hey, the Illustrated Man!"

A calliope screamed, and Mr. William Philippus Phelps stood, arms folded, high on the summer-night platform, a crowd unto himself.

He was an entire civilization. In the Main Country, his chest, the Vasties lived—nipple-eyed dragons swirling over his fleshpot, his almost feminine breasts. His navel was the mouth of a slit-eyed monster—an obscene, in-sucked mouth, toothless as a witch. And there were secret caves where Darklings lurked, his armpits, adrip with slow subterranean liquors, where the Darklings, eyes jealously ablaze, peered out through rank creeper and hanging vine.

Mr. William Philippus Phelps leered down from his freak platform with a thousand peacock eyes. Across the sawdust meadow he saw his wife, Lisabeth, far away, ripping tickets in half, staring at the silver belt buckles of passing men.

Mr. William Philippus Phelps' hands were tattooed roses. At the sight of his wife's interest, the roses shriveled, as with the passing of sunlight.

A year before, when he had led Lisabeth to the marriage bureau to watch her work her name in ink, slowly, on the form, his skin had been pure and white and clean. He glanced down at himself in sudden horror. Now he was like a great painted canvas, shaken in the night wind! How had it happened? Where had it all begun?

It had started with the arguments, and then the flesh, and then the pictures. They had fought deep into the summer nights, she like a brass trumpet forever blaring at him. And he had gone out to eat five thousand steaming hot dogs, ten million hamburgers, and a forest of green onions, and to drink vast red seas of orange juice. Peppermint candy formed his brontosaur bones, the hamburgers shaped his balloon flesh, and strawberry pop pumped in and out of his heart valves sickeningly, until he weighed three hundred pounds.

"William Philippus Phelps," Lisabeth said to him in the eleventh month of their marriage, "you're dumb and fat."

That was the day the carnival boss handed him the blue envelope. "Sorry, Phelps. You're no good to me with all that gut on you."

"Wasn't I always your best tent man, boss?"

"Once. Not anymore. Now you sit, you don't get the work out."

"Let me be your Fat Man."

"I got a Fat Man. Dime a dozen." The boss eyed him up and down. "Tell you what, though. We ain't had a Tattooed Man since Gallery Smith died last year. . . ."

That had been a month ago. Four short weeks. From someone, he had learned of a tattoo artist far out in the rolling Wisconsin country, an old woman, they said, who knew her trade. If he took the dirt road and turned right at the river and then left . . .

He had walked out across a yellow meadow, which was crisp from the sun. Red flowers blew and bent in the wind as he walked, and he came to the old shack, which looked as if it had stood in a million rains.

Inside the door was a silent, bare room, and in the center of the bare room sat an ancient woman.

Her eyes were stitched with red resin-thread. Her nose was sealed with black wax-twine. Her ears were sewn, too, as if a darning-needle dragonfly had stitched all her senses shut. She sat, not moving, in the vacant room. Dust lay in a yellow flour all about, unfootprinted in many weeks; if she had moved it would have shown, but she had not moved. Her hands touched each other like thin, rusted instruments. Her feet were naked and obscene as rain rubbers, and near them sat vials of tattoo milk—red, lightning-blue, brown, cat-yellow. She was a thing sewn tight into whispers and silence.

Only her mouth moved, unsewn: "Come in. Sit down. I'm lonely here."

He did not obey.

"You came for the pictures," she said in a high voice. "I have a picture to show you first."

She tapped a blind finger to her thrust-out palm. "See!" she cried.

It was a tattoo-portrait of William Philippus Phelps.

"Me!" he said.

Her cry stopped him at the door. "Don't run."

He held to the edges of the door, his back to her. "That's me, that's me on your hand!"

"It's been there fifty years." She stroked it like a cat, over and over.

He turned. "It's an *old* tattoo." He drew slowly nearer. He edged forward and bent to blink at it. He put out a trembling finger to brush the picture. "Old. That's impossible! You don't know *me*. I don't know *you*. Your eyes, all sewed shut."

"I've been waiting for you." she said. "And many people." She displayed her arms and legs, like the spindles of an antique chair. "I have pictures on me of people who have already come here to see me. And there are other pictures of other people who are coming to see me in the next one hundred years. And you, you have come."

"How do you know it's me? You can't see!"

"You *feel* like the lions, the elephants, and the tigers to me. Unbutton your shirt. You need me. Don't be afraid. My needles are as clean as a doctor's fingers. When I'm finished with illustrating you, I'll wait for someone else to walk along out here and find me. And someday, a hundred summers from now, perhaps, I'll just go lie down in the forest under some white mushrooms, and in the spring you won't find anything but a small blue cornflower. . . ."

He began to unbutton his sleeves.

"I know the Deep Past and the Clear Present and the even Deeper Future," she whispered, eyes knotted into blindness, face lifted to this unseen man. "It is on my flesh. I will paint it on yours, too. You will be the only *real* illustrated Man in the universe. I'll give you special pictures you will never forget. Pictures of the Future on your skin."

She pricked him with a needle.

✳ He ran back to the carnival that night in a drunken terror and elation. Oh, how quickly the old dust-witch had stitched him with color and design. At the end of a long afternoon of being bitten by a silver snake, his body was alive with portraiture. He looked as if he had dropped and been crushed between the steel rollers of a print press, and come out like an incredible rotogravure. He was clothed in a garment of trolls and scarlet dinosaurs.

"Look!" he cried to Lisabeth. She glanced up from her cosmetics table as he tore his shirt away. He stood in the naked bulb-light of their car-trailer, expanding his impossible chest. Here, the Tremblies, half-maiden, half-goat, leaping when his biceps flexed. Here, the Country of Lost Souls, his chins. In so many accordion pleats of fat, numerous small scorpions, beetles, and mice were crushed, held, hid, darting into view, vanishing, as he raised or lowered his chins.

"My God," said Lisabeth. "My husband's a freak."

She ran from the trailer and he was left alone to pose before the mirror. Why had he done it? To have a job, yes, but, most of all, to cover the fat that had larded itself impossibly over his bones. To hide the fat under a layer of color and fantasy, to hide it from his wife, but most of all from himself.

He thought of the old woman's last words. She had needled him two *special* tattoos, one on his chest, another for his back, which she would not let him see. She covered each with cloth and adhesive.

"You are not to look at these two," she had said.

"Why?"

"Later, you may look. The Future is in these pictures. You can't look now or it may spoil them. They are not quite finished. I put ink on your flesh, and the sweat of you forms the rest of the picture, the Future—your sweat and your thought." Her empty mouth grinned. "Next Saturday night, you may advertise! The Big Unveiling! Come see the Illustrated Man unveil his picture! You can make money in that way. You can charge admission to the Unveiling, like to an art gallery. Tell them you have a picture that even *you* never have seen, that *nobody* has seen yet. The most unusual picture ever painted. Almost alive. And it tells the Future. Roll the drums and blow the trumpets. And you can stand there and unveil at the Big Unveiling."

"That's a good idea," he said.

"But only unveil the picture on your chest," she said. "That is first. You must save the picture on your back, under the adhesive, for the following week. Understand?"

"How much do I owe you?"

"Nothing," she said. "If you walk with these pictures on you, I will be repaid with my own satisfaction. I will sit here for the next two weeks and think how clever my pictures are, for I make them fit each man himself and what is inside him. Now, walk out of this house and never come back. Good-bye."

* "Hey! The Big Unveiling!"

The red signs blew in the night wind: NO ORDINARY TATTOOED MAN!

THIS ONE IS "ILLUSTRATED"! GREATER THAN MICHELANGELO! TONIGHT!
ADMISSION 10 CENTS!

Now the hour had come. Saturday night, the crowd stirring their animal feet in the hot sawdust.

"In one minute—" the carny boss pointed his cardboard megaphone—
"in the tent immediately to my rear, we will unveil the Mysterious Portrait
upon the Illustrated Man's chest! Next Saturday night, the same hour, same
location, we'll unveil the Picture upon the Illustrated Man's *back*! Bring
your friends!"

There was a stuttering roll of drums.

Mr. William Philippus Phelps jumped back and vanished; the crowd
poured into the tent, and, once inside, found him re-established upon
another platform, the band brassing out a jig-time melody.

He looked for his wife and saw her, lost in the crowd, like a stranger,
come to watch a freakish thing, a look of contemptuous curiosity upon her
face. For, after all, he was her husband, this was a thing she didn't know
about him herself. It gave him a feeling of great height and warmness and
light to find himself the center of the jangling universe, the carnival
world, for one night. Even the other freaks—the Skeleton, the Seal Boy, the
Yoga, the Magician, and the Balloon—were scattered through the crowd.

"Ladies and gentlemen, the great moment!"

A trumpet flourish, a hum of drumsticks on tight cowhide.

Mr. William Philippus Phelps let his cape fall. Dinosaurs, trolls, and
half-women-half-snakes writhed on his skin in the stark light.

Ah, murmured the crowd, for surely there had never been a tattooed
man like this! The beast eyes seemed to take red fire and blue fire, blinking
and twisting. The roses on his fingers seemed to expel a sweet pink bouquet.
The Tyrannosaurus rex reared up along his leg, and the sound of the brass
trumpet in the hot tent heavens was a prehistoric cry from the red monster
throat. Mr. William Philippus Phelps was a museum jolted to life. Fish
swam in seas of electric-blue ink. Fountains sparkled under yellow suns.
Ancient buildings stood in meadows of harvest wheat. Rockets burned
across spaces of muscle and flesh. The slightest inhalation of his breath
threatened to make chaos of the entire printed universe. He seemed afire,
the creatures flinching from the flame, drawing back from the great heat of
his pride, as he expanded under the audience's rapt contemplation.

The carny boss laid his fingers to the adhesive. The audience rushed forward, silent in the oven vastness of the night tent.

"You ain't seen nothing yet!" cried the carny boss.

The adhesive ripped free.

There was an instant in which nothing happened. An instant in which the Illustrated Man thought that the Unveiling was a terrible and irrevocable failure.

But then the audience gave a low moan.

The carny boss drew back, his eyes fixed.

Far out at the edge of the crowd, a woman, after a moment, began to cry, began to sob, and did not stop.

Slowly, the Illustrated Man looked down at his naked chest and stomach.

The thing that he saw made the roses on his hands discolor and die. All of his creatures seemed to wither, turn inward, shrivel with the arctic coldness that pumped from his heart outward to freeze and destroy them. He stood trembling. His hands floated up to touch that incredible picture, which lived, moved and shivered with life. It was like gazing into a small room, seeing a thing of someone else's life so intimate, so impossible that one could not believe and one could not long stand to watch without turning away.

It was a picture of his wife, Lisabeth, and himself.

And he was killing her.

Before the eyes of a thousand people in a dark tent in the center of a black-forested Wisconsin land, he was killing his wife.

His great flowered hands were upon her throat, and her face was turning dark and he killed her and he killed her and did not ever in the next minute stop killing her. It was real. While the crowd watched, she died, and he turned very sick. He was about to fall straight down into the crowd. The tent whirled like a monster bat wing, flapping grotesquely. The last thing he heard was a woman, sobbing, far out on the shore of the silent crowd.

And the crying woman was Lisabeth, his wife.

In the night, his bed was moist with perspiration. The carnival sounds had melted away, and his wife, in her own bed, was quiet now, too. He fumbled with his chest. The adhesive was smooth. They had made him put it back.

He had fainted. When he revived, the carny boss had yelled at him, "Why didn't you say what the picture was like?"

"I didn't know, I didn't," said the Illustrated Man.

"Good God!" said the boss. "Scare hell outa everyone. Scared hell outa Lizzie, scared hell outa me. Christ, where'd you *get* that damn tattoo?" He shuddered. "Apologize to Lizzie, now."

His wife stood over him.

"I'm sorry, Lisabeth," he said, weakly, his eyes closed. "I didn't know."

"You did it on purpose," she said. "To scare me."

"I'm sorry."

"Either it goes or I go," she said.

"Lisabeth."

"You heard me. That picture comes off or I quit this show."

"Yeah, Phil," said the boss. "That's how it is."

"Did you lose money? Did the crowd demand refunds?"

"It ain't the money, Phil. For that matter, once the word got around, hundreds of people wanted in. But I'm runnin' a clean show. That tattoo comes off! Was this your idea of a practical joke, Phil?"

He turned in the warm bed. No, not a joke. Not a joke at all. He had been as terrified as anyone. Not a joke. That little old dust-witch, what had she *done* to him and how had she done it? Had she put the picture there? No; she had said that the picture was unfinished, and that he himself, with his thoughts and perspiration, would finish it. Well, he had done the job all right.

But what, if anything, was the significance? He didn't want to kill anyone. He didn't want to kill Lisabeth. Why should such a silly picture burn here on his flesh in the dark?

He crawled his fingers softly, cautiously down to touch the quivering place where the hidden portrait lay. He pressed tight, and the temperature of that spot was enormous. He could almost feel that little evil picture killing and killing and killing all through the night.

I don't wish to kill her, he thought, insistently, looking over at her bed. And then, five minutes later, he whispered aloud: "Or *do* I?"

"What?" she cried, awake.

"Nothing," he said, after a pause, "Go to sleep."

✳ The man bent forward, a buzzing instrument in his hand. "This cost five bucks an inch. Costs more to peel tattoos off than put 'em on. Okay, jerk the adhesive."

The Illustrated Man obeyed.

The skin man sat back. "Christ! No wonder you want that off! That's ghastly. *I* don't even want to look at it." He flicked his machine. "Ready? This won't hurt."

The carny boss stood in the tent flap, watching. After five minutes, the skin man changed the instrument head, cursing. Ten minutes later he scraped his chair back and scratched his head. Half an hour passed and he got up, told Mr. William Philippus Phelps to dress, and packed his kit.

"Wait a minute," said the carny boss. "You ain't done the job."

"And I ain't going to," said the skin man.

"I'm paying good money. What's wrong?"

"Nothing, except that damn picture just won't come off. Damn thing must go right down to the bone."

"You're crazy."

"Mister, I'm in business thirty years and never seen a tattoo like this. An inch deep, if it's anything."

"But I've got to get it off!" cried the Illustrated Man.

The skin man shook his head. "Only one way to get rid of that."

"How?"

"Take a knife and cut off your chest. You won't live long, but the picture'll be gone."

"Come back here!"

But the skin man walked away.

They could hear the big Sunday-night crowd, waiting.

"That's a big crowd," said the Illustrated Man.

"But they ain't going to see what they came to see," said the carny boss. "You ain't going out there, except with the adhesive. Hold still now, I'm curious about this *other* picture, on your back. We might be able to give 'em an Unveiling on this one instead."

"She said it wouldn't be ready for a week or so. The old woman said it would take time to set, make a pattern."

There was a soft ripping as the carny boss pulled aside a flap of white tape on the Illustrated Man's spine.

"What do you see?" gasped Mr. Phelps, bent over.

The carny boss replaced the tape. "Buster, as a Tattooed Man, you're a washout, ain't you? Why'd you let that old dame fix you up this way?"

"I didn't know who she was."

"She sure cheated you on this one. No design to it. Nothing. No picture at all."

"It'll come clear. You wait and see."

The boss laughed. "Okay. Come on. We'll show the crowd part of you, anyway."

They walked out into an explosion of brassy music.

✳ He stood monstrous in the middle of the night, putting out his hands like a blind man to balance himself in a world now tilted, now rushing, now threatening to spin him over and down into the mirror before which he raised his hands. Upon the flat, dimly lighted tabletop were peroxide, acids, silver razors, and squares of sandpaper. He took each of them in turn. He soaked the vicious tattoo upon his chest, he scraped at it. He worked steadily for an hour.

He was aware, suddenly, that someone stood in the trailer door behind him. It was three in the morning. There was a faint odor of beer. She had come home from town. He heard her slow breathing. He did not turn. "Lisabeth?" he said.

"You'd better get rid of it," she said, watching his hands move the sandpaper. She stepped into the trailer.

"I didn't want the picture this way," he said.

"You did," she said. "You planned it."

"I didn't."

"I know you," she said. "Oh, I know you hate me. Well, that's nothing. I hate you. I've hated you a long time now. Good God, when you started putting on the fat, you think anyone could love you then? I could teach you some things about hate. Why don't you ask me?"

"Leave me alone," he said.

"In front of that crowd, making a spectacle out of me!"

"I didn't know what was under the tape."

She walked around the table, hands fitted to her hips talking to the beds, the walls, the table, talking it all out of her. And he thought: *Or did I know? Who made this picture, me or the witch? Who formed it? How? Do I really want her dead? No! And yet.* . . . He watched his wife draw nearer, nearer, he saw the ropy strings of her throat vibrate to her shouting. This and this and *this* was wrong with him! That and that and *that* was unspeakable about him! He was a liar, a schemer, a fat, lazy, ugly man, a child. Did he think he could compete with the carny boss or the tentpeggers? Did he think he was sylphine and graceful, did he think he was a framed El Greco? DaVinci, huh! Michelangelo, my eye! She brayed. She showed her teeth. "Well, you can't scare me into staying with someone I don't want touching me with their slobby paws!" she finished, triumphantly.

"Lisabeth," he said.

"Don't Lisabeth me!" she shrieked. "I know your plan. You had that picture put on to scare me. You thought I wouldn't *dare* leave you. Well!"

"Next Saturday night, the Second Unveiling," he said. "You'll be proud of me."

"Proud! You're silly and pitiful. God, you're like a whale. You ever see a beached whale? I saw one when I was a kid. There it was, and they came and shot it. Some lifeguards shot it. Jesus, a whale!"

"Lisabeth."

"I'm leaving, that's all, and getting a divorce."

"Don't."

"And I'm marrying a man, not a fat woman—that's what you are, so much fat on you there ain't no sex!"

"You can't leave me," he said.

"Just watch!"

"I love you," he said.

"Oh," she said. "Go look at your pictures."

He reached out.

"Keep your hands off," she said.

"Lisabeth."

"Don't come near. You turn my stomach."

"Lisabeth."

All the eyes of his body seemed to fire, all the snakes to move, all the monsters to seethe, all the mouths to widen and rage. He moved toward her—not like a man, but a crowd.

He felt the great blooded reservoir of orangeade pump through him now, the sluice of cola and rich lemon pop pulse in sickening sweet anger through his wrists his legs, his heart. All of it, the oceans of mustard and relish and all the million drinks he had drowned himself in in the last year were aboil; his face was the color of a steamed beef. And the pink roses of his hands became those hungry, carnivorous flowers kept long years in tepid jungle and now let free to find their way on the night air before him.

He gathered her to him, like a great beast gathering in a struggling animal. It was a frantic gesture of love, quickening and demanding, which, as she struggled, hardened to another thing. She beat and clawed at the picture on his chest.

"You've got to love me, Lisabeth."

"Let go!" she screamed. She beat at the picture that burned under her fists. She slashed at it with her fingernails.

"Oh, Lisabeth," he said, his hands moving up her arms.

"I'll scream," she said, seeing his eyes.

"Lisabeth." The hands moved up to her shoulders, to her neck. "Don't go away."

"Help!" she screamed. The blood ran from the picture on his chest.

He put his fingers about her neck and squeezed.

She was a calliope cut in mid-shriek.

Outside, the grass rustled. There was the sound of running feet.

Mr. William Philippus Phelps opened the trailer door and stepped out.

They were waiting for him. Skeleton, Midget, Balloon, Yoga, Electra, Pop-eye, Seal Boy. The freaks, waiting in the middle of the night, in the dry grass.

He walked toward them. He moved with a feeling that he must get away; these people would understand nothing, they were not thinking people. And because he did not flee, because he only walked, balanced, stunned, between the tents, slowly, the freaks moved to let him pass. They watched him, because their watching guaranteed that he would not escape. He walked out across the black meadow, moths fluttering in his face. He walked steadily as long as he was visible, not knowing where he was going. They watched him go, and then they turned and all of them shuffled to the silent car-trailer together and pushed the door slowly wide. . . .

The Illustrated Man walked steadily in the dry meadows beyond the town.

"He went that way!" a faint voice cried. Flashlights bobbled over the hills. There were dim shapes, running.

Mr. William Philippus Phelps waved to them. He was tired. He wanted only to be found now. He was tired of running away. He waved again.

"There he is!" The flashlights changed direction. "Come on! We'll get the bastard!"

When it was time, the Illustrated Man ran again. He was careful to run slowly. He deliberately fell down twice. Looking back, he saw the tent stakes they held in their hands.

He ran toward a far crossroads lantern, where all the summer night seemed to gather: merry-go-rounds of fireflies whirling, crickets moving their song toward that light, everything rushing, as if by some midnight attraction, toward that one high-hung lantern—the Illustrated Man first, the others close at his heels.

As he reached the light and passed a few yards under and beyond it, he did not need to look back. On the road ahead, in silhouette, he saw the upraised tent stakes sweep violently up, up, and then *down*!

A minute passed.

In the country ravines, the crickets sang. The freaks stood over the sprawled Illustrated Man, holding their tent stakes loosely.

Finally they rolled him over on his stomach. Blood ran from his mouth.

They ripped the adhesive from his back. They stared down for a long moment at the freshly revealed picture. Someone whispered. Someone else swore, softly. The Thin Man pushed back and walked away and was sick. Another and another of the freaks stared, their mouths trembling, and moved away, leaving the Illustrated Man on the deserted road, the blood running from his mouth.

In the dim light, the unveiled Illustration was easily seen.

It showed a crowd of freaks bending over a dying fat man on a dark and lonely road, looking at a tattoo on his back which illustrated a crowd of freaks bending over a dying fat man on a . . .

THE DEAD MAN

THAT'S THE MAN, RIGHT OVER THERE," said Mrs. Ribmoll, nodding across the street. "See that man perched on the tar barrel afront Mr. Jenkins' Odd Martin."

Odd Martin.

"The one that says he's dead?" cried Arthur.

Mrs. Ribmoll nodded. "Crazy as a weasel down a chimney. Carries on firm about how he's been dead since the flood and nobody appreciates."

"I see him sitting there every day," cried Arthur.

"Oh yes, he sits there, he does. Sits there and stares at nothing. I say it's a crying shame they don't throw him in jail."

Arthur made a face at the man. "Yah!"

"Never mind, he won't notice you. Most uncivil man I ever seen. Nothing pleased him." She yanked Arthur's arm. "Come on, sonny, we got shopping to do."

They passed on up the street past the barber shop. In the window, after they'd gone by, stood Mr. Simpson, sniping his blue shears and chewing his tasteless gum. He squinted thoughtfully out through the fly-specked glass, looking at the man sitting over there on the tar barrel. "I figure the best thing could happen to Odd Martin would be to get married," he figured. His eyes glinted slyly. Over his shoulder he looked at his manicurist, Miss Weldon, who was busy burnishing the scraggly fingernails of a farmer named Gilpatrick. Miss Weldon, at this suggestion, did not look up. She had heard it often. They were always ragging her about Odd Martin.

Mr. Simpson walked back and started work on Gilpatrick's dusty hair again. Gilpatrick chuckled softly. "What woman would marry Odd? Sometimes I almost believe he *is* dead. He's got an awful odor to him."

Miss Weldon looked up into Mr. Gilpatrick's face and carefully cut his finger with one of her little scalpels. "Gol darn it!" "Watch what you're doing, woman!"

Miss Weldon looked at him with calm little blue eyes in a small white face. Her hair was mouse-brown; she wore no make-up and talked to no one most of the time.

Mr. Simpson cackled and snicked his blue steel shears. "Hope, hope, hope!" he laughed like that. "Miss Weldon, she knows what she's doin', Gilpatrick. You just be careful. Miss Weldon, she give a bottle of eau de cologne to Odd Martin last Christmas. It helped cover up his smell."

Miss Weldon laid down her instruments.

"Sorry, Miss Weldon," apologized Mr. Simpson. "I won't say no more."

Reluctantly, she took up her instruments again.

"Hey, there he goes again!" cried one of the four other men waiting in the shop. Mr. Simpson whirled, almost taking Gilpatrick's pink ear with him in his shears. "Come look, boys!"

✳ Across the street the sheriff stepped out of his office door just then and he saw it happen, too. He saw what Odd Martin was doing.

Everybody came running from all the little stores.

The sheriff arrived and looked down into the gutter.

"Come on now, Odd Martin, come on now," he shouted. He poked down into the gutter with his shiny black boot-tip. "Come on, get up. You're not dead. You're good as me. You'll catch your death of cold there with all them gum wrappers and cigar butts! Come on, get up!"

Mr. Simpson arrived on the scene and looked at Odd Martin lying there. "He looks like a carton of milk."

"He's takin' up valuable parkin' space for cars, this bein' Friday mornin'," whined the sheriff. "And lots of people needin' the area. Here now, Odd. Hmm. Well, give me a hand here, boys."

They laid the body on the sidewalk.

"Let him stay here," declared the sheriff, jostling around in his boots. "Just let him stay till he gets tired of layin'. He's done this a million times before. Likes the publicity. *Git*, you kids!"

He sent a bunch of children scuttling ahead of his cheek of tobacco.

Back in the barber shop, Simpson looked around. "Where's Miss Weldon? Unh." He looked through the glass. "There she is, brushing him off again, while he lies there. Fixing his coat, buttoning it up. Here she comes back. Don't nobody fun with her, she resents it."

The barber clock said twelve o'clock and then one and then two and then three. Mr. Simpson kept track of it. "I make you a bet that Odd Martin lies over there 'till four o'clock," he said.

Someone else said, "I'll bet he's there until four-thirty."

"Last time—" a snickering of the shears "—he was there four hours. Nice warm day today. He may nap there until five. I'll say five. Let's see your money, gents or maybe later."

The money was collected and put on a shelf by the hair-ointments.

One of the younger men began shaving a stick with his pocketknife. "It's sorta funny how we joke about Odd. We're scared of him, inside. I mean we won't let ourselves believe he's really dead. We don't dare believe it. We'd never get over it if we knew. So we make him a joke. We let him lie around. He don't hurt nobody. He's just there. But I notice Doc Hudson has never really touched Odd's heart with his stethoscope. Scared of what he'd find, I bet."

"Scared of what he'd find!" Laughter. Simpson laughed and snished his shears. Two men with crusty beards laughed, a little too loud. The laughter didn't last long. "Great one for jokin', you are!" they all said, slapping their gaunt knees.

Miss Weldon, she went on manicuring her client.

"He's getting up!"

There was a general scramble to the plate glass window to watch Odd Martin gain his feet. "He's up on one knee, now up on the other, now someone's givin' him a hand."

"It's Miss Weldon. She sure got over there in a rush."

"What time is it?"

"Five o'clock. Pay me, boys!"

"That Miss Weldon's a queer nut herself. Takin' after a man like Odd."

Simpson clicked his scissors. "Being an orphan, she's got quiet ways. She likes men who don't say much. Odd, he don't say hardly anything. Just the opposite of us crude men, eh, fellows? We talk too much. Miss Weldon don't like our way of talking."

"There they go, the two of 'em, Miss Weldon and Odd Martin."

"Say, take a little more off around my ears, will you, Simp?"

✳ Skipping down the street, bouncing a red rubber ball, came little Charlie Bellows, his blond hair flopping in a yellow fringe over his blue eyes. He bounced the ball abstractedly, tongue between lips, and the ball fell under Odd Martin's feet where he sat once more on the tar barrel. Inside the grocery, Miss Weldon was doing her supper shopping, putting soup cans and vegetable cans into a basket.

"Can I have my ball?" asked little Charlie Bellows upward at the six feet, two inches of Odd Martin. No one was within hearing distance.

"Can you have your ball?" said Odd Martin haltingly. He turned it over inside his head, it appeared. His level gray eyes shaped up Charlie like one would shape up a little ball of clay. "You can have your ball; yes, take it."

Charlie bent slowly and took hold of the bright red rubber globe and arose slowly, a secretive look in his eyes. He looked north and south and then up at Odd's bony pale brown face. "I know something."

Odd Martin looked down. "You know something?"

Charlie leaned forward. "You're dead."

Odd Martin sat there.

"You're really dead," whispered little Charlie Bellows. "But I'm the only one who really knows. I believe you, Mr. Odd. I tried it once myself. Dying, I mean. It's hard. It's work. I laid on the floor for an hour. But I blinked and my stomach itched, so I scratched it. Then— I quit. Why?" He looked at his shoes. "'Cause I had to go to the bathroom."

A slow, understanding smile formed in the soft pallid flesh of Odd Martin's long, bony face. "It is work. It isn't easy."

"Sometimes I think about you," said Charlie. "I see you walking by my house at night. Sometimes at two in the morning. Sometimes at four. I wake up and I know you're out walking around. I know I should look out, and I do, and, gee, there you are, walking and walking. Not going hardly any place."

"There's no place to go." Odd sat with his large square, calloused hands on his knees. "I try thinking of some—place to—go—" He slowed, like a horse to a bit-pull. "—but it's hard to think. I try and—try. Sometimes I almost know what to do, where to go. Then I forget. Once I had an idea to go to a doctor and have him declare me dead, but somehow—" his voice was slow and husky and low "—I never got there."

Charlie looked straight at him. "If you want, I'll take you."

Odd Martin looked leisurely at the setting sun. "No. I'm weary-tired, but I'll—wait. Now I've gone this far, I'm curious to see what happens next. After the flood that washed away my farm and all my stock and put me under water, like a chicken in a bucket, I filled up like you'd fill a Thermos with water, and I came walking out of the flood, anyhow. But I knew I was dead. Late of nights I lay listening in my room, but there's no heartbeat in my ears or in my chest or in my wrists, though I lie still as a cold cricket. Nothing inside me but a darkness and a relaxation and an understanding. There must be a reason for me still walking, though. Maybe it was because I was still young when I died. Only twenty-eight, and not married yet. I always wanted to marry. Never got around to it. Here I am, doing odd jobs around town, saving my money, 'cause I never eat, heck, I *can't* eat, and sometimes getting so discouraged and downright bewildered that I lie down in the gutter and hope they'll take me and poke me in a pine box and lay me away forever. Yet at the same time—I don't want that. I want a little more. I know that whenever Miss Weldon walks by and I see the wind playing her hair like a little brown feather—" He sighed away into silence.

Charlie Bellows waited politely a minute, then cleared his throat and darted away, bouncing his ball. "See you later!"

Odd stared at the spot where Charlie'd been. Five minutes later he blinked. "Eh? Somebody here? Somebody speak?"

Miss Weldon came out of the grocery with a basket full of food.

"Would you like to walk me home, Odd?"

They walked along in an easy silence, she careful not to walk too fast, because he set his legs down carefully. The wind rustled in the cedars and in the elms and the maples all along the way. Several times his lips parted and he glanced aside at her, and then he shut his mouth tight and stared ahead, as if looking at something a million miles away.

Finally, he said. "Miss Weldon?"

"Yes, Odd?"

"I been saving and saving up my money. I've got quite a handsome sum.

I don't spend much for anything, and—you'd be surprised," he said, sincerely. "I got about a thousand dollars. Maybe more. Some times I count it and get tired and I can't count no more. And—" he seemed baffled and a little angry with her suddenly. "Why do you like me, Miss Weldon?" he demanded.

She looked a little surprised, then smiled up at him. It was almost a child-like look of liking she gave him. "Because you're quiet. Because you're not loud and mean like the men at the barber shop. Because I'm lonely, and you've been kind. Because you're the first one that ever liked me. The others don't even look at me once. They say I can't think. They say I'm a moron, because I didn't finish the sixth grade. But I'm so lonely, Odd, and talking to you means so much."

He held her small white hand, tight.

She moistened her lips. "I wish we could do something about the way people talk about you. I don't want to sound mean, but if you'd only stop telling them you're dead, Odd."

He stopped walking. "Then you don't believe me, either," he said remotely.

"You're 'dead' for want of a good woman's cooking, for loving, for living right, Odd. That's what you mean by 'dead'; nothing else!"

His gray eyes were deep and lost. "Is that what I mean?" He saw her eager, shiny face. "Yes, that's what I mean. You guessed it right. That's what I mean."

Their footsteps went alone together, drifting in the wind, like leaves floating, and the night got darker and softer and the stars came out.

＊ Two boys and two girls stood under a street lamp about nine o'clock that evening. Far away down the street someone walked along slowly, quietly, alone.

"There he is," said one of the boys. "You ask him, Tom."

Tom scowled uneasily. The girls laughed at him. Tom said, "Oh, okay, but you come along."

The wind flung the trees right and left, shaking down leaves in singles and clusters that fell past Odd Martin's head as he approached.

"Mr. Odd? Hey there, Mr. Odd?"

"Eh? Oh, hello."

"We—uh—that is—" gulped Tom, looking around for assistance. "We want to know if—well—we want you to come to our party!"

A minute later, after looking at Tom's clean, soap-smelling face and seeing the pretty blue jacket his sixteen-year-old girl friend wore, Odd Martin answered. "Thank you. But I don't know. I might forget to come."

"No, you wouldn't," insisted Tom. "You'd remember this one, because it's Hallowe'en!"

One of the girls yanked Tom's arm and hissed. "Let's not, Tom. Let's not. Please. He won't do, Tom. He isn't scary enough."

Tom shook her off. "Let *me* handle this."

The girl pleaded. "Please, no. He's just a dirty old man. Bill can put candle tallow on his fingers and those horrible porcelain teeth in his mouth and the green chalk marks under his eyes, and scare the ducks out of us. We don't need *him*?" And she jerked her rebellious head at Odd.

Odd Martin stood there. He heard the wind in the high tree-tops for ten minutes before he knew that the four young people were gone. A small dry laugh came up in his mouth like a pebble. Children. Hallowe'en. Not scary enough. Bill would do better. Just an old man. He tasted the laughter and found it both strange and bitter.

✳ The next morning little Charlie Bellows flung his ball against the store front, retrieved it flung it again. He heard someone humming behind him, turned. "Oh, hello, Mr. Odd!"

Odd Martin was walking along, with green paper dollars in his fingers, counting it. He stopped, suddenly. His eyes were blank.

"Charlie," he cried out. "Charlie!" His hands groped.

"Yes, sir, Mr. Odd!"

"Charlie, where was I going? Where was I going? Going somewhere to buy something for Miss Weldon! Here, Charlie, help me!"

"Yes, sir, Mr. Odd." Charlie ran up and stood in his shadow.

A hand came down, money in it, seventy dollars of money. "Charlie, run buy a dress for—Miss Weldon—" His mind was grasping, clutching, seizing, wrestling in a web of forgetfulness. There was stark terror and longing and fear in his face. "I can't remember the place, oh God, help me remember. A dress and a coat, for Miss Weldon, at—at—"

"Krausmeyer's Department Store?" asked Charlie, helpfully.

"No!"

"Fieldman's?"

"No!"

"Mr. Leiberman's?"

"Leiberman! That's it! Leiberman, Leiberman! Here, here, Charlie, here, run down there to—"

"Leiberman's."

"—and get a new green dress for—Miss Weldon, and a coat. A new green dress with yellow roses painted on it. You get them and bring them to me here. Oh, Charlie, wait."

"Yes, sir, Mr. Odd?"

"Charlie—you think, maybe I could clean up at your house?" asked Odd quietly. "I need a—a bath."

"Gee, I don't know, Mr. Odd. My folks are funny. I don't know."

"That's all right, Charlie. I understand. Run now!"

Charlie ran on the double, clutching the money. He ran by the barber shop. He poked his head in. Mr. Simpson stopped snipping on Mr. Trumbull's hair and glared at him. "Hey!" cried Charlie. Odd Martin's humming a tune!"

"What tune?" asked Mr. Simpson.

"It goes like this," said Charlie, and hummed it.

"Yee Gods Amaughty!" bellowed Simpson. "So that's why Miss Weldon ain't here manicurin' this morning! That there tune's the Wedding March!"

Charlie ran on. Pandemonium!

✳ Shouting, laughter, the sound of water squishing and pattering. The back of the barber shop steamed. They took turns. First, Mr. Simpson got a bucket of hot water and tossed it down in a flap over Odd Martin, who sat in the tub, saying nothing, just sitting there, and then Mr. Trumbull scrubbed Odd Martin's pale back with a big brush and lots of cow-soap, and every once in a while Shorty Phillips doused Odd with a jigger of eau de cologne. They all laughed and ran around in the steam. "Gettin' married, hunh, Odd? Congratulations, boy!" More water. "I always said that's what you needed," laughed Mr. Simpson, hitting Odd in the chest with a bunch of cold water this time. Odd Martin pretended not to even notice the shock. "You'll smell better now!"

Odd sat there. "Thanks. Thanks so very much for doing this. Thanks for helping me. Thanks for giving me a bath this way. I needed it."

Simpson laughed behind his hand. "Sure thing, anything for you, Odd."

Someone whispered in the steamy background, "Imagine her and him married? A moron married to an idiot!"

Simpson frowned. "Shut up back there!"

Charlie rushed in. "Here's the green dress, Mr. Odd!"

An hour later they had Odd in the barber chair. Someone had lent him a new pair of shoes. Mr. Trumbull was polishing them vigorously, winking at everybody Mr. Simpson snipped Odd's hair for him, would not take money for it. "No, no, Odd, you keep that as a wedding present from me to you. Yes, sir." And he spat. Then he shook some rose-water all over Odd's dark hair. "There. Moonlight and roses!"

Martin looked around. "You won't tell nobody about this marriage," he asked, "until tomorrow? Me and Miss Weldon sort of want a marriage without the town poking fun. You understand?"

"Why sure, sure, Odd," said Simpson, finishing the job. "Mum's the word. Where you going to live? You buying a new farm?"

"Farm?" Odd Martin stepped down from the chair. Somebody lent him a nice new coat and someone else had pressed his pants for him. He looked fine. "Yes, I'm going to buy the property now. Have to pay extra for it, but it's worth it. Extra. Come along now. Charlie Bellows." He went to the door. "I bought a house out on the edge of town. I have to go make the payment on it now. Come on, Charlie."

Simpson stopped him. "What's it like? You didn't have much money; you couldn't afford much."

"No," said Odd, "you're right. It's a small house. But it'll do. Some folks built it awhile back, then moved away East somewheres, it was up for sale for only five hundred, so I got it. Miss Weldon and I are moving out there tonight, after our marriage. But don't tell nobody, please, until tomorrow."

"Sure thing, Odd. Sure thing."

Odd went away into the four o'clock light, Charlie at his side, and the men in the barber shop went and sat down, laughing.

The wind sighed outside, and slowly the sun went down and the snipping of the shears went on, and the men sat around, laughing and talking . . .

❋ The next morning at breakfast, little Charlie Bellows sat thoughtfully spooning his cereal. Father folded his newspaper across the table and looked at Mother. "Everybody in town's talking about the quiet elopement of Odd Martin and Miss Weldon," said Father. "People, looking for them, can't find them."

"Well," said Mother, "I hear he bought a house for her."

"I heard that, too," said Father. "I phoned Carl Rogers this morning. He says he didn't sell any house to Odd. And Carl is the only real estate dealer in town."

Charlie Bellows swallowed some cereal. He looked at his father. "Oh, no, he's not the only real estate dealer in town?"

"What do you mean?" demanded Father.

"Nothing, except that I looked out the window at midnight, and I saw something."

"You saw *what*?"

"It was all moonlight. And you know what I saw? Well, I saw two people walking up the Elm Grade road. A man and a woman. A man in a new dark coat, and a woman in a green dress. Walking real slow. Holding hands." Charlie took a breath. "And the two people were Mr. Odd Martin and Miss Weldon. And walking out the Elm Grade road there ain't any houses out that way at all. Only the Trinity Park Cemetery. And Mr. Gustavsson, in town, he sells tombs in the Trinity Park Cemetery. He's got an office in town. Like I said, Mr. Carl Rogers ain't the *only* real estate man in town. So—"

"Oh," snorted Father, irritably, "you were dreaming!"

Charlie bent his head over his cereal and looked out from the corners of his eyes.

"Yes, sir," he said finally, sighing. "I was only dreaming."

JUNE 2001: AND THE MOON BE STILL AS BRIGHT

It was so cold when they first came from the rocket into the night that Spender began to gather the dry Martian wood and build a small fire. He didn't say anything about a celebration; he merely gathered the wood, set fire to it, and watched it burn.

In the flare that lighted the thin air of this dried-up sea of Mars he looked over his shoulder and saw the rocket that had brought them all, Captain Wilder and Cheroke and Hathaway and Sam Parkhill and himself, across a silent black space of stars to land upon a dead, dreaming world.

Jeff Spender waited for the noise. He watched the other men and waited for them to jump around and shout. It would happen as soon as the numbness of being the "first" men to Mars wore off. None of them said anything, but many of them were hoping, perhaps, that the other expeditions had failed and that this, the Fourth, would be the one. They meant nothing evil by it. But they stood thinking it, nevertheless, thinking of the honor and fame, while their lungs became accustomed to the thinness of the atmosphere, which almost made you drunk if you moved too quickly.

Gibbs walked over to the freshly ignited fire and said, "Why don't we use the ship chemical fire instead of that wood?"

"Never mind," said Spender, not looking up.

It wouldn't be right, the first night on Mars, to make a loud noise, to introduce a strange, silly bright thing like a stove. It would be a kind of imported blasphemy. There'd be time for that later; time to throw condensed-milk cans in the proud Martian canals; time for copies of the New York Times to blow and caper and rustle across the lone gray Martian sea bottoms; time for banana peels and picnic papers in the fluted, delicate ruins of the old Martian valley towns. Plenty of time for that. And he gave a small inward shiver at the thought.

He fed the fire by hand, and it was like an offering to a dead giant. They had landed on an immense tomb. Here a civilization had died. It was only simple courtesy that the first night be spent quietly.

"This isn't my idea of a celebration." Gibbs turned to Captain Wilder. "Sir, I thought we might break out rations of gin and meat and whoop it up a bit."

Captain Wilder looked off toward a dead city a mile away. "We're all tired," he said remotely, as if his whole attention was on the city and his men forgotten. "Tomorrow night, perhaps. Tonight we should be glad we got across all that space without getting a meteor in our bulkhead or having one man of us die."

The men shifted around. There were twenty of them, holding to each other's shoulders or adjusting their belts. Spender watched them. They were not satisfied. They had risked their lives to do a big thing. Now they wanted to be shouting drunk, firing off guns to show how wonderful they were to have kicked a hole in space and ridden a rocket all the way to Mars.

But nobody was yelling.

The captain gave a quiet order. One of the men ran into the ship and brought forth food tins which were opened and dished out without much noise. The men were beginning to talk now. The captain sat down and recounted the trip to them. They already knew it all, but it was good to hear about it, as something over and done and safely put away. They would not talk about the return trip. Someone brought that up, but they told him to keep quiet. The spoons moved in the double moonlight; the food tasted good and the wine was even better.

There was a touch of fire across the sky, and an instant later the auxiliary rocket landed beyond the camp. Spender watched as the small port opened and Hathaway, the physician-geologist—they were all men of twofold ability, to conserve space on the trip—stepped out. He walked slowly over to the captain.

"Well?" said Captain Wilder.

Hathaway gazed out at the distant cities twinkling in the starlight. After swallowing and focusing his eyes he said, "That city there, Captain, is dead and has been dead a good many thousand years. That applies to those three cities in the hills also. But that fifth city, two hundred miles over, sir—"

"What about it?"

"People were living in it last week, sir."

Spender got to his feet.

"Martians," said Hathaway.

"Where are they now?"

"Dead," said Hathaway. "I went into a house on one street. I thought that it, like the other towns and houses, had been dead for centuries. My God, there were bodies there. It was like walking in a pile of autumn leaves. Like sticks and pieces of burned newspaper, that's all. And *fresh*. They'd been dead ten days at the outside."

"Did you check other towns? Did you see *anything* alive?"

"Nothing whatever. So I went out to check the other towns. Four out of five have been empty for thousands of years. What happened to the original inhabitants I haven't the faintest idea. But the fifth city always contained the same thing. Bodies. Thousands of bodies."

"What did they die of?" Spender moved forward.

"You won't believe it."

"What killed them?"

Hathaway said simply, "Chicken pox."

"My God, no!"

"Yes. I made tests. Chicken pox. It did things to the Martians it never did to Earth Men. Their metabolism reacted differently, I suppose. Burned them black and dried them out to brittle flakes. But it's chicken pox, nevertheless. So York and Captain Williams and Captain Black must have got through to Mars, all three expeditions. God knows what happened to them. But we at least know what they unintentionally did to the Martians."

"You saw no other life?"

"Chances are a few of the Martians, if they were smart, escaped to the mountains. But there aren't enough, I'll lay you money, to be a native problem. This planet is through."

Spender turned and went to sit at the fire, looking into it. Chicken pox, God, chicken pox, think of it! A race builds itself for a million years, refines itself, erects cities like those out there, does everything it can to give itself respect and beauty, and then it dies. Part of it dies slowly, in its own time, before our age, with dignity. But the rest! Does the rest of Mars die of a disease with a fine name or a terrifying name or a majestic name? No, in the name of all that's holy, it has to be chicken pox, a child's disease, a disease that doesn't even kill *children* on Earth! It's not right and it's not fair. It's like saying the Greeks died of mumps, or the proud Romans died on their beautiful hills of athlete's foot! If only we'd given the Martians time to arrange their death robes, lie down, look fit, and think up some other excuse for dying. It can't be a dirty, silly thing like chicken pox. It doesn't fit the architecture; it doesn't fit this entire world!

"All right, Hathaway, get yourself some food."

"Thank you, Captain."

And as quickly as that it was forgotten. The men talked among themselves.

Spender did not take his eyes off them. He left his food on his plate under his hands. He felt the land getting colder. The stars drew closer, very clear.

When anyone talked too loudly the captain would reply in a low voice that made them talk quietly from imitation.

The air smelled clean and new. Spender sat for a long time just enjoying the way it was made. It had a lot of things in it he couldn't identify: flowers, chemistries, dusts, winds.

"Then there was that time in New York when I got that blonde, what's her name?—Ginnie!" cried Biggs. "*That* was it!"

Spender tightened in. His hand began to quiver. His eyes moved behind the thin, sparse lids.

"And Ginnie said to me—" cried Biggs.

The men roared.

"So I smacked her!" shouted Biggs with a bottle in his hand.

Spender set down his plate. He listened to the wind over his ears, cool and whispering. He looked at the cool ice of the white Martian buildings over there on the empty sea lands.

"What a woman, what a woman!" Biggs emptied his bottle in his wide mouth. "Of all the women I ever knew!"

The smell of Biggs's sweating body was on the air. Spender let the fire die. "Hey, kick her up there, Spender!" said Biggs, glancing at him for a moment, then back to his bottle. "Well, one night Ginnie and me—"

A man named Schoenke got out his accordion and did a kicking dance, the dust springing up around him.

"Ahoo—I'm alive!" he shouted.

"Yay!" roared the men. They threw down their empty plates. Three of them lined up and kicked like chorus maidens, joking loudly. The others, clapping hands, yelled for something to happen. Cheroke pulled off his shirt and showed his naked chest, sweating as he whirled about. The moonlight shone on his crew-cut hair and his young, clean-shaven cheeks.

In the sea bottom the wind stirred along faint vapors, and from the mountains great stone visages looked upon the silvery rocket and the small fire.

The noise got louder, more men jumped up, someone sucked on a mouth organ, someone else blew on a tissue-papered comb. Twenty more bottles were opened and drunk. Biggs staggered about, wagging his arms to direct the dancing men.

"Come on, sir!" cried Cheroke to the captain, wailing a song.

The captain had to join the dance. He didn't want to. His face was solemn. Spender watched, thinking: You poor man, what a night this is! They don't know what they're doing. They should have had an orientation program before they came to Mars to tell them how to look and how to walk around and be good for a few days.

"That does it." The captain begged off and sat down, saying he was exhausted. Spender looked at the captain's chest. It wasn't moving up and down very fast. His face wasn't sweaty, either.

Accordion, harmonica, wine, shout, dance, wail, roundabout, clash of pan, laughter.

Biggs weaved to the rim of the Martian canal. He carried six empty bottles and dropped them one by one into the deep blue canal waters. They made empty, hollow, drowning sounds as they sank.

"I christen thee, I christen thee, I christen thee—" said Biggs thickly. "I christen thee Biggs, Biggs, Biggs Canal—"

Spender was on his feet, over the fire, and alongside Biggs before anyone moved. He hit Biggs once in the teeth and once in the ear. Biggs toppled and fell down into the canal water. After the splash Spender waited silently for Biggs to climb back up onto the stone bank. By that time the men were holding Spender.

"Hey, what's eating you, Spender? Hey?" they asked.

Biggs climbed up and stood dripping. He saw the men holding Spender. "Well," he said, and started forward.

"That's enough," snapped Captain Wilder. The men broke away from Spender. Biggs stopped and glanced at the captain.

"All right, Biggs, get some dry clothes. You men, carry on your party! Spender, come with me!"

The men took up the party. Wilder moved off some distance and confronted Spender. "Suppose you explain what just happened," he said.

Spender looked at the canal. "I don't know. I was ashamed. Of Biggs and us and the noise. Christ, what a spectacle."

"It's been a long trip. They've got to have their fling."

"Where's their respect, sir? Where's their sense of the right thing?"

"You're tired, and you've a different way of seeing things, Spender. That's a fifty-dollar fine for you."

"Yes, sir. It was just the idea of Them watching us make fools of ourselves."

"Them?"

"The Martians, whether they're dead or not."

"Most certainly dead," said the captain. "Do you think They know we're here?"

"Doesn't an old thing always know when a new thing comes?"

"I suppose so. You sound as if you believe in spirits."

"I believe in the things that were done, and there are evidences of many things done on Mars. There are streets and houses, and there are books, I imagine, and big canals and clocks and places for stabling, if not horses, well, then some domestic animal, perhaps with twelve legs, who knows? Everywhere I look I see things that were used. They were touched and handled for centuries.

"Ask me, then, if I believe in the spirit of the things as they were used, and I'll say yes. They're all here. All the things which had uses. All the mountains which had names. And we'll never be able to use them without feeling uncomfortable. And somehow the mountains will never sound right to us; we'll give them new names, but the old names are there, somewhere in time, and the mountains were shaped and seen under those names. The names we'll give to the canals and mountains and cities will fall like so much water on the back of a mallard. No matter how we touch Mars, we'll never touch it. And then we'll get mad at it, and you know what we'll do? We'll rip it up, rip the skin off, and change it to fit ourselves."

"We won't ruin Mars," said the captain. "It's too big and too good."

"You think not? We Earth Men have a talent for ruining big, beautiful things. The only reason we didn't set up hot-dog stands in the midst of the Egyptian temple of Karnak is because it was out of the way and served no large commercial purpose. And Egypt is a small part of Earth. But here, this whole thing is ancient and different, and we have to set down somewhere and start fouling it up. We'll call the canal the Rockefeller Canal and the mountain King George Mountain and the sea the Dupont Sea, and there'll be Roosevelt and Lincoln and Coolidge cities and it won't ever be right, when there are the proper names for these places."

"That'll be your job, as archaeologist, to find out the old names, and we'll use them."

"A few men like us against all the commercial interests." Spender looked at the iron mountains. "They know we're here tonight, to spit in their wine, and I imagine they hate us."

The captain shook his head. "There's no hatred here." He listened to the wind. "From the look of their cities they were a graceful, beautiful, and philosophical people. They accepted what came to them. They acceded to racial death, that much we know, and without a last-moment war of frustration to tumble down their cities. Every town we've seen so far has been flawlessly intact. They probably don't mind us being here anymore than they'd mind children playing on the lawn, knowing and understanding children for what they are. And, anyway, perhaps all this will change us for the better.

"Did you notice the peculiar quiet of the men, Spender, until Biggs forced them to get happy? They looked pretty humble and frightened. Looking at all this, we know we're not so hot; we're kids in rompers, shouting with our play rockets and atoms, loud and alive. But one day Earth will be as Mars is today. This will sober us. It's an object lesson in civilizations.

We'll learn from Mars. Now suck in your chin. Let's go back and play happy. That fifty-dollar fine still goes."

❋ The party was not going too well. The wind kept coming in off the dead sea. It moved around the men and it moved around the captain and Jeff Spender as they returned to the group. The wind pulled at the dust and the shining rocket and pulled at the accordion, and the dust got into the vamped harmonica. The dust got in their eyes and the wind made a high singing sound in the air. As suddenly as it had come the wind died.

But the party had died too.

The men stood upright against the dark cold sky.

"Come on, gents, come on!" Biggs bounded from the ship in a fresh uniform, not looking at Spender even once. His voice was like someone in an empty auditorium. It was alone. "Come on!"

Nobody moved.

"Come on, Whitie, your harmonica!"

Whitie blew a chord. It sounded funny and wrong. Whitie knocked the moisture from his harmonica and put it away.

"What kinda party is this?" Biggs wanted to know.

Someone hugged the accordion. It gave a sound like a dying animal. That was all.

"Okay, me and my bottle will go have our own party." Biggs squatted against the rocket, drinking from a flask.

Spender watched him. Spender did not move for a long time. Then his fingers crawled up along his trembling leg to his holstered pistol, very quietly, and stroked and tapped the leather sheath.

"All those who want to can come into the city with me," announced the captain. "We'll post a guard here at the rocket and go armed, just in case."

The men counted off. Fourteen of them wanted to go, including Biggs, who laughingly counted himself in, waving his bottle. Six others stayed behind.

"Here we go!" Biggs shouted.

The party moved out into the moonlight, silently. They made their way to the outer rim of the dreaming dead city in the light of the racing twin moons. Their shadows, under them, were double shadows. They did not breathe, or seemed not to, perhaps, for several minutes. They were waiting for something to stir in the dead city, some gray form to rise, some ancient, ancestral shape to come galloping across the vacant sea bottom on an ancient, armored steed of impossible lineage, of unbelievable derivation.

Spender filled the streets with his eyes and his mind. People moved like blue vapor lights on the cobbled avenues, and there were faint murmurs of sound, and odd animals scurrying across the gray-red sands. Each window was given a person who leaned from it and waved slowly, as if under a timeless water, at some moving form in the fathoms of space below the moon-silvered towers. Music was played on some inner ear, and Spender imagined the shape of such instruments to evoke such music. The land was haunted.

"Hey!" shouted Biggs, standing tall, his hands around his open mouth. "Hey, you people in the city there, you!"

"Biggs!" said the captain.

Biggs quieted.

They walked forward on a tiled avenue. They were all whispering now, for it was like entering a vast open library or a mausoleum in which the wind lived and over which the stars shone. The captain spoke quietly. He wondered where the people had gone, and what they had been, and who their kings were, and how they had died. And he wondered, quietly aloud, how they had built this city to last the ages through, and had they ever come to Earth? Were they ancestors of Earth Men ten thousand years removed? And had they loved and hated similar loves and hates, and done similar silly things when silly things were done?

Nobody moved. The moons held and froze them; the wind beat slowly around them.

"Lord Byron," said Jeff Spender.

"Lord who?" The captain turned and regarded him.

"Lord Byron, a nineteenth-century poet. He wrote a poem a long time ago that fits this city and how the Martians must feel, if there's anything left of them to feel. It might have been written by the last Martian poet."

The men stood motionless, their shadows under them.

The captain said, "How does the poem go, Spender?"

Spender shifted, put out his hand to remember, squinted silently a moment; then, remembering, his slow quiet voice repeated the words and the men listened to everything he said:

> "So we'll go no more a-roving
>   So late into the night,
>   Though the heart be still as loving,
>   And the moon be still as bright."

The city was gray and high and motionless. The men's faces were turned in the light.

> "For the sword outwears its sheath,
>   And the soul wears out the breast,
>   And the heart must pause to breathe,
>   And love itself must rest.
> "Though the night was made for loving,
>   And the day returns too soon,
>   Yet we'll go no more a-roving
>   By the light of the moon."

Without a word the Earth Men stood in the center of the city. It was a clear night. There was not a sound except the wind. At their feet lay a tile court worked into the shapes of ancient animals and peoples. They looked down upon it.

Biggs made a sick noise in his throat. His eyes were dull. His hands went to his mouth; he choked, shut his eyes, bent, and a thick rush of fluid filled his mouth, spilled out, fell to splash on the tiles, covering the designs. Biggs did this twice. A sharp winy stench filled the cool air.

No one moved to help Biggs. He went on being sick.

Spender stared for a moment, then turned and walked off into the avenues of the city, alone in the moonlight. Never once did he pause to look back at the gathered men there.

✳ They turned in at four in the morning. They lay upon blankets and shut their eyes and breathed the quiet air. Captain Wilder sat feeding little sticks into the fire.

McClure opened his eyes two hours later. "Aren't you sleeping, sir?"

"I'm waiting for Spender." The captain smiled faintly.

McClure thought it over. "You know, sir, I don't think he'll ever come back. I don't know how I know, but that's the way I feel about him, sir; he'll never come back."

McClure rolled over into sleep. The fire crackled and died.

✳ Spender did not return in the following week. The captain sent searching parties, but they came back saying they didn't know where Spender could have gone. He would be back when he got good and ready. He was a sorehead, they said. To the devil with him!

The captain said nothing but wrote it down in his log. . . .

It was a morning that might have been a Monday or a Tuesday or any day on Mars. Biggs was on the canal rim; his feet hung down into the cool water, soaking, while he took the sun on his face.

A man walked along the bank of the canal. The man threw a shadow down upon Biggs. Biggs glanced up.

"Well, I'll be damned!" said Biggs.

"I'm the last Martian," said the man, taking out a gun.

"What did you say?" asked Biggs.

"I'm going to kill you."

"Cut it. What kind of joke's that, Spender?"

"Stand up and take it in the stomach."

"For Christ's sake, put that gun away."

Spender pulled the trigger only once. Biggs sat on the edge of the canal for a moment before he leaned forward and fell into the water. The gun had made only a whispering hum. The body drifted with slow unconcern under the slow canal tides. It made a hollow bubbling sound that ceased after a moment.

Spender shoved his gun into its holster and walked soundlessly away. The sun was shining down upon Mars. He felt it burn his hands and slide over the sides of his tight face. He did not run; he walked as if nothing were new except the daylight. He walked down to the rocket, and some of the men were eating a freshly cooked breakfast under a shelter built by Cookie.

"Here comes The Lonely One," someone said.

"Hello, Spender! Long time no see!"

The four men at the table regarded the silent man who stood looking back at them.

"You and them goddamn ruins," laughed Cookie, stirring a black substance in a crock. "You're like a dog in a bone yard."

"Maybe," said Spender, "I've been finding out things. What would you say if I said I'd found a Martian prowling around?"

The four men laid down their forks.

"Did you? Where?"

"Never mind. Let me ask you a question. How would you feel if you were a Martian and people came to your land and started tearing it up?"

"I know exactly how I'd feel," said Cheroke. "I've got some Cherokee blood in me. My grandfather told me lots of things about Oklahoma Territory. If there's a Martian around, I'm all for him."

"What about you other men?" asked Spender carefully.

Nobody answered; their silence was talk enough. Catch as catch can, finder's keepers, if the other fellow turns his cheek slap it hard, etc. . . .

"Well," said Spender, "I've found a Martian."

The men squinted at him.

"Up in a dead town. I didn't think I'd find him. I didn't intend looking him up. I don't know what he was doing there. I've been living in a little valley town for about a week, learning how to read the ancient books and looking at their old art forms. And one day I saw this Martian. He stood there for a moment and then he was gone. He didn't come back for another day. I sat around, learning how to read the old writing, and the Martian came back, each time a little nearer, until on the day I learned how to decipher the Martian language—it's amazingly simple and there are picture-graphs to help you—the Martian appeared before me and said, 'Give me your boots.' And I gave him my boots and he said, 'Give me your uniform and all the rest of your apparel.' And I gave him all of that, and then he said, 'Give me your gun,' and I gave him my gun. Then he said, 'Now come along and watch what happens.' And the Martian walked down into camp and he's here now."

"I don't see any Martian," said Cheroke.

"I'm sorry."

Spender took out his gun. It hummed softly. The first bullet got the man on the left; the second and third bullets took the men on the right and the center of the table. Cookie turned in horror from the fire to receive the fourth bullet. He fell back into the fire and lay there while his clothes caught fire.

The rocket lay in the sun. Three men sat at breakfast, their hands on the table, not moving, their food getting cold in front of them. Cheroke, untouched, sat alone, staring in numb disbelief at Spender.

"You can come with me," said Spender.

Cheroke said nothing.

"You can be with me on this." Spender waited.

Finally Cheroke was able to speak. "You killed them," he said, daring to look at the men around him.

"They deserved it."

"You're crazy!"

"Maybe I am. But you can come with me."

"Come with you, for what?" cried Cheroke, the color gone from his face, his eyes watering. "Go on, get out!"

Spender's face hardened. "Of all of them, I thought you would understand."

"Get out!" Cheroke reached for his gun.

Spender fired one last time. Cheroke stopped moving.

Now Spender swayed. He put his hand to his sweating face. He glanced at the rocket and suddenly began to shake all over. He almost fell, the physical reaction was so overwhelming. His face held an expression of one awakening from hypnosis, from a dream. He sat down for a moment and told the shaking to go away.

"Stop it, stop it!" he commanded of his body. Every fiber of him was quivering and shaking. "Stop it!" He crushed his body with his mind until all the shaking was squeezed out of it. His hands lay calmly now upon his silent knees.

He arose and strapped a portable storage locker on his back with quiet efficiency. His hand began to tremble again, just for a breath of an instant, but he said, "No!" very firmly, and the trembling passed. Then, walking stiffly, he moved out between the hot red hills of the land, alone.

✳ The sun burned farther up the sky. An hour later the captain climbed down out of the rocket to get some ham and eggs. He was just saying hello to the four men sitting there when he stopped and noticed a faint smell of gun fumes on the air. He saw the cook lying on the ground, with the campfire under him. The four men sat before food that was now cold.

A moment later Parkhill and two others climbed down. The captain stood in their way, fascinated by the silent men and the way they sat at their breakfast.

"Call the men, all of them," said the captain.

Parkhill hurried off down the canal rim.

The captain touched Cheroke. Cheroke twisted quietly and fell from his chair. Sunlight burned in his bristled short hair and on his high cheekbones.

The men came in.

"Who's missing?"

"It's still Spender, sir. We found Biggs floating in the canal."

"Spender!"

The captain saw the hills rising in the daylight. The sun showed his teeth in a grimace. "Damn him," he said tiredly. "Why didn't he come and talk to me?"

"He should've talked to me," cried Parkhill, eyes blazing. "I'd have shot his bloody brains out, that's what I'd have done, by God!"

Captain Wilder nodded at two of his men. "Get shovels," he said.

It was hot digging the graves. A warm wind came from over the vacant sea and blew the dust into their faces as the captain turned the Bible pages. When the captain closed the book someone began shoveling slow streams of sand down upon the wrapped figures.

They walked back to the rocket, clicked the mechanisms of their rifles, put thick grenade packets on their backs, and checked the free play of pistols in their holsters. They were each assigned a certain part of the hills. The captain directed them without raising his voice or moving his hands where they hung at his sides.

"Let's go," he said.

✳ Spender saw the thin dust rising in several places in the valley and he knew the pursuit was organized and ready. He put down the thin silver book that he had been reading as he sat easily on a flat boulder. The book's pages were tissue-thin, pure silver, hand-painted in black and gold. It was a book of philosophy at least ten thousand years old he had found in one of the villas of a Martian valley town. He was reluctant to lay it aside.

For a time he had thought, What's the use? I'll sit here reading until they come along and shoot me.

The first reaction to his killing the six men this morning had caused a period of stunned blankness, then sickness, and now, a strange peace. But the peace was passing, too, for he saw the dust billowing from the trails of the hunting men, and he experienced the return of resentment.

He took a drink of cool water from his hip canteen. Then he stood up, stretched, yawned, and listened to the peaceful wonder of the valley around him. How very fine if he and a few others he knew on Earth could be here, live out their lives here, without a sound or a worry.

He carried the book with him in one hand, the pistol ready in his other. There was a little swift-running stream filled with white pebbles and rocks where he undressed and waded in for a brief washing. He took all the time he wanted before dressing and picking up his gun again.

The firing began about three in the afternoon. By then Spender was high in the hills. They followed him through three small Martian hill towns. Above the towns, scattered like pebbles, were single villas where ancient families had found a brook, a green spot, and laid out a tile pool, a library, and a court with a pulsing fountain. Spender took half an hour, swimming in one of the pools which was filled with the seasonal rain, waiting for the pursuers to catch up with him.

Shots rang out as he was leaving the little villa. Tile chipped up some twenty feet behind him, exploded. He broke into a trot, moved behind a series of small bluffs, turned, and with his first shot dropped one of the men dead in his tracks.

They would form a net, a circle; Spender knew that. They would go around and close in and they would get him. It was a strange thing that the grenades were not used. Captain Wilder could easily order the grenades tossed.

But I'm much too nice to be blown to bits, thought Spender. That's what the captain thinks. He wants me with only one hole in me. Isn't that odd? He wants my death to be clean. Nothing messy. Why? Because he understands me. And because he understands, he's willing to risk good men to give me a clean shot in the head. Isn't that it?

Nine, ten shots broke out in a rattle. Rocks around him jumped up. Spender fired steadily, sometimes while glancing at the silver book he carried in his hand.

The captain ran in the hot sunlight with a rifle in his hands. Spender followed him in his pistol sights but did not fire. Instead he shifted and blew the top off a rock where Whitie lay, and heard an angry shout.

Suddenly the captain stood up. He had a white handkerchief in his hands. He said something to his men and came walking up the mountain after putting aside his rifle. Spender lay there, then got to his feet, his pistol ready.

The captain came up and sat down on a warm boulder, not looking at Spender for a moment.

The captain reached into his blouse pocket. Spender's fingers tightened on the pistol.

The captain said, "Cigarette?"

"Thanks." Spender took one.

"Light?"

"Got my own."

They took one or two puffs in silence.

"Warm," said the captain.

"It is."

"You comfortable up here?"

"Quite."

"How long do you think you can hold out?"

"About twelve men's worth."

"Why didn't you kill all of us this morning when you had the chance? You could have, you know."

"I know. I got sick. When you want to do a thing badly enough you lie to yourself. You say the other people are all wrong. Well, soon after I started killing people I realized they were just fools and I shouldn't be killing them. But it was too late. I couldn't go on with it then, so I came up here where I could lie to myself some more and get angry, to build it all up again."

"Is it built up?"

"Not very high. Enough."

The captain considered his cigarette. "Why did you do it?"

Spender quietly laid his pistol at his feet. "Because I've seen that what these Martians had was just as good as anything we'll ever hope to have. They stopped where we should have stopped a hundred years ago. I've walked in their cities and I know these people and I'd be glad to call them my ancestors."

"They have a beautiful city there." The captain nodded at one of several places.

"It's not that alone. Yes, their cities are good. They knew how to blend art into their living. It's always been a thing apart for Americans. Art was something you kept in the crazy son's room upstairs. Art was something you took in Sunday doses, mixed with religion, perhaps. Well, these Martians have art and religion and everything."

"You think they knew what it was all about, do you?"

"For my money."

"And for that reason you started shooting people."

"When I was a kid my folks took me to visit Mexico City. I'll always remember the way my father acted—loud and big. And my mother didn't like the people because they were dark and didn't wash enough. And my sister wouldn't talk to most of them. I was the only one really liked it. And I can see my mother and father coming to Mars and acting the same way here.

"Anything that's strange is no good to the average American. If it doesn't have Chicago plumbing, it's nonsense. The thought of that! Oh God, the thought of that! And then—the war. You heard the congressional speeches before we left. If things work out they hope to establish three atomic research and atom bomb depots on Mars. That means Mars is finished; all this wonderful stuff gone. How would you feel if a Martian vomited stale liquor on the White House floor?"

The captain said nothing but listened.

Spender continued: "And then the other power interests coming up. The mineral men and the travel men. Do you remember what happened to Mexico when Cortéz and his very fine good friends arrived from Spain? A whole civilization destroyed by greedy, righteous bigots. History will never forgive Cortéz."

"You haven't acted ethically yourself today," observed the captain.

"What could I do? Argue with you? It's simply me against the whole crooked grinding greedy setup on Earth. They'll be flopping their filthy atom bombs up here, fighting for bases to have wars. Isn't it enough they've ruined one planet, without ruining another; do they have to foul someone else's manger? The simple-minded windbags. When I got up here I felt I was not only free of their so-called culture, I felt I was free of their ethics and their customs. I'm out of their frame of reference, I thought. All I have to do is kill you all off and live my own life."

"But it didn't work out," said the captain.

"No. After the fifth killing at breakfast, I discovered I wasn't all new, all Martian, after all. I couldn't throw away everything I had learned on Earth so easily. But now I'm feeling steady again. I'll kill you all off. That'll delay the next trip in a rocket for a good five years. There's no other rocket in existence today, save this one. The people on Earth will wait a year, two years, and then when they hear nothing from us, they'll be very afraid to build a new rocket. They'll take twice as long and make a hundred extra experimental models to insure themselves against another failure."

"You're correct."

"A good report from you, on the other hand, if you returned, would hasten the whole invasion of Mars. If I'm lucky I'll live to be sixty years old. Every expedition that lands on Mars will be met by me. There won't be more than one ship at a time coming up, one every year or so, and never more than twenty men in the crew. After I've made friends with them and explained that our rocket exploded one day—I intend to blow it up after I finish my job this week—I'll kill them off, every one of them. Mars will be untouched for the next half century. After a while, perhaps the Earth people will give up trying. Remember how they grew leery of the idea of building Zeppelins that were always going down in flames?"

"You've got it all planned," admitted the captain.

"I have."

"Yet you're outnumbered. In an hour we'll have you surrounded. In an hour you'll be dead."

"I've found some underground passages and a place to live you'll never find. I'll withdraw there to live for a few weeks. Until you're off guard. I'll come out then to pick you off, one by one."

The captain nodded. "Tell me about your civilization here," he said, waving his hand at the mountain towns.

"They knew how to live with nature and get along with nature. They didn't try too hard to be all men and no animal. That's the mistake we made when Darwin showed up. We embraced him and Huxley and Freud, all smiles. And then we discovered that Darwin and our religions didn't mix. Or at least we didn't think they did. We were fools. We tried to budge Darwin and Huxley and Freud. They wouldn't move very well. So, like idiots, we tried knocking down religion.

"We succeeded pretty well. We lost our faith and went around wondering what life was for. If art was no more than a frustrated outflinging of desire, if religion was no more than self-delusion, what good was life? Faith had always given us answers to all things. But it all went down the drain with Freud and Darwin. We were and still are a lost people."

"And these Martians are a *found* people?" inquired the captain.

"Yes. They knew how to combine science and religion so the two worked side by side, neither denying the other, each enriching the other."

"That sounds ideal."

"It was. I'd like to show you how the Martians did it."

"My men are waiting."

"We'll be gone half an hour. Tell them that, sir."

The captain hesitated, then rose and called an order down the hill.

Spender led him over into a little Martian village built all of cool perfect marble. There were great friezes of beautiful animals, white-limbed cat things and yellow-limbed sun symbols, and statues of bull-like creatures and statues of men and women and huge fine-featured dogs.

"There's your answer, Captain."

"I don't see."

"The Martians discovered the secret of life among animals. The animal does not question life. It lives. Its very reason for living is life; it enjoys and relishes life. You see—the statuary, the animal symbols, again and again."

"It looks pagan."

"On the contrary, those are God symbols, symbols of life. Man had become too much man and not enough animal on Mars too. And the men of Mars realized that in order to survive they would have to forgo asking that one question any longer: *Why live?* Life was its own answer. Life was the propagation of more life and the living of as good a life as possible. The Martians realized that they asked the question 'Why live at all?' at the height of some period of war and despair, when there was no answer. But once the civilization calmed, quieted, and wars ceased, the question became senseless in a new way. Life was now good and needed no arguments."

"It sounds as if the Martians were quite naïve."

"Only when it paid to be naïve. They quit trying too hard to destroy everything, to humble everything. They blended religion and art and science because, at base, science is no more than an investigation of a miracle we can never explain, and art is an interpretation of that miracle. They never let science crush the aesthetic and the beautiful. It's all simply a matter of degree. An Earth Man thinks: 'In that picture, color does not exist, really. A scientist can prove that color is only the way the cells are placed in a certain material to reflect light. Therefore, color is not really an actual part of things I happen to see.' A Martian, far cleverer, would say: 'This is a fine picture. It came from the hand and the mind of a man inspired. Its idea and its color are from life. This thing is good.'"

There was a pause. Sitting in the afternoon sun, the captain looked curiously around at the little silent cool town.

"I'd like to live here," he said.

"You may if you want."

"You ask me that?"

"Will any of those men under you ever really understand all this? They're professional cynics, and it's too late for them. Why do you want to go back with them? So you can keep up with the Joneses? To buy a gyro just like Smith has? To listen to music with your pocketbook instead of your glands? There's a little patio down here with a reel of Martian music in it at least fifty thousand years old. It still plays. Music you'll never hear in your life. You could hear it. There are books. I've gotten on well in reading them already. You could sit and read."

"It all sounds quite wonderful, Spender."

"But you won't stay?"

"No. Thanks, anyway."

"And you certainly won't let me stay without trouble. I'll have to kill you all."

"You're optimistic."

"I have something to fight for and live for; that makes me a better killer. I've got what amounts to a religion, now. It's learning how to breathe all over again. And how to lie in the sun getting a tan, letting the sun work into you. And how to hear music and how to read a book. What does your civilization offer?"

The captain shifted his feet. He shook his head. "I'm sorry this is happening. I'm sorry about it all."

"I am too. I guess I'd better take you back now so you can start the attack."

"I guess so."

"Captain, I won't kill you. When it's all over, you'll still be alive."

"What?"

"I decided when I started that you'd be untouched."

"Well . . ."

"I'll save you out from the rest. When they're dead, perhaps you'll change your mind."

"No," said the captain. "There's too much Earth blood in me. I'll have to keep after you."

"Even when you have a chance to stay here?"

"It's funny, but yes, even with that. I don't know why. I've never asked myself. Well, here we are." They had returned to their meeting place now. "Will you come quietly, Spender? This is my last offer."

"Thanks, no." Spender put out his hand. "One last thing. If you win, do me a favor. See what can be done to restrict tearing this planet apart, at least for fifty years, until the archaeologists have had a decent chance, will you?"

"Right."

"And last—if it helps any, just think of me as a very crazy fellow who went berserk one summer day and never was right again. It'll be a little easier on you that way."

"I'll think it over. So long, Spender. Good luck."

"You're an odd one," said Spender as the captain walked back down the trail in the warm-blowing wind.

The captain returned like something lost to his dusty men. He kept squinting at the sun and breathing hard.

"Is there a drink?" he said. He felt a bottle put cool into his hand. "Thanks." He drank. He wiped his mouth.

"All right," he said. "Be careful. We have all the time we want. I don't want any more lost. You'll have to kill him. He won't come down. Make it a clean shot if you can. Don't mess him. Get it over with."

"I'll blow his damned brains out," said Sam Parkhill.

"No, through the chest," said the captain. He could see Spender's strong, clearly determined face.

"His bloody brains," said Parkhill.

The captain handed him the bottle jerkingly. "You heard what I said. Through the chest."

Parkhill muttered to himself.

"Now," said the captain.

✳ They spread again, walking and then running, and then walking on the hot hillside places where there would be sudden cool grottoes that smelled of moss, and sudden open blasting places that smelled of sun on stone.

I hate being clever, thought the captain, when you don't really feel clever and don't want to be clever. To sneak around and make plans and feel big about making them. I hate this feeling of thinking I'm doing right when I'm not really certain I am. Who are we, anyway? The majority? Is that the answer? The majority is always holy, is it not? Always, always; just never wrong for one little insignificant tiny moment, is it? Never ever wrong in ten million years? He thought: What is this majority and who are in it? And what do they think and how did they get that way and will they ever change and how the devil did I get caught in this rotten majority? I don't feel comfortable. Is it claustrophobia, fear of crowds, or common sense? Can one man be right, while all the world thinks they are right? Let's not think about it. Let's crawl around and act exciting and pull the trigger. There, and there!

The men ran and ducked and ran and squatted in shadows and showed their teeth, gasping, for the air was thin, not meant for running; the air was thin and they had to sit for five minutes at a time, wheezing and seeing black lights in their eyes, eating at the thin air and wanting more, tightening their eyes, and at last getting up, lifting their guns to tear holes in that thin summer air, holes of sound and heat.

Spender remained where he was, firing only on occasion.

"Damned brains all over!" Parkhill yelled, running uphill.

The captain aimed his gun at Sam Parkhill. He put it down and stared at it in horror. "What were you doing?" he asked of his limp hand and the gun.

He had almost shot Parkhill in the back.

"God help me."

He saw Parkhill still running, then falling to lie safe.

Spender was being gathered in by a loose, running net of men. At the hilltop, behind two rocks, Spender lay, grinning with exhaustion from the thin atmosphere, great islands of sweat under each arm. The captain saw the two rocks. There was an interval between them of some four inches, giving free access to Spender's chest.

"Hey, you!" cried Parkhill. "Here's a slug for your head!"

Captain Wilder waited. Go on, Spender, he thought. Get out, like you said you would. You've only a few minutes to escape. Get out and come back later. Go on. You said you would. Go down in the tunnels you said you found, and lie there and live for months and years, reading your fine books and bathing in your temple pools. Go on, now, man, before it's too late.

Spender did not move from his position.

"What's wrong with him?" the captain asked himself.

The captain picked up his gun. He watched the running, hiding men. He looked at the towers of the little clean Martian village, like sharply carved chess pieces lying in the afternoon. He saw the rocks and the interval between where Spender's chest was revealed.

Parkhill was charging up, screaming in fury.

"No, Parkhill," said the captain. "I can't let you do it. Nor the others. No, none of you. Only me." He raised the gun and sighted it.

Will I be clean after this? he thought. Is it right that it's me who does it? Yes, it is. I know what I'm doing for what reason and it's right, because I think I'm the right person. I hope and pray I can live up to this.

He nodded his head at Spender. "Go on," he called in a loud whisper which no one heard. "I'll give you thirty seconds more to get away. Thirty seconds!"

The watch ticked on his wrist. The captain watched it tick. The men were running. Spender did not move. The watch ticked for a long time, very loudly in the captain's ears. "Go on, Spender, go on, get away!"

The thirty seconds were up.

The gun was sighted. The captain drew a deep breath. "Spender," he said, exhaling.

He pulled the trigger.

All that happened was that a faint powdering of rock went up in the sunlight. The echoes of the report faded.

The captain arose and called to his men: "He's dead."

The other men did not believe it. Their angles had prevented their seeing that particular fissure in the rocks. They saw their captain run up the hill, alone, and thought him either very brave or insane.

The men came after him a few minutes later.

They gathered around the body and someone said, "In the chest?"

The captain looked down. "In the chest," he said. He saw how the rocks had changed color under Spender. "I wonder why he waited. I wonder why he didn't escape as he planned. I wonder why he stayed on and got himself killed."

"Who knows?" someone said.

Spender lay there, his hands clasped, one around the gun, the other around the silver book that glittered in the sun.

Was it because of me? thought the captain. Was it because I refused to give in myself? Did Spender hate the idea of killing me? Am I any different from these others here? Is that what did it? Did he figure he could trust me? What other answer is there?

None. He squatted by the silent body.

I've got to live up to this, he thought. I can't let him down now. If he figured there was something in me that was like himself and couldn't kill me because of it, then what a job I have ahead of me! That's it, yes, that's it. I'm Spender all over again, but I think before I shoot. I don't shoot at all, I don't kill. I do things with people. And he couldn't kill me because I was himself under a slightly different condition.

The captain felt the sunlight on the back of his neck. He heard himself talking: "If only he had come to me and talked it over before he shot anybody, we could have worked it out somehow."

"Worked what out?" said Parkhill. "What could we have worked out with *his* likes?"

There was a singing of heat in the land, off the rocks and off the blue sky. "I guess you're right," said the captain. "We could never have got together. Spender and myself, perhaps. But Spender and you and the others, no, never. He's better off now. Let me have a drink from that canteen."

It was the captain who suggested the empty sarcophagus for Spender. They had found an ancient Martian tomb yard. They put Spender into a silver case with waxes and wines which were ten thousand years old, his hands folded on his chest. The last they saw of him was his peaceful face.

They stood for a moment in the ancient vault. "I think it would be a good idea for you to think of Spender from time to time," said the captain.

They walked from the vault and shut the marble door.

The next afternoon Parkhill did some target practice in one of the dead cities, shooting out the crystal windows and blowing the tops off the fragile towers. The captain caught Parkhill and knocked his teeth out.

THE BURNING MAN

THE RICKETY FORD CAME ALONG A ROAD that plowed up dust in yellow plumes which took an hour to lie back down and move no more in that special slumber that stuns the world in mid-July. Far away, the lake waited, a cool-blue gem in a hot-green lake of grass, but it was indeed still far away, and Neva and Doug were bucketing along in their barrelful of red-hot bolts with lemonade slopping around in a thermos on the back seat and deviled-ham sandwiches fermenting on Doug's lap. Both boy and aunt sucked in hot air and talked out even hotter.

"Fire-eater," said Douglas. "I'm eating fire. Heck, I can hardly *wait* for that lake!"

Suddenly, up ahead, there was a man by the side of the road.

Shirt open to reveal his bronzed body to the waist, his hair ripened to wheat color by July, the man's eyes burned fiery blue in a nest of sun wrinkles. He waved, dying in the heat.

Neva tromped on the brake. Fierce dust clouds rose to make the man vanish. When the golden dust sifted away his hot yellow eyes glared balefully, like a cat's, defying the weather and the burning wind.

He stared at Douglas.

Douglas glanced away, nervously.

For you could see where the man had come across a field high with yellow grass baked and burned by eight weeks of no rain. There was a path where the man had broken the grass and cleaved a passage to the road. The path went as far as one could see down to a dry swamp and an empty creek bed with nothing but baked hot stones in it and fried rock and melting sand.

"I'll be damned, you stopped!" cried the man, angrily.

"I'll be damned, I did," Neva yelled back. "Where you going?"

"I'll think of someplace." The man hopped up like a cat and swung into the rumble seat. "Get going. It's *after* us! The sun, I mean, of course!" He pointed straight up. "Git! Or we'll *all* go mad!"

Neva stomped on the gas. The car left gravel and glided on pure white-hot dust, coming down only now and then to careen off a boulder or kiss a stone. They cut the land in half with racket. Above it, the man shouted:

"Put'er up to seventy, eighty, hell, why not ninety!"

Neva gave a quick, critical look at the lion, the intruder in the back seat, to see if she could shut his jaws with a glance. They shut.

And that, of course, is how Doug felt about the beast. Not a stranger, no, not hitchhiker, but intruder. In just two minutes of leaping into the red-hot car, with his jungle hair and jungle smell, he had managed to disingratiate himself with the climate, the automobile, Doug, and the honorable and perspiring aunt. Now she hunched over the wheel and nursed the car through further storms of heat and backlashes of gravel.

Meanwhile, the creature in the back, with his great lion ruff of hair and mint-fresh yellow eyes, licked his lips and looked straight on at Doug in the rearview mirror. He gave a wink. Douglas tried to wink back, but somehow the lid never came down.

"You ever try to figure—" yelled the man.

"What?" cried Neva.

"You ever try to figure," shouted the man, leaning forward between them "—whether or not the weather is driving you crazy, or you're crazy *already*?"

It was a surprise of a question, which suddenly cooled them on this blast-furnace day.

"I don't quite understand—" said Neva.

"Nor does anyone!" The man smelled like a lion house. His thin arms hung over and down between them, nervously tying and untying an invisible string. He moved as if there were nests of burning hair under each armpit. "Day like today, all hell breaks loose inside your head. Lucifer was born on a day like this, in a wilderness like this," said the man. "With just fire and flame and smoke everywhere," said the man. "And everything so hot you can't touch it, and people not wanting to be touched," said the man.

He gave a nudge to her elbow, a nudge to the boy.

They jumped a mile.

"You see?" The man smiled. "Day like today, you get to thinking lots of things." He smiled. "Ain't this the summer when the seventeen-year locusts are supposed to come back like pure holocaust? Simple but multitudinous plagues?"

"Don't know!" Neva drove fast, staring ahead.

"This *is* the summer. Holocaust just around the bend. I'm thinking so swift it hurts my eyeballs, cracks my head. I'm liable to explode in a fireball with just plain disconnected thought. Why—why—why—"

Neva swallowed hard. Doug held his breath.

Quite suddenly they were terrified. For the man simply idled on with his talk, looking at the shimmering green fire trees that burned by on both sides, sniffing the rich hot dust that flailed up around the tin car, his voice neither high nor low, but steady and calm now in describing his life:

"Yes, sir, there's more to the world than people appreciate. If there can be seventeen-year locusts, why not seventeen-year people? Ever *thought* of that?"

"Never did," said someone.

Probably me, thought Doug, for his mouth had moved like a mouse.

"Or how about twenty-four-year people, or fifty-seven-year people? I mean, we're all so used to people growing up, marrying, having kids, we never stop to think maybe there's other ways for people coming into the world, maybe like locusts, once in a while, who can tell, one hot day, middle of summer!"

"Who can tell?" There was the mouse again. Doug's lips trembled.

"And who's to say there ain't genetic evil in the world?" asked the man of the sun, glaring right up at it without blinking.

"*What* kind of evil?" asked Neva.

"Genetic, ma'am. In the blood, that is to say. People born evil, growed evil, died evil, no changes all the way down the line."

"Whew!" said Douglas. "You mean people who start out mean and stay *at it?*"

"You got the sum, boy. Why not? If there are people everyone thinks are angel-fine from their first sweet breath to their last pure declaration, why not sheer orneriness from January first to December, three hundred sixty-five days later?"

"I never thought of that," said the mouse.

"Think," said the man. "*Think.*"

They thought for above five seconds.

"Now," said the man, squinting one eye at the cool lake five miles

ahead, his other eye shut into darkness and ruminating on coal-bins of fact
there, "listen. What if the intense heat, I mean the really hot hot heat of a
month like this, week like this, day like today, just baked the Ornery Man
right out of the river mud. Been there buried in the mud for forty-seven
years, like a damn larva, waiting to be born. And he shook himself awake
and looked around, full grown, and climbed out of the hot mud into the
world and said, 'I think I'll eat me some summer.'"

"How's that again?"

"Eat me some summer, boy, summer, ma'am. Just devour it whole. Look
at them trees, ain't they a whole dinner? Look at that field of wheat, ain't
that a feast? Them sunflowers by the road, by golly, there's breakfast.
Tarpaper on top that house, there's lunch. And the lake, way up ahead,
Jehoshaphat, that's dinner wine, drink it all!"

"I'm thirsty, all right," said Doug.

"Thirsty, hell, boy, thirst don't begin to describe the state of a man,
come to think about him, come to talk, who's been waiting in the hot mud
thirty years and is born but to die in one day! Thirst! Ye Gods! Your ignorance is complete."

"Well," said Doug.

"Well," said the man. "Not only thirst but hunger. Hunger. Look around.
Not only eat the trees and then the flowers blazing by the roads but then the
white-hot panting dogs. There's one. There's another! And all the cats in the
country. There's two, just passed three! And then just glutton-happy begin to
why, why not, begin to get around to, let me tell you, how's this strike you,
eat people? I mean—people! Fried, cooked, boiled, and parboiled people.
Sunburned beauties of people. Old men, young. Old ladies' hats and then old
ladies under their hats and then young ladies' scarves and young ladies, and
then young boys' swim-trunks, by God, and young boys, elbows, ankles, ears,
toes, and eyebrows! Eyebrows, by God, men, women, boys, ladies, dogs, fill
up the menu, sharpen your teeth, lick your lips, dinner's on!"

"Wait!" someone cried.

Not me, thought Doug. I said nothing.

"Hold on!" someone yelled.

It was Neva.

He saw her knee fly up as if by intuition and down as if by finalized
gumption.

Stomp! went her heel on the floor.

The car braked. Neva had the door open, pointing, shouting, pointing, shouting, her mouth flapping, one hand seized out to grab the man's shirt and rip it.

"Out! Get out!"

"*Here*, ma'am?" The man was astonished.

"Here, here, here, out, out, out!"

"But, ma'am . . . !"

"Out, or you're finished, through!" cried Neva, wildly. "I got a load of Bibles in the back trunk, a pistol with a silver bullet here under the steering wheel. A box of crucifixes under the seat! A wooden stake taped to the axle, with a hammer. I got holy water in the carburetor, blessed before it boiled early this morning at three churches on the way: St. Matthew's Catholic, the Green Town Baptist, and the Zion City High Episcopal. The steam from that will get you alone. Following us, one mile behind, and due to arrive in one minute, is the Reverend Bishop Kelly from Chicago. Up at the lake is Father Rooney from Milwaukee, and Doug, why, Doug here has in his back pocket at this minute one sprig of wolfsbane and two chunks of mandrake root. Out! out! out!"

"Why, ma'am," cried the man. "I *am*!"

And he was.

He landed and fell rolling in the road.

Neva banged the car into full flight.

Behind, the man picked himself up and yelled, "You must be nuts. You must be crazy. Nuts. Crazy."

"*I'm* nuts? *I'm* crazy?" said Neva, and hooted. "Boy!"

". . . nuts . . . crazy . . ." The voice faded.

Douglas looked back and saw the man shaking his fist, then ripping off his shirt and hurling it to the gravel and jumping big puffs of white-hot dust out of it with his bare feet.

The car exploded, rushed, raced, banged pell-mell ahead, his aunt ferociously glued to the hot wheel, until the little sweating figure of the talking man was lost in sun-drenched marshland and burning air. At last Doug exhaled:

"Neva, I never heard you talk like that before."

"And never will again, Doug."

"Was what you said *true*?"

"Not a word."

"You lied, I mean, you *lied*?"

"I lied." Neva blinked. "Do you think *he* was lying, too?"

"I don't know."

"All I know is sometimes it takes a lie to kill a lie, Doug. This time, any-way. Don't let it become customary."

"No, ma'am." He began to laugh. "Say the thing about mandrake root again. Say the thing about wolfsbane in my pocket. Say it about a pistol with a silver bullet, say it."

She said it. They both began to laugh.

Whooping and shouting, they went away in their tin-bucket-junking car over the gravel ruts and humps, her saying, him listening, eyes squeezed shut, roaring, snickering, raving.

They didn't stop laughing until they hit the water in their bathing suits and came up all smiles.

The sun stood hot in the middle of the sky and they dog-paddled hap-pily for five minutes before they began to really swim in the menthol-cool waves.

Only at dusk when the sun was suddenly gone and the shadows moved out from the trees did they remember that now they had to go *back* down that lonely road through all the dark places and past that empty swamp to get to town.

They stood by the car and looked down that long road. Doug swallowed hard.

"*Nothing* can happen to us going home."

"Nothing."

"Jump!"

They hit the seats and Neva kicked the starter like it was a dead dog and they were off.

They drove along under plum-colored trees and among velvet purple hills.

And nothing happened.

They drove along a wide raw gravel road that was turning the color of plums and smelled the warm-cool air that was like lilacs and looked at each other, waiting.

And nothing happened.

Neva began at last to hum under her breath.

The road was empty.

And then it was not empty.

Neva laughed. Douglas squinted and laughed with her.

For there was a small boy, nine years old maybe, dressed in a vanilla-white summer suit, with white shoes and a white tie and his face pink and scrubbed, waiting by the side of the road. He waved.

Neva braked the car.

"Going in to town?" called the boy, cheerily. "Got lost. Folks at a picnic, left without me. Sure glad you came along. It's *spooky* out here."

"Climb in!"

The boy climbed and they were off, the boy in the back seat, and Doug and Neva up front glancing at him, laughing, and then getting quiet.

The small boy kept silent for a long while behind them, sitting straight upright and clean and bright and fresh and new in his white suit.

And they drove along the empty road under a sky that was dark now with a few stars and the wind getting cool.

And at last the boy spoke and said something that Doug didn't hear but he saw Neva stiffen and her face grow as pale as the ice cream from which the small boy's suit was cut.

"What?" asked Doug, glancing back.

The small boy stared directly at him, not blinking, and his mouth moved all to itself as if it were separate from his face.

The car's engine missed fire and died.

They were slowing to a dead stop.

Doug saw Neva kicking and fiddling at the gas and the starter. But most of all he heard the small boy say, in the new and permanent silence:

"Have either of you ever wondered—"

The boy took a breath and finished:

"—if there is such a thing as genetic evil in the world?"

G.B.S.—MARK V

"CHARLIE! WHERE YOU GOING?"

Members of the rocket crew, passing, called.

Charles Willis did not answer.

He took the vacuum tube down through the friendly humming bowels of the spaceship. He fell, thinking: This is the grand hour.

"Chuck! Where traveling?" someone called.

To meet someone dead but alive, cold but warm, forever untouchable but reaching out somehow to touch.

"Idiot! Fool!"

The voice echoed. He smiled.

Then he saw Clive, his best friend, drifting up in the opposite chute. He averted his gaze, but Clive sang out through his seashell ear-pack radio:

"I want to see you!"

"Later!" Willis said.

"I *know* where you're going. Stupid!"

And Clive was gone up away while Willis fell softly down, his hands trembling.

His boots touched surface. On the instant he suffered renewed delight.

He walked down through the hidden machineries of the rocket. Lord, he thought, crazy. Here we are one hundred days gone away from the Earth in Space, and, this very hour, most of the crew, in fever, dialing their aphrodisiac animatronic devices that touched and hummed to them in their shut clamshell beds. While, what do I do? he thought. *This.*

He moved to peer into a small storage pit.

There, in an eternal dusk, sat the old man.

"Sir," he said, and waited.

"Shaw," he whispered. "Oh, Mr. George Bernard Shaw."

The old man's eyes sprang wide as if he had swallowed an Idea.

He seized his bony knees and gave a sharp cry of laughter.

"By God, I *do* accept it *all!*"

"Accept *what,* Mr. Shaw?"

Mr. Shaw flashed his bright blue gaze upon Charles Willis.

"The Universe! *It* thinks, therefore I *am!* So I had *best* accept, eh? Sit."

Willis sat in the shadowed areaway, clasping his knees and his own warm delight with being here again.

"Shall I read your mind, young Willis, and tell you what you've been up to since last we conversed?"

"*Can* you read minds, Mr. Shaw?"

"No, thank God. Wouldn't it be awful if I were not only the cuneiform-tablet robot of Geroge Bernard Shaw, but could also scan your head-bumps and spell your dreams? Unbearable."

"You already *are,* Mr. Shaw."

"*Touché!* Well, now." The old man raked his reddish beard with his thin fingers, then poked Willis gently in the ribs. "How is it you are the only one aboard this starship who ever visits me?"

"Well, sir, you see—"

The young man's cheeks burned themselves to full blossom.

"Ah, yes, I do see," said Shaw. "Up through the honeycomb of the ship, all the happy male bees in their hives with their syrupy wind-up soft-singing nimble-nibbling toys, their bright female puppets."

"Mostly *dumb*."

"Ah, well. It was not always thus. On my last trip the Captain wished to play Scrabble using only names of characters, concepts and ideas from my plays. Now, strange boy, why do *you* squat here with this hideous old ego? Have you no need for that soft and gentle company abovestairs?"

"It's a long journey, Mr. Shaw, two years out beyond Pluto and back. Plenty of time for abovestairs company. Never enough for this. I have the dreams of a goat but the genetics of a saint."

"Well said!" The old man sprang lightly to his feet and paced about, pointing his beard now toward Alpha Centauri, now toward the nebula in Orion.

"How runs our menu today, Willis? Shall I preface *Saint Joan* for you? Or . . . ?"

"Chuck . . . ?"

Willis's head jerked. His seashell radio whispered in his ear. "Willis! Clive calling. You're late for dinner. I know where you are. I'm coming down. Chuck—"

Willis thumped his ear. The voice cut off.

"Quick, Mr. Shaw! Can you—well—*run*?"

"Can Icarus fall from the Sun? Jump! I shall pace you with these spindly cricket legs!"

They ran.

Taking the corkscrew staircase instead of the air-tube, they looked back from the top platform in time to see Clive's shadow dart into that tomb where Shaw had died but to wake again.

"Willis!" cried his voice.

"To hell with him," said Willis.

Shaw beamed. "Hell? I know it well. Come. I'll show you around!"

Laughing, they jumped into the feather-tube and fell *up*.

※ This was the place of stars.

Which is to say the one place in all the ship where, if one wished, one could come and truly look at the Universe and the billion billion stars which poured across it and never stopped pouring, cream from the mad dairies of the gods. Delicious frights or outcrops, on the other hand, if you thought it so, from the sickness of Lord God Jehovah turned in his sleep, upset with Creation, and birthing dinosaur worlds spun about satanic suns.

"It's all in the thinking," observed Mr. Shaw, sidling his eyes at his young consort.

"Mr. Shaw! You *can* read minds?"

"Poppycock. I merely read faces. Yours is clear glass. I glanced just now and saw Job afflicted, Moses and the Burning Bush. Come. Let us look at the Deeps and see what God has been up to in the ten billion years since He collided with Himself and procreated Vastness."

They stood now, surveying the Universe, counting the stars to a billion and beyond.

"Oh," moaned the young man, suddenly, and tears fell from his eyes. "How I wish I had been alive when you were alive, sir. How I wish I had *truly* known you."

"*This* Shaw is best," retorted the old man, "all of the mincemeat and none of the tin. The coattails are better than the man. Hang to them and survive."

Space lay all about, as vast as God's first thought, as deep as His primal breathing.

They stood, one of them tall, one short, by the scanning window, with a fine view of the great Andromeda Nebula whenever they wished to focus it near with a touch of the button which made the Eye magnify and suck things close.

After a long moment of drinking stars, the young man let out his breath.

"Mr. Shaw . . . ? *Say* it. You know what I like to hear."

"Do I, my boy?" Mr. Shaw's eyes twinkled.

All of Space was around them, all of the Universe, all of the night of the celestial Being, all the stars and all the places between the stars, and the ship moving on its silent course, and the crew of the ship busy at work or games or touching their amorous toys, so these two were alone with their talk, these two stood viewing the Mystery and saying what must be said.

"Say it, Mr. Shaw."

"Well, now . . ."

Mr. Shaw fixed his eyes on a star some twenty light-years away.

"What *are* we?" he asked. "Why, we are the miracle of force and matter making itself over into imagination and will. Incredible. The Life Force experimenting with forms. You for one. Me for another. The Universe has shouted itself alive. We are one of the shouts. Creation turns in its abyss. We have bothered it, dreaming ourselves to shapes. The void is filled with slumbers; ten billion on a billion on a billion bombardments of light and material that know not themselves, that sleep moving and move but finally to make an eye and waken on themselves. Among so much that is flight and ignorance, we are the blind force that gropes like Lazarus from a billion-light-year tomb. We summon ourselves. We say, O Lazarus Life Force, truly come ye forth. So the Universe, a motion of deaths, fumbles to reach across Time to feel its own flesh and know it to be ours. We touch both ways and find each other miraculous because we are One."

Mr. Shaw turned to glance at his young friend.

"There you have it. Satisfied?"

"Oh, yes! I—"

The young man stopped.

Behind them, in the viewing-cabin door, stood Clive. Beyond him, they could hear music pulsing from the far cubicles where crewmen and their huge toys played at amorous games.

"Well," said Clive, "what goes on—?"

"Here?" interjected Shaw, lightly. "Why, only the confounding of two energies making do with puzzlements. This contraption—" he touched his own breast, "speaks from computerized elations. That genetic conglomeration—" he nodded at his young friend, "responds with raw, beloved, and true emotions. The sum of us? Pandemonium spread on biscuits and devoured at high tea."

Clive swiveled his gaze to Willis.

"Damn, you're nuts. At dinner you should have *heard* the laughter! You and this old man, and just talk! they said. Just talk, talk! Look, idiot, it's your stand-watch in ten minutes. Be there! God!"

And the door was empty. Clive was gone.

Silently, Willis and Mr. Shaw floated down the drop-tube to the storage pit beneath the vast machineries.

The old man sat once again on the floor.

"Mr. Shaw." Willis shook his head, snorting softly. "Hell. Why is it you seem more alive to me than anyone I have ever known?"

"Why, my dear young friend," replied the old man, gently, "what you warm your hands at are Ideas, eh? I am a walking monument of concepts, scrimshaws of thought, electric deliriums of philosophy and wonder. You love concepts. I am their receptacle. You love dreams in motion. I move. You love palaver and jabber. I am the consummate palaverer and jabberer. You and I, together, masticate Alpha Centauri and spit forth universal myths. We chew upon the tail of Halley's Comet and worry the Horsehead Nebula until it cries a monstrous Uncle and gives over to our creation. You love libraries. I am a library. Tickle my ribs and I vomit forth Melville's Whale, Spirit Spout and all. Tic my ear and I'll build Plato's Republic with my tongue for you to run and live in. You love Toys. I am a Toy, a fabulous plaything, a computerized—"

"—friend," said Willis, quietly.

Mr. Shaw gave him a look less of fire than of hearth.

"—friend," he said.

Willis turned to leave, then stopped to gaze back at that strange old figure propped against the dark storage wall.

"I—I'm afraid to go. I have this fear something may *happen* to you."

"I shall survive," replied Shaw tartly, "but only if you warn your Captain that a vast meteor shower approaches. He must shift course a few hundred thousand miles. Done?"

"Done." But still Willis did not leave.

"Mr. Shaw," he said, at last. "What . . . what do you *do* while the rest of us sleep?"

"Do? Why, bless you. I listen to my tuning fork. Then, I write symphonies between my ears."

Willis was gone.

In the dark, alone, the old man bent his head. A soft hive of dark bees began to hum under his honey-sweet breath.

* Four hours later, Willis, off watch, crept into his sleep-cubicle.

In half-light, the mouth was waiting for him.

Clive's mouth. It licked its lips and whispered:

"Everyone's talking. About you making an ass out of yourself visiting a two-hundred-year-old intellectual relic, you, you, you. Jesus, the psycho-med'll be out tomorrow to X-ray your stupid skull!"

"Better that than what you men do all night every night," said Willis.

"What we do is us."

"Then why not let me be *me*?"

"Because it's unnatural." The tongue licked and darted. "We all *miss* you. Tonight we piled all the grand toys in the midst of the wild room and—"

"I don't want to hear it!"

"Well, then," said the mouth, "I might just trot down and tell all this to your old gentleman friend—"

"Don't go *near* him!"

"I might." The lips moved in the shadows. "You can't stand guard on him forever. Some night soon, when you're asleep, someone might—tamper with him, eh? Scramble his electronic eggs so he'll talk vaudeville instead of *Saint Joan*? Ha, yes. Think. Long journey. Crew's bored. Practical joke like that, worth a million to see you froth. Beware, Charlie. Best come play with us."

Willis, eyes shut, let the blaze out of him.

"Whoever dares to touch Mr. Shaw, so help me God, I'll kill!"

He turned violently on his side, gnawing the back of his fist.

In the half-dark, he could sense Clive's mouth still moving.

"Kill? Well, well. Pity. Sweet dreams."

An hour later, Willis gulped two pills and fell stunned into sleep.

✳ In the middle of the night he dreamed that they were burning good Saint Joan at the stake and, in the midst of burning, the plain-potato maiden turned to an old man stoically wrapped around with ropes and vines. The old man's beard was fiery red even before the flames reached it, and his bright blue eyes were fixed fiercely upon Eternity, ignoring the fire.

"Recant!" cried a voice. "Confess and recant! Recant!"

"There is nothing to confess, therefore no need for recantation," said the old man quietly.

The flames leaped up his body like a mob of insane and burning mice.

"Mr. Shaw!" screamed Willis.

He sprang awake.

Mr. Shaw.

The cabin was silent. Clive lay asleep.

On his face was a smile.

The smile made Willis pull back, with a cry. He dressed. He ran.

Like a leaf in autumn he fell down the air-tube, growing older and heavier with each long instant.

The storage pit where the old man "slept" was much more quiet than it had a right to be.

Willis bent. His hand trembled. At last, he touched the old man.

"Sir—?"

There was no motion. The beard did not bristle. Nor the eyes fire themselves to blue flames. Nor the mouth tremble with gentle blasphemies . . .

"Oh, Mr. Shaw," he said. "Are you dead, then, oh God, are you really dead?"

The old man was what they called dead when a machine no longer spoke or tuned an electric thought or moved. His dreams and philosophies were snow in his shut mouth.

Willis turned the body this way and that looking for some cut, wound, or bruise on the skin.

He thought of the years ahead, the long traveling years and no Mr. Shaw to walk with, gibber with, laugh with. Women in the storage shelves, yes, women in the cots late at night, laughing their strange taped laughters and moving their strange machined motions, and saying the same dumb things that were said on a thousand worlds on a thousand nights.

"Oh, Mr. Shaw," he murmured at last. "Who *did* this to you?"

Silly boy, whispered Mr. Shaw's memory voice. You *know*.

I know, thought Willis.

He whispered a name and ran away.

---

* "Damn you, you killed him!"

Willis seized Clive's bedclothes, at which instant Clive, like a robot, popped wide his eyes. The smile remained constant.

"You can't kill what was never alive," he said.

"Son of a bitch!"

He struck Clive once in the mouth, after which Clive was on his feet, laughing in some strange wild way, wiping blood from his lips.

"What did you do to him?" cried Willis.

"Not much, just—"

But that was the end of their conversation.

"On posts!" a voice cried. "Collision course!"

Bells rang. Sirens shrieked.

In the midst of their shared rage, Willis and Clive turned cursing to seize emergency spacesuits and helmets off the cabin walls.

"Damn, oh, damn, oh—d—"

Half-through his last damn, Clive gasped. He vanished out a sudden hole in the side of the rocket.

The meteor had come and gone in a billionth of a second. On its way out, it had taken all the air in the ship with it through a hole the size of a small car.

My God, thought Willis, he's gone forever.

What saved Willis was a ladder he stood near, against which the swift river of air crushed him on its way into Space. For a moment he could not move or breathe. Then the suction was finished, all the air in the ship gone. There was only time to adjust the pressure in his suit and helmet, and glance wildly around at the veering ship which was being bombarded now as in a space war. Men ran, or rather floated, shouting wildly, everywhere.

Shaw, thought Willis unreasonably, and had to laugh. Shaw.

A final meteor in a tribe of meteors struck the motor section of the rocket and blew the entire ship apart. Shaw, Shaw, oh, Shaw, thought Willis.

He saw the rocket fly apart like a shredded balloon, all its gases only impelling it to more disintegration. With the bits and pieces went wild crowds of men, dismissed from school, from life, from all and everything, never to meet face to face again, not even to say farewell, the dismissal was so abrupt and their deaths and isolation such a swift surprise.

Good-bye, thought Willis.

But there was no true good-bye. He could hear no weeping and no laments over his radio. Of all the crew, he was the last and final and only one alive, because of his suit, his helmet, his oxygen, miraculously spared. For what? To be alone and fall?

To be alone. To fall.

Oh, Mr. Shaw, oh, sir, he thought.

"No sooner called than delivered," whispered a voice.

It was impossible, but . . .

Drifting, spinning, the ancient doll with the wild red beard and blazing blue eyes fell across darkness as if impelled by God's breath, on a whim.

Instinctively, Willis opened his arms.

And the old party landed there, smiling, breathing heavily, or pretending to breathe heavily, as was his bent.

"Well, well, Willis! Quite a treat, eh?"

"Mr. Shaw! You were *dead!*"

"Poppycock! Someone bent some wires in me. The collision knocked things back together. The disconnection is here below my chin. A villain cut me there. So if I fall dead again, jiggle under my jaw and wire me up, eh?"

"Yes, sir!"

"How much food do you carry at this moment, Willis?"

"Enough to last two hundred days in Space."

"Dear me, that's fine, fine! And self-recycling oxygen units, also, for two hundred days?"

"Yes, sir. Now, how long will your batteries last, Mr. Shaw?"

"Ten thousand years!" the old man sang out happily. "Yes, I vow, I swear! I am fitted with solar-cells which will collect God's universal light until I wear out my circuits."

"Which means you will outtalk me, Mr. Shaw, long after I have stopped eating and breathing."

"At which point you must dine on conversation, and breathe past participles instead of air. But, we must hold the thought of rescue uppermost. Are not the chances good?"

"Rockets *do* come by. And I am equipped with radio signals—"

"Which even now cry out into the deep night: I'm here with ramshackle Shaw, eh?"

I'm here with ramshackle Shaw, thought Willis, and was suddenly warm in winter.

"Well, then, while we're waiting to be rescued, Charles Willis, what next?"

"Next? Why—"

They fell away down Space alone but not alone, fearful but elated, and now grown suddenly quiet.

"*Say* it, Mr. Shaw."

"Say what?"

"You know. Say it again."

"Well, then." They spun lazily, holding to each other. "Isn't life miraculous? Matter and force, yes, matter and force making itself over into intelligence and will."

"Is *that* what we are, sir?"

"We are, bet ten thousand bright tin-whistles on it, we are. Shall I say *more*, young Willis?"

"Please, sir," laughed Willis. "I want some more!"

And the old man spoke and the young man listened and the young man spoke and the old man hooted and they fell around a corner of Universe away out of sight, eating and talking, talking and eating, the young man biting gumball foods, the old man devouring sunlight with his solar-cell eyes, and the last that was seen of them they were gesticulating and babbling and conversing and waving their hands until their voices faded into Time and the solar system turned over in its sleep and covered them with a blanket of dark and light, and whether or not a rescue ship named *Rachel*, seeking her lost children, ever came by and found them, who can tell, who would truly ever want to know?

A BLADE OF GRASS

IT HAD BEEN DECIDED ALREADY that Ultar was guilty. The members of the Council sat, luxuriously relaxing as the attendants lubricated and oiled their viselike hands and their slender metal joints.

Kront was most vehement of the seventeen. His steel hand snapped and his round gray visuals flamed red.

"He's an insufferable experimentalist," said Kront. "I recommend the Rust!"

"The Rust?" exclaimed Ome. "Isn't that too drastic?"

Kront thrust his alloyed skull-case forward.

"No. Not for ones like him. He'll undermine the entire Obot State before he's finished."

"Come now," suggested Lione, philosophically. "It would be better to short-circuit him for a few years, as punishment. Why be so sadistic and bitter about it, Kront?"

"In the name of the Great Obot!" said Kront. "Don't you see the danger? Experimenting with protoplasm!"

"I agree," said one of the others. "Nothing is too severe a punishment. If Ultar insists on concluding his present experiments, he may undermine a civilization that has existed for three hundred thousand years. Take Ultar out to sea, unoiled, and fully aware. Drop him in. It will take him many years to Rust, and he will be aware, all of those years, of crumbling and rusting. Be sure that his skull-case is intact, so his awareness will not be short-circuited by water." The others trembled a quiet, metal, hidden trembling.

Kront swayed to his feet, his oblong face gleaming ice-blue and hard. "I want a show of opinion, a vote. The Rust for Ultar. Vote!"

There was an indecisive moment. Kront's fifteen feet of towering, alloyed metal shifted uneasily in the lubrication cell.

Vises came up, arms came up. Six at first. Then four more. Ome and five others declined to vote. Kront counted the vises with an instantaneous flare of his visuals.

"Good. There's an express rocket for Ultar's laboratory in one hundred seconds from Level CV. If we hurry we'll make it!"

Huge, magnetic plates clung to the floor as metal bodies heaved upward with oiled quiet.

They hurried to a wide portal. Ome and the five dissenters followed. He stopped Kront at the portal. "There's a thing I want to ask you, Kront."

"Hurry. We haven't time."

"You've—*seen* it."

"Protoplasm?"

"Yes. You've looked at it?"

Kront nodded. "Yes. I have seen."

Ome said, "What is it *like?*"

Kront did not answer for a long moment and then he said, very slowly. "It is enough to freeze the motion of all Obot Things. It is horror. It is unbelievable. I think you had better come and see this for yourself."

Ome deliberated. "I'll come."

"Hurry then. We have fifty seconds."

They followed the others.

The sea lay quietly as a huge, pallidly relaxed hand. In the vein and artery of that vast hand nothing moved but the gray blood tides. Moved silently and with the motion of one lunar tide against another. The deeps were not stirred by any other thing. The sea was lifeless and clear of any gill or eye or fin or any moving thing save the soft sea dust which arose, filtering, when the tides changed. The sea was dead.

The forests were silent. The brush was naked, the trees high and forlorn in a wilderness of quiet. There were no bird songs, or cracklings of sly animal paws in autumnal leaves, there were no loon cries or far off calls of moose or chipmunk. Only the wind sang little songs of memory it had learned three hundred thousand years before from things called birds. The forest and the land under the forest was dead. The trees were dead, turned to stone, upright, shading the hard stony soil forever. There was no grass and no flowers. The land was dead, as dead as the sea.

Now, over the dead land, in the birdless sky, came a metal sound. The sound of a rocket singing in the dead air.

Then it was gone, leaving a vein of pale gold powder in its wake. Kront and his fellows, on their way to the fortress of Ultar. . . .

A door opened as the ship landed. Kront and the others came forth from the ship.

"I've been waiting for you," said Ultar, standing in the open portal of the laboratory. "I knew you'd bring the Council with you, Kront. Step in, all of you. I can tell by the immediate temperature of your bodies, that I am already condemned to Rust. We shall see. Step in, anyway."

The door rang shut behind the Council. Ultar led the way down a tubular hall which issued forth into a dark room.

"Be seated, Obot Rulers. It is an unusual thing, this reception for the Great. I am flattered."

Kront clicked angrily. "Before you die, you must show us this protoplasm, so it can be judged and destroyed."

"Must I? Must you? Must it?"

"Where is it?"

"Here."

"Where!"

"Patience, Kront."

"I've no patience with blasphemers!"

"That is apparent."

In one corner of the room was a large square box, from which a glow illumined the nearby walls. Over the box hung a yellow cloth which hid the contents from view.

Ultar, with a certain sure sense of the dramatic, moved to this box and made several adjustments of heat-dials. His visuals were glowing. Grasping the yellow cloth, he lifted it up and away from the box.

A hard, rattling tremor passed through the group. Visuals blinked and changed color. Bodies made an uneasy whining of metal. What lay before them was not pleasant. They drifted forward until they circled the box and peered into it. What they saw was blasphemous and sacrilegious and more than horrible.

Something that *grew*.

Something that expanded and built upon itself, changed and reproduced. Something that actually lived and died.

Died.

How silly! No one need die, ever, ever!

Something that could rot away into nothingness and run blood and be tortured. Something that felt and could be burned or hurt or made to feel hot or cold. Silly, silly something, horrid, horrid something, all incomprehensible and nightmarish and unpredictable!

Pink flesh formed six feet tall with long, long fleshy arms and flesh hands and two long flesh legs. And—they remembered from myth-dreams—those two unnecessary things—a mouth and nose!

✳ Ome felt the silent coggery within himself grind slow. It was unbelievable! Like the half-heard myths of an Age of Flesh and Darkness. All those little half-truths, rumors, those dim little mutterings and whispers of creatures that grew instead of being built!

Who ever heard of such blasphemy? To grow instead of being built? How could a thing be perfect unless it was built and tendered every aid to perfection by an Obot scientist? This fleshy pulp was imperfect. The least jar and it broke, the least heat and it melted, the least cold and it froze. And as for the amazing fact that it grew, well, what of that? It was only luck that it grew to be anything. Sheer luck.

Not so the inhabitants of the Obot State! They were perfect to begin with and grew, paradoxically, more perfect as time progressed. It was nothing, nothing at all for them to exist one hundred thousand years, two hundred thousand years. Ome himself was past thirty-thousand, a youth, still a youth!

But—flesh? Depending upon the whims of some cosmic Nature to give it intellect, health, longevity? How silly a joke, how pointless, when it could be installed in parcels and packages, in wheels and cogs and red and blue wires and sparkling currents!

"Here it is," said Ultar, simply, and with pride. He said it with a firmness that was unafraid. "A body of bone and flesh and blood and fantasy."

There was a long silence in which the metal whining did not cease among the stricken Council. There was hardly a flicker of movement among them. They stared.

Ome said, "It is frightening. Where did you get it?"

"I made it."

"How could you bring yourself to think of it?"

"It is hard to say. It was long ago. Ten thousand years ago, when I was walking over the stony forests, alone, one day, as I have often done, I found a blade of grass. Yes, one last small blade of green grass, the last one in all of this world. You can't imagine how unbearably excited I was. I held it up and I examined it and it was a small green miracle. I felt as if I might explode into a million bits. I took the grass blade home with me, carefully, and telling no one. Oh, what a beautiful treasure it was."

"That was a direct violation of the law," said Kront.

"Yes, the law," said Ultar remembering. "Three hundred thousand years ago when we burned the birds in the air, like cinders, and killed the foxes and the snakes in their burrows, and killed fish in the sea, and all animals, including man—"

"Forbidden names!"

"Remembered names, nevertheless. Remembered. And then we saw the forests still grew and reminded us of growing things, so we turned the forests to stone, and killed the grass and flowers, and we've lived on a barren stony world ever since. Why, we even destroyed the microbes that we couldn't *see*, that's how afraid we were of *growing things!*"

✳ Kront rasped out, "We weren't afraid!"

"Weren't we? Never mind. Let me complete my story. We shot the birds from the sky, sprayed insects from the air, killed the flowers and grass, but yet one small blade survived and I found it and brought it here, and nurtured it, and it grew for hundreds of years until it was ten million blades of grass which I studied because it had cells that grew. I cannot tell you with what excitement I greeted the blossoming of the first *flower*."

"Flower!"

"A little thing. A blue flower, after a thousand years of experiment. And from that flower more flowers, and from those flowers, five centuries later, a bush, and from that bush, four hundred years later, a tree. Oh, it's been a strange long time of working and watching, I'll tell you."

"But *this*," cried Kront. "How did it evolve to this?"

"I went looking. I scoured the world. If I found one precious blade of grass, I reasoned, then perhaps I can find another thing, a lizard that had escaped, or a snake, or some such thing. I was more than lucky. I found a small monkey. From there to this is another thousand years and more. Artificial breeding, insemination, a study of genes and cells, well, it is here now, and it is good."

"It is forbidden!"

"Yes. Damnably forbidden. Look, Ome, do you know why flesh was eradicated from the Earth?"

Ome deliberated. "Because it threatened Obot Rule."

"How did it threaten it?"

"With the Rust."

"With more than the Rust," replied Ultar, quietly. "Flesh threatened us with another way of life and thought. It threatened us with delightful imperfection, unpredictability, art, and literature, and we slaughtered flesh and made it blasphemy and forbidden to see flesh or speak of it."

"Liar!"

"Am I?" demanded Ultar. "Who owned the world before us?"

"We've always owned it. Always."

"What about flesh? Explain it?"

"It was an experiment that got away from us for a time. Some insane Obot scientist created monster flesh and it bred, and it was the servant of the Obots, and it overthrew Obot Rule for a time. Finally, the Obots had to destroy it."

"Religious dogmatism!" replied Ultar. "You've been taught to think that. But, know the truth. There must've been a Beginning, do you agree?"

"Yes. There was a Beginning. The Book of Metal says that all the Universe was turned out on one Lathe of one Huge Machine. And we the small Obots of that Lathe and that Machine."

"There had to be a first Obot, did there not?"

"Yes."

"And who built him?"

"Another machine."

"But before that, at the very beginning? Who built the machine that built the Obot? I'll tell you. Flesh. Flesh built the first machine. Flesh once ruled this continent and all continents. Because flesh grows. Machines do not grow. They are made piece by piece—they are *built*. It took a *growing* creature to build them!"

Ome went wild. "No, no. That is a terrible thought!"

"Listen," said Ultar. "We could not stand man and his imperfect ways. We thought him silly and ridiculous with his art and music. He could die. We could not. So we destroyed him because he was in the way, he cluttered up our perfect universe. And then, we had to lie to ourselves. In our own way we are colossally vain. Just as man fashioned God in his own image, so we had to fashion our God in our image. We couldn't stand the thought of Man being our God, so we eradicated every vestige of protoplasm on Earth, and forbade speaking of it. We were Machines, made by Machines, that was the All, and the Truth."

He was finished with his speaking. The others looked at him, and at last Kront said, "Why did you do it? Why have you made this thing of flesh and imperfection?"

"Why?" Ultar turned to the box. "Look at him, this creature, this man, so small, so vulnerable. His life is worth something because of his very vulnerability. Out of his fear and terror and uncertainty he once created great art, great music and great literature. Do we? We do not.

"How can a civilization create when it lives forever and nothing is of value? Things only take value from their evanescence, things are only appreciated because they vanish. How beautiful a summer day is that is only one of a kind; you all have seen such days—one of the few things of beauty that we know, the weather, which *changes*. We do not change, therefore there is no beauty and no art.

"See him here, in his box, dreaming, about to wake. Little frightened man, on the edge of death, but writing fine books to live long after. I've seen those books in forbidden libraries, full of love and tenderness and terror. And what was his music but a proclamation against the uncertainty of living and the sureness of death and dissolution? What perfect things came from such imperfect creatures. They were sublimely delicate and sublimely wrong, and they waged wars and did many bad things, which we, in our perfectness cannot understand.

"We cannot understand death, really, for it is so rare among us, and has no value. But this man knows death and beauty and for that reason I created him so that some of the beauty and uncertainty would return to the world. Only then could life have any meaning to me, little as I can appreciate it with my limited faculties.

"He had the pleasure of pain, yes, even pain a pleasure, in its own way, for it is feeling and being alive; he lived, and he ate, which we do not do, and knew the goodness of love and raising others like himself and he knew a thing called sleep, and in those sleepings he dreamed, a thing we never do, and here he is now, dreaming fine things we could never hope to know or understand. And you are here, afraid of him and afraid of beauty and meaning and value."

The others stiffened. Kront turned to them and said, "Listen, all of you. You will say nothing of what you've seen today, you will tell no one. Understand?"

The others swayed and moaned in a dazed, wavering anger.

The sleeper in the long oblong box stirred, fitfully, the eyelids quivered, the lips moved. The man was waking.

"The Rust!" screamed Kront, rushing forward. "Seize Ultar! The Rust! The Rust!"

THE SOUND OF SUMMER RUNNING

LATE THAT NIGHT, GOING HOME from the show with his mother and father and his brother Tom, Douglas saw the tennis shoes in the bright store window. He glanced quickly away, but his ankles were seized, his feet suspended, then rushed. The earth spun; the shop awnings slammed their canvas wings overhead with the thrust of his body running. His mother and father and brother walked quietly on both sides of him. Douglas walked backward, watching the tennis shoes in the midnight window left behind.

"It was a nice movie," said Mother.

Douglas murmured, "It was. . . ."

It was June and long past time for buying the special shoes that were quiet as a summer rain falling on the walks. June and the earth full of raw power and everything everywhere in motion. The grass was still pouring in from the country, surrounding the sidewalks, stranding the houses. Any moment the town would capsize, go down and leave not a stir in the clover and weeds. And here Douglas stood, trapped on the dead cement and the red-brick streets, hardly able to move.

"Dad!" He blurted it out. "Back there in that window, those Cream-Sponge Para Litefoot Shoes . . ."

His father didn't even turn. "Suppose you tell me why you need a new pair of sneakers. Can you do that?"

"Well . . ."

It was because they felt the way it feels every summer when you take off your shoes for the first time and run in the grass. They felt like it feels sticking your feet out of the hot covers in wintertime to let the cold wind from the open window blow on them suddenly and you let them stay out a long time until you pull them back in under the covers again to feel them, like packed snow. The tennis shoes felt like it always feels the first time every year wading in the slow waters of the creek and seeing your feet below, half an inch farther downstream, with refraction, than the real part of you above water.

"Dad," said Douglas, "it's hard to explain."

Somehow the people who made tennis shoes knew what boys needed and wanted. They put marshmallows and coiled springs in the soles and they wove the rest out of grasses bleached and fired in the wilderness. Somewhere deep in the soft loam of the shoes the thin hard sinews of the buck deer were hidden. The people that made the shoes must have watched a lot of winds blow the trees and a lot of rivers going down to the lakes. Whatever it was, it was in the shoes, and it was summer.

Douglas tried to get all this in words.

"Yes," said Father, "but what's wrong with last year's sneakers? Why can't you dig *them* out of the closet?"

Well, he felt sorry for boys who lived in California where they wore tennis shoes all year and never knew what it was to get winter off your feet, peel off the iron leather shoes all full of snow and rain and run barefoot for a day and then lace on the first new tennis shoes of the season, which was better than barefoot. The magic was always in the new pair of shoes. The magic might die by the first of September, but now in late June there was still plenty of magic, and shoes like these could jump you over trees and rivers and houses. And if you wanted, they could jump you over fences and sidewalks and dogs.

"Don't you see?" said Douglas. "I just *can't* use last year's pair."

For last year's pair were dead inside. They had been fine when he started them out, last year. But by the end of summer, every year, you always found out, you always knew, you couldn't really jump over rivers and trees and houses in them, and they were dead. But this was a new year, and he felt that this time, with this new pair of shoes, he could do anything, anything at all.

They walked up on the steps to their house. "Save your money," said Dad. "In five or six weeks—"

"Summer'll be over!"

Lights out, with Tom asleep, Douglas lay watching his feet, far away down there at the end of the bed in the moonlight, free of the heavy iron shoes, the big chunks of winter fallen away from them.

"Reasons. I've got to think of reasons for the shoes."

Well, as anyone knew, the hills around town were wild with friends putting cows to riot, playing barometer to the atmospheric changes, taking sun, peeling like calendars each day to take more sun. To catch those friends, you must run much faster than foxes or squirrels. As for the town, it steamed with enemies grown irritable with heat, so remembering every winter argument and insult. *Find friends, ditch enemies!* That was the Cream-Sponge Para Litefoot motto. *Does the world run too fast? Want to be alert, stay alert? Litefoot, then! Litefoot!*

He held his coin bank up and heard the faint small tinkling, the airy weight of money there.

Whatever you want, he thought, you got to make your own way. During the night now, let's find that path through the forest. . . .

Downtown, the store lights went out, one by one. A wind blew in the window. It was like a river going downstream and his feet wanting to go with it.

In his dreams he heard a rabbit running running running in the deep warm grass.

✳ Old Mr. Sanderson moved through his shoe store as the proprietor of a pet shop must move through his shop where are kenneled animals from everywhere in the world, touching each one briefly along the way. Mr. Sanderson brushed his hands over the shoes in the window, and some of them were like cats to him and some were like dogs; he touched each pair with concern, adjusting laces, fixing tongues. Then he stood in the exact center of the carpet and looked around, nodding.

There was a sound of growing thunder.

One moment, the door to Sanderson's Shoe Emporium was empty. The next, Douglas Spaulding stood clumsily there, staring down at his leather shoes as if these heavy things could not be pulled up out of the cement. The thunder had stopped when his shoes stopped. Now, with painful slowness, daring to look only at the money in his cupped hand, Douglas moved out of the bright sunlight of Saturday noon. He made careful stacks of nickels, dimes, and quarters on the counter, like someone playing chess and worried if the next move carried him out into sun or deep into shadow.

"Don't say a word!" said Mr. Sanderson.

Douglas froze.

"First, I know just what you want to buy," said Mr. Sanderson. "Second, I see you every afternoon at my window; you think I don't see? You're wrong. Third, to give it its full name, you want the Royal Crown Cream-Sponge Para Litefoot Tennis Shoes: 'LIKE MENTHOL ON YOUR FEET!' Fourth, you want credit."

"No!" cried Douglas, breathing hard, as if he'd run all night in his dreams. "I got something better than credit to offer!" he gasped. "Before I tell, Mr. Sanderson, you got to do me one small favor. Can you remember when was the last time you yourself wore a pair of Litefoot sneakers, sir?"

Mr. Sanderson's face darkened. "Oh, ten, twenty, say, thirty years ago. Why . . . ?"

"Mr. Sanderson, don't you think you owe it to your customers, sir, to at least try the tennis shoes you sell, for just one minute, so you know how they feel? People forget if they don't keep testing things. United Cigar Store man smokes cigars, don't he? Candy-store man samples his own stuff, I should think. So . . ."

"You may have noticed," said the old man, "I'm wearing shoes."

"But not sneakers, sir! How you going to sell sneakers unless you can rave about them and how you going to rave about them unless you know them?"

Mr. Sanderson backed off a little distance from the boy's fever, one hand to his chin. "Well . . ."

"Mr. Sanderson," said Douglas, "you sell me something and I'll sell you something just as valuable."

"Is it absolutely necessary to the sale that I put on a pair of the sneakers, boy?" said the old man.

"I sure wish you could, sir!"

The old man sighed. A minute later, seated panting quietly, he laced the tennis shoes to his long narrow feet. They looked detached and alien down there next to the dark cuffs of his business suit. Mr. Sanderson stood up.

"How do they *feel*?" asked the boy.

"How do they feel, he asks; they feel fine." He started to sit down.

"Please!" Douglas held out his hand. "Mr. Sanderson, now could you kind of rock back and forth a little, sponge around, bounce kind of, while I tell you the rest? It's this: I give you my money, you give me the shoes, I owe you a dollar. But, Mr. Sanderson, but—soon as I get those shoes on, you know what *happens*?"

"What?"

"Bang! I deliver your packages, pick up packages, bring you coffee, burn your trash, run to the post office, telegraph office, library! You'll see twelve of me in and out, in and out, every minute. Feel those shoes, Mr. Sanderson, *feel* how fast they'd take me? All those springs inside? Feel all the running inside? Feel how they kind of grab hold and can't let you alone and don't like you just *standing* there? Feel how quick I'd be doing the things you'd rather not bother with? You stay in the nice cool store while I'm jumping all around town! But it's not me really, it's the shoes. They're going like mad down alleys, cutting corners, and back! There they go!"

Mr. Sanderson stood amazed with the rush of words. When the words got going the flow carried him; he began to sink deep in the shoes, to flex his toes, limber his arches, test his ankles. He rocked softly, secretly, back and forth in a small breeze from the open door. The tennis shoes silently hushed themselves deep in the carpet, sank as in a jungle grass, in loam and resilient clay. He gave one solemn bounce of his heels in the yeasty dough, in the yielding and welcoming earth. Emotions hurried over his face as if many colored lights had been switched on and off. His mouth hung slightly open. Slowly he gentled and rocked himself to a halt, and the boy's voice faded and they stood there looking at each other in a tremendous and natural silence.

A few people drifted by on the sidewalk outside, in the hot sun.

Still the man and boy stood there, the boy glowing, the man with revelation in his face.

"Boy," said the old man at last, "in five years, how would you like a job selling shoes in this emporium?"

"Gosh, thanks, Mr. Sanderson, but I don't know what I'm going to be yet."

"Anything you want to be, son," said the old man, "you'll be. No one will ever stop you."

The old man walked lightly across the store to the wall of ten thousand boxes, came back with some shoes for the boy, and wrote up a list on some paper while the boy was lacing the shoes on his feet and then standing there, waiting.

The old man held out his list. "A dozen things you got to do for me this afternoon. Finish them, we're even Stephen, and you're fired."

"Thanks, Mr. Sanderson!" Douglas bounded away.

"Stop!" cried the old man.

Douglas pulled up and turned.

Mr. Sanderson leaned forward. "How do they *feel*?"

The boy looked down at his feet deep in the rivers, in the fields of wheat, in the wind that already was rushing him out of the town. He looked up at the old man, his eyes burning, his mouth moving, but no sound came out.

"Antelopes?" said the old man, looking from the boy's face to his shoes. "Gazelles?"

The boy thought about it, hesitated, and nodded a quick nod. Almost immediately he vanished. He just spun about with a whisper and went off. The door stood empty. The sound of the tennis shoes faded in the jungle heat.

Mr. Sanderson stood in the sun-blazed door, listening. From a long time ago, when he dreamed as a boy, he remembered the sound. Beautiful creatures leaping under the sky, gone through brush, under trees, away, and only the soft echo their running left behind.

"Antelopes," said Mr. Sanderson. "Gazelles."

He bent to pick up the boy's abandoned winter shoes, heavy with forgotten rains and long-melted snows. Moving out of the blazing sun, walking softly, lightly, slowly, he headed back toward civilization. . . .

AND THE SAILOR, HOME FROM THE SEA

"Good morning, Captain."

"Good morning, Hanks."

"Coffee's ready, sir, sit down."

"Thank you, Hanks."

The old man sat by the galley table, his hands in his lap. He looked at them and they were like speckled trout idling beneath frosty waters, the exhalations of his faint breath on the air. He had seen such trout as these surfacing in the mountain streams when he was ten. He became fascinated with their trembling motion there below, for as he watched they seemed to grow paler.

"Captain," said Hanks, "you all right?"

The captain jerked his head up and flashed his old burning glance.

"Of course! What do you mean, am I all right?"

The cook put down the coffee from which rose warm vapors of women so far gone in his past they were only dark musk and rubbed incense to his nose. Quite suddenly he sneezed, and Hanks was there with a cloth.

"Thank you, Hanks." He blew his nose and then tremblingly drank the brew.

"Hanks?"

"Yes, sir, Captain?"

"The barometer is falling."

Hanks turned to stare at the wall.

"No, sir, it's fair and mild, that's what it says, fair and mild!"

"The storm is rising and it will be a long time and a hard pull before another calm."

"I won't have that kind of talk!" said Hanks, circling him.

"I must say what I feel. The calm had to end one day. The storm had to come. I've been ready now a long time."

A long time, yes. How many years? The sand fell through the glass beyond counting. The snows fell through the glass, too, applying and reapplying whiteness to whiteness, burying deeper and yet deeper winters beyond recall.

He got up, swaying, moved to the galley door, opened it, and stepped forth . . .

. . . onto the porch of a house built like the prow of a ship, onto a porch whose deck was tarred ship's timbers. He looked down upon not water but the summer-baked dirt of his front yard. Moving to the rail, he gazed upon gently rolling hills that spread forever in any direction you wheeled to strike your eye.

What am I doing here, he thought with sudden wildness, on a strange ship-house stranded without canvas in the midst of lonesome prairies where the only sound is bird shadow one way in autumn, another way come spring!

What indeed!

He quieted, raising the binoculars which hung from the rail, to survey the emptiness of land as well as life.

Kate Katherine Katie, where are you?

He was always forgetting by night, drowned deep in his bed, remembering by day when he came forth from memory. He was alone and had been alone for twenty years now, save for Hanks, the first face at dawn, the last at sundown.

And Kate?

A thousand storms and a thousand calms ago there had been a calm and a storm that had stayed on the rest of his life.

"There she is, Kate!" He heard his early-morning voice, running along the dock. "There's the ship will take us wherever we want to go!"

And again they moved, incredible pair, Kate miraculously what? twenty-five at most: and himself leaned far into his forties, but no more than a child holding her hand, drawing her up the gangplank.

Then, hesitant, Kate turned to face the Alexandrian hills of San Francisco and said half aloud to herself or no one, "I shall never touch land again."

"The trip's not that long!"

"Oh, yes," she said quietly. "It will be a very long journey."

And for a moment all he heard was the immense creaking of the ship like a Fate turning in its sleep.

"Now, why did I say that?" she asked. "Silly."

She put her foot out and down and stepped aboard the ship.

They sailed that night for the Southern Isles, a groom with the skin of a tortoise and a bride lithe as a salamander dancing on the fiery hearth of the afterdeck on August afternoons.

Then, midway in the voyage, a calm fell upon the ship like a great warm breath, an exhalation that collapsed the sails in a mournful yet a peaceful sigh.

Perhaps this sigh wakened him, or perhaps it was Katie, rising up to listen.

Not a rat-scurry of rope, not a whisper of canvas, not a rustle of naked feet on the deck. The ship was spelled for certain. It was as if the moon rising had said a single silver word: Peace.

The men, fastened to their stations by the incantation of the word, did not turn when the captain moved to the rail with his wife and sensed that Now had become Eternity.

And then, as if she could read the future in the mirror that held the ship fast, she said, fervently, "There's never been a finer night, nor two happier people on a better ship. Oh, I wish we could stay here a thousand years, this is perfect, our own world where we make our own laws and live by them. Promise you'll never let me die."

"Never," he said. "Shall I tell you why?"

"Yes, and make me believe it."

He remembered then, and told her, of a story he had heard once of a woman so lovely the gods were jealous of Time and put her to sea and said she might never touch shore again where the earth might burden her with gravity and weaken her with vain encounters, senseless excursions, and wild alarms that would cause her death. If she stayed on the water she would live forever and be beautiful. So she sailed many years, passing the island where her lover grew old. Time and again she called to him, demanding that he summon her ashore. But, fearful of her destruction, he refused, and one day she took it on herself to land and run to him. And they had one night together, a night of beauties and wonder, before he found her, when the sun rose, a very old woman, a withered leaf, at his side.

"Did I hear the story once?" he asked. "Or will someone tell it later, and are we part of it? Is that why I've carried you off from the land, so the noise and traffic and millions of people and things can't wear you away?"

But Kate was laughing at him now. She threw her head back and let the sound out, for every man's head turned and every mouth smiled.

"Tom, Tom, remember what I said before we sailed? I'd never touch land again? I must have guessed your reason for running off with me. All right, then, I'll stay on board wherever we go, around the world. Then I'll never change, and you won't either, will you?"

"I'll always be forty-eight!"

And he laughed, too, glad he had got the darkness out of himself, holding her shoulders and kissing her throat which was like bending to winter at the heart of August. And that night, in the blazing calm that would last forever, she was a fall of snow in his bed. . . .

"Hanks, do you remember the calm in August ninety-seven?" The old man examined his faraway hands. "How long did it last?"

"Nine, ten days, sir."

"No, Hanks. I swear it, we lived nine full years in those days of the calm."

Nine days, nine years. And in the midst of those days and years he thought, Oh, Kate, I'm glad I brought you, I'm glad I didn't let the others joke me out of making myself younger by touching you. Love is everywhere, they said, waiting on the docks, underneath the trees, like warm coconuts to be fondled, nuzzled, drunk. But, God, they wrong. Poor drunken souls, let them wrestle apes in Borneo, melons in Sumatra, what could they build with dancing monkeys and dark rooms? Sailing home, those captains slept with themselves. Themselves! Such sinful company, ten thousand miles! No, Kate, no matter what, there's us!

And the great deep breathing calm went on at the center of the ocean world beyond which lay nothing, the dreadnought continents foundered and sunk by time.

But on the ninth day the men themselves let down the boats and sat in them waiting for orders, and there was nothing for it but to row for a wind, the captain joining his men.

Toward the end of the tenth day, an island came slowly up over the horizon.

He called to his wife, "Kate, we'll row in for provisions. Will you come along?"

She stared at the island as if she had seen it somewhere long before she was born, and shook her head, slowly, no.

"Go on! I won't touch land until we're home!"

And looking up at her he knew that she was, by instinct, living the legend he had so lightly spun and told. Like the golden woman in the myth, she sensed some secret evil on a lonely swelter of sand and coral that might diminish or, more, destroy her.

"God bless you, Kate! Three hours!"

And he rowed away to the island with his men.

Late in the day they rowed back with five kegs of fresh sweet water and the boats odorous with warm fruit and flowers.

And waiting for him was Kate who would not go ashore, who would not, she said, touch ground.

She was first to drink the clear cool water.

Brushing her hair, looking out at the unmoved tides that night, she said, "It's almost over. There'll be a change by morning. Oh, Tom, hold me. After its being so warm, it'll be so cold."

In the night he woke. Kate, breathing in the dark, murmured. Her hand fell upon his, white hot. She cried out in her sleep. He felt her wrist and there first heard the rising of the storm.

As he sat by her, the ship lifted high on a great slow breast of water, and the spell was broken.

The slack canvas shuddered against the sky. Every rope hummed as if a huge hand had passed down the ship as over a silent harp, calling forth fresh sounds of voyaging.

The calm over, one storm began.

Another followed.

Of the two storms, one ended abruptly—the fever that raged in Kate and burned her to a white dust. A great silence moved in her body and then did not move at all.

The sail mender was brought to dress her for the sea. The motion of his needle flickering in the underwater light of the cabin was like a tropic fish, sharp, thin, infinitely patient, nibbling away at the shroud, skirting the dark, sealing the silence in.

In the final hours of the vast storm above, they brought the white calm from below and let her free in a fall that tore the sea only a moment. Then, without trace, Kate and life were gone.

"Kate, Kate, oh, Kate!"

He could not leave her here, lost to the tidal flows between the Japan Sea and the Golden Gate. Weeping that night, he stormed himself out of the storm. Gripped to the wheel, he circled the ship again and again around that wound that had healed with untimely swiftness. Then he knew a calm that lasted the rest of his days. He never raised his voice or clenched his fist again to any man. And with that pale voice and unclenched fist, he turned the ship away at last from the unscarred ground, circled the earth, delivered his goods, then turned his face from the sea for all time. Leaving his ship to nudge the green-mantled dock, he walked and rode inland twelve hundred miles. Blindly, he bought land, blindly he built, with Hanks, not knowing for a long while what he had bought or built. Only knowing that he had always been too old, and had been young for a short hour with Kate, and now was very old indeed and would never chance such an hour again.

So, in mid-continent, a thousand miles from the sea on the east, a thousand miles from the hateful sea on the west, he damned the life and the water he had known, remembering not what had been given but what had been so swiftly taken away.

On this land, then, he walked out and cast forth seed, prepared himself for his first harvest and called himself farmer.

But one night in that first summer of living as far from the sea as any man could get, he was waked by an incredible, a familiar, sound. Trembling in his bed, he whispered, No, no, it can't be—I'm mad! But . . . listen!

He opened the farmhouse door to look upon the land. He stepped out on the porch, spelled by this thing he had done without knowing it. He held to the porch rail and blinked, wet-eyed, out beyond his house.

There, in the moonlight, hill after slow-rising hill of wheat blew in tidal winds with the motion of waves. An immense Pacific of grain shimmered off beyond seeing, with his house, his now-recognized ship, becalmed in its midst.

He stayed out half the night, striding here, standing there, stunned with the discovery, lost in the deeps of this inland sea. And with the following years, tackle by tackle, timber by timber, the house shaped itself to the size, feel, and thrust of ships he had sailed in crueler winds and deeper waters.

"How long, Hanks, since we last saw water?"

"Twenty years, Captain."

"No, yesterday morning."

Coming back through the door, his heart pounded. The wall barometer clouded over, flickered with a faint lightning that played along the rims of his eyelids.

"No coffee, Hanks. Just—a cup of clear water."

Hanks went away and came back.

"Hanks? Promise. Bury me where she is."

"But, Captain, she's—" Hanks stopped. He nodded. "Where she is. Yes, sir."

"Good. Now give me the cup."

The water was fresh. It came from the islands beneath the earth. It tasted of sleep.

"One cup. She was right, Hanks, you know. Not to touch land, ever again. She was right. But I brought her one cup of water from the land, and the land was in water that touched her lips. One cup. Oh, if *only* . . . !"

He shifted it in his rusted hands. A typhoon swarmed from nowhere, filling the cup. It was a black storm raging in a small place.

He raised the cup and drank the typhoon.

"Hanks!" someone cried.

But not he. The typhoon, storming, had gone, and he with it.

The cup fell empty to the floor.

✳ It was a mild morning. The air was sweet and the wind steady. Hanks had worked half the night digging and half the morning filling. Now the work was done. The town minister helped, and then stood back as Hanks jigsawed the final square of sod into place. Piece after piece, he fitted neatly and tamped and joined. And on each piece, as Hanks had made certain, was the golden, the full rich ripe-grained wheat, as high as a ten-year-old boy.

Hanks bent and put the last piece to rest.

"No marker?" asked the minister.

"Oh, no, sir, and never will be one."

The minister started to protest, when Hanks took his arm, and walked him up the hill a way, then turned and pointed back.

They stood a long moment. The minister nodded at last, smiled quietly and said, "I see. I understand."

For there was just the ocean of wheat going on and on forever, vast tides of it blowing in the wind, moving east and ever east beyond, and not a line or seam or ripple to show where the old man sank from sight.

"It was a sea burial," said the minister.

"It was," said Hanks. "As I promised. It was, indeed."

Then they turned and walked off along the hilly shore, saying nothing again until they reached and entered the creaking house.

THE LONELY ONES

THEY ATE SIX SUPPERS IN THE OPEN, talking back and forth over the small campfire. The light shone high on the silver rocket in which they had traveled across space. From a long way off in the blue hills, their campfire seemed like a star that had landed beside the long Martian canals under the clear and windless Martian sky.

On the sixth night the two men sat by the fire, looking tensely in all directions.

"Cold?" asked Drew, for the other was shivering.

"What?" Smith looked at his arms. "No."

Drew looked at Smith's forehead. It was covered with sweat.

"Too warm?"

"No, not that either."

"Lonely?"

"Maybe." His hand jerked as he put another piece of wood on the fire.

"Game of cards?"

"Can't concentrate."

Drew listened to Smith's quick shallow breathing. "We've our information. Each day we took pictures and ore samples. We're about loaded. Why don't we start the trip home tonight?"

Smith laughed. "You're not *that* lonely, are you?"

"Cut it."

They shifted their boots in the cool sand. There was no wind. The fire burned steadily, straight up, fed by the oxygen hose from the ship. They themselves wore transparent glass masks over their faces, very thin, through which a soft oxygen film pulsed up from the oxygen vests under their jackets. Drew checked his wrist dial. Six more hours of oxygen in his jacket. Fine.

He pulled out his ukelele and started to strum on it carelessly, eyes half closed, leaning back to look at the stars.

> The girl of my dreams is the sweetest girl
> Of all the girls I know—
> Each sweet coed, like a rainbow red
> Fades in the afterglow.
> The blue of her eyes and the gold of her hair. . . .

The sound of the ukelele came up Drew's arms into his earphones. Smith could not hear the instrument, only Drew's singing. The atmosphere was too thin.

"She's the sweetheart of Sigma Chi—"

"Aw, cut it out!" cried Smith.

"What's eating you?"

"I said cut it out, is all!" Smith sat back, glaring at the other man.

"Okay, okay, don't get excited."

Drew put the ukelele down and lay back, thinking. He knew what it was. It was in him, too. The cold loneliness, the midnight loneliness, the loneliness of distance and time and space, of stars and travel and months and days.

Only too well he remembered Anna's face looking in at him through the space port of the rocket a minute before blast-off time. It was like a vivid, clear-cut blue cameo—the blue round glass and her lovely face, her hand uplifted to wave, her smiling lips and her bright eyes. She had kissed her hand to him. Then she had vanished.

He looked idly over at Smith. Smith's eyes were closed. He was turning over a thought of his own in his mind. Marguerite, of course. Wonderful Marguerite, the brown eyes and the soft brown hair. Sixty million miles away on some improbable world where they had been born.

"I wonder what they're doing tonight?" Drew said.

Smith opened his eyes and looked across the fire. Without even questioning Drew's meaning, he replied, "Going to a television concert, swimming, playing badminton, lots of things."

Drew nodded. He withdrew into himself again and he felt the sweat starting to come out in his hands and his face. He began to tremble and there was a shrill whining emotion deep inside himself. He didn't want to sleep tonight. It would be like other nights. Out of nothing, the lips and the warmth and the dream. And, all too soon, the empty morning, the arising into the nightmare of reality.

He jumped up violently.

Smith fell back, staring.

"Let's take a walk, do something," said Drew heartily.

"All right."

They walked through the pink sands of the empty sea bottom, saying nothing, only walking. Drew felt part of the tightness vanish. He cleared his throat.

"Suppose," he said, "just to be supposing, of course, you met up with a Martian woman? Now. Some time in the next hour?"

Smith snorted. "Don't be silly. There aren't any."

"But just suppose."

"I don't know," replied Smith, looking ahead as he walked. He put his head down and rubbed his hand along the thin warm glass mask over his face. "Marguerite's waiting for me in New York."

"And Anna's waiting for me. But let's be practical. Here we are, two very human men, a year away from earth, cold, lonely, isolated, in need of consolation, hand-holding. No wonder we're brooding over the women we left behind."

"It's plain silly to brood, and we ought to quit it. There's no women around anyway, drat it!"

They walked onward for a distance.

"Anyway," Smith continued at last, after a time of thinking, "If we did find a woman here, I'm sure Marguerite would be the first to comprehend the situation and forgive me."

"Are you sure?"

"Absolutely!"

"Or are you rationalizing?"

"No!"

"Let me show you something, then. Turn back. Over there." Drew took

Smith's arm and guided him back and to one side about fifty paces. "The reason I brought the whole subject up is this." He pointed.

Smith gasped.

A footprint lay like a tiny soft valley in the sand.

The two men bent, put their fingers eagerly down, brushing nervously to each side of it. Their breath hissed in their nostrils. Smith's eyes glittered.

They looked into each other's faces for a long time.

"A woman's footstep!" cried Smith.

"Perfect in every detail," said Drew, nodding solemnly. "I happen to know. I once worked in a shoe store. I'd know a woman's print anywhere. Perfect, perfect!"

✳ They swallowed the thickened knots in their dry throats. Their hearts began to beat wildly.

Smith opened and closed his hands into fists. "Glory, it's small! Look at the toes! Gosh, it's dainty!"

He stood up and looked ahead, eyes squinted. Then, crying out, he began to run. "Here's another, and another. More. They go on, that way!"

"Take it easy," Drew caught up with him. He took hold of Smith's arm. "Where you think you're going?"

"Let go; blast it!" Smith pointed. "I'm following them up, of course.

"What about Marguerite?"

"This is a devil of a time to talk of her. Let go before I crack you one!"

Musingly, Drew dropped his hand. "Okay. Go ahead."

They ran together. . . .

Fresh footsteps, fresh and deep and delicately defined. Footsteps that rushed, swirled, pelted on before them, coming and going, alone, across the dry sea bottom. Glance at the wrist watch. Five minutes, then. Hurry. Rush. Run. Drew panted, laughing. Ridiculous. Silly. Two men plunging forward. Really, if it weren't such a lonely, serious thing, he would sit down and laugh until he cried. Two supposedly intelligent men, two Robinson Crusoes racing after a feminine and as yet invisible girl Friday! Ha!

"What's funny?" shouted Smith, far ahead.

"Nothing. Watch the time. Oxygen gives out, you know."

"We've plenty."

"Watch it, though!"

Did she realize when she came by here, thought Drew amusedly, putting her footfalls so delicately into the earth, that by so doing, so innocently laying her gentle small feet, she would cause a crisis among men? No. Totally unaware. Totally.

He must run anyway and keep up with that insane Smith. Silly, silly. And yet—not so silly.

As Drew ran, a warmness filled his head. After all, it would be swell to sit by the fire tonight beside a beautiful woman, holding her hand, kissing her and touching her.

"What if she's blue?"

Smith turned as he ran. "What?"

"What if her skin's blue? Like the hills? What then?"

"Blast you, Drew!"

"Ha!" Drew shouted his laugh and they pelted into an old river draw and along a canal, both lying empty in the seasonless time.

The footprints moved delicately on and on to the foothills. They had to stop when they reached the climb.

"Dibs," said Drew, eyes sharp and yellow.

"What?"

"I said 'Dibs on her.' That means I get to speak to her first. Remember when we were kids? We said 'Dibs.' Okay. I just said 'Dibs.' That makes it official."

Smith was not smiling.

"What's wrong, Smith? 'Fraid of competition?" said Drew.

Smith did not speak.

"I've got quite a profile," Drew pointed out. "Also, I'm four inches taller."

Smith looked coldly at him. His eyes were still.

"Yes, sir, competition," Drew went on. "Tell you what, Smith—if she's got a friend, I'll let you have the friend."

"Shut up," said Smith glaring at him.

Drew stopped smiling and stood back. "Look here, Smith, you better take it slow. You're getting all het up. I don't like to see you this way. Everything's been fine until now."

"I'll act anyway I please. You just keep out of my business. After all, I found the footprints!"

"Say that again."

"Well, you found them, maybe, but it was *my* idea to follow them up!"

"*Was* it?" Drew said slowly.

"You know it was."

"*Do* I?"

"Holy Pete, a year in space, no company, nothing, traveling, and now when something like this happens, someone human—"

"Someone *feminine*."

✳ Smith cocked his fist. Drew caught it, twisted it, slapped Smith's face.

"Wake up!" he shouted into the blank face. "Wake up!" He seized Smith's shirt front. He shook him like a kid. "Listen, listen, you fool! Maybe she's somebody else's woman. Think of that. Where there's a Martian woman, there's going to be a Martian man, you chump."

"Let go of me!"

"Think of it, you idiot, that's all." Drew gave Smith a shove. Smith toppled, almost fell, reached for his gun, thought better of it, shoved it back.

But Drew had seen the gesture. He looked at Smith. "So it's come to that, has it? You really are in a bad way, aren't you? The old cave man himself."

"Shut up!" Smith started to walk on, climbing. "You don't understand."

"No, I've been nowhere the last year. I've been home with Anna every night. I've been warm and safe in New York. You went on the trip all by your lonely little self!" Drew snorted violently and swore. "You sure are an egocentric little squirt!"

They climbed a hill of sand and were among other hills where the footprints led them. They found an abandoned fireplace, charred sticks of wood, a small metal tin which had once, from its arrangement, contained oxygen to feed the fire. They looked new.

"She can't be much farther on." Smith was ready to drop, but still he ran. He slugged his feet into the sand and gasped.

I wonder what she's like, thought Drew, moving in his thoughts, freely, wonderingly. I wonder if she's tall and slender or small and very thin. I wonder what color eyes, what color hair she has? I wonder what her voice is like? Sweet, high? Or soft and very low?

I wonder a lot of things. So does Smith. Smith's wondering, too, now. Listen to him wonder and gasp and run and wonder some more. This isn't any good. It'll lead us to something bad, I know. Why do we go on? A silly question. We go on, of course, because we're only human, no more, no less.

I just hope, he thought, that she doesn't have snakes for hair.

"A cave!"

They had come to the side of a small mountain, into which a cave went back through darkness. The footprints vanished within.

Smith snatched forth his electric torch and sent the beam inside, flashing it swiftly about, grinning with apprehension. He moved forward cautiously, his breath rasping in the earphones.

"It won't be long now," said Drew.

Smith didn't look at him.

They walked together, elbows bumping. Every time Drew tried to draw ahead, Smith grunted and increased his pace; his face angry with color.

The tunnel twisted, but the footprints still appeared as they flicked the torch beam down.

Suddenly they came out into an immense cave. Across it, by a campfire which had gone out, a figure lay.

"There she is!" shouted Smith. "There she is!"

"Dibs," whispered Drew quietly.

Smith turned, the gun was in his hand. "Get out," he said.

"What?" Drew blinked at the gun.

"You heard what I said, get out!"

"Now, wait a minute—"

"Get back to the ship, wait for me there!"

"If you think you're going to—"

"I'll count to ten, if you haven't moved by then, I'll burn you where you stand—"

"You're crazy!"

"One, two, three, better start moving."

"Listen to me, Smith, for Heaven's sake!"

"Four, five, six, I warned you—ah!"

The gun went off.

⁕ The bullet struck Drew in the hip, whirling him about to fall face down, crying out with pain. He lay in darkness.

"I didn't mean it, Drew, I didn't!" Smith cried. "It went off; my finger, my hand, nervous; I didn't mean it!" A figure bent down in the blazing light, turned him over. "I'l fix you up, I'm sorry. I'll get her to help us. Just a second!"

The pain in his side, Drew lay watching as the torch turned and Smith rushed loudly across the long cave toward the sleeping figure by the black fire. He heard Smith call out once or twice, saw him approach and bend down to the figure, touch it.

For a long time, Drew waited.

Smith turned the figure over.

From a distance, Drew heard Smith say, "She's dead."

"What!" called Drew. With fumbling hands he was taking out a small kit of medicine. He broke open a vial of white powder which he swallowed. The pain in his side stopped instantly. Now he went about bandaging the wound. It was bad enough, but not too bad. In the middle distance he saw Smith standing all alone, his torch senselessly in his numb hand, looking down at the woman's figure.

Smith came back and sat down and looked at nothing.

"She's—she's been dead a long long time."

"But the footprints? What about them?"

"This world, of course, this world. We didn't stop to think. We just ran. I just ran. Like a fool. This world, I didn't think until now. Now I know."

"What is it?"

"There's no wind, nothing. No seasons, no rain, no storms, no nothing. Ten thousand years ago, in a dying world, that woman there walked across the sands, alone. Maybe the last one alive. With a few oxygen tins to keep her going. Something happened to the planet. The atmosphere drained off into space. No wind, no oxygen, no seasons. And her walking alone." Smith shaped it in his mind before telling it quietly to Drew, not looking at him. "And she came to this cave and lay down and died."

"Ten thousand years ago?"

"Ten thousand years. And she's been here ever since. Perfect. Lying here, waiting for us to come and make fools of ourselves. A cosmic joke. Ah, yes! Very funny."

"But the footprints?"

"No wind. No rain. The footprints look just as fresh as the day she made them, naturally. Everything looks new and fresh. Even her. Except there's something about her. Just by seeing her you know she's been dead a long long while. I don't know what it is."

His voice faded away.

Suddenly he remembered Drew. "My gun. You. Can I help?"

"I got it all dressed. It was an accident. Let's put it that way."

"Does it hurt?"

"No."

"You won't try and kill me for this?"

"Shut your mouth. Your finger slipped."

"It did—it really did! I'm sorry."

"I know it did. Shut up." Drew finished packing the wound. "Give me a hand now, we've got to get back to the ship." Smith helped him grunt to his feet and stand swaying. "Now walk me over so I can take a look at Miss Mars, ten thousand B.C. After all that running and this trouble I ought to get a look at her, anyway."

Smith helped him slowly over to stand above the sprawling form. "Looks like she's only sleeping," said Smith. "But she's dead, awful dead. Isn't she pretty?"

She looks just like Anna, thought Drew, with a sense of shock. Anna sleeping there, ready to wake and smile and say hello.

"She looks just like Marguerite," Smith said.

Drew's mouth twitched. "Marguerite?" He hesitated. "Yes. Y-yes, I guess she does." He shook his head. "All depends on how you look at it. I was just thinking myself—"

"What?"

"Never mind. Let her lie. Leave her there. Now, we've got to hurry. Back to the ship for us."

"I wonder who she was?"

"We'll never know. A princess maybe. A stenographer in some ancient city, a dancing maid? Come on, Smith."

They made it back to the rocket in half an hour, slowly and painfully.

"Aren't we fools, though? Really prime fools?"

The rocket door slammed.

The rocket fired up on fountains of red and blue flame.

Below, the sand was stirred and blasted and blown. The footprints, for the first time in ten thousands years were disturbed. They blew away in fine particles. When the fire wind died, the prints were gone.

THE FINNEGAN

To say that I have been haunted for the rest of my life by the affair Finnegan is to grossly understate the events leading up to that final melancholy. Only now, at threescore and ten, can I write these words for an astonished constabulary who may well run with picks and shovels to unearth my truths or bury my lies.

The facts are these:

Three children went astray and were missed. Their bodies were found in the midst of Chatham Forest and each bore no marks of criminal assassination, but all had suffered their lifeblood to be drained. Only their skin remained like that of some discolored vineyard grapes withered by sunlight and no rain.

From the withered detritus of these innocents rose fresh rumors of vampires or similar beasts with similar appetites. Such myths always pursue the facts to stun them in their tracks. It could only have been a tombyard beast, it was said, that fed on and destroyed three lives and ruined three dozen more.

The children were buried in the most holy ground. Soon after, Sir Robert Merriweather, pretender to the throne of Sherlock Holmes but modestly refusing the claim, moved through the ten dozen doors of his antique house to come forth to search for this terrible thief of life. With myself, I might add, to carry his brandy and bumbershoot and warn him of underbrush pitfalls in that dark and mysterious forest.

Sir Robert Merriweather, you say?

Just that. Plus the ten times ten plus twelve amazing doors in his shut-up house.

Were the doors used? Not one in nine. How had they appeared in Sir Robert's old manse? He had shipped them in, as a collector of doors, from Rio, Paris, Rome, Tokyo, and mid-America. Once collected, he had stashed them, hinged, to be seen from both sides, on the walls of his upper and lower chambers. There he conducted tours of these odd portals for such antique fools as were ravished by the sight of the curiously overdone, the undersimplified, the rococo, or some First Empire cast aside by Napoleon's nephews or seized from Hermann Goering, who had in turn ransacked the Louvre. Others, pelted by Oklahoma dust storms, were jostled home in flatbeds cushioned by bright posters from carnivals buried in the wind-blown desolations of 1936 America. Name your least favorite door, it was *his.* Name the best quality, he owned it also, hidden and safe, true beauties behind oblivion's portals.

I had come to see his doors, not the deaths. At his behest, which was a command, I had bought my curiosity a steamship ticket and arrived to find Sir Robert involved not with ten dozen doors, but some great *dark* door. A mysterious portal, still un-found. And beneath? A tomb.

Sir Robert hurried the grand tour, opening and shutting panels rescued from Peking, long buried near Etna, or filched from Nantucket. But his heart, gone sick, was not in this, what should have been delightful, tour.

He described the spring rains that drenched the country to make things green, only to have people to walk out in that fine weather and one week find the body of a boy emptied of life through two incisions in his neck, and in the next weeks, the bodies of the two girls. People shouted for the police and sat drinking in pubs, their faces long and pale, while mothers locked their children home where fathers lectured on the dooms that lay in Chatham Forest.

"Will you come with me," said Sir Robert at last, "on a very strange, sad picnic?"

"I will," I said.

So we snapped ourselves in weather-proofs, lugged a hamper of sandwiches and red wine, and plunged into the forest on a drear Sunday.

There was time, as we moved down a hill into the dripping gloom of the trees, to recall what the papers had said about the vanished children's bloodless flesh, the police thrashing the forest ten dozen times, clueless, while the surrounding estates slammed their doors drum-tight at sunset.

"Rain. Damn. Rain!" Sir Robert's pale face stared up, his gray mustache quivering over his thin mouth. He was sick and brittle and old. "Our picnic will be *ruined!*"

"Picnic?" I said. "Will our killer join us for eats?"

"I pray to God he will," Sir Robert said. "Yes, pray to God he will."

We walked through a land that was now mists, now dim sunlight, now forest, now open glade, until we came into a silent part of the woods, a silence made of the way the trees grew wetly together and the way the green moss lay in swards and hillocks. Spring had not yet filled the empty trees. The sun was like an arctic disk, withdrawn, cold, and almost dead.

"This is the place," said Sir Robert at last.

"Where the children were found?" I inquired.

"Their bodies empty as empty can be."

I looked at the glade and thought of the children and the people who had stood over them with startled faces and the police who had come to whisper and touch and go away, lost.

"The murderer was never apprehended?"

"Not this clever fellow. How observant are you?" asked Sir Robert.

"What do you want observed?"

"There's the catch. The police slipped up. They were stupidly anthropomorphic about the whole bloody mess, seeking a killer with two arms, two legs, a suit of clothes, and a knife. So hypnotized with their human concept of the killer that they overlooked one obvious unbelievable fact about this place. So!"

He gave his cane a quick light tap on the earth.

Something happened. I stared at the ground. "Do that again," I whispered.

"You saw it?"

"I thought I saw a small trapdoor open and shut. May I have your cane?"

He gave me the cane. I tapped the ground.

It happened again.

"A spider!" I cried. "Gone! God, how quick!"

"Finnegan," Sir Robert muttered.

"What?"

"You know the old saying: in again, out again, Finnegan. Here."

With his penknife, Sir Robert dug in the soil to lift an entire clod of earth, breaking off bits to show me the tunnel. The spider, in panic, leaped out its small wafer door and fell to the ground.

Sir Robert handed me the tunnel. "Like gray velvet. Feel. A model builder, that small chap. A tiny shelter, camouflaged, and him alert. He could hear a fly walk. Then pounce out, seize, pop back, slam the lid!"

"I didn't know you loved Nature."

"Loathe it. But this wee chap, there's much we share. Doors. Hinges. Wouldn't consider other arachnids. But my love of portals drew me to study this incredible carpenter." Sir Robert worked the trap on its cobweb hinges. "What craftsmanship! And it *all* ties to the tragedies!"

"The murdered children?"

Sir Robert nodded. "Notice any special thing about this forest?"

"It's too quiet."

"Quiet!" Sir Robert smiled weakly. "Vast *quantities* of silence. No familiar birds, beetles, crickets, toads. Not a rustle or stir. The police didn't notice. Why should they? But it was this absence of sound and motion in the glade that prompted my wild theory about the murders."

He toyed with the amazing structure in his hands.

"What would you say if you could imagine a spider *large* enough, in a hideout *big* enough, so that a running child might hear a vacuumed sound, be seized, and vanish with a soft thud below. How say you?" Sir Robert stared at the trees. "Poppycock and bilge? Yet, why *not*? Evolution, selection, growth, mutations, and—*pfft!*"

Again he tapped with his cane. A trapdoor flew open, shut.

"Finnegan," he said.

The sky darkened.

"Rain!" Casting a cold gray eye at the clouds, he stretched his frail hand to touch the showers. "Damn! Arachnids *hate* rain. And so will our huge dark Finnegan."

"Finnegan!" I cried irritably.

"I *believe* in him, yes."

"A spider larger than a *child*?!"

"*Twice* as large."

The cold wind blew a mizzle of rain over us. "Lord, I hate to leave. Quick, before we go. *Here*."

Sir Robert raked away the old leaves with his cane, revealing two globular gray-brown objects.

"What *are* they?" I bent. "Old cannonballs?"

"No." He cracked the grayish globes. "Soil, through and through."

I touched the crumbled bits.

"Our Finnegan excavates," said Sir Robert. "To make his tunnel. With his large rakelike chelicerae he dislodges soil, works it into a ball, carries it in his jaws, and drops it beyond his hole."

Sir Robert displayed half a dozen pellets on his trembling palm. "Normal balls evicted from a tiny trapdoor tunnel. Toy-size." He knocked his cane on the huge globes at our feet. "Explain *those*!"

I laughed. "The *children* must've made them with mud!"

"Nonsense!" cried Sir Robert irritably, glaring about at trees and earth. "By God, somewhere, our dark beast lurks beneath his velvet lid. We might be *standing* on it. Christ, don't stare! His door has beveled rims. Some architect, this Finnegan. A genius at camouflage."

Sir Robert raved on and on, describing the dark earth, the arachnid, its fiddling legs, its hungry mouth, as the wind roared and the trees shook.

Suddenly, Sir Robert flung up his cane.

"No!" he cried.

I had no time to turn. My flesh froze, my heart stopped.

Something snatched my spine.

I thought I heard a huge bottle uncorked, a lid sprung. Then this monstrous thing crawled down my back.

"Here!" cried Sir Robert. "Now!"

He struck with his cane. I fell, dead weight. He thrust the thing from my spine. He lifted it.

The wind had cracked the dead tree branch and knocked it onto my back.

Weakly, I tried to rise, shivering. "Silly," I said a dozen times. "Silly. Damn awful silly!"

"Silly, no. Brandy, yes!" said Sir Robert. "Brandy?"

The sky was very black now. The rain swarmed over us.

✳ Door after door after door, and at last into Sir Robert's country house study. A warm, rich room, where a fire smoldered on a drafty hearth. We devoured our sandwiches, waiting for the rain to cease. Sir Robert estimated that it would stop by eight o'clock, when, by moonlight, we might return, ever so reluctantly, to Chatham Forest. I remembered the fallen branch, its spidering touch, and drank both wine and brandy.

"The silence in the forest," said Sir Robert, finishing his meal. "What murderer could achieve such a silence?"

"An insanely clever man with a series of baited, poisoned traps, with liberal quantities of insecticide, might kill off every bird, every rabbit, every insect," I said.

"Why should he do that?"

"To convince us that there is a large spider nearby. To perfect his act."

"We are the only ones who have noticed this silence; the police did not. Why should a murderer go to all that trouble for nothing?"

"Why *is* a murderer? you might well ask."

"I am not convinced." Sir Robert topped his food with wine. "This creature, with a voracious mouth, has cleansed the forest. With nothing left, he
seized the children. The silence, the murders, the prevalence of trapdoor
spiders, the large earth balls, it all *fits*."

Sir Robert's fingers crawled about the desktop, quite like a washed,
manicured spider in itself. He made a cup of his frail hands, held them up.

"At the bottom of a spider's burrow is a dustbin into which drop insect
remnants on which the spider has dined. Imagine the dustbin of our Grand
Finnegan!"

I imagined. I visioned a Great Legged thing fastened to its dark lid under
the forest and a child running, singing in the half-light. A brisk insucked
whisk of air, the song cut short, then nothing but an empty glade and the
echo of a softly dropped lid, and beneath the dark earth the spider, fiddling,
cabling, spinning the stunned child in its silently orchestrating legs.

What would the dustbin of such an incredible spider resemble? What
the remnants of many banquets? I shuddered.

"Rain's letting up." Sir Robert nodded his approval. "Back to the forest.
I've mapped the damned place for weeks. All the bodies were found in one
half-open glade. That's where the assassin, if it was a man, arrives! Or
where the unnatural silk-spinning, earth-tunneling architect of special
doors abides his tomb."

"*Must* I hear all this?" I protested.

"Listen more." Sir Robert downed the last of his burgundy. "The poor
children's prolapsed corpses were found at thirteen-day intervals. Which
means that every two weeks our loathsome eight-legged hide-and-seeker
must feed. Tonight is the fourteenth night after the last child was found,
nothing but skin. Tonight our hidden friend *must* hunger afresh. So! Within
the hour, I shall introduce you to Finnegan the great and horrible!"

"All of which," I said, "makes me want to drink."

"Here I go." Sir Robert stepped through one of his Louis the Fourteenth
portals. "To find the last and final and most awful door in all my life. You
will follow."

Damn, *yes*! I followed.

✳ The sun had set, the rain was gone, and the clouds cleared off to show a
cold and troubled moon. We moved in our own silence and the silence of
the exhausted paths and glades while Sir Robert handed me a small silver
pistol.

"Not that that would help. Killing an outsize arachnid is sticky. Hard to know where to fire the first shot. If you miss, there'll be no time for a second. Damned things, large or small, move in the *instant!*"

"Thanks." I took the weapon. "I need a drink."

"Done." Sir Robert handed me a silver brandy flask. "Drink as needed."

I drank. "What about you?"

"I have my own special flask." Sir Robert lifted it. "For the right time."

"Why wait?"

"I must surprise the beast and mustn't be drunk at the encounter. Four seconds before the thing grabs me, I will imbibe of this dear Napoleon stuff, spiced with a rude surprise."

"Surprise?"

"Ah, wait. You'll see. So will this dark thief of life. Now, dear sir, here we part company. I this way, you yonder. Do you mind?"

"Mind when I'm scared gutless? What's that?"

"Here. If I should vanish." He handed me a sealed letter. "Read it aloud to the constabulary. It will help them locate me and Finnegan, lost and found."

"Please, no details. I feel like a damned fool following you while Finnegan, if he exists, is underfoot snug and warm, saying, 'Ah, those idiots above running about, freezing. I think I'll *let* them freeze.'"

"One hopes not. Get away now. If we walk together, he won't jump up. Alone, he'll peer out the merest crack, glom the scene with a huge bright eye, flip down again, *ssst*, and one of us gone to darkness."

"Not me, please. Not me."

We walked on about sixty feet apart and beginning to lose one another in the half moonlight.

"Are you there?" called Sir Robert from half the world away in leafy dark.

"I wish I weren't," I yelled back.

"Onward!" cried Sir Robert. "Don't lose sight of me. Move closer. We're near on the site. I can intuit, I almost *feel*—"

As a final cloud shifted, moonlight glowed brilliantly to show Sir Robert waving his arms about like antennae, eyes half shut, gasping with expectation.

"Closer, closer," I heard him exhale. "Near on. Be still. Perhaps . . ."

He froze in place. There was something in his aspect that made me want to leap, race, and yank him off the turf he had chosen.

"Sir Robert, oh, God!" I cried. "Run!"

He froze. One hand and arm orchestrated the air, feeling, probing, while his other hand delved, brought forth his silver-coated flask of brandy. He held it high in the moonlight, a toast to doom. Then, afflicted with need, he took one, two, three, my God, *four* incredible swigs!

Arms out, balancing the wind, tilting his head back, laughing like a boy, he swigged the last of his mysterious drink.

"All right, Finnegan, below and beneath!" he cried. "Come *get* me!"

He stomped his foot.

Cried out victorious.

And *vanished*.

It was all over in a second.

A flicker, a blur, a dark bush had grown up from the earth with a whisper, a suction, and the thud of a body dropped and a door shut.

The glade was empty.

"Sir Robert. Quick!"

But there was no one to quicken.

Not thinking that I might be snatched and vanished, I lurched to the spot where Sir Robert had drunk his wild toast.

I stood staring down at earth and leaves with not a sound save my heart beating while the leaves blew away to reveal only pebbles, dry grass, and earth.

I must have lifted my head and bayed to the moon like a dog, then fell to my knees, fearless, to dig for lids, for tunneled tombs where a voiceless tangle of legs wove themselves, binding and mummifying a thing that had been my friend. This is his final door, I thought insanely, crying the name of my friend.

I found only his pipe, cane, and empty brandy flask, flung down when he had escaped night, life, everything.

Swaying up, I fired the pistol six times here into the unanswering earth, a dumb thing gone stupid as I finished and staggered over his instant graveyard, his locked-in tomb, listening for muffled screams, shrieks, cries, but heard none. I ran in circles, with no ammunition save my weeping shouts. I would have stayed all night, but a downpour of leaves, a great spidering flourish of broken branches, fell to panic and suffer my heart. I fled, still calling his name to a silence lidded by clouds that hid the moon.

At his estate, I beat on the door, wailing, yanking, until I recalled: it opened inward, it was unlocked.

Alone in the library, with only liquor to help me live, I read the letter that Sir Robert had left behind:

My dear Douglas:

I am old and have seen much but am not mad. Finnegan exists. My chemist had provided me with a sure poison that I will mix in my brandy for our walk. I will drink all. Finnegan, not knowing me as a poisoned morsel, will give me a swift invite. Now you see me, now you don't. I will then be the weapon of his death, minutes after my own. I do not think there is another outsize nightmare like him on earth. Once gone, that's the end.

Being old, I am immensely curious. I fear not death, for my physicians tell me that if no accidents kill me, cancer will.

I thought of giving a poisoned rabbit to our nightmare assassin. But then I'd never know where he was or if he really existed. Finnegan would die unseen in his monstrous closet, and I never the wiser. This way, for one victorious moment, I will *know* Fear for me. Envy me. Pray for me. Sorry to abandon you without farewells. Dear friend, carry on.

I folded the letter and wept.

No more was ever heard of him.

Some say Sir Robert killed himself, an actor in his own melodrama, and that one day we shall unearth his brooding, lost, and Gothic body and that it was he who killed the children and that his preoccupation with doors and hinges, and more doors, led him, crazed, to study this one species of spider, and wildly plan and build the most amazing door in history, an insane burrow into which he popped to die, before my eyes, thus hoping to perpetuate the incredible Finnegan.

But I have found no burrow. I do not believe a man could construct such a pit, even given Sir Robert's overwhelming passion for doors.

I can only ask, would a man murder, draw his victims' blood, build an earthen vault? For what motive? Create the *finest* secret exit in all time? Madness. And what of those large grayish balls of earth supposedly tossed forth from the spider's lair?

Somewhere, Finnegan and Sir Robert lie clasped in a velvet-lined unmarked crypt, deep under. Whether one is the paranoiac alter ego of the other, I cannot say. But the murders have ceased, the rabbits once more rush in Chatham Forest, and its bushes teem with butterflies and birds. It is another spring, and the children run again through a loud glade, no longer silent.

Finnegan and Sir Robert, *requiescat in pace*.

ON THE ORIENT, NORTH

It was on the Orient Express heading north from Venice to Paris to Calais that the old woman noticed the ghastly passenger.

He was a traveler obviously dying of some dread disease.

He occupied compartment 22 on the third car back, and had his meals sent in and only at twilight did he rouse to come sit in the dining car surrounded by the false electric lights and the sound of crystal and women's laughter.

He arrived this night, moving with a terrible slowness to sit across the aisle from this woman of some years, her bosom like a fortress, her brow serene, her eyes with a kindness that had mellowed with time.

There was a black medical bag at her side, and a thermometer tucked in her mannish lapel pocket.

The ghastly man's paleness caused her left hand to crawl up along her lapel to touch the thermometer.

"Oh, dear," whispered Miss Minerva Halliday.

The maître d' was passing. She touched his elbow and nodded across the aisle.

"Pardon, but where is that poor man going?"

"Calais and London, madame. If God is willing."

And he hurried off.

Minerva Halliday, her appetite gone, stared across at that skeleton made of snow.

The man and the cutlery laid before him seemed one. The knives, forks and spoons jingled with a silvery cold sound. He listened, fascinated, as if to the sound of his inner soul as the cutlery crept, touched, chimed; a tintinnabulation from another sphere. His hands lay in his lap like lonely pets, and when the train swerved around a long curve his body, mindless, swayed now this way, now that, toppling.

At which moment the train took a greater curve and knocked the silverware, chittering. A woman at a far table, laughing, cried out:

"I don't *believe* it!"

To which a man with a louder laugh shouted:

"Nor do *I*!"

The coincidence caused, in the ghastly passenger, a terrible melting. The doubting laughter had pierced his ears.

He visibly shrank. His eyes hollowed and one could almost imagine a cold vapor gasped from his mouth.

Miss Minerva Halliday, shocked, leaned forward and put out one hand. She heard herself whisper:

"*I believe!*"

The effect was instantaneous.

The ghastly passenger sat up. Color returned to his white cheeks. His eyes glowed with a rebirth of fire. His head swiveled and he stared across the aisle at this miraculous woman with words that cured.

Blushing furiously, the old nurse with the great warm bosom caught hold, rose, and hurried off.

Not five minutes later, Miss Minerva Halliday heard the maître d' hurrying along the corridor, tapping on doors, whispering. As he passed her open door, he glanced at her.

"Could it be that you are—"

"No," she guessed, "not a doctor. But a registered nurse. Is it that old man in the dining car?"

"Yes, yes! Please, madame, this way!"

The ghastly man had been carried back to his own compartment.

Reaching it, Miss Minerva Halliday peered within.

And there the strange man lay strewn, his eyes wilted shut, his mouth a bloodless wound, the only life in him the joggle of his head as the train swerved.

My God, she thought, he's *dead*!

Out loud she said, "I'll call if I need you."

The maître d' went away.

Miss Minerva Halliday quietly shut the sliding door and turned to examine the dead man—for surely he was dead. And yet. . . .

But at last she dared to reach out and touch the wrists in which so much ice-water ran. She pulled back, as if her fingers had been burned by dry ice. Then she leaned forward to whisper into the pale man's face.

"Listen very carefully. *Yes?*"

For answer, she thought she heard the coldest throb of a single heartbeat.

She continued. "I do not know how I guess this. I know who you are, and what you are sick of—"

The train curved. His head lolled as if his neck had been broken.

"I'll tell you what you're dying from!" she whispered. "You suffer a disease—of *people!*"

His eyes popped wide, as if he had been shot through the heart. She said:

"The people on this train are killing you. *They* are your affliction."

Something like a breath stirred behind the shut wound of the man's mouth.

"Yesssss . . . ssss."

Her grip tightened on his wrist, probing for some pulse:

"You are from some middle European country, yes? Somewhere where the nights are long and when the wind blows, people *listen*? But now things have changed, and you have tried to escape by travel, but . . ."

Just then, a party of young, wine-filled tourists bustled along the outer corridor, firing off their laughter.

The ghastly passenger withered.

"How do . . . you . . ." he whispered, ". . . know . . . thissss?"

"I am a special nurse with a special memory. I saw, I met, someone like you when I was six—"

"Saw?" the pale man exhaled.

"In Ireland, near Kileshandra. My uncle's house, a hundred years old, full of rain and fog and there was walking on the roof late at night, and sounds in the hall as if the storm had come in, and then at last this shadow entered my room. It sat on my bed and the cold from his body made *me* cold. I remember and know it was no dream, for the shadow who came to sit on my bed and whisper . . . was much . . . like you."

Eyes shut, from the depths of his arctic soul, the old sick man mourned in response:

"And who . . . and *what* . . . am I?"

"You are not sick. And you are not dying. . . . You *are*—"

The whistle on the Orient Express wailed a long way off.

"—a ghost," she said.

"Yesssss!" he cried.

It was a vast shout of need, recognition, assurance. He almost bolted upright.

"Yes!"

At which moment there arrived in the doorway a young priest, eager to perform. Eyes bright, lips moist, one hand clutching his crucifix, he stared at the collapsed figure of the ghastly passenger and cried, "May I—?"

"Last rites?" The ancient passenger opened one eye like the lid on a silver box. "From you? No." His eye shifted to the nurse. "*Her!*"

"Sir!" cried the young priest.

He stepped back, seized his crucifix as if it were a parachute ripcord, spun, and scurried off.

Leaving the old nurse to sit examining her now even more strange patient until at last he said:

"How," he gasped, "can *you* nurse *me?*"

"Why—" she gave a small self-deprecating laugh. "We must *find* a way."

With yet another wail, the Orient Express encountered more mileages of night, fog, mist, and cut through it with a shriek.

"You are going to Calais?" she said.

"And beyond, to Dover, London, and perhaps a castle outside Edinburgh, where I will be safe—"

"That's almost impossible—" She might as well have shot him through the heart. "No, no, wait, wait!" she cried. "Impossible . . . without *me*! I will travel with you to Calais and across to Dover."

"But you do not *know* me!"

"Oh, but I dreamed you as a child, long before I met someone like you, in the mists and rains of Ireland. At age nine I searched the moors for the Baskerville Hound."

"Yes," said the ghastly passenger. "You are English and the English *believe!*"

"True. Better than Americans, who *doubt*. French? Cynics! English is best. There is hardly an old London house that does not have its sad lady of mists crying before dawn."

At which moment the compartment door, shaken by a long curve of track, sprang wide. An onslaught of poisonous talk, of delirious chatter, of what could only be irreligious laughter poured in from the corridor. The ghastly passenger wilted.

Springing to her feet, Minerva Halliday slammed the door and turned to look with the familiarity of a lifetime of sleep-tossed encounters at her traveling companion.

"You, now," she asked, "who exactly are *you?*"

The ghastly passenger, seeing in her face the face of a sad child he might have encountered long ago, now described his life:

"I have 'lived' in one place outside Vienna for two hundred years. To survive, assaulted by atheists as well as true believers, I have hidden in libraries in dust-filled stacks there to dine on myths and moundyard tales. I have taken midnight feasts of panic and terror from bolting horses, baying dogs, catapulting tomcats . . . crumbs shaken from tomb lids. As the years passed, my compatriots of the unseen world vanished one by one as castles tumbled or lords rented out their haunted gardens to women's clubs or bed-and-breakfast entrepreneurs. Evicted, we ghastly wanderers of the world have sunk in tar, bog, and fields of disbelief, doubt, scorn, or outright derision. With the populations and disbeliefs doubling by the day, all of my specter friends have fled. I am the last, trying to train across Europe to some safe, rain-drenched castle-keep where men are properly frightened by soots and smokes of wandering souls. England and Scotland for me!"

His voice faded into silence.

"And your name?" she said, at last.

"I have no name," he whispered. "A thousand fogs have visited my family plot. A thousand rains have drenched my tombstone. The chisel marks were erased by mist and water and sun. My name has vanished with the flowers and the grass and the marble dust." He opened his eyes.

"*Why* are you doing this?" he said. "*Helping* me?"

And at last she smiled, for she heard the right answer fall from her lips: "I have never in my life had a *lark*."

"Lark!"

"My life was that of a stuffed owl. I was not a nun, yet never married. Treating an invalid mother and a half-blind father, I gave myself to hospitals, tombstone beds, cries at night, and medicines that are not perfume to passing men. So, I am something of a ghost myself, yes? And now, tonight, sixty-six years on, I have at last found in you a patient, magnificently different, fresh, absolutely new. Oh, Lord, what a challenge. A race! I will pace you, to face people off the train, through the crowds in Paris, then the trip to the sea, off the train, on to the ferry! It will indeed be a—"

"Lark!" cried the ghastly passenger. Spasms of laughter shook him.

"Larks? Yes, *that* is what we are!"

"But," she said, "in Paris, do they not *eat* larks even while they roast priests?"

He shut his eyes and whispered, "Paris? Ah, yes."

The train wailed. The night passed.

And they arrived in Paris.

And even as they arrived, a boy, no more than six, ran past and froze. He stared at the ghastly passenger and the ghastly passenger shot back a remembrance of antarctic ice floes. The boy gave a cry and fled. The old nurse flung the door wide to peer out.

The boy was gibbering to his father at the far end of the corridor. The father charged along the corridor, crying:

"What goes *on* here? Who has frightened my—?"

The man stopped. Outside the door he now fixed his gaze on this ghastly passenger on the slowing, braking Orient Express. He braked his own tongue. "—my son," he finished.

The ghastly passenger looked at him quietly with fog-gray eyes.

"I—" The Frenchman drew back, sucking his teeth in disbelief. "Forgive me!" He gasped. "Regrets!"

And he turned to run, shove at his son. "Troublemaker. "Get!" Their door slammed.

"Paris!" echoed through the train.

"Hush and hurry!" advised Minerva Halliday as she bustled her ancient friend out on to a platform milling with bad tempers and misplaced luggage.

"I am *melting*!" cried the ghastly passenger.

"Not where *I'm* taking you!" She displayed a picnic hamper and flung him forth to the miracle of a single remaining taxi. And they arrived under a stormy sky at the Père Lachaise cemetery. The great gates were swinging shut. The nurse waved a handful of francs. The gate froze.

Inside, they wandered at peace among ten thousand monuments. So much cold marble was there, and so many hidden souls, that the old nurse felt a sudden dizziness, a pain in one wrist, and a swift coldness on the left side of her face. She shook her head, refusing this. And they walked on among the stones.

"Where do we picnic?" he said.

"Anywhere," she said. "But carefully! For this is a *French* cemetery! Packed with cynics! *Armies* of egotists who burned people for their faith one year only to be burned for *their* faith the next! So, pick. Choose!" They walked. The ghastly passenger nodded. "This first stone. Beneath it: *nothing*. Death final, not a *whisper* of time. The *second* stone: a woman, a secret believer because she loved her husband and hoped to see him again in eternity . . . a murmur of spirit here, the turning of a heart. *Better*. Now this third gravestone: a writer of thrillers for a French magazine. But he *loved* his nights, his fogs, his castles.

This stone is a proper temperature, like a good wine. So here we shall sit, dear lady, as you decant the champagne and we wait to go back to the train."

She offered a glass, happily. "*Can you drink?*"

"One can try." He took it. "One can only try."

❊ The ghastly passenger almost "died" as they left Paris. A group of intellectuals, fresh from seminars about Sartre's "nausea," and hot-air ballooning about Simone de Beauvoir, streamed through the corridors, leaving the air behind them boiled and empty.

The pale passenger became paler.

The second stop beyond Paris, another invasion! A group of Germans surged aboard, loud in their disbelief of ancestral spirits, doubtful of politics, some even carrying books titled *Was God Ever Home?*

The Orient ghost sank deeper in his X-ray image bones.

"Oh, dear," cried Miss Minerva Halliday, and ran to her own compartment to plunge back and toss down a cascade of books.

"*Hamlet!*" she cried, "his father, yes? *A Christmas Carol.* Four ghosts! *Wuthering Heights.* Kathy *returns,* yes? To haunt the snows? Ah, *The Turn of the Screw,* and . . . *Rebecca!* Then—my favorite! *The Monkey's Paw! Which?*"

But the Orient ghost said not a Marley word. His eyes were locked, his mouth sewn with icicles.

"Wait!" she cried.

And opened the first book . . .

Where Hamlet stood on the castle wall and heard his ghost-of-a-father moan and so she said these words:

" 'Mark me . . . my hour is almost come . . . when I to sulfurous and tormenting flames . . . must render up myself . . . ' "

And then she read:

" 'I am thy father's spirit,/Doomed for a certain term to walk the night . . . ' "

And again:

" ' . . . If thou didst ever thy dear father love . . . O, God! . . . Revenge his foul and most unnatural murder . . . ' "

And yet again:

" ' . . . Murder most foul . . . ' "

And the train ran in the night as she spoke the last words of Hamlet's father's ghost:

" ' . . . Fare thee well at once . . . ' "

"' . . . Adieu, adieu! Remember me.' "

And she repeated:

"' . . . remember me!' "

And the Orient ghost quivered. She pretended not to notice but seized a further book:

"' . . . Marley was dead, to begin with . . .' "

As the Orient train thundered across a twilight bridge above an unseen stream.

Her hands flew like birds over the books.

"'I am the Ghost of Christmas Past!' "

Then:

"'The Phantom Rickshaw glided from the mist and clop-clopped off into the fog—' "

And wasn't there the faintest echo of a horse's hooves behind, within the Orient ghost's mouth?

"'The beating beating beating, under the floorboards of the Old Man's Telltale Heart!' " she cried, softly.

And there! like the leap of a frog. The first faint pulse of the Orient ghost's heart in more than an hour.

The Germans down the corridor fired off a cannon of disbelief.

But she poured the medicine:

"'The Hound bayed out on the Moor—' "

And the echo of that bay, that most forlorn cry, came from her traveling companion's soul, wailed from his throat.

And the night grew on and the moon arose and a Woman in White crossed a landscape, as the old nurse said and told, and a bat that became a wolf that became a lizard scaled a wall on the ghastly passenger's brow.

And at last the train was silent with sleeping, and Miss Minerva Halliday let the last book drop with the thump of a body to the floor.

"*Requiescat in pace?*" whispered the Orient traveler, eyes shut.

"Yes." She smiled, nodding. "*Requiescat in pace.*" And they slept.

And at last they reached the sea.

✳ And there was mist, which became fog, which became scatters of rain, like a proper drench of tears from a seamless sky.

Which made the ghastly passenger open, ungum his mouth, and murmur thanks for the haunted sky and the shore visited by phantoms of tide as the train slid into the shed where the mobbed exchange would be made, a full train becoming a full boat.

The Orient ghost who stood well back, the last figure on a now self-haunted train.

"Wait," he cried, softly, piteously. "That boat! There's no place on it to hide! And the *customs!*"

But the customs men took one look at the pale face snowed under the dark cap and earmuffs, and swiftly flagged the wintry soul on to the ferry.

To be surrounded by dumb voices, ignorant elbows, layers of people shoving as the boat shuddered and moved and the nurse saw her fragile icicle melt yet again.

It was a mob of children shrieking by that made her say: "Quickly!"

And she all but lifted and carried the wicker man in the wake of the boys and girls.

"No," cried the old passenger. "The noise!"

"It's special!" The nurse hustled him through a door. "A medicine! Here!"

The old man stared around.

"Why," he murmured. "This is—a playroom."

And she steered him into the midst of all the screams and running.

"Children!" she called.

The children froze.

"Story-telling time!"

They were about to run again when she added, "*Ghost* story-telling time!"

She pointed casually to the ghastly passenger, whose pale moth fingers grasped the scarf about his icy throat.

"All fall *down!*" said the nurse.

The children plummeted with squeals to the floor. All about the Orient traveler, like Indians around a tepee, they stared up along his body to where blizzards ran odd temperatures in his gaping mouth.

He wavered. She quickly said:

"You *do* believe in ghosts, *yes?*"

"Oh, *yes!*" was the shout. "Yes!"

It was as if a ramrod had shot up his spine. The Orient traveler stiffened. The most brittle of tiny flinty sparks fired his eyes. Winter roses budded in his cheeks. And the more the children leaned, the taller he grew, and the warmer his complexion. With one icicle finger he pointed at their faces.

"I," he whispered, "I," a pause. "Shall tell you a frightful tale. About a *real* ghost!"

"Oh, yes!" cried the children.

And he began to talk and as the fever of his tongue conjured fogs, lured mists and invited rains, the children hugged and crowded close, a bed of charcoals on which he happily baked. And as he talked Nurse Halliday, backed off near the door, saw what he saw across the haunted sea, the ghost cliffs, the chalk cliffs, the safe cliffs of Dover and not so far beyond, waiting, the whispering towers, the murmuring castle-keeps, where phantoms were as they had always been, with the still attics waiting. And staring, the old nurse felt her hand creep up her lapel toward her thermometer. She felt her own pulse. A brief darkness touched her eyes.

And then one child said: "Who *are* you?"

And gathering his gossamer shroud, the ghastly passenger whetted his imagination, and replied.

It was only the sound of the ferry landing whistle that cut short the long telling of midnight tales. And the parents poured in to seize their lost children, away from the Orient gentleman with the ghastly eyes whose gently raving mouth shivered their marrows as he whispered and whispered until the ferry nudged the dock and the last boy was dragged, protesting, away, leaving the old man and his nurse alone in the children's playroom as the ferry stopped shuddering its delicious shudders, as if it had listened, heard, and deliriously enjoyed the long-before-dawn tales.

At the gangplank, the Orient traveler said, with a touch of briskness, "No. I'll need no help going down. Watch!"

And he strode down the plank. And even as the children had been tonic for his color, height and vocal cords, so the closer he came to England, pacing, the firmer his stride, and when he actually touched the dock, a small happy burst of sound erupted from his thin lips and the nurse, behind him, stopped frowning, and let him run toward the train.

And seeing him dash, like a child before her, she could only stand, riven with delight and something more than delight. And he ran and her heart ran with him and suddenly knew a stab of amazing pain, and a lid of darkness struck her, and she swooned.

Hurrying, the ghastly passenger did not notice that the old nurse was not beside or behind him, so eagerly did he go.

At the train he gasped, "There!" safely grasping the compartment handle. Only then did he sense a loss, and turned.

Minerva Halliday was not there.

And yet, an instant later, she arrived, looking paler than before, but with an incredibly radiant smile. She wavered and almost fell. This time it was he who reached out.

"Dear lady," he said, "you have been so kind."

"But," she said, quietly, looking at him, waiting for him to truly see her, "I am not leaving."

"You . . . ?"

"I am going with you," she said.

"But your plans?"

"Have changed. Now, I have nowhere *else* to go."

She half-turned to look over her shoulder.

At the dock, a swiftly gathering crowd peered down at someone lying on the planks. Voices murmured and cried out. The word "doctor" was called several times.

The ghastly passenger looked at Minerva Halliday. Then he looked at the crowd and the object of the crowd's alarm lying on the dock: a medical thermometer lay broken under their feet. He looked back at Minerva Halliday, who still stared at the broken thermometer.

"Oh, my dear kind lady," he said, at last. "Come."

She looked into his face. "Larks?" she said.

He nodded and said, "Larks!"

And he helped her up into the train, which soon jolted and then dinned and whistled away along the tracks toward London and Edinburgh and moors and castles and dark nights and long years.

"I wonder who she was?" said the ghastly passenger looking back at the crowd on the dock.

"Oh, Lord," said the old nurse. "I never really knew."

And the train was gone.

It took a full twenty seconds for the tracks to stop trembling.

THE SMILING PEOPLE

It was the sensation of silence that was the most notable aspect of the house. As Mr. Greppin came through the front door the oiled silence of it opening and swinging closed behind him was like an opening and shutting dream, a thing accomplished on rubber pads, bathed in lubricant, slow and unmaterialistic. The double carpet in the hall, which he himself had so recently laid, gave off no sound from his movements. And when the wind shook the house late of nights there was not a rattle of eave or tremor of loose sash. He had himself checked the storm windows. The screen doors were securely hooked with bright new, firm hooks, and the furnace did not knock but sent a silent whisper of warm wind up the throats of the heating system that sighed ever so quietly, moving the cuffs of his trousers as he stood, now, warming himself from the bitter afternoon.

Weighing the silence with the remarkable instruments of pitch and balance in his small ears, he nodded with satisfaction that the silence was so unified and finished. Because there *had* been nights when rats had walked between wall-layers and it had taken baited traps and poisoned food before the walls were mute. Even the grandfather clock had been stilled, its brass pendulum hung frozen and gleaming in its long cedar, glass-fronted coffin.

They were waiting for him in the dining room.

He listened. They made no sound. Good. Excellent, in fact. They had learned, then, to be silent. You had to teach people, but it was worthwhile— there was not a rattle of knife or fork from the dining table. He worked off his thick gray gloves, hung up his cold armor of overcoat and stood there with an expression of urgency yet indecisiveness . . . thinking of what had to be done.

Mr. Greppin proceeded with familiar certainty and economy of motion into the dining room, where the four individuals seated at the waiting table did not move or speak a word. The only sound was the merest allowable pad of his shoes on the deep carpet.

His eyes, as usual, instinctively, fastened upon the lady heading the table. Passing, he waved a finger near her cheek. She did not blink.

Aunt Rose sat firmly at the head of the table and if a mote of dust floated lightly down out of the ceiling spaces, did her eye trace its orbit? Did the eye revolve in its shellacked socket, with glassy cold precision? And if the dust mote happened upon the shell of her wet eye did the eye batten? Did the muscles clinch, the lashes close?

No.

Aunt Rose's hand lay on the table like cutlery, rare and fine and old; tarnished. Her bosom was hidden in a salad of fluffy linen.

Beneath the table her stick legs in high-buttoned shoes went up into a pipe of dress. You felt that the legs terminated at the skirt line and from there on she was a department store dummy, all wax and nothingness responding, probably, with much the same chill waxen movements, with as much enthusiasm and response as a mannequin.

So here was Aunt Rose, staring straight at Greppin—he choked out a laugh and clapped hands derisively shut—there were the first hints of a dust mustache gathering across her upper lip!

"Good evening, Aunt Rose," he said, bowing. "Good evening, Uncle Dimity," he said, graciously. "No, not a word," he held up his hand. "Not a word from any of you." He bowed again. "Ah, good evening, cousin Lila, and you, cousin Sam."

Lila sat upon his left, her hair like golden shavings from a tube of lathed brass. Sam, opposite her, told all directions with his hair.

They were both young, he fourteen, she sixteen. Uncle Dimity, their father (but "father" was a nasty word!) sat next to Lila, placed in this secondary niche long, long ago because Aunt Rose said the window draft might get his neck if he sat at the head of the table. Ah, Aunt Rose!

Mr. Greppin drew the chair under his tight-clothed little rump and put a casual elbow to the linen.

"I've something to say," he said. "IT's very important. This has gone on for weeks now. It can't go any further. I'm in love. Oh, but I've told you that long ago. On the day I made you all smile, remember?"

The eyes of the four seated people did not blink, the hands did not move.

Greppin became introspective. The day he had made them smile. Two weeks ago it was. He had come home, walked in, looked at them and said, "I'm to be married!"

They had all whirled with expressions as if someone had just smashed the window.

"You're WHAT?" cried Aunt Rose.

"To Alice Jane Ballard!" he had said, stiffening somewhat.

"Congratulations," said Uncle Dimity. "I guess," he added, looking at his wife. He cleared his throat. "But isn't it a little early, son?" He looked at his wife again. "Yes. Yes, I think it's a little early. I wouldn't advise it yet, not just yet, no."

"The house is in a terrible way," said Aunt Rose. "We won't have it fixed for a year yet."

"That's what you said last year and the year before," said Mr. Greppin. "And anyway," he said bluntly, "this is *my* house."

Aunt Rose's jaw had clamped at that. "After all these years for us to be bodily thrown out, why I—"

"You won't be thrown out, don't be idiotic," said Greppin, furiously.

"Now, Rose—" said Uncle Dimity in a pale tone.

Aunt Rose dropped her hands. "After all I've done—"

In that instant Greppin had known they would *have* to go, all of them. First he would make them silent, then he would make them smile, then, later, he would move them out like luggage. He couldn't bring Alice Jane into a house full of grims such as these, where Aunt Rose followed you wherever you went even when she wasn't following you, and the children performed indignities upon you at a glance from their maternal parent, and the father, no better than a third child, carefully rearranged his advice to you on being a bachelor. Greppin stared at them. It was their fault that his loving and living was all wrong. If he did something about them—then his warm bright dreams of soft bodies glowing with an anxious perspiration of love might become tangible and near. Then he would have the house all to himself and—and Alice Jane. Yes, Alice Jane.

They would have to go. Quickly. If he told them to go, as he had often done, twenty years might pass as Aunt Rose gathered sunbleached sachets and Edison phonographs. Long before then Alice Jane herself would be moved and gone.

Greppin looked at them as he picked up the carving knife.

✳ Greppin's head snapped with tiredness.

He flicked his eyes open. Eh? Oh, he had been drowsing, thinking.

All *that* had occurred two weeks ago. Two weeks ago this very night that conversation about marriage, moving, Alice Jane, had come about. Two weeks ago it had been. Two weeks ago he had made them smile.

Now, recovering from his reverie, he smiled around at the silent and motionless figures. They smiled back in peculiarly pleasing fashion.

"I hate you, old woman," he said to Aunt Rose, directly. "Two weeks ago I wouldn't have dared say that. Tonight, ah, well—" he lazed his voice, turning. "Uncle Dimity, let me give you a little advice, old man—"

He talked small talk, picked up a spoon, pretended to eat peaches from an empty dish. He had already eaten downtown in a tray cafeteria; pork, potatoes, apple pie, string beans, beets, potato salad. But now he made dessert-eating motions because he enjoyed this little act. He made as if he were chewing.

"So—tonight you are finally, once and for all, moving out. I've waited two weeks, thinking it all over. In a way I guess I've kept you here this long because I wanted to keep an eye on you. Once you're gone, I can't be sure—" And here his eyes gleamed with fear. "You might come prowling around, making noises at night, and I couldn't stand that. I can't ever have noises in this house, not even when Alice moves in. . . ."

The double carpet was thick and soundless underfoot, reassuring.

"Alice wants to move in day after tomorrow. We're getting married."

Aunt Rose winked evilly, doubtfully at him.

"Ah!" he cried, leaping up, then, staring, he sank down, mouth convulsing. He released the tension in him, laughing. "Oh, I see. It was a fly." He watched the fly crawl with slow precision on the ivory cheek of Aunt Rose and dart away. Why did it have to pick that instant to make her eye appear to blink, to doubt. "Do you doubt I ever will marry, Aunt Rose? Do you think me incapable of marriage, of love and love's duties? Do you think me immature, unable to cope with a woman and her ways of living? Do you think me a child, only daydreaming? Well!" He calmed himself with an effort, shaking his head. "Man, man," he argued to himself. "It was only a fly, and does a fly make doubt of love, or did you make it into a fly and a wink? Damn it!" He pointed at the four of them.

"I'm going to fix the furnace hotter. In an hour I'll be moving you out of the house once and for all. You comprehend? Good. I see you do."

Outside, it was beginning to rain, a cold drizzling downpour that drenched the house. A look of irritation came to Greppin's face. The sound of the rain was the one thing he couldn't stop, couldn't be helped. No way to buy new hinges or lubricants or hooks for that. You might tent the house-top with lengths of cloth to soften the sound, mightn't you? That's going a bit far. No. No way of preventing the rain sounds.

He wanted silence now, where he had never wanted it before in his life so much. Each sound was a fear. So each sound had to be muffled, gotten to and eliminated.

The drum of rain was like the knuckles of an impatient man on a surface. He lapsed again into remembering.

He remembered the rest of it. The rest of that hour on that day two weeks ago when he had made them smile. . . .

He had taken up the carving knife and prepared to cut the bird upon the table. As usual the family had been gathered, all wearing their solemn, puritanical masks. If the children smiled the smiles were stepped on like nasty bugs by Aunt Rose.

Aunt Rose criticized the angle of Greppin's elbows as he cut the bird. The knife, she made him understand also, was not sharp enough. Oh, yes, the sharpness of the knife. At this point in his memory he stopped, rolled-tilted his eyes, and laughed. Dutifully, then, he had crisped the knife on the sharpening rod and again set upon the fowl.

He had severed away much of it in some minutes before he slowly looked up at their solemn, critical faces, like puddings with agate eyes, and after staring at them a moment, as if discovered with a naked woman instead of a naked-limbed partridge, he lifted the knife and cried hoarsely, "Why in God's name can't you, any of you, ever smile? I'll *make* you smile!"

He raised the knife a number of times like a magician's wand.

And, in a short interval—behold! they were *all* of them smiling!

❋ He broke that memory in half, crumpled it, balled it, tossed it down. Rising briskly, he went to the hall, down the hall to the kitchen, and from there down the dim stairs into the cellar where he opened the furnace door and built the fire steadily and expertly into wonderful flame.

Walking upstairs again he looked about him. He would have cleaners come and clean the empty house, redecorators slide down the dull drapes and hoist new shimmery banners up. New thick Oriental rugs purchased for the floors would subtly insure the silence he desired and would need at least for the next month, if not for the entire year.

He put his hands to his face. What if Alice Jane made noise moving about the house? Some noise, some how, some place!

And then he laughed. It was quite a joke. That problem was already solved. Yes, it was solved. He need fear no noise from Alice Jane. It was all absurdly simple. He would have all the pleasure of Alice Jane and none of the dream-destroying distractions and discomforts.

There was one other addition needed to the quality of silence. Upon the tops of the doors that the wind sucked shut with a bang at frequent intervals he would install air-compression brakes, those kind they have on library doors that hiss gently as their levers seal.

He passed through the dining room. The figures had not moved from their tableau. Their hands remained affixed in familiar positions, and their indifference to him was not impoliteness.

He climbed the hall stairs to change his clothing, preparatory to the task of moving the family. Taking the links from his fine cuffs, he swung his head to one side. Music. At first he paid it no mind. Then, slowly, his face swinging to the ceiling, the color drained out of his cheeks.

At the very apex of the house the music began, note by note, one note following another, and it terrified him.

Each note came like a plucking of one single harp thread. In the complete silence the small sound of it was made larger until it grew all out of proportion to itself, gone mad with all this soundlessness to stretch about in.

The door opened in an explosion from his hands, the next thing his feet were trying the stairs to the third level of the house, the banister twisted in a long polished snake under his tightening, relaxing, reaching-up, pulling-hands! The steps went under to be replaced by longer, higher, darker steps. He had started the game at the bottom with a slow stumbling, now he was running with full impetus and if a wall had suddenly confronted him he would not have stopped for it until he saw blood on it and fingernail scratches where he tried to pass through.

He felt like a mouse running in a great clear space of a bell. And high in the bell sphere the one harp thread hummed. It drew him on, caught him up with an unbilical of sound, gave his fear sustenance and life, mothered him. Fears passed between mother and groping child. He sought to shear the connection with his hands, could not. He felt as if someone had given a heave on the cord, wriggling.

Another clear threaded tone. And another.

"No, keep quiet," he shouted. "There can't be noise in my house. Not since two weeks ago. I said there would be no more noise. So it can't be—it's impossible! Keep quiet!"

He burst upward into the attic.

Relief can be hysteria.

Teardrops fell from a vent in the roof and struck, shattering upon a tall neck of Swedish cut-glass flowerware with resonant tone.

He shattered the vase with one swift move of his triumphant foot!

✳ Picking out and putting on an old shirt and old pair of pants in his room, he chuckled. The music was gone, the vent plugged, the silence again insured. There are silences and silences. Each with its own identity. There were summer night silences, which weren't silences at all, but layer on layer of insect chorals and the sound of electric arc lamps swaying in lonely small orbits on lonely country roads, casting out feeble rings of illumination upon which the night fed—summer night silence which, to be a silence, demanded an indolence and a neglect and an indifference upon the part of the listener. Not a silence at all! And there was a winter silence, but it was an incoffined silence, ready to burst out at the first touch of spring, things had a compression, a not-for-long feel, the silence made a sound unto itself, the freezing was so complete it made chimes of everything or detonations of a single breath or word you spoke at midnight in the diamond air. No, it was not a silence worthy of the name. A silence between two lovers, when there need be no words. Color came in his cheeks, he shut his eyes. It was a most pleasant silence, a perfect silence with Alice Jane. He had seen to that. *Everything* was perfect.

Whispering.

He hoped the neighbors hadn't heard him shrieking like a fool.

A faint whispering.

Now, about silences. The best silence was one conceived in every aspect by an individual, himself, so that there could be no bursting of crystal bonds, or electric-insect hummings, the human mind could cope with each sound, each emergency, until such a complete silence was achieved that one could hear ones cells adjust in ones hand.

A whispering.

He shook his head. There was no whispering. There could be none in *his* house. Sweat began to seep down his body, he began to shake in small, imperceptible shakings, his jaw loosened, his eyes were turned free in their sockets.

Whispering. Low rumors of talk.

"I tell you I'm getting married," he said, weakly, loosely.

"You're lying," said the whispers.

His head fell forward on its neck as if hung, chin on chest.

"Her name is Alice Jane Ballard—" he mouthed it between soft, wet lips and the words were formless. One of his eyes began to jitter its lid up and down as if blinking out a message to some unseen guest. "You can't stop me from loving her, I love her—"

Whispering.

He took a blind step forward.

The cuff of his pants leg quivered as he reached the floor grille of the ventilator. A hot rise of air followed his cuffs. Whispering.

The furnace.

✳ He was on his way downstairs when someone knocked on the front door. He leaned against it. "Who is it?"

"Mr. Greppin?"

Greppin drew in his breath. "Yes?"

"Will you let us in, please?"

"Well, who is it?"

"The police," said the man outside.

"What do you want, I'm just sitting down to supper!"

"Just want a talk with you. The neighbors phoned. Said they hadn't seen your aunt and uncle for two weeks. Heard a noise awhile ago—"

"I assure you everything is all right." He forced a laugh.

"Well, then," continued the voice outside, "we can talk it over in friendly style if you'll only open the door."

"I'm sorry," insisted Greppin. "I'm tired and hungry, come back tomorrow. I'll talk to you then, if you want me to."

"I'll have to insist, Mr. Greppin."

They began to beat against the door.

Greppin turned automatically, stiffly, walked down the hall past the old clock, into the dining room, without a word. He seated himself without looking at any one in particular and then he began to talk, slowly at first, then more rapidly.

"Some pests at the door. You'll talk to them, won't you, Aunt Rose? You'll tell them to go away, won't you, we're eating dinner? Everyone else go on eating and look pleasant and they'll go away, if they do come in. Aunt Rose you *will* talk to them, won't you? And now that things are happening I have something to tell you." A few hot tears fell for no reason. He looked at them as they soaked and spread in the white linen, vanishing. "I don't know anyone named Alice Jane Ballard. I never knew anyone named Alice Jane Ballard. It was all—all—I don't know. I said I loved her and wanted to marry her to get around somehow to make you smile. Yes, I said it because I planned to make you smile, that was the only reason. I'm never going to have a woman, I always knew for years I never would have. Will you please pass the potatoes, Aunt Rose?"

 The front door splintered and fell. A heavy softened rushing filled the hall. Men broke into the dining room.

A hesitation.

The police inspector hastily removed his hat.

"Oh, I beg your pardon," he apologized. "I didn't mean to intrude upon your supper, I—"

The sudden halting of the police was such that their movement shook the room. The movement catapulted the bodies of Aunt Rose and Uncle Dimity straight away to the carpet, where they lay, their throats severed in a half moon from ear to ear—which caused them, like the children seated at the table, to have what was the horrid illusion of a smile under their chins, ragged smiles that welcomed in the late arrivals and told them everything with a simple grimace. . . .

✳

THE FRUIT AT THE BOTTOM
OF THE BOWL

WILLIAM ACTON ROSE TO HIS FEET. The clock on the mantel ticked midnight.

He looked at his fingers and he looked at the large room around him and he looked at the man lying on the floor. William Acton, whose fingers had stroked typewriter keys and made love and fried ham and eggs for early breakfasts, had now accomplished a murder with those same ten whorled fingers.

He had never thought of himself as a sculptor and yet, in this moment, looking down between his hands at the body upon the polished hardwood floor, he realized that by some sculptural clenching and remodeling and twisting of human clay he had taken hold of this man named Donald Huxley and changed his physiognomy, the very frame of his body.

With a twist of his fingers he had wiped away the exacting glitter of Huxley's eyes; replaced it with a blind dullness of eye cold in socket. The lips, always pink and sensuous, were gaped to show the equine teeth, the yellow incisors, the nicotined canines, the gold-inlaid molars. The nose, pink also, was now mottled, pale, discolored, as were the ears. Huxley's hands, upon the floor, were open, pleading for the first time in their lives, instead of demanding.

Yes, it was an artistic conception. On the whole, the change had done Huxley a share of good. Death made him a handsomer man to deal with. You could talk to him now and he'd have to listen.

William Acton looked at his own fingers.

It was done. He could not change it back. Had anyone heard? He listened. Outside, the normal late sounds of street traffic continued. There was no banging of the house door, no shoulder wrecking the portal into kindling, no voices demanding entrance. The murder, the sculpturing of clay from warmth to coldness was done, and nobody knew.

Now what? The clock ticked midnight. His every impulse exploded him in a hysteria toward the door. Rush, get away, run, never come back, board a train, hail a taxi, get, go, run, walk, saunter, but get the blazes out of here!

His hands hovered before his eyes, floating, turning.

He twisted them in slow deliberation; they felt airy and feather-light. Why was he staring at them this way? he inquired of himself. Was there something in them of immense interest that he should pause now, after a successful throttling, and examine them whorl by whorl?

They were ordinary hands. Not thick, not thin, not long, not short, not hairy, not naked, not manicured and yet not dirty, not soft and yet not callused, not wrinkled and yet not smooth; not murdering hands at all—and yet not innocent. He seemed to find them miracles to look upon.

It was not the hands as hands he was interested in, nor the fingers as fingers. In the numb timelessness after an accomplished violence he found interest only in the *tips* of his fingers.

The clock ticked upon the mantel.

He knelt by Huxley's body, took a handkerchief from Huxley's pocket, and began methodically to swab Huxley's throat with it. He brushed and massaged the throat and wiped the face and the back of the neck with fierce energy. Then he stood up.

He looked at the throat. He looked at the polished floor. He bent slowly and gave the floor a few dabs with the handkerchief, then he scowled and swabbed the floor; first, near the head of the corpse; secondly, near the arms. Then he polished the floor all around the body. He polished the floor one yard from the body on all sides. Then he polished the floor two yards from the body on all sides. The he polished the floor three yards from the body in all directions. Then he—

He stopped.

✳ There was a moment when he saw the entire house, the mirrored halls, the carved doors, the splendid furniture; and, as clearly as if it were being repeated word for word, he heard Huxley talking and himself just the way they had talked only an hour ago.

Finger on Huxley's doorbell. Huxley's door opening.

"Oh!" Huxley shocked. "It's *you*, Acton."

"Where's my wife, Huxley?"

"Do you think I'd tell you, really? Don't stand out there, you idiot. If you want to talk business, come in. Through that door. There. Into the library."

Acton had *touched* the library door.

"Drink?"

"I need one. I can't believe Lily is gone, that she—"

"There's a bottle of burgundy, Acton. Mind fetching it from that cabinet?"

Yes, fetch it. *Handle* it. *Touch* it. He did.

"Some interesting first editions there, Acton. Feel this binding. *Feel* of it."

"I didn't come to see books, I—"

He had *touched* the books and the library table and *touched* the burgundy bottle and burgundy glasses.

Now, squatting on the floor beside Huxley's cold body with the polishing handkerchief in his fingers, motionless, he stared at the house, the walls, the furniture about him, his eyes widening, his mouth dropping, stunned by what he realized and what he saw. He shut his eyes, dropped his head, crushed the handkerchief between his hands, wadding it, biting his lips with his teeth, pulling in on himself.

The fingerprints were everywhere, *everywhere*!

"Mind getting the burgundy, Acton, eh? The burgundy bottle, eh? With your fingers, eh? I'm terribly tired. You understand?"

A pair of gloves.

Before he did one more thing, before he polished another area, he must have a pair of gloves, or he might unintentionally, after cleaning a surface, redistribute his identity.

He put his hands in his pockets. He walked through the house to the hall umbrella stand, the hatrack. Huxley's overcoat. He pulled out the overcoat pockets.

No gloves.

His hands in his pockets again, he walked upstairs, moving with a controlled swiftness, allowing himself nothing frantic, nothing wild. He had made the initial error of not wearing gloves (but, after all, he hadn't *planned* a murder, and his subconscious, which may have known of the crime before its commitment, had not even hinted he might need gloves before the night was finished), so now he had to sweat for his sin of omission. Somewhere in the house there must be at least one pair of gloves. He would have to hurry; there was every chance that someone might visit Huxley, even at this hour. Rich friends drinking themselves in and out the door, laughing, shouting, coming and going without so much as hello–good-bye. He would have until six in the morning, at the outside, when Huxley's friends were to pick Huxley up for the trip to the airport and Mexico City. . . .

Acton hurried about upstairs opening drawers, using the handkerchief as blotter. He untidied seventy or eighty drawers in six rooms, left them with their tongues, so to speak, hanging out, ran on to new ones. He felt naked, unable to do anything until he found gloves. He might scour the entire house with the handkerchief, buffing every possible surface where fingerprints might lie, then accidentally bump a wall here or there, thus sealing his own fate with one microscopic, whorling symbol! It would be putting his stamp of approval on the murder, that's what it would be! Like those waxen seals in the old days when they rattled papyrus, flourished ink, dusted all with sand to dry the ink, and pressed their signet rings in hot crimson tallow at the bottom. So it would be if he left one, mind you, one fingerprint upon the scene! His approval of the murder did not extend as far as affixing said seal.

More drawers! Be quiet, be curious, be careful, he told himself.

At the bottom of the eighty-fifth drawer he found gloves.

"Oh, my Lord, my Lord!" He slumped against the bureau, sighing. He tried the gloves on, held them up, proudly flexed them, buttoned them. They were soft, gray, thick, impregnable. He could do all sorts of tricks with hands now and leave no trace. He thumbed his nose in the bedroom mirror, sucking his teeth.

✳ "NO!" cried Huxley.

What a wicked plan it had been.

Huxley had fallen to the floor, *purposely*! Oh, what a wickedly clever man! Down onto the hardwood floor had dropped Huxley, with Acton after him. They had rolled and tussled and clawed at the floor, printing and printing it with their frantic fingertips! Huxley had slipped away a few feet, Acton crawling after to lay hands on his neck and squeeze until the life came out like paste from a tube!

Gloved, William Acton returned to the room and knelt down upon the floor and laboriously began the task of swabbing every wildly infested inch of it. Inch by inch, inch by inch, he polished and polished until he could almost see his intent, sweating face in it. Then he came to a table and polished the leg of it, on up its solid body and along the knobs and over the top. He came to a bowl of wax fruit, burnished the filigree silver, plucked out the wax fruit and wiped them clean, leaving the fruit at the bottom unpolished.

"I'm *sure* I didn't touch *them*," he said.

After rubbing the table he came to a picture frame hung over it.

"I'm certain I didn't touch *that*," he said.

He stood looking at it.

He glanced at all the doors in the room. Which doors had he used tonight? He couldn't remember. Polish all of them, then. He started on the doorknobs, shined them all up, and then he curried the doors from head to foot, taking no chances. Then he went to all the furniture in the room and wiped the chair arms.

"That chair you're sitting in, Acton, is an old Louis XIV piece. *Feel* that material," said Huxley.

"I didn't come to talk furniture, Huxley! I came about Lily."

"Oh, come off it, you're not that serious about her. She doesn't love you, you know. She's told me she'll go with me to Mexico City tomorrow."

"You and your money and your damned furniture!"

"It's nice furniture, Acton; be a good guest and feel of it."

Fingerprints can be found on fabric.

"Huxley!" William Acton stared at the body. "Did you guess I was going to kill you? Did your subconscious suspect, just as my subconscious suspected? And did your subconscious tell you to make me run about the house handling, touching, *fondling* books, dishes, doors, chairs? Were you *that* clever and *that* mean?"

He washed the chairs dryly with the clenched handkerchief. Then he remembered the body—he hadn't dry-washed it. He went to it and turned it now this way, now that, and burnished every surface of it. He even shined the shoes, charging nothing.

While shining the shoes his face took on a little tremor of worry, and after a moment he got up and walked over to that table.

He took out and polished the wax fruit at the bottom of the bowl.

"Better," he whispered, and went back to the body.

But as he crouched over the body his eyelids twitched and his jaw moved from side to side and he debated, then he got up and walked once more to the table.

He polished the picture frame.

While polishing the picture frame he discovered—

The wall.

"That," he said, "is *silly*."

"Oh!" cried Huxley, fending him off. He gave Acton a shove as they struggled. Acton fell, got up, *touching* the wall, and ran toward Huxley again. He strangled Huxley. Huxley died.

Acton turned steadfastly from the wall, with equilibrium and decision. The harsh words and the action faded in his mind; he hid them away. He glanced at the four walls.

"Ridiculous!" he said.

From the corners of his eyes he saw something on one wall.

"I refuse to pay attention," he said to distract himself. "The next room, now! I'll be methodical. Let's see—altogether we were in the hall, the library, *this* room, and the dining room and the kitchen."

There was a spot on the wall behind him.

Well, *wasn't* there?

He turned angrily. "All right, all right, just to be *sure*," and he went over and couldn't find any spot. Oh, a *little* one, yes, right—*there*. He dabbed it. It wasn't a fingerprint anyhow. He finished with it, and his gloved hand leaned against the wall and he looked at the wall and the way it went over to his right and over to his left and how it went down to his feet and up over his head and he said softly, "No." He looked up and down and over and across and he said quietly, "That would be too much." How many square feet? "I don't give a good damn," he said. But unknown to his eyes, his gloved fingers moved in a little rubbing rhythm on the wall.

He peered at his hand and the wallpaper. He looked over his shoulder at the other room. "I must go in there and polish the essentials," he told himself, but his hand remained, as if to hold the wall, or himself, up. His face hardened.

Without a word he began to scrub the wall, up and down, back and forth, up and down, as high as he could stretch and as low as he could bend.

"Ridiculous, oh my Lord, ridiculous!"

But you must be certain, his thought said to him.

"Yes, one *must* be certain," he replied.

He got one wall finished, and then . . .

He came to another wall.

"What time *is* it?"

He looked at the mantel clock. An hour gone. It was five after one.

The doorbell rang.

Acton froze, staring at the door, the clock, the door, the clock.

Someone rapped loudly.

A long moment passed. Acton did not breathe. Without new air in his body he began to fail away, to sway; his head roared a silence of cold waves thundering onto heavy rocks.

"Hey, in there!" cried a drunken voice. "I know you're in there, Huxley! Open up, dammit! This is Billy-boy, drunk as an owl, Huxley, old pal, drunker than two owls."

"Go away," whispered Acton soundlessly, crushed.

"Huxley, you're in there, I hear you *breathing*!" cried the drunken voice.

"Yes, I'm in here," whispered Acton, feeling long and sprawled and clumsy on the floor, clumsy and cold and silent. "Yes."

"Hell!" said the voice, fading away into mist. The footsteps shuffled off. "Hell . . ."

Acton stood a long time feeling the red heart beat inside his shut eyes, within his head. When at last he opened his eyes he looked at the new fresh wall straight ahead of him and finally got courage to speak. "Silly," he said. "This wall's flawless. I won't touch it. Got to hurry. Got to hurry. Time, time. Only a few hours before those damn-fool friends blunder in!" He turned away.

From the corners of his eyes he saw the little webs. When his back was turned the little spiders came out of the woodwork and delicately spun their fragile little half-invisible webs. Not upon the wall at his left, which was already washed fresh, but upon the three walls as yet untouched. Each time he stared directly at them the spiders dropped back into the wood-work, only to spindle out as he retreated. "Those walls are all right," he insisted in a half shout. "I won't *touch* them!"

He went to a writing desk at which Huxley had been seated earlier. He opened a drawer and took out what he was looking for. A little magnifying glass Huxley sometimes used for reading. He took the magnifier and approached the wall uneasily.

Fingerprints.

"But those aren't mine!" He laughed unsteadily. "I *didn't* put them there! I'm *sure* I didn't! A servant, a butler, or a maid perhaps!"

The wall was full of them.

"Look at this one here," he said. "Long and tapered, a woman's, I'd bet money on it."

"Would you?"

"I would!"

"Are you certain?"

"Yes!"

"Positive?"

"Well—yes."

"Absolutely?"

"Yes, damn it, yes!"

"Wipe it out, anyway, why don't you?"

"There, by God!"

"Out damned spot, eh, Acton?"

"And this one, over here," scoffed Acton. "That's the print of a fat man."

"Are you sure?"

"Don't start *that* again!" he snapped, and rubbed it out. He pulled off a glove and held his hand up, trembling, in the glary light.

"Look at it, you idiot! See how the whorls go? See?"

"That proves nothing!"

"Oh, all right!" Raging, he swept the wall up and down, back and forth, with gloved hands, sweating, grunting, swearing, bending, rising, and getting redder of face.

He took off his coat, put it on a chair.

"Two o'clock," he said, finishing the wall, glaring at the clock.

He walked over to the bowl and took out the wax fruit and polished the ones at the bottom and put them back, and polished the picture frame.

He gazed up at the chandelier.

His fingers twitched at his sides.

His mouth slipped open and the tongue moved along his lips and he looked at the chandelier and looked away and looked back at the chandelier and looked at Huxley's body and then at the crystal chandelier with its long pearls of rainbow glass.

He got a chair and brought it over under the chandelier and put one foot up on it and took it down and threw the chair, violently, laughing, into a corner. Then he ran out of the room, leaving one wall as yet unwashed.

In the dining room he came to a table.

"I want to show you my Gregorian cutlery, Acton," Huxley had said. Oh, that casual, that *hypnotic* voice!

"I haven't time," Acton said. "I've got to see Lily—"

"Nonsense, look at this silver, this exquisite craftsmanship."

Acton paused over the table where the boxes of cutlery were laid out, hearing once more Huxley's voice, remembering all the touchings and gesturings.

Now Acton wiped the forks and spoons and took down all the plaques and special ceramic dishes from the wall itself. . . .

"Here's a lovely bit of ceramics by Gertrude and Otto Natzler, Acton. Are you familiar with their work?"

"It *is* lovely."

"Pick it up. Turn it over. See the fine thinness of the bowl, hand-thrown on a turntable, thin as eggshell, incredible. And the amazing volcanic glaze. Handle it, *go* ahead. *I* don't mind."

HANDLE IT. GO AHEAD. PICK IT UP!

Acton sobbed unevenly. He hurled the pottery against the wall. It shattered and spread, flaking wildly, upon the floor.

An instant later he was on his knees. Every piece, every shard of it, must be found. Fool, fool, fool! he cried to himself, shaking his head and shutting and opening his eyes and bending under the table. Find every piece, idiot, not one fragment of it must be left behind. Fool, fool! He gathered them. Are they all here? He looked at them on the table before him. He looked under the table again and under the chairs and the service bureaus, and found one more piece by match light and started to polish each little fragment as if it were a precious stone. He laid them all out neatly upon the shining polished table.

"A lovely bit of ceramics, Acton. Go ahead—*handle* it."

He took out the linen and wiped it and wiped the chairs and tables and doorknobs and windowpanes and ledges and drapes and wiped the floor and found the kitchen, panting, breathing violently, and took off his vest and adjusted his gloves and wiped the glittering chromium. . . . "I want to show you my house, Acton," said Huxley. "Come along. . . ." And he wiped all the utensils and the silver faucets and the mixing bowls, for now he had forgotten what he had touched and what he had not. Huxley and he had lingered here, in the kitchen, Huxley prideful of its array, covering his nervousness at the presence of a potential killer, perhaps wanting to be near the knives if they were needed. They had idled, touched this, that, something else—there was no remembering what or how much or how many—and he finished the kitchen and came through the hall into the room where Huxley lay.

He cried out.

He had forgotten to wash the fourth wall of the room! And while he was gone the little spiders had popped from the fourth, unwashed wall and swarmed over the already clean walls, dirtying them again! On the ceilings, from the chandelier, in the corners, on the floor, a million little whorled webs hung billowing at his scream! Tiny, tiny little webs, no bigger than, ironically, your—finger!

As he watched, the webs were woven over the picture frame, the fruit bowl, the body, the floor. Prints wielded the paper knife, pulled out drawers, touched the tabletop, touched, touched, touched everything everywhere.

He polished the floor wildly, wildly. He rolled the body over and cried on it while he washed it, and got up and walked over and polished the fruit at the bottom of the bowl. Then he put a chair under the chandelier and got up and polished each little hanging fire of it, shaking it like a crystal tambourine until it tilted bellwise in the air. Then he leaped off the chair and gripped the doorknobs and got up on other chairs and swabbed the walls higher and higher and ran to the kitchen and got a broom and wiped the webs down from the ceiling and polished the bottom fruit of the bowl and washed the body and doorknobs and silverware and found the hall banister and followed the banister upstairs.

Three o'clock! Everywhere, with a fierce, mechanical intensity, clocks ticked! There were twelve rooms downstairs and eight above. He figured the yards and yards of space and time needed. One hundred chairs, six sofas, twenty-seven tables, six radios. And under and on top and behind. He yanked furniture out away from walls and, sobbing, wiped them clean of years-old dust, and staggered and followed the banister up, up the stairs, handling, erasing, rubbing, polishing, because if he left one little print it would reproduce and make a million more!—and the job would have to be done all over again and now it was four o'clock!—and his arms ached and his eyes were swollen and staring and he moved sluggishly about, on strange legs, his head down, his arms moving, swabbing and rubbing, bedroom by bedroom, closet by closet. . . .

They found him at six-thirty that morning.

In the attic.

The entire house was polished to a brilliance. Vases shone like glass stars. Chairs were burnished. Bronzes, brasses, and coppers were all aglint. Floors sparkled. Banisters gleamed.

Everything glittered. Everything shone, everything was bright!

They found him in the attic, polishing the old trunks and the old frames and the old chairs and the old carriages and toys and music boxes and vases and cutlery and rocking horses and dusty Civil War coins. He was half through the attic when the police officer walked up behind him with a gun.

"Done!"

On the way out of the house Acton polished the front doorknob with his handkerchief and slammed it in triumph!

BUG

Looking back now, I can't remember a time when Bug wasn't dancing. Bug is short for jitterbug and, of course, those were the days in the late thirties, our final days in high school and our first days out in the vast world looking for work that didn't exist when jitterbugging was all the rage. And I can remember Bug (his real name was Bert Bagley, which shortens to Bug nicely), during a jazz-band blast at our final aud-call for our high school senior class, suddenly leaping up to dance with an invisible partner in the middle of the front aisle of the auditorium. That brought the house down. You never heard such a roar or such applause. The bandleader, stricken with Bug's oblivious joy, gave an encore and Bug did the same and we all exploded. After that the band played "Thanks for the Memory" and we all sang it, with tears pouring down our cheeks. Nobody in all the years after could forget: Bug dancing in the aisle, eyes shut, hands out to grasp his invisible girlfriend, his legs not connected to his body, just his heart, all over the place. When it was over, nobody, not even the band, wanted to leave. We just stood there in the world Bug had made, hating to go out into that other world that was waiting for us.

It was about a year later when Bug saw me on the street and stopped his roadster and said come on along to my place for a hot dog and a Coke, and I jumped in and we drove over with the top down and the wind really hitting us and Bug talking and talking at the top of his lungs, about life and the times and what he wanted to show me in his front parlor—front parlor, hell, dining room, kitchen, and bedroom.

What was it he wanted me to see?

Trophies. Big ones, little ones, solid gold and silver and brass trophies with his name on them. Dance trophies. I mean they were everywhere, on the floor by his bed, on the kitchen sink, in the bathroom, but in the parlor, especially, they had settled like a locust plague. There were so many of them on the mantel, and in bookcases instead of books, and on the floor, you had to wade through, kicking some over as you went. They totaled, he said, tilting his head back and counting inside his eyelids, to about three hundred and twenty prizes, which means grabbing onto a trophy almost every night in the past year.

"All this," I gasped, "just since we left high school?"

"Ain't I the cat's pajamas?" Bug cried.

"You're the whole darned department store! Who was your partner, all those nights?"

"Not partner, partners," Bug corrected. "Three hundred, give or take a dozen, different women on three hundred different nights."

"Where do you find three hundred women, all talented, all good enough, to win prizes?"

"They weren't talented or all good," said Bug, glancing around at his collection. "They were just ordinary, good, every-night dancers. I won the prizes. I made them good. And when we got out there dancing, we cleared the floor. Everyone else stopped, to watch us there out in the middle of nowhere, and we never stopped."

He paused, blushed, and shook his head. "Sorry about that. Didn't mean to brag."

But he wasn't bragging. I could see. He was just telling the truth.

"You want to know how this all started?" said Bug, handing over a hot dog and a Coke.

"Don't tell me," I said. "I know."

"How could you?" said Bug, looking me over.

"The last aud-call at L.A. High, I think they played 'Thanks for the Memory,' but just before that—"

" 'Roll Out the Barrel'—"

"—'the Barrel,' yes, and there you were in front of God and everyone, jumping."

"I never stopped," said Bug, eyes shut, back in those years. "Never," he said, "stopped."

"You got your life all made," I said.

"Unless," said Bug, "something *happens*."

What happened was, of course, the war.

Looking back, I remember that in that last year in school, sap that I was, I made up a list of my one hundred and sixty-five *best* friends. Can you imagine that? One hundred and sixty-five, count 'em, best *friends*! It's a good thing I never showed that list to anyone. I would have been hooted out of school.

Anyway, the war came and went and took with it a couple dozen of those listed friends and the rest just disappeared into holes in the ground or went east or wound up in Malibu or Fort Lauderdale. Bug was on that list, but I didn't figure out I didn't really *know* him until half a lifetime later. By that time I was down to half a dozen pals or women I might turn to if I needed, and it was then, walking down Hollywood Boulevard one Saturday afternoon, I heard someone call:

"How about a hot dog and a Coke?"

Bug, I thought without turning. And that's who it was, standing on the Walk of Stars with his feet planted on Mary Pickford and Ricardo Cortez just behind and Jimmy Stewart just ahead. Bug had taken off some hair and put on some weight, but it *was* Bug and I was overjoyed, perhaps too much, and showed it, for he seemed embarrassed at my enthusiasm. I saw then that his suit was not half new enough and his shirt frayed, but his tie was neatly tied and he shook my hand off and we popped into a place where we stood and had that hot dog and that Coke.

"Still going to be the world's greatest writer?" said Bug.

"Working at it," I said.

"You'll get there," said Bug and smiled, meaning it. "You were always good."

"So were you," I said.

That seemed to pain him slightly, for he stopped chewing for a moment and took a swig of Coke. "Yes, sir," he said. "I surely *was*."

"God," I said, "I can still remember the day I saw all those trophies for the first time. What a family! Whatever—?"

Before I could finish asking, he gave the answer.

"Put 'em in storage, some. Some wound up with my first wife. Goodwill got the rest."

"I'm sorry," I said, and truly was.

Bug looked at me steadily. "How come *you're* sorry?"

"Hell, I dunno," I said. "It's just, they seemed such a part of you. I haven't thought of you often the last few years or so, to be honest, but when I do, there you are knee-deep in all those cups and mugs in your front room, out in the kitchen, hell, in your *garage!*"

"I'll be damned," said Bug. "What a memory you got."

We finished our Cokes and it was almost time to go. I couldn't help myself, even seeing that Bug had fleshed himself out over the years.

"When—" I started to say, and stopped.

"When what?" said Bug.

"When," I said with difficulty, "when was the last time you danced?"

"Years," said Bug.

"But how long ago?"

"Ten years. Fifteen. Maybe twenty. Yeah, twenty. I don't dance anymore."

"I don't believe that. Bug not dance? Nuts."

"Truth. Gave my fancy night-out shoes to the Goodwill, too. Can't dance in your socks."

"*Can*, and barefoot, too!"

Bug had to laugh at that. "You're really something. Well, it's been nice." He started edging toward the door. "Take care, genius—"

"Not so fast." I walked him out into the light and he was looking both ways as if there were heavy traffic. "You know one thing I never saw and wanted to see? You bragged about it, said you took three hundred ordinary girls out on the dance floor and turned them into Ginger Rogers inside three minutes. But I only saw you once at that aud-call in '38, so I don't believe you."

"What?" said Bug. "You saw the trophies!"

"You could have had those made up," I pursued, looking at his wrinkled suit and frayed shirt cuffs. "Anyone can go in a trophy shop and buy a cup and have his name put on it!"

"You think I did that?" cried Bug.

"I think that, yes!"

Bug glanced out in the street and back at me and back in the street and back to me, trying to decide which way to run or push or shout.

"What's got into you?" said Bug. "Why're you talking like that?"

"God, I don't know," I admitted. "It's just, we might not meet again and I'll never have the chance, or you to prove it. I'd like, after all this time, to see what you talked about. I'd love to see you dance again, Bug."

"Naw," said Bug. "I've forgotten how."

"Don't hand me that. You may have forgotten, but the rest of you knows how. Bet you could go down to the Ambassador Hotel this afternoon, they still have tea dances there, and clear the floor, just like you said. After you're out there nobody else dances, they all stop and look at you and her just like thirty years ago."

"No," said Bug, backing away but coming back. "No, no."

"Pick a stranger, any girl, any woman, out of the crowd, lead her out, hold her in your arms and just skim her around as if you were on ice and dream her to Paradise."

"If you write like that, you'll never sell," said Bug.

"Bet you, Bug."

"I don't bet."

"All right, then. Bet you you can't. Bet you, By God, that you've lost your stuff!"

"Now, hold on," said Bug.

"I mean it. Lost your stuff forever, for good. Bet you. Wanna bet?"

Bug's eyes took on a peculiar shine and his face was flushed. "How much?"

"Fifty bucks!"

"I don't have—"

"Thirty bucks, then. Twenty! You can afford to lose that, *can't* you?"

"Who says I'd lose, dammit?"

"I say. Twenty. Is it a deal?"

"You're throwing your money away."

"No, I'm a sure winner, because you can't dance worth shoats and shinola!"

"Where's your money?" cried Bug, incensed now.

"Here!"

"Where's your car!?"

"I don't own a car. Never learned to drive. Where's yours?"

"Sold it! Jesus, no cars. How do we get to the tea dance!?"

We got. We grabbed a cab and I paid and, before Bug could relent, dragged him through the hotel lobby and into the ballroom. It was a nice summer afternoon, so nice that the room was filled with mostly middle-aged men and their wives, a few younger ones with their girlfriends, and some kids out of college who looked out of place, embarrassed by the mostly old-folks music out of another time. We got the last table and when Bug opened his mouth for one last protest, I put a straw in it and helped him nurse a margarita.

"Why are you *doing* this?" he protested again.

"Because you were just one of one hundred sixty-five close friends!" I said.

"We were never friends," said Bug.

"Well, today, anyway. There's 'Moonlight Serenade.' Always liked that, never danced myself, clumsy fool. On your feet, Bug!"

He was on his feet, swaying.

"Who do you pick?" I said. "You cut in on a couple? Or there's a few wallflowers over there, a tableful of women. I dare you to pick the least likely and give her lessons, yes?"

That did it. Casting me a glance of the purest scorn, he charged off half into the pretty teatime dresses and immaculate men, searching around until his eyes lit on a table where a woman of indeterminate age sat, hands folded, face thin and sickly pale, half hidden under a wide-brimmed hat, looking as if she were waiting for someone who never came.

That one, I thought.

Bug glanced from her to me. I nodded. And in a moment he was bowing at her table and a conversation ensued. It seemed she didn't dance, didn't know *how* to dance, didn't *want* to dance. Ah, yes, he seemed to be saying. Ah, *no*, she seemed to reply. Bug turned, holding her hand, and gave me a long stare and a wink. Then, without looking at her, he raised her by her hand and arm and out, with a seamless glide, onto the floor.

What can I say, how can I tell? Bug, long ago, had never bragged, but only told the truth. Once he got hold of a girl, she was weightless. By the time he had whisked and whirled and glided her once around the floor, she almost took off, it seemed he had to hold her down, she was pure gossamer, the closest thing to a hummingbird held in the hand so you cannot feel its weight but only sense its heartbeat sounding to your touch, and there she went out and around and back, with Bug guiding and moving, enticing and retreating, and not fifty anymore, no, but eighteen, his body remembering what his mind thought it had long forgotten, for his body was free of the earth now, too. He carried himself, as he carried her, with that careless insouciance of a lover who knows what will happen in the next hour and the night soon following.

And it happened, just like he said. Within a minute, a minute and a half at most, the dance floor cleared. As Bug and his stranger lady whirled by with a glance, every couple on the floor stood still. The bandleader almost forgot to keep time with his baton, and the members of the orchestra, in a similar trance, leaned forward over their instruments to see Bug and his new love whirl and turn without touching the floor.

When the "Serenade" ended, there was a moment of stillness and then an explosion of applause. Bug pretended it was all for the lady, and helped her curtsy and took her to her table, where she sat, eyes shut, not believing what had happened. By that time Bug was on the floor again, with one of the wives he borrowed from the nearest table. This time, no one even went out on the floor. Bug and the borrowed wife filled it around and around, and this time even Bug's eyes were shut.

I got up and put twenty dollars on the table where he might find it. After all, he *had* won the bet, hadn't he?

Why had I done it? Well, I couldn't very well have left him out in the middle of the high school auditorium aisle dancing *alone*, could I?

On my way out I looked back. Bug saw me and waved, his eyes as brimmed full as mine. Someone passing whispered, "Hey, come on, *lookit* this guy!"

God, I thought, he'll be dancing all night.

Me, I could only walk.

And I went out and walked until I was fifty again and the sun was going down and the low June fog was coming in early over old Los Angeles.

That night, just before going to sleep, I wished that in the morning when Bug woke up he would find the floor around his bed covered with trophies.

Or at the very least he would turn and find a quiet and understanding trophy with her head on his pillow, near enough to touch.

DOWNWIND FROM
GETTYSBURG

AT EIGHT THIRTY THAT NIGHT he heard the sharp crack from the theater down the hall.

Backfire, he thought. No. Gun.

A moment later he heard the great lift and drop of voices like an ocean surprised by a landfall which stopped it dead. A door banged. Feet ran.

An usher burst through his office door, glanced swiftly about as if blind, his face pale, his mouth trying words that would not come.

"Lincoln . . . Lincoln . . ."

Bayes glanced up from his desk.

"What about Lincoln?"

"He . . . he's been *shot*."

"Good joke. Now—"

"Shot. Don't you understand? Shot. Really shot. For the second time, shot!"

The usher wandered out, holding to the wall.

Bayes felt himself rise. "Oh, for Christ—"

And he was running and passed the usher who, feeling him pass, began to run with him.

"No, no," said Bayes. "It didn't happen. It didn't. It couldn't. It didn't, couldn't . . ."

"Shot," said the usher.

As they made the corridor turn, the theater doors exploded wide and a crowd that had turned mob shouted or yelled or screamed or stunned simply said, "Where is he?" "There!" "Is that him?" "Where?" "Who did it?" "He did? *Him?*" "Hold him!" "Watch out!" "Stop!"

Two security guards stumbled to view, pushed, pulled, twisted now this way and that, and between them a man who struggled to heave back from the bodies, the grasping hands and now the upflung and downfell fists. People snatched, pecked, pummeled, beat at him with packages or frail sun parasols which splintered like kites in a great storm. Women turned in dazed circles seeking lost friends, whimpering. Men, crying out, shoved them aside to squirm through to the center of the push and thrust and backward-pumping guards and the assaulted man who now masked his cut face with splayed fingers.

"Oh God, God." Bayes froze, beginning to believe. He stared upon the scene. Then he sprang forward. "This way! Back inside! Clear off! Here! Here!"

And somehow the mob was breached, a door cracked wide to shove flesh through, then slammed.

Outside, the mob hammered, threatening damnations and scourges unheard of by living men. The whole theater structure quaked with their muted wails, cries and estimates of doom.

Bayes stared a long moment at the shaken and twisted doorknobs, the chattering locks, then over to the guards and the man slumped between them.

Bayes leaped back suddenly, as if an even fresher truth had exploded there in the aisle.

Dimly, he felt his left shoe kick something which spun skittering like a rat chasing its tail along the carpeting under the seats. He bent to let his blind hand search, grope, find the still-half-warm pistol which, looked at but disbelieved, he shoved in his coat pocket as he backed down the aisle. It was a full half minute before he forced himself to turn and face the inevitable stage and that figure in the center of the stage.

Abraham Lincoln sat in his carved highback chair, his head bent forward at an unfamiliar angle. Eyes flexed wide, he gazed upon nothing. His large hands rested gently on the chair arms, as if he might momentarily shift weight, rise, and declare this sad emergency at an end.

Moving as under a tide of cold water, Bayes mounted the steps.

"Lights, dammit! Give us more lights!"

Somewhere, an unseen technician remembered what switches were for. A kind of dawn grew in the dim place.

Bayes, on the platform, circled the occupant of the chair, and stopped.

Yes. There it was. A neat bullet hole at the base of the skull, behind the left ear.

"*Sic semper tyrannis,*" a voice murmured somewhere.

Bayes jerked his head up.

The assassin, seated now in the last row of the theater, face down but sensing Bayes' preoccupation with Lincoln, spoke to the floor, to himself:

"Sic—"

He stopped. For there was an outraged stir above him. One security guard's fist flew up, as if the man had nothing to do with it. The fist, urgent to itself, was on its way down to silence the killer when—

"Stop!" said Bayes.

The fist paused halfway, then withdrew to be nursed by the guard with mixtures of anger and frustration.

None, thought Bayes, I believe none of it. Not that man, not the guards and not . . . he turned to again see the bullet hole in the skull of the slain leader.

From the hole a slow trickle of machinery oil dripped.

From Mr. Lincoln's mouth, a similar slow exudation of liquid moved down over the chin and whiskers to rain drop by drop upon his tie and shirt.

Bayes knelt and put his ear to the figure's chest.

Faintly within there was the whine and hum of wheels, cogs, and circuitries still intact but malfunctioning.

For some reason this sound reared him to his feet in alarm.

"Phipps . . . !?"

The guards blinked with incomprehension.

Bayes snapped his fingers. "Is Phipps coming in tonight? Oh God, he mustn't see this! Head him off! Tell him there's an emergency, yes, emergency at the machine plant in Glendale! Move!"

One of the guards hurried out the door.

And watching him run, Bayes thought, please, God, keep Phipps home, keep him off . . .

Strange, at such a time, not your own life but the lives of others flashed by.

Remember . . . that day five years past when Phipps first slung his blueprints, his paintings, his watercolors out on a table and announced his Grand Plan? And how they had all stared at the plans and then up at him and gasped:

Lincoln?

Yes! Phipps had laughed like a father just come from a church where some sweet high vision in some strange Annunciation has promised him a most peculiar son.

Lincoln. That was the idea. Lincoln born again.

And Phipps? He would both engender and nurture this fabulous ever-ready giant robot child.

Wouldn't it be fine . . . if they could stand in the meadow fields of Gettysburg, listen, learn, see, hone the edge of their razor souls, and *live*?

Bayes circled the slumped figure in the chair and, circling, numbered the days and remembered years.

Phipps, holding up a cocktail glass one night, like a lens that simultaneously proportions out the light of the past and the illumination of the future:

"I have always wanted to do a film on Gettysburg and the vast crowd there and far away out at the edge of that sun-drowsed impatient lost thick crowd, a farmer and his son trying so hard to hear, not hearing, trying to catch the wind-blown words from the tall speaker there on the distant stand, that gaunt man in the stovepipe hat who now takes off his hat, looks in it as to his soul rummaged there on scribbled letterbacks and begins to speak.

"And this farmer, in order to get his son up out of the crush, why, he hefts the boy up to sit upon his shoulders. There the boy, nine years old, a frail encumbrance, becomes ears to the man, for the man indeed cannot hear nor see but only guess what the President is speaking far across a sea of people there at Gettysburg and the President's voice is high and drifts now clear, now gone, seized and dispersed by contesting breeze and wind. And there have been too many speakers before him and the crowd all crumpled wool and sweat, all mindless stockyard squirm and jostled elbow, and the farmer talks up to his son on his shoulders in a yearning whisper: What? What's he *say*? And the boy, tilting his head, leaning his peach-fuzz ear to the wind, replies:

" 'Fourscore and seven years . . . ' "

"Yes?"

" ' . . . ago, our fathers brought forth . . . ' "

"Yes, yes!?"

" ' . . . on this continent . . . ' "

"Eh?"

"Continent! 'A new nation, conceived in liberty, and dedicated to the proposition that all men are . . . '

"And so it goes, the wind leaning against the frail words, the far man uttering, the farmer never tiring of his sweet burden of son and the son obedient cupping and catching and telling it all down in a fierce good whisper and the father hearing the broken bits and some parts missing and some whole but all fine somehow to the end . . .

" ' . . . of the people, by the people, for the people, shall not perish from the earth.'

"The boy stops whispering.

"It is done.

"And the crowd disperses to the four directions. And Gettysburg is history.

"And for a long time the father cannot bring himself to ease his translator of the wind down to set him on the earth, but the boy, changed, comes down at last . . ."

Bayes sat looking at Phipps.

Phipps slugged down his drink, suddenly chagrined at his own expansiveness, then snorted:

"I'll never make that film. But I will make *this*!"

And that was the moment he pulled forth and unfolded the blueprints of the Phipps Eveready Salem, Illinois, and Springfield Ghost Machine, the Lincoln mechanical, the electro-oil-lubricated plastic India-rubber perfect-motioned and outspoken dream.

Phipps and his born-full-tall-at-birth Lincoln. Lincoln. Summoned live from the grave of technology, fathered by a romantic, drawn by need, slapped to life by small lightnings, given voice by an unknown actor, to be placed there to live forever in this far southwest corner of old-new America! Phipps and Lincoln.

And that was the day, yes, of the first wild bursts of laughter which Phipps ignored by simply saying, "We must, oh we must, stand all of us, downwind from Gettysburg. It's the only hearing place."

And he shared out his pride among them. This man he gave armatures, to that the splendid skull, another must trap the Ouija-spirit voice and sounding word, yet others must grow the precious skin, hair, and finger-prints. Yes, even Lincoln's *touch* must be borrowed, copied, the same!

Derision then was their style of life.

Abe would never really speak, they all knew that, nor move. It would all be summed and written off with taxes as a loss.

But as the months lengthened into years, their outcries of hilarity turned to accepting smiles and stunned wild grins. They were a gang of boys caught up in some furtive but irritably joyous mortuary society who met midnights in marble vaults to disperse through graveyards at dawn.

The Lincoln Resurrection Brigade yeasted full and prospered. Instead of one mad fool, a dozen maniacs fell to rifling old mummy-dust newsfiles, begging and then pilfering death masks, burying and then digging up new plastic bones.

Some toured the Civil War battlefields in hopes that history, borne on some morning wind, might whip their coats like flags. Some prowled the October fields of Salem, starched brown with farewell summer, sniffing airs, pricking ears, alert for some lank lawyer's unrecorded voice, anxious for echoes, pleading their case.

And none more anxious nor paternal-proud worrying than Phipps until the month when the robot was spread out on delivery tables, there to be ball and socketed, voice box locked in, rubber eyelids peeled back to sink therein the deep sad eyes which, gazing out, had seen too much. The generous ears were appended that might hear only time lost. The large-knuckled hands were hung like pendulums to guess that time. And then upon the tall man's nakedness they shucked on suiting, buttoned buttons, fixed his tie, a gathering of tailors, no, Disciples now on a bright and glorious Easter morn and them on Jerusalem's hills ready to roll aside the rock and stand Him forth at their cry.

And in the last hour of the last day Phipps had locked them all out as he finished the final touches on the recumbent flesh and spirit and at last opened the door and, not literally, no, but in some metaphoric sense, asked them to hoist him on their shoulders a last time.

And in silence watched as Phipps called across the old battlefield and beyond, saying the tomb was not his place; arise.

And Lincoln, deep in his cool Springfield marbled keep, turned in his slumbers and dreamed himself awake.

And rose up.

And spoke.

A phone rang.

Bayes jerked.

The memories fell away.

The theater phone on one far stage wall buzzed.

Oh, God, he thought, and ran to lift the phone.

"Bayes? This is Phipps. Buck just called and told me to get over there! Said something about Lincoln—"

"No," said Bayes. "You know Buck. Must have called from the nearest bar. I'm here in the theater. Everything's fine. One of the generator's acted up. We just finished repairs—"

"*He's* all right, then?"

"He's great." He could not take his eyes off the slumped body. Oh Christ. Oh God. Absurd.

"I—I'm coming over."

"No, don't!"

"Jesus, why are you *shouting*?"

Bayes bit his tongue, took a deep breath, shut his eyes so he could not see the thing in the chair and said, slowly:

"Phipps, I'm not shouting. There. The lights just came back on. I can't keep the crowd waiting. I swear to you—"

"You're lying."

"Phipps!"

But Phipps had hung up.

Ten minutes, thought Bayes wildly, oh God, he'll be here in ten minutes. Ten minutes before the man who brought Lincoln out of the grave meets the man who put him back in it . . .

He moved. A mad impulse made him wish to run backstage, start the tapes, see how much of the fallen creature would motivate, which limbs jerk, which lie numb—more madness. Time for that tomorrow.

There was only time now for the mystery.

And the mystery was enclosed in the man who sat in the third seat over in the last row back from the stage.

The assassin—he was an assassin, wasn't he? The assassin, what did he look like?

He had seen his face, some few moments ago, hadn't he? And wasn't it a face from an old, a familiar, a faded and put-away daguerreotype? Was there a full mustache? Were there dark and arrogant eyes?

Slowly Bayes stepped down from the stage. Slowly he moved up the aisle and stopped, looking in at that man with his head bent into clutching fingers.

Bayes inhaled then slowly exhaled a question in two words:

"Mr. . . . Booth?"

The strange faraway man stiffened, then shuddered and let forth a terrible whisper:

"Yes . . ."

Bayes waited. Then he dared ask:

"Mr. . . . John *Wilkes* Booth?"

To this the assassin laughed quietly. The laugh faded into a kind of dry croak.

"Norman Llewellyn Booth. Only the last name is . . . the same."

Thank God, thought Bayes. I couldn't have stood the other.

Bayes spun and paced up the aisle, stopped, and fixed his eyes to his watch. No time. Phipps was on the freeway now. Any moment, he'd be hammering at the door. Bayes spoke rigidly to the theater wall directly in front of him:

"Why?"

And it was an echo of the affrighted cry of three hundred people who had sat here not ten minutes ago and jumped to terror at the shot.

"Why!?"

"I don't know!" cried Booth.

"Liar!" cried Bayes, in the same breath and instant.

"Too good a chance to miss."

"What?!" Bayes whirled.

". . . nothing."

"You don't dare say that again!"

"Because," said Booth, head down, half hid, now light, now dark, jerking into and out of emotions he only sensed as they came, went, rose, faded with barks of laughter and then silence. "Because . . . it's the truth." In awe, he whispered, stroking his cheeks. "I did it. I actually *did* it."

"Bastard!"

Bayes had to keep walking up, around, down the aisles, circling, afraid to stop, afraid he might rush and strike and keep on striking this stupid genius, this bright killer—

Booth saw this and said:

"What are you waiting for? Get it over."

"I will not—!" Bayes forced his yell down to a steady calmness. "I will not be tried for murder because I killed a man who killed another man who wasn't really a man at all, but a machine. It's enough to shoot a thing that seems alive. I won't have some judge or jury trying to figure a law for a man who kills because a humanoid computer was shot. I won't repeat your stupidity."

"Pity," mourned the man named Booth, and saying it, the light went out of his face.

"Talk," said Bayes, gazing through the wall, imagining the night roads, Phipps in his car, and time running out. "You've got five minutes, maybe more, maybe less. Why did you do it, why? Start somewhere. Start with the fact you're a coward."

He waited. The security guard waited behind Booth, creaking uneasily in his shoes.

"Coward, yes," said Booth. "How did you know?"

"I know."

"Coward," said Booth. "That's me. Always afraid. You name it. Things. People. Places. Afraid. People I wanted to hit, but never hit. Things I always wanted, never had. Places I wanted to go, never went. Always wanted to be big, famous, why not? That didn't work either. So, I thought, if you can't find something to be glad about, find something to be sad. Lots of ways to enjoy being sad. Why? Who knows? I just had to find something awful to do and then cry about what I had done. That way you felt you had accomplished something. So, I set out to do something bad."

"You've succeeded."

Booth gazed down at his hands hung between his knees as if they held an old but suddenly remembered and simple weapon.

"Did you ever kill a turtle?"

"What?"

"When I was ten I found out about death. I found out that the turtle, that big dumb rocklike thing, was going to live long after I was dead. I figured if I had to go, the turtle went first. So I took a brick and hit him on the back until I broke his shell and he died . . ."

Bayes slowed in his constant pacing and said, "For the same reason, I once let a butterfly live."

"No," said Booth, quickly, then added, "no, not for the same reason. A butterfly lit on my hand once. The butterfly opened and shut its wings, just resting there. I knew I could crush it. But I didn't because I knew that in ten minutes or an hour some bird would eat it. So I let it just fly away. But turtles?! They lie around backyards and live forever. So I went and got a brick and I was sorry for months after. Maybe I still am. Look . . ."

His hands trembled before him.

"And what," said Bayes, "has all this to do with your being here tonight?"

"Do? What!" cried Booth, looking at Bayes as if *he* were mad. "Haven't you been *listening*? Great God, I'm jealous! Jealous of anything that works right, anything that's perfect, anything that's beautiful all to itself, anything that lasts I don't care what it is! Jealous!"

"You can't be jealous of machines."

"Why not, dammit?" Booth clutched the back of the seat in front of him and slowly pulled himself forward staring at the slumped figure in that highback chair in the center of the stage. "Aren't machines more perfect, ninety-nine times out of a hundred than most people you've ever known? I mean *really*? Don't they do things right? How many people can you name do things right one third, one half the time? That damned thing up there, that machine, not only looks perfection, but speaks and acts perfection. More, if you keep it oiled and wound and fixed it'll be looking, speaking, acting right and grand and beautiful a hundred, two hundred years after I'm in the earth! "Jealous? Damn right I am!"

"But a machine doesn't *know* what it is."

"*I* know, *I* feel!" said Booth. "I'm outside it looking in. I'm always outside things like that. I've never been in. The machine has it. I don't. It was built to do one or two things exactly on the nose. No matter how much I learned or knew or tried the rest of my life, no matter what I did, I could never be as perfect, as fine, as maddening, as deserving of destruction as that thing up there, that man, that thing, that creature, that president . . ."

He was on his feet now, shouting at the stage eighty feet away.

Lincoln said nothing. Machinery oil gathered glistening on the floor under the chair.

"That president—" murmured Booth, as if he had come upon the real truth at last. "That president. Yes. Lincoln. Don't you see? He died a long time ago. He can't be alive. He just can't be. It's not right. A hundred years ago and yet here he is. He was shot once, buried once, yet here he is going on and on and on. Tomorrow and the day after that and all the days. So his name being Lincoln and mine Booth . . . I just *had* to come . . ."

His voice faded. His eyes had glazed over.

"Sit down," said Bayes, quietly.

Booth sat, and Bayes nodded to the remaining security guard. "Wait outside, please."

When the guard was gone and there were only Booth and himself and the quiet thing waiting up there in the chair, Bayes turned slowly at last and looked at the assassin. He weighed his words carefully and said:

"Good but not good enough."

"What?"

"You haven't given all the reasons why you came here tonight."

"I have!"

"You just think you have. You're kidding yourself. All Romantics do. One way or the other. Phipps when he invented this machine. You when you destroyed it. But it all comes down to this . . . very plain and very simple, you'd love to have your picture in the papers, wouldn't you?"

Booth did not answer, but his shoulder straightened, imperceptibly.

"Like to be seen coast-to-coast on magazine covers?"

"No."

"Get free time on TV?"

"No."

"Be interviewed on radio?"

"No!"

"Like to have trials and lawyers arguing whether a man can be tried for proxy-murder . . ."

"No!"

". . . that is, attacking, shooting a humanoid machine . . ."

"No!"

Booth was breathing fast now, his eyes moving wildly in his face. Bayes let more out:

"Great to have two hundred million people talking about you tomorrow morning, next week, next month, next year!"

Silence.

But a smile appeared, like the faintest drip of saliva, at the corner of Booth's mouth. He must have felt it. He raised a hand to touch it away.

"Fine to sell your personal true real story to the international syndicates for a fine chunk?"

Sweat moved down Booth's face and itched in his palms.

"Shall I give you the answer to all, all the questions I have just asked? Eh? Eh? Well," said Bayes, "the answer is—"

Someone rapped on a far theater door.

Bayes jumped. Booth turned to stare.

The knock came, louder.

"Bayes, let me in, this is Phipps," a voice cried outside in the night.

Hammering, pounding, then silence. In the silence, Booth and Bayes looked at each other like conspirators.

"Let me in, oh Christ, let me in!"

More hammering, then a pause and again the insistent onslaught, a crazy drum and tattoo, then silence again, the man outside panting, circling perhaps to find another door.

"Where was I?" said Bayes. "No. Yes. The answer to all those questions? Do you get worldwide TV radio film magazine newspaper gossip broadcast publicity . . . ?"

A pause.

"No."

Booth's mouth jerked but he stayed silent.

"N," Bayes spelled it, "O."

He reached in, found Booth's wallet, snapped out all the identity cards, pocketed them, and handed the empty wallet back to the assassin.

"No?" said Booth, stunned.

"No, Mr. Booth. No pictures. No coast-to-coast TV. No magazines. No columns. No papers. No advertisement. No glory. No fame. No fun. No self-pity. No resignation. No immortality. No nonsense about triumphing over the dehumanization of man by machines. No martyrdom. No respite from your own mediocrity. No splendid suffering. No maudlin tears. No renunciation of possible futures. No trial. No lawyers. No analysts speeding you up this month, this year, thirty years, sixty years, ninety years after, no stories with double spreads, no money, no."

Booth rose up as if a rope had hauled him tall and stretched him gaunt and washed him pale.

"I don't understand. I—"

"You went to all this trouble? Yes. And I'm ruining the game. For when all is said and done, Mr. Booth, all the reasons listed and all the sums summed, you're a has-been that never was. And you're going to stay that way, spoiled and narcissistic and small and mean and rotten. You're a short man and I intend to squash and squeeze and press and batter you an inch shorter instead of force-growing you, helping you gloat nine feet tall."

"You can't!" cried Booth.

"Oh, Mr. Booth," said Bayes, on the instant, almost happy, "I *can*. I can do anything with this case I wish, and I wish not to press charges. More than that, Mr. Booth, it *never happened*."

The hammering came again, this time on a locked door up on the stage.

"Bayes, for God's sake, let me in! This is Phipps! Bayes! Bayes!"

Booth stared at the trembling, the thundershaken, the rattling door, even while Bayes called very calmly and with an ease that was beautiful:

"Just a moment."

He knew that in a few minutes this calm would pass, something would break, but for now there was this splendidly serene thing he was doing; he must play it out. With fine round tones he addressed the assassin and watched him dwindle and spoke further and watched him shrink.

"It never happened, Mr. Booth. Tell your story, but we'll deny it. You were never here, no gun, no shot, no computerized data-processed assassination, no outrage, no shock, no panic, no mob. Why now, look at your face. Why are you falling back? Why are you sitting down? Why do you shake? Is it the disappointment? Have I turned your fun the wrong way? Good." He nodded at the aisle. "And now, Mr. Booth, get out."

"You can't make—"

"Sorry you said that, Mr. Booth." Bayes took a soft step in, reached down, took hold of the man's tie and slowly pulled him to his feet so he was breathing full in his face.

"If you ever tell your wife, any friend, employer, child, man, woman, stranger, uncle, aunt, cousin, if you ever tell even yourself out loud going to sleep some night about this thing you did, do you know what I am going to do to you, Mr. Booth? If I hear one whisper, one word, one breath, I shall stalk you, I shall follow you for a dozen or a hundred or two hundred days, you'll never know what day, what night, what noon, where, when or how but suddenly I'll be there when you least expect and then do you know what I am going to do to you, Mr. Booth? I won't say, Mr. Booth, I can't tell. But it will be awful and it will be terrible and you'll wish you had never been born, that's how awful and terrible it will be."

Booth's pale face shook, his head bobbed, his eyes peeled wide, his mouth open like one who walks in a heavy rain.

"What did I just say, Mr. Booth? Tell me!"

"You'll kill me?"

"Say it again!"

He shook Booth until the words fell out of his chattered teeth:

"Kill me!"

He held tight, shaking and shaking the man firmly and steadily, holding and massaging the shirt and the flesh beneath the shirt, stirring up the panic beneath the cloth.

So long, Mr. Nobody, and no magazine stories and no fun and no TV, no celebrity, an unmarked grave and you not in the history books, no, now get out of here, get out, run, run before I kill you.

He shoved Booth. Booth ran, fell, picked himself up, and lunged toward a theater door which, on the instant, from outside, was shaken, pounded, riven.

Phipps was there, calling in the darkness.

"The other door," said Bayes.

He pointed and Booth wheeled to stumble in a new direction to stand swaying by yet another door, putting one hand out—

"Wait," said Bayes.

He walked across the theater and when he reached Booth raised his flat hand up and hit Booth once, hard, a slapping strike across the face. Sweat flew in a rain upon the air.

"I," said Bayes, "I just had to do that. Just once."

He looked at his hand, then turned to open the door.

They both looked out into a world of night and cool stars and no mob.

Booth pulled back, his great dark liquid eyes the eyes of an eternally wounded and surprised child, with the look of the self-shot deer that would go on wounding, being shot by itself forever.

"Get," said Bayes.

Booth darted. The door slammed shut. Bayes fell against it, breathing hard.

Far across the arena at another locked door, the hammering, pounding, the crying out began again. Bayes stared at that shuddering but remote door. Phipps. But Phipps would have to wait. Now . . .

The theater was as vast and empty as Gettysburg in the late day with the crowd gone home and the sun set. Where the crowd had been and was no more, where the Father had lifted the Boy high on his shoulders and where the Boy had spoken and said the words, but the words now, also, gone . . .

On the stage, after a long moment, he reached out. His fingers brushed Lincoln's shoulder.

Fool, he thought standing there in the dusk. Don't. Now, don't. Stop it. Why are you doing this? Silly. Stop. Stop.

And what he had come to find he found. What he needed to do he did.

For tears were running down his face.

He wept. Sobs choked his mouth. He could not stop them. They would not cease.

Mr. Lincoln was dead. Mr. Lincoln was *dead*!

And *he* had let his murderer go.

TIME IN THY FLIGHT

A WIND BLEW THE LONG YEARS AWAY past their hot faces.

The Time Machine stopped.

"Nineteen hundred and twenty-eight," said Janet. The two boys looked past her.

Mr. Fields stirred. "Remember, you're here to observe the behavior of those ancient people. Be inquisitive, be intelligent, observe."

"Yes," said the girl and the two boys in crisp khaki uniforms. They wore identical haircuts, had identical wristwatches, sandals, and coloring of hair, eyes, teeth, and skin, though they were not related.

"Shh!" said Mr. Fields.

They looked out at a little Illinois town in the spring of the year. A cool mist lay on the early morning streets.

Far down the street a small boy came running in the last light of the marble-cream moon. Somewhere a great clock struck 5 A.M. far away. Leaving tennis-shoe prints softly in the quiet lawns, the boy stepped near the invisible Time Machine and cried up to a high dark house window.

The house window opened. Another boy crept down the roof to the ground. The two boys ran off with banana-filled mouths into the dark cold morning.

"Follow them," whispered Mr. Fields. "Study their life patterns. Quick!"

Janet and William and Robert ran on the cold pavements of spring, visible now, through the slumbering town, through a park. All about, lights flickered, doors clicked, and other children rushed alone or in gasping pairs down a hill to some gleaming blue tracks.

"Here it comes!" The children milled about before dawn. Far down the shining tracks a small light grew seconds later into steaming thunder.

"What is it?" screamed Janet.

"A train, silly, you've seen pictures of them!" shouted Robert.

And as the Time Children watched, from the train stepped gigantic gray elephants, steaming the pavements with their mighty waters, lifting question-mark nozzles to the cold morning sky. Cumbrous wagons rolled from the long freight flats, red and gold. Lions roared and paced in boxed darkness.

"Why—*this* must be a—circus!" Janet trembled.

"You think so? Whatever happened to them?"

"Like Christmas, I guess. Just vanished, long ago."

Janet looked around. "Oh, it's awful, isn't it."

The boys stood numbed. "It sure is."

Men shouted in the first faint gleam of dawn. Sleeping cars drew up, dazed faces blinked out at the children. Horses clattered like a great fall of stones on the pavement.

Mr. Fields was suddenly behind the children. "Disgusting, barbaric, keeping animals in cages. If I'd known this was here, I'd never let you come see. This is a terrible ritual."

"Oh, yes." But Janet's eyes were puzzled. "And yet, you know, it's like a nest of maggots. I want to study it."

"I don't know," said Robert, his eyes darting, his fingers trembling. "It's pretty crazy. We might try writing a thesis on it if Mr. Fields says it's all right . . ."

Mr. Fields nodded. "I'm glad you're digging in here, finding motives, studying this horror. All right—we'll see the circus this afternoon."

"I think I'm going to be sick," said Janet.

The Time Machine hummed.

"So that was a circus," said Janet, solemnly.

The trombone circus died in their ears. The last thing they saw was candy-pink trapeze people whirling while baking powder clowns shrieked and bounded.

"You must admit psychovision's better," said Robert slowly.

"All those nasty animal smells, the excitement." Janet blinked. "That's bad for children, isn't it? And those older people seated with the children. Mothers, fathers, they called them. Oh, that *was* strange."

Mr. Fields put some marks in his class grading book.

Janet shook her head numbly. "I want to see it all again. I've missed the motives somewhere. I want to make that run across town again in the early morning. The cold air on my face—the sidewalk under my feet—the circus train coming in. Was it the air and the early hour that made the children get up and run to see the train come in? I want to retrace the entire pattern. Why should they be excited? I feel I've missed out on the answer."

"They all smiled so much," said William.

"Manic-depressives," said Robert.

"What are summer vacations? I heard them talk about it." Janet looked at Mr. Fields.

"They spent their summers racing about like idiots, beating each other up," replied Mr. Fields seriously.

"I'll take our State Engineered summers of work for children anytime," said Robert, looking at nothing, his voice faint.

The Time Machine stopped again.

"The Fourth of July," announced Mr. Fields. "Nineteen hundred and twenty-eight. An ancient holiday when people blew each other's fingers off."

They stood before the same house on the same street but on a soft summer evening. Fire wheels hissed, on front porches laughing children tossed things out that went bang!

"Don't run!" cried Mr. Fields. "It's not war, don't be afraid!"

But Janet's and Robert's and William's faces were pink, now blue, now white with fountains of soft fire.

"We're all right," said Janet, standing very still.

"Happily," announced Mr. Fields, "they prohibited fireworks a century ago, did away with the whole messy explosion."

Children did fairy dances, weaving their names and destinies on the dark summer air with white sparklers.

"I'd like to do that," said Janet, softly. "Write my name on the air. See? I'd like that."

"What?" Mr. Fields hadn't been listening.

"Nothing," said Janet.

"Bang!" whispered William and Robert, standing under the soft summer trees, in shadow, watching, watching the red, white, and green fires on the beautiful summer night lawns. "Bang!"

October.

The Time Machine paused for the last time, an hour later in the month of burning leaves. People bustled into dim houses carrying pumpkins and corn shocks. Skeletons danced, bats flew, candles flamed, apples swung in empty doorways.

"Halloween," said Mr. Fields. "The acme of horror. This was the age of superstition, you know. Later they banned the Grimm Brothers, ghosts, skeletons, and all that claptrap. You children, thank God, were raised in an antiseptic world of no shadows or ghosts. You had decent holidays like William C. Chatterton's Birthday, Work Day, and Machine Day."

They walked by the same house in the empty October night, peering in at the triangle-eyed pumpkins, the masks leering in black attics and damp cellars. Now, inside the house, some party children squatted telling stories, laughing!

"I want to be inside with them," said Janet at last.

"Sociologically, of course," said the boys.

"No," she said.

"What?" asked Mr. Fields.

"No, I just want to be inside, I just want to stay here, I want to see it all and be here and never be anywhere else, I want firecrackers and pumpkins and circuses, I want Christmases and Valentines and Fourths, like we've seen."

"This is getting out of hand . . ." Mr. Fields started to say.

But suddenly Janet was gone. "Robert, William, come on!" She ran. The boys leaped after her.

"Hold on!" shouted Mr. Fields. "Robert! William, I've got you!" He seized the last boy, but the other escaped. "Janet, Robert—come back here! You'll never pass into the seventh grade! You'll fail, Janet, Bob—*Bob!*"

An October wind blew wildly down the street, vanishing with the children off among moaning trees.

William twisted and kicked.

"No, not you, too, William, you're coming home with me. We'll teach those other two a lesson they won't forget. So they want to stay in the past, do they?" Mr. Fields shouted so everyone could hear. "All right, Janet, Bob, stay in this horror, in this chaos! In a few weeks you'll come sniveling back here to me. But I'll be gone! I'm leaving you here to go mad in this world!"

He hurried William to the Time Machine. The boy was sobbing. "Don't make me come back here on any more Field Excursions ever again, please, Mr. Fields, please—"

"Shut up!"

Almost instantly the Time Machine whisked away toward the future, toward the underground hive cities, the metal buildings, the metal flowers, the metal lawns.

"Good-bye, Janet, Bob!"

A great cold October wind blew through the town like water. And when it had ceased blowing it had carried all the children, whether invited or uninvited, masked or unmasked, to the doors of houses which closed upon them. There was not a running child anywhere in the night. The wind whined away in the bare treetops.

And inside the big house, in the candlelight, someone was pouring cold apple cider all around, to everyone, no matter *who* they were.

CHANGELING

By EIGHT O'CLOCK SHE HAD PLACED the long cigarettes and the wine crystals and the silver bucket of thin shaved ice packed around the green bottle. She stood looking at the room, each picture neat, ashtrays conveniently disposed. She plumped a lounge pillow and stepped back, her eyes squinting. Then she hurried into the bathroom and returned with the strychnine bottle, which she laid under a magazine on an end table. She had already hidden a hammer and an ice pick.

She was ready.

Seeming to know this, the phone rang. When she answered, a voice said:

"I'm coming up."

He was in the elevator now, floating silently up the iron throat of the house, fingering his accurate little mustache, adjusting his white summer evening coat and black tie. He would be smoothing his gray-blond hair, that handsome man of fifty still able to visit handsome women of thirty-three, fresh, convivial, ready for the wine and the rest of it.

"You're a faker!" she whispered to the closed door a moment before he rapped.

"Good evening, Martha," he said. "Are you just going to stand there, looking?" She kissed him quietly. "Was that a kiss?" he wondered, his blue eyes warmly amused. "Here." He gave her a better one.

Her eyes closed, she thought, is this different from last week, last month, last year? What makes me suspicious? Some little thing. Something she couldn't even tell, it was so minor. He had changed subtly and drastically. So drastically in fact, so completely that she had begun to stay awake nights two months ago. She had taken to riding the helicopters at three in the morning out to the beach and back to see all-night films projected on the clouds near The Point, films that had been made way back in 1955, huge memories in the ocean mist over the dark waters, with the voices drifting in like gods' voices with the tide. She was constantly tired.

"Not much response." He held her away and surveyed her critically. "Is anything wrong, Martha?"

"Nothing," she said. Everything she thought. You, she thought. Where are you tonight, Leonard? Who are you dancing with far away, or drinking with in an apartment on the other side of town, who are you being lovably polite with? For you most certainly are not here in this room, and I intend to prove it.

"What's this?" he said, looking down. "A hammer? Have you been hanging pictures, Martha?"

"No, I'm going to hit you with it," she said, and laughed.

"Of course," he said, smiling. "Well, perhaps this will make you change your mind." He drew forth a plush case, inside which was a pearl necklace.

"Oh, Leonard!" She put it on with trembling fingers and turned to him, excited. "You are good to me."

"It's nothing at all," he said.

At these times, she almost forgot her suspicions. She had everything with him, didn't she? There was no sign of his losing interest, was there? Certainly not. He was just as kind and gentle and generous. He never came without something for her wrist or her finger. Why did she feel so lonely with him then? Why didn't she feel with him? Perhaps it had started with that picture in the paper two months ago. A picture of him and Alice Summers in The Club on the night of April 17th. She hadn't seen the picture until a month later and then she had spoken of it to him:

"Leonard, you didn't tell me you took Alice Summers to The Club on the night of April seventeenth."

"Didn't I, Martha? Well, I did."

"But wasn't that one of the nights you were here with me?"

"I don't see how it could have been. We have supper and play symphonies and drink wine until early morning."

"I'm sure you were here with me April seventeenth, Leonard."

"You're a little drunk, my dear. Do you keep a diary?"

"I'm not a child."

"There you are then. No diary, no record. I was here the night before or the night after. Come on now, Martha, drink up."

But that hadn't settled it. She had not gone to sleep that night with thinking and being positive he had been with her on April 17th. It was impossible, of course. He couldn't be in two places.

They both stood looking down at the hammer on the floor. She picked it up and put it on a table. "Kiss me," she said, quite suddenly, for she wanted now, more than ever, to be certain of this thing. He evaded her and said, "First, the wine." "No," she insisted, and kissed him.

There it was. The difference. The little change. There was no way to tell anyone, or even describe it. It would be like trying to describe a rainbow to a blind man. But there was a subtle chemical difference to his kiss. It was no longer the kiss of Mr. Leonard Hill. It approximated the kiss of Leonard Hill but was sufficiently different to set a subconscious wheel rolling in her. What would an analysis of the faint moisture on his lips reveal? Some bacterial lack? And as for the lips themselves, were or were they not harder, or softer, than before? Some small difference.

"All right, now the wine," she said, and opened it. She poured his glass full. "Oh, will you get some mats from the kitchen to set them on?" While he was gone she poured the strychnine in his glass. He returned with the mats to set the glasses on and picked up his drink.

"To us," he said.

✳ Good Lord, she thought, what if I'm wrong? What if this is really him? What if I'm just some wild paranoid sort of creature, really insane and not aware of it?

"To us." She raised her glass.

He drained his at a gulp, as always. "My God," he said, wincing. "That's horrible stuff. Where did you get it?"

"At Modesti's."

"Well, don't get any more. Here, I'd better ring for more."

"Never mind, I have more in the refrigerator."

When she brought the new bottle in, he was sitting there, clever and alive and fresh. "You look wonderful," she said.

"Feel fine. You're beautiful. I think I love you more tonight than ever."

She waited for him to fall sidewise and stare the stare of the dead. "Here we go," he said, opening the second bottle.

When the second bottle was empty, an hour had passed. He was telling witty little stories and holding her hand and kissing her gently now and again. At last he turned to her and said, "You seem quiet tonight, Martha? Anything wrong?"

"No," she said.

She had seen the news item last week, the item that had finally set her worrying and planning, that had explained her loneliness in his presence. About the Marionettes. Marionettes, Incorporated. Not that they really existed, surely not. But there was a rumor. Police were investigating.

Life-size marionettes, mechanical, stringless, secretive, duplicates of real people. One might buy them for ten thousand dollars on some distant black market. One could be measured for a replica of one's self. If one grew weary of social functions, one could send the replica out to wine, to dine, to shake hands, to trade gossip with Mrs. Rinehart on your left, Mr. Simmons on your right, Miss Glenner across the table.

Think of the political tirades one might miss! Think of the bad shows one need never see. Think of the dull people one could snub without actually snubbing. And, last of all, think of the jeweled loved ones you could ignore, yet not ignore. What would a good slogan be? She Need Never Know? Don't Tell Your Best Friends? It Walks, It Talks, It Sneezes, It Says "Mama"?

When she thought of this she became almost hysterical. Of course it had not been proven that such things as Marionettes existed. Just a sly rumor, with enough to it to make a sensitive person crawl with horror.

"Abstracted again," he said, interrupting her quietness. "There you go, wandering off. What's in that pretty head of yours?"

She looked at him. It was foolish; at any moment he might convulse and die. Then she would be sorry for her jealousy.

Without thinking, she said, "Your mouth; it tastes funny."

"Dear me," he said. "I shall have to see to that, eh?"

"It's tasted funny for some time."

For the first time he seemed concerned. "Has it? I'm sorry. I'll see my doctor."

"It's not that important." She felt her heart beating quickly and she was cold. It was his mouth. After all, no matter how perfect chemists were, could they analyze and reproduce the exact taste? Hardly. Taste was individual. Taste was one thing to her, something else to another. There was where they had fallen down. She would not put up with it another minute. She walked over to the other couch, reached down and drew out the gun.

"What's that?" he said, looking at it. "Oh my God," he laughed. "A gun. How dramatic."

"I've caught on to you," she said.

"Is there anything to catch on to?" he wanted to know, calmly, his mouth straight, his eyes twinkling.

"You've been lying to me. You haven't been here in eight weeks or more," she said.

"Is that true? Where have I been then?"

"With Alice Summers, I wouldn't doubt. I'll bet you're with her right now."

"Is that possible?" he asked.

"I don't know Alice Summers, I've never met her, but I think I'll call her apartment right now."

"Do that," he said, looking straight at her.

"I will," she said, moving to the phone. Her hand shook so that she could hardly dial information. While waiting for the number to come through she watched Leonard and he watched her with the eye of a psychiatrist witnessing a not-unusual phenomenon.

"You are badly off," he said. "My dear Martha—"

"Sit down!"

"My dear Martha," he moved back in the couch, chuckling softly. "What have you been reading?"

"About the Marionettes is all."

"That poppycock? Good God, Martha, I'm ashamed of you. It's not true. I looked into it!"

"What!"

"Of course!" he cried, in delight. "I have so many social obligations, and then my first wife came back from India as you know and demanded my time and I thought how fine it would be if I had a replica of myself made, as bait you might say, to turn my wife off my trail, to keep her busy, how nice, eh? But it was all false. Just me. I thought I needed a change. So I went on to Alice and tired of her. And went on to Helen Kingsley, you remember her, don't you? And tired of her. And on to Ann Montgomery. And that didn't last. Oh, Martha, there are at least six duplicates of me, mechanical hypocrites, ticking away tonight, in all parts of the town, keeping six people happy. And do you know what I am doing, the real I?

"I'm home in bed early for the first time in thirty years, reading my little book of Montaigne's essays and enjoying it and drinking a hot glass of chocolate milk and turning out the lights at ten o'clock. I've been asleep for an hour now, and I shall sleep the sleep of the innocent until morning and arise refreshed and free."

"Stop!" she shrieked.

"I've got to tell you," he said. "You've cut several of my ligaments with your bullets. I can't get up. The doctors, if they came, would find me out anyway, I'm not that perfect. Perfect enough, but not that good. Oh, Martha, I didn't want to hurt you. Believe me. I wanted only your happiness. That's why I was so careful with my planned withdrawal. I spent fifteen thousand dollars for this replica, perfect in every detail. There are variables. The saliva for one. A regrettable error. It set you off. But you must know that I loved you."

She would fall at any moment, writhing into insanity, she thought. He had to be stopped from talking.

"And when I saw how the others loved me," he whispered to the ceiling, eyes wide, "I had to provide replicas for them, poor dears. They love me so. You won't tell them, will you, Martha? Promise me you won't give the show away. I'm a very tired old man, and I want only peace, a book, some milk and a lot of sleep. You won't call them up and give it away?"

"All this year, this whole year, I've been alone, alone every night," she said, the coldness filling her. "Talking to a mechanical horror! In love with nothingness! Alone all that time, when I could have been out with someone real!"

"I can still love you, Martha."

"Oh God!" she cried, and seized up the hammer.

"Don't, Martha!"

She smashed his head in and beat at his chest and his thrashing arms and wild legs. She beat at the soft head until steel shone through, and sudden explosions of wire and brass coggery showered about the room with metal tinkles.

"I love you," said the man's mouth. She struck it with the hammer and the tongue fell out. The glass eyes rolled on the carpet. She pounded at the thing until it was strewn like the remains of a child's electric train on the floor. She laughed while she was doing it.

In the kitchen she found several cardboard boxes. She loaded the cogs and wires and metal into these and sealed the tops. Ten minutes later she had summoned the houseboy from below.

"Deliver these packages to Mr. Leonard Hill, 17 Elm Drive," she said, and tipped the boy. "Right now, tonight. Wake him up, tell him it's a surprise package from Martha."

"A surprise package from Martha," said the boy.

After the door closed, she sat on the couch with the gun in her hand, turning it over and over, listening. The last thing she heard in her life was the sound of the packages being carried down the hall, the metal jingling softly, cog against cog, wire against wire, fading.

THE DRAGON

THE NIGHT BLEW IN THE SHORT GRASS on the moor; there was no other motion. It had been years since a single bird had flown by in the great blind shell of sky. Long ago a few small stones had simulated life when they crumbled and fell into dust. Now only the night moved in the souls of the two men bent by their lonely fire in the wilderness; darkness pumped quietly in their veins and ticked silently in their temples and their wrists.

Firelight fled up and down their wild faces and welled in their eyes in orange tatters. They listened to each other's faint, cool breathing and the lizard blink of their eyelids. At last, one man poked the fire with his sword.

"Don't, idiot; you'll give us away!"

"No matter," said this second man. "The dragon can smell us miles off anyway. God's breath, it's cold. I wish I was back at the castle."

"It's death, not sleep we're after. . . ."

"Why? Why? The dragon never sets foot in the town!"

"Quiet, fool! He eats men traveling alone from our town to the next!"

"Let them be eaten and let us get home!"

"Wait now; listen!"

The two men froze.

They waited a long time, but there was only the shake of their horses' nervous skin like black velvet tambourines jingling the silver stirrup buckles, softly, softly.

"Ah." The second man sighed. "What a land of nightmares. Everything happens here. Someone blows out the sun; it's night. And then, and *then*, oh, sweet mortality, listen! This dragon, they say his eyes are fire. His breath a white gas; you can see him burn across the dark lands. He runs with sulfur and thunder and kindles the grass. Sheep panic and die insane. Women deliver forth monsters. The dragon's fury is such that tower walls shake back to dust. His victims, at sunrise, are strewn hither thither on the hills. How many knights, I ask, have gone for this monster and failed, even as we shall fail?"

"Enough of that!"

"More than enough! Out here in this desolation I cannot tell what year this is!"

"Nine hundred years since the Nativity."

"No, no," whispered the second man, eyes shut. "On this moor is no Time, is only Forever. I feel if I ran back on the road the town would be gone, the people yet unborn, things changed, the castles unquarried from the rocks, the timbers still uncut from the forests; don't ask how I know; the moor knows and tells me. And here we sit alone in the land of the fire dragon, God save us!"

"Be you afraid, then gird on your armor!"

"What use? The dragon runs from nowhere; we cannot guess its home. It vanishes in fog; we know not where it goes. Aye, on with our armor, we'll die well dressed."

Half into his silver corselet, the second man stopped again and turned his head.

Across the dim country, full of night and nothingness from the heart of the moor itself, the wind sprang full of dust from clocks that used dust for telling time. There were black suns burning in the heart of this new wind and a million burned leaves shaken from some autumn tree beyond the horizon. The wind melted landscapes, lengthened bones like white wax, made the blood roil and thicken to a muddy deposit in the brain. The wind was a thousand souls dying and all Time confused and in transit. It was a fog inside of a mist inside of a darkness, and this place was no man's place and there was no year or hour at all, but only these men in a faceless emptiness of sudden frost, storm and white thunder which moved behind the great falling pane of green glass that was the lightning. A squall of rain drenched the turf; all faded away until there was unbreathing hush and the two men waiting alone with their warmth in a cool season.

"There," whispered the first man, "Oh, *there* . . ."

Miles off, rushing with a great chant and a roar—the dragon.

In silence the men buckled on their armor and mounted their horses. The midnight wilderness was split by a monstrous gushing as the dragon roared nearer, nearer; its flashing yellow glare spurted above a hill and then, fold on fold of dark body, distantly seen, therefore indistinct, flowed over that hill and plunged vanishing into a valley.

"Quick!"

They spurred their horses forward to a small hollow.

"This is where it passes!"

They seized their lances with mailed fists and blinded their horses by flipping the visors down over their eyes.

"Lord!"

"Yes, let us use His name."

On the instant, the dragon rounded a hill. Its monstrous amber eye fed on them, fired their armor in red glints and glitters. With a terrible wailing cry and a grinding rush it flung itself forward.

"Mercy, mercy!"

The lance struck under the unlidded yellow eye, buckled, tossed the man through the air. The dragon hit, spilled him over, down, ground him under. Passing, the black brunt of its shoulder smashed the remaining horse and rider a hundred feet against the side of a boulder, wailing, wailing, the dragon shrieking, the fire all about, around, under it, a pink, yellow, orange sun-fire with great soft plumes of blinding smoke.

"Did you *see* it?" cried a voice. "Just like I told you!"

"The same! The same! A knight in armor, by the Lord Harry! We *hit* him!"

"You goin' to stop?"

"Did once; found nothing. Don't like to stop on this moor. I get the willies. Got a *feel*, it has."

"But we hit *something*!"

"Gave him plenty of whistle; chap wouldn't budge!"

A steaming blast cut the mist aside.

"We'll make Stokely on time. More coal, eh, Fred?"

Another whistle shook dew from the empty sky. The night train, in fire and fury, shot through a gully, up a rise, and vanished away over cold earth toward the north, leaving black smoke and steam to dissolve in the numbed air minutes after it had passed and gone forever.

LET'S PLAY "POISON"

"WE HATE YOU!" CRIED THE SIXTEEN BOYS and girls rushing and crowding about Michael in the school room. Michael screamed. Recess was over, Mr. Howard, the teacher, was still absent from the filling room. "We hate you!" and the sixteen boys and girls, bumping and clustering and breathing, raised a window. It was three flights down to the sidewalk. Michael flailed.

They took hold of Michael and pushed him out the window.

Mr. Howard, their teacher, came into the room. "Wait a minute!" he shouted.

Michael fell three flights. Michael died.

Nothing was done about it. The police shrugged eloquently. These children were all eight or nine, they didn't understand what they were doing. So.

Mr. Howard's breakdown occurred the next day. He refused ever again, to teach! "But, why?" asked his friends. Mr. Howard gave no answer. He remained silent and a terrible light filled his eyes, and later he remarked that if he told them the truth they would think him quite insane.

Mr. Howard left Madison City. He went to live in a small nearby town, Green Bay, for seven years, on an income managed from writing stories and poetry.

He never married. The few women he approached always desired—children.

In the autumn of his seventh year of self-enforced retirement, a good friend of Mr. Howard's, a teacher, fell ill. For lack of a proper substitute,

Mr. Howard was summoned and convinced that it was his duty to take over the class. Because he realized the appointment could last no longer than a few weeks, Mr. Howard agreed, unhappily.

"Sometimes," announced Mr. Howard, slowly pacing the aisles of the school room on that Monday morning in September, "sometimes, I actually believe that children are invaders from another dimension."

He stopped, and his shiny dark eyes snapped from face to face of his small audience. He held one hand behind him, clenched. The other hand, like a pale animal, climbed his lapel as he talked and later climbed back down to toy with his ribboned glasses.

"Sometimes," he continued, looking at William Arnold and Russell Newell, and Donald Bowers and Charlie Hencoop, "sometimes I believe children are little monsters thrust out of hell, because the devil could no longer cope with them. And I certainly believe that everything should be done to reform their uncivil little minds."

Most of his words ran unfamiliarly into the washed and unwashed ears of Arnold, Newell, Bowers and Company. But the tone inspired one to dread. The little girls lay back in their seats, against their pigtails, lest he yank them like bell ropes, to summon the dark angels. All stared at Mr. Howard, as if hypnotized.

"You are another race entirely, your motives, your beliefs, your disobediences," said Mr. Howard. "You are not human. You are—children. Therefore, until such time as you are adults, you have no right to demand privileges or question your elders, who know better."

He paused, and put his elegant rump upon the chair behind the neat, dustless desk.

"Living in your world of fantasy," he said, scowling darkly. "Well, there'll be no fantasy here. You'll soon discover that a ruler on your hand is no dream, no faerie frill, no Peter Pan excitement." He snorted. "Have I frightened you? I have. Good! Well and good. You deserve to be. I want you to know where we stand. I'm not afraid of you, remember that. I'm not afraid of you." His hand trembled and he drew back in his chair as all their eyes stared as him. "Here!" He flung a glance clear across the room. "What're you whispering about, back there? Some necromancy or other?"

A little girl raised her hand, "What's necromancy?"

"We'll discuss that when our two young friends, Mr. Arnold and Mr. Bowers, explain their whispers. Well, young men?"

Donald Bowers arose. "We don't like you. That's all we said." He sat down again.

Mr. Howard raised his brows, "I like frankness, truth. Thank you for your honesty. But, simultaneously, I do not tolerate flippant rebellion. You'll stay an hour after school tonight and wash the boards."

﹡ After school, walking home, with autumn leaves falling both before and after his passing, Mr. Howard caught up with four of his students. He rapped his cane sharply on the sidewalk. "Here, what are you children doing?"

The startled boys and girls jerked as if struck upon their shoulders by his cane. "Oh," they all said.

"Well," demanded the man. "Explain. What were you doing here when I came up?"

William Arnold said, "Playing poison."

"Poison!" Their teacher's face twisted. He was carefully sarcastic. "Poison, poison, playing poison. Well. And how does one play poison?"

Reluctantly, William Arnold ran off.

"Come back here!" shouted Mr. Howard.

"I'm only showing you," said the boy, hopping over a cement block of the sidewalk. "How we play poison. Whenever we come to a dead man we jump over him."

"One does, does one?" said Mr. Howard.

"If you jump on a dead man's grave, then you're poisoned and fall down and die," expained Isabel Skelton, much too brightly.

"Dead men, graves poisoned," Mr. Howard said, mockingly. "Where do you get this dead man idea?"

"See?" said Clara Parris, pointing with her arithmetic. "On this square, the names of the two dead men."

"Ridiculous," retorted Mr. Howard, squinting down. "Those are simply the names of the contractors who mixed and laid the cement sidewalk."

Isabel and Clara both gasped wildly and turned accusing eyes to the boys. "You said they were gravestones!" they cried, almost together.

William Arnold looked at his feet. "Yeah. They are. Well, almost. Anyway." He looked up. "It's late. I gotta go home. So long."

Clara Parris looked at the two little names cut into the sidewalk. "Mr. Kelly and Mr. Terrill," she read the names. "Then these aren't graves? Mr. Kelly and Mr. Terrill aren't buried here? See, Isabel, that's what I told you, a dozen times I did."

"You did not," sulked Isabel.

"Deliberate lies," Mr. Howard tapped his cane in an impatient code. "Falsification of the highest caliber. Good God, Mr. Arnold, Mr. Bowers, there'll be no more of this, do you understand?"

"Yes, sir," mumbled the boys.

"Speak up!"

"Yes, sir," they replied, again.

"Mr. Howard swung off swiftly down the street. William Arnold waited until he was out of sight before he said, "I hope a bird drops something right smack on his nose—"

"Come on, Clara, let's play poison," said Isabel, hopefully.

Clara pouted. "It's been spoiled. I'm going home."

"I'm poisoned!" cried Donald Bowers, falling to the earth and frothing merrily. "Look, I'm poisoned! Gahhh!"

"Oh," cried Clara, angrily, and ran away.

✳ Saturday morning Mr. Howard glanced out his front window and swore when he saw Isabel Skelton making chalk marks on his sidewalk and then hopping about, making a monotonous sing-song with her voice.

"Stop that!"

Rushing out, he almost flung her to the pavement in his emotion. He grabbed her and shook her violently and let her go and stood over her and the chalk marks.

"I was only playing hopscotch," she sobbed, hands over her eyes.

"I don't care, you can't play it here," he declared. Bending, he erased the chalk marks with his handkerchief, muttering. "Young witch. Pentagrams. Rhymes and incantations, and all looking perfectly innocent, God, how innocent. You little *fiend*!" He made as if to strike her, but stopped. Isabel ran off, wailing. "Go ahead, you little fool!" he screamed furiously. "Run off and tell your little cohorts that you've failed. They'll have to try some other way! They won't get around me, they won't, oh, no!"

He stalked back into his house and poured himself a stiff drink of brandy and drank it down. The rest of the day he heard the children playing kick-the-can, hide-and-seek, Over-Annie-Over, jacks, tops, mibs, and the sound of the little monsters in every shrub and shadow would not let him rest. "Another week of this," he thought, "and I'll be stark staring." He flung his hand to his aching head. "God in heaven, why weren't we all born adults?"

Another week, then. And the hatred growing between him and the children. The hate and the fear growing apace. The nervousness, the sudden tantrums over nothing, and then—the silent waiting, the way the children climbed the trees and looked at him as they swiped late apples, the melancholy smell of autumn settling in around the town, the days growing short, the night coming too soon.

"But they won't touch me, they won't *dare* touch me," thought Mr. Howard sucking down one glass of brandy after another. "It's all very silly anyhow, and there's nothing to it. I'll soon be away from here, and—them. I'll soon—"

There was a white skull at the window.

It was eight o'clock of a Thursday evening. It had been a long week, with the angry flares and the accusations. He had had to continually chase the children away from the water-main excavation in front of his house. Children loved excavations, hiding places, pipes and conduits and trenches, and they were ever ascramble over and on and down in and up out of the holes where the new pipes were being laid. It was all finished, thank the Lord, and tomorrow the workmen would shovel in the earth and tamp it down and put in a new cement sidewalk, and that would eliminate the children. But, right now—

There was a white skull at the window!

There could be no doubt that a boy's hand held the skull against the glass, tapping and moving it. There was a childish tittering from outside.

Mr. Howard burst from the house. "Hey, you!" He exploded into the midst of the three running boys. He leaped after them, shouting and yelling. The street was dark, but he saw the figures dart beyond and below him. He saw them sort of bound and could not remember the reason for this, until too late.

The earth opened under him. He fell and lay in a pit, his head taking a terrific blow from a laid water-pipe, and as he lost consciousness he had an impression as of an avalanche, set off by his fall, cascading down cool moist pellets of dirt upon his pants, his shoes, upon his coat, upon his spine, upon the back of his neck, his head, filling his mouth, his ears, his eyes, his nostrils . . .

✳ The neighbor lady with the eggs wrapped in a napkin, knocked on Mr. Howard's door the next day for five minutes. When she opened the door, finally, and walked in, she found nothing but specules of rugdust floating in the sunny air, the big halls were empty, the cellar smelled of coal and clinkers, and the attic had nothing in it but a rat, a spider, and a faded letter. "Funniest thing," she said many times in the following years, "what ever happened to Mr. Howard."

And adults, being what they are, never observant, paid no attention to the children playing "Poison" on Oak Bay Street, in all the following autumns. Even when the children leaped over one particular square of cement, twisted about and glanced at the marks on it which read:

"M. HOWARD—R.I.P."

"Who's Mr. Howard, Billy?"

"Aw, I guess he's the guy who laid the cement."

"What does R.I.P. mean?"

"Aw, who knows? You're poison! You stepped on it!"

"Get along, get along, children; don't stand on Mother's path! Get along now!"

THE COLD WIND
AND THE WARM

"GOOD GOD IN HEAVEN, WHAT'S THAT?"

"What's what?"

"Are you blind, man, look!"

And Garrity, elevator operator, looked out to see what the hall porter was staring at.

And in out of the Dublin morn, sweeping through the front doors of the Royal Hibernian Hotel, along the entryway and to the registry was a tall willowy man of some forty years followed by five short willowy youths of some twenty years, a burst of bird song, their hands flapping all about on the air as they passed, their eyes squinching, batting, and flickering, their mouths pursed, their brows enlightened and then dark, their color flushed and then pale, or was it both?, their voices now flawless piccolo, now flute, now melodious oboe but always tuneful. Carrying six monologues, all sprayed forth upon each other at once, in a veritable cloud of self-commiseration, peeping and twitting the discouragements of travel and the ardors of weather, the *corps de ballet* as it were flew, cascaded, flowed eloquently in a greater bloom of cologne by astonished hall porter and transfixed elevator man. They collided deliciously to a halt at the desk where the manager glanced up to be swarmed over by their music. His eyes made nice round o's with no centers in them.

"What," whispered Garrity, "was that?"

"You may well ask," said the porter.

At which point the elevator lights flashed and the buzzer buzzed. Garrity had to tear his eyes off the summery crowd and heft himself skyward.

"We," said the tall slender man with a touch of gray at the temples, "should like a room, please."

The manager remembered where he was and heard himself say, "Do you have reservations, sir?"

"Dear me, no," said the older man as the others giggled. "We flew in unexpectedly from Taormina," the tall man with the chiseled features and the moist flower mouth continued. "We were getting so awfully bored, after a long summer, and someone said, Let's have a complete change, let's do something wild. What? I said. Well, where's the most improbable place in the world? Let's name it and go there. Somebody said the North Pole, but that was silly. Then I cried, Ireland! Everyone fell down. When the pandemonium ceased we just scrambled for the airport. Now sunshine and Sicilian shorelines are like yesterday's lime sherbet to us, all melted to nothing. And here we are to do . . . something *mysterious!*"

"Mysterious?" asked the manager.

"We don't know what it is," said the tall man. "But we shall know it when we see it, or it happens, or perhaps we shall have to make it happen, right, cohorts?"

The cohorts responded with something vaguely like tee-hee.

"Perhaps," said the manager, with good grace, "if you gave me some idea what you're looking for in Ireland, I could point out—"

"Goodness, no," said the tall man. "We shall just plummet forth with our intuitions scarved about our necks, taking the wind as 'twere and see what we shall tune in on. When we solve the mystery and find what we came to find, you will know of our discovery by the ululations and cries of awe and wonder emanating from our small tourist group."

"You can say *that* again," said the hall porter, under his breath.

"Well, comrades, let us sign in."

The leader of the encampment reached for a scratchy hotel pen, found it filthy, and flourished forth his own absolutely pure 14-carat solid gold pen with which in an obscure but rather pretty cerise calligraphy he inscribed the name DAVID followed by SNELL followed by dash and ending with ORKNEY. Beneath, he added "and friends."

The manager watched the pen, fascinated, and once more recalled his position in all this. "But, sir, I haven't said if we have space—"

"Oh, surely you must, for six miserable wanderers in sore need of respite from overfriendly airline stewardesses—one room would do it!"

"One?" said the manager, aghast.

"We wouldn't mind the crowd, would we, chums?" asked the older man, not looking at his friends.

No, they wouldn't mind.

"Well," said the manager, uneasily fumbling at the registry. "We just happen to have two adjoining—"

"*Perfecto!*" cried David Snell-Orkney.

And the registration finished, the manager behind the desk and the visitors from a far place stood regarding each other in a prolonged silence. At last the manager blurted, "Porter! Front! Take these gentlemen's luggage—"

But just then the hall porter ran over to look at the floor.

Where there was no luggage.

"No, no, none." David Snell-Orkney airily waved his hand. "We travel light. We're here only for twenty-four hours, or perhaps only twelve, with a change of underwear stuffed in our overcoats. Then back to Sicily and warm twilights. If you want me to pay in advance—"

"That won't be necessary," said the manager, handing the keys to the hall porter. "Forty-six and forty-seven, please."

"It's done," said the porter.

And like a collie dog silently nipping the hooves of some woolly long-haired, bleating, dumbly smiling sheep, he herded the lovely bunch toward the elevator which wafted down just at that precise moment.

At the desk, the manager's wife came up, steel-eyed behind him. "Are you mad?" she whispered, wildly. "Why? Why?"

"All my life," said the manager, half to himself, "I have wished to see not one Communist but ten close by, not two Nigerians but twenty in their skins, not three cowboy Americans but a gross fresh from the saddle. So when six hothouse roses come in a bouquet, I could not resist potting them. The Dublin winter is long, Meg; this may be the only lit fuse in the whole year. Stand by for the lovely concussion."

"Fool," she said.

As they watched, the elevator, freighted with hardly more than the fluff from a blown dandelion, whisked up the shaft, away.

✳ It was exactly at high noon that a series of coincidences occurred that tottered and swerved toward the miraculous.

Now the Royal Hibernian Hotel lies half between Trinity College, if you'll excuse the mention, and St. Stephen's Green, which is more like it, and around behind is Grafton Street, where you can buy silver, glass, and linen, or pink hacking coats, boots, and caps to ride off to the goddamned hounds, or better still duck in to Heeber Finn's pub for a proper proportion of drink and talk—an hour of drink to two hours of talk is about the best prescription.

Now the boys most often seen in Finn's are these: Nolan, you know Nolan; Timulty, who could forget Timulty; Mike MaGuire, surely *everyone's* friend; then there's Hannahan, Flaherty, Kilpatrick, and, on occasion, when God seems a bit untidy and Job comes to mind, Father Liam Leary himself, who strides in like Justice and glides forth like Mercy.

Well, that's the lot, and it's high noon, and out of the Hibernian Hotel front who should come now but Snell-Orkney and his canary five.

Which resulted in the first of a dumbfounding series of confrontations.

For passing below, sore torn between the sweet shops and Heeber Finn's, was *Timulty* himself.

Timulty, as you recall, when Blight, Famine, Starvation, and other mean Horsemen drive him, works a day here or there at the post office. Now, idling along between dread employments, he smelled a smell as if the gates of Eden had swung wide again and him invited back in after a hundred million years. So Timulty looked up to see what made the wind blow out of the Garden.

And the wind, of course, was in tumult about Snell-Orkney and his uncaged pets.

"I tell you," said Timulty, years later, "I felt my eyes start as if I'd been given a good bash on the skull. A new part ran down the center of my hair."

Timulty, frozen to the spot, watched the Snell-Orkney delegation flow down the steps and around the corner. At which point he decided on sweeter things than candy and rushed the long way to Finn's.

At that instant, rounding the corner, Mr. David Snell-Orkney-plus-five passed a beggar-lady playing a harp in the street. And there, with nothing else to do but dance the time away, was Mike MaGuire himself, flinging his feet about in a self-involved rigadoon to "Lightly o'er the Lea." Dancing, Mike MaGuire heard a sound that was like the passing by of warm weather from the Hebrides. It was not quite a twittering nor a whirr, and it was not unlike a pet shop when the bell tinkles as you step in and a chorus of parakeets and doves start up in coos and light shrieks. But hear he did, above the sound of his own shoes and the pringle of harp. He froze in mid-jig.

As David Snell-Orkney-plus-five swept by all tropic smiled and gave him a wave.

Before he knew what he was doing, Mike waved back, then stopped and seized his wounded hand to his breast. "What the hell am I waving for?" he cried to no one. "I don't know them, *do* I?"

"Ask God for strength!" said the harpist to her harp and flung her fingers down the strings.

Drawn as by some strange new vacuum cleaner that swept all before it, Mike followed the Team down the street.

Which takes care of two senses now, the sense of smell and the use of the ears.

It was at the *next* corner that Nolan, leaving Finn's pub because of an argument with Finn himself, came around the bend fast and ran bang into David Snell-Orkney. Both swayed and grabbed each other for support.

"Top of the afternoon!" said David Snell-Orkney.

"The Back Side of Something!" replied Nolan, and fell away, gaping to let the circus by. He had a terrible urge to rush back to Finn's. His fight with the owner of the pub was obliterated. He wished now to report upon this fell encounter with a feather duster, a Siamese cat, a spoiled Pekingese, and three others gone ghastly frail from undereating and overwashing.

The six stopped outside the pub looking up at the sign.

Ah, God, thought Nolan. They're going in. What will *come* of it? Who do I warn first? Them? Or Finn?

Then, the door opened. Finn himself looked out. Damn, thought Nolan, that spoils it! Now we won't be allowed to describe this adventure. It will be Finn this, Finn that, and shut up to us all! There was a long moment when Snell-Orkney and his cohorts looked at Finn. Finn's eyes did not fasten on them. He looked above. He looked over. He looked beyond.

But he *had* seen them, this Nolan knew. For now a lovely thing happened.

All the color went out of Finn's face.

Then an even lovelier thing happened.

All the color rushed back into Finn's face.

Why, cried Nolan to himself, he's . . . *blushing!*

But still Finn refused to look anywhere save the sky, the lamps, the street, until Snell-Orkney trilled, "Sir, which way to St. Stephen's Green?"

"Jesus," said Finn and turned away. "Who knows *where* they put it, *this* week!" and slammed the door.

The six went on up the street, all smiles and delight, and Nolan was all for heaving himself through the door when a worse thing happened.

Garrity, the elevator operator from the Royal Hibernian Hotel, whipped across the sidewalk from nowhere. His face ablaze with excitement, he ran first into Finn's to spread the word.

By the time Nolan was inside, and Timulty rushing in next, Garrity was all up and down the length of the bar while Finn stood behind it suffering concussions from which he had not as yet recovered.

"It's a shame you missed it!" cried Garrity to all. "I mean it was the next thing to one of them fiction-and-science fillums they show at the Gayety Cinema!"

"How do you mean?" asked Finn, shaken out of his trance.

"*Nothing* they weigh!" Garrity told them. "Lifting them in the elevator was throwing a handful of chaff up a chimney! And you should have *heard.* They're here in Ireland for . . ." He lowered his voice and squinched his eyes. ". . . for *mysterious reasons!*"

"Mysterious!" Everyone leaned in at him.

"They'll put no name to it, but, mark my declaration, they're up to no good! Have you ever seen the like?"

"Not since the great fire at the convent," said Finn. "I—"

✳ But the word "convent" seemed one more magic touch. The doors sprang wide at this. Father Leary entered in reverse. That is to say he backed into the pub one hand to his cheek as if the Fates had dealt him a proper blow unbewares.

Reading the look of his spine, the men shoved their noses in their drinks until such time as the father had put a bit of the brew into himself, still staring as if the door were the gates of Hell ajar.

"Beyond," said the father, at last, "not two minutes gone, I saw a sight as would be hard to credit. In all the days of her collecting up the grievances of the world, has Ireland indeed gone mad?"

Finn refilled the priest's glass. "Was you standing in the blast of *The Invaders from the Planet Venus,* Father?"

"Have you seen them, then, Finn?" the father said.

"Yes, and do you guess them bad, your Holiness?"

"It's not so much bad or good as strange and *outré*, Finn, and words like rococo, I should guess, and baroque if you go with my drift?"

"I lie easy in the tide, sir."

"When last seen, where heading?" asked Timulty.

"On the edge of the Green," said the priest. "You don't imagine there'll be a bacchanal in the park now?"

"The weather won't allow, beg your pardon, Father," said Nolan, "but it strikes me, instead of standing with the gab in our mouth we should be out on the spy—"

"You move against my ethics," said the priest.

"A drowning man clutches at anything," said Nolan, "and ethics may drown with him if *that's* what he grabs instead of a lifebelt."

"Off the Mount, Nolan," said the priest, "and enough of the Sermon. What's your point?"

"The point is, Father, we have had no such influx of honorary Sicilians since the mind boggles to remember. For all we know, at this moment, they may be reading aloud to Mrs. Murphy, Miss Clancy, or Mrs. O'Hanlan in the midst of the park. And reading aloud from *what*, I ask you?"

"*The Ballad of Reading Gaol?*" asked Finn.

"You have rammed the target and sunk the ship," said Nolan, mildly irritated the point had been plucked from him. "How do we know these imps out of bottles are not selling real-estate tracts in a place called Fire Island? Have you *heard* of it, Father?"

"The American gazettes come often to my table, man."

"Well, do you remember the great hurricane of nineteen-and-fifty-six when the waves washed over Fire Island there in New York? An uncle of mine, God save his sanity and sight, was with the Coast Guard there which evacuated the entirety of the population of Fire Island. It was worse than the twice-a-year showing at Fennelly's dressworks, he said. It was more terrible than a Baptist Convention. Ten thousand men came rushing down to the stormy shore carrying bolts of drape material, cages full of parakeets, tomato-and-tangerine-colored sport coats, and lime-colored shoes. It was the most tumultuous scene since Hieronymus Bosch laid down his palette after he painted Hell for all generations to come. You do not easily evacuate ten thousand Venetian-glass boyos with their great blinky cow-eyes and their phonograph symphonic records in their hands and their rings in their ears, without tearing down the middle. My uncle, soon after, took to the heavy drink."

"Tell us *more* about that night," said Kilpatrick, entranced.

"More, hell," said the priest. "Out, I say. Surround the park. Keep your eyes peeled. And meet me back here in an hour."

"That's more like it," cried Kelly. "Let's *really* see what dread thing they're up to!"

The doors banged wide.

On the sidewalk, the priest gave directions. "Kelly, Murphy, you around the north side of the park. Timulty, you to the south. Nolan and Garrity, the east; Moran, MaGuire, and Kilpatrick, the west. Git!" But somehow or other in all the ruction, Kelly and Murphy wound up at the Four Shamrocks pub halfway to the Green and fortified themselves for the chase, and Nolan and Moran each met their wives on the street and had to run the other way, and MaGuire and Kilpatrick, passing the Elite Cinema and hearing Lawrence Tibbett singing inside, cadged their way in for a few half-used cigarettes.

So it wound up with just two, Garrity on the east and Timulty on the south side of the park, looking in at the visitors from another world.

After half an hour of freezing weather, Garrity stomped up to Timulty and said, "What's *wrong* with the fiends? They're just *standing* there in the midst of the park. They haven't moved half the afternoon. And it's cut to the bone is my toes. I'll nip around to the hotel, warm up, and rush back to stand guard with you, Tim."

"Take your time," called Timulty in a strange sad wandering, philosophical voice as the other charged away.

Left alone, Timulty walked in and sat for a full hour watching the six men who, as before, did not move. You might almost have thought to see Timulty there, with his eyes brooding, and, his mouth gone into a tragic crease, that he was some Irish neighbor of Kant or Schopenhauer, or had just read something by a poet or thought of a song that declined his spirits. And when at last the hour was up and he had gathered his thoughts like a handful of cold pebbles, he turned and made his way out of the park. Garrity was there, pounding his feet and swinging his hands but before he could explode with questions, Timulty pointed in and said, "Go sit. Look. Think. Then *you* tell *me*."

Everyone at Finn's looked up sheepishly when Timulty made his entrance. The priest was still off on errands around the city, and after a few walks about the Green to assuage their consciences, all had returned, nonplussed, to intelligence headquarters.

"Timulty!" they cried. "Tell us! What? What?"

Timulty took his time walking to the bar and sipping his drink. Silently, he observed his own image remotely buried beneath the lunar ice of the barroom mirror. He turned the subject this way. He twisted it inside out. He put it back wrong-side-to. Then he shut his eyes and said:

"It strikes me as how—"

Yes, said all silently, about him.

"From a lifetime of travel and thought, it comes to the top of my mind," Timulty went on, "there is a strange resemblance between the likes of them and the likes of us."

There was such a gasp as changed the scintillation, the goings and comings of light in the prisms of the little chandeliers over the bar. When the schools of fish-light had stopped swarming at this exhalation, Nolan cried, "Do you mind putting your hat on so I can knock it off!?"

"Consider," Timulty calmly said. "Are we or are we not great ones for the poem and the song?"

Another kind of gasp went through the crowd. There was a warm burst of approval. "Oh, sure, we're *that*!" "My God, is *that* all you're up to?" "We were afraid—"

"Hold it!" Timulty raised a hand, eyes still closed.

And all shut up.

"If we're not singing the songs, we're writing them, and if not writing, dancing them, and aren't *they* fond admirers of the song and the writing of same and the dancing out the whole? Well, just now, I heard them at a distance reciting poems and singing, to themselves, in the Green."

Timulty had something there. Everyone had to paw everybody and admit it.

"Do you find any *other* resemblances?" asked Finn, heavily, glowering.

"I do," said Timulty, with a judge's manner.

There was a still more fascinated indraw of breath and the crowd drew nearer.

"They do not mind a drink now and then," said Timulty.

"By God, he's right!" cried Murphy.

"Also," intoned Timulty, "they do not marry until very late, if ever at all! And—"

But here the tumult was such he had to wait for it to subside before he could finish:

"And they—ah—have very little to do with women."

✳ After that there was a great clamor, a yelling and shoving about and ordering of drinks and someone invited Timulty outside. But Timulty wouldn't even lift one eyelid, and the brawler was held off and when everyone had a new drink in them and the near-fistfights had drained away, one loud clear voice, Finn's, declared:

"Now would you mind explaining the criminal comparison you have just made in the clean air of my honorable pub?"

Timulty sipped his drink slowly and then at last opened his eyes and looked at Finn steadily, and said, with a clear bell-trumpet tone and wondrous enunciation:

"Where in all of Ireland can a man lie down with a woman?"

He let that sink in.

"Three hundred twenty-nine days a damn year it rains. The rest it's so wet there's no dry piece, no bit of land you would dare trip a woman out flat on for fear of her taking root and coming up in leaves, do you deny that?"

The silence did not deny.

"So when it comes to places to do sinful evils and perform outrageous acts of the flesh, it's to Arabia the poor damn fool Irishman must take himself. It's Arabian dreams we have, of warm nights, dry land, and a decent place not just to sit down but to lie down on, and not just lie down on but to roister joyfully about on in clinches and clenches of outrageous delight."

"Ah, Jaisus," said Flynn, "you can say *that* again."

"Ah, Jaisus," said everyone, nodding.

"That's number one." Timulty ticked it off on his fingers. "Place is lacking. Then, second, time and circumstances. For say you should sweet talk a fair girl into the field, eh? in her rainboots and slicker and her shawl over her head and her umbrella over that and you making noises like a stuck pig half over the sty gate, which means you've got one hand in her bosom and the other wrestling with her boots, which is as far as you'll damn well get, for who's standing there behind you, and you feel his sweet spearmint breath on your neck?"

"The father from the local parish?" offered Garrity.

"The father from the local parish," said everyone, in despair.

"There's nails number two and three in the cross on which all Ireland's males hang crucified," said Timulty.

"Go on, Timulty, go on."

"Those fellows visiting here from Sicily run in teams. *We* run in teams. Here we are, the gang, in Finn's, are we *not*?"

"Be damned and we are!"

"*They* look sad and are melancholy half the time and then spitting like happy demons the rest, either up or down, never in between, and who does *that* remind you of?"

Everyone looked in the mirror and nodded.

"If we had the choice," said Timulty, "to go home to the dire wife and the dread mother-in-law and the old-maid sister all sour sweats and terrors, or stay here in Finn's for one more song or one more drink or one more story, *which* would all of us men choose?"

Silence.

"Think on that," said Timulty. "Answer the truth. Resemblances. Similarities. The long list of them runs off one hand and up the other arm. And well worth the mulling over before we leap about crying Jaisus and Mary and summoning the Guard."

Silence.

"I," said someone, after a long while, strangely, curiously, "would like . . . to see them closer."

"I think you'll get your wish. Hist!"

All froze in a tableau.

And far off they heard a faint and fragile sound. It was like the wondrous morning you wake and lie in bed and know by a special feel that the first fall of snow is in the air, on its way down, tickling the sky, making the silence to stir aside and fall back in on nothing.

"Ah, God," said Finn, at last, "it's the first day of spring . . ."

And it was that, too. First the dainty snowfall of feet drifting on the cobbles, and then a choir of bird song.

And along the sidewalk and down the street and outside the pub came the sounds that were winter *and* spring. The doors sprang wide. The men reeled back from the impact of the meeting to come. They steeled their nerves. They balled their fists. They geared their teeth in their anxious mouths, and into the pub like children come into a Christmas place and everything a bauble or a toy, a special gift or color, there stood the tall thin older man who looked young and the small thin younger men who had old things in their eyes. The sound of snowfall stopped. The sound of spring birds ceased.

The strange children herded by the strange shepherd found themselves suddenly stranded as if they sensed a pulling away of a tide of people, even though the men at the bar had flinched but the merest hair.

The children of a warm isle regarded the short child-size and runty fullgrown men of this cold land and the full-grown men looked back in mutual assize.

Timulty and the men at the bar breathed long and slow. You could smell the terrible clean smell of the children way over here. There was too much spring in it.

Snell-Orkney and his young-old boy-men breathed swiftly as the heart-beats of birds trapped in a cruel pair of fists. You could smell the dusty, impacted, prolonged, and dark-clothed smell of the little men way over here. There was too much winter in it.

Each might have commented upon the other's choice of scent, but—

At this moment the double doors at the side banged wide and Garrity charged in full-blown, crying the alarm:

"Jesus, I've seen everything! Do you know where they are *now*, and what *doing*?"

Every hand at the bar flew up to shush him.

By the startled look in their eyes, the intruders knew they were being shouted about.

"They're still at St. Stephen's Green!" Garrity, on the move, saw naught that was before him. "I stopped by the hotel to spread the news. Now it's your turn. Those fellows—"

"Those fellows," said David Snell-Orkney, "are here in—" He hesitated.

"Heeber Finn's pub," said Heeber Finn, looking at his shoes.

"Heeber Finn's," said the tall man, nodding his thanks.

"Where," said Garrity, gone miserable, "we will all be having a drink instantly."

He flung himself at the bar.

But the six intruders were moving, also. They made a small parade to either side of Garrity and just by being amiably there made him hunch three inches smaller.

"Good afternoon," said Snell-Orkney.

"It is and it isn't," said Finn, carefully, waiting.

"It seems," said the tall man surrounded by the little boy-men, "there is much talk about what we are doing in Ireland."

"That would be putting the mildest interpretation on it," said Finn.

"Allow me to explain," said the stranger.

"Have you ever," continued Mr. David Snell-Orkney, "heard of the Snow Queen and the Summer King?"

Several jaws trapped wide down.

Someone gasped as if booted in the stomach.

Finn, after a moment in which he considered just where a blow might have landed upon him, poured himself a long slow drink with scowling precision. He took a stiff snort of the stuff and with the fire in his mouth, replied, carefully, letting the warm breath out over his tongue:

"Ah . . . *what* Queen is that again, *and* the King?"

"Well," said the tall pale man, "there was this Queen who lived in Iceland who had never seen summer, and this King who lived in the Isles of Sun who had never seen winter. The people under the King almost died of heat in the summers, and the people under the Snow Queen almost died of ice in the winters. But the people of both countries were saved from their terrible weathers. The Snow Queen and the Sun King met and fell in love and every summer when the sun killed people in the islands they moved North to the lands of ice and lived temperately. And every winter when the snow killed people in the North, all of the Snow Queen's people moved South and lived in the mild island sun. So there were no longer two nations, two peoples, but *one* race which commuted from land to land with the strange weathers and wild seasons. *The end.*"

There was a round of applause, not from the canary boys, but from the men lined up at the bar who had been spelled. Finn saw his own hands out clapping on the air, and put them down. The others saw their own hands and dropped them.

But Timulty summed it up, "God, if you only had a brogue! What a teller of tales you would make."

"Many thanks, many thanks," said David Snell-Orkney.

"All of which brings us around to the point of the story," Finn said. "I mean, well, about that Queen and the King and all."

"The point is," said Snell-Orkney, "that we have not seen a leaf fall in five years. We hardly know a cloud when we see it. We have not felt snow in ten years, or hardly a drop of rain. Our story is the reverse. We must have rain or we'll perish, right, chums?"

"Oh, yes, right," said all five, in a sweet chirruping.

"We have followed summer around the world for six or seven years. We have lived in Jamaica and Nassau and Port-au-Prince and Calcutta, and Madagascar and Bali and Taormina but finally just today we said we must go north, we must have cold again. We didn't quite know what we were looking for, but we found it in St. Stephen's Green."

"The *mysterious* thing?" Nolan burst out. "I mean—"

"Your friend here will tell you," said the tall man.

"Our friend? You mean—Garrity?"

Everyone looked at Garrity.

"As I was going to say," said Garrity, "when I came in the door. They was in the park standing there . . . *watching the leaves turn colors.*"

"Is that *all*?" said Nolan, dismayed.

"It seemed sufficient unto the moment," said Snell-Orkney.

"*Are* the leaves changing color up at St. Stephen's?" asked Kilpatrick.

"Do you know," said Timulty numbly, "it's been twenty years since I *looked.*"

"The most beautiful sight in all the world," said David Snell-Orkney, "lies up in the midst of St. Stephen's this very hour."

"He speaks deep," murmured Nolan.

"The drinks are on me," said David Snell-Orkney.

"He's touched *bottom,*" said MaGuire.

"Champagne all around!"

"Don't mind if I do!" said everyone.

And not ten minutes later they were all up at the park, together.

And well now, as Timulty said years after, did you ever see as many damned leaves on a tree as there was on the first tree just inside the gate at St. Stephen's Green? No! cried all. And what, though, about the *second* tree? Well, that had a *billion* leaves on it. And the more they looked the more they saw it was a wonder. And Nolan went around craning his neck so hard he fell over on his back and had to be helped up by two or three others, and there were general exhalations of awe and proclamations of devout inspiration as to the fact that as far as they could remember there had never *been* any goddamn leaves on the trees to begin with, but now they were there! Or if they had been there they had *never* had any color, or if they *had* had color, well, it was so long ago . . . Ah, what the hell, shut up, said everyone, and look!

Which is exactly what Nolan and Timulty and Kelly and Kilpatrick and Garrity and Snell-Orkney and his friends did for the rest of the declining afternoon. For a fact, autumn had taken the country, and the bright flags were out by the millions through the park.

Which is exactly where Father Leary found them.

But before he could say anything, three out of the six summer invaders asked him if he would hear their confessions.

And next thing you know with a look of great pain and alarm the father was taking Snell-Orkney & Co. back to see the stained glass at the church and the way the apse was put together by a master architect, and they liked his church so much and said so out loud again and again that he cut way down on their Hail Marys and the rigamaroles that went with.

But the top of the entire day was when one of the young-old boy-men back at the pub asked what would it be? Should he sing "Mother Machree" or "My Buddy"?

Arguments followed, and with polls taken and results announced, he sang both.

He had a dear voice, all said, eyes melting bright. A sweet high clear voice.

And as Nolan put it, "He wouldn't make much of a son. But there's a great daughter there somewhere!"

And all said "aye" to that.

And suddenly it was time to leave.

"But great God!" said Finn, "you just arrived!"

"We found what we came for, there's no need to stay," announced the tall sad happy old young man. "It's back to the hothouse with the flowers . . . or they wilt overnight. We never stay. We are always flying and jumping and running. We are always on the move."

The airport being fogged-in, there was nothing for it but the birds cage themselves on the Dun Laoghaire boat bound for England, and there was nothing for it but the inhabitants of Finn's should be down at the dock to watch them pull away in the middle of the evening. There they stood, all six, on the top deck, waving their thin hands down, and there stood Timulty and Nolan and Garrity and the rest waving their thick hands up. And as the boat hooted and pulled away the keeper-of-the-birds nodded once, and winged his right hand on the air and all sang forth: "*As I was walking through Dublin City, about the hour of twelve at night, I saw a maid, so fair was she . . . combing her hair by candlelight.*"

"Jesus," said Timulty, "do you *hear*?"

"Sopranos, every *one* of them!" cried Nolan.

"Not Irish sopranos, but real *real* sopranos," said Kelly.

"Damn, why didn't they *say*? If we'd known, we'd have had a good hour of *that* out of them before the boat."

Timulty nodded and added, listening to the music float over the waters. "Strange. Strange. I hate to see them go. Think. Think. For a hundred years or more people have said we had none. But now they have returned, if but for a little time."

"We had none of *what*?" asked Garrity. "And *what* returned?"

"Why," said Timulty, "the fairies, of course, the fairies that once lived in Ireland, and live here no more, but who came this day and changed our weather, and there they go again, who once stayed all the while."

"Ah, shut up!" cried Kilpatrick. "And listen!"

And listen they did, nine men on the end of a dock as the boat sailed out and the voices sang and the fog came in and they did not move for a long time until the boat was far gone and the voices faded like a scent of papaya on the mist.

By the time they walked back to Finn's it had begun to rain.

THE MEADOW

A WALL COLLAPSES, FOLLOWED BY ANOTHER and another; with dull thunder, a city falls into ruin.

The night wind blows.

The world lies silent.

London was torn down during the day. Port Said was destroyed. The nails were pulled out of San Francisco. Glasgow is no more.

They are gone, forever.

Boards clatter softly in the wind, sand whines and trickles in small storms upon the still air.

Along the road toward the colorless ruins comes the old night watchman to unlock the gate in the high barbed-wire fence and stand looking in.

There in the moonlight lie Alexandria and Moscow and New York. There in the moonlight lie Johannesburg and Dublin and Stockholm. And Clearwater, Kansas, and Provincetown, and Rio de Janeiro.

Just this afternoon the old man saw it happen, saw the car roaring outside the barbed-wire fence, saw the lean, sun-tanned men in that car, the men with their luxurious charcoal-flannel suits, and winking gold-mask cuff links, and their burning-gold wristwatches, and eye-blinding rings, lighting their cork-tipped cigarettes with engraved lighters. . . .

"There it is, gentlemen. What a mess. Look what the weather's done to it."

"Yes, sir, it's bad, Mr. Douglas!"

"We just *might* save Paris."

"Yes, *sir!*"

"But, hell! The rain's warped it. That's Hollywood for you! Tear it down! Clear it out! We can use that land. Send a wrecking crew in today!"

"Yes, *sir*, Mr. Douglas!"

The car roaring off and gone away.

✳ And now it is night. And the old night watchman stands inside the gate.

He remembers what happened this same still afternoon when the wreckers came.

A hammering, ripping, clattering; a collapse and a roar. Dust and thunder, thunder and dust!

And the whole of the entire world shook loose its nails and lath and plaster and sill and celluloid window as town after town following town banged over flat and lay still.

A shuddering, a thunder fading away, and then, once more, only the quiet wind.

The night watchman now walks slowly forward along the empty streets.

And one moment he is in Baghdad, and beggars loll in wondrous filth, and women with clear sapphire eyes give veiled smiles from high thin windows.

The wind blows sand and confetti.

The women and beggars vanish.

And it is all strutworks again, it is all papier-mâché and oil-painted canvas and props lettered with the name of this studio, and there is nothing behind any of the building fronts but night and space and stars.

The old man pulls a hammer and a few long nails from his tool chest; he peers around in the junk until he finds a dozen good strong boards and some untorn canvas. And he takes the bright steel nails in his blunt fingers, and they are single-headed nails.

And he begins to put London back together again, hammering and hammering, board by board, wall by wall, window by window, hammering, hammering, louder, louder, steel on steel, steel in wood, wood against sky, working the hours toward midnight, with no end to his striking and fixing and striking again.

"Hey there, *you!*"

The old man pauses.

"You, night *watchman!*"

Out of the shadows hurries a stranger in overalls, calling:

"Hey, what's-your-name!"

The old man turns. "The name's Smith."

"Okay, Smith, what in hell's the idea!"

The watchman eyes the stranger quietly. "Who are *you*?"

"Kelly, foreman of the wrecking gang."

The old man nods. "Ah. The ones who tear everything down. You've done plenty today. Why aren't you home bragging about it?"

Kelly hawks and spits. "There was some machinery over on the Singapore set I had to check." He wipes his mouth. . . . "Now, Smith, what in Christ's name you think you're doing? Drop that hammer. You're building it all up again! We tear it down and you put it up. You crazy?"

The old man nods. "Maybe I am. But somebody has to put it up again."

"Look, Smith. I do *my* work, you do yours, everyone's happy. But I can't have you messing, see? I'm turning you in to Mr. Douglas."

The old man goes on with his hammering. "Call him up. Send him around. I want to talk to him. *He's* the crazy one."

Kelly laughs. "You kidding? Douglas don't see nobody." He jerks his hand, then bends to examine Smith's newly finished work. "Hey, wait a minute! What *kind* of nails you using? Single-heads! Now, *cut that*! It'll be hell to pay tomorrow, trying to pull 'em out!"

Smith turns his head and looks for a moment at the other man swaying there. "Well, it stands to reason you can't put the world together with double-headed nails. They're too easy to yank out. You got to use single-headed nails and hammer 'em way in. Like *this*!"

He gives a steel nail one tremendous blow that buries it completely in the wood.

Kelly works his hands on his hips. "I'll give you one more chance. Quit putting things back together and I'll play ball with you."

"Young man," says the night watchman, and keeps on hammering while he talks, and thinks about it, and talks some more, "I was here long before you were born. I was here when all *this* was only a meadow. And there was a wind set the meadow running in waves. For more than thirty years I watched it grow, until it was all of the world together. I lived here *with* it. I lived nice. This is the *real* world to me now. That world out there, beyond the fence, is where I spend time sleeping. I got a little room on a little street, and I see headlines and read about wars and strange, bad people. But here? Here I have the whole world together and it's all peace. I been walking through the cities of *this* world since 1920. Any night I feel like it, I have a one-o'clock snack at a bar on the Champs Élysées! I can get me some fine amontillado sherry at a sidewalk café in Madrid, if I want. Or else me and the stone gargoyles, high up there—you *see* them, on top Notre Dame?—we can turn over great state matters and reach big political decisions!"

"Yeah, Pop, sure." Kelly waves impatiently.

"And now you come and kick it down and leave only that world out there which hasn't learned the *first thing* about peace that I know from seeing this land here inside the barbed wire. And so you come and rip it up and there's no peace anymore, anywhere. You and your wreckers so proud of your wrecking. Pulling down towns and cities and whole lands!"

"A guy's got to live," says Kelly. "I got a wife and kids."

"That's what they all say. They got wives and kids. And they go on, pulling apart, tearing down, killing. They had *orders*! Somebody *told* them. They *had* to do it!"

"Shut up and gimme that hammer!"

"Don't come any closer!"

"Why, you crazy old—"

"This hammer's good for more than nails!" The old man whistles the hammer through the air; the wrecker jumps back.

"Hell," says Kelly, "you're insane! I'm putting a call through to the main studio; we'll get some cops here quick. My God, one minute you're building things up and talking crazy, but how do I know two minutes from now you won't run wild and start pouring kerosene and lighting matches!"

"I wouldn't harm the smallest piece of kindling in this place, and you know it," says the old man.

"Might burn the whole goddam place down, hell," says Kelly. "Listen, old man, you just wait right *there*!"

The wrecker spins about and runs off into the villages and the ruined cities and the sleeping two-dimensional towns of this night world, and after his footsteps fade there is a music that the wind plays on the long silver barbed wires of the fence, and the old man hammering and hammering and selecting long boards and rearing walls until a time finally comes when his mouth is gasping, his heart is exploding; the hammer drops from his open fingers, steel nails tinkle like coins on the pavement, and the old man cries out to himself alone:

"It's no use, no use. I can't put it all back up before they come. I need so very much help I don't know what to do."

The old man leaves his hammer lying on the road and begins to walk with no direction, with no purpose, it seems, save that he is thinking to make one last round and take one last look at everything and say good-bye to whatever there is or was in this world to say good-bye to. And so he walks with the shadows all around and the shadows all through this land where time has grown late indeed, and the shadows are of all kinds and types and sizes, shadows of buildings, and shadows of people. And he doesn't look straight at them, no, because if he looked at them straight, they would all blow away. No, he just walks, down the middle of Piccadilly Circus . . . the echo of his steps . . . or the Rue de la Paix . . . the sound of him clearing his throat . . . or Fifth Avenue . . . and he doesn't look right or left. And all around him, in dark doorways and empty windows, are his many friends, his good friends, his very good friends. Far away there are the hiss and steam and soft whispering of a *caffè espresso* machine, all silver and chrome, and soft Italian singing . . . the flutter of hands in darkness over the open mouths of balalaikas, the rustle of palm trees, a touching of drums with the chimes chiming and small bells belling, and a sound of summer apples dropped in soft night grass which are not apples at all but the motion of women's bared feet slowly dancing a circle to the chimes' faint chiming and the belling of the tiny golden bells. There is the munch of maize kernels crushed on black volcanic stone, the sizzle of tortillas drowned in hot fat, the whisk of charcoals tossing up a thousand fireflies of spark at the blowing of a mouth and the wave of a papaya frond; everywhere faces and forms, everywhere stirs and gestures and ghost fires which float the magical torch-colored faces of Spanish gypsies in air as on a fiery water, the mouths crying out the songs that tell of the oddness and the strangeness and the sadness of living. Everywhere shadows and people, everywhere people and shadows and singing to music.

Just that very trite thing—the wind?

No. The people are all here. They have been here for many years. And tomorrow?

The old man stops, presses his hands to his chest.

They will not be here anymore.

* A horn blows!

Outside the barbed-wire gate—the enemy! Outside the gate a small black police car and a large black limousine from the studio itself, three miles away.

The horn blares!

The old man seizes the rungs of a ladder and climbs, the sound of the horn pushing him higher and higher. The gate crashes wide; the enemy roars in.

"There he goes!"

The glaring lights of the police shine in upon the cities of the meadow; the lights reveal the stark canvas set-pieces of Manhattan, Chicago, and Chungking! The light glitters on the imitation stone towers of Notre Dame Cathedral, fixes on a tiny figure balancing on the catwalks of Notre Dame, climbing and climbing up where the night and the stars are turning slowly by.

"There he is, Mr. Douglas, at the top!"

"Good God. It's getting so a man can't spend an evening at a quiet party without—"

"He's striking a match! Call the fire department!"

On top of Notre Dame, the night watchman, looking down, shielding the match from the softly blowing wind, sees the police, the workmen, and the producer in a dark suit, a big man, gazing up at him. Then the night watchman slowly turns the match, cupping it, applies it to the tip of his cigar. He lights the cigar in slow puffs.

He calls: "Is Mr. Douglas down there?"

A voice calls back: "What do you want with me?"

The old man smiles. "Come up, alone! Bring a gun if you want! I just want a little talk!"

The voices echo in the vast churchyard:

"Don't *do* it, Mr. Douglas!"

"Give me your gun. Let's get this *over* with so I can get back to the party. Keep me covered, I'll play it safe. I don't want these sets burned. There's two million dollars in lumber alone here. *Ready?* I'm on my way."

The producer climbs high on the night ladders, up through the half shell of Notre Dame to where the old man leans against a plaster gargoyle, quietly smoking a cigar. The producer stops, gun pointed, half through an open trapdoor.

"All right, Smith. Stay where you are."

Smith removes the cigar from his mouth quietly. "Don't you be afraid of me. I'm all right."

"I wouldn't bet money on that."

"Mr. Douglas," says the night watchman, "did you ever read that story about the man who traveled to the future and found everyone there insane? *Everyone.* But since they were all insane they didn't *know* they were insane. They all acted alike and so they thought themselves normal. And since our hero was the only sane one among them, he was abnormal; therefore, *he* was the insane one. To *them*, at least. Yes, Mr. Douglas, insanity is relative. It depends on who has who locked in what cage."

The producer swears under his breath. "I didn't climb up here to talk all night. What do you want?"

"I want to talk with the Creator. That's you, Mr. Douglas. You created all this. You came here one day and struck the earth with a magical checkbook and cried, 'Let there be Paris!' And there *was* Paris: streets, bistros, flowers, wine, outdoor bookshops and all. And you clapped your hands again: 'Let there be Constantinople!' And there *it* was! You clapped your hands a thousand times, and each time made something new, and now you think just by clapping your hands one *last* time you can drop it all down in ruins. But, Mr. Douglas, it's not as easy as that!"

"I own fifty-one percent of the stock in this studio!"

"But did the studio ever belong to you, really? Did you ever think to drive here late some night and climb up on this cathedral and see what a *wonderful* world you created? Did you ever wonder if it might not be a good idea for you to sit up here with me and my friends and have a cup of amontillado sherry with us? All right—so the amontillado smells and looks and tastes like coffee. Imagination, Mr. Creator, imagination. But no, you never came around, you never climbed up, you never looked or listened or cared. There was always a party somewhere else. And now, very late, without asking us, you want to destroy it all. You may own fifty-one percent of the studio stock, but you don't own *them*."

"Them!" cries the producer. "What's all this business about 'them'?"

"It's hard to put in words. The people who *live* here." The night watchman moves his hand in the empty air toward the half-cities and the night. "So many films were made here in all the long years. Extras moved in the streets in costumes, they talked a thousand tongues, they smoked cigarettes and meerschaums and Persian hookahs, even. Dancing girls danced. They *glittered*, oh, how they glittered! Women with veils smiled down from high balconies. Soldiers marched. Children played. Knights in silver armor fought. There were orange-tea shops. People sipped tea in them and dropped their *h*'s Gongs were beaten. Viking ships sailed the inland seas."

The producer lifts himself up through the trapdoor and sits on the plankings, the gun cradled more easily in his hand. He seems to be looking at the old man first with one eye, then the other, listening to him with one ear, then the other, shaking his head a little to himself.

The night watchman continues:

"And somehow, after the extras and the men with the cameras and microphones and all the equipment walked away and the gates were shut and they drove off in big cars, somehow something of all those thousands of different people remained. The things they had been, or *pretended* to be, stayed on. The foreign languages, the costumes, the things they did, the things they thought about, their religions and their music, all those little things and big things stayed on. The sights of far places. The smells. The salt wind. The sea. It's all here tonight if you *listen*."

The producer listens and the old man listens in the drafty strutworks of the cathedral, with the moonlight blinding the eyes of the plaster gargoyles and the wind making the false stone mouths to whisper, and the sound of a thousand lands within a land below blowing and dusting and leaning in that wind, a thousand yellow minarets and milk-white towers and green avenues yet untouched among the hundred new ruins, and all of it murmuring its wires and lathings like a great steel-and-wooden harp touched in the night, and the wind bringing that self-made sound high up here in the sky to these two men who stand listening and apart.

The producer laughs shortly and shakes his head.

"You *heard*," says the night watchman. "You *did* hear, didn't you? I see it in your face."

Douglas shoves the gun in his coat pocket. "Anything you listen for you can hear. I made the mistake of listening. You should have been a writer. You could throw six of my best ones out of work. Well, what about it—are you ready to come down out of here now?"

"You sound almost polite," says the night watchman.

"Don't know why I should. You ruined a good evening for me."

"Did I? It hasn't been that bad, has it? A bit different, I should say. Stimulating, maybe."

Douglas laughs quietly. "You're not dangerous at all. You just need company. It's your job and everything going to hell and you're lonely. I can't quite figure you, though."

"Don't tell me I've got you thinking?" asks the old man.

Douglas snorts. "After you've lived in Hollywood long enough, you meet all kinds. Besides, I've never been up here before. It's a real view, like you say. But I'll be damned if I can figure why you should worry about all this junk. What's it to you?"

The night watchman gets down on one knee and taps one hand into the palm of the other, illustrating his points. "Look. As I said before, you came here years ago, clapped your hands, and three hundred cities jumped up! Then you added a half-thousand other nations, and states and peoples and religions and political setups inside the barbed-wire fence. And there was trouble! Oh, nothing you could see. It was all in the wind and the spaces between. But it was the same kind of trouble the world out there beyond the fence has—squabbles and riots and invisible wars. But at last the trouble died out. You want to know why?"

"If I didn't, I wouldn't be sitting up here freezing."

A little night music, please, thinks the old man, and moves his hand on the air like someone playing the proper and beautiful music to background all that he has to tell. . . .

"Because you got Boston joined to Trinidad," he says softly, "part of Trinidad poking out of Lisbon, part of Lisbon leaning on Alexandria, Alexandria tacked onto Shanghai, and a lot of little pegs and nails between, like Chattanooga, Oshkosh, Oslo, Sweet Water, Soissons, Beirut, Bombay, and Port Arthur. You shoot a man in New York and he stumbles forward and drops dead in Athens. You take a political bribe in Chicago and somebody in London goes to jail. You hang a Negro man in Alabama and the people of Hungary have to bury him. The dead Jews of Poland clutter the streets of Sydney, Portland, and Tokyo. You push a knife into a man's stomach in Berlin and it comes out the back of a farmer in Memphis. It's all so *close*, so very *close*. That's why we have peace here. We're all so crowded there *has got to be peace*, or nothing would be left! One fire would destroy all of us, no matter who started it, for what reason. So all of the people, the memories, whatever you want to call them, that are here, have settled down, and this is their world, a good world, a fine world."

The old man stops and licks his lips slowly and takes a breath. "And tomorrow," he says, "you're going to stomp it down."

The old man crouches there a moment longer, then gets to his feet and gazes out at the cities and the thousand shadows in those cities. The great plaster cathedral whines and sways in the night air, back and forth, rocking on the summer tides.

"Well," says Douglas at last, "shall—shall we go down now?"

Smith nods. "I've had my say."

Douglas vanishes, and the watchman listens to the younger man going down and down through the ladders and catwalks of the night. Then, after a reasonable hesitation, the old man takes hold of the ladder, breathes something to himself, and begins the long descent in shadow.

✳ The studio police and the few workers and some minor executives all drive away. Only one large dark car waits outside the barbed-wire gate as the two men stand talking in the cities of the meadow.

"What are you going to do now?" asks Smith.

"Go back to my party, I suppose," says the producer.

"Will it be fun?"

"Yes." The producer hesitates. "Sure, it'll be fun!" He glances at the night watchman's right hand. "Don't tell me you've found that hammer Kelly told me you were using? You going to start building again? You don't give up, do you?"

"Would you, if you were the last builder and everybody else was a wrecker?"

Douglas starts to walk with the old man. "Well, maybe I'll see you again, Smith."

"No," says Smith, "I won't be here. This all won't be here. If you come back again, it'll be too late."

Douglas stops. "Hell, hell! What do you want me to do?"

"A simple thing. Leave all this standing. Leave these cities up."

"I can't do that! Damn it. Business reasons. It has to go."

"A man with a real nose for business and some imagination could think up a profitable reason for it to stay," says Smith.

"My car's waiting! How do I get out of here?"

The producer strikes off over a patch of rubble, cuts through half of a tumbled ruin, kicking boards aside, leaning for a moment on plaster façades and strutworks. Dust rains from the sky.

"Watch out!"

The producer stumbles in a thunder of dust and avalanching brick; he gropes, he topples, he is seized upon by the old man and yanked forward.

"Jump!"

They jump, and half the building slides to ruin, crashes into hills and mountains of old paper and lathing. A great bloom of dust strikes out upon the air.

"You all right?"

"Yes. Thanks. Thanks." The producer looks at the fallen building. The dust clears. "You probably saved my life."

"Hardly that. Most of those are papier-mâché bricks. You might have been cut and bruised a little."

"Nevertheless, thanks. What building was that that fell?"

"Norman village tower, built in 1925. Don't get near the rest of it; it might go down."

"I'll be careful." The producer moves carefully in to stand by the set-piece. "Why—I could push this whole damn building over with one hand." He demonstrates; the building leans and quivers and groans. The producer steps quickly back. "I could knock it down in a second."

"But you wouldn't want to do that," says the watchman.

"Oh, wouldn't I? What's one French house more or less, this late in the day?"

The old man takes his arm. "Walk around here to the other side of the house."

They walk to the other side.

"Read that sign," says Smith.

The producer flicks his cigarette lighter, holds the fire up to help him squint, and reads:

" 'THE FIRST NATIONAL BANK MELLIN TOWN.' " He pauses. " 'ILLINOIS,' " he says, very slowly.

The building stands there in the sharp light of the stars and the bland light of the moon.

"On one side"—Douglas balances his hands like a scales—"a French tower. On the other side—" He walks seven steps to the right, seven steps to the left, peering. " 'THE FIRST NATIONAL BANK.' Bank. Tower. Tower. Bank. Well, I'll be *damned*."

Smith smiles and says, "Still want to push the French tower down, Mr. Douglas?"

"Wait a minute, wait a minute, hold on, hold on," says Douglas, and suddenly begins to see the buildings that stand before him. He turns in a slow circle; his eyes move up and down and across and over; his eyes flick here, flick there, see this, see that, examine, file, put away, and re-examine. He begins to walk in silence. They move in the cities of the meadow, over grasses and wild flowers, up to and into and through ruins and half-ruins and up to and into and through complete avenues and villages and towns.

They begin a recital which goes on and on as they walk, Douglas asking, the night watchman answering, Douglas asking, the night watchman answering.

"What's this over here?"

"A Buddhist temple."

"And on the other side of it?"

"The log cabin where Lincoln was born."

"And here?"

"St. Patrick's church, New York."

"And on the reverse?"

"A Russian Orthodox church in Rostov!"

"What's *this*?"

"The door of a castle on the Rhine!"

"And *inside*?"

"A Kansas City soda fountain!"

"And here? And here? And over *there*? And what's *that*?" asks Douglas. "What's this! What about that one! And over *there*?"

It seems as if they are running and rushing and yelling all through the cities, here, there, everywhere, up, down, in, out, climbing, descending, poking, stirring, opening-shutting doors.

"And this, and this, and this, and *this*?"

The night watchman tells all there is to tell.

Their shadows run ahead in narrow alleys, and avenues as broad as rivers made of stone and sand.

They make a great talking circle; they hurry all around and back to where they started.

They are quiet again. The old man is quiet from having said what there was to say, and the producer is quiet from listening and remembering and fitting it all together in his mind. He stands, absentmindedly fumbling for his cigarette case. It takes him a full minute to open it, examining every action, thinking about it, and to offer the case to the watchman.

"Thanks."

They light up thoughtfully. They puff on their cigarettes and watch the smoke blow away.

Douglas says, "Where's that damned hammer of yours?"

"Here," says Smith.

"You got your nails with you?"

"Yes, sir."

Douglas takes a deep drag on his cigarette and exhales. "Okay, Smith, get to work."

"What?"

"You heard me. Nail what you can back up, on your own time. Most of the stuff that's already torn down is a complete loss. But any bits and pieces that fit and will look decent, put 'em together. Thank God there's a lot still standing. It took me a long time to get it through my head. A man with a nose for business and some imagination, you said. That *is* the world, you said. I should have seen it years ago. Here it all is inside the fence, and me too blind to see what could be done with it. The World Federation in my own back yard and me kicking it over. So help me God, we need more crazy people and night watchmen."

"You know," says the night watchman, "I'm getting old and I'm getting strange. You wouldn't be fooling an old and strange man, would you?"

"I'll make no promises I can't keep," says the producer. "I'll only promise to try. There's a good chance we can go ahead. It would make a beautiful film, there's no doubt of that. We could make it all here, inside the fence, photograph it ten ways from Christmas. There's no doubt about a story, either. You provided it. It's yours. It wouldn't be hard to put some writers to work on it. Good writers. Perhaps only a short subject, twenty minutes, but we could show all the cities and countries here, leaning on and holding each other up. I *like* the idea. I like it very much, believe me. We could show a film like that to anyone anywhere in the world and they'd like it. They couldn't pass it up, it would be too important."

"It's good to hear you talk this way."

"I hope I keep on talking this way," says the producer. "I can't be trusted. I don't trust myself. Hell, I get excited, up one day, down the next. Maybe you'll have to hit me on the head with that hammer to keep me going."

"I'd be pleased," says Smith.

"And *if* we do the film," says the younger man, "I suppose you could help. You know the sets, probably better than anyone. Any suggestions you might want to make, we'd be glad to have. Then, after we do the film, I suppose you won't mind letting us tear the rest of the world down, right?"

"I'd give my permission," says the watchman.

"Well, I'll call off the hounds for a few days and see what happens. Send out a camera crew tomorrow to see what we can line up for shots. Send out some writers. Maybe you can *all* gab. Hell, hell. We'll work it out." Douglas turns toward the gate. "In the meantime, use your hammer all you want. I'll be seeing you. My God, I'm *freezing!*"

They hurry toward the gate. On the way, the old man finds his lunch box where he abandoned it some hours ago. He picks it up, takes out the thermos, and shakes it. "How about a drink before you go?"

"What've you got? Some of that amontillado you were yelling about?"

"1876."

"Let's have some of that, sure."

The thermos is opened and the liquid poured steaming from it into the cup.

"There you are," says the old man.

"Thanks. Here's to you." The producer drinks. "That's good. Ah, that's damned good!"

"It might taste like coffee, but I tell you it's the finest amontillado ever put under a cork."

"You can say *that* again."

The two of them stand among the cities of the world in the moonlight, drinking the hot drink, and the old man remembers something: "There's an old song fits here, a drinking song, I think, a song that all of us who live inside the fence sing, when we're of a mind, when I listen right, and the wind's just right in the telephone wires. It goes like this:

> *"We all go the same way home,*
> *All the same collection, in the same direction,*
> *All go the same way home.*
> *So there's no need to part at all,*
> *And we'll all cling together like the ivy on the old garden wall . . ."*

They finish drinking the coffee in the middle of Port-au-Prince.

"Hey!" says the producer suddenly. "Take it easy with that cigarette! You want to burn down the whole darn *world*?"

They both look at the cigarette and smile.

"I'll be careful," says Smith.

"So long," says the producer. "I'm *really* late for that party."

"So long, Mr. Douglas."

The gate hasp clicks open and shut, the footsteps die away, the limousine starts up and drives off in the moonlight, leaving behind the cities of the world and an old man standing in the middle of these cities of the world raising his hand to wave.

"So long," says the night watchman.

And then there is only the wind.

THE KILIMANJARO DEVICE

I ARRIVED IN THE TRUCK VERY EARLY in the morning. I had been driving all night, for I hadn't been able to sleep at the motel so I thought I might as well drive and I arrived among the mountains and hills near Ketchum and Sun Valley just as the sun came up and I was glad I had kept busy with driving.

I drove into the town itself without looking up at that one hill. I was afraid if I looked at it, I would make a mistake. It was very important not to look at the grave. At least that is how I felt. And I had to go on my hunch.

I parked the truck in front of an old saloon and walked around the town and talked to a few people and breathed the air and it was sweet and clear. I found a young hunter, but he was wrong; I knew that after talking to him for a few minutes. I found a very old man, but he was no better. Then I found me a hunter about fifty, and he was just right. He knew, or sensed, everything I was looking for.

I bought him a beer and we talked about a lot of things, and then I bought him another beer and led the conversation around to what I was doing here and why I wanted to talk to him. We were silent for a while and I waited, not showing my impatience, for the hunter, on his own, to bring up the past, to speak of other days three years ago, and of driving toward Sun Valley at this time or that and what he saw and knew about a man who had once sat in this bar and drunk beer and talked about hunting or gone hunting out beyond.

And at last, looking off at the wall as if it were the highway and the mountains, the hunter gathered up his quiet voice and was ready to speak.

"That old man," he said. "Oh, that old man on the road. Oh, that poor old man."

I waited.

"I just can't get over that old man on the road," he said, looking down now into his drink.

I drank some more of my beer, not feeling well, feeling very old myself and tired.

When the silence prolonged itself, I got out a local map and laid it on the wooden table. The bar was quiet. It was midmorning and we were completely alone there.

"This is where you saw him most often?" I asked.

The hunter touched the map three times. "I used to see him walking here. And along there. Then he'd cut across the land here. That poor old man. I wanted to tell him to keep off the road. I didn't want to hurt or insult him. You don't tell a man like that about roads or that maybe he'll be hit. If he's going to be hit, well that's it. You figure it's his business, and you go on. Oh, but he was old there at the last."

"He was," I said, and folded the map and put it in my pocket.

"You another of those reporters?" said the hunter.

"Not quite *those*," I said.

"Didn't mean to lump you in with them," he said.

"No apology needed," I said. "Let's just say I was one of his readers."

"Oh, he had readers all right, all kinds of readers. Even me. I don't touch books from one autumn to the next. But I touched his. I think I liked the Michigan stories best. About the fishing. I think the stories about the fishing are good. I don't think anybody ever wrote about fishing that way and maybe won't ever again. Of course, the bullfight stuff is good, too. But that's a little far off. Some of the cowpokes like them; they been around the animals all their life. A bull here or a bull there, I guess it's the same. I know one cowpoke has read just the bull stuff in the Spanish stories of the old man's forty times. He could go over there and fight, I swear."

"I think all of us felt," I said, "at least once in our lives, when we were young, we could go over there, after reading the bull stuff in the Spanish stories, that we could go over there and fight. Or at least jog ahead of the running of the bulls, in the early morning, with a good drink waiting at the other end of the run, and your best girl with you there for the long weekend."

I stopped. I laughed quietly. For my voice had, without knowing, fallen into the rhythm of his way of saying, either out of his mouth, or from his hand. I shook my head and was silent.

"You been up to the grave yet?" asked the hunter, as if he knew I would answer yes.

"No," I said.

That really surprised him. He tried not to show it.

"They all go up to the grave," he said.

"Not this one."

He explored around in his mind for a polite way of asking. "I mean . . ." he said. "Why not?"

"Because it's the wrong grave," I said.

"All graves are wrong graves when you come down to it," he said.

"No," I said. "There are right graves and wrong ones, just as there are good times to die and bad times."

He nodded at this. I had come back to something he knew, or at least smelled was right.

"Sure, I knew men," he said, "died just perfect. You always felt, yes, that was good. One man I knew, sitting at the table waiting for supper, his wife in the kitchen, when she came in with a big bowl of soup there he was sitting dead and neat at the table. Bad for her, but, I mean, wasn't that a good way for him? No sickness. No nothing but sitting there waiting for supper to come and never knowing if it came or not. Like another friend. Had an old dog. Fourteen years old. Dog was going blind and tired. Decided at last to take the dog to the pound and have him put to sleep. Loaded the old blind tired dog on the front seat of his car. The dog licked his hand, once. The man felt awful. He drove toward the pound. On the way there, with not one sound, the dog passed away, died on the front seat, as if he knew and, knowing, picked the better way, just handed over his ghost, and there you are. That's what you're talking about, right?"

I nodded.

"So you think that grave up on the hill is a wrong grave for a right man, do you?"

"That's about it," I said.

"You think there are all kinds of graves along the road for all of us?"

"Could be," I said.

"And if we could see all our life one way or another, we'd choose better? At the end, looking back," said the hunter, "we'd say, hell, *that* was the year and the place, not the *other* year and the other place, but that one year, that one place. Would we say that?"

"Since we have to choose or be pushed finally," I said, "yes."

"That's a nice idea," said the hunter. "But how many of us have that much sense? Most of us don't have brains enough to leave a party when the gin runs out. We hang around."

"We hang around," I said, "and what a shame."

We ordered some more beer.

The hunter drank half the glass and wiped his mouth.

"So what can you do about wrong graves?" he said.

"Treat them as if they didn't exist," I said. "And maybe they'll go away, like a bad dream."

The hunter laughed once, a kind of forlorn cry. "God, you're crazy. But I like listening to crazy people. Blow some more."

"That's all," I said.

"Are you the Resurrection and the Life?" said the hunter.

"No."

"You going to say Lazarus come forth?"

"No."

"What then?"

"I just want, very late in the day," I said, "to choose right places, right times, right graves."

"Drink that drink," said the hunter. "You need it. Who in hell sent you?"

"Me," I said. "I did. And some friends. We all chipped in and picked one out of ten. We bought that truck out on the street and I drove it across country. On the way I did a lot of hunting and fishing to put myself in the right frame. I was in Cuba last year. Spain the summer before. Africa the summer before that. I got a lot to think about. That's why they picked me."

"To do *what*, to do *what*, goddammit?" said the hunter urgently, half wildly, shaking his head. "You can't do anything. It's all over."

"Most of it," I said. "Come on."

I walked to the door. The hunter sat there. At last, examining the fires lit in my face by my talking, he grunted, got up, walked over, and came outside with me.

I pointed at the curb. We looked together at the truck parked there.

"I've seen those before," he said. "A truck like that, in a movie. Don't they hunt rhino from a truck like that? And lions and things like that? Or at least travel in them around Africa?"

"You remember right."

"No lions around here," he said. "No rhino, no water buffalo, nothing."

"No?" I asked.

He didn't answer that.

I walked over and touched the open truck.

"You know what this is?"

"I'm playing dumb from here on," said the hunter. "What is it?"

I stroked the fender for a long moment.

"A Time Machine," I said.

His eyes widened and then narrowed and he sipped the beer he was carrying in one large hand. He nodded me on.

"A Time Machine," I repeated.

"I heard you," he said.

He walked out around the safari truck and stood in the street looking at it. He wouldn't look at me. He circled the truck one entire round and stood back on the curb and looked at the cap on the gas tank.

"What kind of mileage you get?" he said.

"I don't know yet."

"You don't know anything," he said.

"This is the first trip," I said. "I won't know until it's over."

"What do you fuel a thing like that with?" he said.

I was silent.

"What kind of stuff you put in?" he asked.

I could have said: Reading late at night, reading many nights over the years until almost morning, reading up in the mountains in the snow or reading at noon in Pamplona, or reading by the streams or out in a boat somewhere along the Florida coast. Or I could have said: All of us put our hands on this Machine, all of us thought about it and bought it and touched it and put our love in it and our remembering what his words did to us twenty years or twenty-five or thirty years ago. There's a lot of life and remembering and love put by here, and that's the gas and the fuel and the stuff or whatever you want to call it; the rain in Paris, the sun in Madrid, the snow in the high Alps, the smoke off the guns in the Tyrol, the shine of light off the Gulf Stream, the explosion of bombs or explosions of leaped fish, that's the gas and the fuel and the stuff here; I should have said that, I thought it, but I let it stay unsaid.

The hunter must have smelled my thought, for his eyes squinted up and, telepath that he was from long years in the forest, chewed over my thinking.

Then he walked over and did an unexpected thing. He reached out and . . . *touched* . . . my Machine.

He laid his hand on it and left it there, as if feeling for the life, and approving what he sensed beneath his hand. He stood that way for a long time.

Then he turned without a word, not looking at me, and went back into the bar and sat drinking alone, his back turned toward the door.

I didn't want to break the silence. It seemed a good time to go, to try.

I got in the truck and started the motor.

What kind of mileage? What kind of fuel? I thought. And drove away.

* I kept on the road and didn't look right or left and I drove for what must have been an hour, first this direction and then that, part of the time my eyes shut for full seconds, taking a chance I might go off and get hurt or killed.

And then, just before noon, with the clouds over the sun, suddenly I knew it was all right.

I looked up at the hill and I almost yelled.

The grave was gone.

I drove down into a little hollow just then and on the road ahead, wandering along by himself, was an old man in a heavy sweater.

I idled the safari truck along until I was pacing him as he walked. I saw he was wearing steel-rimmed glasses and for a long moment we moved together, each ignoring the other until I called his name.

He hesitated, and then walked on.

I caught up with him in the truck and said again, "Papa."

He stopped and waited.

I braked the car and sat there in the front seat.

"Papa," I said.

He came over and stood near the door.

"Do I know you?"

"No. But I know you."

He looked me in the eyes and studied my face and mouth. "Yes. I think you do."

"I saw you on the road. I think I'm going your way. Want a lift?"

"It's good walking this time of day," he said. "Thanks."

"Let me tell you where I'm going," I said.

He had started off but now stopped and, without looking at me, said, "Where?"

"A long way," I said.

"It sounds long, the way you tell it. Can't you make it shorter?"

"No. A long way," I said. "About two thousand six hundred days, give or take some days, and half an afternoon."

He came back and looked into the car.

"Is that how far you're going?"

"That's how far."

"In which direction? Ahead?"

"Don't you want to go ahead?"

He looked at the sky. "I don't know. I'm not sure."

"It's not ahead," I said. "It's back."

His eyes took on a different color. It was a subtle shift, a flex, like a man stepping out from the shade of a tree into sunlight on a cloudy day.

"Back."

"Somewhere between two thousand and three thousand days, split half a day, give or take an hour, borrow or loan a minute, haggle over a second," I said.

"You really talk," he said.

"Compulsive," I said.

"You'd make a lousy writer," he said. "I never knew a writer yet was a good talker."

"That's my albatross," I said.

"Back?" He weighed the word.

"I'm turning the car around," I said. "And I'm going back down the road."

"Not miles but days?"

"Not miles but days."

"Is it that kind of car?"

"That's how it's built."

"You're an inventor then?"

"A reader who happens to invent."

"If the car works, that's some car you got there."

"At your service," I said.

"And when you get where you're going," said the old man, putting his hand on the door and leaning and then, seeing what he had done, taking his hand away and standing taller to speak to me, "where will you be?"

"January 10, 1954."

"That's quite a date," he said.

"It is, it was. It can be more of a date."

Without moving, his eyes took another step out into fuller light.

"And where will you be on that day?"

"Africa," I said.

He was silent. His mouth did not work. His eyes did not shift.

"Not far from Nairobi," I said.

He nodded, once, slowly.

"Africa, not far from Nairobi."

I waited.

"And when we get there, if we go?" he said.

"I leave you there."

"And then?"

"You stay there."

"And then?"

"That's all."

"That's all?"

"Forever," I said.

The old man breathed out and in, and ran his hand over the edge of the doorsill.

"This car," he said, "somewhere along the way does it turn into a plane?"

"I don't know," I said.

"Somewhere along the way do you turn into my pilot?"

"It could be. I've never done this before."

"But you're willing to try?"

I nodded.

"Why?" he said, and leaned in and stared me directly in the face with a terrible, quietly wild intensity. *"Why?"*

Old man, I thought, I can't tell you why. Don't ask me.

He withdrew, sensing he had gone too far.

"I didn't say that," he said.

"You didn't say it," I said.

"And when you bring the plane in for a forced landing," he said, "will you land a little differently this time?"

"Different, yes."

"A little harder?"

"I'll see what can be done."

"And will I be thrown out but the rest of you okay?"

"The odds are in favor."

He looked up at the hill where there was no grave. I looked at the same hill. And maybe he guessed the digging of it there.

He gazed back down the road at the mountains and the sea that could not be seen beyond the mountains and a continent beyond the sea. "That's a good day you're talking about."

"The best."

"And a good hour and a good second."

"Really, nothing better."

"Worth thinking about."

His hand lay on the doorsill, not leaning, but testing, feeling, touching, tremulous, undecided. But his eyes came full into the light of African noon.

"Yes."

"Yes?" I said.

"I think," he said, "I'll grab a lift with you."

I waited one heartbeat, then reached over and opened the door.

Silently he got in the front seat and sat there and quietly shut the door without slamming it. He sat there, very old and very tired. I waited. "Start her up," he said.

I started the engine and gentled it.

"Turn her around," he said.

I turned the car so it was going back on the road.

"Is this really," he said, "that kind of car?"

"Really, that kind of car."

He looked out at the land and the mountains and the distant house.

I waited, idling the motor.

"When we get there," he said, "will you remember something . . . ?"

"I'll try."

"There's a mountain," he said, and stopped and sat there, his mouth quiet, and he didn't go on.

But I went on for him. There is a mountain in Africa named Kilimanjaro, I thought. And on the western slope of that mountain was once found the dried and frozen carcass of a leopard. No one has ever explained what the leopard was seeking at that altitude.

We will put you up on that same slope, I thought, on Kilimanjaro, near the leopard, and write your name and under it say nobody knew what he was doing here so high, but here he is. And write the date born and died, and go away down toward the hot summer grass and let mainly dark warriors and white hunters and swift okapis know the grave.

The old man shaded his eyes, looking at the road winding away over the hills. He nodded.

"Let's go," he said.

"Yes, Papa," I said.

And we motored away, myself at the wheel, going slow, and the old man beside me, and as we went down the first hill and topped the next, the sun came out full and the wind smelled of fire. We ran like a lion in the long grass. Rivers and streams flashed by. I wished we might stop for one hour and wade and fish and lie by the stream frying the fish and talking or not talking. But if we stopped we might never go on again. I gunned the engine. It made a great fierce wondrous animal's roar. The old man grinned.

"It's going to be a great day!" he shouted.

"A great day."

Back on the road, I thought, How must it be now, and now, us disappearing? And now, us gone? And now, the road empty. Sun Valley quiet in the sun. What must it be, having us gone?

I had the car up to ninety.

We both yelled like boys.

After that I didn't know anything.

"By God," said the old man, toward the end. "You know? I think we're . . . flying?"

THE MAN IN
THE RORSCHACH SHIRT

Brokaw.

What a name!

Listen to it bark, growl, yip, hear the bold proclamation of:

Immanuel Brokaw!

A fine name for the greatest psychiatrist who ever tread the waters of existence without capsizing.

Toss a pepper-ground Freud casebook in the air and all students sneezed:

Brokaw!

What ever happened to him?

One day, like a high-class vaudeville act, he vanished.

With the spotlight out, his miracles seemed in danger of reversal. Psychotic rabbits threatened to leap back into hats. Smokes were sucked back into loud-powder gun muzzles. We all waited.

Silence for ten years. And more silence.

Brokaw was lost, as if he had thrown himself with shouts of laughter into mid-Atlantic. For what? To plumb for Moby-Dick? To psychoanalyze that colorless fiend and see what he really had against Mad Ahab?

Who knows?

I last saw him running for a twilight plane, his wife and six Pomeranian dogs yapping far behind him on the dusky field.

"Good-bye forever!"

His happy cry seemed a joke. But I found men flaking his gold-leaf name from his office door next day, as his great fat-women couches were hustled out into the raw weather toward some Third Avenue auction.

So the giant who had been Gandhi-Moses-Christ-Buddha-Freud all layered in one incredible Armenian dessert had dropped through a hole in the clouds. To die? To live in secret?

Ten years later I rode on a California bus along the lovely shores of Newport.

The bus stopped. A man in his seventies bounced on, jingling silver into the coin box like manna. I glanced up from the rear of the bus and gasped.

"Brokaw! By the saints!"

And with or without sanctification, there he stood. Reared up like God manifest, bearded, benevolent, pontifical, erudite, merry, accepting, forgiving, messianic, tutorial, forever and eternal . . .

Immanuel Brokaw.

But not in a dark suit, no.

Instead, as if they were vestments of some proud new church, he wore:

Bermuda shorts. Black leather Mexican sandals. A Los Angeles Dodgers' baseball cap. French sunglasses. And . . .

The shirt! Ah God! The shirt!

A wild thing, all lush creeper and live flytrap undergrowth, all Pop-Op dilation and contraction, full flowered and crammed at every interstice and crosshatch with mythological beasts and symbols!

Open at the neck, this vast shirt hung wind-whipped like a thousand flags from a parade of united but neurotic nations.

But now, Dr. Brokaw tilted his baseball cap, lifted his French sunglasses to survey the empty bus seats. Striding slowly down the aisle, he wheeled, he paused, he lingered, now here, now there. He whispered, he murmured, now to this man, this woman, that child.

I was about to cry out when I heard him say:

"Well, what do you make of it?"

A small boy, stunned by the circus-poster effect of the old man's attire, blinked, in need of nudging. The old man nudged:

"My *shirt*, boy! What do you *see*!?"

"Horses!" the child blurted, at last. "Dancing horses!"

"Bravo!" The doctor beamed, patted him, and strode on. "And you, sir?"

A young man, quite taken with the forthrightness of this invader from some summer world, said:

"Why . . . clouds, of course."

"Cumulus or nimbus?"

"Er . . . not storm clouds, no, no. Fleecy, sheep clouds."

"Well done!"

The psychiatrist plunged on.

"Mademoiselle?"

"Surfers!" A teen-age girl stared. "They're the waves, big ones. Surf-boards. Super!"

And so it went, on down the length of the bus and as the great man progressed a few scraps and titters of laughter sprang up, then, grown infectious, turned to roars of hilarity. By now, a dozen passengers had heard the first responses and so fell in with the game. This woman saw skyscrapers! The doctor scowled at her suspiciously. The doctor winked. That man saw crossword puzzles. The doctor shook his hand. This child found zebras all optical illusion on an African wild. The doctor slapped the animals and made them jump! This old woman saw vague Adams and misty Eves being driven from half-seen Gardens. The doctor scooched in on the seat with her awhile; they talked in fierce whispered elations, then up he jumped and forged on. Had the old woman seen an eviction? This young one saw the couple invited back in!

Dogs, lightnings, cats, cars, mushroom clouds, man-eating tiger lilies!

Each person, each response, brought greater outcries. We found ourselves all laughing together. This fine old man was a happening of nature, a caprice, God's rambunctious Will, sewing all our separateness up in one.

Elephants! Elevators! Alarums! Dooms!

When first he had bounded aboard we had wanted naught of each other. But now like an immense snowfall which we must gossip on or an electrical failure that blacked out two million homes and so thrown us all together in communal chat, laugh, guffaw, we felt the tears clean up our souls even as they cleaned down our cheeks.

Each answer seemed funnier than the previous, and no one shouted louder his great torments of laughter than this grand tall and marvelous physician who asked for, got, and cured us of our hairballs on the spot. Whales. Kelp. Grass meadows. Lost cities. Beauteous women. He paused. He wheeled. He sat. He rose. He flapped his wildly colored shirt, until at last he towered before me and said:

"Sir, what do you find?"

"Why, Dr. Brokaw, of course!"

The old man's laughter stopped as if he were shot. He seized his dark glasses off, then clapped them on and grabbed my shoulders as if to wrench me into focus.

"Simon Wincelaus, is that *you*?"

"Me, me!" I laughed. "Good grief, doctor, I thought you were dead and buried years ago. What's this you're up to?"

"Up to?" He squeezed and shook my hands and pummeled my arms and cheeks gently. Then he snorted a great self-forgiving laugh as he gazed down along the acreage of ridiculous shirting. "Up to? Retired. Swiftly gone. Overnight traveled three thousand miles from where last you saw me . . ." His peppermint breath warmed my face. "And now best known hereabouts as . . . listen! . . . the Man in the Rorschach Shirt."

"In the what?" I cried.

"Rorschach Shirt."

Light as a carnival gas balloon he touched into the seat beside me.

I sat stunned and silent.

We rode along by the blue sea under a bright summer sky.

The doctor gazed ahead as if reading my thoughts in vast skywriting among the clouds.

"Why, you ask, why? I see your face, startled, at the airport years ago. My Going Away Forever day. My plane should have been named the *Happy Titanic*. On it I sank forever into the traceless sky. Yet here I am in the absolute flesh, yes? Not drunk, nor mad, nor riven by age and retirement's boredom. Where, what, why, how come?"

"Yes," I said, "why *did* you retire, with everything pitched for you? Skill, reputation, money. Not a breath of—"

"Scandal? None! Why, then? Because, this old camel had not one but two humps broken by two straws. Two amazing straws. Hump Number One—"

He paused. He cast me a sidelong glance from under his dark glasses.

"This is a confessional," I said. "Mum's the word."

"Confessional. Yes. Thanks."

The bus hummed softly on the road.

His voice rose and fell with the hum.

"You know my photographic memory? Blessed, cursed, with total recall. Anything said, seen, done, touched, heard, can be snapped back to focus by me, forty, fifty, sixty years later. All, all of it, trapped in here."

He stroked his temples lightly with the fingers of both hands.

"Hundreds of psychiatric cases, delivered through my door, day after day, year on year. And never once did I check my notes on any of those sessions. I found, early on, I need only play back what I had heard inside my head. Sound tapes, of course, were kept as a double-check, but never listened to. There you have the stage set for the whole shocking business.

"One day in my sixtieth year a woman patient spoke a single word. I asked her to repeat it. Why? Suddenly I had felt my semicircular canals shift as if some valves had opened upon cool fresh air at a subterranean level.

"'Best,' she said.

"'I thought you said, 'beast,'" I said.

"'Oh, no, doctor, 'best.'"

"One word. One pebble dropped off the edge. And then—the avalanche. For, distinctly, I had heard her claim: 'He loved the beast in me,' which is one kettle of sexual fish, eh? When in reality she had said, 'He loved the best in me,' which is quite another pan of cold cod, you must agree.

"That night I could not sleep. I smoked, I stared from windows. My head, my ears, felt strangely clear, as if I had just gotten over a thirty years' cold. I suspected myself, my past, my senses, so at three in the deadfall morning I motored to my office and found the worst:

"The recalled conversations of hundreds of cases in my mind were not the same as those recorded on my tapes or typed out in my secretary's notes!"

"You mean . . . ?"

"I mean when I heard beast it was truly best. Dumb was really numb. Ox were cocks and vice-versa. I heard bed and someone had said head. Sleep was creep. Lay was day. Paws were really pause. Rump was merely jump. Fiend was only leaned. Sex was hex or mix or, God knows, *perplex*! Yes-mess. No-slow. Binge-hinge. Wrong-long. Side-hide. Name a name, I'd heard it wrong. Ten million dozen misheard nouns! I panicked through my files! Good Grief! Great Jumping Josie!

"All those years, those people! Holy Moses, Brokaw, I cried, all these years down from the Mount, the word of God like a flea in your ear. And now, late in the day, old wise one, you think to consult your lightning-scribbled stones. And find your Laws, your Tables, *different*!

"Moses fled his offices that night. I ran in dark, unraveling my despair. I trained to Far Rockaway, perhaps because of its lamenting name.

"I walked by a tumult of waves only equaled by the tumult in my breast. How? I cried, how can you have been half-deaf for a lifetime and not known it! And known it only now when through some fluke, the sense, the gift, returned, how, how?!

"My only answer was a great stroke of thunder wave upon the sands.

"So much for straw number one that broke Hump Number One of this odd-shaped human camel."

There was a moment of silence.

We rode swaying on the bus. The bus moved along the golden shore road, through a gentle breeze.

"Straw number two?" I asked, quietly, at last.

Dr. Brokaw held his French sunglasses up so sunlight struck fish-glitters all about the cavern of the bus. We watched the swimming rainbow patterns, he with detachment and at last half-amused concern.

"Sight. Vision. Texture. Detail. Aren't they miraculous. Aweful in the sense of meaning true awe? What is sight, vision, insight? Do we really want to see the world?"

"Oh, yes," I cried, promptly.

"A young man's unthinking answer. No, my dear boy, we do not. At twenty, yes, we think we wish to see, know, be all. So thought I once. But I have had weak eyes most of my life, spent half my days being fitted out with new specs by oculists, hee? Well, comes the dawn of the corneal lens! At last, I decided, I will fit myself with those bright little teardrop miracles, those invisible discs! Coincidence? Psychosomatic cause and effect? For, that same week I got my contact lenses was the week my hearing cleared up! There must be some physio-mental connection, but don't hazard me into an informed guess.

"All I know is I had my little crystal corneal lenses ground and installed upon my weak baby blue eyes and—*voilà!*

"There was the world!

"THERE were people!

"And there, God save us, was the dirt, and the multitudinous pores upon the people.

"Simon," he added, grieving gently, eyes shut for a moment behind his dark glasses, "have you ever thought, did you know, that people are for the most part pores?"

He let that sink in. I thought about it.

"Pores?" I said, at last.

"Pores! But who thinks of it? Who bothers to go look? But with my restored vision I saw! A thousand, a million, ten billion . . . pores. Large, small, pale, crimson . . . pores. Everyone and on everyone. People passing. People crowding buses, theaters, telephone booths, all pore and little substance. Small pores on tiny women. Big pores on monster men. Or vice versa. Pores as numerous as that foul dust which slides pell-mell down church-nave sunbeams late afternoons. Pores. They became my utter and riven fascination. I stared at fine ladies' complexions, not their eyes, mouths, or earlobes. Shouldn't a man watch a woman's skeleton hinge and unhinge itself within that sweet pincushion flesh? Yes! But no, I saw only cheese-grater, kitchen-sieve skins. All Beauty turned sour Grotesque. Swiveling my gaze was like swiveling the 200-inch Palomar telescope in my damned skull. Everywhere I looked I saw the meteor-bombarded moon, in dread super closeup!

"Myself? God, shaving mornings was exquisite torture. I could not pluck my eyes from my lost battle-pitted face. Damnation, Immanuel Brokaw, I soughed, you are the Grand Canyon at high noon, an orange with a billion navels, a pomegranate with the skin stripped off.

"In sum, my contact lenses had made me fifteen years old again. That is: festering, self-crucified bundle of doubt, horror, and absolute imperfection. The worst age in all one's life had returned to haunt me with its pimpled, bumpy ghost.

"I lay, a sleepless wreck. Ah, second Adolescence, take pity, I cried. How could I have been so blind, so many years? Blind, yes, and knew it, and always said it was of no importance. So I groped about the world as lustful myope, nearsightedly missing the holes, rips, tears, and bumps on others as well as myself. Now, Reality had run me down in the street. And the Reality was: Pores.

"I shut my eyes and went to bed for several days. Then I sat up in bed and proclaimed, wide-eyed: Reality is not all! I refuse this knowledge. I legislate against Pores! I accept instead those truths we intuit, or make up to live by.

"I traded in my eyeballs.

"That is I handed my corneal-contact lenses to a sadist nephew who thrives on garbages and lumpy people and hairy things.

"I clapped back on my old undercorrected specs. I strolled through a world of returned and gentle mists. I saw enough but not too much. I found half-discerned ghost peoples I could love again. I saw the 'me' in the morning glass I could once more bed with, admire and take as chum. I began to laugh each day with new happiness. Softly. Then, very loud.

"What a joke, Simon, life is.

"From vanity we buy lenses that see all and so lose everything!

"And by giving up some small bit-piece of so-called wisdom, reality, truth, we gain back an entirety of life! Who does not know this? Writers do! Intuited novels are far more 'true' than all your scribbled data-fact reportage in the history of the world!

"But then at last I had to face the great twin fractures lying athwart my conscience. My eyes. My ears. Holy Cow, I said, softly. The thousand folk who tread my offices and creaked my couches and looked for echoes in my Delphic Cave, why, why, preposterous! I had seen none of them, nor heard any clear!

"Who was that Miss Harbottle?

"What of old Dinsmuir?

"What was the real color, look, size of Miss Grimes?

"Did Mrs. Scrapwight really resemble and speak like an Egyptian papyrus mummy fallen out of a rug at my desk?

"I could not even guess. Two thousand days of fogs surrounded my lost children, mere voices calling, fading, gone.

"My God, I had wandered the marketplace with an invisible sign BLIND AND DEAF and people had rushed to fill my beggar's cup with coins and rush off cured. Cured! Isn't that miraculous, strange? Cured by an old ricket with one arm gone, as 'twere, and one leg missing. What? What did I say right to them out of hearing wrong? Who indeed were those people? I will never know.

"And then I thought: there are a hundred psychiatrists about town who see and hear more clearly than I. But whose patients walk naked into high seas or leap off playground slides at midnight or truss women up and smoke cigars over them.

"So I had to face the irreducible fact of a successful career.

"The lame do not lead the lame, my reason cried, the blind and halt do not cure the halt and the blind! But a voice from the far balcony of my soul replied with immense irony: Bee'swax and Bull-Durham! You, Immanuel Brokaw, are a porcelain genius, which means cracked but brilliant! Your occluded eyes see, your corked ears hear. Your fractured sensibilities cure at some level below consciousness! Bravo!

"But no, I could not live with my perfect imperfections. I could not understand nor tolerate this smug secret thing which, through screens and obfuscations, played meadow doctor to the world and cured field beasts.

"I had several choices then. Put my corneal lenses back in? Buy ear radios to help my rapidly improving sense of sound? And then? Find I had lost touch with my best and hidden mind which had grown comfortably accustomed to thirty years of bad vision and lousy hearing? Chaos for both curer and cured.

"Stay blind and deaf and work? It seemed a dreadful fraud, though my record was laundry-fresh, pressed white and clean.

"So I retired.

"Packed my bags and ran off into golden oblivion to let the incredible wax collect in my most terrible strange ears . . ."

We rode in the bus along the shore in the warm afternoon. A few clouds moved over the sun. Shadows misted on the sands and the people strewn on the sands under the colored umbrellas.

I cleared my throat.

"Will you ever return to practice again, doctor?"

"I practice now."

"But you just said—"

"Oh, not officially, and not with an office or fees, no, never that again." The doctor laughed quietly. "I am sore beset by the mystery anyway. That is, of how I cured all those people with a laying on of hands even though my arms were chopped off at the elbows. Still, now, I do keep my 'hand' in."

"How?"

"This shirt of mine. You saw. You heard."

"Coming down the aisle?"

"Exactly. The colors. The patterns. One thing to that man, another to the girl, a third to the boy. Zebras, goats, lightnings, Egyptian amulets. What, what, what? I ask. And: answer, answer, answer. The Man in the Rorschach Shirt.

"I have a dozen such shirts at home.

"All colors, all different pattern mixes. One was designed for me by Jackson Pollack before he died. I wear each shirt for a day, or a week, if the going, the answers, are thick, fast, full of excitement and reward. Then off with the old and on with the new. Ten billion glances, ten billion startled responds!

"Might I not market these Rorschach shirts to your psychoanalyst on vacation? Test your friends? Shock your neighbors? Titillate your wife? No, no. This is my own special private most dear fun. No one must share it. Me and my shirts, the sun, the bus, and a thousand afternoons ahead. The beach waits. And on it, my people!

"So I walk the shores of this summer world. There is no winter here, amazing, yes, no winter of discontent it would almost seem, and death a rumor beyond the dunes. I walk along in my own time and way and come on people and let the wind flap my great sailcloth shirt now veering north, south or south-by-west and watch their eyes pop, glide, leer, squint, wonder. And when a certain person says a certain word about my ink-slashed cotton colors I give pause. I chat. I walk with them awhile. We peer into the great glass of the sea. I sidewise peer into their soul. Sometimes we stroll for hours, a longish session with the weather. Usually it takes but that one day and, not knowing with whom they walked, scot-free, they are discharged all unwitting patients. They walk on down the dusky shore toward a fairer brighter eve. Behind their backs, the deaf-blind man waves them bon voyage and trots home there to devour happy suppers, brisk with fine work done.

"Or sometimes I meet some half-slumberer on the sand whose troubles cannot all be fetched out to die in the raw light of one day. Then, as by accident, we collide a week later and walk by the tidal churn doing what has always been done; we have our traveling confessional. For long before pent-up priests and whispers and repentances, friends walked, talked, listened, and in the listening-talk cured each other's sour despairs. Good friends trade hairballs all the time, give gifts of mutual dismays and so are rid of them.

"Trash collects on lawns and in minds. With bright shirt and nail-tipped trash stick I set out each dawn to . . . clean up the beaches. So many, oh, so many bodies lying out there in the light. So many minds lost in the dark. I try to walk among them all, without . . . stumbling . . ."

The wind blew in the bus window cool and fresh, making a sea of ripples through the thoughtful old man's patterned shirt.

The bus stopped.

Dr. Brokaw suddenly saw where he was and leaped up. "Wait!"

Everyone on the bus turned as if to watch the exit of a star performer. Everyone smiled.

Dr. Brokaw pumped my hand and ran. At the far front end of the bus he turned, amazed at his own forgetfulness, lifted his dark glasses and squinted at me with his weak baby-blue eyes.

"You—" he said.

Already, to him, I was a mist, a pointillist dream somewhere out beyond the rim of vision.

"You . . ." he called into that fabulous cloud of existence which surrounded and pressed him warm and close, "you never *told* me. What? *What?!*"

He stood tall to display that incredible Rorschach shirt which fluttered and swarmed with everchanging line and color.

I looked. I blinked. I answered.

"A sunrise!" I cried.

The doctor reeled with this gentle friendly blow.

"Are you sure it isn't a sunset?" he called, cupping one hand to his ear.

I looked again and smiled. I hoped he saw my smile a thousand miles away within the bus.

"No," I said. "A sunrise. A beautiful sunrise."

He shut his eyes to digest the words. His great hands wandered along the shore of his wind-gentled shirt. He nodded. Then he opened his pale eyes, waved once, and stepped out into the world.

The bus drove on. I looked back once.

And there went Dr. Brokaw advancing straight out and across a beach where lay a random sampling of the world, a thousand bathers in the warm light.

He seemed to tread lightly upon a water of people.

The last I saw of him, he was still gloriously afloat.

✳

BLESS ME, FATHER, FOR I HAVE SINNED

IT WAS JUST BEFORE MIDNIGHT on Christmas Eve when Father Mellon woke, having slept for only a few minutes. He had a most peculiar urge to rise, go, and swing wide the front door of his church to let the snow in and then go sit in the confessional to wait.

Wait for what? Who could say? Who might tell? But the urge was so incredibly strong it was not to be denied.

"What's going on here?" he muttered quietly to himself, as he dressed. "I am going mad, am I not? At this hour, who could possibly want or need, and why in blazes should I—"

But dress he did and down he went and opened wide the front door of the church and stood in awe of the great artwork beyond, better than any painting in history, a tapestry of snow weaving in laces and gentling to roofs and shadowing the lamps and putting shawls on the huddled masses of cars waiting to be blessed at the curb. The snow touched the pavements and then his eyelids and then his heart. He found himself holding his breath with the fickle beauties and then, turning, the snow following at his back, he went to hide in the confessional.

Damn fool, he thought. Stupid old man. *Out* of here! Back to your bed!

But then he heard it; a sound at the door, and footsteps scraping on the pavestones of the church, and at last the damp rustle of some invader fresh to the other side of the confessional. Father Mellon waited.

"Bless me," a man's voice whispered, "for I have sinned!"

Stunned at the quickness of this asking, Father Mellon could only retort:

"How *could* you know the church would be open and I here?"

"I prayed, Father," was the quiet reply. "God *made* you come open up."

There seemed no answer to this, so the old priest, and what sounded like a hoarse old sinner, sat for a long cold moment as the clock itched on toward midnight, and at last the refugee from darkness repeated:

"*Bless* this sinner, Father!"

But in place of the usual unguents and ointments of words, with Christmas hurrying fast through the snow, Father Mellon leaned toward the lattice window and could not help saying:

"It must be a terrible load of sin you carry to have driven you out on such a night on an impossible mission that turned possible only because God heard and pushed me out of bed."

"It *is* a terrible list, Father, as you will find!"

"Then speak, son," said the priest, "before we both freeze—"

"Well, it was this way—" whispered the wintry voice behind the thin paneling. "—Sixty years back—"

"Speak up! Sixty?!" The priest gasped. "That *long* past?"

"Sixty!" And there was a tormented silence.

"Go on," said the priest, ashamed of interrupting.

"Sixty years this week, when I was twelve," said the gray voice, "I Christmas-shopped with my grandmother in a small town back East. We walked both ways. In those days, who had a car? We walked, and coming home with the wrapped gifts, my grandma said something, I've long since forgotten what, and I got mad and ran ahead, away from her. Far off, I could hear her call and then cry, terribly, for me to come back, come back, but I wouldn't. She wailed so, I knew I had hurt her, which made me feel strong and good, so I ran even more, laughing, and beat her to the house and when she came in she was gasping and weeping as if never to stop. I felt ashamed and ran to hide . . ."

There was a long silence.

The priest prompted, "Is that it?"

"The list is long," mourned the voice beyond the thin panel.

"Continue," said the priest, eyes shut.

"I did much the same to my mother, before New Year's. She angered me. I ran. I heard her cry out behind me. I smiled and ran faster. Why? Why, oh God, why?"

The priest had no answer.

"Is that it, then?" he murmured, at last, feeling strangely moved toward the old man beyond.

"One summer day," said the voice, "some bullies beat me. When they were gone, on a bush I saw two butterflies, embraced, lovely. I hated their happiness. I grabbed them in my fist and pulverized them to dust. Oh, Father, the shame!"

The wind blew in the church door at that moment and both of them glanced up to see a Christmas ghost of snow turned about in the door and falling away in drifts of whiteness to scatter on the pavings.

"There's one last terrible thing," said the old man, hidden away with his grief. And then he said:

"When I was thirteen, again in Christmas week, my dog Bo ran away and was lost three days and nights. I loved him more than life itself. He was special and loving and fine. And all of a sudden the beast was gone, and all his beauty with him. I waited. I cried. I waited. I prayed. I shouted under my breath. I knew he would never, never come back! And then, oh, then, that Christmas Eve at two in the morning, with sleet on the pavements and icicles on roofs and snow falling, I heard a sound in my sleep and woke to hear him scratching the door! I bounded from bed so fast I almost killed myself! I yanked the door open and there was my miserable dog, shivering, excited, covered with dirty slush. I yelled, pulled him in, slammed the door, fell to my knees, grabbed him and wept. What a gift, what a gift! I called his name over and over, and he wept with me, all whines and agonies of joy. And then I stopped. Do you know what I did then? Can you guess the terrible thing? I beat him. Yes, beat him. With my fists, my hands, my palms, and my fists again, crying: how dare you leave, how dare you run off, how dare you do that to me, how dare you, how dare!? And I beat and beat until I was weak and sobbed and had to stop for I saw what I'd done, and he just stood and took it all as if he knew he deserved it, he had failed my love and now I was failing his, and I pulled off and tears streamed from my eyes, my breath strangled, and I grabbed him again and crushed him to me but this time cried: forgive, oh please, Bo, forgive. I didn't mean it. Oh, Bo, forgive . . .

"But, oh, Father, he couldn't forgive me. Who was he? A beast, an animal, a dog, my love. And he looked at me with such great dark eyes that it locked my heart and it's been locked forever after with shame. I could not then forgive myself. All these years, the memory of my love and how I failed him, and every Christmas since, not the rest of the year, but every Christmas Eve, his ghost comes back, I see the dog, I hear the beating, I know my failure. Oh, God!"

The man fell silent, weeping.

And at last the old priest dared a word: "And that is why you are here?"

"Yes, Father. Isn't it awful? Isn't it terrible?"

The priest could not answer, for tears were streaming down his face, too, and he found himself unaccountably short of breath.

"Will God forgive me, Father?" asked the other.

"Yes."

"Will you forgive me, Father?"

"Yes. But let me tell you something now, son. When I was ten, the same things happened. My parents, of course, but then—my dog, the love of my life, who ran off and I hated him for leaving me, and when he came back I, too, loved and beat him, then went back to love. Until this night, I have told no one. The shame has stayed put all these years. I have confessed all to my priest-confessor. But never that. So—"

There was a pause.

"So, Father?"

"Lord, Lord, dear man, God will forgive us. At long last, we have brought it out, dared to say. And I, I will forgive you. But finally—"

The old priest could not go on, for new tears were really pouring down his face now.

The stranger on the other side guessed this and very carefully inquired, "Do you want my forgiveness, Father?"

The priest nodded, silently. Perhaps the other felt the shadow of the nod, for he quickly said, "Ah, well. It's *given*."

And they both sat there for a long moment in the dark and another ghost moved to stand in the door, then sank to snow and drifted away.

"Before you go," said the priest, "come share a glass of wine."

The great clock in the square across from the church struck midnight.

"It's Christmas, Father," said the voice from behind the panel.

"The finest Christmas ever, I think."

"The finest."

The old priest rose and stepped out.

He waited a moment for some stir, some movement from the opposite side of the confessional.

There was no sound.

Frowning, the priest reached out and opened the confessional door and peered into the cubicle.

There was nothing and no one there.

His jaw dropped. Snow moved along the back of his neck.

He put his hand out to feel the darkness.

The place was empty.

Turning, he stared at the entry door, and hurried over to look out.

Snow fell in the last tones of far clocks late-sounding the hour. The streets were deserted.

Turning again, he saw the tall mirror that stood in the church entry.

There was an old man, himself, reflected in the cold glass.

Almost without thinking, he raised his hand and made the sign of blessing. The reflection in the mirror did likewise.

Then the old priest, wiping his eyes, turned a last time, and went to find the wine.

Outside, Christmas, like the snow, was everywhere.

THE PEDESTRIAN

To ENTER OUT INTO THAT SILENCE that was the city at eight o'clock of a misty evening in November, to put your feet upon that buckling concrete walk, to step over grassy seams and make your way, hands in pockets, through the silences, that was what Mr. Leonard Mead most dearly loved to do. He would stand upon the corner of an intersection and peer down long moonlit avenues of sidewalk in four directions, deciding which way to go, but it really made no difference; he was alone in this world of A.D. 2053, or as good as alone, and with a final decision made, a path selected, he would stride off, sending patterns of frosty air before him like the smoke of a cigar.

Sometimes he would walk for hours and miles and return only at midnight to his house. And on his way he would see the cottages and homes with their dark windows, and it was not unequal to walking through a graveyard where only the faintest glimmers of firefly light appeared in flickers behind the windows. Sudden gray phantoms seemed to manifest upon inner room walls where a curtain was still undrawn against the night, or there were whisperings and murmurs where a window in a tomb-like building was still open.

Mr. Leonard Mead would pause, cock his head, listen, look, and march on, his feet making no noise on the lumpy walk. For long ago he had wisely changed to sneakers when strolling at night, because the dogs in intermittent squads would parallel his journey with barkings if he wore hard heels, and lights might click on and faces appear and an entire street be startled by the passing of a lone figure, himself, in the early November evening.

On this particular evening he began his journey in a westerly direction, toward the hidden sea. There was a good crystal frost in the air; it cut the nose and made the lungs blaze like a Christmas tree inside; you could feel the cold light going on and off, all the branches filled with invisible snow. He listened to the faint push of his soft shoes through autumn leaves with satisfaction, and whistled a cold quiet whistle between his teeth, occasionally picking up a leaf as he passed, examining its skeletal pattern in the infrequent lamplights as he went on, smelling its rusty smell.

"Hello, in there," he whispered to every house on every side as he moved. "What's up tonight on Channel 4, Channel 7, Channel 9? Where are the cowboys rushing, and do I see the United States Cavalry over the next hill to the rescue?"

The street was silent and long and empty, with only his shadow moving like the shadow of a hawk in midcountry. If he closed his eyes and stood very still, frozen, he could imagine himself upon the center of a plain, a wintry, windless American desert with no house in a thousand miles, and only dry riverbeds, the streets, for company.

"What is it now?" he asked the houses, noticing his wrist watch. "Eight-thirty P.M.? Time for a dozen assorted murders? A quiz? A revue? A comedian falling off the stage?"

Was that a murmur of laughter from within a moon-white house? He hesitated, but went on when nothing more happened. He stumbled over a particularly uneven section of sidewalk. The cement was vanishing under flowers and grass. In ten years of walking by night or day, for thousands of miles, he had never met another person walking, not once in all that time.

He came to a cloverleaf intersection which stood silent where two main highways crossed the town. During the day it was a thunderous surge of cars, the gas stations open, a great insect rustling and a ceaseless jockeying for position as the scarab-beetles, a faint incense puttering from their exhausts, skimmed homeward to the far directions. But now these highways, too, were like streams in a dry season, all stone and bed and moon radiance.

He turned back on a side street, circling around toward his home. He was within a block of his destination when the lone car turned a corner quite suddenly and flashed a fierce white cone of light upon him. He stood entranced, not unlike a night moth, stunned by the illumination, and then drawn toward it.

A metallic voice called to him:

"Stand still. Stay where you are! Don't move!"

He halted.

"Put up your hands!"

"But—" he said.

"Your hands up! Or we'll shoot!"

The police, of course, but what a rare, incredible thing; in a city of three million, there was only *one* police car left, wasn't that correct? Ever since a year ago, 2052, the election year, the force had been cut down from three cars to one. Crime was ebbing; there was no need now for the police, save for this one lone car wandering and wandering the empty streets.

"Your name?" said the police car in a metallic whisper. He couldn't see the men in it for the bright light in his eyes.

"Leonard Mead," he said.

"Speak up!"

"Leonard Mead!"

"Business or profession?"

"I guess you'd call me a writer."

"No profession," said the police car, as if talking to itself. The light held him fixed, like a museum specimen, needle thrust through chest.

"You might say that," said Mr. Mead. He hadn't written in years. Magazines and books didn't sell anymore. Everything went on in the tomblike houses at night now, he thought, continuing his fancy. The tombs, ill-lit by television light, where the people sat like the dead, the gray or multicolored lights touching their faces, but never really touching *them*.

"No profession," said the phonograph voice, hissing. "What are you doing out?"

"Walking," said Leonard Mead.

"Walking!"

"Just walking," he said simply, but his face felt cold.

"Walking, just walking, walking?"

"Yes, sir."

"Walking where? For what?"

"Walking for air. Walking to see."

"Your address!"

"Eleven South Saint James Street."

"And there is air *in* your house, you have an *air conditioner*, Mr. Mead?"

"Yes."

"And you have a viewing screen in your house to see with?"

"No."

"No?" There was a crackling quiet that in itself was an accusation.

"Are you married, Mr. Mead?"

"No."

"Not married," said the police voice behind the fiery beam. The moon was high and clear among the stars and the houses were gray and silent.

"Nobody wanted me," said Leonard Mead with a smile.

"Don't speak unless you're spoken to!"

Leonard Mead waited in the cold night.

"Just *walking*, Mr. Mead?"

"Yes."

"But you haven't explained for what purpose."

"I explained; for air, and to see, and just to walk."

"Have you done this often?"

"Every night for years."

The police car sat in the center of the street with its radio throat faintly humming.

"Well, Mr. Mead," it said.

"Is that all?" he asked politely.

"Yes," said the voice. "Here." There was a sigh, a pop. The back door of the police car sprang wide. "Get in."

"Wait a minute, I haven't done anything!"

"Get in."

"I protest!"

"Mr. Mead."

He walked like a man suddenly drunk. As he passed the front window of the car he looked in. As he had expected there was no one in the front seat, no one in the car at all.

"Get in."

He put his hand to the door and peered into the back seat, which was a little cell, a little black jail with bars. It smelled of riveted steel. It smelled of harsh antiseptic; it smelled too clean and hard and metallic. There was nothing soft there.

"Now if you had a wife to give you an alibi," said the iron voice. "But—"

"Where are you taking me?"

The car hesitated, or rather gave a faint whirring click, as if information, somewhere, was dropping card by punch-slotted card under electric eyes. "To the Psychiatric Center for Research on Regressive Tendencies."

He got in. The door shut with a soft thud. The police car rolled through the night avenues, flashing its dim lights ahead.

They passed one house on one street a moment later, one house in an entire city of houses that were dark, but this one particular house had all of its electric lights brightly lit, every window a loud yellow illumination, square and warm in the cool darkness.

"That's my house," said Leonard Mead.

No one answered him.

The car moved down the empty riverbed streets and off away, leaving the empty streets with the empty sidewalks, and no sound and no motion all the rest of the chill November night.

TRAPDOOR

CLARA PECK HAD LIVED IN THE OLD HOUSE for some ten years before she made the strange discovery. Halfway upstairs to the second floor, on the landing, in the ceiling—

The trapdoor.

"Well, my God!"

She stopped dead, midstairs, to glare at the surprise, daring it to be true.

"It can't be! How could I have been so blind? Good grief, there's an *attic* in my house!"

She had marched up and downstairs a thousand times on a thousand days and never *seen*.

"Damned old fool."

And she almost tripped going down, having forgotten what she had come up for in the first place.

Before lunch, she arrived to stand under the trapdoor again, like a tall, thin, nervous child with pale hair and cheeks, her too-bright eyes darting, fixing, staring.

"Now I've discovered the damn thing, what do I *do* with it? Storage room up there, I bet. Well—"

And she went away, vaguely troubled, feeling her mind slipping off out of the sun.

"To hell with that, Clara Peck!" she said, vacuuming the parlor. "You're only fifty-seven. Not senile, yet, by God!"

But still, why hadn't she *noticed*?

It was the quality of the silence, that was it. Her roof had never leaked, so no water had ever tapped the ceilings; the high beams had never shifted in any wind, and there were no mice. If the rain had whispered, or the beams groaned, or the mice danced in her attic, she would have glanced up and *found* the trapdoor.

But the house had stayed silent, and she had stayed blind.

"Bosh!" she cried, at supper. She finished the dishes, read until ten, went to bed early.

It was during that night that she heard the first, faint, Morse-code tapping, the first graffiti-scratching above, behind the blank ceiling's pale, lunar face.

Half asleep, her lips whispered: Mouse?

And then it was dawn.

✳ Going downstairs to fix breakfast, she fixed the trapdoor with her steady, small-girl's stare and felt her skinny fingers twitch to go fetch the stepladder.

"Hell," she muttered. "Why bother to look at an empty attic? Next week, maybe."

For about three days after that, the trapdoor vanished.

That is, she forgot to look at it. So it might as well not have been there.

But around midnight on the third night, she heard the mouse sounds or the whatever-they-were sounds drifting across her bedroom ceiling like milkweed ghosts touching the lost surfaces of the moon.

From that odd thought she shifted to tumbleweeds or dandelion seeds or just plain dust shaken from an attic sill.

She thought of sleep, but the thought didn't take.

Lying flat in her bed, she watched the ceiling so fixedly she felt she could x-ray whatever it was that cavorted behind the plaster.

A flea circus? A tribe of gypsy mice in exodus from a neighbor's house? Several had been shrouded, recently, to look like dark circus tents, so that pest-killers could toss in killer bombs and run off to let the secret life in the places die.

That secret life had most probably packed its fur luggage and fled. Clara Peck's boarding house attic, free meals, was their new home away from home.

And yet. . . .

As she stared, the sounds began again. They shaped themselves into patterns across the wide ceiling's brow; long fingernails that, scraping, wandered to this corner and that of the shut-away chamber above.

Clara Peck held her breath.

The patterns increased. The soft prowlings began to cluster toward an area above and beyond her bedroom door. It was as if the tiny creatures, whatever they were, were nuzzling another secret door, above, wanting out.

Slowly, Clara Peck sat up in bed, and slowly put her weight to the floor, not wanting it to creak. Slowly she cracked her bedroom door. She peered out into a hall flooded with cold light from a full moon, which poured through the landing window to show her—

The trapdoor.

Now, as if summoned by her warmth, the sounds of the tiny lost ghost feet above rushed to cluster and fret at the trapdoor rim itself.

Christ! thought Clara Peck. They *hear* me. They want me to—

The trapdoor shuddered gently with the tiny rocking weights of whatever it was arustle there.

And more and more of the invisible spider feet or rodent feet of the blown curls of old and yellowed newspapers touched and rustled the wooden frame.

Louder, and still louder.

Clara was about to cry: Go! Git!

When the phone rang.

"Gah!" gasped Clara Peck.

She felt a ton of blood plunge like a broken weight down her frame to crush her toes.

"Gah!"

She ran to seize, lift and strangle the phone.

"Who!?" she cried.

"Clara! It's Emma Crowley! What's *wrong?!*"

"My God!" shouted Clara. "You scared the hell out of me! Emma, why are you calling this late?"

There was a long silence as the woman across town found her own breath.

"It's silly, I couldn't sleep. I had this hunch—"

"Emma—"

"No, let me finish. All of a sudden I thought, Clara's not well, or Clara's hurt, or—"

Clara Peck sank to the edge of the bed, the weight of Emma's voice pulling her down. Eyes shut, she nodded.

"Clara," said Emma, a thousand miles off, "you—all *right*?"

"All right," said Clara, at last.

"Not sick? House ain't on fire?"

"No, no. No."

"Thank God. Silly me. Forgive?"

"Forgiven."

"Well, then . . . good night."

And Emma Crowley hung up.

Clara Peck sat looking at the receiver for a full minute, listening to the signal that said that someone had gone away, and then at last placed the phone blindly back in its cradle.

She went back out to look up at the trapdoor.

It was quiet. Only a pattern of leaves, from the window, flickered and tossed on its wooden frame.

Clara blinked at the trapdoor.

"Think you're *smart*, don't you?" she said.

There were no more prowls, dances, murmurs or mouse-pavanes for the rest of that night.

✳ The sounds returned, three nights later, and they were—*larger*.

"Not *mice*," said Clara Peck. "Good-sized *rats*. Eh?"

In answer, the ceiling above executed an intricate crosscurrenting ballet, without music. This toe dancing, of a most peculiar sort, continued until the moon sank. Then, as soon as the light failed, the house grew silent and only Clara Peck took up breathing and life, again.

By the end of the week, the patterns were more geometrical. The sounds echoed in every upstairs room; the sewing room, the old bedroom, and in the library where some former occupant had once turned pages and gazed over a sea of chestnut trees.

On the tenth night, all eyes and no face, with the sounds coming in drumbeats and weird syncopations, at three in the morning, Clara Peck flung her sweaty hand at the telephone to dial Emma Crowley:

"Clara! I *knew* you'd call!"

"Emma, it's three A.M. Aren't you surprised?"

"No, I been lying here thinking of you. I wanted to call, but felt a fool. Something *is* wrong, yes?"

"Emma, answer me this. If a house has an empty attic for years, and all of a sudden has an attic *full* of things, *how come?*"

"I didn't know you *had* an attic—"

"Who *did?* Listen, what started as mice then sounded like rats and now sounds like cats running around up there. What'll I do?"

"The telephone number of the Ratzaway Pest Team on Main Street is— wait. Here. MAIN seven-seven-nine-nine. You *sure* something's *in* your attic?"

"The whole damned high school track team."

"Who used to live in your house, Clara?"

"Who—"

"I mean, it's been clean all this time, right, and now, well, *infested.* Anyone ever *die* there?"

"Die?"

"Sure, if someone died there, maybe you haven't got mice, at *all.*"

"You trying to tell me—ghosts?"

"Don't you believe—"

"Ghosts, or so-called friends who try spooking me with them. Don't call again, Emma!"

"But, *you* called *me!*"

"Hang up, Emma!!"

Emma Crowley hung up.

In the hall at three fifteen in the cold morning, Clara Peck glided out, stood for a moment, then pointed up at the ceiling, as if to provoke it.

"Ghosts?" she whispered.

The trapdoor's hinges, lost in the night above, oiled themselves with wind.

Clara Peck turned slowly and went back, and thinking about every movement, got into bed.

She woke at four twenty in the morning because a wind shook the house.

Out in the hall, could it be?

She strained. She tuned her ears.

Very softly, very quietly, the trapdoor in the stairwell ceiling squealed. And opened wide.

Can't be! she thought.

The door fell up, in, and down, with a thud.

Is! she thought.

I'll go make sure, she thought.

No!

She jumped, ran, locked the door, leaped back in bed.

"Hello, Ratzaway!" she heard herself call, muffled, under the covers.

✳ Going downstairs, sleepless, at six in the morning, she kept her eyes straight ahead, so as not to see that dreadful ceiling.

Halfway down she glanced back, started, and laughed.

"Silly!" she cried.

For the trapdoor was not open at all.

It was shut.

"Ratzaway?" she said, into the telephone receiver, at seven thirty on a bright morning.

✳ It was noon when the Ratzaway inspection truck stopped in front of Clara Peck's house.

In the way that Mr. Timmons, the young inspector, strolled with insolent disdain up the walk, Clara saw that he knew everything in the world about mice, termites, old maids, and odd late-night sounds. Moving, he glanced around at the world with that fine masculine hauteur of the bullfighter midring or the skydiver fresh from the sky, or the womanizer lighting his cigarette, back turned to the poor creature in the bed behind him. As he pressed her doorbell, he was God's messenger. When Clara opened the door she almost slammed it for the way his eyes peeled away her dress, her flesh, her thoughts. His smile was the alcoholic's smile. He was drunk on himself. There was only one thing to do:

"Don't just stand there!" she shouted. "Make yourself useful!" She spun around and marched away from his shocked face.

She glanced back to see if it had had the right effect. Very few women had ever talked this way to him. He was studying the door. Then, curious, he stepped in.

"This way!" said Clara.

She paraded through the hall, up the steps to the landing, where she had placed a metal stepladder. She thrust her hand up, pointing.

"There's the attic. See if you can make sense out of the damned noises up there. And don't overcharge me when you're done. Wipe your feet when you come down. I got to go shopping. Can I trust you not to steal me blind while I'm gone?"

With each blow, she could see him veer off balance. His face flushed. His eyes shone. Before he could speak, she marched back down the steps to shrug on a light coat.

"Do you know what mice sound like in attics?" she said, over her shoulder.

"I damn well do, lady," he said.

"Clean up your language. You know rats? These could be rats or bigger. What's bigger in an attic?"

"You got any raccoons around here?" he said.

"How'd they get in?"

"Don't you know your own house, lady? I—"

But here they both stopped.

For a sound had come from above.

It was a small itch of a sound at first. Then it scratched. Then it gave a thump like a heart.

Something moved in the attic.

Timmons blinked up at the shut trapdoor and snorted.

"Hey!"

Clara Peck nodded, satisfied, pulled on her gloves, adjusted her hat, watching.

"It sounds like—" drawled Mr. Timmons.

"Yes?"

"Did a sea captain ever live in this house?" he asked, at last.

The sound came again, louder. The whole house seemed to drift and whine with the weight which was shifted above.

"Sounds like cargo." Timmons shut his eyes to listen. "Cargo on a ship, sliding when the ship changes course." He broke into a laugh and opened his eyes.

"Good God," said Clara, and tried to imagine that.

"On the other hand," said Mr. Timmons, half-smiling up at that ceiling, "you got a greenhouse up there, or something? Sounds like plants growing. Or a yeast, maybe, big as a doghouse, getting out of hand. I heard of a man once, raised yeast in his cellar. It—"

The front screen door slammed.

Clara Peck, outside glaring in at his jokes, said:

"I'll be back in an hour. Jump!"

She heard his laughter follow her down the walk as she marched. She hesitated only once to look back.

The damn fool was standing at the foot of the ladder, looking up. Then he shrugged, gave a what-the-hell gesture with his hands, and—

Scrambled up the stepladder like a sailor.

✳ When Clara Peck marched back an hour later, the Ratzaway truck still stood silent at the curb.

"Hell," she said to it. "Thought he'd be done by now. Strange man tromping around, swearing—"

She stopped and listened to the house.

Silence.

"Odd," she muttered.

"Mr. Timmons!?" she called.

And realizing she was still twenty feet from the open front door, she approached to call through the screen.

"Anyone *home?*"

She stepped through the door into a silence like the silence in the old days before the mice had begun to change to rats and the rats had danced themselves into something larger and darker on the upper attic decks. It was a silence that, if you breathed it in, smothered you.

She swayed at the bottom of the flight of stairs, gazing up, her groceries hugged like a dead child in her arms.

"Mr. Timmons—?"

But the entire house was still.

The portable ladder still stood waiting on the landing.

But the trapdoor was shut.

Well, he's *obviously* not up in there! she thought. He wouldn't climb and shut himself in. Damn fool's just gone away.

She turned to squint out at his truck abandoned in the bright noon's glare.

Truck's broke down, I imagine. He's gone for help.

She dumped her groceries in the kitchen and for the first time in years, not knowing why, lit a cigarette, smoked it, lit another, and made a loud lunch, banging skillets and running the can opener overtime.

The house listened to all this, and made no response.

By two o'clock the silence hung about her like a cloud of floor polish.

"Ratzaway," she said, as she dialed the phone.

The Pest Team owner arrived half an hour later, by motorcycle, to pick up the abandoned truck. Tipping his cap, he stepped in through the screen door to chat with Clara Peck and look at the empty rooms and weigh the silence.

"No sweat, ma'am," he said, at last. "Charlie's been on a few benders, lately. He'll show up to be fired, tomorrow. What was he *doing* here?"

With this, he glanced up the stairs at the stepladder.

"Oh," said Clara Peck, quickly, "he was just looking at—everything."

"I'll come, myself, tomorrow," said the owner.

And as he drove away in the afternoon, Clara Peck slowly moved up the stairs to lift her face toward the ceiling and watch the trapdoor.

"*He* didn't see you, *either*," she whispered.

Not a beam stirred, not a mouse danced, in the attic.

She stood like a statue, feeling the sunlight shift and lean through the front door.

Why? she wondered. Why did I lie?

Well, for one thing, the trapdoor's shut, isn't it?

And, I don't know why, she thought, but I won't want anyone going up that ladder, ever again. Isn't that silly? Isn't that strange?

✳ She ate dinner early, listening.

She washed the dishes, alert.

She put herself to bed at ten o'clock, but in the old downstairs maid's room, for long years unused. Why she chose to lie in this downstairs room, she did not know, she simply did it, and lay there with aching ears, and the pulse moving in her neck and in her brow.

Rigid as a tomb carving under the sheet, she waited.

Around midnight, a wind passed, shook a pattern of leaves on her counterpane. Her eyes flicked wide.

The beams of the house trembled.

She lifted her head.

Something whispered ever so softly in the attic.

She sat up.

The sound grew louder, heavier, like a large but shapeless animal, prowling the attic dark.

She placed her feet on the floor and sat looking at them. The noise came again, far up, a scramble like rabbits' feet here, a thump like a large heart there.

THE SWAN

AND OUT THERE IN THE MIDDLE of the first day of August, just getting into his car, was Bill Forrester, who shouted he was going downtown for some extraordinary ice cream or other and would anyone join him? So, not five minutes later, jiggled and steamed into a better mood, Douglas found himself stepping in off the fiery pavements and moving through the grotto of soda-scented air, of vanilla freshness at the drugstore, to sit at the snow-marble fountain with Bill Forrester. They then asked for a recital of the most unusual ices and when the fountain man said, "Old fashioned lime-vanilla ice . . ."

"That's it!" said Bill Forrester.

"Yes, sir!" said Douglas.

And, while waiting, they turned slowly on their rotating stools. The silver spigots, the gleaming mirrors, the hushed whirl-around ceiling fans, the green shades over the small windows, the harp-wire chairs, passed under their moving gaze. They stopped turning. Their eyes had touched upon the face and form of Miss Helen Loomis, ninety-five years old, ice-cream spoon in hand, ice cream in mouth.

"Young man," she said to Bill Forrester, "you are a person of taste and imagination. Also, you have the will power of ten men; otherwise you would not dare veer away from the common flavors listed on the menu and order, straight out, without quibble or reservation, such an unheard-of thing as lime-vanilla ice."

He bowed his head solemnly to her.

"Come sit with me, both of you," she said. "We'll talk of strange ice creams and such things as we seem to have a bent for. Don't be afraid; I'll foot the bill."

Smiling, they carried their dishes to her table and sat.

"You look like a Spaulding," she said to the boy. "You've got your grandfather's head. And you, you're William Forrester. You write for the

Chronicle, a good enough column. I've heard more about you than I'd care to tell."

"I know you," said Bill Forrester. "You're Helen Loomis." He hesitated, then continued. "I was in love with you once," he said.

"Now that's the way I like a conversation to open." She dug quietly at her ice cream. "That's grounds for another meeting. No—don't tell me where or when or how you were in love with me. We'll save that for next time. You've taken away my appetite with your talk. Look there now! Well, I must get home anyway. Since you're a reporter, come for tea tomorrow between three and four; it's just possible I can sketch out the history of this town, since it was a trading post, for you. And, so we'll both have something for our curiosity to chew on, Mr. Forrester, you remind me of a gentleman I went with seventy, yes, seventy years ago."

She sat across from them and it was like talking with a gray and lost quivering moth. The voice came from far away inside the grayness and the oldness, wrapped in the powders of pressed flowers and ancient butterflies.

"Well." She arose. "Will you come tomorrow?"

"I most certainly will," said Bill Forrester.

And she went off into the town on business, leaving the young boy and the young man there, looking after her, slowly finishing their ice cream.

✳ William Forrester spent the next morning checking some local news items for the paper, had time after lunch for some fishing in the river outside town, caught only some small fish which he threw back happily, and, without thinking about it, or at least not noticing that he had thought about it, at three o'clock he found his car taking him down a certain street. He watched with interest as his hands turned the steering wheel and motored him up a vast circular drive where he stopped under an ivy-covered entry. Letting himself out, he was conscious of the fact that his car was like his pipe—old, chewed-on, unkempt in this huge green garden by this freshly painted, three-story Victorian house. He saw a faint ghostlike movement at the far end of the garden, heard a whispery cry, and saw that Miss Loomis was there, removed across time and distance, seated alone, the tea service glittering its soft silver surfaces, waiting for him.

"This is the first time a woman has ever been ready and waiting," he said, walking up. "It is also," he admitted, "the first time in my life I have been on time for an appointment."

"Why is that?" she asked, propped back in her wicker chair.

"I don't know," he admitted.

"Well." She started pouring tea. "To start things off, what do you think of the world?"

"I don't know anything."

"The beginning of wisdom, as they say. When you're seventeen you know everything. When you're twenty-seven if you still know everything you're still seventeen."

"You seem to have learned quite a lot over the years."

"It is the privilege of old people to seem to know everything. But it's an act and a mask, like every other act and mask. Between ourselves, we old ones wink at each other and smile, saying, How do you like my mask, my act, my certainty? Isn't life a play? Don't I play it well?"

They both laughed quietly. He sat back and let the laughter come naturally from his mouth for the first time in many months. When they quieted she held her teacup in her two hands and looked into it. "Do you know, it's lucky we met so late. I wouldn't have wanted you to meet me when I was twenty-one and full of foolishness."

"They have special laws for pretty girls twenty-one."

"So you think I was pretty?"

He nodded good-humoredly.

"But how can you tell?" she asked. "When you meet a dragon that has eaten a swan, do you guess by the few feathers left around the mouth? That's what it is—a body like this is a dragon, all scales and folds. So the dragon ate the white swan. I haven't seen her for years. I can't even remember what she looks like. I feel her, though. She's safe inside, still alive; the essential swan hasn't changed a feather. Do you know, there are some mornings in spring or fall, when I wake and think, I'll run across the fields into the woods and pick wild strawberries! Or I'll swim in the lake, or I'll dance all night tonight until dawn! And then, in a rage, discover I'm in this old and ruined dragon. I'm the princess in the crumbled tower, no way out, waiting for her Prince Charming."

"You should have written books."

"My dear boy, I have written. What else was there for an old maid? I was a crazy creature with a headful of carnival spangles until I was thirty, and then the only man I ever really cared for stopped waiting and married someone else. So in spite, in anger at myself, I told myself I deserved my fate for not having married when the best chance was at hand. I started traveling. My luggage was snowed under blizzards of travel stickers. I have been alone in Paris, alone in Vienna, alone in London, and all in all, it is very much like being alone in Green Town, Illinois. It is, in essence, being alone. Oh, you have plenty of time to think, improve your manners, sharpen your conversations. But I sometimes think I could easily trade a verb tense or a curtsy for some company that would stay over for a thirty-year weekend."

They drank their tea.

"Oh, such a rush of self-pity," she said good-naturedly. "About yourself, now. You're thirty-one and still not married?"

"Let me put it this way," he said. "Women who act and think and talk like you are rare."

"My," she said seriously, "you mustn't expect young women to talk like me. That comes later. They're much too young, first of all. And secondly, the average man runs helter-skelter the moment he finds anything like a brain in a lady. You've probably met quite a few brainy ones who hid it most successfully from you. You'll have to pry around a bit to find the odd beetle. Lift a few boards."

They were laughing again.

"I shall probably be a meticulous old bachelor," he said.

"No, no, you mustn't do that. It wouldn't be right. You shouldn't even be here this afternoon. This is a street which ends only in an Egyptian pyramid. Pyramids are all very nice, but mummies are hardly fit companions. Where would you like to go, what would you really like to do with your life?"

"See Istanbul, Port Said, Nairobi, Budapest. Write a book. Smoke too many cigarettes. Fall off a cliff, but get caught in a tree halfway down. Get shot at a few times in a dark alley on a Moroccan midnight. Love a beautiful woman."

"Well, I don't think I can provide them all," she said. "But I've traveled and I can tell you about many of those places. And if you'd care to run across my front lawn tonight about eleven and if I'm still awake, I'll fire off a Civil War musket at you. Will that satisfy your masculine urge for adventure?"

"That would be just fine."

"Where would you like to go first? I can take you there, you know. I can weave a spell. Just name it. London? Cairo? Cairo makes your face turn on like a light. So let's go to Cairo. Just relax now. Put some of that nice tobacco in that pipe of yours and sit back."

He sat back, lit his pipe, half smiling, relaxing, and listened, and she began to talk. "Cairo . . ." she said.

✳ The hour passed in jewels and alleys and winds from the Egyptian desert. The sun was golden and the Nile was muddy where it lapped down to the deltas, and there was someone very young and very quick at the top of the pyramid, laughing, calling to him to come on up the shadowy side into the sun, and he was climbing, she putting her hand down to help him up the last step, and then they were laughing on camel back, loping toward the great stretched bulk of the Sphinx, and late at night, in the native quarter, there was the tinkle of small hammers on bronze and silver, and music from some stringed instruments fading away and away and away. . . .

✳ William Forrester opened his eyes. Miss Helen Loomis had finished the adventure and they were home again, very familiar to each other, on the best of terms, in the garden, the tea cold in the silver pourer, the biscuits dried in the latened sun. He sighed and stretched and sighed again.

"I've never been so comfortable in my life."

"Nor I."

"I've kept you late. I should have gone an hour ago."

"You know I love every minute of it. But what you should see in an old silly woman . . ."

He lay back in his chair and half closed his eyes and looked at her. He squinted his eyes so the merest filament of light came through. He tilted his head ever so little this way, then that.

"What are you doing?" she asked uncomfortably.

He said nothing, but continued looking.

"If you do this just right," he murmured, "you can adjust, make allowances. . . ." To himself he was thinking, You can erase lines, adjust the time factor, turn back the years.

Suddenly he started.

"What's wrong?" she asked.

But then it was gone. He opened his eyes to catch it. That was a mistake. He should have stayed back, idling, erasing, his eyes gently half closed.

"For just a moment," he said, "I saw it."

"Saw what?"

"The swan, of course," he thought. His mouth must have pantomimed the words.

The next instant she was sitting very straight in her chair. Her hands were in her lap, rigid. Her eyes were fixed upon him and as he watched, feeling helpless, each of her eyes cupped and brimmed itself full.

"I'm sorry," he said, "terribly sorry."

"No, don't be." She held herself rigid and did not touch her face or her eyes; her hands remained, one atop the other, holding on. "You'd better go now. Yes, you may come tomorrow, but go now, please, and don't say any more."

He walked off through the garden, leaving her by her table in the shade. He could not bring himself to look back.

❋ Four days, eight days, twelve days passed, and he was invited to teas, to suppers, to lunches. They sat talking through the long green afternoons—they talked of art, of literature, of life, of society and politics. They ate ice creams and squabs and drank good wines.

"I don't care what anyone says," she said. "And people are saying things, aren't they?"

He shifted uneasily.

"I knew it. A woman's never safe, even when ninety-five, from gossip."

"I could stop visiting."

"Oh, no," she cried, and recovered. In a quieter voice she said, "You know you can't do that. You know you don't care what they think, do you? So long as we know it's all right?"

"I don't care," he said.

"Now"—she settled back—"let's play our game. Where shall it be this time? Paris? I think Paris."

"Paris," he said, nodding quietly.

"Well," she began, "it's the year 1885 and we're boarding the ship in New York harbor. There's our luggage, here are our tickets, there goes the sky line. Now we're at sea. Now we're coming into Marseilles. . . ."

Here she was on a bridge looking into the clear waters of the Seine, and here he was, suddenly, a moment later, beside her, looking down at the tides of summer flowing past. Here she was with an apéritif in her talcum-white fingers, and here he was, with amazing quickness, bending toward her to tap her wineglass with his. His face appeared in mirrored halls at Versailles, over steaming *smörgåsbords* in Stockholm, and they counted the barber poles in the Venice canals. The things she had done alone, they were now doing together.

✳ In the middle of August they sat staring at one another one late afternoon.

"Do you realize," he said, "I've seen you nearly every day for two and a half weeks?"

"Impossible!"

"I've enjoyed it immensely."

"Yes, but there are so many young girls . . ."

"You're everything they are not—kind, intelligent, witty."

"Nonsense. Kindness and intelligence are the preoccupations of age. Being cruel and thoughtless is far more fascinating when you're twenty." She paused and drew a breath. "Now, I'm going to embarrass you. Do you recall that first afternoon we met in the soda fountain, you said that you had had some degree of—shall we say affection for me at one time? You've purposely put me off on this by never mentioning it again. Now I'm forced to ask you to explain the whole uncomfortable thing."

He didn't seem to know what to say. "That's embarrassing," he protested.

"Spit it out!"

"I saw your picture once, years ago."

"I never let my picture be taken."

"This was an old one, taken when you were twenty."

"Oh, that. It's quite a joke. Each time I give to a charity or attend a ball they dust that picture off and print it. Everyone in town laughs; even I."

"It's cruel of the paper."

"No. I told them, If you want a picture of me, use the one taken back in 1853. Let them remember me that way. Keep the lid down, in the name of the good Lord, during the service."

"I'll tell you all about it." He folded his hands and looked at them and paused a moment. He was remembering the picture now and it was very clear in his mind. There was time, here in the garden to think of every aspect of the photograph and of Helen Loomis, very young, posing for her picture the first time, alone and beautiful. He thought of her quiet, shyly smiling face.

It was the face of spring, it was the face of summer, it was the warmness of clover breath. Pomegranate glowed in her lips, and the noon sky in her eyes. To touch her face was that always new experience of opening your window one December morning, early, and putting out your hand to the first white cool powdering of snow that had come, silently, with no announce-ment, in the night. And all of this, this breath-warmness and plum-tenderness was held forever in one miracle of photographic chemistry which no clock winds could blow upon to change one hour or one second; this fine first cool white snow would never melt, but live a thousand summers.

That was the photograph; that was the way he knew her. Now he was talking again, after the remembering and the thinking over and the hold-ing of the picture in his mind. "When I first saw that picture—it was a sim-ple, straightforward picture with a simple hairdo—I didn't know it had been taken that long ago. The item in the paper said something about Helen Loomis marshaling the Town Ball that night. I tore the picture from the paper. I carried it with me all that day. I intended going to the ball. Then, late in the afternoon, someone saw me looking at the picture, and told me about it. How the picture of the beautiful girl had been taken so long ago and used every year since by the paper. And they said I shouldn't go to the Town Ball that night, carrying that picture and looking for you."

They sat in the garden for a long minute. He glanced over at her face. She was looking at the farthest garden wall and the pink roses climbing there. There was no way to tell what she was thinking. Her face showed nothing. She rocked for a little while in her chair and then said softly, "Shall we have some more tea? There you are."

They sat sipping the tea. Then she reached over and patted his arm. "Thank you."

"For what?"

"For wanting to come to find me at the dance, for clipping out my pic-ture, for everything. Thank you so very much."

They walked about the garden on the paths.

"And now," she said, "it's my turn. Do you remember, I mentioned a cer-tain young man who once attended me, seventy years ago? Oh, he's been dead fifty years now, at least, but when he was very young and very hand-some he rode a fast horse off for days, or on summer nights over the mead-ows around town. He had a healthy, wild face, always sunburned, his hands were always cut and he fumed like a stovepipe and walked as if he were going to fly apart; wouldn't keep a job, quit those he had when he felt like it, and one day he sort of rode off away from me because I was even wilder than he and wouldn't settle down, and that was that. I never thought the day would come when I would see him alive again. But you're pretty much alive, you spill ashes around like he did, you're clumsy and graceful com-bined, I know everything you're going to do before you do it, but after you've done it I'm always surprised. Reincarnation's a lot of milk-mush to me, but the other day I felt, What if I called Robert, Robert, to you on the street, would William Forrester turn around?"

"I don't know," he said.

"Neither do I. That's what makes life interesting."

✳ August was almost over. The first cool touch of autumn moved slowly through the town and there was a softening and the first gradual burning fever of color in every tree, a faint flush and coloring in the hills, and the color of lions in the wheat fields. Now the pattern of days was familiar and repeated like a penman beautifully inscribing again and again, in practice, a series of *l*'s and *w*'s and *m*'s, day after day the line repeated in delicate rills.

William Forrester walked across the garden one early August afternoon to find Helen Loomis writing with great care at the tea table.

She put aside her pen and ink.

"I've been writing you a letter," she said.

"Well, my being here saves you the trouble."

"No, this is a special letter. Look at it." She showed him the blue envelope, which she now sealed and pressed flat. "Remember how it looks. When you receive this in the mail, you'll know I'm dead."

"That's no way to talk, is it?"

"Sit down and listen to me."

He sat.

"My dear William," she said, under the parasol shade. "In a few days I will be dead. No." She put up her hand. "I don't want you to say a thing. I'm not afraid. When you live as long as I've lived you lose that, too. I never liked lobster in my life, and mainly because I'd never tried it. On my eightieth birthday I tried it. I can't say I'm greatly excited over lobster still, but I have no doubt as to its taste now, and I don't fear it. I dare say death will be a lobster, too, and I can come to terms with it." She motioned with her hands. "But enough of that. The important thing is that I shan't be seeing you again. There will be no services. I believe that a woman who has passed through that particular door has as much right to privacy as a woman who has retired for the night."

"You can't predict death," he said at last.

"For fifty years I've watched the grandfather clock in the hall, William. After it is wound I can predict to the hour when it will stop. Old people are no different. They can feel the machinery slow down and the last weights shift. Oh, please don't look that way—please don't."

"I can't help it," he said.

"We've had a nice time, haven't we? It has been very special here, talk-ing every day. It was that much-overburdened and worn phrase referred to as a 'meeting of the minds.'" She turned the blue envelope in her hands. "I've always known that the quality of love was the mind, even though the body sometimes refuses this knowledge. The body lives for itself. It lives only to feed and wait for the night. It's essentially nocturnal. But what of the mind which is born of the sun, William, and must spend thousands of hours of a lifetime awake and aware? Can you balance off the body, that pitiful, selfish thing of night against a whole lifetime of sun and intellect? I don't know. I only know there has been your mind here and my mind here, and the afternoons have been like none I can remember. There is still so much to talk about, but we must save it for another time."

"We don't seem to have much time now."

"No, but perhaps there will be another time. Time is so strange and life is twice as strange. The cogs miss, the wheels turn, and lives interlace too early or too late. I lived too long, that much is certain. And you were born either too early or too late. It was a terrible bit of timing. But perhaps I am being punished for being a silly girl. Anyway, the next spin around, wheels might function right again. Meantime you must find a nice girl and be mar-ried and be happy. But you must promise me one thing."

"Anything."

"You must promise me not to live to be too old, William. If it is at all convenient, die before you're fifty. It may take a bit of doing. But I advise this simply because there is no telling when another Helen Loomis might be born. It would be dreadful, wouldn't it, if you lived on to be very, very old and some afternoon in 1999 walked down Main Street and saw me standing there, aged twenty-one, and the whole thing out of balance again? I don't think we could go through any more afternoons like these we've had, no matter how pleasant, do you? A thousand gallons of tea and five hundred biscuits is enough for one friendship. So you must have an attack of pneumonia some time in about twenty years. For I don't know how long they let you linger on the other side. Perhaps they send you back immedi-ately. But I shall do my best, William, really I shall. And everything put right and in balance, do you know what might happen?"

"You tell me."

"Some afternoon in 1985 or 1990 a young man named Tom Smith or John Green, or a name like that, will be walking downtown and will stop in the drugstore and order, appropriately, a dish of some unusual ice cream. A young girl the same age will be sitting there and when she hears the name of that ice cream, something will happen. I can't say what or how. *She* won't know why or how, assuredly. Nor will the young man. It will simply be that the name of that ice cream will be a very good thing to both of them. They'll talk. And later, when they know each other's names, they'll walk from the drugstore together."

She smiled at him.

"This is all very neat, but forgive an old lady for tying things in neat packets. It's a silly trifle to leave you. Now let's talk of something else. What shall we talk about? Is there any place in the world we haven't traveled to yet? Have we been to Stockholm?"

"Yes, it's a fine town."

"Glasgow? Yes? Where then?"

"Why not Green Town, Illinois?" he said. "Here. We haven't really visited our own town together at all."

She settled back, as did he, and she said, "I'll tell you how it was, then, when I was only nineteen, in this town, a long time ago. . . ."

It was a night in winter and she was skating lightly over a pond of white moon ice, her image gliding and whispering under her. It was a night in summer in this town of fire in the air, in the cheeks, in the heart, your eyes full of the glowing and shutting-off color of fireflies. It was a rustling night in October, and there she stood, pulling taffy from a hook in the kitchen, singing, and there she was, running on the moss by the river, and swimming in the granite pit beyond town on a spring night, in the soft deep warm waters, and now it was the Fourth of July with rockets slamming the sky and every porch full of now red-fire, now blue-fire, now white-fire faces, hers dazzling bright among them as the last rocket died.

"Can you see all these things?" asked Helen Loomis. "Can you see me doing them and being with them?"

"Yes," said William Forrester, eyes closed. "I can see you."

"And then," she said, "and then . . ."

Her voice moved on and on as the afternoon grew late and the twilight deepened quickly, but her voice moved in the garden and anyone passing on the road, at a far distance, could have heard its moth sound, faintly, faintly. . . .

✳ Two days later William Forrester was at his desk in his room when the letter came. Douglas brought it upstairs and handed it to Bill and looked as if he knew what was in it.

William Forrester recognized the blue envelope, but did not open it. He simply put it in his shirt pocket, looked at the boy for a moment, and said, "Come on, Doug; my treat."

They walked downtown, saying very little, Douglas preserving the silence he sensed was necessary. Autumn, which had threatened for a time, was gone. Summer was back full, boiling the clouds and scouring the metal sky. They turned in at the drugstore and sat at the marble fountain. William Forrester took the letter out and laid it before him and still did not open it.

He looked out at the yellow sunlight on the concrete and on the green awnings and shining on the gold letters of the window signs across the street, and he looked at the calendar on the wall. August 27, 1928. He looked at his wrist watch and felt his heartbeat slowly, saw the second hand of the watch moving moving with no speed at all, saw the calendar frozen there with its one day seeming forever, the sun nailed to the sky with no motion toward sunset whatever. The warm air spread under the sighing fans over his head. A number of women laughed by the open door and were gone through his vision, which was focused beyond them at the town itself and the high courthouse clock. He opened the letter and began to read.

He turned slowly on the revolving chair. He tried the words again and again, silently, on his tongue, and at last spoke them aloud and repeated them.

"A dish of lime-vanilla ice," he said. "A dish of lime-vanilla ice."

THE SEA SHELL

HE WANTED TO GET OUT AND RUN, bounding over hedges, kicking tin cans down the alley, shouting at all the windows for the gang to come and play. The sun was up and the day was bright, and here he was swaddled with bed clothes, sweating and scowling, and not liking it at all.

Johnny Bishop sat up in bed, sniffling. Orange juice, cough medicine and the perfume of his mother, lately gone from the room, hung in a shaft of sunlight that struck down to heat his toes. The entire lower half of the patch-work quilt was a circus banner of red, green, purple and blue. It practically yelled color into his eyes. Johnny fidgeted.

"I wanna go out," he complained softly. "Darn it. Darn it."

A fly buzzed, bumping again and again at the window pane with a dry staccato of its transparent wings.

Johnny looked at it, understanding how it wanted out, too.

He coughed a few times and decided that it was not the cough of a decrepit old man, but a youngster of eleven years who, next week this time, would be loose again to filch apples from the orchard trees or bean teacher with spit-balls.

He heard the trot of crisp footsteps in the freshly polished hall, the door opened, and mother was there. "Young man," she said, "what are you doing sitting up in bed? Lie down."

"I feel better already. Honest."

"The doctor said two more days."

"Two!" Consternation was the order of the moment. "Do I hafta be sick that long?"

Mom laughed. "Well—not *sick*. But in bed, anyway." She spanked his left cheek very lightly. "Want some more orange juice?"

"With or without medicine?"

"Medicine?"

"I know you. You put medicine in my orange juice so I can't taste it. but I taste it anyway."

"This time—no medicine."

"What's that in your hand?"

"Oh, this?" Mother held out a round gleaming object. Johnny took it. It was hard and shiny and—pretty. "Doctor Hull dropped by a few minutes ago and left it. He thought you might have fun with it."

* Johnny looked palely dubious. His small hands brushed the slick surface. "How can I have fun with it? I don't even know what it is!"

Mother's smile was better than sunshine. "It's a shell from the sea, Johnny. Doctor Hull picked it up on the Pacific shore last year when he was out there."

"Hey, that's all right. What kind of shell is it?"

"Oh, I don't know. Some form of sea life probably lived in it once, a long time ago."

Johnny's brows went up. "Lived in this? Made it a home?"

"Yes."

"Aw—really?"

She adjusted it in his hand. "If you don't believe me, listen for yourself, young man. Put this end—here—against your ear."

"Like this?" He raised the shell to his small pink ear and pressed it tight. "Now, what do I do?"

Mother smiled. "Now, if you're very quiet, and listen closely, you'll hear something very, very familiar."

Johnny listened. His ear opened imperceptibly like a small flower opening, waiting.

A titanic wave came in on a rocky shore and smashed itself down.

"The sea!" cried Johnny Bishop. "Oh, Mom! The ocean! The waves! The sea!"

Wave after wave came in on that distant, craggy shore. Johnny closed his eyes tight black and a smile folded his small face exactly in half. Wave after pounding wave roared in his small pinkly alert ear.

"Yes, Johnny," said mother. "The sea."

✳ It was late afternoon. Johnny lay back on his pillow, cradling the sea shell in his small hands, smiling, and looking out the large window just to the right side of the bed. He had a good view of the vacant lot across the street. The kids were scuddling around over there like a cluster of indignant beetles, each one complaining, "Aw, I shot you dead first! Now, I got you first! Aw, you don't play fair! I won't play unless I can be Captain!"

Their voices seemed so far away, lazy, drifting on a tide of sun. The sunlight was just like deep yellow, lambent water, lapping at the summer, full tide. Slow, languorous, warm, lazy. The whole world was over its head in that tide and everything was slowed down. The clock ticked slower. The street car came down the avenue in warm metal slow motion. It was almost like seeing a motion film that is losing speed and noise. Everything was softer. Nothing seemed to count as much.

He wanted to get out and play, badly. He kept watching the kids climbing the fences, playing soft ball, roller skating in the warm languor. His head felt heavy, heavy, heavy. His eyelids were window sashes pulling down, down. The sea shell lay against his ear. He pressed it close.

Pounding, drumming, waves broke on a shore. A yellow sand shore. And when the waves went back out they left foam, like the suds of beer, on the sand. The suds broke and vanished, like dreams. And more waves came with more foam. And the sand crabs tumbled, salt-wet, scuttling brown, in the ripples. Cool green water pounding cold on the sand. The very sound of it conjured up visions; the ocean breeze soothed Johnny Bishop's small body. Suddenly the hot afternoon was no longer hot and depressing. The clock started ticking faster. The street cars clanged metal quickly. The slowness of the summer world was spanked to crisp life by the pound-pound of waves on an unseen and brilliant beach.

This sea shell would be a valuable thing in the days to come. Whenever the afternoons stretched long and tiresome, he would press it around the lobe and rim of his ear and vacation on a wind-blown peninsula far, far off.

Four thirty, said the clock. Time for medicine, said mother's exact trot in the gleaming hall.

She offered the medicine in a silver spoon. It tasted like, unfortunately—medicine. Johnny made a special kind of bitter face. Then when the taste was modified by a drink of refrigerated milk he looked up at the nice soft white face of mom and said, "Can we go to the seashore some day, huh?"

"I think we can. Maybe the Fourth of July, if your father gets his two weeks then. We can drive to the coast in two days, stay a week, and come back."

Johnny settled himself, his eyes funny. "I've never really seen the ocean, except in movies. It smells different and looks different than Fox Lake, I bet. It's bigger, and a heck of a lot better. Gosh, I wish I could go now."

"It won't be long. You children are so impatient."

"I can't help it."

Mother sat down on the bed and held his hand. The things she said he couldn't understand fully, but some of them made sense. "If I had to write a philosophy of children, I guess I'd title it impatience. Impatience with everything in life. You must have things—*right now*—or else. Tomorrow's so far away, and yesterday is nothing. You're a tribe of potential Omar Khayyam's, that's what. When you're older, you'll understand that waiting, planning, being patient, are attributes of maturity; that is, of being grown up."

"I don't wanna be patient. I don't like being in bed. I want to go to the sea shore."

"And last week it was a catcher's mitt you wanted—*right now*. Please, pretty please, you said. Oh, gosh, Mom, it's elegant. It's the last one at the store."

Mom was very strange, all right. She talked some more:

"I remember, I saw a doll once when I was a girl. I told my mother about it, said it was the last one for sale. I said I was afraid it would be sold before I could get it. The truth of the matter is there were a dozen others just like it. I couldn't wait. I was impatient, too."

Johnny shifted on the bed. His eyes widened and got full of blue light. "But, Mom, I don't want to wait. If I wait too long, I'll be grown up, and then it won't be any fun."

That silenced mother. She just sort of sat there, her hands tightened, her eyes got all wet after a while, because she was thinking, maybe, to herself. She closed her eyes, opened them again, and said, "Sometimes—I think children know more about living than we do. Sometimes I think you're—right. But I don't dare tell you. It isn't according to the rules—"

"What rules, Mom?"

"Civilization's. Enjoy yourself, while you are young. Enjoy yourself, Johnny." She said it strong, and funnylike.

Johnny put the shell to his ear. "Mom. Know what I'd like to do? I'd like to be at the seashore right now, running toward the water, holding my nose and yelling, 'Last one in is a double-darned monkey!'" Johnny laughed.

The phone rang downstairs. Mother walked to answer it.

Johnny lay there, quietly, listening.

✳ Two more days. Johnny tilted his head against the shell and sighed. Two more whole days. It was dark in his room. Stars were caught in the square glass corrals of the big window. A wind moved the trees. Roller skates rotated, scraping, on the cement sidewalks below.

Johnny closed his eyes. Downstairs, silverware was being clattered at the dinner table. Mom and Pop were eating. He heard Pop laughing his deep laughter.

The waves still came in, over and over, on the shore inside the sea shell. And—something else.

"Down where the waves lift, down where the waves play, down where the gulls swoop low on a summer's day—"

"Huh?" Johnny listened. His body stiffened. He blinked his eyes.

Softly, way off.

"Stark ocean sky, sunlight on waves. Yo ho, heave ho, heave ho, my braves—"

It sounded like a hundred voices singing to the creak of oarlocks.

"Come down to the sea in ships—"

And then another voice, all by itself, soft against the sound of waves and ocean wind. "Come down to the sea, the contortionist sea, where the great tides wrestle and swell. Come down to the salt in the glittering brine, on a trail that you'll soon know well—"

Johnny pulled the shell from his head, stared at it.

"Do you want to come down to the sea, my lad, do you want to come down to the sea? Well, take me by the hand, my lad, just take me by the hand, my lad, and come along with me!"

Trembling, Johnny clamped the shell to his ear again, sat up in bed, breathing fast. His small heart leaped and hit the wall of his chest.

Waves pounded, crashing on a distant shore.

"Have you ever seen a fine conch-shell shaped and shined like a pearl corkscrew? It starts out big and it ends up small, seemingly ending with nothing at all, but aye lad, it ends where the sea-cliffs fall; where the sea-cliffs fall to the blue!"

Johnny's fingers tightened on the circular marks of the shell. That was right. It went around and around and around until you couldn't see it going around anymore.

Johnny's lips tightened. What was it Mother had said? Children. The—the philosophy—what a big word! Of children! Impatience. Impatience! Yes, yes, he was impatient! Why not? His free hand clenched into a tiny hard white fist, pounding against the quilted covers.

"Johnny!"

Johnny yanked the shell from his ear, hid it quickly under the sheets. Father was coming down the hall from the stairs.

"Hi there, son."

"Hi, Dad!"

Mother and Father were fast asleep. It was long after midnight. Very softly Johnny extracted the precious shell from under the covers and raised it to his ear.

Yes. The waves were still there. And far off, the creening of oarlocks, the snap of wind in the stomach of a mainsail, the singing chant of boatmen faintly drifting on a salt sea wind.

He held the shell closer and yet closer.

✳ Mother's footsteps came along the hall. She turned in at Johnny's room. "Good morning, son! Wake yet?"

The bed was empty. There was nothing but sunlight and silence in the room. Sunlight lay abed, like a bright patient with its brilliant head on the pillow. The quilt, a red-blue circus banner, was thrown back. The bed was wrinkled like the face of a pale old man, and it was very empty.

Mother looked at it and scowled and stamped her crisp heel. "Darn that little scamp!" she cried, to nobody. "Gone out to play with those neighbor ruffians, sure as the day I was born! Wait'll I catch him, I'll—" She stopped and smiled. "I'll love the little scamp to death. Children are so—impatient."

Walking to the bedside she began brushing, adjusted the quilt into place when her knuckles rapped against a lump in the sheet. Reaching under the quilt, she brought forth a shining object into the sun.

She smiled. It was the sea shell.

She grasped it, and, just for fun, lifted it to her ear. Her eyes widened. Her jaw dropped.

The room whirled around in a bright swaying merry-go-round of bannered quilts and glassed run.

The sea shell roared in her ear.

Waves thundered on a distant shore. Waves foamed cool on a far off beach.

Then the sound of small feet crunching swiftly in the sand. A high young voice yelling:

"Hi! Come on, you guys! Last one in is a double-darned monkey!"

And the sound of a small body diving, splashing, into those waves . . .

ONCE MORE, LEGATO

FENTRISS SAT UP IN HIS CHAIR in the garden in the middle of a fine autumn and listened. The drink in his hand remained unsipped, his friend Black unspoken to, the fine house unnoticed, the very weather itself neglected, for there was a veritable fountain of sound in the air above them.

"My God," he said. "Do you hear?"

"What, the birds?" asked his friend Black, doing just the opposite, sipping his drink, noticing the weather, admiring the rich house, and neglecting the birds entirely until this moment.

"Great God in heaven, listen to them!" cried Fentriss.

Black listened. "Rather nice."

"Clean out your ears!"

Black made a halfhearted gesture, symbolizing the cleaning out of ears. "Well?"

"Damn it, don't be funny. I mean really *listen*! They're singing a tune!"

"Birds usually do."

"No, they don't; birds paste together bits and pieces maybe, five or six notes, eight at the most. Mockingbirds have repertoires that change, but not entire melodies. *These* birds are different. Now shut up and give over!"

Both men sat, enchanted. Black's expression melted.

"I'll be damned," he said at last. "They *do* go on." He leaned forward and listened intently.

"Yes . . ." murmured Fentriss, eyes shut, nodding to the rhythms that sprang like fresh rain from the tree just above their heads. ". . . ohmigod . . . indeed."

Black rose as if to move under the tree and peer up. Fentriss protested with a fierce whisper:

"Don't spoil it. Sit. Be very still. Where's my pencil? Ah . . ."

Half peering around, he found a pencil and notepad, shut his eyes, and began to scribble blindly.

The birds sang.

"You're not *actually* writing down their song?" said Black.

"What does it look like? Quiet."

And with eyes now open, now shut, Fentriss drew scales and jammed in the notes.

"I didn't know you read music," said Black, astonished.

"I played the violin until my father broke it. Please! There. There. Yes!

"Slower," he whispered. "Wait for me."

As if hearing, the birds adjusted their lilt, moving toward *piano* instead of *bravado*.

A breeze stirred the leaves, like an invisible conductor, and the singing died.

Fentriss, perspiration beading his forehead, stopped scribbling and fell back.

"I'll be damned." Black gulped his drink. "What was *that* all about?"

"Writing a song." Fentriss stared at the scales he had dashed on paper. "Or a tone poem."

"Let me *see* that!"

"Wait." The tree shook itself gently, but produced no further notes. "I want to be sure they're done."

Silence.

Black seized the pages and let his eyes drift over the scales. "Jesus, Joseph, and Mary," he said, aghast. "It *works*." He glanced up at the thick green of the tree, where no throat warbled, no wing stirred. "What kind of birds *are* those?"

"The birds of forever, the small beasts of an Immaculate Musical Conception. Something," said Fentriss, "has made them with child and its name is song—"

"Hogwash!"

"*Is* it?! Something in the air, in the seeds they ate at dawn, some whim of climate and weather, God! But now they're mine, *it's* mine. A fine tune."

"It *is*," said Black. "But *can't* be!"

"Never question the miraculous when it happens. Good grief, maybe those damned wonderful creatures have been throwing up incredible songs for months, years, but no one *listened*. Today, for the first time, someone *did*. Me! Now, what to *do* with the gift?"

"You don't seriously mean—?"

"I've been out of work for a year. I quit my computers, retired early, I'm only forty-nine, and have been threatening to knit macramé to give friends to spoil their walls, day after day. Which shall it be, friend, macramé or Mozart?"

"Are *you* Mozart?"

"Just his bastard son."

"Nonsense," cried Black, pointing his face like a blunderbuss at the trees as if he might blast the choir. "That tree, those birds, are a Rorschach test. Your subconscious is picking and choosing notes from pure chaos. There's no discernible tune, no special rhythm. You had me fooled, but I see and hear it now: you've had a repressed desire since childhood to compose. And you've let a clutch of idiot birds grab you by the ears. Put down that pen!"

"Nonsense right back at you." Fentriss laughed. "You're jealous that after twelve layabout years, thunderstruck with boredom, one of us has found an occupation. I shall follow it. Listen and write, write and listen. Sit down, you're obstructing the acoustics!"

"I'll sit," Black exclaimed, "but—" He clapped his hands over his ears.

"Fair enough," said Fentriss. "Escape fantastic reality while I change a few notes and finish out this unexpected birth."

Glancing up at the tree, he whispered:

"Wait for me."

The tree rustled its leaves and fell quiet.

"Crazy," muttered Black.

✳ One, two, three hours later, entering the library quietly and then loudly, Black cried out:

"What *are* you doing?"

Bent over his desk, his hand moving furiously, Fentriss said:

"Finishing a symphony!"

"The same one you began in the garden?"

"No, the birds began, the birds!"

"The birds, then." Black edged closer to study the mad inscriptions. "How do you know *what* to do with that stuff?"

"They did most. I've added variations!"

"An arrogance the ornithologists will resent and attack. Have you composed before?"

"Not"—Fentriss let his fingers roam, loop, and scratch—"until today!"

"You realize, of course, you're plagiarizing those songbirds?"

"Borrowing, Black, borrowing. If a milkmaid, singing at dawn, can have her hum borrowed by Berlioz, *well*! Or if Dvorak, hearing a Dixie banjo plucker pluck 'Goin' Home,' steals the banjo to eke out his New World, why can't I weave a net to catch a tune? There! Finito. Done! Give us a title, Black!"

"I? Who sings off-key?"

"What about 'The Emperor's Nightingale'?"

"Stravinsky."

"'The Birds'?"

"Hitchcock."

"Damn. How's this: 'It's Only John Cage in a Gilded Bird'?"

"Brilliant. But no one knows who John Cage *was*."

"Well, then, I've *got* it!"

And he wrote:

"'Forty-seven Magpies Baked in a Pie.'"

"*Blackbirds*, you mean; go back to John Cage."

"Bosh!" Fentriss stabbed the phone. "Hello, Willie? Could you come over? Yes, a small job. Symphonic arrangement for a friend, or friends. What's your usual Philharmonic fee? Eh? Good enough. Tonight!"

Fentriss disconnected and turned to gaze at the tree with wonder in it.

"What *next*?" he murmured.

✳ "Forty-seven Magpies," with title shortened, premiered at the Glendale Chamber Symphony a month later with standing ovations, incredible reviews.

Fentriss, outside his skin with joy, prepared to launch himself atop large, small, symphonic, operatic, whatever fell on his ears. He had listened to the strange choirs each day for weeks, but had noted nothing, waiting to see if the "Magpie" experiment was to be repeated. When the applause rose in storms and the critics hopped when they weren't skipping, he knew he must strike again before the epilepsy ceased.

There followed: "Wings," "Flight," "Night Chorus," "The Fledgling Madrigals," and "Dawn Patrol," each greeted by new thunderstorms of acclamation and critics angry at excellence but forced to praise.

"By now," said Fentriss, "I should be unbearable to live with, but the birds caution modesty."

"Also," said Black, seated under the tree, waiting for a sprig of benison and the merest touch of symphonic manna, "shut up! If all those sly dimwit composers, who will soon be lurking in the bushes, cop your secret, you're a gone poacher."

"Poacher! By God, yes!" Fentriss laughed. "Poacher."

And damn if the first poacher didn't arrive!

Glancing out at three in the morning, Fentriss witnessed a runty shadow stretching up, handheld tape recorder poised, warbling and whistling softly at the tree. When this failed, the half-seen poacher tried dove-coos and then orioles and roosters, half dancing in a circle.

"Damn it to hell!" Fentriss leaped out with a shotgun cry: "Is that Wolfgang Prouty poaching my garden? Out, Wolfgang! Go!"

Dropping his recorder, Prouty vaulted a bush, impaled himself on thorns, and vanished.

Fentriss, cursing, picked up an abandoned notepad.

"Nightsong," it read. On the tape recorder he found a lovely Satie-like bird-choir.

After that, more poachers arrived midnight to depart at dawn. Their spawn, Fentriss realized, would soon throttle his creativity and still his voice. He loitered full-time in the garden now, not knowing what seed to give his beauties, and heavily watered the lawn to fetch up worms. Wearily he stood guard through sleepless nights, nodding off only to find Wolfgang Prouty's evil minions astride the wall, prompting arias, and one night, by God, perched in the tree itself, humming in hopes of sing-alongs.

A shotgun was the final answer. After its first fiery roar, the garden was empty for a week. That is, until—

Someone came very late indeed and committed mayhem.

As quietly as possible, he cut the branches and sawed the limbs.

"Oh, envious composers, dreadful murderers!" cried Fentriss.

And the birds were gone.

And the career of Amadeus Two with it.

"Black!" cried Fentriss.

"Yes, dear friend?" said Black, looking at the bleak sky where once green was.

"Is your car outside?"

"When last I looked."

"Drive!"

But driving in search didn't do it. It wasn't like calling in lost dogs or telephone-poled cats. They must find and cage an entire Mormon tabernacle team of soprano springtime-in-the-Rockies birdseed lovers to prove one in the hand is worth two in the bush.

But still they hastened from block to block, garden to garden, lurking and listening. Now their spirits soared with an echo of "Hallelujah Chorus" oriole warbling, only to sink in a drab sparrow twilight of despair.

Only when they had crossed and recrossed interminable mazes of asphalt and greens did one of them finally (Black) light his pipe and emit a theory.

"Did you ever think to wonder," he mused behind a smoke-cloud, "what *season* of the year this *is*?"

"Season of the year?" said Fentriss, exasperated.

"Well, coincidentally, wasn't the night the tree fell and the wee songsters blew town, was not that the first fall night of autumn?"

Fentriss clenched a fist and struck his brow.

"You *mean*?"

"Your friends have flown the coop. Their migration must be above San Miguel Allende just now."

"If they are migratory birds!"

"Do you *doubt* it?"

Another pained silence, another blow to the head.

"Shit!"

"Precisely," said Black.

"Friend," said Fentriss.

"Sir?"

"Drive home."

✳ It was a long year, it was a short year, it was a year of anticipation, it was the burgeoning of despair, it was the revival of inspiration, but at its heart, Fentriss knew, just another Tale of Two Cities, but he did not know what the other city was!

How stupid of me, he thought, not to have guessed or imagined that my songsters were wanderers who each autumn fled south and each springtime swarmed north in a cappella choirs of sound.

"The waiting," he told Black, "is madness. The phone never stops—"

The phone rang. He picked it up and addressed it like a child. "Yes. Yes. Of course. Soon. When? Very soon." And put the phone down. "You see? That was Philadelphia. They want another Cantata as good as the first. At dawn today it was Boston. Yesterday the Vienna Philharmonic. *Soon*, I say. When? God knows. Lunacy! Where are those angels that once sang me to my rest?"

He threw down maps and weather charts of Mexico, Peru, Guatemala, and the Argentines.

"How far south? Do I scour Buenos Aires or Rio, Mazatlán or Cuernavaca? And then? Wander about with a tin ear, standing under trees waiting for bird-drops like a spotted owl? Will the Argentine critics trot by scoffing to see me leaning on trees, eyes shut, waiting for the quasi-melody, the lost chord? I'd let no one know the cause of my journey, my search, otherwise pandemoniums of laughter. But in what city, under what kind of tree would I wander to stand? A tree like mine? Do they seek the same roosts? or will anything do in Ecuador or Peru? God, I could waste months guessing and come back with birdseed in my hair and bird bombs on my lapels. What to do, Black? *Speak!*"

"Well, for one thing"—Black stuffed and lit his pipe and exhaled his aromatic concepts—"you might clear off this stump and plant a new tree."

They had been circling the stump and kicking it for inspiration. Fentriss froze with one foot raised. "Say that *again?!*"

"I said—"

"Good grief, you genius! Let me kiss you!"

"Rather not. Hugs, maybe."

Fentriss hugged him, wildly. "Friend!"

"Always was."

"Let's get a shovel and spade."

"You get. I'll watch."

Fentriss ran back a minute later with a spade and pickax. "Sure you won't join me?"

Black sucked his pipe, blew smoke. "Later."

"How much would a full-*grown* tree cost?"

"Too much."

"Yes, but if it were *here* and the birds *did* return?"

Black let out more smoke. "Might be worth it. Opus Number Two: 'In the Beginning' by Charles Fentriss, stuff like that."

" 'In the Beginning,' or maybe '*The Return*.' "

"One of those."

"Or—" Fentriss struck the stump with the pickax. " 'Rebirth.' " He struck again. " '*Ode to Joy*.' " Another strike. " '*Spring Harvest*.' " Another. " '*Let the Heavens Resound*.' How's that, Black?"

"I prefer the other," said Black.

✳ The stump was pulled and the new tree bought.

"Don't show me the bill," Fentriss told his accountant. "Pay it."

And the tallest tree they could find, of the same family as the one dead and gone, was planted.

"What if *it* dies before my choir returns?" said Fentriss.

"What if it *lives*," said Black, "and your choir goes *elsewhere*?"

The tree, planted, seemed in no immediate need to die. Neither did it look particularly vital and ready to welcome small singers from some far southern places.

Meanwhile, the sky, like the tree, was empty.

"Don't they know I'm *waiting*?" said Fentriss.

"Not unless," offered Black, "you majored in cross-continental telepathy."

"I've checked with Audubon. They say that while the swallows *do* come back to Capistrano on a special day, give or take a white lie, other migrating species are often one or two weeks late."

"If I were you," said Black, "I would plunge into an intense love affair to distract you while you wait."

"I am fresh out of love affairs."

"Well, then," said Black, "suffer."

The hours passed slower than the minutes, the days passed slower than the hours, the weeks passed slower than the days. Black called. "No birds?"

"No birds."

"Pity. I can't stand watching you lose weight." And Black disconnected.

On a final night, when Fentriss had almost yanked the phone out of the wall, fearful of another call from the Boston Symphony, he leaned an ax against the trunk of the new tree and addressed it and the empty sky.

"Last chance," he said. "If the dawn patrol doesn't show by seven A.M., it's quits."

And he touched ax-blade against the tree-bole, took two shots of vodka so swiftly that the spirits squirted out both eyes, and went to bed.

He awoke twice during the night to hear nothing but a soft breeze outside his window, stirring the leaves, with not a ghost of song.

And awoke at dawn with tear-filled eyes, having dreamed that the birds had returned, but knew, in waking, it was only a dream.

And yet . . . ?

Hark, someone might have said in an old novel. List! as in an old play.

Eyes shut, he fine-tuned his ears . . .

The tree outside, as he arose, looked fatter, as if it had taken on invisible ballasts in the night. There were stirrings there, not of simple breeze or probing winds, but of something in the very leaves that knitted and purled them in rhythms. He dared not look but lay back down to ache his senses and try to *know*.

A single chirp hovered in the window.

He waited.

Silence.

Go on, he thought.

Another chirp.

Don't breathe, he thought; don't let them know you're listening.

Hush.

A fourth sound, then a fifth note, then a sixth and seventh.

My God, he thought, is this a substitute orchestra, a replacement choir come to scare off my loves?

Another five notes.

Perhaps, he prayed, they're only tuning *up*!

Another twelve notes, of no special timbre or pace, and as he was about to explode like a lunatic conductor and fire the bunch—

It happened.

Note after note, line after line, fluid melody following spring freshet melody, the whole choir exhaled to blossom the tree with joyous proclamations of return and welcome in chorus.

And as they sang, Fentriss sneaked his hand to find a pad and pen to hide under the covers so that its scratching might not disturb the choir that soared and dipped to soar again, firing the bright air that flowed from the tree to tune his soul with delight and move his hand to remember.

The phone rang. He picked it up swiftly to hear Black ask if the waiting was over. Without speaking, he held the receiver in the window.

"I'll be damned," said Black's voice.

"No, *anointed*," whispered the composer, scribbling Cantata No. 2. Laughing, he called softly to the sky.

"Please. More slowly. *Legato*, not *agitato*."

And the tree and the creatures within the tree obeyed.

Agitato ceased.

Legato prevailed.

JUNE 2003: WAY IN THE MIDDLE OF THE AIR

"Did you hear about it?"

"About what?"

"The niggers, the niggers!"

"What about 'em?"

"Them leaving, pulling out, going away; did you hear?"

"What you mean, pulling out? How can they do that?"

"They can, they will, they are."

"Just a couple?"

"Every single one here in the South!"

"No."

"Yes!"

"I got to see that. I don't believe it. Where they going—Africa?"

A silence.

"Mars."

"You mean the planet Mars?"

"That's right."

The men stood up in the hot shade of the hardware porch. Someone quit lighting a pipe. Somebody else spat out into the hot dust of noon.

"They can't leave, they can't do that."

"They're doing it, anyways."

"Where'd you hear this?"

"It's everywhere, on the radio a minute ago, just come through."

Like a series of dusty statues, the men came to life.

Samuel Teece, the hardware proprietor, laughed uneasily. "I wondered what happened to Silly. I sent him on my bike an hour ago. He ain't come back from Mrs. Bordman's yet. You think that black fool just pedaled off to Mars?"

The men snorted.

"All I say is, he better bring back my bike. I don't take stealing from no one, by God."

"Listen!"

The men collided irritably with each other, turning.

Far up the street the levee seemed to have broken. The black warm waters descended and engulfed the town. Between the blazing white banks of the town stores, among the tree silences, a black tide flowed. Like a kind of summer molasses, it poured turgidly forth upon the cinnamon-dusty road. It surged slow, slow, and it was men and women and horses and barking dogs, and it was little boys and girls. And from the mouths of the people partaking of this tide came the sound of a river. A summer-day river going somewhere, murmuring and irrevocable. And in that slow, steady channel of darkness that cut across the white glare of day were touches of alert white, the eyes, the ivory eyes staring ahead, glancing aside, as the river, the long and endless river, took itself from old channels into a new one. From various and uncountable tributaries, in creeks and brooks of color and motion, the parts of this river had joined, become one mother current, and flowed on. And brimming the swell were things carried by the river: grandfather clocks chiming, kitchen clocks ticking, caged hens screaming, babies wailing; and swimming among the thickened eddies were mules and cats, and sudden excursions of burst mattress springs floating by, insane hair stuffing sticking out, and boxes and crates and pictures of dark grand-fathers in oak frames—the river flowing it on while the men sat like nervous hounds on the hardware porch, too late to mend the levee, their hands empty.

Samuel Teece wouldn't believe it. "Why, hell, where'd they get the transportation? How they goin' to get to Mars?"

"Rockets," said Grandpa Quartermain.

"All the damn-fool things. Where'd they get rockets?"

"Saved their money and built them."

"I never heard about it."

"Seems these niggers kept it secret, worked on the rockets all themselves, don't know where—in Africa, maybe."

"Could they do that?" demanded Samuel Teece, pacing about the porch. "Ain't there a law?"

"It ain't as if they're declarin' war," said Grandpa quietly.

"Where do they get off, God damn it, workin' in secret, plottin'?" shouted Teece.

"Schedule is for all this town's niggers to gather out by Loon Lake. Rockets be there at one o'clock, pick 'em up, take 'em to Mars."

"Telephone the governor, call out the militia," cried Teece. "They should've given notice!"

"Here comes your woman, Teece."

The men turned again.

As they watched, down the hot road in the windless light first one white woman and then another arrived, all of them with stunned faces, all of them rustling like ancient papers. Some of them were crying, some were stern. All came to find their husbands. They pushed through barroom swing doors, vanishing. They entered cool, quiet groceries. They went in at drug shops and garages. And one of them, Mrs. Clara Teece, came to stand in the dust by the hardware porch, blinking up at her stiff and angry husband as the black river flowed full behind her.

"It's Lucinda, Pa; you got to come home!"

"I'm not comin' home for no damn darkie!"

"She's leaving. What'll I do without her?"

"Fetch for yourself, maybe. I won't get down on my knees to stop her."

"But she's like a family member," Mrs. Teece moaned.

"Don't shout! I won't have you blubberin' in public this way about no goddamn—"

His wife's small sob stopped him. She dabbed at her eyes. "I kept telling her, 'Lucinda,' I said, 'you stay on and I raise your pay, and you get two nights off a week, if you want,' but she just looked set! I never seen her so set, and I said, 'Don't you love me, Lucinda?' and she said yes, but she had to go because that's the way it was, is all. She cleaned the house and dusted it and put luncheon on the table and then she went to the parlor door and—and stood there with two bundles, one by each foot, and shook my hand and said, 'Good-bye, Mrs. Teece.' And she went out the door. And there was her luncheon on the table, and all of us too upset to even eat it. It's still there now, I know; last time I looked it was getting cold."

Teece almost struck her. "God damn it, Mrs. Teece, you get the hell home. Standin' there makin' a sight of yourself!"

"But, Pa . . ."

He strode away into the hot dimness of the store. He came back out a few seconds later with a silver pistol in his hand.

His wife was gone.

The river flowed black between the buildings, with a rustle and a creak and a constant whispering shuffle. It was a very quiet thing, with a great certainty to it; no laughter, no wildness, just a steady, decided, and cease-less flow.

Teece sat on the edge of his hardwood chair. "If one of 'em so much as laughs, by Christ, I'll kill 'em."

The men waited.

The river passed quietly in the dreamful noon.

"Looks like you goin' to have to hoe your own turnips, Sam," Grandpa chuckled.

"I'm not bad at shootin' white folks neither." Teece didn't look at Grandpa. Grandpa turned his head away and shut up his mouth.

"Hold on there!" Samuel Teece leaped off the porch. He reached up and seized the reins of a horse ridden by a tall Negro man. "You, Belter, come down off there!"

"Yes, sir." Belter slid down.

Teece looked him over. "Now, just what you think you're doin'?"

"Well, Mr. Teece . . ."

"I reckon you think you're goin', just like that song—what's the words? 'Way up in the middle of the air'; ain't that it?"

"Yes, sir." The Negro waited.

"You recollect you owe me fifty dollars, Belter?"

"Yes, sir."

"You tryin' to sneak out? By God, I'll horsewhip you!"

"All the excitement, and it slipped my mind, sir."

"It slipped his mind." Teece gave a vicious wink at his men on the hardware porch. "God damn, mister, you know what you're goin' to do?"

"No, sir."

"You're stayin' here to work out that fifty bucks, or my name ain't Samuel W. Teece." He turned again to smile confidently at the men in the shade.

Belter looked at the river going along the street, that dark river flowing and flowing between the shops, the dark river on wheels and horses and in dusty shoes, the dark river from which he had been snatched on his journey. He began to shiver. "Let me go, Mr. Teece. I'll send your money from up there, I promise!"

"Listen, Belter." Teece grasped the man's suspenders like two harp strings, playing them now and again, contemptuously, snorting at the sky, pointing one bony finger straight at God. "Belter, you know anything about what's up there?"

"What they tells me."

"What they tells him! Christ! Hear that? What they tells him!" He swung the man's weight by his suspenders, idly, ever so casual, flicking a finger in the black face. "Belter, you fly up and up like a July Fourth rocket, and bang! There you are, cinders, spread all over space. Them crackpot scientists, they don't know nothin', they kill you all off!"

"I don't care."

"Glad to hear that. Because you know what's up on that planet Mars? There's monsters with big raw eyes like mushrooms! You seen them pictures on those future magazines you buy at the drugstore for a dime, ain't you? Well! Them monsters jump up and suck marrow from your bones!"

"I don't care, don't care at all, don't care." Belter watched the parade slide by, leaving him. Sweat lay on his dark brow. He seemed about to collapse.

"And it's cold up there; no air, you fall down, jerk like a fish, gaspin', dyin', stranglin', stranglin' and dyin'. You *like* that?"

"Lots of things I don't like, sir. Please, sir, let me go. I'm late."

"I'll let you go when I'm ready to let you go. We'll just talk here polite until I say you can leave, and you know it damn well. You want to travel, do you? Well, Mister Way up in the Middle of the Air, you get the hell home and work out that fifty bucks you owe me! Take you two months to do that!"

"But if I work it out, I'll miss the rocket, sir!"

"Ain't that a shame now?" Teece tried to look sad.

"I give you my horse, sir."

"Horse ain't legal tender. You don't move until I get my money." Teece laughed inside. He felt very warm and good.

A small crowd of dark people had gathered to hear all this. Now as Belter stood, head down, trembling, an old man stepped forward.

"Mister?"

Teece flashed him a quick look. "Well?"

"How much this man owe you, mister?"

"None of your damn business!"

The old man looked at Belter. "How much, son?"

"Fifty dollars."

The old man put out his black hands at the people around him. "There's twenty-five of you. Each give two dollars; quick now, this no time for argument."

"Here, now!" cried Teece, stiffening up, tall, tall.

The money appeared. The old man fingered it into his hat and gave the hat to Belter. "Son," he said, "you ain't missin' no rocket."

Belter smiled into the hat. "No, sir, I guess I ain't!"

Teece shouted: "You give that money back to them!"

Belter bowed respectfully, handing the money over, and when Teece would not touch it he set it down in the dust at Teece's feet. "There's your money, sir," he said. "Thank you kindly." Smiling, he gained the saddle of his horse and whipped his horse along, thanking the old man, who rode with him now until they were out of sight and hearing.

"Son of a bitch," whispered Teece, staring blind at the sun. "Son of a bitch."

"Pick up the money, Samuel," said someone from the porch.

It was happening all along the way. Little white boys, barefoot, dashed up with the news. "Them that has helps them that hasn't! And that way they *all* get free! Seen a rich man give a poor man two hundred bucks to pay off some'un! Seen some'un else give some'un else ten bucks, five bucks, sixteen, lots of that, all over, everybody!"

The white men sat with sour water in their mouths. Their eyes were almost puffed shut, as if they had been struck in their faces by wind and sand and heat.

The rage was in Samuel Teece. He climbed up on the porch and glared at the passing swarms. He waved his gun. And after a while when he had to do something, he began to shout at anyone, any Negro who looked up at him. "Bang! There's another rocket out in space!" he shouted so all could hear. "Bang! By God!" The dark heads didn't flicker or pretend to hear, but their white eyes slid swiftly over and back. "Crash! All them rockets fallin'! Screamin', dyin'! Bang! God Almighty, I'm glad I'm right here on old terra firma. As they says in that old joke, the more firma, the less terra! Ha, ha!"

Horses clopped along, shuffling up dust. Wagons bumbled on ruined springs.

"Bang!" His voice was lonely in the heat, trying to terrify the dust and the blazing sun sky. "Wham! Niggers all over space! Jerked outa rockets like so many minnows hit by a meteor, by God! Space fulla meteors. You know that? Sure! Thick as buckshot; powie! Shoot down them tin-can rockets like so many ducks, so many clay pipes! Ole sardine cans full of black cod! Bangin' like a stringa ladyfingers, bang, bang, bang! Ten thousand dead here, ten thousand there. Floatin' in space, around and around earth, ever and ever, cold and way out, Lord! You hear that, you there!"

Silence. The river was broad and continuous. Having entered all cotton shacks during the hour, having flooded all the valuables out, it was now carrying the clocks and the washboards, the silk bolts and curtain rods on down to some distant black sea.

High tide passed. It was two o'clock. Low tide came. Soon the river was dried up, the town silent, the dust settling in a film on the stores, the seated men, the tall hot trees.

Silence.

The men on the porch listened.

Hearing nothing, they extended their thoughts and their imaginations out and out into the surrounding meadows. In the early morning the land had been filled with its usual concoctions of sound. Here and there, with stubborn persistence to custom, there had been voices singing, the honey laughter under the mimosa branches, the pickaninnies rushing in clear water laughter at the creek, movements and bendings in the fields, jokes and shouts of amusement from the shingle shacks covered with fresh green vine.

Now it was as if a great wind had washed the land clean of sounds. There was nothing. Skeleton doors hung open on leather hinges. Rubber-tire swings hung in the silent air, uninhibited. The washing rocks at the river were empty, and the watermelon patches, if any, were left alone to

heat their hidden liquors in the sun. Spiders started building new webs in
abandoned huts; dust started to sift in from unpatched roofs in golden
spicules. Here and there a fire, forgotten in the last rush, lingered and in a
sudden access of strength fed upon the dry bones of some littered shack.
The sound of a gentle feeding burn went up through the silenced air.

The men sat on the hardware porch, not blinking or swallowing.

"I can't figure why they left now. With things lookin' up. I mean, every
day they got more rights. What they want, anyway? Here's the poll tax
gone, and more and more states passin' anti-lynchin' bills, and all kinds of
equal rights. What *more* they want? They make almost as good money as a
white man, but there they go."

Far down the empty street a bicycle came.

"I'll be goddamned, Teece, here comes your Silly now."

The bicycle pulled up before the porch, a seventeen-year-old colored boy
on it, all arms and feet and long legs and round watermelon head. He
looked up at Samuel Teece and smiled.

"So you got a guilty conscience and came back," said Teece.

"No, sir, I just brought the bicycle."

"What's wrong, couldn't get it on the rocket?"

"That wasn't it, sir."

"Don't tell me what it was! Get off, you're not goin' to steal my property!" He gave the boy a push. The bicycle fell. "Get inside and start cleaning the brass."

"Beg pardon?" The boy's eyes widened.

"You heard what I said. There's guns need unpacking there, and a crate
of nails just come from Natchez—"

"Mr. Teece."

"And a box of hammers need fixin'—"

"Mr. Teece, sir?"

"You *still* standin' there!" Teece glared.

"Mr. Teece, you don't mind I take the day off," he said apologetically.

"And tomorrow and day after tomorrow and the day after the day after
that," said Teece.

"I'm afraid so, sir."

"You *should* be afraid, boy. Come here." He marched the boy across the
porch and drew a paper out of a desk. "Remember this?"

"Sir?"

"It's your workin' paper. You signed it, there's your X right there, ain't
it? Answer me."

"I didn't sign that, Mr. Teece." The boy trembled. "Anyone can make an X."

"Listen to this, Silly. Contract: 'I will work for Mr. Samuel Teece two years, starting July 15, 2001, and if intending to leave will give four weeks' notice and continue working until my position is filled.' There." Teece slapped the paper, his eyes glittering. "You cause trouble, we'll take it to court."

"I can't do that," wailed the boy, tears starting to roll down his face. "If I don't go today, I don't go."

"I know just how you feel, Silly; yes, sir, I sympathize with you, boy. But we'll treat you good and give you good food, boy. Now you just get inside and start working and forget all about that nonsense, eh, Silly? Sure." Teece grinned and patted the boy's shoulder.

The boy turned and looked at the old men sitting on the porch. He could hardly see now for his tears. "Maybe—maybe one of these gentlemen here . . ." The men looked up in the hot, uneasy shadows, looking first at the boy and then at Teece.

"You meanin' to say you think a *white man* should take your place, boy?" asked Teece coldly.

Grandpa Quartermain took his red hands off his knees. He looked out at the horizon thoughtfully and said, "Teece, what about me?"

"What?"

"I'll take Silly's job."

The porch was silent.

Teece balanced himself in the air. "Grandpa," he said warningly.

"Let the boy go. I'll clean the brass."

"Would you, would you, really?" Silly ran over to Grandpa, laughing, tears on his cheeks, unbelieving.

"Sure."

"Grandpa," said Teece, "keep your damn trap outa this."

"Give the kid a break, Teece."

Teece walked over and seized the boy's arm. "He's mine. I'm lockin' him in the back room until tonight."

"Don't, Mr. Teece!"

The boy began to sob now. His crying filled the air of the porch. His eyes were tight. Far down the street an old tin Ford was choking along, approaching, a last load of colored people in it. "Here comes my family, Mr. Teece, oh, please, please, oh God, please!"

"Teece," said one of the other men on the porch, getting up, "let him go."

Another man rose also. "That goes for me too."

"And me," said another.

"What's the use?" The men all talked now. "Cut it out, Teece."

"Let him go."

Teece felt for his gun in his pocket. He saw the men's faces. He took his hand away and left the gun in his pocket and said, "So that's how it is?"

"That's how it is," someone said.

Teece let the boy go. "All right. Get out." He jerked his hand back in the store. "But I hope you don't think you're gonna leave any trash behind to clutter my store."

"No, sir!"

"You clean everything outa your shed in back, burn it."

Silly shook his head. "I'll take it with."

"They won't let you put it on that damn rocket."

"I'll take it with," insisted the boy softly.

He rushed back through the hardware store. There were sounds of sweeping and cleaning out, and a moment later he appeared, his hands full of tops and marbles and old dusty kites and junk collected through the years. Just then the old tin Ford drove up and Silly climbed in and the door slammed. Teece stood on the porch with a bitter smile. "What you goin' to do up *there*?"

"Startin' new," said Silly. "Gonna have my own hardware."

"God damn it, you been learnin' my trade so you could run off and use it!"

"No, sir, I never thought one day this'd happen, sir, but it did. I can't help it if I learned, Mr. Teece."

"I suppose you got names for your rockets?"

They looked at their one clock on the dashboard of the car.

"Yes, sir."

"Like Elijah and the Chariot, The Big Wheel and The Little Wheel, Faith, Hope, and Charity, eh?"

"We got names for the ships, Mr. Teece."

"God the Son and the Holy Ghost, I wouldn't wonder? Say, boy, you got one named the First Baptist Church?"

"We got to leave now, Mr. Teece."

Teece laughed. "You got one named Swing Low, and another named Sweet Chariot?"

The car started up. "Good-bye, Mr. Teece."

"You got one named Roll Dem Bones?"

"Good-bye, mister!"

"And another called Over Jordan! Ha! Well, tote that rocket, boy, lift that rocket, boy, go on, get blown up, see if I care!"

The car churned off into the dust. The boy rose and cupped his hands to his mouth and shouted one last time at Teece: "Mr. Teece, Mr. Teece, what you goin' to do nights from now on? What you goin' to do nights, Mr. Teece?"

Silence. The car faded down the road. It was gone. "What in hell did he mean?" mused Teece. "What am I goin' to do nights?"

He watched the dust settle, and it suddenly came to him.

He remembered nights when men drove to his house, their knees sticking up sharp and their shotguns sticking up sharper, like a carful of cranes under the night trees of summer, their eyes mean. Honking the horn and him slamming his door, a gun in his hand, laughing to himself, his heart racing like a ten-year-old's, driving off down the summer-night road, a ring of hemp rope coiled on the car floor, fresh shell boxes making every man's coat look bunchy. How many nights over the years, how many nights of the wind rushing in the car, flopping their hair over their mean eyes, roaring, as they picked a tree, a good strong tree, and rapped on a shanty door!

"So that's what the son of a bitch meant?" Teece leaped out into the sunlight. "Come back, you bastard! What am I goin' to do nights? Why, that lousy, insolent son of a . . ."

It was a good question. He sickened and was empty. Yes, What *will* we do nights? he thought. Now *they're* gone, what? He was absolutely empty and numb.

He pulled the pistol from his pocket, checked its load.

"What you goin' to do, Sam?" someone asked.

"Kill that son of a bitch."

Grandpa said, "Don't get yourself heated."

But Samuel Teece was gone around behind the store. A moment later he drove out the drive in his open-top car. "Anyone comin' with me?"

"I'd like a drive," said Grandpa, and got up.

"Anyone else?"

Nobody replied.

Grandpa got in and slammed the door. Samuel Teece gutted the car out in a great whorl of dust. They didn't speak as they rushed down the road under the bright sky. The heat from the dry meadows was shimmering.

They stopped at a crossroad. "Which way'd they go, Grandpa?"

Grandpa squinted. "Straight on ahead, I figure."

They went on. Under the summer trees their car made a lonely sound. The road was empty, and as they drove along they began to notice something. Teece slowed the car and bent out, his yellow eyes fierce.

"God damn it, Grandpa, you see what them bastards did?"

"What?" asked Grandpa, and looked.

Where they had been carefully set down and left, in neat bundles every few feet along the empty country road, were old roller skates, a bandanna full of knicknacks, some old shoes, a cartwheel, stacks of pants and coats and ancient hats, bits of oriental crystal that had once tinkled in the wind, tin cans of pink geraniums, dishes of waxed fruit, cartons of Confederate money, washtubs, scrubboards, wash lines, soap, somebody's tricycle, someone else's hedge shears, a toy wagon, a jack-in-the-box, a stained-glass window from the Negro Baptist Church, a whole set of brake rims, inner tubes, mattresses, couches, rocking chairs, jars of cold cream, hand mirrors. None of it flung down, no, but deposited gently and with feeling, with decorum, upon the dusty edges of the road, as if a whole city had walked here with hands full, at which time a great bronze trumpet had sounded, the articles had been relinquished to the quiet dust, and one and all, the inhabitants of the earth had fled straight up into the blue heavens.

"Wouldn't burn them, they said," cried Teece angrily. "No, wouldn't burn them like I said, but had to take them along and leave them where they could see them for the last time, on the road, all together and whole. Them niggers think they're smart."

He veered the car wildly, mile after mile, down the road, tumbling, smashing, breaking, scattering bundles of paper, jewel boxes, mirrors, chairs. "There, by damn, and there!"

The front tire gave a whistling cry. The car spilled crazily off the road into a ditch, flinging Teece against the glass.

"Son of a bitch!" He dusted himself off and stood out of the car, almost crying with rage.

He looked at the silent, empty road. "We'll never catch them now, never, never." As far as he could see there was nothing but bundles and stacks and more bundles neatly placed like little abandoned shrines in the late day, in the warm-blowing wind.

Teece and Grandpa came walking tiredly back to the hardware store an hour later. The men were still sitting there, listening, and watching the sky. Just as Teece sat down and eased his tight shoes off someone cried, "Look!"

"I'll be *damned* if I will," said Teece.

But the others looked. And they saw the golden bobbins rising in the sky, far away. Leaving flame behind, they vanished.

In the cotton fields the wind blew idly among the snow clusters. In still farther meadows the watermelons lay, unfingerprinted, striped like tortoise cats lying in the sun.

The men on the porch sat down, looked at each other, looked at the yellow rope piled neat on the store shelves, glanced at the gun shells glinting shiny brass in their cartons, saw the silver pistols and long black metal shotguns hung high and quiet in the shadows. Somebody put a straw in his mouth. Someone else drew a figure in the dust.

Finally Samuel Teece held his empty shoe up in triumph, turned it over, stared at it, and said, "Did you notice? Right up to the very last, by God, he said 'Mister'!"

THE WONDERFUL DEATH
OF DUDLEY STONE

"Alive!"

"Dead!"

"Alive in New England, damn it."

"Died twenty years ago!"

"Pass the hat, I'll go myself and bring back his head!"

That's how the talk went that night. A stranger set it off with his mouthings about Dudley Stone dead. Alive! we cried. And shouldn't we know? Weren't we the last frail remnants of those who had burned incense and read his books by the light of blazing intellectual votives in the twenties?

The Dudley Stone. That magnificent stylist, that proudest of literary lions. Surely you recall the head-pounding, the cliff-jumping, the whistlings of doom that followed on his writing his publishers this note:

sirs: Today, aged 30, I retire from the field, renounce writing, burn all my effects, toss my latest manuscript on the dump, cry hail and fare thee well. Yrs., affect.

Dudley Stone

Earthquakes and avalanches, in that order.

"*Why?*" we asked ourselves, meeting down the years.

In fine soap-opera fashion we debated if it was women caused him to hurl his literary future away. Was it the Bottle. Or Horses that outran him and stopped a fine pacer in his prime?

We freely admitted to one and all, that were Stone writing now, Faulkner, Hemingway, and Steinbeck would be buried in his lava. All the sadder that Stone, on the brink of his greatest work, turned one day and went off to live in a town we shall call Obscurity by the sea best named The Past.

"*Why?*"

That question forever lived with those of us who had seen the glints of genius in his piebald works.

One night a few weeks ago, musing off the erosion of the years, finding each others' faces somewhat more pouched and our hairs more conspicuously in absence, we became enraged over the typical citizen's ignorance of Dudley Stone.

At least, we muttered, Thomas Wolfe had had a full measure of success before he seized his nose and jumped off the rim of Eternity. At least the critics gathered to stare after his plunge into darkness as after a meteor that made much fire in its passing. But who now remembered Dudley Stone, his coteries, his frenzied followers of the twenties?

"Pass the hat," I said. "I'll travel three hundred miles, grab Dudley Stone by the pants and say: 'Look here, Mr. Stone, why did you let us down so badly? Why haven't you written a book in twenty-five years?'"

The hat was lined with cash; I sent a telegram and took a train.

I do not know what I expected. Perhaps to find a doddering and frail praying mantis, whisping about the station, blown by seawinds, a chalk-white ghost who would husk at me with the voices of grass and reeds blown in the night. I clenched my knees in agony as my train chuffed into the station. I let myself down into a lonely country-side, a mile from the sea, like a man foolishly insane, wondering why I had come so far.

On a bulletin board in front of the boarded-up ticket office I found a cluster of announcements, inches thick, pasted and nailed one upon another for uncountable years. Leafing under, peeling away anthropological layers of printed tissue I found what I wanted. Dudley Stone for alderman, Dudley Stone for Sheriff, Dudley Stone for Mayor! On up through the years his photograph, bleached by sun and rain, faintly recognizable, asked for ever more responsible positions in the life of this world near the sea. I stood reading them.

"Hey!"

And Dudley Stone plunged across the station platform behind me suddenly. "Is that you, Mr. Douglas!" I whirled to confront this great architecture of a man, big but not in the least fat, his legs huge pistons thrusting him on, a bright flower in his lapel, a bright tie at his neck. He crushed my hand, looked down upon me like Michelangelo's God creating Adam with a mighty touch. His face was the face of those illustrated North Winds and South Winds that blow hot and cold in ancient mariners' charts. It was the face that symbolizes the sun in Egyptian carvings, ablaze with life!

My God! I thought. And this is the man who hasn't written in twenty-odd years. Impossible. He's so alive it's sinful. I can hear his *heartbeat*!

I must have stood with my eyes very wide to let the look of him cram in upon my startled senses.

"You thought you'd find Marley's Ghost," he laughed. "Admit it."

"I—"

"My wife's waiting with a New England boiled dinner, we've plenty of ale and stout. I like the ring of those words. To *ale* is not to sicken, but to revive the flagging spirit. A tricky word, that. And *stout*? There's a nice ruddy sound to it. Stout!" A great golden watch bounced on his vestfront, hung in bright chains. He vised my elbow and charmed me along, a magician well on his way back to his cave with a luckless rabbit. "Glad to see you! I suppose you've come, as the others came, to ask the same question, eh! Well, this time I'll tell everything!"

My heart jumped. "Wonderful!"

Behind the empty station sat an open-top 1927-vintage Model-T Ford. "Fresh air. Drive at twilight like this, you get all the fields, the grass, the flowers, coming at you in the wind. I hope you're not one of those who tip-toe around shutting windows! Our house is like the top of a mesa. We let the weather do our broom-work. Hop in!"

❋ Ten minutes later we swung off the highway onto a drive that had not been leveled or filled in years. Stone drove straight on over the pits and bumps, smiling steadily. Bang! We shuddered the last few yards to a wild, unpainted two-story house. The car was allowed to gasp itself away into mortal silence.

"Do you want the truth?" Stone turned to look me in the face and hold my shoulder with an earnest hand. "I was murdered by a man with a gun twenty-five years ago almost to this very day."

I sat staring after him as he leaped from the car. He was solid as a ton of rock, no ghost to him, but yet I knew that somehow the truth was in what he had told me before firing himself like a cannon at the house.

✳ "This is my wife, and this is the house, and that is our supper waiting for us! Look at our view. Windows on three sides of the living room, a view of the sea, the shore, the meadows. We nail the windows open three out of four seasons. I swear you get a smell of limes here midsummer, and something from Antarctica, ammonia and ice cream, come December. Sit down! Lena, isn't it *nice* having him here?"

"I hope you like New England boiled dinner," said Lena, now here, now there, a tall, firmly-built woman, the sun in the East, Father Christmas' daughter, a bright lamp of a face that lit our table as she dealt out the heavy useful dishes made to stand the pound of giants' fists. The cutlery was solid enough to take a lion's teeth. A great whiff of steam rose up, through which we gladly descended, sinners into Hell. I saw the seconds-plate skim by three times and felt the ballast gather in my chest, my throat, and at last my ears. Dudley Stone poured me a brew he had made from wild Concords that had cried for mercy, he said. The wine bottle, empty, had its green glass mouth blown softly by Stone, who summoned out a rhythmic one-note tune that was quickly done.

"Well, I've kept you waiting long enough," he said, peering at me from that distance which drinking adds between people and which, at odd turns in the evening, seems closeness itself. "I'll tell you about my murder. I've never told anyone before; believe me. Do you know John Oatis Kendall?"

"A minor writer in the twenties, wasn't he?" I said. "A few books. Burned out by '31. Died last week."

"God rest him." Mr. Stone lapsed into a special brief melancholy from which he revived as he began to speak again.

"Yes. John Oatis Kendall, burned out by the year 1931, a writer of great potentialities."

"Not as great as yours," I said, quickly.

"Well, just wait. We were boys together, John Oatis and I, born where the shade of an oak tree touched my house in the morning and his house at night, swam every creek in the world together, got sick on sour apples and cigarettes together, saw the same lights in the same blond hair of the same young girl together, and in our late teens went out to kick Fate in the stomach and get beat on the head together. We both did fair, and then I better and still better as the years ran. If his first book got one good notice, mine got six, if I got one bad notice, he got a dozen. We were like two friends on a train which the public has uncoupled. There went John Oatis on the caboose, left behind, crying out, 'Save me! You're leaving me in Tank Town, Ohio; we're on the same track!' And the conductor saying, 'Yes, but not the same *train!*' And myself yelling, 'I believe in you, John, be of good heart, I'll come back for you!' And the caboose dwindling behind with its red and green lamps like cherry and lime pops shining in the dark and we yelling our friendship to each other: 'John, old man!' 'Dudley, old pal!' while John Oatis went out on a dark siding behind a tin baling-shed at midnight and my engine, with all the flag-wavers and brass bands, boiled on toward dawn."

Dudley Stone paused and noticed my look of general confusion.

"All this to lead up to my murder," he said. "For it was John Oatis Kendall who, in 1930, traded a few old clothes and some remaindered copies of his books for a gun and came out to this house and this room."

"He really meant to kill you?"

"Meant to, hell! He did! Bang! Have some more wine? That's better."

A strawberry shortcake was set upon the table by Mrs. Stone, while he enjoyed my gibbering suspense. Stone sliced it into three huge chunks and served it around, fixing me with his kindly approximation of the Wedding Guest's eye.

"There he sat, John Oatis, in that chair where you sit now. Behind him, outside, in the smokehouse, seventeen hams; in our wine cellars, five hundred bottles of the best; beyond the window open country, the elegant sea in full lace; overhead a moon like a dish of cool cream, everywhere the full panoply of spring, and Lena across the table, too, a willow tree in the wind, laughing at everything I said or did not choose to say, both of us thirty, mind you, thirty years old, life our magnificent carousel, our fingers playing full chords, my books selling well, fan mail pouring upon us in crisp white founts, horses in the stables for moonlight rides to coves where either we or the sea might whisper all we wished in the night. And John

Oatis seated there where you sit now, quietly taking the little blue gun from his pocket."

"I laughed, thinking it was a cigar lighter of some sort," said his wife.

"But John Oatis said quite seriously: 'I'm going to kill you, Mr. Stone.'"

"What did you do?"

"Do? I sat there, stunned, riven; I heard a terrible slam! the coffin lid in my face! I heard coal down a black chute; dirt on my buried door. They say all your *past* hurtles by at such times. Nonsense. The *future* does. You see your face a bloody porridge. You sit there until your fumbling mouth can say, 'But why, John, what have I *done* to you?'

"'Done!' he cried.

"And his eye skimmed along the vast bookshelf and the handsome brigade of books drawn stiffly to attention there with my name on each blazing like a panther's eye in the Moroccan blackness. 'Done!' he cried, mortally. And his hand itched the revolver in a sweat. 'Now, John,' I cautioned. 'What do you want?'

"'One thing more than anything else in the world,' he said, 'to kill you and be famous. Get my name in headlines. Be famous as you are famous. Be known for a lifetime and beyond as the man who killed Dudley Stone!'

"'You can't mean that!'

"'I do. I'll be very famous. Far more famous than I am today, in your shadow. Oh, listen here, no one in the world knows how to hate like a writer does. God, how I love your work and God, how I hate you because you write so well. Amazing ambivalence. But I can't take it anymore, not being able to write as you do, so I'll take my fame the easy way. I'll cut you off before you reach your prime. They say your next book will be your very finest, your most brilliant!'

"'They exaggerate.'

"'My guess is they're right!' he said.

"I looked beyond him to Lena who sat in her chair, frightened, but not frightened enough to scream or run and spoil the scene so it might end inadvertently.

"'Calm,' I said. 'Calmness. Sit there, John. I ask only one minute. Then pull the trigger.'

"'No!' Lena whispered.

"'Calmness,' I said to her, to myself, to John Oatis.

"I gazed out the open windows, I felt the wind, I thought of the wine in the cellar, the coves at the beach, the sea, the night moon like a disc of menthol cooling the summer heavens, drawing clouds of flaming salt, the stars, after it in a wheel toward morning. I thought of myself only thirty, Lena thirty, our whole lives ahead. I thought of all the flesh of life hung high and waiting for me to really *start* banqueting! I had never climbed a mountain, I had never sailed an ocean, I had never run for mayor, I had never dived for pearls, I had never owned a telescope, I had never acted on a stage or built a house or read all the classics I had so *wished* to read. All the *actions* waiting to be done!

"So in that almost instantaneous sixty seconds, I thought at last of my career. The books I had written, the books I *was* writing, the books I intended to write. The reviews, the sales, our huge balance in the bank. And, believe or disbelieve me, for the first time in my life I got free of it all. I became, in one moment, a critic. I cleared the scales. On one hand I put all the boats I hadn't taken, the flowers I hadn't planted, the children I hadn't raised, all the hills I hadn't looked at, with Lena there, goddess of the harvest. In the middle I put John Oatis Kendall with his gun—the upright that held the balances. And on the empty scale a dozen books. I made some minor adjustments. The sixty opposite I laid my pen, my ink, my empty paper, my seconds were ticking by. The sweet night wind blew across the table. It touched a curl of hair on Lena's neck, oh Lord, how softly, softly it touched . . .

"The gun pointed at me. I have seen the moon craters in photographs, and that hole in space called the Great Coal Sack Nebula, but neither was as big, take my word, as the mouth of that gun across the room from me.

" 'John,' I said at last, 'do you hate me *that* much? Because I've been lucky and you not?'

" 'Yes, damn it!' he cried.

"It was almost funny he should envy me. I was not that much better a writer than he. A flick of the wrist made the difference.

" 'John,' I said quietly to him, 'if you want me dead, I'll *be* dead. Would you like for me to never write again?'

" 'I'd like nothing better!' he cried. 'Get ready!' He aimed at my heart!

" 'All right,' I said, 'I'll never write again.'

" 'What?' he said.

" 'We're old old friends, we've never lied to each other, have we? Then take my word, from this night on I'll never put pen to paper.'

" 'Oh God,' he said, and laughed with contempt and disbelief.

" 'There,' I said, nodding my head at the desk near him, 'are the only original copies of the two books I've been working on for the last three years. I'll burn one in front of you now. The other you yourself may throw in the sea. Clean out the house, take everything faintly resembling literature, burn my published books, too. Here.' I got up. He could have shot me then, but I had him fascinated. I tossed one manuscript on the hearth and touched a match to it.

" 'No!' Lena said. I turned. 'I know what I'm doing,' I said. She began to cry. John Oatis Kendall simply stared at me, bewitched. I brought him the other unpublished manuscript. 'Here,' I said, tucking it under his right shoe so his foot was a paper weight. I went back and sat down. The wind was blowing and the night was warm and Lena was white as apple-blossoms there across the table.

"I said, 'From this day forward I will not write ever again.'

"At last John Oatis managed to say, 'How can you do this?'

" 'To make everyone happy,' I said. 'To make you happy because we'll be friends again, eventually. To make Lena happy because I'll be just her husband again and no agent's performing seal. And myself happy because I'd rather be a live man than a dead author. A dying man will do anything, John. Now take my last novel and get along with you.'

"We sat there, the three of us, just as we three are sitting tonight. There was a smell of lemons and limes and camellias. The ocean roared on the stony coastland below; God, what a lovely moonlit sound. And at last, picking up the manuscripts, John Oatis took them, like my body, out of the room. He paused at the door and said, 'I believe you.' And then he was gone. I heard him drive away. I put Lena to bed. That was one of the few nights in my life I ever walked down by the shore, but walk I did, taking deep breaths and feeling my arms and legs and my face with my hands, crying like a child, walking and wading in the surf to feel the cold salt water foaming about me in a million suds."

Dudley Stone paused. Time had made a stop in the room. Time was in another year, the three of us sitting there, enchanted with his telling of the murder.

"And did he destroy your last novel?" I asked.

Dudley Stone nodded. "A week later one of the pages drifted up on the shore. He must have thrown them over the cliff, a thousand pages, I see it in my mind's eye, a flock of white sea-gulls it might seem, flying down to the water and going out with the tide at four in the black morning. Lena ran up the beach with that single page in her hand, crying, 'Look, look!' And when I saw what she handed me, I tossed it back in the ocean."

"Don't tell me you honored your promise!"

Dudley Stone looked at me steadily. "What would *you* have done in a similar position? Look at it this way: John Oatis did me a favor. He didn't kill me. He didn't shoot me. He took my word. He honored my word. He let me live. He let me go on eating and sleeping and breathing. Quite suddenly he had broadened my horizons. I was so grateful that standing on the beach hip-deep in water that night, I cried. I was grateful. Do you really understand that word? Grateful he had let me live when he had had it in his hand to annihilate me forever."

Mrs. Stone rose up, the dinner was ended. She cleared the dishes, we lit cigars; and Dudley Stone strolled me over to his office-at-home, a rolltop desk, its jaws propped wide with parcels and papers and ink bottles, a typewriter, documents, ledgers, indexes.

"It was all rolling to a boil in me. John Oatis simply spooned the froth off the top so I could see the brew. It was very clear," said Dudley Stone. "Writing was always so much mustard and gallweed to me; fidgeting words on paper, experiencing vast depressions of heart and soul. Watching the greedy critics graph me up, chart me down, slice me like sausage, eat me at midnight breakfasts. Work of the worst sort. I was *ready* to fling the pack. My trigger was set. Boom! There was John Oatis! Look here."

He rummaged in the desk and brought forth handbills and posters. "I had been *writing* about living. Now I wanted to live. *Do* things instead of tell about things. I ran for the board of education. I won. I ran for alderman. I won. I ran for mayor. I won! Sheriff! Town librarian! Sewage disposal official. I shook a lot of hands, saw a lot of life, did a lot of things. We've lived every way there is to live, with our eyes and noses and mouths, with our ears and hands. We've climbed hills and painted pictures, there are some on the wall! We've been three times around the world! I even delivered our baby son, unexpectedly. He's grown and married now—lives in New York! We've done and done again." Stone paused and smiled. "Come on out in the yard; we've set up a telescope, would you like to see the rings of Saturn?"

We stood in the yard, and the wind blew from a thousand miles at sea and while we were standing there, looking at the stars through the telescope, Mrs. Stone went down into the midnight cellar after a rare Spanish wine.

✳ It was noon the next day when we reached the lonely station after a hurricane trip across the jouncing meadows from the sea. Mr. Dudley Stone let the car have its head, while he talked to me, laughing, smiling, pointing to this or that outcrop of Neolithic stone, this or that wild flower, falling silent again only as we parked and waited for the train to come and take me away.

"I suppose," he said, looking at the sky, "you think I'm quite insane."

"No, I'd never say that."

"Well," said Dudley Stone, "John Oatis Kendall did me one other favor."

"What was that?"

Stone hitched around conversationally in the patched leather seat.

"He helped me get out when the going was good. Deep down inside I must have guessed that my literary success was something that would melt when they turned off the cooling system. My subconscious had a pretty fair picture of my future. I knew what none of my critics knew, that I was headed nowhere but down. The two books John Oatis destroyed were very bad. They would have killed me deader than Oatis possibly could. So he helped me decide, unwittingly, what I might not have had the courage to decide myself, to bow gracefully out while the cotillion was still on, while the Chinese lanterns still cast flattering pink lights on my Harvard complexion. I had seen too many writers up, down, and out, hurt, unhappy, suicidal. The combination of circumstance, coincidence, subconscious knowledge, relief, and gratitude to John Oatis Kendall to just *be alive*, were fortuitous, to say the least."

We sat in the warm sunlight another minute.

"And then I had the pleasure of seeing myself compared to all the greats when I announced my departure from the literary scene. Few authors in recent history have bowed out to such publicity. It was a lovely funeral. I looked, as they say, natural. And the echoes lingered. 'His *next* book!' the critics cried, 'would have been *it*! A masterpiece!' I had them panting, waiting. Little did they know. Even now, a quarter-century later, my readers who were college boys then, make sooty excursions on drafty kerosene-stinking shortline trains to solve the mystery of why I've made them wait so long for my 'masterpiece.' And thanks to John Oatis Kendall I still have a little reputation; it has receded slowly, painlessly. The next year I might have died by my own writing hand. How much better to cut your own caboose off the train, before others do it for you.

"My friendship with John Oatis Kendall? It came back. It took time, of course. But he was out here to see me in 1947; it was a nice day, all around, like old times. And now he's dead and at last I've told someone everything. What will you tell your friends in the city? They won't believe a word of this. But it *is* true, I swear it, as I sit here and breathe God's good air and look at the calluses on my hands and begin to resemble the faded handbills I used when I ran for county treasurer."

We stood on the station platform.

"Good-by, and thanks for coming and opening your ears and letting my world crash in on you. God bless to all your curious friends. Here comes the train! I've got to run; Lena and I are going to a Red Cross drive down the coast this afternoon! Good-by!"

I watched the dead man stomp and leap across the platform, felt the plankings shudder, saw him jump into his Model-T, heard it lurch under his bulk, saw him bang the floor-boards with a big foot, idle the motor, roar it, turn, smile, wave to me, and then roar off and away toward that suddenly brilliant town called Obscurity by a dazzling seashore called The Past.

BY THE NUMBERS!

"COMPANY, TENSHUN!"

Snap.

"Company, forward— *Harch!*"

Tromp, tromp.

"Company *halt!*"

Tromp, rattle, clump.

"Eyes right."

Whisper.

"Eyes left."

Rustle.

"About face!"

Tromp, scrape, tromp.

In the sunlight, a long time ago, the man shouted and the company obeyed. By a hotel pool under a Los Angeles sky in the summer of '52, there was the drill sergeant and there stood his team.

"Eyes front! Head up! Chin in! Chest out! Stomach sucked! Shoulders back, dammit, *back*!

Rustle, whisper, murmur, scratch, silence.

And the drill sergeant walking forward, dressed in bathing trunks by the edge of that pool to fix his cold bluewater gaze on his company, his squad, his team, his—

Son.

A boy of nine or ten, standing stiffly upright, staring arrow-straight ahead at military nothings, shoulders starched, as his father paced, circling him, barking commands, leaning in at him, mouth crisply enunciating the words. Both father and son were dressed in bathing togs and, a moment before, had been cleaning the pool area, arranging towels, sweeping with brooms. But now, just before noon:

"Company! By the numbers! One, two!"

"Three, four!" cried the boy.

"One, two!" shouted the father.

"Three, *four*!"

"Company halt, shoulder arms, present arms, tuck that chin, square those toes, hup!"

The memory came and went like a badly projected film in an old rerun cinema. Where had it come from, and why?

I was on a train heading north from Los Angeles to San Francisco. I was in the bar-car, alone, late at night, save for the barman and a young-old stranger who sat directly across from me, drinking his second martini.

The old memory had come from him.

Nine feet away, his hair, his face, his startled blue and wounded eyes had suddenly cut the time stream and sent me back.

In and out of focus, I was on the train, then beside that pool, watching the hurt bright gaze of this man across the aisle, hearing his father thirty years lost, and watching the son, five thousand afternoons ago, wheeling and pivoting, turning and freezing, presenting imaginary arms, shouldering imaginary rifles.

"Tenshun!!" barked the father.

"Shun!" echoed the son.

"My God," whispered Sid, my best friend, lying beside me in the hot noon light, staring.

"My God, indeed," I muttered.

"How long has *this* been going on?"

"Years, maybe. Looks that way. Years."

"Hut, two!"

"Three, four!"

A church clock nearby struck noon; time to open the pool liquor bar.

"Company . . . *harch!*"

A parade of two, the man and boy strode across the tiles toward the half-locked gates on the open-air bar.

"Company, halt. Ready! Free locks! Hut!"

The boy snapped the locks wide.

"Hut!"

The boy flung the gate aside, jumped back, stiffened, waiting.

"Bout face, forward, harch!"

When the boy had almost reached the rim of the pool and was about to fall in, the father, with the wryest of smiles, called, quietly: ". . . halt."

The son teetered on the edge of the pool.

"God damn," whispered Sid.

The father left his son standing there skeleton stiff and flagpole erect, and went away.

Sid jumped up suddenly, staring at this.

"Sit down," I said.

"Christ, is he going to leave the kid just *waiting* there?!"

"Sit down, Sid."

"Well, for God's sake, that's inhuman!"

"He's not your son, Sid," I said, quietly. "You want to start a real fight?"

"Yeah!" said Sid. "Dammit!"

"It wouldn't do any good."

"Yes, it would. I'd like to beat hell—"

"Look at the boy's *face*, Sid."

Sid looked and began to slump.

The son, standing there in the burning glare of sun and water, was proud. The way he held his head, the way his eyes took fire, the way his naked shoulders carried the burden of goad or instruction, was all pride.

It was the logic of that pride which finally caved Sid in. Weighted with some small despair, he sank back down to his knees.

"Are we going to have to sit here all afternoon, and watch this dumb game of—" Sid's voice rose in spite of himself "—Simon Says?!"

The father heard. In the midst of stacking towels on the far side of the pool, he froze. The muscles on his back played like a pinball machine, making sums. Then he turned smartly, veered past his son who still stood balanced a half inch from the pool's rim, gave him a glance, nodded with intense, scowling approval, and came to cast his iron shadow over Sid and myself.

"I will thank you, sir," he said, quietly, "to keep your voice down, to not confuse my son—"

"I'll say any damn thing I want!" Sid started to get up.

"No, sir, you will not." The man pointed his nose at Sid; it might just as well have been a gun. "This is my pool, my turf, I have an agreement with the hotel, their territory stops out there by the gate. If I'm to run a clean, tucked-in shop, it is to be with total authority. Any dissidents—*out. Bodily.* On the gymnasium wall inside you'll find my ju-jitsu black belt, boxing, and rifle-marksman certificates. If you try to shake my hand, I will break your wrist. If you sneeze, I will crack your nose. One word and your dental surgeon will need two years to reshape your smile. Company, *tenshun!*"

The words all flowed together.

His son stiffened at the rim of the pool.

"Forty laps! Hut!"

"Hut!" cried the boy, and leaped.

His body striking the water and his beginning to swim furiously stopped Sid from any further outrage. Sid shut his eyes.

The father smiled at Sid, and turned to watch the boy churning the summer waters to a foam.

"There's everything I never was," he said. "Gentlemen."

He gave us a curt nod and stalked away.

Sid could only run and jump in the pool. He did twenty laps himself. Most of the time, the boy beat him. When Sid came out, the blaze was gone from his face and he threw himself down.

"Christ," he muttered, his face buried in his towel, "someday that boy *must* haul off and murder that son of a bitch!"

"As a Hemingway character once said," I replied, watching the son finish his thirty-fifth lap, "wouldn't it be nice to *think* so?"

✳ The final time, the last day I ever saw them, the father was still marching about briskly, emptying ashtrays (no one could empty them the way *he* could), straightening tables, aligning chairs and loungers in military rows, and arranging fresh white towels on benches in crisp mathematical stacks.

Even the way he swabbed the deck was geometrical. In all his marching and going, fixing and realigning, only on occasion did he snap his head up, flick a gaze to make sure his squad, his platoon, his company still stood frozen by the hour, a boy like a ramrod guidon, his hair blowing in the summer wind, eyes straight on the late afternoon horizon, mouth clamped, chin tucked, shoulders back.

I could not help myself. Sid was long gone. I waited on the balcony of the hotel overlooking the pool, having a final drink, not able to take my gaze off the marching father and the statue son. At dusk, the father double-timed it to the outer gate and almost as an afterthought called over his shoulder:

"Tenshun! Squad right. One, two—"

"Three, four!" cried the boy.

The boy strode through the gate, feet clubbing the cement as if he wore boots. He marched off toward the parking lot as his father snap-locked the gate with a robot's ease, took a fast scan around, raised his stare, saw me, and hesitated. His eyes burned over my face. I felt my shoulders go back, my chin drop, my shoulders flinch. To stop it, I lifted my drink, waved it carelessly at him, and drank.

What will happen, I thought, in the years ahead? Will the son grow up to kill his old man, or beat him up, or just run away to know a ruined life, always marching to some unheard shout of "Hut" or "harch!" but never "at ease!"?

Or, I thought, drinking, would the boy raise sons himself and just yell at *them* on hot noons by far pools in endless years? Would he one day stick a pistol in his mouth and kill his father the only way he knew how? Or would he marry and have *no* sons and thus bury all shouts, all drills, all sergeants? Questions, half-answers, more questions.

My glass was empty. The sun had gone, and the father and his son with it.

But now, in the flesh, straight across from me on this late night train, heading north for unlit destinations, one of them had returned. There he was, the kid himself, the raw recruit, the child of the father who shouted at noon and told the sun to rise or set.

Merely alive? *half* alive? *all* alive?

I wasn't sure.

But there he sat, thirty years later, a young-old or old-young man, sipping on his third martini.

By now, I realized that my glances were becoming much too constant and embarrassing. I studied his bright blue, wounded eyes, for that is what they were: wounded, and at last took courage and spoke:

"Pardon me," I said. "This may seem silly, but—thirty years back, I swam weekends at the Ambassador Hotel where a military man tended the pool with his son. He—well. Are *you* that son?"

The young-old man across from me thought for a moment, looked me over with his shifting eyes and at last smiled, quietly.

"I," he said, "*am* that son. Come on over."

We shook hands. I sat and ordered a final round for us, as if we were celebrating something, or holding a wake, nobody seemed to know which. After the barman delivered the drinks, I said, "To nineteen fifty-two, a toast. A good year? Bad year? Here's to it, anyway!"

We drank and the young-old man said, almost immediately, "You're wondering what ever happened to my father."

"My God," I sighed.

"No, no," he assured me, "it's all right. A lot of people have wondered, have asked, over the years."

The boy inside the older man nursed his martini and remembered the past.

"Do you *tell* people when they ask?" I said.

"I do."

I took a deep breath. "All right, then. What *did* happen to your father?"

"He died."

There was a long pause.

"Is that *all*?"

"Not quite." The young-old man arranged his glass on the table in front of him, and placed a napkin at a precise angle to it, and fitted an olive to the very center of the napkin, reading the past there. "You remember what he was like?"

"Vividly."

"Oh, what a world of meaning you put into that 'vividly'!" The young-old man snorted faintly. "You remember his marches up, down, around the pool, left face, right, tenshun, don't move, chin-stomach in, chest out, harch two, hut?"

"I remember."

"Well, one day in nineteen fifty-three, long after the old crowd was gone from the pool, and you with them, my dad was drilling me outdoors one late afternoon. He had me standing in the hot sun for an hour or so and he yelled in my face, I can remember the saliva spray on my chin, my nose, my eyelids when he yelled: don't move a muscle! don't blink! don't twitch! don't breathe till I *tell* you! You hear, soldier? Hear? You hear? Hear?!

"'Sir!' I gritted between my teeth.

"As my father turned, he slipped on the tiles and fell in the water."

The young-old man paused and gave a strange small bark of a laugh.

"Did you *know*? Of course you didn't. I didn't either . . . that in all those years of working at various pools, cleaning out the showers, replacing the towels, repairing the diving boards, fixing the plumbing, he had never, my God, never learned to swim! *Never!* Jesus. It's unbelievable. Never.

"He had never *told* me. Somehow, I had never guessed! And since he had just yelled at me, instructed me, *ordered* me: eyes right! don't twitch! don't *move*! I just *stood* there staring straight ahead at the late afternoon sun. I didn't let my eyes drop to see, even once. Just straight ahead, by the numbers, as told.

"I heard him thrashing around in the water, yelling. But I couldn't understand what he said. I heard him suck and gasp and gargle and suck again, going down, shrieking, but I stood straight, chin up, stomach tight, eyes level, sweat on my brow, mouth firm, buttocks clenched, ramrod spine, and him yelling, gagging, taking water. I kept waiting for him to yell, 'At ease!' 'At ease!' he should have yelled, but he never did. So what could I do? I just stood there, like a statue, until the shrieking stopped and the water lapped the pool rim and everything got quiet. I stood there for ten minutes, maybe twenty, half an hour, until someone came out and found me there, and they looked down in the pool and saw something deep under and said Jesus Christ and finally turned and came up to me, because they knew me and my father, and at last said, At Ease.

"And then I cried."

The young-old man finished his drink.

"You see, the thing is, I couldn't be sure he wasn't faking. He'd done tricks like that before, to get me off guard, make me relax. He'd go around a corner, wait, duck back, to see if I was ramrod tall. Or he'd pretend to go into the men's room, and jump back to find me wrong. Then he'd punish me. So, standing there by the pool that day, I thought, it's a trick, to make me fall out. So I had to wait, didn't I, to be sure? . . . to be sure."

Finished, he put his empty martini glass down on the tray and sat back in his own silence, eyes gazing over my shoulder at nothing in particular. I tried to see if his eyes were wet, or if his mouth gave some special sign now that the tale was told, but I saw nothing.

"Now," I said, "I know about your father. But . . . what ever happened to you?"

"As you see," he said, "I'm here."

He stood up and reached over and shook my hand.

"Good night," he said.

I looked straight up in his face and saw the young boy there waiting for orders five thousand afternoons back. Then I looked at his left hand; no wedding ring there. Which meant what? No sons, no future? But I couldn't ask.

"I'm glad we met again," I heard myself say.

"Yes." He nodded, and gave my hand a final shake. "It's good to see you made it through."

Me, I thought. My God! *Me?!*

But he had turned and was walking off down the aisle, beautifully balanced, not swaying with the train's motion, this way or that. He moved in a clean, lithe, well-cared-for body, which the train's swerving could do nothing to as he went away.

As he reached the door, he hesitated, his back to me, and he seemed to be waiting for some final word, some order, some shout from someone.

Forward, I wanted to say, by the numbers! *March!*

But I said nothing.

Not knowing if it would kill him, or release him, I simply bit my tongue, and watched him open the door, slip silently through, and stride down the corridor of the next sleeping car toward a past I just might have imagined, toward a future I could not guess.

APRIL 2005: USHER II

"'DURING THE WHOLE OF A DULL, DARK, and soundless day in the autumn of the year, when the clouds hung oppressively low in the heavens, I had been passing alone, on horseback, through a singularly dreary tract of country, and at length found myself, as the shades of evening drew on, within view of the melancholy House of Usher. . . .'"

Mr. William Stendahl paused in his quotation. There, upon a low black hill, stood the House, its cornerstone bearing the inscription 2005 A.D.

Mr. Bigelow, the architect, said, "It's completed. Here's the key, Mr. Stendahl."

The two men stood together silently in the quiet autumn afternoon. Blueprints rustled on the raven grass at their feet.

"The House of Usher," said Mr. Stendahl with pleasure. "Planned, built, bought, paid for. Wouldn't Mr. Poe be *delighted*?"

Mr. Bigelow squinted. "Is it everything you wanted, sir?"

"Yes!"

"Is the color right? Is it desolate and *terrible*?"

"Very desolate, very terrible!"

"The walls are—*bleak*?"

"Amazingly so!"

"The tarn, is it 'black and lurid' enough?"

"Most incredibly black and lurid."

"And the sedge—we've dyed it, you know—is it the proper gray and ebon?"

"Hideous!"

Mr. Bigelow consulted his architectural plans. From these he quoted in part: "Does the whole structure cause an 'iciness, a sickening of the heart, a dreariness of thought'? The House, the lake, the land, Mr. Stendahl?"

"Mr. Bigelow, it's worth every penny! My God, it's beautiful!"

"Thank you. I had to work in total ignorance. Thank the Lord you had your own private rockets or we'd never have been allowed to bring most of the equipment through. You notice, it's always twilight here, this land, always October, barren, sterile, dead. It took a bit of doing. We killed everything. Ten thousand tons of DDT. Not a snake, frog, or Martian fly left! Twilight always, Mr. Stendahl; I'm proud of that. There are machines, hidden, which blot out the sun. It's always properly 'dreary.'"

Stendahl drank it in, the dreariness, the oppression, the fetid vapors, the whole "atmosphere," so delicately contrived and fitted. And that House! That crumbling horror, that evil lake, the fungi, the extensive decay! Plastic or otherwise, who could guess?

He looked at the autumn sky. Somewhere above, beyond, far off, was the sun. Somewhere it was the month of April on the planet Mars, a yellow month with a blue sky. Somewhere above, the rockets burned down to civilize a beautifully dead planet. The sound of their screaming passage was muffled by this dim, soundproofed world, this ancient autumn world.

"Now that my job's done," said Mr. Bigelow uneasily, "I feel free to ask what you're going to do with all this."

"With Usher? Haven't you guessed?"

"No."

"Does the name Usher mean nothing to you?"

"Nothing."

"Well, what about *this* name: Edgar Allan Poe?"

Mr. Bigelow shook his head.

"Of course." Stendahl snorted delicately, a combination of dismay and contempt. "How could I expect you to know blessed Mr. Poe? He died a long while ago, before Lincoln. All of his books were burned in the Great Fire. That's thirty years ago—1975."

"Ah," said Mr. Bigelow wisely. "*One of those!*"

"Yes, one of those, Bigelow. He and Lovecraft and Hawthorne and Ambrose Bierce and all the tales of terror and fantasy and horror and, for that matter, tales of the future were burned. Heartlessly. They passed a law. Oh, it started very small. In 1950 and '60 it was a grain of sand. They began by controlling books of cartoons and then detective books and, of course, films, one way or another, one group or another, political bias, religious prejudice, union pressures; there was always a minority afraid of something, and a great majority afraid of the dark, afraid of the future, afraid of the past, afraid of the present, afraid of themselves and shadows of themselves."

"I see."

"Afraid of the word 'politics' (which eventually became a synonym for Communism among the more reactionary elements, so I hear, and it was worth your life to use the word!), and with a screw tightened here, a bolt fastened there, a push, a pull, a yank, art and literature were soon like a great twine of taffy strung about, being twisted in braids and tied in knots and thrown in all directions, until there was no more resiliency and no more savor to it. Then the film cameras chopped short and the theaters turned dark, and the print presses trickled down from a great Niagara of reading matter to a mere innocuous dripping of 'pure' material. Oh, the word 'escape' was radical, too, I tell you!"

"Was it?"

"It was! Every man, they said, must face reality. Must face the Here and Now! Everything that was *not* so must go. All the beautiful literary lies and flights of fancy must be shot in mid-air! So they lined them up against a library wall one Sunday morning thirty years ago, in 1975; they lined them

up, St. Nicholas and the Headless Horseman and Snow White and Rumpelstiltskin and Mother Goose—oh, what a wailing!—and shot them down,
and burned the paper castles and the fairy frogs and old kings and the people who lived happily ever after (for of course it was a fact that *nobody* lived
happily ever after!), and Once Upon A Time became No More! And they
spread the ashes of the Phantom Rickshaw with the rubble of the Land of
Oz; they filleted the bones of Glinda the Good and Ozma and shattered Poly-
chrome in a spectroscope and served Jack Pumpkinhead with meringue at
the Biologists' Ball! The Beanstalk died in a bramble of red tape! Sleeping
Beauty awoke at the kiss of a scientist and expired at the fatal puncture of
his syringe. And they made Alice drink something from a bottle which
reduced her to a size where she could no longer cry 'Curiouser and curiouser,' and they gave the Looking Glass one hammer blow to smash it and
every Red King and Oyster away!"

He clenched his fists. Lord, how immediate it was! His face was red and
he was gasping for breath.

As for Mr. Bigelow, he was astounded at this long explosion. He blinked
and at last said, "Sorry. Don't know what you're talking about. Just names
to me. From what I hear, the Burning was a good thing."

"Get out!" screamed Stendahl. "You've done your job, now let me alone,
you idiot!"

Mr. Bigelow summoned his carpenters and went away.

Mr. Stendahl stood alone before his House.

"Listen here," he said to the unseen rockets. "I came to Mars to get away
from you Clean-Minded people, but you're flocking in thicker every day,
like flies to offal. So I'm going to show you. I'm going to teach you a fine lesson for what you did to Mr. Poe on Earth. As of this day, beware. The House
of Usher is open for business!"

He pushed a fist at the sky.

The rocket landed. A man stepped out jauntily. He glanced at the House,
and his gray eyes were displeased and vexed. He strode across the moat to
confront the small man there.

"Your name Stendahl?"

"Yes."

"I'm Garrett, Investigator of Moral Climates."

"So you finally got to Mars, you Moral Climate people? I wondered when
you'd appear."

"We arrived last week. We'll soon have things as neat and tidy as Earth." The man waved an identification card irritably toward the House. "Suppose you tell me about that place, Stendahl?"

"It's a haunted castle, if you like."

"I don't like, Stendahl, I don't like. The sound of that word 'haunted.'"

"Simple enough. In this year of our Lord 2005 I have built a mechanical sanctuary. In it copper bats fly on electronic beams, brass rats scuttle in plastic cellars, robot skeletons dance; robot vampires, harlequins, wolves, and white phantoms, compounded of chemical and ingenuity, live here."

"That's what I was afraid of," said Garrett, smiling quietly. "I'm afraid we're going to have to tear your place down."

"I knew you'd come out as soon as you discovered what went on."

"I'd have come sooner, but we at Moral Climates wanted to be sure of your intentions before we moved in. We can have the Dismantlers and Burning Crew here by supper. By midnight your place will be razed to the cellar. Mr. Stendahl, I consider you somewhat of a fool, sir. Spending hard-earned money on a folly. Why, it must have cost you three million dollars—"

"Four million! But, Mr. Garrett, I inherited twenty-five million when very young. I can afford to throw it about. Seems a dreadful shame, though, to have the House finished only an hour and have you race out with your Dismantlers. Couldn't you possibly let me play with my Toy for just, well, twenty-four hours?"

"You know the law. Strict to the letter. No books, no houses, nothing to be produced which in any way suggests ghosts, vampires, fairies, or any creature of the imagination."

"You'll be burning Babbitts next!"

"You've caused us a lot of trouble, Mr. Stendahl. It's in the record. Twenty years ago. On Earth. You and your library."

"Yes, me and my library. And a few others like me. Oh, Poe's been forgotten for many years now, and Oz and the other creatures. But I had my little cache. We had our libraries, a few private citizens, until you sent your men around with torches and incinerators and tore my fifty thousand books up and burned them. Just as you put a stake through the heart of Halloween and told your film producers that if they made anything at all they would have to make and remake Ernest Hemingway. My God, how many times have I seen *For Whom the Bell Tolls* done! Thirty different versions. All realistic. Oh, realism! Oh, here, oh, now, oh hell!"

"It doesn't pay to be bitter!"

"Mr. Garrett, you must turn in a full report, mustn't you?"

"Yes."

"Then, for curiosity's sake, you'd better come in and look around. It'll take only a minute."

"All right. Lead the way. And no tricks. I've a gun with me."

The door to the House of Usher creaked wide. A moist wind issued forth. There was an immense sighing and moaning, like a subterranean bellows breathing in the lost catacombs.

A rat pranced across the floor stones. Garrett, crying out, gave it a kick. It fell over, the rat did, and from its nylon fur streamed an incredible horde of metal fleas.

"Amazing!" Garrett bent to see.

An old witch sat in a niche, quivering her wax hands over some orange-and-blue tarot cards. She jerked her head and hissed through her toothless mouth at Garrett, tapping her greasy cards.

"Death!" she cried.

"Now that's the sort of thing I mean," said Garrett. "Deplorable!"

"I'll let you burn her personally."

"Will you, really?" Garrett was pleased. Then he frowned. "I must say you're taking this all so well."

"It was enough just to be able to create this place. To be able to say I did it. To say I nurtured a medieval atmosphere in a modern, incredulous world."

"I've a somewhat reluctant admiration for your genius myself, sir." Garrett watched a mist drift by, whispering and whispering, shaped like a beautiful and nebulous woman. Down a moist corridor a machine whirled. Like the stuff from a cotton-candy centrifuge, mists sprang up and floated, murmuring, in the silent halls.

An ape appeared out of nowhere.

"Hold on!" cried Garrett.

"Don't be afraid." Stendahl tapped the animal's black chest. "A robot. Copper skeleton and all, like the witch. See?" He stroked the fur, and under it metal tubing came to light.

"Yes." Garrett put out a timid hand to pet the thing. "But why, Mr. Stendahl, why all this? What obsessed you?"

"Bureaucracy, Mr. Garrett. But I haven't time to explain. The government will discover soon enough." He nodded to the ape. "All right. Now."

The ape killed Mr. Garrett.

✳ "Are we almost ready, Pikes?"

Pikes looked up from the table. "Yes, sir."

"You've done a splendid job."

"Well, I'm paid for it, Mr. Stendahl," said Pikes softly as he lifted the plastic eyelid of the robot and inserted the glass eyeball to fasten the rubberoid muscles neatly. "There."

"The spitting image of Mr. Garrett."

"What do we do with him, sir?" Pikes nodded at the slab where the real Mr. Garrett lay dead.

"Better burn him, Pikes. We wouldn't want two Mr. Garretts, would we?"

Pikes wheeled Mr. Garrett to the brick incinerator. "Good-bye." He pushed Mr. Garrett in and slammed the door.

Stendahl confronted the robot Garrett. "You have your orders, Garrett?"

"Yes, sir." The robot sat up. "I'm to return to Moral Climates. I'll file a complimentary report. Delay action for at least forty-eight hours. Say I'm investigating more fully."

"Right, Garrett. Good-bye."

The robot hurried out to Garrett's rocket, got in, and flew away.

Stendahl turned. "Now, Pikes, we send the remainder of the invitations for tonight. I think we'll have a jolly time, don't you?"

"Considering we waited twenty years, quite jolly!"

They winked at each other.

❋ Seven o'clock. Stendahl studied his watch. Almost time. He twirled the sherry glass in his hand. He sat quietly. Above him, among the oaken beams, the bats, their delicate copper bodies hidden under rubber flesh, blinked at him and shrieked. He raised his glass to them. "To our success." Then he leaned back, closed his eyes, and considered the entire affair. How he would savor this in his old age. This paying back of the antiseptic government for its literary terrors and conflagrations. Oh, how the anger and hatred had grown in him through the years. Oh, how the plan had taken a slow shape in his numbed mind, until that day three years ago when he had met Pikes.

Ah yes, Pikes. Pikes with the bitterness in him as deep as a black, charred well of green acid. Who was Pikes? Only the greatest of them all! Pikes, the man of ten thousand faces, a fury, a smoke, a blue fog, a white rain, a bat, a gargoyle, a monster, that was Pikes! Better than Lon Chaney, the father? Stendahl ruminated. Night after night he had watched Chaney in the old, old films. Yes, better than Chaney. Better than that other ancient mummer? What was his name? Karloff? Far better! Lugosi? The comparison was odious! No, there was only one Pikes, and he was a man stripped of his fantasies now, no place on Earth to go, no one to show off to. Forbidden even to perform for himself before a mirror!

Poor impossible, defeated Pikes! How must it have felt, Pikes, the night they seized your films, like entrails yanked from the camera, out of your guts, clutching them in roils and wads to stuff them up a stove to burn away? Did it feel as bad as having some fifty thousand books annihilated with no recompense? Yes. Yes. Stendahl felt his hands grow cold with the senseless anger. So what more natural than they would one day talk over endless coffeepots into innumerable midnights, and out of all the talk and the bitter brewings would come—the House of Usher.

A great church bell rang. The guests were arriving.

Smiling, he went to greet them.

✳ Full grown without memory, the robots waited. In green silks the color of forest pools, in silks the color of frog and fern, they waited. In yellow hair the color of the sun and sand, the robots waited. Oiled, with tube bones cut from bronze and sunk in gelatin, the robots lay. In coffins for the not dead and not alive, in planked boxes, the metronomes waited to be set in motion. There was a smell of lubrication and lathed brass. There was a silence of the tomb yard. Sexed but sexless, the robots. Named but unnamed, and borrowing from humans everything but humanity, the robots stared at the nailed lids of their labeled F.O.B. boxes, in a death that was not even a death, for there had never been a life. And now there was a vast screaming of yanked nails. Now there was a lifting of lids. Now there were shadows on the boxes and the pressure of a hand squirting oil from a can. Now one clock was set in motion, a faint ticking. Now another and another, until this was an immense clock shop, purring. The marble eyes rolled wide their rubber lids. The nostrils winked. The robots, clothed in hair of ape and white of rabbit, arose: Tweedledum following Tweedledee, Mock-Turtle, Dormouse, drowned bodies from the sea compounded of salt and whiteweed, swaying; hanging blue-throated men with turned-up, clam-flesh eyes, and creatures of ice and burning tinsel, loam-dwarfs and pepper-elves, Tik-Tok, Ruggedo, St. Nicholas with a self-made snow flurry blowing on before him, Bluebeard with whiskers like acetylene flame, and sulfur clouds from which green fire snouts protruded, and, in scaly and gigantic serpentine, a dragon with a furnace in its belly reeled out the door with a scream, a tick, a bellow, a silence, a rush, a wind. Ten thousand lids fell back. The clock shop moved out into Usher. The night was enchanted.

* A warm breeze came over the land. The guest rockets, burning the sky and turning the weather from autumn to spring, arrived.

The men stepped out in evening clothes and the women stepped out after them, their hair coiffed up in elaborate detail.

"So *that's* Usher!"

"But where's the door?"

At this moment Stendahl appeared. The women laughed and chattered. Mr. Stendahl raised a hand to quiet them. Turning, he looked up to a high castle window and called:

"Rapunzel, Rapunzel, let down your hair."

And from above, a beautiful maiden leaned out upon the night wind and let down her golden hair. And the hair twined and blew and became a ladder upon which the guests might ascend, laughing, into the House.

What eminent sociologists! What clever psychologists! What tremendously important politicians, bacteriologists, and neurologists! There they stood, within the dank walls.

"Welcome, all of you!"

Mr. Tryon, Mr. Owen, Mr. Dunne, Mr. Lang, Mr. Steffens, Mr. Fletcher, and a double-dozen more.

"Come in, come in!"

Miss Gibbs, Miss Pope, Miss Churchil, Miss Blunt, Miss Drummond, and a score of other women, glittering.

Eminent, eminent people, one and all, members of the Society for the Prevention of Fantasy, advocators of the banishment of Halloween and Guy Fawkes, killers of bats, burners of books, bearers of torches; good clean citizens, every one, who had waited until the rough men had come up and buried the Martians and cleansed the cities and built the towns and repaired the highways and made everything safe. And then, with everything well on its way to Safety, the Spoil-Funs, the people with mercurochrome for blood and iodine-colored eyes, came now to set up their Moral Climates and dole out goodness to everyone. And they were his friends! Yes, carefully, carefully, he had met and befriended each of them on Earth in the last year!

"Welcome to the vasty halls of Death!" he cried.

"Hello, Stendahl, what *is* all this?"

"You'll see. Everyone off with their clothes. You'll find booths to one side there. Change into costumes you find there. Men on this side, women on that."

The people stood uneasily about.

"I don't know if we should stay," said Miss Pope. "I don't like the looks of this. It verges on—blasphemy."

"Nonsense, a costume ball!"

"Seems quite illegal." Mr. Steffens sniffed about.

"Come off it." Stendahl laughed. "Enjoy yourselves. Tomorrow it'll be a ruin. Get in the booths!"

The House blazed with life and color; harlequins rang by with belled caps and white mice danced miniature quadrilles to the music of dwarfs who tickled tiny fiddles with tiny bows, and flags rippled from scorched beams while bats flew in clouds about gargoyle mouths which spouted down wine, cool, wild, and foaming. A creek wandered through the seven rooms of the masked ball. Guests sipped and found it to be sherry. Guests poured from the booths, transformed from one age into another, their faces covered with dominoes, the very act of putting on a mask revoking all their licenses to pick a quarrel with fantasy and horror. The women swept about in red gowns, laughing. The men danced them attendance. And on the walls were shadows with no people to throw them, and here or there were mirrors in which no image showed. "All of us vampires!" laughed Mr. Fletcher. "Dead!"

There were seven rooms, each a different color, one blue, one purple, one green, one orange, another white, the sixth violet, and the seventh shrouded in black velvet. And in the black room was an ebony clock which struck the hour loud. And through these rooms the guests ran, drunk at last, among the robot fantasies, amid the Dormice and Mad Hatters, the Trolls and Giants, the Black Cats and White Queens, and under their dancing feet the floor gave off the massive pumping beat of a hidden and telltale heart.

"Mr. Stendahl!"

A whisper.

"Mr. Stendahl!"

A monster with the face of Death stood at his elbow. It was Pikes. "I must see you alone."

"What is it?"

"Here." Pikes held out a skeleton hand. In it were a few half-melted, charred wheels, nuts, cogs, bolts.

Stendahl looked at them for a long moment. Then he drew Pikes into a corridor. "Garrett?" he whispered.

Pikes nodded. "He sent a robot in his place. Cleaning out the incinerator a moment ago, I found these."

They both stared at the fateful cogs for a time.

"This means the police will be here any minute," said Pikes. "Our plan will be ruined."

"I don't know." Stendahl glanced in at the whirling yellow and blue and orange people. The music swept through the misting halls. "I should have guessed Garrett wouldn't be fool enough to come in person. But wait!"

"What's the matter?"

"Nothing. There's nothing the matter. Garrett sent a robot to us. Well, we sent one back. Unless he checks closely, he won't notice the switch."

"Of course!"

"Next time he'll come *himself*. Now that he thinks it's safe. Why, he might be at the door any minute, in *person*! More wine, Pikes!"

The great bell rang.

"There he is now, I'll bet you. Go let Mr. Garrett in."

Rapunzel let down her golden hair.

"Mr. Stendahl?"

"Mr. Garrett. The *real* Mr. Garrett?"

"The same." Garrett eyed the dank walls and the whirling people. "I thought I'd better come see for myself. You can't depend on robots. Other people's robots, especially. I also took the precaution of summoning the Dismantlers. They'll be here in one hour to knock the props out from under this horrible place."

Stendahl bowed. "Thanks for telling me." He waved his hand. "In the meantime, you might as well enjoy this. A little wine?"

"No, thank you. What's going on? How low can a man sink?"

"See for yourself, Mr. Garrett."

"Murder," said Garrett.

"Murder most foul," said Stendahl.

A woman screamed. Miss Pope ran up, her face the color of a cheese. "The most horrid thing just happened! I saw Miss Blunt strangled by an ape and stuffed up a chimney!"

They looked and saw the long yellow hair trailing down from the flue. Garrett cried out.

"Horrid!" sobbed Miss Pope, and then ceased crying. She blinked and turned. "Miss Blunt!"

"Yes," said Miss Blunt, standing there.

"But I just saw you crammed up the flue!"

"No," laughed Miss Blunt. "A robot of myself. A clever facsimile!"

"But, but . . ."

"Don't cry, darling. I'm quite all right. Let me look at myself. Well, so there I *am*! Up the chimney. Like you said. Isn't that funny?"

Miss Blunt walked away, laughing.

"Have a drink, Garrett?"

"I believe I will. That unnerved me. My God, what a place. This does deserve tearing down. For a moment there . . ."

Garrett drank.

Another scream. Mr. Steffens, borne upon the shoulders of four white rabbits, was carried down a flight of stairs which magically appeared in the floor. Into a pit went Mr. Steffens, where, bound and tied, he was left to face the advancing razor steel of a great pendulum which now whirled down, down, closer and closer to his outraged body.

"Is that me down there?" said Mr. Steffens, appearing at Garrett's elbow. He bent over the pit. "How strange, how odd, to see yourself die."

The pendulum made a final stroke.

"How realistic," said Mr. Steffens, turning away.

"Another drink, Mr. Garrett?"

"Yes, please."

"It won't be long. The Dismantlers will be here."

"Thank God!"

And for a third time, a scream.

"What now?" said Garrett apprehensively.

"It's my turn," said Miss Drummond. "Look."

And a second Miss Drummond, shrieking, was nailed into a coffin and thrust into the raw earth under the floor.

"Why, I remember *that*," gasped the Investigator of Moral Climates. "From the old forbidden books. The Premature Burial. And the others. The Pit, the Pendulum, and the ape, the chimney, the Murders in the Rue Morgue. In a book I burned, yes!"

"Another drink, Garrett. Here, hold your glass steady."

"My lord, you *have* an imagination, haven't you?"

They stood and watched five others die, one in the mouth of a dragon, the others thrown off into the black tarn, sinking and vanishing.

"Would you like to see what we have planned for you?" asked Stendahl.

"Certainly," said Garrett. "What's the difference? We'll blow the whole damn thing up, anyway. You're nasty."

"Come along then. This way."

And he led Garrett down into the floor, through numerous passages and down again upon spiral stairs into the earth, into the catacombs.

"What do you want to show me down here?" said Garrett.

"Yourself killed."

"A duplicate?"

"Yes. And also something else."

"What?"

"The Amontillado," said Stendahl, going ahead with a blazing lantern which he held high. Skeletons froze half out of coffin lids. Garrett held his hand to his nose, his face disgusted.

"The what?"

"Haven't you ever heard of the Amontillado?"

"No!"

"Don't you recognize this?" Stendahl pointed to a cell.

"Should I?"

"Or this?" Stendahl produced a trowel from under his cape smiling.

"What's that thing?"

"Come," said Stendahl.

They stepped into the cell. In the dark, Stendahl affixed the chains to the half-drunken man.

"For God's sake, what are you doing?" shouted Garrett, rattling about.

"I'm being ironic. Don't interrupt a man in the midst of being ironic, it's not polite. There!"

"You've locked me in chains!"

"So I have."

"What are you going to do?"

"Leave you here."

"You're joking."

"A very good joke."

"Where's my duplicate? Don't we see him killed?"

"There is no duplicate."

"But the others?"

"The others are dead. The ones you saw killed were the real people. The duplicates, the robots, stood by and watched."

Garrett said nothing.

"Now you're supposed to say, 'For the love of God, Montresor!'" said Stendahl. "And I will reply, 'Yes, for the love of God.' Won't you say it? Come on. Say it."

"You fool."

"Must I coax you? Say it. Say 'For the love of God, Montresor!'"

"I won't, you idiot. Get me out of here." He was sober now.

"Here. Put this on." Stendahl tossed in something that belled and rang.

"What is it?"

"A cap and bells. Put it on and I might let you out."

"Stendahl!"

"Put it on, I said!"

Garrett obeyed. The bells tinkled.

"Don't you have a feeling that this has all happened before?" inquired Stendahl, setting to work with trowel and mortar and brick now.

"What're you doing?"

"Walling you in. Here's one row. Here's another."

"You're insane!"

"I won't argue that point."

"You'll be prosecuted for this!"

He tapped a brick and placed it on the wet mortar, humming.

Now there was a thrashing and pounding and a crying out from within the darkening place. The bricks rose higher. "More thrashing, please," said Stendahl. "Let's make it a good show."

"Let me out, let me out!"

There was one last brick to shove into place. The screaming was continuous.

"Garrett?" called Stendahl softly. Garrett silenced himself. "Garrett," said Stendahl, "do you know why I've done this to you? Because you burned Mr. Poe's books without really reading them. You took other people's advice that they needed burning. Otherwise you'd have realized what I was going to do to you when we came down here a moment ago. Ignorance is fatal, Mr. Garrett."

Garrett was silent.

"I want this to be perfect," said Stendahl, holding his lantern up so its light penetrated in upon the slumped figure. "Jingle your bells softly." The bells rustled. "Now, if you'll please say, 'For the love of God, Montresor,' I might let you free."

The man's face came up in the light. There was a hesitation. Then grotesquely the man said, "For the love of God, Montresor."

"Ah," said Stendahl, eyes closed. He shoved the last brick into place and mortared it tight. "*Requiescat in pace*, dear friend."

He hastened from the catacomb.

In the seven rooms the sound of a midnight clock brought everything to a halt.

The Red Death appeared.

Stendahl turned for a moment at the door to watch. And then he ran out of the great House, across the moat, to where a helicopter waited.

"Ready, Pikes?"

"Ready."

"There it goes!"

They looked at the great House, smiling. It began to crack down the middle, as with an earthquake, and as Stendahl watched the magnificent sight he heard Pikes reciting behind him in a low, cadenced voice:

" ' . . . my brain reeled as I saw the mighty walls rushing asunder— there was a long tumultuous shouting sound like the voice of a thousand waters—and the deep and dank tarn at my feet closed sullenly and silently over the fragments of the House of Usher.' "

The helicopter rose over the steaming lake and flew into the west.

THE SQUARE PEGS

LISABETH STOPPED SCREAMING BECAUSE SHE WAS TIRED. Also, there was this room to consider. There was a vast vibration, like being plunged about in the loud interior of a bell. The room was filled with sighs and murmurs of travel. She was in a rocket. Suddenly she recalled the explosion, the plummeting, the Moon riding by in cool space, the Earth gone. Lisabeth turned to a round window deep and blue as a mountain well. It was filled to its brim with evil swift life, movement, vast space monsters lurking with fiery arms, hurrying to some unscheduled destruction. A meteor school flashed by, blinking insane dot-dash codes. She put her hand out after them.

Then she heard the voices. Sighing, whispering voices.

Quietly, she moved to an iron barred door and peered without a sound through the little window of the locked frame.

"Lisabeth's stopped screaming," a tired woman's voice said. It was Helen.

"Thank heaven," a man's voice sighed. "I'll be raving myself before we reach Asteroid Thirty-six."

A second woman's voice said, irritably, "Are you sure this will work? Is it the *best* thing for Lisabeth?"

"She'll be better off than she was on Earth," cried the man.

"We might have asked her if she wanted to *take* this trip, at least, John."

John swore. "You can't ask an insane sister what she wants!"

"Insane? Don't use that word!"

"Insane she is," John said, bluntly. "For honesty's sake, call a spade a spade. There was no question of asking her to come on this trip. We simply had to *make* her do it, that's all."

Listening to them talk, Lisabeth's white fingers trembled on the caged room wall. They were like voices from some warm dream, far away, on a telephone, talking in another language.

"The sooner we get her there and settled on Asteroid Thirty-six, the sooner I can get back to New York," the man was saying in this incomprehensible telephone talk she was eavesdropping on. "After all, when you have a woman thinking she's Catherine the Great—"

"I am, I am, I am!" screamed Lisabeth out of her window into their midst. "I am Catherine!" It was as if she had shot a lightning bolt into the room. The three people almost flew apart. Now Lisabeth raved and cried and clung drunkenly to the cell bars and shouted out her belief in herself. "I am, oh, I am!" she sobbed.

"Good heavens," said Alice.

"Oh, Lisabeth!"

✳ The man, with a look of startled concern, came to the window and looked in with the false understanding of a person looking down upon a wounded rabbit. "Lisabeth we're sorry. We understand. You *are* Catherine, Lisabeth."

"Then call me Catherine!" screamed the wild thing in the room.

"Of course, Catherine," insisted the man, swiftly. "Catherine, your Highness, we await your commands."

This only made the pale thing writhing against the door the wilder. "You don't believe, you don't really believe. I can tell by your awful faces, I can tell by your eyes and your mouths. Oh, you don't really believe. I want to kill you!" She blazed her hatred out at them so the man fell away from the door. "You're lying, and I know it's a lie. But I *am* Catherine and you'll never in all your years understand!"

"No," said the man, turning. He went and sat down and put his hands to his face. "I guess we don't understand."

"Good grief," said Alice.

Lisabeth slipped to the red velvet floor and lay there, sobbing away her great unhappiness. The room moved on in space, the voices outside the room murmured and argued and talked on and on through the next half hour.

They placed a food tray inside her door an hour later. It was a simple tray with simple bowls of cereal and milk and hot buns on it. Lisabeth did not move from where she lay. There was one regal thing in the room—this red velvet on which she sprawled in silent rebellion. She would not eat their nasty food for it was most probably poisoned. And it did not come in monogrammed dishes with monogrammed napkins on a regally monogrammed tray for Catherine, Empress of All the Russias! Therefore she would not eat.

"Catherine! Eat your food, Catherine."

Lisabeth said nothing. They could go on insisting. She wanted only to die now. Nobody understood. There was an evil plan to oust her from her throne. These dark, wicked people were part of the plan.

The voices murmured again.

"I have important business in New York, too, just as important as yours. Alice," said the man. "The Amusement Park for one; those rides have to be installed next week, and the gambling equipment I bought in Reno, that has to be shipped East by next Saturday. If I'm not there to do it, who'll attend to the job?"

Murmur, murmur, dream soft, listen, far away voices.

Alice said, "Here it is autumn and the big fashion show tomorrow and here I am going off in space to some ridiculous planet for heaven knows what reason. I don't see why one of us couldn't have committed her."

"We're her brother and sisters, that's why," the man snapped.

"Well, now that we're talking about it, I don't understand it all. About Lisabeth and where we're taking her. What *is* this Asteroid Thirty-six?"

"A civilization."

"It's an insane asylum, I thought."

"Nonsense, it's not." He struck a cigarette into fire, puffing. "We discovered, a century ago, that the asteroids were inhabited, inside. They're really a series of small planets, inside of which people breathe and walk around."

"And they'll cure Lisabeth?"

"No, they won't cure her at all."

"Then, why are we taking her there?" Helen was mixing a drink with a brisk shaking of her hands, the ice rattling in the container. She poured and drank. "Why?"

"Because she will be happy there, because it will be the environment for her."

"Won't she ever come back to Earth?"

"Never."

"But how silly. I thought she'd be cured and come home."

✳ He crushed out one cigarette, snapped another into light, smoked it hungrily, lines under his eyes, his hands trembling.

"Don't ask questions. I've got some radioing to do back to New York." He walked across the cabin and fussed with some equipment. There was a buzzing and a bell sound. He shouted, "Hello, New York! Hang it. Get me through to Sam Norman on Eighth Avenue, Apartment C." He waited. Finally. "Hello, Sam. My, but that was a slow connection. Look, Sam, about that equipment—*What* equipment? The gambling equipment, where's your brain!"

"While you have the contact through to Earth—" said Helen.

"What? Sam—What?" He turned to glare at Helen.

"While you've the contact through," said Helen, holding his elbow urgently, "let me call my beauty operator, I want an appointment for Monday. My hair's a mess."

"I'm trying to talk to Sam Norman," John objected. To Sam he said. "What did you say?" To Helen: "Go away."

"But I want to talk—"

"You can when I'm finished!" He talked with Sam for five minutes, very loud, and then hung up.

"Oh." Helen gasped.

"I'm sorry," he said, tiredly. "Call Earth back yourself and get your fool hairdresser." He lighted another cigarette while she dialed and called into the speaker.

He looked at Alice who was emptying her fourth cocktail glass. "Alice, you know, Lisabeth's not really insane."

Helen, who was calling Earth, said "*Shh!*" then turned to her brother blankly. "Not insane?" To the space phone: "Hold on a minute, there." To her brother: "What do you mean, not insane?"

"It's relative. She is insane to us. She wants to be Catherine of Russia. That's illogical, to us. To her it is logical in the extreme. We are now taking her to a planet where it will be logic itself."

He got up, walked to the door and looked in at the lovely pale recumbent Catherine the Great. He put his hand to the bars, the cigarette tremoring out nervous smoke. He spoke quietly:

"Some times, I envy her. I'll envy her even more every hour. She'll stay and be happy. And we? We'll go back, back to New York, back to big roulettes and big dice." He looked at Helen. "Back to hairdressers and men." He looked at Alice, "Back to cocktails and straight gin."

"I don't like insults," cried Alice.

"I wasn't insulting anybody," he replied.

"Just a moment!" said Helen. "New York?"

John sat wearily down. "Anyway, it's all relative. These asteroids are amazing places; all kinds of cultures. You *know* that."

Lisabeth leaned against the cell door which swayed ever so quietly outward. It was unlocked. Her gaze dropped to the catch and her eyes widened. Escape. These talking fools, who didn't understand, were trying to kill her. She might run out of the cell quickly, across the room and into the other little room, where there were all kinds of weird mechanisms. If she managed to reach that room, she could smash and tangle wires and boxes with her hands!

"I don't even know what insanity is," said Alice, far away.

"It's a rebellion. Against the mores or ethical setup in a society. That's what it is," said the man.

Lisabeth opened the door slowly, gathering herself.

Helen was still on the phone, her back turned.

Lisabeth ran, laughing. The three people looked up and cried out as she darted by them. She was across the room and into the automatic pilot room in an instant, lightly. There was a hammer and she snatched it up, shout-

ing against all of them, and crashed it down upon the wires and the mechanisms. There were explosions, dancing lights, the shuddering of the ship
in space, a revolving, a flying free. The man rushed into the room as she
hammered and rehammered the controls into dented masses of fusing
metal!

"Lisabeth!" a woman screamed.

"Lisabeth!" The man struck at her, missed, then struck again. The hammer flew from her fingers. She collapsed into dizziness. In the darkness, in
the pain, she felt him groping with the controls, trying to make amends.

He was babbling hysterically.

"Ah! The control!"

* Alice and Helen were swaying against the wildly rocking walls of the
ship. Gravity suddenly went insane and shot them against the ceiling.

"Down!" cried the man. "Strap yourselves. We're crashing! There's a
planetoid!"

A dark shape ran up onto the port of the ship, black and swift. The two
women were sobbing hysterically, calling out to him to do something.

"Shut up, shut up, and let me think!" he cried. He did something with a
control, the ship righted itself.

"We'll be killed, we'll be killed!" wailed the sisters. "No, no," he said,
and before the planetoid loomed too close he threw his whole body against
the one metal rod that was stuck and would not give. But it gave now, with
a shudder of grating metal, as he fell forward.

The ship blacked out, something hit, struck, twisted, turning, shook
them around. Lisabeth felt herself lifted, whirled, and brought down with
stunning force upon the floor. That was all. She remembered no more. . . .

A voice was saying, "Where are we, where are we—where?"

Dimly, Lisabeth heard the voice. There was a smell of alien atmosphere.
Words came in over a muffled phone: "Planetoid One-Oh-One. Planetoid
One-Oh-One. Calling crashed ship *Earth Two*! Crash ship *Earth Two*! Can you
give us a bearing on you? We'll try to send a rescue craft along."

"Hello, hello, Planetoid One-Oh-One, Radio." Lisabeth opened her eyes.
John and the two women were huddled about the radio set, working it in
the dim light. Through the port she could see the bleak and cold asteroid
plain.

"You'd better try to get up from there," said the radio voice. "That's bad
territory you're in."

"What does he mean?" asked Alice, leaning down over the man.

"This is killing land."

"Killing?"

"Killers, from Earth. Insane killers. Brought here. Dropped off to spend the rest of their lives, killing. They're happy that way."

"You're—you're joking."

"Oh, *am* I?"

The radio voice said. "We'll run through as soon as possible. Don't go outside, whatever you do. There's an atmosphere, yes, but there's likely to be some of the Inmates, too."

Alice ran to the port. "John!" She pointed down. "Down there! There are some men out there now!"

Helen seized John's arm. "Get us out of here, get us out of here!"

"They can't hurt us. Let go of me, for Pete's sake! They can't get inside." John stood staring moodily out the port.

Lisabeth lay easily, luxuriating in the nearness of death. Outside the ship. Killing Land. Killers. *Her* men, of course. Catherine of Russia's bodyguard! Come to rescue her!

She arose. Silently she tiptoed across the room. The man and the two women still stared fascinated out the port. They did not hear her. What would it be like to go below, to open the air lock wide to the terrible killers outside? Wouldn't that be fine? Let them in to kill, to destroy, to annihilate her captors! How wonderful, how simple.

Where was the air lock? Below somewhere. She was out of the room with no sound. She slipped through the lounge on the soft blue carpeting, came to the spiral ladder and descended it, smiling quietly to herself. She reached the lower deck. The air lock stood shining there.

She stabbed her hands at all kinds of red buttons, trying to find the one that yanked the lock open.

Above, she heard a frantic, surprised voice: "Where's Lisabeth?"

"Below!" Feet began running. "Lisabeth!"

"Quick!" cried Lisabeth to her hands. "Quick!"

Click! A hiss. The air lock groaned open.

Behind her, on the ladder, John leaped down. "Lisabeth!"

The lock was open. The smell of an alien world came in.

The men who had been waiting outside rushed forward, silently. They filled the lock, ten, twelve of them! They were pale and thin and trembling.

Lisabeth smiled, jerking her hand at John and crying out to the alien men. "This man held me prisoner!" she said. "Kill him!"

The alien men seemed stupefied. They stood. Their full eyes only gazed at Lisabeth and John.

"No," one of them said, at last, as John waited for them to rush forward in the silent room. "No," the alien man said, dully. "We do not kill. We are the ones who are killed. We die. We wish to die. We do not care to live anymore, ever."

There was a silence.

"You heard what I said!" cried Lisabeth.

"No," the men replied. They stood, swaying in the silence.

John fell back against a wall, sighing. Then, after a time he began to laugh with exhausted moves of his body. "Ah-ha! I see. I see!"

The men blinked in bewilderment at him.

Lisabeth's eyes flashed. She made a helpless gesture.

John recovered. He slapped his hands together and made a pushing motion, talking as a man does to a pack of dogs.

"Go on, now," he said, quietly. "Get out." He waved to the men. "Go on, move!"

The men did not believe him at first and then, reluctantly, whimpering in their throats, they walked from the rocket. Several of them turned and pleaded with their eyes.

"No," said John coldly. "Move out. We won't have anything to do with you."

He shut the air lock door on them.

Taking Lisabeth's pale hand John said, "It didn't work. Come along. Upstairs with you, scheming lady."

"What happened?" Alice and Helen waited as he brought Lisabeth up the ladder.

"They wanted to die," John said, smiling tiredly. "They weren't Killers, but the Ones to Be Killed. I see it all now." He laughed sharply. "To make an insane killer happy, you have to provide him a culture where people like and approve of being killed. This is such a culture. Those men wanted to be shot."

For a moment Helen stared at him. Then she said one word:

"Wanted?"

"Yes. I've read about it. They're peculiar to this planetoid. After propagating, at the age of twenty-one, they have a death drive, just as many insects and fish do. To balance this drive, we bring in a bunch of insane murderers from Earth. In this culture, a killer becomes the norm, accepted, happy. Thus we transform insanity into sanity. Roughly, anyway. If you *like* that kind of sanity." He slapped his knee, went to the radio. "Hello, Planetoid One-Oh-One, Radio! A bit of trouble. All okay. We met the Ones Who Want to Die, rather than the Killers. Lucky, I'd say."

"Very," said the radio. "We've got your bearing. There should be a ship to you in an hour. Hold on."

Helen was by the port, staring out. "Insane. Insane, all of them."

"To us, yes," said John. "To themselves no. Their culture is sane to itself and all inhabitants within it. That's all that counts."

"I don't understand."

"Take a man who wants eighty-nine wives. On Earth he goes insane because he can't have them. He's frustrated. Bring him out here to the asteroids, put him on a planet full of women where marriage in triplicate is okay, and he becomes the norm, becomes happy."

"Oh."

"On Earth we tend to try to fit square pegs in round holes. It doesn't work. In the asteroids we've got a hole for every peg, no matter what shape. On Earth if pegs don't fit we hammer them until they split. We can't change our culture to fit them, that would be silly and inconvenient. But we can bring them out to the asteroids. There are cultures here, thousands of years old, convenient, preferable." He got up. "I need a drink. I feel terrible."

The rescue ship arrived within the hour. It came down out of space and landed neatly on the asteroid plateau. "Hello there," the pilot said.

"Hello yourself!"

✳ They got aboard, Alice, John, Helen, and—Lisabeth.

Their ship was to be towed into a repair port and returned to them later, on Earth.

"I want to call Chicago," said Helen, instantly, when they reached port.

John sighed. "We have us a close shave and all you want to do is call Chicago. William, again?"

"Suppose it is?" she snapped.

"Nothing. Go ahead. I suppose they'll let you use the space phone." He nodded at the captain of the rescue ship, who said, "Certainly. Right over here."

Lisabeth did not move. They had taken her to a little room and locked her in once more. There would be no more mistakenly unlocked doors. It was all over. Now there was nothing.

"Hello, Chicago. William? This is Helen!" Laughter.

A pouring of drinks. "I," said Alice, "am going," she lifted the glass, "to," she went on, "get very drunk."

The captain of the ship came in. "We'll be landing on Thirty-six in about ten minutes. You've had bad luck."

"It's all right now. A bit thick for me." John nodded at Helen cooing and stroking the phone, at Alice mixing a drink, and at Lisabeth standing, white and silent, in her little cell.

The captain raised his brows and nodded, wryly.

John lighted a cigarette and moved forward. "Suppose I thought I was Christ, captain? Would you take me to a planetoid where everybody thought *they* were saviors of the world?"

"Heavens, no." The captain laughed. "You'd kill each other off as 'impostors.' No, we'd take you to a culture prepared to accept and take you in as the *only* world savior."

"One that would *lie* to me, say they believed I was a savior?"

"No. No lies. Only the truth. The people must really *believe* in order that you, as a messiah, may be happy. The entire idea of sending insane people out here to various planets is to be sure they'll live happily the rest of their lives. So such a complex must live in a culture where people actually think he *is* a savior."

"It must be difficult to find enough room on your planets for all those who think they're saviors, mustn't it?"

"We've a Charting Committee for that. Nine thousand Earthmen, hopelessly insane, beyond treatment on Earth, think they're messiahs. That means a waiting list. There are only forty-seven thousand available cultures on forty-seven thousand planetoids between here and Saturn, and in the other sun systems. And only two thousand of these cultures are gullible enough to accept a false redeemer. Therefore, there's a long list of such applicants waiting to travel to some culture when an older savior dies. We couldn't possibly introduce two self-deluded Gautama Buddhas into one culture simultaneously. Oh! what dissension that would cause! But in event of one John, the Baptist, for instance, we could, at the same time, accommodate one Caesar, one Pontius Pilate, one Matthew, one Mark, one Luke, one John, along with him. You see?"

"I think so."

"When you put one Mohammed into juxtaposition with one pseudo-contempory of ancient times, history repeats itself. All the drama of ancient times is being re-enacted here on these planetoids. Everybody's happy, insanity is banished, drama lives."

"Sounds faintly blasphemous."

"Hardly. They're happy, normal, to themselves. See that planet, there? Somewhere on it is a Joan of Arc listening for angel voices. Over there, see! A Mecca waits for a Mohammed to appear so they may finish out their acts."

"It's frightening."

"Somewhat." The captain walked off, away. Lisabeth watched him go.

Asteroid Number Thirty-six swung up and under the ship!

Other planetoids whirled by. Lisabeth watched them from her cell. They moved on the deep ocean blackness, full of some hidden drama and tragedy she could not fathom.

"There's Othello's planet!" cried John. "I read about that one."

"Oh." Alice was drinking steadily. She sat in a rubberoid chair, her eyes glazed. "Oh. Well, well. Isn't that nice, isn't it?"

"Othello and Desdemona and Iago! Warriors and banners and trumpets. Gosh, what it must be like down there."

More planetoids, more, more. Lisabeth counted them with her simple, moving, pink lips. Moving, moving. More. There, and there!

"Down there somewhere is a man who thinks he's Shakespeare!"

"Good for him, good," murmured Alice, putting down her drink, lazily.

"Stratford on Avon's down there, and strolling minstrels. All you do is bring some crazy fellow from Maine who thinks he's Shakespeare up here and there's the culture waiting for him, to really make him into Shakespeare! And do you know, Alice—Alice, are you listening?" John breathed swiftly. "They live and die just as the famous men lived and died. They die the same deaths, in imitation. A woman who thinks she is Cleopatra puts an asp to her flesh. A man, who thinks he is Socrates, quaffs the hemlock! They live out old lives and die the old deaths. What an immensely beautiful insanity it is."

"William, the things you say!" cooed Helen into the space phone. "I'll be in Chicago next week, William. Yes, I'm all right. I'll see you then, sweets."

"Oh, pish," said Alice.

"This is the best thing for Lizabeth," John said. "We shouldn't feel badly."

"We certainly had to wait long enough." Alice dropped her glass. "Put in application six months ago."

"There were one thousand Catherines of Russia. One died yesterday. Lisabeth will fill her position. She'll rule unwisely and not too well, but happily."

Helen kissed her lips in front of the phone, pouting her red moist lips. "You *know* I do," she said, eyes shut. "Love you, William, love you." She was speaking softly over a few million miles of space.

"Time!" shouted the audio in the room. "Landing time!"

John got up and smoked a last cigarette nervously, his face wincing.

Catherine of Russia looked out at the three people. She saw Alice drink quietly and stupidly and John standing in a litter of cigarette butts under his shoes. And Helen was lying full length on a rubberoid couch, murmuring softly into the phone, stroking it.

Now John came to the window of the cell. She did not answer when he said hello. He did not believe in her.

"Sometimes I wonder where we'll all wind up," he said, simply, looking at Catherine. "Myself on a planetoid where I can burn gambling machines all day? First chop them with axes, then pour kerosene on them, then burn them? And what about Alice? Will she wind up on a planetoid where oceans of gin and canals of sherry are the rule? And Helen? Will she land on a place full of handsome men, thousands of them? And nobody to reprimand her?"

A bell rang. "Asteroid Thirty-six! Landing! Landing! Time, time!"

John turned and walked to Alice. "Stop drinking." He turned to Helen. "Get off the phone, we're landing!" He took the phone away from her when she would not stop.

Catherine of Russia was ready for the welcome that came as she stepped from the ship. Streets were flooded with people, gilt carriages awaited, banners flew, somewhere a band played, cannons exploded into the roaring atmosphere. She began to cry. They believed in her! They were her friends, all of these persons with smiling faces, all of these people in correct, shining costume. The palace awaited at the end of the avenue.

"Catherine, Catherine!"

"Your Majesty! Welcome Home!"

"Oh, your Majesty!"

"I've been away so long," cried Catherine, holding her hands to her tearful face. She straightened herself. She controlled her voice, finally. "Such a long, long time. And now I'm back. It's good, so good to be home."

"Your Majesty, your Majesty!"

✳ They kissed her hand, before conducting her to a carriage. Smiling, laughing, she called for wine. They brought her vast goblets of clear wine. She drank and threw a goblet shattering on the street! And a band played and drums beat and guns thundered! And just as the horses pranced and the French and English Ambassadors stepped into the carriage, Catherine turned to give one last silent look at the ship from which she had stepped. For a moment she was quiet and for this brief time she knew a silence and a restive sadness. In the open port of the ship were three people, a man and two women, waving, waving at her.

"Who are those people, your Majesty?" asked the Spanish Ambassador.

"I don't know," whispered Catherine.

"Where are they from?"

"Some strange, far away place."

"Do you know them, your Majesty?"

"Know them?" She put her hand out, almost to wave to them, then put her hand down. "No. I don't think so. Odd people. Strange people. From some long ago, some horrible land somewhere. Insane, all three of them. One works big game machines, another talks strangely over phones, and a third drinks, and drinks, forever. Really, quite insane." Her eyes were dull. Now, her attention sharpened. She cracked her hand down. "Give them notice!"

"Your Majesty!"

"An hour's notice to get out of Saint Petersburg!"

"Yes, your Majesty!"

"I won't have strangers here, understand!"

"Yes, your Majesty!"

The carriage moved down the street, the horses dancing, the crowd hallooing, the band playing, leaving the silver rocket ship behind.

She did not look back again, not even when the man in the silver ship cried, "Good-bye, good-bye!" for his voice was drowned when the crowd on all sides rushed warmly in, engulfing her in happiness, shouting, "Catherine, Catherine, Mother of all the Russias!"

THE TROLLEY

THE FIRST LIGHT ON THE ROOF OUTSIDE; very early morning. The leaves on all the trees tremble with a soft awakening to any breeze the dawn may offer. And then, far off, around a curve of silver track, comes the trolley, balanced on four small steel-blue wheels, and it is painted the color of tangerines. Epaulets of shimmery brass cover it, and pipings of gold; and its chrome bell bings if the ancient motorman taps it with a wrinkled shoe. The numerals on the trolley's front and sides are bright as lemons. Within, its seats prickle with cool green moss. Something like a buggy whip flings up from its roof to brush the spider thread high in the passing trees from which it takes its juice. From every window blows an incense, the all-pervasive blue and secret smell of summer storms and lightning.

Down the long, elm-shadowed streets the trolley moves, alone, the motorman's gray gloves touched gently, timelessly, to the controls.

At noon the motorman stopped his car in the middle of the block and leaned out. "Hey!"

And Douglas and Charlie and Tom and all the boys and girls on the block saw the gray glove waving, and dropped from trees and left skip ropes in white snakes on lawns, to run and sit in the green plush seats, and there was no charge. Mr. Tridden, the conductor, kept his glove over the mouth of the money box as he moved the trolley on down the shady block. "Hey," said Charlie. "Where are we going?"

"Last ride," said Mr. Tridden, eyes on the high electric wire ahead. "No more trolley. Bus starts tomorrow. Going to retire me with a pension, they are. So—a free ride for everyone! Watch out!"

He moved the brass handle, the trolley groaned and swung round an endless green curve, and all the time in the world held still, as if only the children and Mr. Tridden and his miraculous machine were riding an endless river, away.

"Last day?" asked Douglas, stunned. "They can't *do* that! They can't take off the trolley! Why," said Douglas, "no matter how you look at it, a bus ain't a trolley. Don't make the same kind of noise. Don't have tracks or wires, don't throw sparks, don't pour sand on the tracks, don't have the same colors, don't have a bell, don't let down a step like a trolley does!"

"Hey, that's right," said Charlie. "I always get a kick watching a trolley let down the step, like an accordion."

"Sure," said Douglas.

And then they were at the end of the line; the tracks, abandoned for thirty years, ran on into rolling country. In 1910 people took the trolley out to Chessman's Park with vast picnic hampers. The track still lay rusting among the hills.

"Here's where we turn around," said Charlie.

"Here's where you're wrong!" Mr. Tridden snapped the emergency generator switch. "Now!"

The trolley, with a bump and a sailing glide, swept past the city limits, turned off the street, and swooped downhill through intervals of odorous sunlight and vast acreages of shadow that smelled of toadstools. Here and there creek waters flushed the tracks and sun filtered through trees like green glass. They slid whispering on meadows washed with wild sunflowers, past abandoned way stations empty of all save transfer-punched confetti, to follow a forest stream into a summer country, while Douglas talked. "Why, just the *smell* of a trolley, *that's* different. I been on Chicago buses; they smell funny."

"Trolleys are too slow," said Mr. Tridden. "Going to put buses on. Buses for people and buses for school."

The trolley whined to a stop. From overhead Mr. Tridden reached down huge picnic hampers. Yelling, the children helped him carry the baskets out by a creek that emptied into a silent lake, where an ancient bandstand stood crumbling into termite dust.

They sat eating ham sandwiches and fresh strawberries and waxy oranges, and Mr. Tridden told them how it had been forty years ago: the band playing on that ornate stand at night, the men pumping air into their brass horns, the plump conductor flinging perspiration from his baton, the children and fireflies running in the deep grass, the ladies with long dresses and high pompadours treading the wooden xylophone walks with men in choking collars. There was the walk now, all softened into a fiber mush through the years. The lake was silent and blue and serene, and fish peacefully threaded the bright reeds, and the motorman murmured on and on, and the children felt it was some other year, with Mr. Tridden looking wonderfully young, his eyes lighted like small bulbs, blue and electric. It was a drifting, easy day, nobody rushing, and the forest all about, the sun held in one position, as Mr. Tridden's voice rose and fell, and a darning needle sewed along the air, stitching, restitching, designs both golden and invisible. A bee settled into a flower, humming and humming. The trolley stood like an enchanted calliope, simmering where the sun fell upon it. The trolley was on their hands, a brass smell, as they ate ripe cherries. The bright odor of the trolley blew from their clothes on the summer wind.

A loon flew over the sky, crying.

Somebody shivered.

Mr. Tridden worked on his gloves. "Well, time to go. Parents'll think I stole you all for good."

The trolley was silent and cool-dark, like the inside of an ice-cream drugstore. With a soft green rustling of velvet buff, the seats were turned by the quiet children so they sat with their backs to the silent lake, the deserted bandstand, and the wooden planks that made a kind of music if you walked down the shore on them into other lands.

Bing! went the soft bell under Mr. Tridden's foot, and they soared back over sun-abandoned, withered flower meadows, through woods, toward a town that seemed to crush the sides of the trolley with bricks and asphalt and wood when Mr. Tridden stopped to let the children out.

Charlie and Douglas were the last to stand near the opened tongue of the trolley, the folding step, breathing electricity, watching Mr. Tridden's gloves on the brass controls.

Douglas ran his fingers over the green creek moss, looked at the silver, the brass, the wine color of the ceiling.

"Well . . . So long again, Mr. Tridden."

"Good-bye, boys."

"See you around, Mr. Tridden."

"See you around."

There was a soft sigh of air; the door collapsed gently shut, tucking up its corrugated tongue. The trolley sailed slowly down the late afternoon, brighter than the sun, all tangerine, all flashing gold and lemon, turned a far corner, wheeling, and vanished, gone away.

"School buses." Charlie walked to the curb. "Won't even give us a chance to be late for school. Come get you at your front door. Never be late again in all our lives. Think of that nightmare, Doug, just think it all over."

But Douglas, standing on the lawn, was seeing how it would be tomorrow, when the men would pour hot tar over the silver tracks so you would never know a trolley had ever run this way. He knew it would take as many years as he could think of now to forget the tracks, no matter how deeply buried. Some morning in autumn, spring, or winter, he knew he'd wake, and if he didn't go near the window, if he just lay deep and snug and warm in his bed, he would hear it, faint and faraway.

And around the bend of the morning street, up the avenue, between the even rows of sycamore, elm, and maple, in the quietness before the start of living, past his house, he would hear the familiar sounds. Like the ticking of a clock, the rumble of a dozen metal barrels rolling, the hum of a single immense dragonfly at dawn. Like a merry-go-round, like a small electrical storm, the color of blue lightning, coming, here, and gone. The trolley's chime. The hiss like a soda-fountain spigot as it let down and took up its step, and the starting of the dream again, as on it sailed along its way, traveling a hidden and buried track to some hidden and buried destination. . . .

"Kick-the-can after supper?" asked Charlie.

"Sure," said Douglas. "Kick-the-can."

THE SMILE

IN THE TOWN SQUARE THE QUEUE HAD FORMED at five in the morning while cocks were crowing far out in the rimed country and there were no fires. All about, among the ruined buildings, bits of mist had clung at first, but now with the new light of seven o'clock it was beginning to disperse. Down the road, in twos and threes, more people were gathering in for the day of marketing, the day of festival.

The small boy stood immediately behind two men who had been talking loudly in the clear air, and all of the sounds they made seemed twice as loud because of the cold. The small boy stomped his feet and blew on his red, chapped hands, and looked up at the soiled gunny sack clothing of the men and down the long line of men and women ahead.

"Here, boy, what're you doing out so early?" said the man behind him.

"Got my place in line, I have," said the boy.

"Whyn't you run off, give your place to someone who appreciates?"

"Leave the boy alone," said the man ahead, suddenly turning.

"I was joking." The man behind put his hand on the boy's head. The boy shook it away coldly. "I just thought it strange, a boy out of bed so early."

"This boy's an appreciator of arts, I'll have you know," said the boy's defender, a man named Grigsby. "What's your name, lad?"

"Tom."

"Tom here is going to spit clean and true, right, Tom?"

"I sure am!"

Laughter passed down the line.

A man was selling cracked cups of hot coffee up ahead. Tom looked and saw the little hot fire and the brew bubbling in a rusty pan. It wasn't really coffee. It was made from some berry that grew on the meadowlands beyond town, and it sold a penny a cup to warm their stomachs; but not many were buying, not many had the wealth.

Tom stared ahead to the place where the line ended, beyond a bombed-out stone wall.

"They say she *smiles*," said the boy.

"Aye, she does," said Grigsby.

"They say she's made of oil and canvas."

"True. And that's what makes me think she's not the original one. The original, now, I've heard, was painted on wood a long time ago."

"They say she's four centuries old."

"Maybe more. No one knows what year this is, to be sure."

"It's 2061!"

"That's what they say, boy, yes. Liars. Could be 3000 or 5000, for all we know. Things were in a fearful mess there for a while. All we got now is bits and pieces."

They shuffled along the cold stones of the street.

"How much longer before we see her?" asked Tom uneasily.

"Just a few more minutes. They got her set up with four brass poles and velvet rope, all fancy, to keep folks back. Now mind, no rocks, Tom; they don't allow rocks thrown at her."

"Yes, sir."

The sun rose higher in the heavens, bringing heat which made the men shed their grimy coats and greasy hats.

"Why're we all here in line?" asked Tom at last. "Why're we all here to spit?"

Grigsby did not glance down at him, but judged the sun. "Well, Tom, there's lots of reasons." He reached absently for a pocket that was long gone, for a cigarette that wasn't there. Tom had seen the gesture a million times. "Tom, it has to do with hate. Hate for everything in the past. I ask you, Tom, how did we get in such a state, cities all junk, roads like jigsaws from bombs, and half the cornfields glowing with radioactivity at night? Ain't that a lousy stew, I ask you?"

"Yes, sir, I guess so."

"It's this way, Tom. You hate whatever it was that got you all knocked down and ruined. That's human nature. Unthinking, maybe, but human nature anyway."

"There's hardly nobody or nothing we don't hate," said Tom.

"Right! The whole blooming kaboodle of them people in the past who run the world. So here we are on a Thursday morning with our guts plastered to our spines, cold, live in caves and such, don't smoke, don't drink, don't nothing except have our festivals, Tom, our festivals."

And Tom thought of the festivals in the past few years. The year they tore up all the books in the square and burned them and everyone was drunk and laughing. And the festival of science a month ago when they dragged in the last motorcar and picked lots and each lucky man who won was allowed one smash of a sledgehammer at the car.

"Do I remember *that*, Tom? Do I *remember*? Why, I got to smash the front window, the window, you hear? My Lord, it made a lovely sound! *Crash!*"

Tom could hear the glass fall in glittering heaps.

"And Bill Henderson, he got to bash the engine. Oh, he did a smart job of it, with great efficiency. Wham!"

"But best of all," recalled Grigsby, "there was the time they smashed a factory that was still trying to turn out airplanes.

"Lord, did we feel good blowing it up!" said Grigsby. "And then we found that newspaper plant and the munitions depot and exploded them together. Do you understand, Tom?"

Tom puzzled over it. "I guess."

It was high noon. Now the odors of the ruined city stank on the hot air and things crawled among the tumbled buildings.

"Won't it ever come back, mister?"

"What, civilization? Nobody wants it. Not me!"

"I could stand a bit of it," said the man behind another man. "There were a few spots of beauty in it."

"Don't worry your heads," shouted Grigsby. "There's no room for that, either."

"Ah," said the man behind the man. "Someone'll come along someday with imagination and patch it up. Mark my words. Someone with a heart."

"No," said Grigsby.

"I say yes. Someone with a soul for pretty things. Might give us back a kind of limited sort of civilization, the kind we could live in in peace."

"First thing you know there's war!"

"But maybe next time it'd be different."

※ At last they stood in the main square. A man on horseback was riding from the distance into the town. He had a piece of paper in his hand. In the center of the square was the roped-off area. Tom, Grigsby, and the others were collecting their spittle and moving forward—moving forward prepared and ready, eyes wide. Tom felt his heart beating very strongly and excitedly, and the earth was hot under his bare feet.

"Here we go, Tom, let fly!"

Four policemen stood at the corners of the roped area, four men with bits of yellow twine on their wrists to show their authority over other men. They were there to prevent rocks being hurled.

"This way," said Grigsby at the last moment, "everyone feels he's had his chance at her, you see, Tom? Go on, now!"

Tom stood before the painting and looked at it for a long time.

"Tom, spit!"

His mouth was dry.

"Get on, Tom! Move!"

"But," said Tom, slowly, "she's beautiful!"

"Here, I'll spit for you!" Grigsby spat and the missile flew in the sunlight. The woman in the portrait smiled serenely, secretly, at Tom, and he looked back at her, his heart beating, a kind of music in his ears.

"She's beautiful," he said.

"Now get on, before the police—"

"Attention!"

The line fell silent. One moment they were berating Tom for not moving forward, now they were turning to the man on horseback.

"What do they call it, sir?" asked Tom, quietly.

"The picture? *Mona Lisa*, Tom, I think. Yes, the *Mona Lisa*."

"I have an announcement," said the man on horseback. "The authorities have decreed that as of high noon today the portrait in the square is to be given over into the hands of the populace there, so they may participate in the destruction of—"

Tom hadn't even time to scream before the crowd bore him, shouting and pummeling about, stampeding toward the portrait. There was a sharp ripping sound. The police ran to escape. The crowd was in full cry, their hands like so many hungry birds pecking away at the portrait. Tom felt himself thrust almost through the broken thing. Reaching out in blind imitation of the others, he snatched a scrap of oily canvas, yanked, felt the canvas give, then fell, was kicked, sent rolling to the outer rim of the mob. Bloody, his clothing torn, he watched old women chew pieces of canvas, men break the frame, kick the ragged cloth, and rip it into confetti.

Only Tom stood apart, silent in the moving square. He looked down at his hand. It clutched the piece of canvas close to his chest, hidden.

"Hey there, Tom!" cried Grigsby.

Without a word, sobbing, Tom ran. He ran out and down the bomb-pitted road, into a field, across a shallow stream, not looking back, his hand clenched tightly, tucked under his coat.

At sunset he reached the small village and passed on through. By nine o'clock he came to the ruined farm dwelling. Around back, in the half silo, in the part that still remained upright, tented over, he heard the sounds of sleeping, the family—his mother, father, and brother. He slipped quickly, silently, through the small door and lay down, panting.

"Tom?" called his mother in the dark.

"Yes."

"Where've you been?" snapped his father. "I'll beat you in the morning."

Someone kicked him. His brother, who had been left behind to work their little patch of ground.

"Go to sleep," cried his mother, faintly.

Another kick.

Tom lay getting his breath. All was quiet. His hand was pushed to his chest, tight, tight. He lay for half an hour this way, eyes closed.

Then he felt something, and it was a cold white light. The moon rose very high and the little square of light moved in the silo and crept slowly over Tom's body. Then, and only then, did his hand relax. Slowly, carefully, listening to those who slept about him, Tom drew his hand forth. He hesitated, sucked in his breath, and then, waiting, opened his hand and uncrumpled the tiny fragment of painted canvas.

All the world was asleep in the moonlight.

And there on his hand was the Smile.

He looked at it in the white illumination from the midnight sky. And he thought, over and over to himself, quietly, *the Smile, the lovely Smile.*

An hour later he could still see it, even after he had folded it carefully and hidden it. He shut his eyes and the Smile was there in the darkness. And it was still there, warm and gentle, when he went to sleep and the world was silent and the moon sailed up and then down the cold sky toward morning.

THE MIRACLES OF JAMIE

JAMIE WINTERS WORKED HIS FIRST MIRACLE in the morning. The second, third, and various other miracles came later in the day. But the first miracle was always the most important.

It was always the same: "Make Mother well. Put color in her cheeks. Don't let Mom be sick too much longer."

It was Mom's illness that had first made him think about himself and miracles. And because of her he kept on, learning how to be good at them so that he could keep her well and could make life jump through a hoop.

It was not the first day that he had worked miracles. He had done them in the past, but always hesitantly, since sometimes he did not say them right, or Ma and Pa interrupted, or the other kids in the seventh grade at school made noise. They spoiled things.

But in the past month he had felt his power flow over him like cool, certain water; he bathed in it, basked in it, had come from the shower of it beaded with glory water and with a halo of wonder about his dark-haired head.

Five days ago he'd taken down the family Bible, with real color pictures of Jesus as a boy in it, and had compared them with his own face in the bathroom mirror, gasping. He shook all over. There it *was*.

And wasn't Ma getting better every day now? Well—*there*!

Now, on Monday morning, following the first miracle at home, he worked a second one at school. He wanted to lead the Arizona State Day parade as head of his class battalion. And the principal, naturally, selected Jamie to lead. Jamie felt fine. The girls looked up to him, bumping him with their soft, thin little elbows, especially one named Ingrid, whose golden hair rustled in Jamie's face as they all hurried out of the cloakroom.

Jamie Winters held his head so high, and when he drank from the chromium fountain he bent so carefully and twisted the shining handle so exactly, so precisely—so godlike and indomitable.

Jamie knew it would be useless to tell his friends. They'd laugh. After all, Jesus was pounded nail through palm and ankle to a Calvary Hill cross because he told on himself. This time, it would be wise to wait. At least until he was sixteen and grew a beard, thus establishing once and for all the incredible proof of his identity!

Sixteen was somewhat young for a beard, but Jamie felt that he could exert the effort to force one if the time came and necessity demanded.

The children poured from the schoolhouse into the hot spring light. In the distance were the mountains, the foothills spread green with cactus, and overhead was a vast Arizona sky of very fine blue. The children donned paper hats and crepe-paper Sam Browne belts in blue and red. Flags burst open upon the wind; everybody yelled and formed into groups, glad to escape the schoolrooms for one day.

Jamie stood at the head of the line, very calm and quiet. Someone said something, and Jamie realized that it was young Huff who was talking.

"I hope we win the parade prize," said Huff worriedly.

Jamie looked at him. "Oh, we'll win all right. I know we'll win. I'll guarantee it! Heck, yes!"

Huff was brightened by such steadfast faith. "You think so?"

"I *know* so! Leave it to me!"

"What do you mean, Jamie?"

"Nothing. Just watch and see, that's all. Just watch!"

"Now, children!" Mr. Palmborg, the principal, clapped hands; the sun shone on his glasses. Silence came quickly. "Now, children," he said, nodding, "remember what we taught you yesterday about marching. Remember how you pivot to turn a corner, and remember those special routines we practiced, will you?"

"Sure!" everybody said at once.

The principal concluded his brief address and the parade began, Jamie heading it with his hundreds of following disciples.

The feet bent up and straightened down, and the street went under them. The yellow sun warmed Jamie and he, in turn, bade it shine the whole day to make things perfect.

When the parade edged onto Main Street, and the high-school band began pulsing its brass heart and rattling its wooden bones on the drums, Jamie wished they would play "Stars and Stripes Forever."

Later, when they played "Columbia, Gem of the Ocean," Jamie thought quickly, oh, yeah, that's what he'd meant—"Columbia," not "Stars and Stripes Forever"—and was satisfied that his wish had been obeyed.

The street was lined with people, as it was on the Arizona rodeo days in February. People sweated in intent layers, five deep for over a mile; the rhythm of feet came back in reflected cadence from two-story frame fronts. There were occasional glimpses of mirrored armies marching in the tall windows of the J. C. Penney Store or of the Morble Company. Each cadence was like a whip thud on the dusty asphalt, sharp and true, and the band music shot blood through Jamie's miraculous veins.

He concentrated, scowling fiercely. Let us win, he thought. Let everyone march perfectly: chins up, shoulders back, knees high, down, high again, sun upon denimed knees rising in a blue tide, sun upon tanned girl-knees like small, round faces upping and falling. Perfect, perfect, perfect. Perfection surged confidently through Jamie, extending into an encompassing aura that held his own group intact. As he moved, so moved the nation. As his fingers snapped in a brisk pendulum at his sides, so did their fingers, their arms cutting an orbit. And as his shoes trod asphalt, so theirs followed in obedient imitation.

As they reached the reviewing stand, Jamie cued them; they coiled back upon their own lines like bright garlands twining to return again, marching in the original direction, without chaos.

Oh, so darn perfect! cried Jamie to himself.

It was hot. Holy sweat poured out of Jamie, and the world sagged from side to side. Presently the drums were exhausted and the children melted away. Lapping an ice-cream cone, Jamie was relieved that it was all over.

Mr. Palmborg came rushing up, all heated and sweating.

"Children, children, I have an announcement to make!" he cried.

Jamie looked at young Huff, who stood beside him, also with an ice-cream cone. The children shrilled, and Mr. Palmborg patted the noise into a ball which he made vanish like a magician.

"We've won the competition! Our school marched finest of all the schools!"

In the clamor and noise and jumping up and down and hitting one another on the arm muscles in celebration, Jamie nodded quietly over his ice-cream cone, looked at young Huff, and said, "See? I told you so. Now, will you believe in me!"

Jamie continued licking his cold cone with a great, golden peace in him.

✳ Jamie did not immediately tell his friends why they had won the marching competition. He had observed a tendency in them to be suspicious and to ridicule anyone who told them that they were not as good as they thought they were, that their talent had been derived from an outside source.

No, it was enough for Jamie to savor his minor and major victories; he enjoyed his little secret, he enjoyed the things that happened. Such things as getting high marks in arithmetic or winning a basketball game were ample reward. There was always some by-product of his miracles to satisfy his as-yet-small hunger.

He paid attention to blond young Ingrid with the placid gray-blue eyes. She, in turn, favored him with her attentions, and he knew then that his ability was well rooted, established.

Aside from Ingrid, there were other good things. Friendships with several boys came about in wondrous fashion. One case, though, required some little thought and care. The boy's name was Cunningham. He was big and fat and bald because some fever had necessitated shaving his skull. The kids called him Billiard; he thanked them by kicking them in the shins, knocking them down, and sitting on them while he performed quick dentistry with his knuckles.

It was upon this Billiard Cunningham that Jamie hoped to apply his greatest ecclesiastical power. Walking through the rough paths of the desert toward his home, Jamie often conjured up visions of himself picking up Billiard by his left foot and cracking him like a whip so as to shock him senseless. Dad had once done that to a rattlesnake. Of course, Billiard was too heavy for this neat trick. Besides, it might hurt him, and Jamie didn't really want him killed or anything, just dusted off a little to show him where he belonged in the world.

But when he chinned up to Billiard, Jamie got cold feet and decided to wait a day or two longer for meditation. There was no use rushing things, so he let Billiard go free. Boy, Billiard didn't know how lucky he was at such times, Jamie clucked to himself.

One Tuesday, Jamie carried Ingrid's books home. She lived in a small cottage not far from the Santa Catalina foothills. Together they walked in peaceful content, needing no words. They even held hands for a while.

Turning about a clump of prickly pears, they came face to face with Billiard Cunningham.

He stood with his big feet planted across the path, plump fists on his hips, staring at Ingrid with appreciative eyes. Everybody stood still, and Billiard said:

"I'll carry your books, Ingrid. Here."

He reached to take them from Jamie.

Jamie fell back a step. "Oh, no, you don't," he said.

"Oh, yes, I do," retorted Billiard.

"Like heck you do," said Jamie.

"Like heck I don't," exclaimed Billiard, and snatched again, knocking the books into the dust.

Ingrid yelled, then said, "Look here, you can both carry my books. Half and half. That'll settle it."

Billiard shook his head.

"All or nothing," he leered.

Jamie looked back at him.

"Nothing, then!" he shouted.

He summoned up his powers like wrathful storm clouds; lightning crackled hot in each fist. What matter if Billiard loomed four inches taller and some several broader? The fury-wrath lived in Jamie; he would knock Billiard senseless with one clean bolt—maybe two.

There was no room for stuttering fear now; Jamie was cauterized clean of it by a great rage. He pulled away back and let Billiard have it on the chin.

"Jamie!" screamed Ingrid.

The only miracle after that was how Jamie got out of it with his life.

✳ Dad poured Epsom salts into a dishpan of hot water, stirred it firmly, and said, "You oughta known better, darn your hide. Your mother sick an' you comin' home all banged up this way."

Dad made a leathery motion of one brown hand. His eyes were bedded in crinkles and lines, and his mustache was pepper-gray and sparse, as was his hair.

"I didn't know Ma was very sick anymore," said Jamie.

"Women don't talk much," said Dad, dryly. He soaked a towel in steaming Epsom salts and wrung it out. He held Jamie's beaten profile and swabbed it. Jamie whimpered. "Hold still," said Dad. "How you expect me to fix that cut if you don't hold still, darn it."

"What's going on out there?" Mother's voice asked from the bedroom, real tired and soft.

"Nothing," said Dad, wringing out the towel again. "Don't you fret. Jamie just fell and cut his lip, that's all."

"Oh, Jamie," said Mother.

"I'm okay, Ma," said Jamie. The warm towel helped to normalize things. He tried not to think of the fight. It made bad thinking. There were memories of flailing arms, himself pinned down, Billiard whooping with delight and beating downward while Ingrid, crying real tears, threw her books, screaming, at his back.

And then Jamie staggered home alone, sobbing bitterly.

"Oh, Dad," he said now. "It didn't work." He meant his physical miracle on Billiard. "It didn't work."

"What didn't work?" said Dad, applying liniment to bruises.

"Oh, nothing. Nothing." Jamie licked his swollen lip and began to calm down. After all, you can't have a perfect batting average. Even the Lord made mistakes. And—Jamie grinned suddenly—yes, yes, he had *meant* to lose the fight! Yes, he had. Wouldn't Ingrid love him all the more for having fought and lost just for her?

Sure. That was the answer. It was just a reversed miracle, that was all!

"Jamie," Mother called him.

He went in to see her.

✳ With one thing and another, including Epsom salts and a great resurgence of faith in himself because Ingrid loved him now more than ever, Jamie went through the rest of the week without much pain.

He walked Ingrid home, and Billiard didn't bother him again. Billiard played after-school baseball, which was a greater attraction than Ingrid—the sudden sport interest being induced indirectly by telepathy via Jamie, Jamie decided.

Thursday, Ma looked worse. She bleached out to a pallid trembling and a pale coughing. Dad looked scared. Jamie spent less time trying to make things come out wonderful in school and thought more and more of curing Ma.

Friday night, walking alone from Ingrid's house, Jamie watched telegraph poles swing by him very slowly. He thought, If I get to the next telegraph pole before that car behind me reaches me, Mama will be all well.

Jamie walked casually, not looking back, ears itching, legs wanting to run to make the wish come true.

The telegraph pole approached. So did the car behind.

Jamie whistled cautiously. The car was coming too fast!

Jamie jumped past the pole just in time; the car roared by.

There now. Mama would be all well again.

He walked along some more.

Forget about her. Forget about wishes and things, he told himself. But it was tempting, like a hot pie on a windowsill. He had to touch it. He couldn't leave it be, oh, no. He looked ahead on the road and behind on the road.

"I bet I can get down to Schabold's ranch gate before another car comes and do it walking easy," he declared to the sky. "And that will make Mama well all the quicker."

At this moment, in a traitorous, mechanical action, a car jumped over the low hill behind him and roared forward.

Jamie walked fast, then began to run.

I bet I can get down to Schabold's gate, I bet I can—

Feet up, feet down.

He stumbled.

He fell into the ditch, his books fluttering about like dry, white birds. When he got up, sucking his lips, the gate was only twenty yards farther on.

The car motored by him in a large cloud of dust.

"I take it back, I take it back," cried Jamie. "I take it back, what I said, I didn't mean it."

With a sudden bleat of terror, he ran for home. It was all his fault, *all* his fault!

The doctor's car stood in front of the house.

Through the window, Mama looked sicker. The doctor closed up his little black bag and looked at Dad a long time with strange lights in his little black eyes.

Jamie ran out onto the desert to walk alone. He did not cry. He was paralyzed, and he walked like an iron child, hating himself, blundering into the dry riverbed, kicking at prickly pears and stumbling again and again.

Hours later, with the first stars, he came home to find Dad standing beside Mama's bed and Mama not saying much—just lying there like fallen snow, so quiet. Dad tightened his jaw, screwed up his eyes, caved in his chest, and put his head down.

Jamie took up a station at the end of the bed and stared at Mama, shouting instructions in his mind to her.

Get well, get well, Ma, get well, you'll be all right, sure you'll be fine, I command it, you'll be fine, you'll be swell, you just get up and dance around, we need you, Dad and I do, wouldn't be good without you, get well, Ma, get well, Ma. Get well!

The fierce energy lashed out from him silently, wrapping, cuddling her and beating into her sickness, tendering her heart. Jamie felt glorified in his warm power.

She *would* get well. She *must*! Why, it was silly to think any other way. Ma just wasn't the dying sort.

Dad moved suddenly. It was a stiff movement with a jerking of breath. He held Mama's wrists so hard he might have broken them. He lay against her breasts sounding the heart and Jamie screamed inside.

Ma, don't, Ma, don't, oh, Ma, please don't give up.

Dad got up, swaying.

She was dead.

Inside the walls of Jericho that was Jamie's mind, a thought went screaming about in one last drive of power: Yes, she's dead, all right, so she is dead, so what if she is dead? Bring her back to life again, yes, make her live again, Lazarus, come forth, Lazarus, Lazarus, come forth from the tomb, Lazarus, come forth.

He must have been babbling aloud, for Dad turned and glared at him in old, ancient horror and struck him bluntly across the mouth to shut him up.

Jamie sank against the bed, mouthing into the cold blankets, and the walls of Jericho crumbled and fell down about him.

✳ Jamie returned to school a week later. He did not stride into the schoolyard with his old assurance; he did not bend imperiously at the fountain; nor did he pass his tests with anything more than a grade of seventy-five.

The children wondered what had happened to him. He was never quite the same.

They did not know that Jamie had given up his role. He could not tell them. They did not know what they had lost.

A FAR-AWAY GUITAR

Old Miss Bidwell used to sit with a lemonade glass in her hand in her squeaking rocker on the porch of her house on Saint James Street every summer night from seven until nine. At nine, you could hear the front door tap shut, the brass key turn in the lock, the blinds rustle down, and the lights click out.

Her routine varied in no detail; she lived alone with a house full of rococo pictures, a dusty library, a yellow-mouthed piano, and a music box which, when she wound it up and set it going, prickled the air like the bubbles from lemon soda pop. Miss Bidwell had a nod for everyone walking by, and it was interesting that her house had no front steps leading up to its wooden porch. No front steps, and no back steps. For Miss Bidwell hadn't left her house in forty years. In the year 1911, she had had the back and the front steps completely torn down and the porches railed in.

In the autumn—the closing-up, the nailing-in, the hiding-away time— she would have one last lemonade on her cooling, bleak porch; then she would carry her wicker chair inside, and no one would see her again until the next spring.

"There she goes," said Mr. Widmer, the grocer, pointing with the red apple in his hand. "Take a good look at her." He tapped the wall calendar. "Nine o'clock of an evening in the month of September, the day after Labor Day."

Several customers peered over at Miss Bidwell's house. There was the old lady, looking around for a final time; then she went inside.

"Won't see her again until May first," said Mr. Widmer. "There's a trapdoor in her kitchen wall. I unlock that trapdoor and shove the groceries in. There's an envelope there, with money in it and a list of the things she wants. I never see her."

"What's she do all winter?"

"Only the Lord knows. She's had a 'phone for forty years and never used it."

Miss Bidwell's house was dark.

Mr. Widmer bit into his apple, enjoying its crisp succulence. "Forty years ago, she had the front steps taken away."

"Why? Folks die?"

"They died before that."

"Husband or children die?"

"Never had no children nor husband. She held hands with a young man who had all kinds of notions about traveling. They were going to be married. He used to sit and play the guitar and sing to her on that porch. One day he just went to the railway station and bought one ticket for Arizona, California, and China."

"That's a long time for a woman to carry a torch."

They laughed quietly and solemnly, for it was a sad admission they had made.

"Suppose she'll *ever* come out?"

"When you're *seventy*? All I do every year is wait for the first of May. If she don't come out on the porch that day and set up her chair, I'll know for sure she's dead. Then I'll 'phone the police."

"Good night," said everyone, and left Mr. Widmer alone in the gray light of his grocery shop.

Mr. Widmer put on his coat and listened to the whining of the wind grow stronger. Yes, every year. And every year at this time he'd watched the old woman become more of an old woman. She was as remote as one of those barometers where the woman comes out for fair weather and the man appears for bad. But what a broken instrument, with only the woman coming out and coming out alone, and never a man at all, for bad or for better. How many thousands of July and August nights had he seen her there, beyond her moat of green grass which was as impassable as a crocodile stream? Forty years of small-town nights. How much might they weigh if put to the scale? A feather to himself, but how much to *her*?

✳ Mr. Widmer was putting on his hat when he saw the man.

The man came along the street, on the other side: an old man, dim in the light of the single corner street lamp. He was looking at all the house numbers, and when he came to the corner house, number 11, he stopped and looked at the lightless windows.

"It couldn't be," said Mr. Widmer. He turned out the light and stood in the warm grocery smell of his shop, watching the old man through the plate glass. "Not after this much time." He shook his head. It was much more than ridiculous, for hadn't he felt his heart quicken at least once a day, every day, for four decades whenever he saw a man pass or pause by Miss Bidwell's? Every man in the history of the town who so much as tied a shoelace in front of her locked house had been a source of wonder to Mr. Widmer.

"Are you the young man who ran off and left our Miss Bidwell?" he cried to himself.

Once, thirty years ago, white apron flapping, he had run across the brick street to confront a young man. "Well, so you came back!"

"What?" the young man said.

"Aren't you Mr. Robert Farr, the one who brought her red carnations and played the guitar and sang?"

"The name's Corley," and the young man drew forth silk samples to display and sell.

As the years passed, Mr. Widmer had become frightened about one thing: Suppose Mr. Farr *did* come back some day, how was he to be recognized? In his mind, Mr. Widmer remembered the man as striding and young and very clean-faced. But forty years could peel a man away and dry his bones and tighten his flesh into a fine, acid etching. Perhaps some day Mr. Farr might return, like a hound to old trials, and, because of Mr. Widmer's negligence, think the house locked and buried deep in another century, and go away, never the wiser. Perhaps it had happened *already*!

There stood the man, the old man, the unbelievable man, at nine-fifteen in the evening of the day after Labor Day in September. There was a slight bend to his knees and his back, and his face was turned to the Bidwell house.

"One last try," said Mr. Widmer. "Sticking my nose in."

He stepped lightly over the cool brick street and reached the farther curb. The old man turned toward him.

" 'Evening," said Mr. Widmer.

"I wonder if you could help me?" said the old man. "Is this the old Bidwell house?"

"Yes."

"Does anyone live there?"

"Miss Ann Bidwell, she's still there."

"Thank you."

"Good night." And Mr. Widmer walked off, his heart pounding, cursing himself. Why didn't you ask him, you idiot! Why didn't you say, Mr. Farr? Is that you, Mr. Farr?

But he knew the answer. This time, he wanted it to *be* Mr. Farr. And the only way to insure that it *was* Mr. Farr was not to shatter the thin bubble of reality. Asking outright might have evoked an answer which would have crushed him all over again. No, I'm not Mr. Farr; no, I'm not him. But *this* way, by *not* asking, Mr. Widmer could go to his home tonight, could lie in his upstairs bed, and, for an hour or so, could imagine, with an ancient and implausible tinge of romanticism, that at last the wandering man had come home from long trackways of traveling and long years of other cities and other worlds. This sort of lie was the most pleasant in which to indulge. You don't ask a dream if it is real, or you wake up. All right then, let that man—bill collector, dust-man, or whatever—for this night, at least, assume the identity of a lost person.

Mr. Widmer walked back across the street, around the side of his shop, and up the narrow, dark stairs to where his wife was already in bed, asleep.

"Suppose it *is* him," he thought, in bed. "And he's knocking on the house sides, knocking on the back door with a broom handle, tapping at the windows, calling her on the 'phone, leaving his card poked under the doors, suppose?"

He turned on his side.

"Will she answer?" he wondered. "Will she pay attention, will she do anything? Or will she just sit in her house with the fenced-in porch and no steps going up or down to the door, and let him knock and call her name?"

He turned on his other side.

"Will we see her again next May first, and not until then? And will he wait until then . . . six months of knocking and calling her name and waiting?"

He got up and went to the window. There, far away over the green lawns, at the base of the huge, black house, by the porch which had no steps, stood the old man. And was it imagination or was his voice calling, calling there under the autumn trees, at the lightless windows?

＊ The next morning, very early, Mr. Widmer looked down at Miss Bid-well's lawn.

It was empty. "I doubt if he was even there," said Mr. Widmer. "I doubt I even talked to anyone but a lamp post. That apple was half cider; it turned my head."

It was seven o'clock; Mrs. Terle and Mrs. Adams came into the cold shop for bacon and eggs and milk. Mr. Widmer edged round the subject. "Say, you didn't see no prowlers near Miss Bidwell's last night, did you?"

"Were there some?" cried the ladies.

"Thought I saw some."

"I didn't see no one," they said.

"It was the apple," murmured Mr. Widmer. "Pure cider."

The door slammed, and Mr. Widmer felt his spirits slump. Only he had seen, and the seeing must have been the rusted product of too many years of trying to live out another person's life.

The streets were empty, but the town was slowly arising to life. The sun was a reddish ball over the courthouse clock. Dew still lay on everything in a cool blanket. Dew stood in bubbles on every grass blade, on every silent red brick; dripped from the elms and the maples and the empty apple trees.

He walked slowly and carefully across the empty street and stood on Miss Bidwell's sidewalk. Her lawns, a vast green sea of dew that had fallen in the night, lay before him. Mr. Widmer felt again the warm pounding of his heart. For there, in the dew, circling and circling the house, where they had left fine, clear impressions, was a series of endless footprints, round and round, under the windows, near the bushes, at the doors. Footprints in the crystal grass, footprints that melted as the sun rose.

The day was a slow day. Mr. Widmer kept near the front of his shop, but saw nothing. At sunset, he sat smoking under the awning. "Maybe he's gone, maybe he'll never come back. She didn't answer. I know her. She's proud and old. The older the prouder, that's what they say. Maybe he's gone off on the train again. Why didn't I ask him his name? Why didn't I pound on the doors with him!"

But the fact remained that he hadn't asked and he hadn't pounded, and he felt himself the nucleus of a tragedy that was beginning to grow far beyond him.

"He won't come back. Not after all night walking round. He must have left just before dawn. Footsteps still fresh."

Eight o'clock. Eight-thirty. Nothing. Nine o'clock. Nine-thirty. Nothing. Mr. Widmer stayed open until quite late, even though there were no customers.

It was after eleven when he sat by the upstairs window of his home, not watching exactly, but not going to bed either.

At eleven-thirty, the clock struck softly, and the old man came along the street and stood before the house.

"Of course!" said Mr. Widmer to himself. "He's afraid someone will see him. He slept all day somewhere and waited. Afraid of what people might say. Look at him there, going round and round."

He listened. There was the calling again. Like the last cricket of the year, like the last rustle of the last oak leaf of the season. At the front door, at the back, at the bay windows. Oh, there would be a million slow footprints in the meadow lawn tomorrow when the sun rose.

Was she *listening*?

"Ann, Ann, oh, Ann!" was that what he called? "Ann, can you hear me, Ann?"—was that what you called when you came back very late in the day?

And then, suddenly, Mr. Widmer stood up.

Suppose she didn't *hear* him? How could he be sure that she was still *able* to hear? Seventy years make for spider webs in the ears, gray waddings of time which dull everything for some people until they live in a universe of cotton and wool and silence. Nobody had spoken to her in thirty years save to open their mouths to say hello. What if she were deaf, lying there in her cold bed now like a little girl playing out a long and lonely game, never even aware that someone was tapping on the rattling windows, someone was calling through her flake-painted door, someone was walking on the soft grass round her locked house? Perhaps not pride but a physical inability prevented her from answering!

In the living room, Mr. Widmer quietly took the 'phone off the hook, watching the bedroom door to be certain he hadn't wakened his wife. To the operator he said, "Helen? Give me 729."

"That you, Mr. Widmer? Funny time of night to call *her*."

"Never mind."

"All right, but she won't answer, never has. Don't recall she ever *has* used her 'phone in all the years after she had it put in."

The 'phone rang. It rang six times, and nothing happened.

"Keep trying, Helen."

The 'phone rang twelve times more. His face was streaming perspiration. Someone picked up the 'phone at the other end.

"Miss Bidwell!" cried Mr. Widmer, almost collapsing in relief. "Miss Bidwell?" he lowered his voice. "This is Mr. Widmer, the grocer, calling."

No answer. She was on the other end, in her house, standing in the dark. Through his window he could see that her house was still unlit. She hadn't switched on any lights to find the 'phone.

"Miss Bidwell, do you hear me?" he asked.

Silence.

"Miss Bidwell, I want you to do me a favor," he said.

Click.

"I want you to open your front door and look out," he said.

"She's hung up," said Helen. "Want me to call her again?"

"No thanks." He put the receiver back on the hook.

* There was the house, in the morning sun, in the afternoon sun, and in the twilight—silent. Here was the grocery, with Mr. Widmer in it, thinking: she's a fool. No matter what, she's a fool. It's never too late. No matter how old, wrinkled hands are better than none. He's traveled a long way, and, by his look, he's never married but always traveled, as some men do, crazy to change their scenery every week, every month, every year, until they reach an age where they find they are collecting nothing at all but a lot of empty trips and a lot of towns with no more substance to them than movie sets and a lot of people in those towns who are about as real as wax dummies seen in lighted windows late at night as you pass by on a slow, black train.

He's been living with a world of people who didn't care about him because he never stayed anywhere long enough to make anyone worry whether he would rise in the morning or whether he had turned to dust. And then he got to thinking about her and decided that she was the one real person he'd ever known. And just a little too late, he took a train and got off and walked up here, and there he is on her lawn, feeling like a fool, and one more night of this and he won't come back at all.

This was the third night. Mr. Widmer thought of going over, of setting fire to the porch of Miss Bidwell's house, and of causing the firemen to roar up. That would bring her out, right into the old man's arms, by Jupiter!

But wait! Ah, but wait.

Mr. Widmer's eyes went to the ceiling. Up there, in the attic—wasn't there a weapon there to be used against pride and time? In all that dust, wasn't there something with which to strike out? Something as old as all of them—Mr. Widmer, the old man, the old lady? How long since the attic has been cleaned out? Never.

But it was too ridiculous. He wouldn't dare!

And yet, this was the last night. A weapon *must* be provided.

Ten minutes later, he heard his wife cry out to him, "Tom, Tom! What's that noise! What are you doing in the attic?"

At eleven-thirty, there was the old man. He stood in front of the stepless house as if not knowing what to try next. And then he took a quick step and looked down.

Mr. Widmer, from his upstairs window, whispered, "Yes, yes, go ahead."

The old man bent over.

"Pick it up!" cried Mr. Widmer to himself.

The old man extended his hands.

"Brush it off! I know, I know it's dusty; but it's still fair enough. Brush it off, *use* it!"

In the moonlight, the old man held a guitar in his hands. It had been lying in the middle of the lawn. There was a period of long waiting while the old man turned it over with his fingers.

"Go on!" said Mr. Widmer, silently.

There was a tentative chord of music.

"Go on!" said Mr. Widmer. "What voices can't do, music can. That's it. Play! You're right, try it!" urged Mr. Widmer.

And he thought: sing under the windows, sing under the apple trees and near the back porch, sing until the guitar notes shake her, sing until she starts to cry. You get a woman to crying, and you're on safe ground. Her pride will all wash away; and the best thing to start the dissolving and crying is music. Sing songs, sing "Genevieve, Sweet Genevieve, the years may come the years may go," and sing "Meet Me Tonight in Dreamland," and sing "We Were Sailing Along on Moonlight Bay," and sing "There's a Long, Long Trail Awinding," and sing all those old summer songs and old-time songs, any song that's old and quiet and lovely; sing soft and light, with a few notes of the guitar; sing and play and perhaps you'll hear the key turn in the lock!

He listened.

As pure as drops of water falling in the night, the guitar played, softly, softly, and it was half an hour before the old man began to sing, and it was so faint that no one could hear; no one except someone behind a wall in that house, in a bed, or standing in the dark behind a shaded window.

Mr. Widmer went to bed, numb, and lay there for an hour, hearing the far-away guitar.

✳ The next morning, Mrs. Terle said, "I seen that prowler."

"Yes?"

"He was there all night. Playing a guitar. Can you imagine? How silly can old people get? Who *is* he, anyway?"

"I'm sure I don't know," said Mr. Widmer.

"Well, him and his guitar went away down the street at six this morning," said Mrs. Terle.

"Didn't the door open for him?"

"No. Should it?"

"I suppose not. He'll be back tonight."

Tonight will do it, thought Mr. Widmer. Tonight, just one more night. He's not the sort to give up now. Now that he has the guitar, he'll be back, and tonight will do it. Mr. Widmer whistled, moving about the shop.

A van drove up outside, and Mr. Frank Henderson climbed out, a kit of hammers and nails and a saw in his hands. He went round the van and took out a couple of dozen fresh-cut new pieces of raw, good-smelling timber.

"Morning, Frank," called Mr. Widmer. "How's the carpentry business?"

"Picking up this morning," said Frank. He sorted out the good yellow wood and the bright steel nails. "Got a job."

"Where?"

"Miss Bidwell's."

"Yes?" Mr. Widmer felt his heart begin the familiar pounding.

"Yes. She 'phoned an hour ago. Wants me to build a new set of steps on to her front porch. Wants it done today."

Mr. Widmer stood looking at the carpenter's hands, at the hammers and nails, and the good, fresh, clean wood. The sun was rising higher and the day was bright.

"Here," said Mr. Widmer, picking up some of the wood. "Let me help."

They walked together, carrying the fine timber, across the green lawn, under the trees, toward the waiting house and the waiting, stepless porch. And they were smiling.

THE CISTERN

IT WAS AN AFTERNOON OF RAIN, and lamps lighted against the gray. For a long while the two sisters had been in the dining room. One of them, Juliet, embroidered tablecloths; the younger, Anna, sat quietly on the window seat, staring out at the dark street and the dark sky.

Anna kept her brow pressed against the pane, but her lips moved and after reflecting a long moment, she said, "I never thought of that before."

"Of what?" asked Juliet.

"It just came to me. There's actually a city under a city. A dead city, right here, right under our feet."

Juliet poked her needle in and out the white cloth. "Come away from the window. That rain's done something to you."

"No, really. Didn't you ever think of the cisterns before? They're all through the town, there's one for every street, and you can walk in them without bumping your head, and they go everywhere and finally go down to the sea," said Anna, fascinated with the rain on the asphalt pavement out there and the rain falling from the sky and vanishing down the gratings at each corner of the distant intersection. "Wouldn't you like to live in a cistern?"

"I would not!"

"But wouldn't it be fun—I mean, very secret? To live in the cistern and peek up at people through the slots and see them and them not see you? Like when you were a child and played hide-and-seek and nobody found you, and there you were in their midst all the time, all sheltered and hidden and warm and excited. I'd like that. That's what it must be like to live in the cistern."

Juliet looked slowly up from her work. "You *are* my sister, aren't you, Anna? You *were* born, weren't you? Sometimes, the way you talk, I think Mother found you under a tree one day and brought you home and planted you in a pot and grew you to this size and there you are, and you'll never change."

Anna didn't reply, so Juliet went back to her needle. There was no color in the room; neither of the two sisters added any color to it. Anna held her head to the window for five minutes. Then she looked way off into the distance and said, "I guess you'd call it a dream. While I've been here, the last hour, I mean. Thinking. Yes, Juliet, it was a dream."

Now it was Juliet's turn not to answer.

Anna whispered. "All this water put me to sleep a while, I guess, and then I began to think about the rain and where it came from and where it went and how it went down those little slots in the curb, and then I thought about deep under, and suddenly there *they* were. A man . . . and a woman. Down in that cistern, under the road."

"What would they be doing there?" asked Juliet.

Anna said, "Must they have a reason?"

"No, not if they're insane, no," said Juliet. "In that case no reasons are necessary. There they are in their cistern, and let them stay."

"But they aren't just in the cistern," said Anna, knowingly, her head to one side, her eyes moving under the half-down lids. "No, they're in love, these two."

"For heaven's sake," said Juliet, "did love make them crawl down there?"

"No, they've been there for years and years," said Anna.

"You can't tell me they've been in that cistern for years, living together," protested Juliet.

"Did I say they were alive?" asked Anna, surprised. "Oh, but no. They're dead."

The rain scrambled in wild, pushing pellets down the window. Drops came and joined with others and made streaks.

"Oh," said Juliet.

"Yes," said Anna, pleasantly. "Dead. He's dead and she's dead." This seemed to satisfy her; it was a nice discovery, and she was proud of it. "He looks like a very lonely man who never traveled in all his life."

"How do you know?"

"He looks like the kind of man who never traveled but wanted to. You know by his eyes."

"You know what he looks like, then?"

"Yes. Very ill and very handsome. You know how it is with a man made handsome by illness? Illness brings out the bones in the face."

"And he's dead?" asked the older sister.

"For five years." Anna talked softly, with her eyelids rising and falling, as if she were about to tell a long story and knew it and wanted to work into it slowly, and then faster and then faster, until the very momentum of the story would carry her on, with her eyes wide and her lips parted. But now it was slowly, with only a slight fever to the telling. "Five years ago this man was walking along a street and he knew he'd been walking the same street on many nights and he'd go on walking it, so he came to a manhole cover, one of those big iron waffles in the center of the street, and he heard the river rushing under his feet, under the metal cover, rushing toward the sea." Anna put out her right hand. "And he bent slowly and lifted up the cistern lid and looked down at the rushing foam and the water, and he thought of someone he wanted to love and couldn't, and then he swung himself onto the iron rungs and walked down them until he was all gone. . . ."

"And what about her?" asked Juliet, busy. "When'd she die?"

"I'm not sure. She's new. She's just dead, now. But she is dead. Beautifully, beautifully dead." Anna admired the image she had in her mind. "It takes death to make a woman really beautiful, and it takes death by drowning to make her most beautiful of all. Then all the stiffness is taken out of her, and her hair hangs up on the water like a drift of smoke." She nodded her head, amusedly. "All the schools and etiquettes and teachings in the world can't make a woman move with this dreamy ease, supple and ripply and fine." Anna tried to show how fine, how ripply, how graceful, with her broad, coarse hand.

"He'd been waiting for her, for five years. But she hadn't known where he was till now. So there they are, and will be, from now on. . . . In the rainy season they'll live. But in the dry seasons—that's sometimes months—they'll have long rest periods, they'll lie in little hidden niches, like those Japanese water flowers, all dry and compact and old and quiet."

Juliet got up and turned on yet another little lamp in the corner of the dining room. "I wish you wouldn't talk about it."

Anna laughed. "But let me tell you about how it starts, how they come back to life. I've got it all worked out." She bent forward, held onto her knees, staring at the street and the rain and the cistern mouths. "There they are, down under dry and quiet, and up above the sky gets electrical and powdery." She threw back her dull, graying hair with one hand. "At first all the upper world is pellets. Then there's lightning and then thunder and the dry season is over, and the little pellets run along the gutters and get big and fall into the drains. They take gum wrappers and theater tickets with them, and bus transfers!"

"Come away from that window, now."

Anna made a square with her hands and imagined things. "I know just what it's like under the pavement, in the big square cistern. It's huge. It's all empty from the weeks with nothing but sunshine. It echoes if you talk. The only sound you can hear standing down there is an auto passing above. Far up above. The whole cistern is like a dry, hollow camel bone in a desert, waiting."

She lifted her hand, pointing, as if she herself were down in the cistern, waiting. "Now, a little trickle. It comes down on the floor. It's like something was hurt and bleeding up in the outer world. There's some thunder! Or was it a truck going by?"

She spoke a little more rapidly now, but held her body relaxed against the window, breathing out, and in the next words: "It seeps down. Then, into all the other hollows come other seepages. Little twines and snakes. Tobacco-stained water. Then it moves. It joins others. It makes snakes and then one big constrictor which rolls along on the flat, papered floor. From everywhere, from the north and south, from other streets, other streams come and they join and make one hissing and shining coil. And the water writhes into those two little dry niches I told you about. It rises slowly around those two, the man and the woman, lying there like Japanese flowers."

She clasped her hands, slowly, working finger into finger, interlacing.

"The water soaks into them. First, it lifts the woman's hand. In a little move. Her hand's the only live part of her. Then her arm lifts and one foot. And her hair . . ." she touched her own hair as it hung about her shoulders ". . . unloosens and opens out like a flower in the water. Her shut eyelids are blue. . . ."

The room got darker, Juliet sewed on, and Anna talked and told all she saw in her mind. She told how the water rose and took the woman with it, unfolding her out and loosening her and standing her full upright in the cistern. "The water is interested in the woman, and she lets it have its way. After a long time of lying still, she's ready to live again, any life the water wants her to have."

Somewhere else, the man stood up in the water also. And Anna told of that, and how the water carried him slowly, drifting, and her, drifting, until they met each other. "The water opens their eyes. Now they can see but not see each other. They circle, not touching yet." Anna made a little move of her head, eyes closed. "They watch each other. They glow with some kind of phosphorus. They smile. . . . They—touch hands."

At last Juliet, stiffening, put down her sewing and stared at her sister, across the gray, rain-silent room.

"Anna!"

"The tide—makes them touch. The tide comes and puts them together. It's a perfect kind of love, with no ego to it, only two bodies, moved by the water, which makes it clean and all right. It's not wicked, this way."

"It's bad you're saying it!" cried her sister.

"No, it's all right," insisted Anna, turning for an instant. "They're not thinking, are they? They're just so deep down and quiet and not caring."

She took her right hand and held it over her left hand very slowly and gently, quavering and interweaving them. The rainy window, with the pale spring light penetrating, put a movement of light and running water on her fingers, made them seem submerged, fathoms deep in gray water, running one about the other as she finished her little dream:

"Him, tall and quiet, his hands open." She showed with a gesture how tall and how easy he was in the water. "Her, small and quiet and relaxed." She looked at her sister, leaving her hands just that way. "They're dead, with no place to go, and no one to tell them. So there they are, with nothing applying to them and no worries, very secret and hidden under the earth in the cistern waters. They touch their hands and lips and when they come into a cross-street outlet of the cistern, the tide rushes them together. Then, later . . ." she disengaged her hands . . . "maybe they travel together, hand in hand, bobbling and floating, down all the streets, doing little crazy upright dances when they're caught in sudden swirls." She whirled her hands about, a drenching of rain spatted the window. "And they go down to the sea, all across the town, past cross drain and cross drain, street and street. Genesee Avenue, Crenshaw, Edmond Place, Washington, Motor City, Ocean Side and then the ocean. They go anywhere the water wants them, all over the earth, and come back later to the cistern inlet and float back up under the town, under a dozen tobacco shops and four dozen liquor stores, and six dozen groceries and ten theaters, a rail junction, Highway 101, under the walking feet of thirty thousand people who don't even know or think of the cistern."

Anna's voice drifted and dreamed and grew quiet again.

"And then—the day passes and the thunder goes away up on the street. The rain stops. The rain season's over. The tunnels drip and stop. The tide goes down." She seemed disappointed, sad it was over. "The river runs out to the ocean. The man and woman feel the water leave them slowly to the floor. They settle." She lowered her hands in little bobblings to her lap, watching them fixedly, longingly. "Their feet lose the life the water has given them from outside. Now the water lays them down, side by side, and drains away, and the tunnels are drying. And there they lie. Up above, in the world, the sun comes out. There they lie, in the darkness, sleeping, until the next time. Until the next rain."

Her hands were now upon her lap, palms up and open. "Nice man, nice woman," she murmured. She bowed her head over them and shut her eyes tight.

Suddenly Anna sat up and glared at her sister. "Do you know who the man is?" she shouted, bitterly.

Juliet did not reply; she had watched, stricken, for the past five minutes while this thing went on. Her mouth was twisted and pale. Anna almost screamed:

"The man is Frank, that's who he is! And I'm the woman!"

"Anna!"

"Yes, it's Frank, down there!"

"But Frank's been gone for years, and certainly not down there, Anna!"

Now, Anna was talking to nobody, and to everybody, to Juliet, to the window, the wall, the street. "Poor Frank," she cried. "I know that's where he went. He couldn't stay anywhere in the world. His mother spoiled him for all the world! So he saw the cistern and saw how secret and fine it was. Oh, poor Frank. And poor Anna, poor me, with only a sister. Oh, Julie, why didn't I hold on to Frank when he was here? Why didn't I fight to win him from his mother?"

"Stop it, this minute, do you hear, this minute!"

Anna slumped down into the corner, by the window, one hand up on it, and wept silently. A few minutes later she heard her sister say, "Are you finished?"

"What?"

"If you're done, come help me finish this, I'll be forever at it."

Anna raised her head and glided over to her sister. "What do you want me to do?" she sighed.

"This and this," said Juliet, showing her.

"All right," said Anna, and took it and sat by the window looking at the rain, moving her hands with the needle and thread, but watching how dark the street was now, and the room, and how hard it was to see the round metal top of the cistern now—there were just little midnight gleams and glitters out there in the black black late afternoon. Lightning crackled over the sky in a web.

Half an hour passed. Juliet drowsed in her chair across the room, removed her glasses, placed them down with her work and for a moment rested her head back and dozed. Perhaps thirty seconds later she heard the front door open violently, heard the wind come in, heard the footsteps run down the walk, turn, and hurry along the black street.

"What?" asked Juliet, sitting up, fumbling for her glasses. "Who's there? Anna, did someone come in the door?" She stared at the empty window seat where Anna had been. "Anna!" she cried. She sprang up and ran out into the hall.

The front door stood open, rain fell through it in a fine mist.

"She's only gone out for a moment," said Juliet, standing there, trying to peer into the wet blackness. "She'll be right back. *Won't* you be right back, Anna dear? Anna, answer me, you *will* be right back, won't you, sister?"

Outside, the cistern lid rose and slammed down.

The rain whispered on the street and fell upon the closed lid all the rest of the night.

THE MACHINERIES OF JOY

FATHER BRIAN DELAYED GOING BELOW TO BREAKFAST because he thought he heard Father Vittorini down there, laughing. Vittorini, as usual, was dining alone. So who was there to laugh with, or at?

Us, thought Father Brian, *that's who.*

He listened again.

Across the hall Father Kelly too was hiding, or meditating, rather, in his room.

They never let Vittorini finish breakfast, no, they always managed to join him as he chewed his last bit of toast. Otherwise they could not have borne their guilt through the day.

Still, that was laughter, was it not, belowstairs? Father Vittorini had ferreted out something in the morning *Times*. Or, worse, had he stayed up half the night with the unholy ghost, that television set which stood in the entry like an unwelcome guest, one foot in whimsy, the other in the doldrums? And, his mind bleached by the electronic beast, was Vittorini now planning some bright fine new devilment, the cogs wheeling in his soundless mind, seated and deliberately fasting, hoping to lure them down curious at the sound of his Italian humors?

"Ah, God." Father Brian sighed and fingered the envelope he had prepared the previous night. He had tucked it in his coat as a protective measure should he decide to hand it to Pastor Sheldon. Would Father Vittorini detect it through the cloth with his quick dark X-ray vision?

Father Brian pressed his hand firmly along his lapel to squash any merest outline of his request for transferral to another parish.

"Here goes."

And, breathing a prayer, Father Brian went downstairs.

✳ "Ah, Father Brian!"

Vittorini looked up from his still full cereal bowl. The brute had not even so much as sugared his corn flakes yet.

Father Brian felt as if he had stepped into an empty elevator shaft.

Impulsively he put out a hand to save himself. It touched the top of the television set. The set was warm. He could not help saying, "Did you have a séance here last night?"

"I sat up with the set, yes."

"Sat up is right!" snorted Father Brian. "One does sit up, doesn't one, with the sick, or the dead? I used to be handy with the ouija board myself. There was more brains in that." He turned from the electrical moron to survey Vittorini. "And did you hear far cries and banshee wails from, what is it? Canaveral?"

"They called off the shot at three A.M."

"And you here now, looking daisy-fresh." Father Brian advanced, shaking his head. "What's true is not always what's fair."

Vittorini now vigorously doused his flakes with milk. "But you, Father Brian, you look as if you made the grand tour of Hell during the night."

Fortunately, at this point Father Kelly entered. He froze when he too saw how little along Vittorini was with his fortifiers. He muttered to both priests, seated himself, and glanced over at the perturbed Father Brian.

"True, William, you look half gone. Insomnia?"

"A touch."

Father Kelly eyed both men, his head to one side. "What goes on here? Did something happen while I was out last night?"

"We had a small discussion," said Father Brian, toying with the dread flakes of corn.

"Small discussion!" said Father Vittorini. He might have laughed, but caught himself and said simply, "The Irish priest is worried by the Italian Pope."

"Now, Father Vittorini," said Kelly.

"Let him run on," said Father Brian.

"Thank you for your permission," said Vittorini, very politely and with a friendly nod. "Il Papa is a constant source of reverent irritation to at least some if not all of the Irish clergy. Why not a pope named Nolan? Why not a green instead of a red hat? Why not, for that matter, move Saint Peter's Cathedral to Cork or Dublin, come the twenty-fifth century?"

"I hope nobody said *that*," said Father Kelly.

"I am an angry man," said Father Brian. "In my anger I might have *inferred* it."

"Angry, why? And inferred for what reason?"

"Did you hear what he just said about the twenty-fifth century?" asked Father Brian. "Well, it's when Flash Gordon and Buck Rogers fly in through the baptistery transom that yours truly hunts for the exits."

Father Kelly sighed. "Ah, God, is it *that* joke again?"

Father Brian felt the blood burn his cheeks, but fought to send it back to cooler regions of his body.

"Joke? It's off and beyond that. For a month now it's Canaveral this and trajectories and astronauts that. You'd think it was Fourth of July, he's up half each night with the rockets. I mean, now, what kind of life is it, from midnight on, carousing about the entryway with that Medusa machine which freezes your intellect if ever you stare at it? I cannot sleep for feeling the whole rectory will blast off any minute."

"Yes, yes," said Father Kelly. "But what's all this about the Pope?"

"Not the new one, the one before the last," said Brian wearily. "Show him the clipping, Father Vittorini."

Vittorini hesitated.

"Show it," insisted Brian, firmly.

Father Vittorini brought forth a small press clipping and put it on the table.

Upside down, even, Father Brian could read the bad news: "POPE BLESSES ASSAULT ON SPACE."

Father Kelly reached one finger out to touch the cutting gingerly. He intoned the news story half aloud, underlining each word with his fingernail:

CASTEL GANDOLFO, ITALY, SEPT. 20—Pope Pius XII gave his blessing today to mankind's efforts to conquer space.

The Pontiff told delegates to the International Astronautical Congress, "God has no intention of setting a limit to the efforts of man to conquer space."

The 400 delegates to the 22-nation congress were received by the Pope at his summer residence here.

"This Astronautic Congress has become one of great importance at this time of man's exploration of outer space," the Pope said. "It should concern all humanity. . . . Man has to make the effort to put himself in new orientation with God and his universe."

Father Kelly's voice trailed off.

"When did this story appear?"

"In 1956."

"*That* long back?" Father Kelly laid the thing down. "I didn't read it."

"It seems," said Father Brian, "you and I, Father, don't read much of anything."

"Anyone could overlook it," said Kelly. "It's a teeny-weeny article."

"With a very large idea in it," added Father Vittorini, his good humor prevailing.

"The point is—"

"The point is," said Vittorini, "when first I spoke of this piece, grave doubts were cast on my veracity. Now we see I have cleaved close by the truth."

"Sure," said Father Brian quickly, "but as our poet William Blake put it, 'A truth that's told with bad intent beats all the lies you can invent.'"

"Yes." Vittorini relaxed further into his amiability. "And didn't Blake also write.

> *He who doubts from what he sees,*
> *Will ne'er believe, do what you please.*
> *If the Sun and Moon should doubt*
> *They'd immediately go out.*

Most appropriate," added the Italian priest, "for the Space Age."

Father Brian stared at the outrageous man.

"I'll thank you not to quote our Blake at us."

"*Your* Blake?" said the slender pale man with the softly glowing dark hair. "Strange, I'd always thought him English."

"The poetry of Blake," said Father Brian, "was always a great comfort to my mother. It was she told me there was Irish blood on his maternal side."

"I will graciously accept that," said Father Vittorini. "But back to the newspaper story. Now that we've found it, it seems a good time to do some research on Pius the Twelfth's encyclical."

Father Brian's wariness, which was a second set of nerves under his skin, prickled alert.

"What encyclical is that?"

"Why, the one on space travel."

"He *didn't* do that?"

"He did."

"On space travel, a special encyclical?"

"A special one."

Both Irish priests were near onto being flung back in their chairs by the blast.

Father Vittorini made the picky motions of a man cleaning up after a detonation, finding lint on his coat sleeve, a crumb or two of toast on the tablecloth.

"Wasn't it enough," said Brian, in a dying voice, "he shook hands with the astronaut bunch and told them well done and all that, but he had to go on and write at length about it?"

"It was not enough," said Father Vittorini. "He wished, I hear, to comment further on the problems of life on other worlds, and its effect on Christian thinking."

Each of these words, precisely spoken, drove the two other men farther back in their chairs.

"You *hear*?" said Father Brian. "You haven't read it yourself yet?"

"No, but I intend—"

"You intend everything and mean worse. Sometimes, Father Vittorini, you do not talk, and I hate to say this, like a priest of the Mother Church at all."

"I talk," replied Vittorini, "like an Italian priest somehow caught and trying to preserve surface tension treading an ecclesiastical bog where I am outnumbered by a great herd of clerics named Shaughnessy and Nulty and Flannery that mill and stampede like caribou or bison every time I so much as whisper 'papal bull.'"

"There is no doubt in my mind"—and here Father Brian squinted off in the general direction of the Vatican, itself—"that it was you, if you could've been there, might've put the Holy Father up to this whole space-travel monkeyshines."

"I?"

"You! It's you, is it not, certainly not us, that lugs in the magazines by the carload with the rocket ships on the shiny covers and the filthy green monsters with six eyes and seventeen gadgets chasing after half-draped females on some moon or other? You I hear late nights doing the count-downs from ten, nine, eight on down to one, in tandem with the beast TV, so we lie aching for the dread concussions to knock the fillings from our teeth. Between one Italian here and another at Castel Gandolfo, may God forgive me, you've managed to depress the entire Irish clergy!"

"Peace," said Father Kelly at last, "both of you."

"And peace it is, one way or another I'll have it," said Father Brian, taking the envelope from his pocket.

"Put that away," said Father Kelly, sensing what must be in the envelope.

"Please give this to Pastor Sheldon for me."

Father Brian rose heavily and peered about to find the door and some way out of the room. He was suddenly gone.

"Now see what you've done!" said Father Kelly.

Father Vittorini, truly shocked, had stopped eating. "But, Father, all along I thought it was an amiable squabble, with him putting on and me putting on, him playing it loud and me soft."

"Well, you've played it too long, and the blasted fun turned serious!" said Kelly. "Ah, you don't know William like I do. You've really torn him."

"I'll do my best to mend—"

"You'll mend the seat of your pants! Get out of the way, this is my job now." Father Kelly grabbed the envelope off the table and held it up to the light, "The X ray of a poor man's soul. Ah, God."

He hurried upstairs. "Father Brian?" he called. He slowed. "Father?" He tapped at the door. "William?"

In the breakfast room, alone once more, Father Vittorini remembered the last few flakes in his mouth. They now had no taste. It took him a long slow while to get them down.

✳ It was only after lunch that Father Kelly cornered Father Brian in the dreary little garden behind the rectory and handed back the envelope.

"Willy, I want you to tear this up. I won't have you quitting in the middle of the game. How long has all this gone on between you two?"

Father Brian sighed and held but did not rip the envelope. "It sort of crept upon us. It was me at first spelling the Irish writers and him pronouncing the Italian operas. Then me describing the Book of Kells in Dublin and him touring me through the Renaissance. Thank God for small favors, he didn't discover the papal encyclical on the blasted space traveling sooner, or I'd have transferred my self to a monkery where the fathers keep silence as a vow. But even there, I fear, he'd follow and count down the Canaveral blastoffs in sign language. What a Devil's advocate that man would make!"

"Father!"

"I'll do penance for that later. It's just this dark otter, this seal, he frolics with Church dogma as if it was a candy-striped bouncy ball. It's all very well to have seals cavorting, but I say don't mix them with the true fanatics, such as you and me! Excuse the pride, Father, but there does seem to be a variation on the true theme every time you get them piccolo players in among us harpers, and don't you agree?"

"What an enigma, Will. We of the Church should be examples for others on how to get along."

"Has anyone told Father Vittorini that? Let's face it, the Italians are the Rotary of the Church. You couldn't have trusted one of them to stay sober during the Last Supper."

"I wonder if we Irish could?" mused Father Kelly.

"We'd wait until it was over, at least!"

"Well, now, are we priests or barbers? Do we stand here splitting hairs, or do we shave Vittorini close with his own razor? William, have you no plan?"

"Perhaps to call in a Baptist to mediate."

"Be off with your Baptist! Have you researched the encyclical?"

"The encyclical?"

"Have you let grass grow since breakfast between your toes? You have! Let's read that space-travel edict! Memorize it, get it pat, then counterattack the rocket man in his own territory! This way, to the library. What is it the youngsters cry these days? Five, four, three, two, one, blast off?"

"Or the rough equivalent."

"Well, say the rough equivalent, then, man. And follow me!"

✳ They met Pastor Sheldon, going into the library as he was coming out.

"It's no use," said the pastor, smiling, as he examined the fever in their faces. "You won't find it in there."

"Won't find what in there?" Father Brian saw the pastor looking at the letter which was still glued to his fingers, and hid it away, fast. "Won't find what, sir?"

"A rocket ship is a trifle too large for our small quarters," said the pastor in a poor try at the enigmatic.

"Has the Italian bent your ear, then?" cried Father Kelly in dismay.

"No, but echoes have a way of ricocheting about the place. I came to do some checking myself."

"Then," gasped Brian with relief, "you're on our side?"

Pastor Sheldon's eyes became somewhat sad. "Is there a side to this, Fathers?"

They all moved into the little library room, where Father Brian and Father Kelly sat uncomfortably on the edges of the hard chairs. Pastor Sheldon remained standing, watchful of their discomfort.

"Now. Why are you afraid of Father Vittorini?"

"Afraid?" Father Brian seemed surprised at the word and cried softly, "It's more like angry."

"One leads to the other," admitted Kelly. He continued, "You see, Pastor, it's mostly a small town in Tuscany shunting stones at Meynooth, which is, as you know, a few miles out from Dublin."

"I'm Irish," said the pastor, patiently.

"So you are, Pastor, and all the more reason we can't figure your great calm in this disaster," said Father Brian.

"I'm California Irish," said the pastor.

He let this sink in. When it had gone to the bottom, Father Brian groaned miserably. "Ah. We *forgot*."

And he looked at the pastor and saw there the recent dark, the tan complexion of one who walked with his face like a sunflower to the sky, even here in Chicago, taking what little light and heat he could to sustain his color and being. Here stood a man with the figure, still, of a badminton and tennis player under his tunic, and with the firm lean hands of the handball expert. In the pulpit, by the look of his arms moving in the air, you could see him swimming under warm California skies.

Father Kelly let forth one sound of laughter.

"Oh, the gentle ironies, the simple fates. Father Brian, here is our Baptist!"

"Baptist?" asked Pastor Sheldon.

"No offense, Pastor, but we were off to find a mediator, and here you are, an Irishman from California, who has known the wintry blows of Illinois so short a time, you've still the look of rolled lawns and January sunburn. We, we were born and raised as lumps in Cork and Kilcock, Pastor. Twenty years in Hollywood would not thaw us out. And now, well, they do say, don't they, that California is much . . ." here he paused, "like Italy?"

"I see where you're driving," mumbled Father Brian.

Pastor Sheldon nodded, his face both warm and gently sad. "My blood is like your own. But the climate I was shaped in is like Rome's. So you see, Father Brian, when I asked *are* there any sides, I spoke from my heart."

"Irish yet not Irish," mourned Father Brian. "Almost but not quite Italian. Oh, the world's played tricks with our flesh."

"Only if we let it, William, Patrick."

Both men started a bit at the sound of their Christian names.

"You still haven't answered: Why are you afraid?"

Father Brian watched his hands fumble like two bewildered wrestlers for a moment. "Why, it's because just when we get things settled on Earth, just when it looks like victory's in sight, the Church on a good footing, along comes Father Vittorini—"

"Forgive me, Father," said the pastor. "Along comes reality. Along comes space, time, entropy, progress, along come a million things, always. Father Vittorini didn't invent space travel."

"No, but he makes a good thing of it. With him 'everything begins in mysticism and ends in politics.' Well, no matter. I'll stash my shillelagh if he'll put away his rockets."

"No, let's leave them out in the open," replied the pastor. "Best not to hide violence or special forms of travel. Best to work with them. Why don't we climb in that rocket, Father, and learn from it?"

"Learn what? That most of the things we've taught in the past on Earth don't fit out there on Mars or Venus or wherever in hell Vittorini would push us? Drive Adam and Eve out of some new Garden, on Jupiter, with our very own rocket fires? Or worse, find there's no Eden, no Adam, no Eve, no damned Apple nor Serpent, no Fall, no Original Sin, no Annunciation, no Birth, no Son, you go on with the list, no nothing at all! on one blasted world tailing another? Is *that* what we must learn, Pastor?"

"If need be, yes," said Pastor Sheldon. "It's the Lord's space and the Lord's worlds *in* space, Father. We must not try to take our cathedrals with us, when all we need is an overnight case. The Church can be packed in a box no larger than is needed for the articles of the Mass, as much as these hands can carry. Allow Father Vittorini this, the people of the southern climes learned long ago to build in wax which melts and takes its shape in harmony with the motion and need of man. William, William, if you insist on building in hard ice, it will shatter when we break the sound barrier or melt and leave you nothing in the fire of the rocket blast."

"That," said Father Brian, "is a hard thing to learn at fifty years, Pastor."

"But learn, I know you will," said the pastor, touching his shoulder. "I set you a task: to make peace with the Italian priest. Find some way tonight for a meeting of minds. Sweat at it, Father. And, first off, since our library is meager, hunt for and find the space encyclical, so we'll know what we're yelling about."

A moment later the pastor was gone.

Father Brian listened to the dying sound of those swift feet—as if a white ball were flying high in the sweet blue air and the pastor were hurrying in for a fine volley.

"Irish but not Irish," he said. "Almost but not quite Italian. And now what are we, Patrick?"

"I begin to wonder," was the reply.

And they went away to a larger library wherein might be hid the grander thoughts of a Pope on a bigger space.

✳ A long while after supper that night, in fact almost at bedtime, Father Kelly, sent on his mission, moved about the rectory tapping on doors and whispering.

Shortly before ten o'clock, Father Vittorini came down the stairs and gasped with surprise.

Father Brian, at the unused fireplace, warming himself at the small gas heater which stood on the hearth, did not turn for a moment.

A space had been cleared and the brute television set moved forward into a circle of four chairs, among which stood two small taborettes on which stood two bottles and four glasses. Father Brian had done it all, allowing Kelly to do nothing. Now he turned, for Kelly and Pastor Sheldon were arriving.

The pastor stood in the entryway and surveyed the room. "Splendid." He paused and added, "I think. Let me see now . . ." He read the label on one bottle. "Father Vittorini is to sit here."

"By the Irish Moss?" asked Vittorini.

"The same," said Father Brian.

Vittorini, much pleased, sat.

"And the rest of us will sit by the Lachryma Christi, I take it?" said the pastor.

"An *Italian* drink, Pastor."

"I think I've heard of it," said the pastor, and sat.

"Here." Father Brian hurried over and, without looking at Vittorini, poured his glass a good way up with the Moss. "An Irish transfusion."

"Allow me." Vittorini nodded his thanks and arose, in turn, to pour the others' drinks. "The tears of Christ and the sunlight of Italy," he said. "And now, before we drink, I have something to say."

The others waited, looking at him.

"The papal encyclical on space travel," he said at last, "does not exist."

"We discovered that," said Kelly, "a few hours ago."

"Forgive me, Fathers," said Vittorini. "I am like the fisherman on the bank who, seeing fish, throws out more bait. I suspected, all along, there was no encyclical. But every time it was brought up, about town, I heard so many priests from Dublin deny it existed, I came to think it *must!* They would not go check the item, for they feared it existed. I would not, in my pride, do research, for I feared it *did not* exist. So Roman pride or Cork pride, it's all the same. I shall go on retreat soon and be silent for a week, Pastor, and do penance."

"Good, Father, good." Pastor Sheldon rose. "Now I've a small announcement. A new priest arrives here next month. I've thought long on it. The man is Italian, born and raised in Montreal."

Vittorini closed one eye and tried to picture this man to himself.

"If the Church must be all things to all people," said the pastor, "I am intrigued with the thought of hot blood raised in a cold climate, as this new Italian was, even as I find it fascinating to consider myself, cold blood raised in California. We've needed another Italian here to shake things up, and this Latin looks to be the sort will shake even Father Vittorini. Now will someone offer a toast?"

"May I, Pastor?" Father Vittorini rose again, smiling gently, his eyes darkly aglow, looking at this one and now that of the three. He raised his glass. "Somewhere did Blake not speak of the Machineries of Joy? That is, did not God promote environments, then intimidate those Natures by provoking the existence of flesh, toy men and women, such as are we all? And thus happily sent forth, at our best, with good grace and fine wit, on calm noons, in fair climes, are we not God's Machineries of Joy?"

"If Blake said that," said Father Brian, "I take it all back. He never lived in Dublin!"

All laughed together.

Vittorini drank the Irish Moss and was duly speechless.

The others drank the Italian wine and grew mellow, and in his mellowness Father Brian cried softly, "Vittorini, now, will you, unholy as it is, tune on the ghost?"

"Channel Nine?"

"Nine it is!"

And while Vittorini dialed the knobs Father Brian mused over his drink, "Did Blake *really* say that?"

"The fact is, Father," said Vittorini, bent to the phantoms coming and going on the screen, "he might have, if he'd lived today. I wrote it down myself tonight."

All watched the Italian with some awe. Then the TV gave a hum and came clear, showing a rocket, a long way off, getting ready.

"The machineries of joy," said Father Brian. "Is that one of them you're tuning in? And is that another sitting there, the rocket on its stand?"

"It could be, tonight," murmured Vittorini. "If the thing goes up, and a man in it, all around the world, and him still alive, and us with him, though we just sit here. That would be joyful indeed."

The rocket was getting ready, and Father Brian shut his eyes for a moment. Forgive me, Jesus, he thought, forgive an old man his prides, and forgive Vittorini his spites, and help me to understand what I see here tonight, and let me stay awake if need be, in good humor, until dawn, and let the thing go well, going up and coming down, and think of the man in that contraption, Jesus, *think* of and be with him. And help me, God, when the summer is young, for, sure as fate on Fourth of July evening there will be Vittorini and the kids from around the block, on the rectory lawn, lighting skyrockets. All them there watching the sky, like the morn of the Redemption, and help me, O Lord, to be as those children before the great night of time and void where you abide. And help me to walk forward, Lord, to light the next rocket Independence Night, and stand with the Latin father, my face suffused with that same look of the delighted child in the face of the burning glories you put near our hand and bid us savor.

He opened his eyes.

Voices from far Canaveral were crying in a wind of time. Strange phantom powers loomed upon the screen. He was drinking the last of the wine when someone touched his elbow gently.

"Father," said Vittorini, near. "Fasten your seat belt."

"I will," said Father Brian. "I will. And many thanks."

He sat back in his chair. He closed his eyes. He waited for the thunder. He waited for the fire. He waited for the concussion and the voice that would teach a silly, a strange, a wild and miraculous thing:

How to count back, ever backward . . . to zero.

BRIGHT PHOENIX

One day in April 2022 the great library door slammed flat shut. Thunder.

Hullo, I thought.

At the bottom step glowering up at my desk, in a United Legion uniform which no longer hung as neatly upon him as it had twenty years before, stood Jonathan Barnes.

Seeing his bravado momentarily in pause, I recalled ten thousand Veterans' speeches sprayed from his mouth, the endless wind-whipped flag parades he had hustled, panted through, the grease-cold chicken and green-pea patriot banquets he had practically cooked himself; the civic drives stillborn in his hat.

Now Jonathan Barnes stomped up the creaking main library steps, giving each the full downthrust of his power, weight, and new authority. His echoes, rushed back from the vast ceilings, must have shocked even him into better manners, for when he reached my desk, I felt his warmly liquored breath stir mere whispers on my face.

"I'm here for the books, Tom."

I turned casually to check some index cards. "When they're ready, we'll call you."

"Hold on," he said. "Wait—"

"You're here to pick up the Veterans' Salvage books for hospital distribution?"

"No, no," he cried. "I'm here for *all* the books."

I gazed at him.

"Well," he said, "*most* of them."

"Most?" I blinked once, then bent to riffle the files. "Only ten volumes to a person at a time. Let's see. Here! Why, you let your card expire when you were twenty years old, thirty years ago. See?" I held it up.

Barnes put both hands on the desk and leaned his great bulk upon them. "I see you are interfering." His face began to color, his breath to husk and rattle. "I don't need a card for *my* work!"

So loud was his whisper that a myriad of white pages stopped butterflying under far green lamps in the big stone rooms. Faintly, a few books thudded shut.

Reading people lifted their serene faces. Their eyes, made antelope by the time and weather of this place, pleaded for silence to return, as it always must when a tiger has come and gone from a special fresh-water spring, as this surely was. Looking at these upturned, gentle faces I thought of my forty years of living, working, even sleeping here among hidden lives and vellumed, silent, and imaginary people. Now, as always, I considered my library as a cool cavern or fresh, ever-growing forest into which men passed from the heat of the day and the fever of motion to refresh their limbs and bathe their minds an hour in the grass-shade illumination, in the sound of small breezes wandered out from the turning and turning of the pale soft book pages. Then, better focused, their ideas rehung upon their frames, their flesh made easy on their bones, men might walk forth into the blast furnace of reality, noon, mob-traffic, improbable senescence, inescapable death. I had seen thousands career into my library starved, and leave well-fed. I had watched lost people find themselves. I had known realists to dream and dreamers to come awake in this marble sanctuary where silence was a marker in each book.

"Yes," I said at last. "But it will only take a moment to re-register you. Fill in this new card. Give two reliable references—"

"I don't *need* references," said Jonathan Barnes, "to burn books!"

"Contrarily," said I. "You'll need even more, to do that."

"My men are my references. They're waiting outside for the books. They're dangerous."

"Men like that always are."

"No no, I mean the books, idiot. The *books* are dangerous. Good God, no two agree. All the damn double-talk. All the lousy babel and slaver and spit. So, we're out to simplify, clarify, hew to the line. We need—"

"To talk this over," said I, taking up a copy of Demosthenes, tucking it under my arm. "It's time for my dinner. Join me, please—"

I was halfway to the door when Barnes, wide-eyed, suddenly remembered the silver whistle hung from his blouse, jammed it to his wet lips, and gave it a piercing blast.

The library doors burst wide. A flood of black charcoal-burned uniformed men collided boisterously upstairs.

I called, softly.

They stopped, surprised.

"Quietly," I said.

Barnes seized my arm. "Are you opposing due process?"

"No," I said. "I won't even ask to see your property invasion permit. I wish only silence as you work."

The readers at the tables had leaped up at the storm of feet. I patted the air. They sat back down and did not glance up again at these men crammed into their tight dark char-smeared suits who stared at my mouth now as if they disbelieved my cautions. Barnes nodded. The men moved softly, on tiptoe, through the big library rooms. With extra care, with proper stealth, they raised the windows. Soundlessly, whispering, they collected books from the shelves to toss down toward the evening yard below. Now and again they scowled at the readers who calmly went on leafing through their books, but made no move to seize these volumes, and continued emptying the shelves.

"Good," said I.

"Good?" asked Barnes.

"Your men can work without you. Take five."

And I was out in the twilight so quickly he could only follow, bursting with unvoiced questions. We crossed the green lawn where a huge portable

Hell was drawn up hungrily, a fat black tar-daubed oven from which shot red-orange and gaseous blue flames into which men were shoveling the wild birds, the literary doves which soared crazily down to flop broken-winged, the precious flights poured from every window to thump the earth, to be kerosene-soaked and chucked in the gulping furnace. As we passed this destructive if colorful industry, Barnes mused.

"Funny. Should be crowds, a thing like this. But . . . no crowd. How do you figure?"

I left him. He had to run to catch up.

In the small café across the street we took a table and Barnes, irritable for no reason he could say, called out, "Service! I've got to get back to work!"

Walter, the proprietor, strolled over, with some dog-eared menus. Walter looked at me. I winked.

Walter looked at Jonathan Barnes.

Walter said, " 'Come live with me and be my love; and we will all the pleasures prove.' "

"What?" Jonathan Barnes blinked.

" 'Call me Ishmael,' " said Walter.

"Ishmael," I said. "We'll have coffee to start."

Walter came back with the coffee.

" 'Tiger! Tiger! burning bright,' " he said. " 'In the forests of the night.' "

Barnes stared after the man who walked away casually. "What's eating him? Is he nuts?"

"No," I said. "But go on with what you were saying back at the library. Explain."

"Explain?" said Barnes. "My God, you're all sweet reason. All right, I will explain. This is a tremendous experiment. A test town. If the burning works here, it'll work anywhere. We don't burn everything, no no. You noticed, my men cleaned only certain shelves and categories? We'll eviscerate about forty-nine point two percent. Then we'll report our success to the overall government committee—"

"Excellent," I said.

Barnes eyed me. "How can you be so cheerful?"

"Any library's problem," I said, "is where to put the books. You've helped me solve it."

"I thought you'd be . . . afraid."

"I've been around Trash Men all my life."

"I beg pardon?"

"Burning is burning. Whoever does it is a Trash Man."

"Chief Censor, Green Town, Illinois, damn it!"

A new man, a waiter, came with the coffee pot steaming.

"Hullo, Keats," I said.

"'Season of mists and mellow fruitfulness,'" said the waiter.

"Keats?" said the Chief Censor. "His name isn't Keats."

"Silly of me," I said. "This is a Greek restaurant. Right, Plato?"

The waiter refilled my cup. "'The people have always some champion whom they set over them and nurse into greatness . . . This and no other is the root from which a tyrant springs; when he first appears he is a protector.'"

Barnes leaned forward to squint at the waiter, who did not move. Then Barnes busied himself blowing on his coffee: "As I see it, our plan is simple as one and one make two . . ."

The waiter said, "'I have hardly ever known a mathematician who was capable of reasoning.'"

"Damn it!" Barnes slammed his cup down. "Peace! Get away while we eat, you, Keats, Plato, Holdridge, *that's* your name. I remember now, *Holdridge*! What's all this *other* junk?"

"Just fancy," said I. "Conceit."

"Damn fancy, and to hell with conceit, you can eat alone, I'm getting out of this madhouse." And Barnes gulped his coffee as the waiter and proprietor watched and I watched him gulping and across the street the bright bonfire in the gut of the monster device burned fiercely. Our silent watching caused Barnes to freeze at last with the cup in his hand and the coffee dripping off his chin. "Why? Why aren't you yelling? Why aren't you fighting me?"

"But I am fighting," I said, taking the book from under my arm. I tore a page from Demosthenes, let Barnes see the name, rolled it into a fine Havana cigar shape, lit it, puffed it, and said, "'Though a man escape every other danger, he can never wholly escape those who do not want such a person as he is to exist.'"

Barnes was on his feet, yelling, the "cigar" was torn from my mouth, stomped on, and the Chief Censor was out of the door, almost in one motion.

I could only follow.

On the sidewalk, Barnes collided with an old man who was entering the café. The old man almost fell. I grabbed his arm.

"Professor Einstein," I said.

"Mr. Shakespeare," he said.

Barnes fled.

✳ I found him on the lawn by the old and beautiful library where the dark men, who wafted kerosene perfume from their every motion, still dumped vast harvestings of gun-shot dead pigeon, dying pheasant books, all autumn gold and silver from the high windows. But . . . softly. And while this still, almost serene, pantomime continued, Barnes stood screaming silently, the scream clenched in his teeth, tongue, lips, cheeks, gagged back so none could hear. But the scream flew out of his wild eyes in flashes and was held for discharge in his knotted fists, and shuttled in colors about his face, now pale, now red as he glared at me, at the café, at the damned proprietor, at the terrible waiter who now waved amiably back at him. The Baal incinerator rumbled its appetite, spark-burned the lawn. Barnes stared full at the blind yellow-red sun in its raving stomach.

"You," I called up easily at the men who paused. "City Ordinance. Closing time is nine sharp. Please be done by then. Wouldn't want to break the law—Good evening, Mr. Lincoln."

" 'Four score,' " said a man, passing, " 'and seven years—' "

"Lincoln?" The Chief Censor turned slowly. "That's Bowman. Charlie Bowman. I know you, Charlie, come back here, Charlie, Chuck!"

But the man was gone, and cars drove by, and now and again as the burning progressed men called to me and I called back, and whether it was, "Mr. Poe!" or hullo to some small bleak stranger with a name like Freud, each time I called in good humor and they replied, Mr. Barnes twitched as if another arrow had pierced, sunk deep in his quivering bulk and he were dying slowly of a hidden seepage of fire and raging life. And still no crowd gathered to watch the commotion.

Suddenly, for no discernible reason, Mr. Barnes shut his eyes, opened his mouth wide, gathered air, and shouted, "Stop!"

The men ceased shoveling the books out of the window above.

"But," I said, "it's not closing time . . ."

"Closing time! Everybody out!" Deep holes had eaten away the center of Jonathan Barnes' eyes. Within, there was no bottom. He seized the air. He pushed down. Obediently, all the windows crashed like guillotines, chiming their panes.

The dark men, bewildered, came out and down the steps.

"Chief Censor." I handed him a key which he would not take, so I forced his fist shut on it. "Come back tomorrow, observe silence, finish up."

The Chief Censor let his bullet-hole gaze, his emptiness, search without finding me.

"How . . . how long has this gone on . . . ?"

"This?"

"This . . . and . . . that . . . and *them*."

He tried but could not nod at the café, the passing cars, the quiet readers descending from the warm library now, nodding as they passed into cold dark, friends, one and all. His blind man's rictal gaze ate holes where my face was. His tongue, anesthetized, stirred. "Do you think you can all fool me, me, *me*?"

I did not answer.

"How can you be sure," he said, "I won't burn people, as well as books?"

I did not answer.

I left him standing in the complete night.

Inside, I checked out the last volumes of those leaving the library now with night come on and shadows everywhere and the great Baal machinery churning smoke, its fire dying in the spring grass where the Chief Censor stood like a poured cement statue, not seeing his men drive off. His fist suddenly flew high. Something swift and bright flew up to crack the front-door glass. Then Barnes turned and walked after the incinerator as it trundled off, a fat black funeral urn unravelling long tissues and scarves of black bunting smoke and fast-vanishing crêpe.

I sat listening.

In the far rooms, filled with soft jungle illumination, there was a lovely autumnal turning of leaves, faint sifts of breathing, infinitesimal quirks, the gesture of a hand, the glint of a ring, the intelligent squirrel blink of an eye. Some nocturnal voyager sailed between the half-empty stacks. In porcelain serenity, the restroom waters flowed down to a still and distant sea. My people, my friends, one by one, passed from the cool marble, the green glades, out into a night better than we could ever have hoped for.

At nine, I went out to pick up the thrown front-door key. I let the last reader, an old man, out with me, and as I was locking up, he took a deep breath of the cool air, looked at the town, the spark-burned lawn, and said, "Will they come back again, ever?"

"Let them. We're ready for them, aren't we?"

The old man took my hand. " 'The wolf also shall dwell with the lamb, and the leopard shall lie down with the kid; and the calf and the young lion and the fatling together.' "

We moved down the steps.

"Good evening, Isaiah," I said.

"Mr. Socrates," he said. "Good night."

And each walked his own way, in the dark.

THE WISH

A WHISPER OF SNOW TOUCHED THE COLD WINDOW.

The vast house creaked in a wind from nowhere.

"What?" I said.

"I didn't say anything." Charlie Simmons, behind me at the fireplace, shook popcorn quietly in a vast metal sieve. "Not a word."

"Damn it, Charlie, I *heard* you . . ."

Stunned, I watched the snow fall on far streets and empty fields. It was a proper night for ghosts of whiteness to visit windows and wander off.

"You're imagining things," said Charlie.

Am I? I thought. Does the weather have voices? Is there a language of night and time and snow? What goes on between that dark out there and my soul in here?

For there in the shadows, a whole civilization of doves seemed to be landing unseen, without benefit of moon or lamp.

And was it the snow softly whispering out there, or was it the past, accumulations of old time and need, despairs mounding themselves to panics and at last finding tongue?

"God, Charles. Just now, I could have sworn I heard you say—"

"Say what?"

"You said: 'Make a wish.' "

"I did?"

His laughter behind me did not make me turn; I kept on watching the snow fall and I told him what I must tell—

"You said, 'It's a special, fine, strange night. So make the finest, dearest, strangest wish ever in your life, deep from your heart. It will be yours.' That's what I heard you say."

"No." I saw his image in the glass shake its head. "But, Tom, you've stood there hypnotized by the snowfall for half an hour. The fire on the hearth talked. Wishes don't come true, Tom. But—" and here he stopped and added with some surprise, "by God, you *did* hear something, didn't you? Well, here. Drink."

✳ The popcorn was done popping. He poured wine which I did not touch. The snow was falling steadily along the dark window in pale breaths.

"Why?" I asked. "Why would this *wish* jump into my head? If you didn't say it, what did?"

What indeed, I thought; what's out there, and who are we? Two writers late, alone, my friend invited for the night, two old companions used to much talk and gossip about ghosts, who've tried their hands at all the usual psychic stuffs, Ouija boards, tarot cards, telepathies, the junk of amiable friendship over years, but always full of taunts and jokes and idle fooleries.

But this out there tonight, I thought, ends the jokes, erases smiles. The snow—why, look! It's burying our laughter. . . .

"Why?" said Charlie at my elbow, drinking wine, gazing at the red-green-blue Yule-tree lights and now at the back of my neck. "Why a *wish* on a night like this? Well, it is the night before Christmas, right? Five minutes from now, Christ is born. Christ and the winter solstice all in one week. This week, this night, proves that Earth won't die. The winter has touched bottom and now starts upward toward the light. That's special. That's incredible."

"Yes," I murmured, and thought of the old days when cavemen died in their hearts when autumn came and the sun went away and the ape-men cried until the world shifted in its white sleep and the sun rose earlier one fine morning and the universe was saved once more, for a little while. "Yes."

"So—" Charlie read my thoughts and sipped his wine. "Christ always was the promise of spring, wasn't he? In the midst of the longest night of the year, Time shook, Earth shuddered and calved a myth. And what did the myth yell? Happy New Year! God, yes, January first isn't New Year's

Day. Christ's birthday is. His breath, sweet as clover, touches our nostrils, promises spring, this very moment before midnight. Take a deep breath, Thomas."

"Shut up!"

"Why? Do you hear voices again?"

Yes! I turned to the window. In sixty seconds, it would be the morn of His birth. What purer, rarer hour was there, I thought wildly, for wishes.

"Tom—" Charlie seized my elbow. But I was gone deep and very wild indeed. Is this a special time? I thought. Do holy ghosts wander on nights of falling snow to do us favors in this strange-held hour? If I make a wish in secret, will that perambulating night, strange sleeps, old blizzards give back my wish tenfold?

I shut my eyes. My throat convulsed.

"Don't," said Charlie.

But it trembled on my lips. I could not wait. Now, now, I thought, a strange star burns at Bethlehem.

"Tom," gasped Charlie, "for Christ's sake!"

Christ, yes, I thought, and said:

"My wish is, for one hour tonight—"

"No!" Charlie struck me, once, to shut my mouth.

"—please, make my father alive again."

The mantel clock struck twelve times to midnight.

"Oh, Thomas . . ." Charlie grieved. His hand fell away from my arm. "Oh, Tom."

A gust of snow rattled the window, clung like a shroud, unraveled away.

The front door exploded wide.

Snow sprang over us in a shower.

"What a sad wish. And . . . it has just come true."

"True?" I whirled to stare at that open door which beckoned like a tomb.

"Don't go, Tom," said Charlie.

The door slammed. Outside, I ran; oh, God, how I ran.

"Tom, come back!" The voice faded far behind me in the whirling fall of white. "Oh, God, *don't*!"

✳ But in this minute after midnight I ran and ran, mindless, gibbering, yelling my heart on to beat, blood to move, legs to run and keep running, and I thought: Him! Him! I know where *he* is! If the gift is mine! If the wish comes true! I know his *place*! And all about in the night-snowing town the bells of Christmas began to clang and chant and clamor. They circled and paced and drew me on as I shouted and mouthed snow and knew maniac desire.

Fool! I thought. He's dead! Go back!

But what if he is alive, one hour tonight, and I *didn't* go to find him?

I was outside town, with no hat or coat, but so warm from running, a salty mask froze my face and flaked away with the jolt of each stride down the middle of an empty road, with the sound of joyous bells blown away and gone.

A wind took me around a final corner of wilderness where a dark wall waited for me.

The cemetery.

I stood by the heavy iron gates, looking numbly in.

The graveyard resembled the scattered ruins of an ancient fort, blown up lifetimes ago, its monuments buried deep in some new Ice Age.

Suddenly, miracles were not possible.

Suddenly the night was just so much wine and talk and dumb enchantments and I running for no reason save I believed, I truly believed, I had felt something *happen* out here in this snow-dead world. . . .

He remembered.

And he began to melt away. He recalled his body shriveling, his dim heart gone to stillness; the slam of some eternal door of night.

He stood very still in my arms, his eyelids flickering over the stuffs that shifted grotesque furnitures within his head. He must have asked himself the most terrible question of all:

Who has done this thing to me?

He opened his eyes. His gaze beat at me.

You? it said.

Yes, I thought. I wished you alive this night.

You! his face and body cried.

And then, half-aloud, the final inquisition:

"Why . . . ?"

Now it was my turn to be blasted and riven.

Why, indeed, had I done this to him?

How had I dared to wish for this awful, this harrowing, confrontation?

What was I to do now with this man, this stranger, this old, bewildered, and frightened child? Why had I summoned him, just to send him back to soils and graves and dreadful sleeps?

Had I even bothered to think of the consequences? No. Raw impulse had shot me from home to this burial field like a mindless stone to a mindless goal. Why? Why?

My father, this old man, stood in the snow now, trembling, waiting for my pitiful answer.

A child again, I could not speak. Some part of me knew a truth I could not say. Inarticulate with him in life, I found myself yet more mute in his waking death.

The truth raved inside my head, cried along the fibers of my spirit and being, but could not break forth from my tongue. I felt my own shouts locked inside.

The moment was passing. This hour would soon be gone. I would lose the chance to say what must be said, what should have been said when he was warm and above the earth so many years ago.

Somewhere far off across country, the bells sounded twelve-thirty on this Christmas morn. Christ ticked in the wind. Snow flaked away at my face with time and cold, cold and time.

Why? my father's eyes asked me; why have you brought me here?

"I—" and then I stopped.

For his hand had tightened on my arm. His face had found its own reason.

This was his chance, too, *his* final hour to say what he should have said when I was twelve or fourteen or twenty-six. No matter if I stood mute. Here in the falling snow, he could make his peace and go his way.

His mouth opened. It was hard, so dreadfully hard, for him to force the old words out. Only the ghost within the withered shell could dare to agonize and gasp. He whispered three words, lost in the wind.

"Yes?" I urged.

He held me tight and tried to keep his eyes open in the blizzard-night. He wanted to sleep, but first his mouth gaped and whistled again and again:

"... I .... uvvv .... yuuuuuuuu ... !"

He stopped, trembled, wracked his body, and tried to shout it again, failing:

"... I .... vvv .... yyy .... u ... !"

"Oh, Dad!" I cried. "Let me say it *for* you!"

He stood very still and waited.

"Were you trying to say I ... love ... you?"

"Esssss!" he cried. And burst out, very clearly, at long last: "Oh, *yes!*"

"Oh, Dad," I said, wild with miserable happiness, all gain and loss. "Oh, and Pa, dear Pa, I love you."

We fell together. We held.

I wept.

And from some strange dry well within his terrible flesh I saw my father squeeze forth tears which trembled and flashed on his eyelids.

And the final question was thus asked and answered.

Why have you brought me here?

Why the wish, why the gifts, and why this snowing night?

Because we had had to say, before the doors were shut and sealed forever, what we never had said in life.

And now it had been said and we stood holding each other in the wilderness, father and son, son and father, the parts of the whole suddenly interchangeable with joy.

The tears turned to ice upon my cheeks.

✳ We stood in the cold wind and falling snow for a long while until we heard the sound of the bells at twelve forty-five, and still we stood in the snowing night saying no more—no more ever need be said—until at last our hour was done.

All over the white world the clocks of one A.M. on Christmas morn, with Christ new in the fresh straw, sounded the end of that gift which had passed so briefly into and now out of our numb hands.

My father held me in his arms.

The last sound of the one-o'clock bells faded.

I felt my father step back, at ease now.

His fingers touched my cheek.

I heard him walking in the snow.

The sound of his walking faded even as the last of the crying faded within myself.

I opened my eyes only in time to see him, a hundred yards off, walking. He turned and waved, once, at me.

The snow came down in a curtain.

How brave, I thought, to go where you go now, old man, and no complaint.

I walked back into town.

I had a drink with Charles by the fire. He looked in my face and drank a silent toast to what he saw there.

Upstairs, my bed waited for me like a great fold of white snow.

The snow was falling beyond my window for a thousand miles to the north, five hundred miles to the east, two hundred miles west, a hundred miles to the south. The snow fell on everything, everywhere. It fell on two sets of footprints beyond the town: one set coming out and the other going back to be lost among the graves.

I lay on my bed of snow. I remembered my father's face as he waved and turned and went away.

It was the face of the youngest, happiest man I had ever seen.

With that I slept, and gave up weeping.

THE LIFEWORK OF JUAN DÍAZ

FILOMENA FLUNG THE PLANK DOOR SHUT with such violence the candle blew out; she and her crying children were left in darkness. The only things to be seen were through the window—the adobe houses, the cobbled streets, where now the gravedigger stalked up the hill, his spade on his shoulder, moonlight honing the blue metal as he turned into the high cold graveyard and was gone.

"Mamacita, what's wrong?" Filepe, her oldest son, just nine, pulled at her. For the strange dark man had said nothing, just stood at the door with the spade and nodded his head and waited until she banged the door in his face. "Mamacita?"

"That gravedigger." Filomena's hands shook as she relit the candle. "The rent is long overdue on your father's grave. Your father will be dug up and placed down in the catacomb, with a wire to hold him standing against the wall, with the other mummies."

"No, Mamacita!"

"Yes." She caught the children to her. "Unless we find the money. Yes."

"I—I will kill that gravedigger!" cried Filepe.

"It is his job. Another would take his place if he died, and another and another after him."

They thought about the man and the terrible high place where he lived and moved and the catacomb he stood guard over and the strange earth into which people went to come forth dried like desert flowers and tanned like leather for shoes and hollow as drums which could be tapped and beaten, an earth which made great cigar-brown rustling dry mummies that might languish forever leaning like fence poles along the catacomb halls. And, thinking of all this familiar but unfamiliar stuff, Filomena and her children were cold in summer, and silent though their hearts made a vast stir in their bodies. They huddled together for a moment longer and then:

"Filepe," said the mother, "come." She opened the door and they stood in the moonlight listening to hear any far sound of a blue metal spade biting the earth, heaping the sand and old flowers. But there was a silence of stars "You others," said Filomena, "to bed."

The door shut. The candle flickered.

The cobbles of the town poured in a river of gleaming moon-silver stone down the hills, past green parks and little shops and the place where the coffin maker tapped and made the clock sounds of death-watch beetles all day and all night, forever in the life of these people. Up along the slide and rush of moonlight on the stones, her skirt whispering of her need, Filomena hurried with Filepe breathless at her side. They turned in at the Official Palace.

The man behind the small, littered desk in the dimly lit office glanced up in some surprise. "Filomena, my cousin!"

"Ricardo." She took his hand and dropped it. "You must help me."

"If God does not prevent. But ask."

"They—" The bitter stone lay in her mouth; she tried to get it out. "Tonight they are taking Juan from the earth."

Ricardo, who had half risen, now sat back down, his eyes growing wide and full of light, and then narrowing and going dull. "If not God, then God's creatures prevent. Has the year gone so swiftly since Juan's death? Can it truly be the rent has come due?" He opened his empty palms and showed them to the woman. "Ah, Filomena, I have no money."

"But if you spoke to the gravedigger. You are the police."

"Filomena, Filomena, the law stops at the edge of the grave."

"But if he will give me ten weeks, only ten, it is almost the end of summer. The Day of the Dead is coming. I will make, I will sell, the candy skulls, and give him the money, oh, please, Ricardo."

And here at last, because there was no longer a way to hold the coldness in and she must let it free before it froze her so she could never move again, she put her hands to her face and wept. And Filepe, seeing that it was permitted, wept, too, and said her name over and over.

"So," said Ricardo, rising. "Yes, yes. I will walk to the mouth of the cat-acomb and spit into it. But, ah, Filomena, expect no answer. Not so much as an echo. Lead the way." And he put his official cap, very old, very greasy, very worn, upon his head.

The graveyard was higher than the churches, higher than all the build-ings, higher than all the hills. It lay on the highest rise of all, overlooking the night valley of the town.

As they entered the vast ironwork gate and advanced among the tombs, the three were confronted by the sight of the gravedigger's back bent into an ever-increasing hole, lifting out spade after spade of dry dirt onto an ever-increasing mound. The digger did not even look up, but made a quiet guess as they stood at the grave's edge.

"Is that Ricardo Albañez, the chief of police?"

"Stop digging!" said Ricardo.

The spade flashed down, dug, lifted, poured. "There is a funeral tomor-row. This grave must be empty, open and ready."

"No one has died in the town."

"Someone always dies. So I dig. I have already waited two months for Filomena to pay what she owes. I am a patient man."

"Be still more patient." Ricardo touched the moving, hunching shoul-der of the bent man.

"Chief of the police." The digger paused to lean, sweating, upon his spade. "This is my country, the country of the dead. These here tell me nothing, nor does any man. I rule this land with a spade, and a steel mind. I do not like the live ones to come talking, to disturb the silence I have so nicely dug and filled. Do I tell you how to conduct your municipal palace? Well, then. Good night." He resumed his task.

"In the sight of God," said Ricardo, standing straight and stiff, his fists at his sides, "and this woman and her son, you dare to desecrate the husband-father's final bed?"

"It is not final and not his, I but rented it to him." The spade floated high, flashing moonlight. "I did not ask the mother and son here to watch this sad event. And listen to me, Ricardo, police chief, one day you will die. I will bury you. Remember that: I. You will be in my hands. Then, oh, then."

"Then what?" shouted Ricardo. "You dog, do you threaten me?"

"I dig." The man was very deep now, vanishing in the shadowed grave, sending only his spade up to speak for him again and again in the cold light. "Good night, señor, señora, niño. Good night."

Outside her small adobe hut, Ricardo smoothed his cousin's hair and touched her cheek. "Filomena, ah, God."

"You did what you could."

"That terrible one. When I am dead, what awful indignities might he not work upon my helpless flesh? He would set me upside down in the tomb, hang me by my hair in a far, unseen part of the catacomb. He takes on weight from knowing someday he will have us all. Good night, Filomena. No, not even that. For the night is bad."

He went away down the street.

Inside, among her many children, Filomena sat with face buried in her lap.

✳ Late the next afternoon, in the tilted sunlight, shrieking, the schoolchildren chased Filepe home. He fell, they circled him, laughing.

"Filepe, Filepe, we saw your father today, yes!"

"Where?" they asked themselves shyly.

"In the catacomb!" they gave answer.

"What a lazy man! He just stands there!"

"He never works!"

"He don't speak! Oh, that Juan Díaz!"

Filepe stood violently atremble under the blazed sun, hot tears streaming from his wide and half-blinded eyes.

Within the hut, Filomena heard, and the knife sounds entered her heart. She leaned against the cool wall, wave after dissolving wave of remembrance sweeping her.

In the last month of his life, agonized, coughing, and drenched with midnight perspirations, Juan had stared and whispered only to the raw ceiling above his straw mat.

"What sort of man am I, to starve my children and hunger my wife? What sort of death is this, to die in bed?"

"Hush." She placed her cool hand over his hot mouth. But he talked beneath her fingers. "What has our marriage been but hunger and sickness and now nothing? Ah, God, you are a good woman, and now I leave you with no money even for my funeral!"

And then at last he had clenched his teeth and cried out at the darkness and grown very quiet in the warm candleshine and taken her hands into his own and held them and swore an oath upon them, vowed himself with religious fervor.

"Filomena, listen. I will be with you. Though I have not protected in life, I will protect in death. Though I fed not in life, in death I will bring food. Though I was poor, I will not be poor in the grave. This I know. This I cry out. This I assure you of. In death I will work and do many things. Do not fear. Kiss the little ones. Filomena. Filomena . . ."

And then he had taken a deep breath, a final gasp, like one who settles beneath warm waters. And he had launched himself gently under, still holding his breath, for a testing of endurance through all eternity. They waited for a long time for him to exhale. But this he did not do. He did not reappear above the surface of life again. His body lay like a waxen fruit on the mat, a surprise to the touch. Like a wax apple to the teeth, so was Juan Díaz to all their senses.

And they took him away to the dry earth which was like the greatest mouth of all which held him a long time, draining the bright moisture of his life, drying him like ancient manuscript paper, until he was a mummy as light as chaff, an autumn harvest ready for the wind.

From that time until this, the thought had come and come again to Filomena, how will I feed my lost children, with Juan burning to brown crepe in a silver-tinseled box, how lengthen my children's bones and push forth their teeth in smiles and color their cheeks?

The children screamed again outside, in happy pursuit of Filepe.

Filomena looked to the distant hill, up which bright tourists' cars hummed bearing many people from the United States. Even now they paid a peso each to that dark man with the spade so that they might step down throught his catacombs among the standing dead, to see what the sun-dry earth and the hot wind did to *all* bodies in this town.

Filomena watched the tourist cars, and Juan's voice whispered, "Filomena." And again: "This I cry out. In death I will work . . . I will not be poor . . . Filomena . . ." His voice ghosted away. And she swayed and was almost ill, for an idea had come into her mind which was new and terrible and made her heart pound. "Filepe!" she cried suddenly.

And Filepe escaped the jeering children and shut the door on the hot white day and said, "Yes, Mamacita?"

"Sit, niño, we must talk, in the name of the saints, we must!"

She felt her face grow old because the soul grew old behind it, and she said, very slowly, with difficulty, "Tonight we must go in secret to the catacomb."

"Shall we take a knife"—Filepe smiled wildly—"and kill the dark man?"

"No, no, Filepe, listen. . . ."

And he heard the words that she spoke.

And the hours passed and it was a night of churches. It was night of bells, and singing. Far off in the air of the valley you could hear voices chanting the evening Mass, you could see children walking with lit candles, in a solemn file, 'way over there on the side of the dark hill, and the huge bronze bells were tilting up and showering out their thunderous crashes and bangs that made the dogs spin, dance and bark on the empty roads.

The graveyard lay glistening, all whiteness, all marble snow, all sparkle and glitter of harsh gravel like an eternal fall of hail, crunched under their feet as Filomena and Filepe took their shadows with them, ink-black and constant from the unclouded moon. They glanced over their shoulders in apprehension, but one cried Halt! They had seen the gravedigger drift, made footless by shadow, down the hill, in answer to a night summons. Now: "Quick, Filepe, the lock!" Together they inserted a long metal rod between padlock hasps and wooden doors which lay flat to the dry earth. Together they seized and pulled. The wood split. The padlock hasps sprang loose. Together they raised the huge doors and flung them back, rattling. Together they peered down into the darkest, most silent night of all. Below, the catacomb waited.

Filomena straightened her shoulders and took a breath.

"Now."

And put her foot upon the first step.

✳ In the adobe of Filomena Díaz, her children slept sprawled here or there in the cool night room, comforting each other with the sound of their warm breathing.

Suddenly their eyes sprang wide.

Footsteps, slow and halting, scraped the cobbles outside. The door shot open. For an instant the silhouettes of three people loomed in the white evening sky beyond the door. One child sat up and struck a match.

"No!" Filomena snatched out with one hand to claw the light. The match fell away. She gasped. The door slammed. The room was solid black. To this blackness Filomena said at last:

"Light no candles. Your father has come home."

✳ The thudding, the insistent knocking and pounding shook the door at midnight.

Filomena opened the door.

The gravedigger almost screamed in her face. "There you are! Thief! Robber!"

Behind him stood Ricardo, looking very rumpled and very tired and very old. "Cousin, permit us, I am sorry. Our friend here—"

"I am the friend of no one," cried the gravedigger. "A lock has been broken and a body stolen. To know the identity of the body is to know the thief. I could only bring you here. Arrest her."

"One small moment, please." Ricardo took the man's hand from his arm and turned, bowing gravely to his cousin. "May we enter?"

"There, there!" The gravedigger leaped in, gazed wildly about and pointed to a far wall. "You see?"

But Ricardo would look only at this woman. Very gently he asked her, "Filomena?"

Filomena's face was the face of one who has gone through a long tunnel of night and has come to the other end at last, where lives a shadow of coming day. Her eyes were prepared. Her mouth knew what to do. All the terror was gone now. What remained was as light as the great length of autumn chaff she had carried down the hill with her good son. Nothing more could happen to her ever in her life; this you knew from how she held her body as she said, "We have no mummy here."

"I believe you, cousin, but"—Ricardo cleared his throat uneasily and raised his eyes—"what stands there against the wall?"

"To celebrate the festival of the day of the dead ones"—Filomena did not turn to look where he was looking—"I have taken paper and flour and wire and clay and made of it a life-size toy which looks like the mummies."

"Have you indeed done this?" asked Ricardo, impressed.

"No, no!" The gravedigger almost danced in exasperation.

"With your permission." Ricardo advanced to confront the figure which stood against the wall. He raised his flashlight. "So," he said. "And so."

Filomena looked only out the open door into the late moonlight. "The plan I have for this mummy which I have made with my own hands is good."

"What plan, what?" the gravedigger demanded, turning.

"We will have money to eat with. Would you deny my children this?"

But Ricardo was not listening. Near the far wall, he tilted his head this way and that and rubbed his chin, squinting at the tall shape which enwrapped its own shadow, which kept its own silence, leaning against the adobe.

"A toy," mused Ricardo. "The largest death toy I have ever seen. I have seen man-size skeletons in windows, and man-size coffins made of cardboard and filled with candy skulls, yes. But this! I stand in awe, Filomena."

"Awe?" said the gravedigger, his voice rising to a shriek. "This is no toy, this is—"

"Do you swear, Filomena?" said Ricardo, not looking at him. He reached out and tapped a few times on the rust-colored chest of the figure. It made the sound of a lonely drum. "Do you swear this is papier-mâché?"

"By the Virgin, I swear."

"Well, then." Ricardo shrugged, snorted, laughed. "It is simple. If you swear by the Virgin, what more need be said? No court action is necessary. Besides, it might take weeks or months to prove or disprove this is or is not a thing of flour paste and old newspapers colored with brown earth."

"Weeks, months, prove, disprove!" The gravedigger turned in a circle as if to challenge the sanity of the universe held tight and impossible in these four walls. "This 'toy' is my property, mine!"

"The 'toy,'" said Filomena serenely, gazing out at the hills, "if it is a toy, and made by me, must surely belong to me. And even," she went on, quietly communing with the new reserve of peace in her body, "even if it is not a toy, and it is indeed Juan Díaz come home, why, then, does not Juan Díaz belong first to God?"

"How can one argue that?" wondered Ricardo.

The gravedigger was willing to try. But before he had stuttered forth a half-dozen words, Filomena said, "And after God, in God's eyes, and at God's altar and in God's church, on one of God's holiest days, did not Juan Díaz say that he would be mine throughout his days?"

"Throughout his days—ah, ha, there you are!" said the gravedigger. "But his days are over, and now he is mine!"

"So," said Filomena, "God's property first, and then Filomena Díaz' property, that is if this toy is not a toy and is Juan Díaz, and anyway, landlord of the dead, you evicted your tenant, you so much as said you did not want him, if you love him so dearly and want him, will you pay the new rent and tenant him again?"

But so smothered by rage was the landlord of silence that it gave Ricardo time to step in. "Grave keeper, I see many months and many lawyers, and many points, fine points, to argue this way and that, which include real estate, toy manufactories, God, Filomena, one Juan Díaz wherever he is, hungry children, the conscience of a digger of graves, and so much complication that death's business will suffer. Under the circumstances are you prepared for these long years in and out of court?"

"I am prepared—" said the gravedigger, and paused.

"My good man," said Ricardo, "the other night you gave me some small bit of advice, which I now return to you. I do not tell you how to control your dead. You, now, do not say how I control the living. Your jurisdiction ends at the tombyard gate. Beyond stand my citizens, silent or otherwise. So . . ."

Ricardo thumped the upright figure a last time on its hollow chest. It gave forth the sound of a beating heart, a single strong and vibrant thump which made the gravedigger jerk.

"I pronounce this officially fake, a toy, no mummy at all. We waste time here. Come along, citizen gravedigger. Back to your proper land! Good night, Filomena's children, Filomena, good cousin."

"What about *it*, what about *him*?" said the gravedigger, motionless, pointing.

"Why do you worry?" asked Ricardo. "It goes nowhere. It stays, if you should wish to pursue the law. Do you see it running? You do not. Good night. Good night."

The door slammed. They were gone before Filomena could put out her hand to thank anyone.

She moved in the dark to place a candle at the foot of the tall cornhusk-dry silence. This was a shrine now, she thought, yes. She lit the candle.

"Do not fear, children," she murmured. "To sleep now. To sleep." And Filepe lay down and the others lay back, and at last Filomena herself lay with a single thin blanket over her on the woven mat by the light of the single candle, and her thoughts before she moved into sleep were long thoughts of the many days that made up tomorrow. In the morning, she thought, the tourist cars will sound on the road, and Filepe will move among them, telling them of this place. And there will be a painted sign outside this door: MUSEUM—30 CENTAVOS. And the tourists will come in, because the graveyard is on the hill, but we are first, we are here in the valley, and close at hand and easy to find. And one day soon with these tourists' money we shall mend the roof, and buy great sacks of fresh corn flour, and some tangerines, yes, for the children. And perhaps one day we will all travel to Mexico City, to the very big schools because of what has happened on this night.

For Juan Díaz is truly home, she thought. He is here, he waits for those who would come to see him. And at his feet I will place a bowl into which the tourists will place more money that Juan Díaz himself tried so hard to earn in all his life.

Juan. She raised her eyes. The breathing of the children was hearth-warm about her. Juan, do you see? Do you know? Do you truly understand? Do you forgive, Juan, do you forgive?

The candle flame flickered.

She closed her eyes. Behind her lids she saw the smile of Juan Díaz, and whether it was the smile that death had carved upon his lips, or whether it was a new smile she had given him or imagined for him, she could not say. Enough that she felt him standing tall and alone and on guard, watching over them and proud through the rest of the night.

A dog barked far away in a nameless town.

Only the gravedigger, wide awake in his tombyard, heard.

TIME INTERVENING/INTERIM

VERY LATE ON THIS NIGHT, the old man came from his house with a flash-light in his hand and asked of the little boys the object of their frolic. The little boys gave no answer, but tumbled on in the leaves.

The old man went into his house and sat down and worried. It was three in the morning. He saw his own pale, small hands trembling on his knees. He was all joints and angles, and his face, reflected above the man-tel, was no more than a pale cloud of breath exhaled upon the mirror.

The children laughed softly outside, in the leaf piles.

He switched out his flashlight quietly and sat in the dark. Why he should be bothered in any way by playing children he could not know. But it was late for them to be out, at three in the morning, playing. He was very cold.

There was a sound of a key in the door and the old man arose to go see who could possibly be coming into his house. The front door opened and a young man entered with a young woman. They were looking at each other softly and tenderly, holding hands, and the old man stared at them and cried, "What are you *doing* in my house?"

The young man and the young woman replied, "What are *you* doing in *our* house?" The young man said, "Here now, get on out." And he took the old man by the elbow and shoved him out the door and closed and locked it after searching him to see if he had stolen something.

"This is *my* house. You can't lock me out!" The old man beat upon the door. He stood in the dark morning air. Looking up he saw the lights illumine the warm inside window and rooms upstairs and then, with a move of shadows, go out.

The old man walked down the street and came back and still the small boys rolled in the icy morning leaves, not looking at him.

He stood before the house and as he watched the lights turned on and turned off more than a thousand times. He counted softly under his breath.

A young boy of about fourteen ran by to the house, a football in his hand. He opened the door without even trying to unlock it, and went in. The door closed.

Half an hour later, with the morning wind rising, the old man saw a car pull up and a plump woman get out with a little boy three years old. They walked across the wet lawn and went into the house after the woman had looked at the old man and said, "Is that you, Mr. Terle?"

"Yes," said the old man, automatically, for somehow he didn't wish to frighten her. But it was a lie. He knew he was not Mr. Terle at all. Mr. Terle lived down the street.

The lights glowed on and off a thousand more times.

The children rustled softly in the leaves.

A seventeen year old boy bounded across the street, smelling faintly of the smudged lipstick on his cheek, almost knocked the old man down, cried, "Sorry!" and leaped up the steps. Fitting a key to the lock he went in.

The old man stood there with the town lying asleep on all sides of him; the unlit windows, the breathing rooms, the stars all through the trees, liberally caught and held on winter branches, so much snow suspended glittering on the cold air.

"That's *my* house; who are all those people going in it?" cried the old man to the wrestling children.

The wind blew, shaking the empty trees.

✳ In the year which was 1923 the house was dark. A car drove up before it, the mother stepped from the car with her son William, who was three. William looked at the dusky morning world and saw his house and as he felt his mother lead him toward the house he heard her say. "Is that you, Mr. Terle?" and in the shadows by the great wind-filled oak tree an old man stood and replied, "Yes." The door closed.

✳ In the year which was 1934 William came running in the summer night, feeling the football cradled in his hands, feeling the murky night street pass under his running feet, along the sidewalk. He smelled, rather than saw, an old man, as he ran past. Neither of them spoke. And so, on into the house.

✳ In the year 1937 William ran with antelope boundings across the street, a smell of lipstick on his face, a smell of someone young and fresh upon his cheeks; all thoughts of love and deep night. He almost knocked the stranger down, cried, "Sorry!" and ran to fit a key to the front door.

✳ In the year 1947 a car drew up before the house, William relaxed, his wife beside him. He wore a fine tweed suit, it was late, he was tired, they both smelled faintly of so many drinks offered and accepted. For a moment they both heard the wind in the trees. They got out of the car and let themselves into the house with a key. An old man came from the living room and cried, "What are you *doing* in my house?"

"Your house?" said William. "Here now, old man, get on out." And William, feeling faintly sick in his stomach, for there was something about the old man that made him feel all water and nothing, searched the old man and pushed him out the door and closed and locked it. From outside the old man cried, "This is *my* house. You can't lock me out!"

They went up to bed and turned out the lights.

✳ In the year 1928 William and the other small boys wrestled on the lawn, waiting for the time when they would leave to watch the circus come chuffing into the pale-dawn railroad station on the blue metal tracks. In the leaves they lay and laughed and kicked and fought. An old man with a flashlight came across the lawn. "Why are you playing here on my lawn at this time of morning?" asked the old man.

"Who are you?" replied William, looking up a moment from the tangle.

The old man stood over the tumbling children a long moment. Then he dropped his flash. "Oh, my dear boy, I know now, now I know!" He bent to touch the boy. "I am you and you are me. I love you, my dear boy, with all of my heart! Let me tell you what will happen to you in the years to come! If you knew! I am you and you were once me! My name is William—so is yours! And all these people going into the house, they are William, they are you, they are me!" The old man shivered. "Oh, all the long years and the passing of time!"

"Go away," said the boy. "You're crazy."

"But—" said the old man.

"You're crazy. I'll call my father."

The old man turned and walked away.

There was a flickering of the house lights, on and off. The boys wrestled quietly and secretly in the rustling leaves. The old man stood on the dark lawn.

✳ Upstairs, in his bed, William Latting did not sleep, in the year 1947. He sat up, lit a cigarette, and looked out the window. His wife was awake. "What's wrong?" she asked.

"That old man," said William Latting. "I think he's still down there, under the oak tree."

"Oh, he couldn't be," she said.

"I can't see very well, but I think he's there. I can barely make him out, it's so dark."

"He'll go away," she said.

William Latting drew quietly on his cigarette. He nodded. "Who are those kids?"

From her bed his wife said, "What kids?"

"Playing on the lawn out there, what a hell of a time of night to be playing in the leaves."

"Probably the Moran boys."

"Doesn't look like them."

He stood by the window. "You hear something?"

"What?"

"A baby crying. Way off?"

"I don't hear anything," she said.

She lay listening. They both thought they heard running footsteps on the street, a key to the door. William Latting went to the hall and looked down the stairs but saw nothing.

＊ In the year 1937, coming to the door, William saw a man in a dressing gown at the top of the stairs, looking down, with a cigarette in his hand. "That *you*, Dad?" No answer. The man sighed and went back into some room. William went to the kitchen to raid the ice-box.

The children wrestled in the soft, dark leaves of morning.

＊ William Latting said, "Listen."

He and his wife listened.

"It's the old man," said William, "crying."

"Why should he be crying?"

"I don't know. Why does anybody cry? Maybe he's unhappy."

"If he's still there in the morning," said his wife in the dim room, "call the police."

William Latting went away from the window, put out his cigarette, and lay in the bed, his eyes closed. "No," he said quietly. "I won't call the police. Not for him, I won't."

"Why not?"

His voice was certain. "I wouldn't want to do that. I just wouldn't."

They both lay there and faintly there was a sound of crying and the wind blew and William Latting knew that all he had to do if he wanted to watch the boys wrestling in the icy leaves of morning would be to reach out with his hand and lift the shade and look, and there they would be, far below, wrestling and wrestling, as dawn came pale in the Eastern sky.

ALMOST THE END
OF THE WORLD

SIGHTING ROCK JUNCTION, ARIZONA, AT NOON on August 22, 1967, Willy Bersinger let his miner's boot rest easy on the jalopy's accelerator and talked quietly to his partner, Samuel Fitts.

"Yes, sir, Samuel, it's great hitting town. After a couple of months out at the Penny Dreadful Mine, a jukebox looks like a stained-glass window to me. We need the town; without it, we might wake some morning and find ourselves all jerked beef and petrified rock. And then, of course, the town needs us, too."

"How's that?" asked Samuel Fitts.

"Well, we bring things into town that it hasn't got—mountains, creeks, desert night, stars, things like that . . ."

And it was true, thought Willy, driving along. Set a man 'way out in the strange lands and he fills with wellsprings of silence. Silence of sagebrush, or a mountain lion purring like a warm beehive at noon. Silence of the river shallows deep in the canyons. All this a man takes in. Opening his mouth, in town, he breathes it out.

"Oh, how I love to climb into that old barbershop chair," Willy admitted, "and see all those city men lined up under the naked-lady calendars, staring back at me, waiting while I chew over my philosophy of rocks and mirages and the kind of Time that just sits out there in the hills waiting for man to go away. I exhale—and that wilderness settles in a fine dust on the customers. Oh, it's nice, me talking, soft and easy, up and down, on and on . . ."

In his mind he saw the customers' eyes strike fire. Someday they would yell and rabbit for the hills, leaving families and time-clock civilization behind.

"It's good to feel wanted," said Willy. "You and me, Samuel, are basic necessities for those city-dwelling folks. Gangway, Rock Junction!"

And with a tremulous tin whistling they steamed across city limits into awe and wonder.

✳ They had driven perhaps a hundred feet through town when Willy kicked the brakes. A great shower of rust flakes sifted from the jalopy fenders. The car stood cowering in the road.

"Something's wrong," said Willy. He squinted his lynx eyes this way and that. He snuffed his huge nose. "You feel it? You smell it?"

"Sure," said Samuel, uneasily, "but what?"

Willy scowled. "You ever see a sky-blue cigar-store Indian?"

"Never did."

"There's one over there. Ever see a pink dog kennel, an orange outhouse, a lilac-colored birdbath? There, there, and over there!"

Both men had risen slowly now to stand on the creaking floorboards.

"Samuel," whispered Willy, "the whole damn shooting match, every kindling pile, porch rail, gewgaw gingerbread, fence, fireplug, garbage truck, the *whole blasted town*, look at it! It was painted just an hour ago!"

"No!" said Samuel Fitts.

But there stood the band pavilion, the Baptist church, the firehouse, the Oddfellows' orphanage, the railroad depot, the county jail, the cat hospital and all the bungalows, cottages, greenhouses, gazebos, shop signs, mailboxes, telephone poles and trashbins, around and in between, and they all blazed with corn yellow, crab-apple greens, circus reds. From water tank to tabernacle, each building looked as if God had jigsawed it, colored it and set it out to dry a moment ago.

Not only that, but where weeds had always been, now cabbages, green onions, and lettuce crammed every yard, crowds of curious sunflowers clocked the noon sky, and pansies lay under unnumbered trees cool as summer puppies, their great damp eyes peering over rolled lawns mint-green as Irish travel posters. To top it all, ten boys, faces scrubbed, hair brilliantined, shirts, pants and tennis shoes clean as chunks of snow, raced by.

"The town," said Willy, watching them run, "has gone mad. Mystery. Mystery everywhere. Samuel, what kind of tyrant's come to power? What law was passed that keeps boys clean, drives people to paint every toothpick, every geranium pot? Smell that smell? There's fresh wallpaper in all those houses! Doom in some horrible shape has tried and tested these people. Human nature doesn't just get this picky perfect overnight. I'll bet all the gold I panned last month those attics, those cellars are cleaned out, all shipshape. I'll bet you a real Thing fell on this town."[*]

"Why, I can almost hear the cherubim singing in the Garden," Samuel protested. "How you figure Doom? Shake my hand, put 'er there. I'll bet and take your money!"

The jalopy swerved around a corner through a wind that smelled of turpentine and whitewash. Samuel threw out a gum wrapper, snorting. He was somewhat surprised at what happened next. An old man in new overalls, with mirror-bright shoes, ran out into the street, grabbed the crumpled gum wrapper and shook his fist after the departing jalopy.

"Doom . . ." Samuel Fitts looked back, his voice fading. "Well, . . . the bet *still* stands."

✳ They opened the door upon a barbershop teeming with customers whose hair had already been cut and oiled, whose faces were shaved close and pink, yet who sat waiting to vault back into the chairs where three barbers flourished their shears and combs. A stock-market uproar filled the room as customers and barbers all talked at once.

When Willy and Samuel entered, the uproar ceased instantly. It was if they had fired a shotgun blast through the door.

"Sam . . . Willy . . ."

In the silence some of the sitting men stood up and some of the standing men sat down, slowly, staring.

"Samuel," said Willy out of the corner of his mouth, "I feel like the Red Death standing here." Aloud he said, "Howdy! Here I am to finish my lecture on the Interesting Flora and Fauna of the Great American Desert, and—"

"No!"

Antonelli, the head barber, rushed frantically at Willy, seized his arm, clapped his hand over Willy's mouth like a snuffer on a candle. "Willy," he whispered, looking apprehensively over his shoulder at his customers. "Promise me one thing: buy a needle and thread, sew up your lips. Silence, man, if you value your life!"

Willy and Samuel felt themselves hurried forward. Two already neat customers leaped out of the barber chairs without being asked. As they stepped into the chairs, the two miners glimpsed their own images in the flyspecked mirror.

"Samuel, there we are! Look! Compare!"

"Why," said Samuel, blinking, "we're the only men in all Rock Junction who really *need* a shave and a haircut."

"Strangers!" Antonelli laid them out in the chairs as if to anesthetize them quickly. "You don't know what strangers you are!"

"Why, we've only been gone a couple of months—" A steaming towel inundated Willy's face; he subsided with muffled cries. In steaming darkness he heard Antonelli's low and urgent voice.

"We'll fix you to look like everyone else. Not that the way you look is dangerous, no, but the kind of talk you miners talk might upset folks at a time like this."

"Time like this, hell!" Willy lifted the seething towel. One bleary eye fixed Antonelli. "What's wrong with Rock Junction?"

"Not just Rock Junction." Antonelli gazed off at some incredible dream beyond the horizon. "Phoenix, Tucson, Denver. All the cities in America! My wife and I are going as tourists to Chicago next week. Imagine Chicago all painted and clean and new. The Pearl of the Orient, they call it! Pittsburgh, Cincinnati, Buffalo, the same! All because—well, get up now, walk over and switch on that television set against the wall."

Willy handed Antonelli the steaming towel, walked over. switched on the television set, listened to it hum, fiddled with the dials and waited. White snow drifted down the screen.

"Try the radio now," said Antonelli.

Willy felt everyone watch as he twisted the radio dial from station to station.

"Hell," he said at last, "both your television and radio are broken."

"No," said Antonelli simply.

Willy lay back down in the chair and closed his eyes.

Antonelli leaned forward, breathing hard.

"Listen," he said.

"Imagine four weeks ago, a late Saturday morning, women and children staring at clowns and magicians on TV. In beauty shops, women staring at TV fashions. In the barbershop and hardware stores, men staring at baseball or trout fishing. Everybody everywhere in the civilized world staring. No sound, no motion, except on the little black-and-white screens.

"And then, in the middle of all that staring . . ."

Antonelli paused to lift up one corner of the broiling cloth.

"Sunspots on the sun," he said.

Willy stiffened.

"Biggest damn sunspots in the history of mortal man," said Antonelli. "Whole damn world flooded with electricity. Wiped every TV screen clean as a whistle, leaving nothing, and, after that, more nothing."

His voice was remote as the voice of a man describing an arctic land-scape. He lathered Willy's face, not looking at what he was doing. Willy peered across the barbershop at the soft snow falling down and down that humming screen in an eternal winter. He could almost hear the rabbit thumping of all the hearts in the shop.

Antonelli continued his funeral oration.

"It took us all that first day to realize what had happened. Two hours after that first sunspot storm hit, every TV repairman in the United States was on the road. Everyone figured it was just their own set. With the radios conked out, too, it was only that night, when newsboys, like in the old days, ran headlines through the streets, that we got the shock about the sunspots maybe going on—for the rest of our lives!"

The customers murmured.

Antonelli's hand, holding the razor, shook. He had to wait.

"All that blankness, that empty stuff falling down, falling down inside our television sets, oh, I tell you, it gave everyone the willies. It was like a good friend who talks to you in your front room and suddenly shuts up and lies there, pale, and you know he's dead and you begin to turn cold yourself.

"That first night, there was a run on the town's movie houses. Films weren't much, but it was like the Oddfellows' Ball downtown till midnight. Drugstores fizzed up two hundred vanilla, three hundred chocolate sodas that first night of the Calamity. But you can't buy movies and sodas every night. What then? Phone your in-laws for canasta or Parcheesi?"

"Might as well," observed Willy, "blow your brains out."

"Sure, but people had to get out of their haunted houses. Walking through their parlors was like whistling past a graveyard. All that silence . . ."

Willy sat up a little. "Speaking of silence—"

"On the third night," said Antonelli quickly, "we were all still in shock. We were saved from outright lunacy by one woman. Somewhere in this town this woman strolled out of the house, and came back a minute later. In one hand she held a paintbrush. And in the other—"

"A bucket of paint," said Willy.

Everyone smiled, seeing how well he understood.

"If those psychologists ever strike off gold medals, they should pin one on that woman and every woman like her in every little town who saved our world from coming to an end. Those women who instinctively wandered in at twilight and brought us the miracle cure."

Willy imagined it. There were the glaring fathers and the scowling sons slumped by their dead TV sets waiting for the damn things to shout Ball One, or Strike Two! And then they looked up from their wake and there in the twilight saw the fair women of great purpose and dignity standing and waiting with brushes and paint. And a glorious light kindled their cheeks and eyes. . . .

"Lord, it spread like wildfire!" said Antonelli. "House to house, city to city. Jigsaw-puzzle craze, 1932, yo-yo craze, 1928, were nothing compared with the Everybody Do Everything Craze that blew this town to smithereens and glued it back again. Men everywhere slapped paint on anything that stood still ten seconds; men everywhere climbed steeples, straddled fences, fell off roofs and ladders by the hundreds. Women painted cupboards, closets; kids painted Tinkertoys, wagons, kites. If they hadn't kept busy, you could have built a wall around this town, renamed it Babbling Brooks. All towns, everywhere, the same, where people had forgotten how to waggle their jaws, make their own talk. I tell you, men were moving in mindless circles, dazed, until their wives shoved a brush into their hands and pointed them toward the nearest unpainted wall!"

"Looks like you finished the job," said Willy.

"Paint stores ran out of paint three times the first week." Antonelli surveyed the town with pride. "The painting could only last so long, of course, unless you start painting hedges and spraying grass blades one by one. Now that the attics and cellars are cleaned out, too, our fire is seeping off into, well, women canning fruit again, making tomato pickles, raspberry, strawberry preserves. Basement shelves are loaded. Big church doings, too. Organized bowling, night donkey baseball, box socials, beer busts. Music shop sold five hundred ukeleles, two hundred and twelve steel guitars, four hundred and sixty ocarinas and kazoos in four weeks. I'm studying trombone. Mac, there, the flute. Band Concerts Thursday and Sunday nights. Hand-crank ice-cream machines? Bert Tyson's sold two hundred last week alone. Twenty-eight days, Willie, Twenty-eights Days That Shook the World!"

Willy Bersinger and Samuel Fitts sat there, trying to imagine and feel the shock, the crushing blow.

"Twenty-eight days, the barbershop jammed with men getting shaved twice a day so they can sit and stare at customers like they might say something," said Antonelli, shaving Willy now. "Once, remember, before TV, barbers were supposed to be great talkers. Well, this month it took us one whole week to warm up, get the rust out. Now we're spouting fourteen to the dozen. No quality, but our quantity is ferocious. When you came in you heard the commotion. Oh, it'll simmer down when we get used to the great Oblivion."

"Is *that* what everyone calls it?"

"It sure looked that way to most of us, there for a while."

Willy Bersinger laughed quietly and shook his head. "Now I know why you didn't want me to start lecturing when I walked in that door."

Of course, thought Willy, why didn't I see it right off? Four short weeks ago the wilderness fell on this town and shook it good and scared it plenty. Because of the sunspots, all the towns in all the Western world have had enough silence to last them ten years. And here I come by with another dose of silence, my easy talk about deserts and nights with no moon and only stars and just the little sound of the sand blowing along the empty river bottoms. No telling what might have happened if Antonelli hadn't shut me up. I see me, tarred and feathered, leaving town.

"Antonelli," he said aloud. "Thanks."

"For nothing," said Antonelli. He picked up his comb and shears. "Now, short on the sides, long in back?"

"Long on the sides," said Willy Bersinger, closing his eyes again, "short in back."

✳ An hour later Willy and Samuel climbed back into their jalopy, which someone, they never knew who, had washed and polished while they were in the barbershop.

"Doom." Samuel handed over a small sack of gold dust. "With a capital D."

"Keep it." Willy sat, thoughtful, behind the wheel. "Let's take this money and hit out for Phoenix, Tucson, Kansas City, why not? Right now we're a surplus commodity around here. We won't be welcome again until those little sets begin to herringbone and dance and sing. Sure as hell, if we stay, we'll open our traps and the gila monsters and chicken hawks and the wilderness will slip out and make us trouble."

Willy squinted at the highway straight ahead.

"Pearl of the Orient, that's what he said. Can you imagine that dirty old town, Chicago, all painted up fresh and new as a babe in the morning light? We just got to go see Chicago, by God!"

He started the car, let it idle, and looked at the town.

"Man survives," he murmured. "Man endures. Too bad we missed the big change. It must have been a fierce thing, a time of trials and testings. Samuel, I don't recall, do you? What have *we* ever seen on TV?"

"Saw a woman wrestle a bear two falls out of three, one night."

"Who won?"

"Damned if I know. She—"

But then the jalopy moved and took Willy Bersinger and Samuel Fitts with it, their hair cut, oiled and neat on their sweet-smelling skulls, their cheeks pink-shaven, their fingernails flashing the sun. They sailed under clipped green, fresh-watered trees, through flowered lanes, past daffodil-, lilac-, violet-, rose- and peppermint-colored houses on the dustless road.

"Pearl of the Orient, here we come!"

A perfumed dog with permanented hair ran out, nipped their tires and barked, until they were gone away and completely out of sight.

THE GREAT COLLISION
OF MONDAY LAST

THE MAN STAGGERED THROUGH THE FLUNG-WIDE DOORS of Heber Finn's pub as if struck by lightning. Reeling, blood on his face, coat, and torn pants, his moan froze every customer at the bar. For a time you heard only the soft foam popping in the lacy mugs, as the customers turned, some faces pale, some pink, some veined and wattle-red. Every eyelid down the line gave a blink.

The stranger swayed in his ruined clothes, eyes wide, lips trembling. The drinkers clenched their fist. Yes! they cried, silently—go on, man! what *happened?*

The stranger leaned far out on the air.

"Collision," he whispered. "Collision on the road."

Then, chopped at the knees, he fell.

"Collision!" A dozen men rushed at the body.

"Kelly!" Heber Finn vaulted the bar. "Get to the road! Mind the victim; easy does it! Joe, run for the Doc!"

"Wait!" said a quiet voice.

From the private stall at the dark end of the pub, the cubby where a philosopher might brood, a dark man blinked out at the crowd.

"Doc!" cried Heber Finn. "It's you!"

Doctor and men hustled out into the night.

"Collision . . ." The man on the floor twitched his lips.

"Softly, boys." Heber Finn and two others gentled the victim atop the bar. He looked handsome as death on the fine inlaid wood with the prismed mirror making him two dread calamities for the price of one.

Outside on the steps, the crowd halted, shocked as if an ocean had sunk Ireland in the dusk and now bulked all about them. Fog in fifty-foot rollers and breakers put out the moon and stars. Blinking, cursing, the men leaped out to vanish in the deeps.

Behind, in the bright doorframe, a young man stood. He was neither red enough nor pale enough of face, nor dark enough or light enough in spirit to be Irish, and so must be American. He was. That established, it follows he dreaded interfering with what seemed village ritual. Since arriving in Ireland, he could not shake the feeling that at all times he was living stage center of the Abbey Theatre. Now, not knowing his lines, he could only stare after the rushing men.

"But," he protested weakly, "I didn't hear any cars on the road."

"You did not!" said an old man almost pridefully. Arthritis limited him to the top step where he teetered, shouting at the white tides where his friends had submerged. "Try the crossroad, boys! That's where it most often does!"

"The crossroad!" Far and near, footsteps rang.

"Nor," said the American, "did I hear a collision."

The old man snorted with contempt. "Ah, we don't be great ones for commotion, nor great crashing sounds. But collision you'll see if you step on out there. Walk, now, don't run! It's the devil's own night. Running blind you might hit into Kelly, beyond, who's a great one for running just to squash his lungs. Or you might head on with Feeney, too drunk to find any road, never mind what's on it! You got a torch, a flash? Blind you'll be, but use it. Walk now, you *hear*?"

The American groped through the fog to his car, found his flashlight, and, immersed in the night beyond Heber Finn's, made direction by the heavy clubbing of shoes and a rally of voices ahead. A hundred yards off in eternity the men approached, grunting whispers: "Easy now!" "Ah, the shameful blight!" "Hold on, don't jiggle him!"

The American was flung aside by a steaming lump of men who swept suddenly from the fog, bearing atop themselves a crumpled object. He glimpsed a bloodstained and livid face high up there, then someone cracked his flashlight down.

By instinct, sensing the far whiskey-colored light of Heber Finn's, the catafalque surged on toward that fixed and familiar harbor.

Behind came dim shapes and a chilling insect rattle.

"Who's that!" cried the American.

"Us, with the vehicles," someone husked. "You might say—we got the collision."

The flashlight fixed them. The American gasped. A moment later, the battery failed.

But not before he had seen two village lads jogging along with no trouble at all, easily, lightly, toting under their arms two ancient black bicycles minus front and tail lights.

"What . . . ?" said the American.

But the lads trotted off, the accident with them. The fog closed in. The American stood abandoned on an empty road, his flashlight dead in his hand.

By the time he opened the door at Heber Finn's, both "bodies" as they called them, had been stretched on the bar.

"We got the bodies on the bar," said the old man, turning as the American entered.

And there was the crowd lined up not for drinks, but blocking the way so the Doc had to shove sidewise from one to another of these relics of blind driving by night on the misty roads.

"One's Pat Nolan," whispered the old man. "Not working at the moment. The other's Mr. Peevey from Meynooth, in candy and cigarettes mostly." Raising his voice, "Are they dead now, Doc?"

"Ah, be still, won't you?" The Doc resembled a sculptor troubled at finding some way to finish up two full-length marble statues at once. "Here, let's put one victim on the floor!"

"The floor's a tomb," said Heber Finn. "He'll catch his death down there. Best leave him up where the warm air gathers from our talk."

"But," said the American quietly, confused, "I've never heard of an acci-

dent like this in all my life. Are you sure there were absolutely no cars?
Only these two men on their *bikes*?"

"Only!" The old man shouted. "Great God, man, a fellow working up a
drizzling sweat can pump along at sixty kilometers. With a long downhill
glide his bike hits ninety or ninety-five! So here they come, these two, no
front or tail lights—"

"Isn't there a law against that?"

"To hell with government interference! So here the two come, no lights,
flying home from one town to the next. Thrashing like Sin Himself's at
their behinds! Both going opposite ways but both on the same side of the
road. Always ride the wrong side of the road, it's safer, they say. But look on
these lads, fair destroyed by all that official palaver. Why? Don't you see?
One remembered it, but the other didn't! Better if the officials kept their
mouths shut! For here the two be, dying."

"Dying?" The American stared.

"Well, think on it, man! What stands between two able-bodied hell-bent
fellas jumping along the path from Kilcock to Meynooth? Fog! Fog is all!
Only fog to keep their skulls from bashing together. Why, look when two
chaps hit at a cross like that, it's like a strike in bowling alleys, tenpins flying! Bang! There go your friends, nine feet up, heads together like dear
chums met, flailing the air, their bikes clenched like two tomcats. Then
they all fall down and just lay there, feeling around for the Dark Angel."

"Surely these men won't—"

"Oh, won't they? Why, last year alone in all the Free State no night
passed some soul did not meet in fatal collision with another!"

"You mean to say over three hundred Irish bicyclists die every year, hitting each other?"

"God's truth and a pity."

"I never ride my bike nights." Heber Finn eyed the bodies. "I walk."

"But still then the damn bikes run you down!" said the old man.
"Awheel or afoot, some idiot's always panting up Doom the other way.
They'd sooner split you down the seam than wave hello. Oh, the brave men
I've seen ruined or half-ruined or worse, and headaches their lifetimes
after." The old man trembled his eyelids shut. "You might almost think,
mightn't you, that human beings was not made to handle such delicate
instruments of power."

"Three hundred dead each year." The American seemed dazed.

"And that don't count the 'walking wounded' by the thousands every fortnight who, cursing, throw their bikes in the bog forever and take government pensions to salve their all-but-murdered bodies."

"Should we stand here talking?" The American gestured helplessly toward the victims. "Is there a hospital?"

"On a night with no moon," Heber Finn continued, "best walk out through the middle of fields and be damned to the evil roads! That's how I have survived into this my fifth decade."

"Ah . . ." The men stirred restlessly.

The Doc, sensing he had withheld information too long, feeling his audience drift away, now snatched their attention back by straightening up briskly and exhaling.

"Well!"

The pub quickened into silence.

"This chap here—" The Doc pointed. "Bruises, lacerations, and agonizing backaches for two weeks running. As for the other lad, however—" And here the Doc let himself scowl for a long moment at the paler one there looking rouged, waxed, and ready for final rites. "Concussion."

"Concussion!"

The quiet wind rose and fell in the silence.

"He'll survive if we run him quick now to Meynooth Clinic. So whose car will volunteer?"

The crowd turned as a staring body toward the American. He felt the gentle shift as he was drawn from outside the ritual to its deep and innermost core. He flushed, remembering the front of Heber Finn's pub, where seventeen bicycles and one automobile were parked at this moment. Quickly, he nodded.

"There! A volunteer, lads! Quick now, hustle this boy—gently!—to our good friend's vehicle!"

The men reached out to lift the body, but froze when the American coughed. They saw him circle his hand to all, and tip his cupped fingers to his lips. They gasped in soft surprise. The gesture was not done when drinks foamed down the bar.

"For the road!"

And now even the luckier victim, suddenly revived, face like cheese, found a mug gentled to his hand with whispers.

"Here, lad, here . . . tell us . . ."

". . . what happened, eh? eh?"

Then the body was gone off the bar, the potential wake over, the room

empty save for the American, the Doc, the revived lad, and two softly cudg-
eling friends. Outside you could hear the crowd putting the one serious
result of the great collision into the volunteer's car.

The Doc said, "Finish your drink, Mr.—?"

"McGuire," said the American.

"By the saints, he's Irish!"

No, thought the American, far away, looking numbly around at the pub,
at the recovered bicyclist seated, waiting for the crowd to come back and
mill about him, seeing the blood-spotted floor, the two bicycles tilted near
the door like props from a vaudeville turn, the dark night waiting outside
with its improbable fog, listening to the roll and cadence and gentle equilibrium of these voices balanced each in its own throat and environment.
No, thought the American named McGuire, I'm almost, but certainly not
quite, Irish . . .

"Doctor," he heard himself say as he placed money on the bar, "do you
often have auto wrecks, collisions, between people in *cars*?"

"Not in our town!" The Doc nodded scornfully east. "If you like that sort
of thing, now, Dublin's the very place for it!"

Crossing the pub together, the Doc took his arm as if to impart some
secret which would change his Fates. Thus steered, the American found the
stout inside himself a shifting weight he must accommodate from side to
side as the Doc breathed soft in his ear.

"Look here now, McGuire, admit it, you've driven but little in Ireland,
right? Then, listen! Driving to Meynooth, fog and all, you'd best take it fast!
Raise a din! Why? Scare the cyclists and cows off the path, both sides! If you
drive slow, why you'll creep up on and do away with dozens before they know
what took them off! And another thing: when a car approaches, douse your
lights! Pass each other, lights out, in safety. Them devil's own lights have put
out more eyes and demolished more innocents than all of seeing's worth. Is
it clear, now? Two things: speed, and douse your lights when cars loom up!"

At the door, the American nodded. Behind him he heard the one victim,
settled easy in his chair, working the stout around on his tongue, thinking,
preparing, beginning his tale:

"Well, I'm on me way home, blithe as you please, asailing downhill near
the cross when—"

Outside in the car with the other collision victim moaning softly in the
back seat, the Doc offered final advice.

"Always wear a cap, lad. If you want to walk nights ever, on the roads, that is. A cap'll save you the frightful migraines should you meet Kelly or Moran or any other hurtling full-tilt the other way, full of fiery moss and hard-skulled from birth. Even on foot, these men are dangerous. So you see, there's rules for pedestrians too in Ireland, and wear a cap at night is Number One!"

Without thinking, the American fumbled under the seat, brought forth a brown tweed cap purchased in Dublin that day, and put it on. Adjusting it, he looked out at the dark mist boiling across the night. He listened to the empty highway waiting for him ahead, quiet, quiet, quiet, but not quiet somehow. For hundreds of long strange miles up and down all of Ireland he saw a thousand crossroads covered with a thousand fogs through which one thousand tweed-capped, gray-mufflered phantoms wheeled along in mid-air, singing, shouting, and smelling of Guinness Stout.

He blinked. The phantoms shadowed off. The road lay empty and dark and waiting.

Taking a deep breath, shutting his eyes, the American named McGuire turned the key in the switch and stepped on the starter.

THE POEMS

It started out to be just another poem. And then David began sweating over it, stalking the rooms, talking to himself more than ever before in the long, poorly-paid years. So intent was he upon the poem's facets that Lisa felt forgotten, left out, put away until such time as he finished writing and could notice her again.

Then, finally—the poem was completed.

With the ink still wet upon an old envelope's back, he gave it to her with trembling fingers, his eyes red-rimmed and shining with a hot, inspired light. And she read it.

"David—" she murmured. Her hand began to shake in sympathy with his.

"It's *good*, isn't it?" he cried. Damn good!"

The cottage whirled around Lisa in a wooden torrent. Gazing at the paper she experienced sensations as if words were melting, flowing into animate things. The paper was a square, brilliantly sunlit casement through which one might lean into another and brighter amber land! Her mind swung pendulum-wise. She had to clutch, crying out fearfully, at the ledges of this incredible window to support herself from being flung headlong into three-dimensional impossibility!

"David, how strange and wonderful and—*frightening*."

It was as if she held a tube of light cupped in her hands, through which she could race into a vast space of singing and color and new sensation. Somehow, David had caught up, netted, skeined, imbedded reality, substance, atoms—mounting them upon paper with a simple imprisonment of ink!

He described the green, moist verdure of the dell, the eucalyptus trees and the birds flowing through their high, swaying branches. And the flowers cupping the propelled humming of bees.

"It *is* good, David. The very finest poem you've ever written!" She felt her heart beat swiftly with the idea and urge that came to her in the next moment. She felt that she must see the dell, to compare its quiet contents with those of this poem. She took David's arm. "Darling, let's walk down the road—now."

In high spirits, David agreed, and they set out together, from their lonely little house in the hills. Half down the road she changed her mind and wanted to retreat, but she brushed the thought aside with a move of her fine, thinly sculptured face. It seemed ominously dark for this time of day, down there toward the end of the path. She talked lightly to shield her apprehension.

"You've worked so hard, so long, to write the perfect poem. I knew you'd succeed some day. I guess this is it."

"Thanks to a patient wife," he said.

They rounded a bend of gigantic rock and twilight came as swiftly as a purple veil drawn down.

"David!"

In the unexpected dimness she clutched and found his arm and held to him. "What's happened? Is this the dell?"

"Yes, of course it is."

"But, it's so dark!"

"Well—yes—it is—" He sounded at a loss.

"The flowers are gone!"

"I saw them early this morning; they can't be gone!"

"You wrote about them in the poem. And where are the grape vines?"

"They *must* be there. It's only been an hour or more. It's too dark. Let's go back." He sounded afraid himself, peering into the uneven light.

"I can't find anything, David. The grass is gone, and the trees and bushes and vines, all gone!"

She cried it out, then stopped, and it fell upon them, the unnatural blank spaced silence, a vague timelessness, windlessness, a vacuumed sucked out feeling that oppressed and panicked them.

He swore softly and there was no echo. "It's too dark to tell now. It'll all be here tomorrow."

"But what if it *never* comes back?" She began to shiver.

"What are you raving about?"

She held the poem out. It glowed quietly with a steady pure yellow shining, like a small niche in which a candle steadily lived.

"You've written the perfect poem. Too perfect. That's what you've done." She heard herself talking, tonelessly, far away.

She read the poem again. And a coldness moved through her.

"The dell is here. Reading this is like opening a gate upon a path and walking knee-high in grass, smelling blue grapes, hearing bees in yellow transits on the air, and the wind carrying birds upon it. The paper dissolves into things, sun, water, colors and life. It's not symbols or reading anymore, it's LIVING!"

"No," he said. "You're wrong. It's crazy."

✳ They ran up the path together. A wind came to meet them after they were free of the lightless vacuum behind them.

In their small, meagerly furnished cottage they sat at the window, staring down at the dell. All around was the unchanged light of mid-afternoon. Not dimmed or diffused or silent as down in the cup of rocks.

"It's not true. Poems don't work that way," he said.

"Words are symbols. They conjure up images in the mind."

"Have I done more than that?" he demanded. "And how did I do it, I ask you?" He rattled the paper, scowling intently at each line. "Have I made more than symbols with a form of matter and energy. Have I compressed, concentrated, dehydrated life? Does matter pass into and through my mind, like light through a magnifying glass to be focused into one narrow, magnificent blazing apex of fire? Can I etch life, burn it onto paper, with that flame? Gods in heaven, I'm going mad with thought!"

A wind circled the house.

"If we are not crazy, the two of us," said Lisa, stiffening at the sound of the wind, "there is one way to prove our suspicions."

"How?"

"Cage the wind."

"Cage it? Bar it up? Build a mortar of ink around it?"

She nodded.

"No, I won't fool myself." He jerked his head. Wetting his lips, he sat for a long while. Then, cursing at his own curiosity, he walked to the table and fumbled self-consciously with pen and ink. He looked at her, then at the windy light outside. Dipping his pen, he flowed it out onto paper in regular dark miracles.

Instantly, the wind vanished.

"The wind," he said. "It's caged. The ink is dry."

✳ Over his shoulder she read it, became immersed in its cool heady current, smelling far oceans tainted on it, odors of distant wheat acres and green corn and the sharp brick and cement smell of cities far away.

David stood up so quickly the chair fell back like an old thin woman. Like a blind man he walked down the hill toward the dell, not turning, even when Lisa called after him, frantically.

When he returned he was by turns hysterical and immensely calm. He collapsed in a chair. By night, he was smoking his pipe, eyes closed, talking on and on, as calmly as possible.

"I've got power now no man ever had. I don't know its extensions, its boundaries or its governing limits. Somewhere, the enchantment ends. Oh, my god, Lisa, you should see what I've done to that dell. Its gone, all gone, stripped to the very raw primordial bones of its former self. And the beauty is here!" He opened his eyes and stared at the poem, as at the Holy Grail. "Captured forever, a few bars of midnight ink on paper! I'll be the greatest poet in history! I've always dreamed of that."

"I'm afraid, David. Let's tear up the poems and get away from here!"

"Move away? Now?"

"It's dangerous. What if your power extends beyond the valley?"

His eyes shone fiercely. "Then I can destroy the universe and immortalize it at one and the same instant. It's in the power of a sonnet, if I choose to write it."

"But you *won't* write it, promise me, David?"

He seemed not to hear her. He seemed to be listening to a cosmic music, a movement of bird wings very high and clear. He seemed to be wondering how long this land had waited here, for centuries perhaps, waiting for a poet to come and drink of its power. This valley seemed like the center of the universe, now.

"It would be a magnificent poem," he said, thoughtfully. "The most magnificent poem ever written, shamming Keats and Shelley and Browning and all the rest. A poem about the universe. But no." He shook his head sadly. "I guess I won't ever write that poem."

Breathless, Lisa waited in the long silence.

Another wind came from across the world to replace the one newly imprisoned. She let out her breath, at ease.

"For a moment I was afraid you'd overstepped the boundary and taken in all the winds of the earth. It's all right now."

"All right, hell," he cried, happily. "It's marvelous!"

And he caught hold of her, and kissed her again and again.

Fifty poems were written in fifty days. Poems about a rock, a stem, a blossom, a pebble, an ant, a dropped feather, a raindrop, an avalanche, a dried skull, a dropped key, a fingernail, a shattered light bulb.

Recognition came upon him like a rain shower. The poems were bought and read across the world. Critics referred to the masterpieces as "—chunks of amber in which are caught whole portions of life and living—" "—each poem a window looking out upon the world—"

He was suddenly a very famous man. It took him many days to believe it. When he saw his name on the printed books he didn't believe it, and said so. And when he read the critics columns he didn't believe them either.

Then it began to make a flame inside him, growing up, climbing and consuming his body and legs and arms and face.

Amidst the sound and glory, she pressed her cheek to his and whispered:

"This is your perfect hour. When will there ever be a more perfect time than this? Never again."

He showed her the letters as they arrived.

"See? This letter. From New York." He blinked rapidly and couldn't sit still. "They want me to write more poems. Thousands more. Look at this letter. Here." He gave it to her. "That editor says that if I can write so fine and great about a pebble or a drop of water, think what I can do when I—well experiment with real life. Real life. Nothing big. An amoeba perhaps. Or, well, just this morning. I saw a bird—"

"A bird?" She stiffened and waited for him to answer.

"Yes, a hummingbird—hovering, settling, rising—"

"You didn't . . . ?"

"Why NOT? Only a bird. One bird out of a billion," he said self-consciously. "One little bird, one little poem. You can't deny me that."

"One amoeba," she repeated, tonelessly. "And then next it will be one dog, one man, one city, one continent, one universe!"

"Nonsense." His cheek twitched. He paced the room, fingering back his dark hair. "You dramatize things. Well, after all what's one dog, even, or to go one step further, one man?"

She sighed. "It's the very thing you talked of with fear, the danger we spoke of that first time we knew your power. Remember, David, it's not really yours, it was only an accident our coming here to the valley house—"

He swore softly. "Who cares whether it was accident or Fate? The thing that counts is that I'm here, now, and they're—they're—" He paused, flushing.

"They're what?" she prompted.

"They're calling me the greatest poet who ever lived!"

"It'll ruin you."

"Let it ruin me, then! Let's have silence, now."

He stalked into his den and sat restlessly studying the dirt road. While in this mood, he saw a small brown dog come patting along the road, raising little dust-tufts behind.

"And a damn good poet I am," he whispered, angrily, taking out pen and paper. He scratched out four lines swiftly.

The dog's barking came in even shrill intervals upon the air as it circled a tree and bounded a green bush. Quite unexpectedly, half over one leap across a vine, the barking ceased, and the dog fell apart in the air, inch by inch, and vanished.

Locked in his den, he composed at a furious pace, counting pebbles in the garden and changing them to stars simply by giving them mention, immortalizing clouds, hornets, bees, lightning and thunder with a few pen flourishes.

It was inevitable that some of his more secret poems should be stumbled upon and read by his wife.

Coming home from a long afternoon walk he found her with the poems lying all unfolded upon her lap.

"David," she demanded. "What does this mean?" She was very cold and shaken by it. "This poem. First a dog. Then a cat, some sheep and—finally—a man!"

He seized the papers from her. "So what!" Sliding them in a drawer, he slammed it, violently. "He was just an old man, they were old sheep, and it was a microbe-infested terrier! The world breathes better without them!"

"But here, THIS poem, too." She held it straight out before her, eyes widened. "A woman. Three children from Charlottesville!"

"All right, so you don't like it!" he said, furiously. "An artist has to experiment. With everything—I can't just stand still and do the same thing over and over. I've got greater plans than you think. Yes, really good, fine plans. I've decided to write about everything. I'll dissect the heavens if I wish, rip down the worlds, toy with suns if I damn please!"

"David," she said, shocked.

"Well, I will! I will!"

"You're such a child, David. I should have known. If this goes on, I can't stay here with you."

"You'll have to stay," he said.

"What do you mean?"

He didn't know what he meant himself. He looked around, helplessly and then declared, "I mean. I mean—if you try to go all I have to do is sit at my desk and describe you in ink . . ."

"You . . ." she said, dazedly.

She began to cry. Very silently, with no noise, her shoulders moved, as she sank down on a chair.

"I'm sorry," he said, lamely, hating the scene. "I didn't mean to say that, Lisa. Forgive me." He came and laid a hand upon her quivering body.

"I won't leave you," she said, finally.

And closing her eyes, she began to think.

* It was much later in the day when she returned from a shopping trip to town with bulging grocery sacks and a large gleaming bottle of champagne.

David looked at it and laughed aloud. "Celebrating, are we?"

"Yes," she said, giving him the bottle and an opener. "Celebrating you as the world's greatest poet!"

"I detect sarcasm, Lisa," he said, pouring drinks. "Here's a toast to the—the universe." He drank. "Good stuff." He pointed at hers. "Drink up. What's wrong?" Her eyes looked wet and sad about something.

She refilled his glass and lifted her own. "May we always be together. Always."

The room tilted. "It's hitting me," he observed very seriously, sitting down so as not to fall. "On an empty stomach I drank. Oh, Lord!"

He sat for ten minutes while she refilled his glass. She seemed very happy suddenly, for no reason. He sat scowling, thinking, looking at his pen and ink and paper, trying to make a decision. "Lisa?"

"Yes?" She was now preparing supper, singing.

"I feel in a mood. I have been considering all afternoon and—"

"And what, darling?"

"I am going to write the greatest poem in history—NOW!"

She felt her heart flutter.

"Will your poem be about the valley?"

He smirked. "No. No! Bigger than that. Much bigger!"

"I'm afraid I'm not much good at guessing," she confessed.

"Simple," he said, gulping another drink of champagne. Nice of her to think of buying it, it stimulated his thoughts. He held up his pen and dipped it in ink. "I shall write my poem about the universe! Let me see now . . ."

"David!"

He winced. "What?"

"Oh, nothing. Just, have some more champagne, darling."

"Eh?" He blinked fuzzily. "Don't mind if I do. Pour."

She sat beside him, trying to be casual.

"Tell me again. What is it you'll write?"

"About the universe, the stars, the epileptic shamblings of comets, the blind black seekings of meteors, the heated embraces and spawnings of giant suns, the cold, graceful excursions of polar planets, asteroids plummeting like paramecium under a gigantic microscope, all and everything and anything my mind lays claim to! Earth, sun, stars!" he exclaimed.

"No!" she said, but caught herself. "I mean, darling, don't do it all at once. One thing at a time—"

"One at a time." He made a face. "That's the way I've been doing things and I'm tied to dandelions and daisies."

He wrote upon the paper with the pen.

"What're you doing?" she demanded, catching his elbow.

"Let me alone!" He shook her off.

She saw the black words form:

"Illimitable universe, with stars and planets and suns—"

She must have screamed.

"No, David, cross it out, before it's too late. Stop it!"

He gazed at her as through a long dark tube, and her far away at the other end, echoing. "Cross it out?" he said. "Why, it's GOOD poetry! Not a line will I cross out. I want to be a GOOD poet!"

She fell across him, groping, finding the pen. With one instantaneous slash, she wiped out the words.

"Before the ink dries, before it dries!"

"Fool!" he shouted. "Let me alone!"

✳ She ran to the window. The first evening stars were still there, and the crescent moon. She sobbed with relief. She swung about to face him and walked toward him. "I want to help you write your poem—"

"Don't need your help!"

"Are you blind? Do you realize the power of your pen!"

To distract him, she poured more champagne, which he welcomed and drank. "Ah," he sighed, dizzily. "My head spins."

But it didn't stop him from writing, and write he did, starting again on a new sheet of paper.

"UNIVERSE—VAST UNIVERSE—BILLION STARRED AND WIDE—"

She snatched frantically at shreds of things to say, things to stave off his writing.

"That's poor poetry," she said.

"What do you mean 'poor'?" he wanted to know, writing.

"You've got to start at the beginning and build up," she explained logically. "Like a watch spring being wound or the universe starting with a molecule building on up through stars into a stellar cartwheel—"

He slowed his writing and scowled with thought.

She hurried on, seeing this. "You see, darling, you've let emotion run off with you. You can't start with the big things. Put them at the end of your poem. Build to a climax!"

The ink was drying. She stared at it as it dried. In another sixty seconds—

He stopped writing. "Maybe you're right. Just maybe you are." He put aside the pen a moment.

"I know I'm right," she said, lightly, laughing. "Here. I'll just take the pen and—there—"

She had expected him to stop her, but he was holding his pale brow and looking pained with the ache in his eyes from the drink.

She drew a bold line through his poem. Her heart slowed.

"Now," she said, solicitously, "you take the pen, and I'll help you. Start out with small things and build, like an artist."

His eyes were gray-filmed. "Maybe you're right, maybe, maybe."

The wind howled outside.

"Catch the wind!" she cried, to give him a minor triumph to satisfy his ego. "Catch the wind!"

He stroked the pen. "Caught it!" he bellowed, drunkenly, weaving. "Caught the wind! Made a cage of ink!"

"Catch the flowers!" she commanded, excitedly. "Every one in the valley! And the grass!"

"There! Caught the flowers!"

"The hill next!" she said.

"The hill!"

"The valley!"

"The valley!"

"The sunlight, the odors, the trees, the shadows, the house and the garden, and the things inside the house!"

"Yes, yes, yes," he cried, going on and on and on.

And while he wrote quickly she said, "David, I love you. Forgive me for what I do next, darling—"

"What?" he asked, not having heard her.

"Nothing at all. Except that we are never satisfied and want to go on beyond proper limits. You tried to do that, David, and it was wrong."

He nodded over his work. She kissed him on the cheek. He reached up and patted her chin. "Know what, lady?"

"What?"

"I think I like you, yes, sir, I think I like you."

She shook him. "Don't go to sleep, David, don't."

"Want to sleep. Want to sleep."

"Later, darling. When you've finished your poem, your last great poem, the very finest one, David. Listen to me—"

He fumbled with the pen. "What'll I say?"

She smoothed his hair, touched his cheek with her fingers and kissed him, tremblingly. Then, closing her eyes, she began to dictate.

"There lived a fine man named David and his wife's name was Lisa and—"

The pen moved slowly, achingly, tiredly forming words.

"Yes?" he prompted.

"—and they lived in a house in the garden of Eden—"

He wrote again, tediously. She watched.

He raised his eyes. "Well? What's next?"

She looked at the house, and the night outside, and the wind returned to sing in her ears and she held his hands and kissed his sleepy lips.

"That's all," she said, "the ink is drying."

✳ The publishers from New York visited the valley months later and went back to New York with only three pieces of paper they had found blowing in the wind around and about the raw, scarred, empty valley.

The publishers stared at one another, blankly:

"Why, why, there was nothing left at all," they said. "Just bare rock, not a sign of vegetation or humanity. The home he lived in—gone! The road, everything! *He* was gone! His wife, *she* was gone, too! Not a word out of them. It was like a river flood had washed through, scraping away the whole countryside! Gone! Washed out! And only three last poems to show for the whole thing!"

No further word was ever received from the poet or his wife. The Agricultural College experts traveled hundreds of miles to study the starkly denuded valley, and went away, shaking their heads and looking pale.

But it is all simply found again.

You turn the pages of his last small thin book and read the three poems.

She is there, pale and beautiful and immortal, you smell the sweet warm flash of her, young forever, hair blowing golden upon the wind.

And next to her, upon the opposite page, he stands gaunt, smiling, firm, hair like raven's hair, hands on hips, face raised to look about him.

And on all sides of them, green with an immortal green, under a sapphire sky, with the odor of fat wine grapes, with the grass knee-high and bending to touch of exploring feet, with the trails waiting for any reader who takes them, one finds the valley, and the house, and the deep rich peace of sunlight and of moonlight and many stars, and the two of them, he and she, walking through it all, laughing together, forever and forever.

APRIL 2026:
THE LONG YEARS

WHENEVER THE WIND CAME THROUGH THE SKY, he and his small family would sit in the stone hut and warm their hands over a wood fire. The wind would stir the canal waters and almost blow the stars out of the sky, but Mr. Hathaway would sit contented and talk to his wife, and his wife would reply, and he would speak to his two daughters and his son about the old days on Earth, and they would all answer neatly.

It was the twentieth year after the Great War. Mars was a tomb planet. Whether or not Earth was the same was a matter for much silent debate for Hathaway and his family on the long Martian nights.

This night one of the violent Martian dust storms had come over the low Martian graveyards, blowing through ancient towns and tearing away the plastic walls of the newer, American-built city that was melting down into the sand, desolated.

The storm abated. Hathaway went out into the cleared weather to see Earth burning green on the windy sky. He put his hand up as one might reach to adjust a dimly burning globe in the ceiling of a dark room. He looked across the long-dead sea bottoms. Not another living thing on this entire planet, he thought. Just myself. And them. He looked back within the stone hut.

What was happening on Earth now? He had seen no visible sign of change in Earth's aspect through his thirty-inch telescope. Well, he thought, I'm good for another twenty years if I'm careful. Someone might come. Either across the dead seas or out of space in a rocket on a little thread of red flame.

He called into the hut, "I'm going to take a walk."

"All right," his wife said.

He moved quietly down through a series of ruins. "Made in New York," he read from a piece of metal as he passed. "And all these things from Earth will be gone long before the old Martian towns." He looked toward the fifty-centuries-old village that lay among the blue mountains.

He came to a solitary Martian graveyard, a series of small hexagonal stones on a hill swept by the lonely wind.

He stood looking down at four graves with crude wooden crosses on them, and names. Tears did not come to his eyes. They had dried long ago.

"Do you forgive me for what I've done?" he asked of the crosses. "I was very much alone. You do understand, don't you?"

He returned to the stone hut and once more, just before going in, shaded his eyes, searching the black sky.

"You keep waiting and waiting and looking," he said, "and one night, perhaps—"

There was a tiny red flame on the sky.

He stepped away from the light of the hut.

"—and you look again," he whispered.

The tiny red flame was still there.

"It wasn't there last night," he whispered.

He stumbled and fell, picked himself up, ran behind the hut, swiveled the telescope, and pointed it at the sky.

A minute later, after a long, wild staring, he appeared in the low door of the hut. The wife and the two daughters and the son turned their heads to him. Finally he was able to speak.

"I have good news," he said. "I have looked at the sky. A rocket is coming to take us all home. It will be here in the early morning."

He put his hands down and put his head into his hands and began to cry gently.

He burned what was left of New New York that morning at three.

He took a torch and moved into the plastic city and with the flame touched the walls here or there. The city bloomed up in great tosses of heat and light. It was a square mile of illumination, big enough to be seen out in space. It would beckon the rocket down to Mr. Hathaway and his family.

His heartbeating rapidly with pain, he returned to the hut. "See?" He held up a dusty bottle into the light. "Wine I saved, just for tonight. I knew that someday someone would find us! We'll have a drink to celebrate!"

He poured five glasses full.

"It's been a long time," he said, gravely looking into his drink. "Remember the day the war broke? Twenty years and seven months ago.

And all the rockets were called home from Mars. And you and I and the children were out in the mountains, doing archaeological work, research on the ancient surgical methods of the Martians. We ran our horses, almost killing them, remember? But we got here to the city a week late. Everyone was gone. America had been destroyed; every rocket had left without waiting for stragglers, remember, remember? And it turned out we were the only ones left? Lord, Lord, how the years pass. I couldn't have stood it without you here, all of you. I'd have killed myself without you. But with you, it was worth waiting. Here's to us, then." He lifted his glass. "And to our long wait together." He drank.

The wife and the two daughters and the son raised their glasses to their lips.

The wine ran down over the chins of all four of them.

✳ By morning the city was blowing in great black soft flakes across the sea bottom. The fire was exhausted, but it had served its purpose; the red spot on the sky grew larger.

From the stone hut came the rich brown smell of baked gingerbread. His wife stood over the table, setting down the hot pans of new bread as Hathaway entered. The two daughters were gently sweeping the bare stone floor with stiff brooms, and the son was polishing the silverware.

"We'll have a huge breakfast for them," laughed Hathaway. "Put on your best clothes!"

He hurried across his land to the vast metal storage shed. Inside was the cold-storage unit and power plant he had repaired and restored with his efficient, small, nervous fingers over the years, just as he had repaired clocks, telephones, and spool recorders in his spare time. The shed was full of things he had built, some senseless mechanisms the functions of which were a mystery even to himself now as he looked upon them.

From the deep freeze he fetched rimed cartons of beans and strawberries, twenty years old. Lazarus come forth, he thought, and pulled out a cool chicken.

The air was full of cooking odors when the rocket landed.

Like a boy, Hathaway raced down the hill. He stopped once because of a sudden sick pain in his chest. He sat on a rock to regain his breath, then ran all the rest of the way.

He stood in the hot atmosphere generated by the fiery rocket. A port opened. A man looked down.

Hathaway shielded his eyes and at last said, "Captain Wilder!"

"Who is it?" asked Captain Wilder, and jumped down and stood there looking at the old man. He put his hand out. "Good lord, it's Hathaway!"

"That's right." They looked into each other's faces.

"Hathaway, from my old crew, from the Fourth Expedition."

"It's been a long time, Captain."

"Too long. It's good to see you."

"I'm old," said Hathaway simply.

"I'm not young myself anymore. I've been out to Jupiter and Saturn and Neptune for twenty years."

"I heard they had kicked you upstairs so you wouldn't interfere with colonial policy here on Mars." The old man looked around. "You've been gone so long you don't know what's happened—"

Wilder said, "I can guess. We've circled Mars twice. Found only one other man, name of Walter Gripp, about ten thousand miles from here. We offered to take him with us, but he said no. The last we saw of him he was sitting in the middle of the highway in a rocking chair, smoking a pipe, waving to us. Mars is pretty well dead, not even a Martian alive. What about Earth?"

"You know as much as I do. Once in a while I get the Earth radio, very faintly. But it's always in some other language. I'm sorry to say I only know Latin. A few words come through. I take it most of Earth's a shambles, but the war goes on. Are you going back, sir?"

"Yes. We're curious, of course. We had no radio contact so far out in space. We'll want to see Earth, no matter what."

"You'll take us with you?"

The captain started. "Of course, your wife, I remember her. Twenty-five years ago, wasn't it? When they opened First Town and you quit the service and brought her up here. And there were children—"

"My son and two daughters."

"Yes, I remember. They're here?"

"Up at our hut. There's a fine breakfast waiting all of you up the hill. Will you come?"

"We would be honored, Mr. Hathaway." Captain Wilder called to the rocket, "Abandon ship!"

✳ They walked up the hill, Hathaway and Captain Wilder, the twenty crew members following, taking deep breaths of the thin, cool morning air. The sun rose and it was a good day.

"Do you remember Spender, Captain?"

"I've never forgotten him."

"About once a year I walk up past his tomb. It looks like he got his way at last. He didn't want us to come here, and I suppose he's happy now that we've all gone away."

"What about—what was his name?—Parkhill, Sam Parkhill?"

"He opened a hot-dog stand."

"It sounds just *like* him."

"And went back to Earth the next week for the war." Hathaway put his hand to his chest and sat down abruptly upon a boulder. "I'm sorry. The excitement. Seeing you again after all these years. Have to rest." He felt his heart pound. He counted the beats. It was very bad.

"We've a doctor," said Wilder. "Excuse me, Hathaway, I know you are one, but we'd better check you with our own—" The doctor was summoned.

"I'll be all right," insisted Hathaway. "The waiting, the excitement." He could hardly breathe. His lips were blue. "You know," he said as the doctor placed a stethoscope to him, "it's as if I kept alive all these years just for this day, and now you're here to take me back to Earth, I'm satisfied and I can just lie down and quit."

"Here." The doctor handed him a yellow pellet. "We'd better let you rest."

"Nonsense. Just let me sit a moment. It's good to see all of you. Good to hear new voices again."

"Is the pellet working?"

"Fine. Here we go!"

They walked on up the hill.

* "Alice, come see who's here!"

Hathaway frowned and bent into the hut. "Alice, did you hear?"

His wife appeared. A moment later the two daughters, tall and gracious, came out, followed by an even taller son.

"Alice, you remember Captain Wilder?"

She hesitated and looked at Hathaway as if for instructions and then smiled. "Of course, Captain Wilder!"

"I remember, we had dinner together the night before I took off for Jupiter, Mrs. Hathaway."

She shook his hand vigorously. "My daughters, Marguerite and Susan. My son, John. You remember the captain, surely?"

Hands were shaken amid laughter and much talk.

Captain Wilder sniffed the air. "Is that gingerbread?"

"Will you have some?"

Everyone moved. Folding tables were hurried out while hot foods were rushed forth and plates and fine damask napkins and good silverware were laid. Captain Wilder stood looking first at Mrs. Hathaway and then at her son and her two tall, quiet-moving daughters. He looked into their faces as they darted past and he followed every move of their youthful hands and every expression of their wrinkleless faces. He sat upon a chair the son brought. "How old are you, John?"

The son replied, "Twenty-three."

Wilder shifted his silverware clumsily. His face was suddenly pale. The man next to him whispered, "Captain Wilder, that can't be right."

The son moved away to bring more chairs.

"What's that, Williamson?"

"I'm forty-three myself, Captain. I was in school the same time as young John Hathaway there, twenty years ago. He says he's only twenty-three now; he only *looks* twenty-three. But that's wrong. He should be forty-two, at least. What's it mean, sir?"

"I don't know."

"You look kind of sick, sir."

"I don't feel well. The daughters, too, I saw them twenty years or so ago; they haven't changed, not a wrinkle. Will you do me a favor? I want you to run an errand, Williamson. I'll tell you where to go and what to check. Late in the breakfast, slip away. It should take you only ten minutes. The place isn't far from here. I saw it from the rocket as we landed."

"Here! What are you talking about so seriously?" Mrs. Hathaway ladled quick spoons of soup into their bowls. "Smile now; we're all together, the trip's over, and it's like home!"

"Yes." Captain Wilder laughed. "You certainly look very well and young, Mrs. Hathaway!"

"Isn't that like a man!"

He watched her drift away, drift with her pink face warm, smooth as an apple, unwrinkled and colorful. She chimed her laugh at every joke, she tossed salads neatly, never once pausing for breath. And the bony son and curved daughters were brilliantly witty, like their father, telling of the long years and their secret life, while their father nodded proudly to each.

Williamson slipped off down the hill.

"Where's *he* going?" asked Hathaway.

"Checking the rocket," said Wilder. "But, as I was saying, Hathaway, there's nothing on Jupiter, nothing at all for men. That includes Saturn and Pluto." Wilder talked mechanically, not hearing his words, thinking only of Williamson running down the hill and climbing back to tell what he had found.

"Thanks." Marguerite Hathaway was filling his water glass. Impulsively he touched her arm. She did not even mind. Her flesh was warm and soft.

Hathaway, across the table, paused several times, touched his chest with his fingers, painfully, then went on listening to the murmuring talk and sudden loud chattering, glancing now and again with concern at Wilder, who did not seem to like chewing his gingerbread.

Williamson returned. He sat picking at his food until the captain whispered aside to him, "Well?"

"I found it, sir."

"And?"

Williamson's cheeks were white. He kept his eyes on the laughing people. The daughters were smiling gravely and the son was telling a joke. Williamson said, "I went into the graveyard."

"The four crosses were there?"

"The four crosses were there, sir. The names were still on them. I wrote them down to be sure." He read from a white paper: "Alice, Marguerite, Susan, and John Hathaway. Died of unknown virus. July 2007."

"Thank you, Williamson." Wilder closed his eyes.

"Nineteen years ago, sir." Williamson's hand trembled.

"Yes."

"Then who are *these!*"

"I don't know."

"What are you going to do?"

"I don't know that either."

"Will we tell the other men?"

"Later. Go on with your food as if nothing happened."

"I'm not very hungry now, sir."

The meal ended with wine brought from the rocket. Hathaway arose. "A toast to all of you; it's good to be with friends again. And to my wife and children, without whom I couldn't have survived alone. It is only through their kindness in caring for me that I've lived on, waiting for your arrival." He moved his wineglass toward his family, who looked back self-consciously, lowering their eyes at last as everyone drank.

Hathaway drank down his wine. He did not cry out as he fell forward onto the table and slipped to the ground. Several men eased him to rest. The doctor bent to him and listened. Wilder touched the doctor's shoulder. The doctor looked up and shook his head. Wilder knelt and took the old man's hand. "Wilder?" Hathaway's voice was barely audible. "I spoiled the breakfast."

"Nonsense."

"Say good-bye to Alice and the children for me."

"Just a moment, I'll call them."

"No, no, don't!" gasped Hathaway. "They wouldn't understand. I wouldn't want them to understand! Don't!"

Wilder did not move.

Hathaway was dead.

Wilder waited for a long time. Then he arose and walked away from the stunned group around Hathaway. He went to Alice Hathaway, looked into her face, and said, "Do you know what has just happened?"

"Something about my husband?"

"He's just passed away; his heart," said Wilder, watching her.

"I'm sorry," she said.

"How do you feel?" he asked.

"He didn't want us to feel badly. He told us it would happen one day and he didn't want us to cry. He didn't teach us how, you know. He didn't want us to know. He said it was the worst thing that could happen to a man to know how to be lonely and know how to be sad and then to cry. So we're not to know what crying is, or being sad."

Wilder glanced at her hands, the soft warm hands and the fine manicured nails and the tapered wrists. He saw her slender, smooth white neck and her intelligent eyes. Finally he said, "Mr. Hathaway did a fine job on you and your children."

"He would have liked to hear you say that. He was so proud of us. After a while he even forgot that he had made us. At the end he loved and took us as his real wife and children. And, in a way, we are."

"You gave him a good deal of comfort."

"Yes, for years on end we sat and talked. He so much loved to talk. He liked the stone hut and the open fire. We could have lived in a regular house in the town, but he liked it up here, where he could be primitive if he liked, or modern if he liked. He told me all about his laboratory and the things he did in it. He wired the entire dead American town below with sound speakers. When he pressed a button the town lit up and made noises as if ten thousand people lived in it. There were airplane noises and car noises and the sounds of people talking. He would sit and light a cigar and talk to us, and the sounds of the town would come up to us, and once in a while the phone would ring and a recorded voice would ask Mr. Hathaway scientific and surgical questions and he would answer them. With the phone ringing and us here and the sounds of the town and his cigar, Mr. Hathaway was quite happy. There's only one thing he couldn't make us do," she said. "And that was to grow old. He got older every day, but we stayed the same. I guess he didn't mind. I guess he wanted us this way."

"We'll bury him down in the yard where the other four crosses are. I think he would like that."

She put her hand on his wrist, lightly. "I'm sure he would."

Orders were given. The family followed the little procession down the hill. Two men carried Hathaway on a covered stretcher. They passed the stone hut and the storage shed where Hathaway, many years before, had begun his work. Wilder paused within the workshop door.

How would it be, he wondered, to live on a planet with a wife and three children and have them die, leaving you alone with the wind and silence? What would a person do? Bury them with crosses in the graveyard and then come back up to the workshop and, with all the power of mind and memory and accuracy of finger and genius, put together, bit by bit, all those things that were wife, son, daughters. With an entire American city below from which to draw needed supplies, a brilliant man might do anything.

The sound of their footsteps was muffled in the sand. At the graveyard, as they turned in, two men were already spading out the earth.

✳ They returned to the rocket in the late afternoon.

Williamson nodded at the stone hut. "What are we going to do about *them*?"

"I don't know," said the captain.

"Are you going to turn them off?"

"Off?" The captain looked faintly surprised. "It never entered my mind."

"You're not taking them back with us?"

"No, it would be useless."

"You mean you're going to leave them here, like t*hat*, as they *are*!"

The captain handed Williamson a gun. "If you can do anything about this, you're a better man than I."

Five minutes later Williamson returned from the hut, sweating. "Here, take your gun. I understand what you mean now. I went in the hut with the gun. One of the daughters smiled at me. So did the others. The wife offered me a cup of tea. Lord, it'd be murder!"

Wilder nodded. "There'll never be anything as fine as them again. They're built to last; ten, fifty, two hundred years. Yes, they've as much right to—to life as you or I or any of us." He knocked out his pipe. "Well, get aboard. We're taking off. This city's done for, we'll not be using it."

It was late in the day. A cold wind was rising. The men were aboard. The captain hesitated. Williamson said, "Don't tell me you're going back to say—good-bye—to them?"

The captain looked at Williamson coldly. "None of your business."

Wilder strode up toward the hut through the darkening wind. The men in the rocket saw his shadow lingering in the stone-hut doorway. They saw a woman's shadow. They saw the captain shake her hand.

Moments later he came running back to the rocket.

On nights when the wind comes over the dead sea bottoms and through the hexagonal graveyard, over four old crosses and one new one, there is a light burning in the low stone hut, and in that hut, as the wind roars by and the dust whirls and the cold stars burn, are four figures, a woman, two daughters, a son, tending a low fire for no reason and talking and laughing.

Night after night for every year and every year, for no reason at all, the woman comes out and looks at the sky, her hands up, for a long moment, looking at the green burning of Earth, not knowing why she looks, and then she goes back and throws a stick on the fire, and the wind comes up and the dead sea goes on being dead.

ICARUS MONTGOLFIER WRIGHT

HE LAY ON HIS BED AND THE WIND BLEW through the window over his ears and over his half-opened mouth so it whispered to him in his dream. It was like the wind of time hollowing the Delphic caves to say what must be said of yesterday, today, tomorrow. Sometimes one voice gave a shout far off away, sometimes two, a dozen, an entire race of men cried out through his mouth, but their words were always the same:

"Look, look, we've done it!"

For suddenly he, they, one or many, were flung in the dream, and flew. The air spread in a soft warm sea where he swam, disbelieving.

"Look, look! It's done!"

But he didn't ask the world to watch, he was only shocking his senses wide to see, taste, smell, touch the air, the wind, the rising Moon. He swam along in the sky. The heavy Earth was gone.

But wait, he thought, wait now!

Tonight—what night is this?

The night before, of course. The night before the first flight of a rocket to the Moon. Beyond this room on the baked desert floor one hundred yards away the rocket waits for me.

Well, does it now? Is there *really* a rocket?

Hold on! he thought, and twisted, turned, sweating, eyes tight, to the wall, the fierce whisper in his teeth. Be certain-sure! You, now, who *are* you?

Me? he thought. *My* name?

Jedediah Prentiss, born 1938, college graduate 1959, licensed rocket pilot, 1971. Jedediah Prentiss . . . Jedediah Prentiss. . . .

The wind whistled his name away! He grabbed for it, yelling.

Then, gone quiet, he waited for the wind to bring his name back. He waited a long while, and there was only silence, and then after a thousand heartbeats he felt motion.

The sky opened out like a soft blue flower. The Aegean Sea stirred soft white fans through a distant wine-colored surf.

In the wash of the waves on the shore, he heard his name.

Icarus.

And again in a breathing whisper.

Icarus.

Someone shook his arm and it was his father saying his name and shaking away the night. And he himself lay small, half-turned to the window and the shore below and the deep sky, feeling the first wind of morning ruffle the golden feathers bedded in amber wax lying by the side of his cot. Golden wings stirred half-alive in his father's arms, and the faint down on his own shoulders quilled trembling as he looked at these wings and beyond them to the cliff.

"Father, how's the wind?"

"Enough for me, but never enough for you. . . ."

"Father, don't worry. The wings seem clumsy now, but my bones in the feathers will make them strong, my blood in the wax will make it live!"

"My blood, my bones too, remember; each man lends his flesh to his children, asking that they tend it well. Promise you'll not go high, Icarus. *The* sun or *my* son, the heat of one, the fever of the other, could melt these wings. Take care!"

And they carried the splendid golden wings into the morning and heard them whisper in their arms, whisper his name or a name or some name that blew, spun, and settled like a feather on the soft air.

Montgolfier.

His hands touched fiery rope, bright linen, stitched thread gone hot as summer. His hands fed wool and straw to a breathing flame.

Montgolfier.

And his eye soared up along the swell and sway, the oceanic tug and pull, the immensely wafted silver pear still filling with the shimmering tidal airs channeled up from the blaze. Silent as a god tilted slumbering above French countryside, this delicate linen envelope, this swelling sack of oven-baked air would soon pluck itself free. Drafting upward to blue worlds of silence, his mind and his brother's mind would sail with it, muted, serene among island clouds where uncivilized lightnings slept. Into that uncharted gulf and abyss where no bird-song or shout of man could follow, the balloon would hush itself. So cast adrift, he, Montgolfier, and all men, might hear the unmeasured breathing of God and the cathedral tread of eternity.

"Ah . . ." He moved, the crowd moved, shadowed by the warm balloon. "Everything's ready, everything's right. . . ."

Right. His lips twitched in his dream. Right. Hiss, whisper, flutter, rush. Right.

From his father's hands a toy jumped to the ceiling, whirled in its own wind, suspended, while he and his brother stared to see it flicker, rustle, whistle, heard it murmuring their names.

Wright.

Whispering: wind, sky, cloud, space, wing, fly . . .

"Wilbur, Orville? Look, how's *that?*"

Ah. In his sleep, his mouth sighed.

The toy helicopter hummed, bumped the ceiling, murmured eagle, raven, sparrow, robin, hawk; murmured eagle, raven, sparrow, robin, hawk. Whispered eagle, whispered raven, and at last, fluttering to their hands with a susurration, a wash of blowing weather from summers yet to come, with a last whir and exhalation, whispered hawk.

Dreaming, he smiled.

He saw the clouds rush down the Aegean sky.

He felt the balloon sway drunkenly, its great bulk ready for the clear running wind.

He felt the sand hiss up the Atlantic shelves from the soft dunes that might save him if he, a fledgling bird, should fall. The framework struts hummed and chorded like a harp, and himself caught up in its music.

Beyond this room he felt the primed rocket glide on the desert field, its fire wings folded, its fire breath kept, held ready to speak for three billion men. In a moment he would wake and walk slowly out to that rocket.

And stand on the rim of the cliff.

Stand cool in the shadow of the warm balloon.

Stand whipped by tidal sands drummed over Kitty Hawk.

And sheathe his boy's wrists, arms, hands, fingers with golden wings in golden wax.

And touch for a final time the captured breath of man, the warm gasp of awe and wonder siphoned and sewn to lift their dreams.

And spark the gasoline engine.

And take his father's hand and wish him well with his own wings, flexed and ready, here on the precipice.

Then whirl and jump.

Then cut the cords to free the great balloon.

Then rev the motor, prop the plane on air.

And crack the switch, to fire the rocket fuse.

And together in a single leap, swim, rush, flail, jump, sail, and glide, upturned to sun, moon, stars, they would go above Atlantic, Mediterranean; over country, wilderness, city, town; in gaseous silence, riffling feather, rattle-drum frame, in volcanic eruption, in timid, sputtering roar; in start, jar, hesitation, then steady ascension, beautifully held, wondrously transported, they would laugh and cry each his own name to himself. Or shout the names of others unborn or others long dead and blown away by the wine wind or the salt wind or the silent hush of balloon wind or the wind of chemical fire. Each feeling the bright feathers stir and bud deep-buried and thrusting to burst from their riven shoulder blades! Each leaving behind the echo of their flying, a sound to encircle, recircle the Earth in the winds and speak again in other years to the sons of the sons of their sons, asleep but hearing the restless midnight sky.

Up, yet farther up, higher, higher! A spring tide, a summer flood, an unending river of wings!

A bell rang softly.

No, he whispered, I'll wake in a moment. Wait . . .

The Aegean slid away below the window, gone; the Atlantic dunes, the French countryside, dissolved down to New Mexico desert. In his room near his cot stirred no plumes in golden wax. Outside, no wind-sculpted pear, no trapdrum butterfly machine. Outside only a rocket, a combustible dream, waiting for the friction of his hand to set it off.

In the last moment of sleep someone asked his name.

Quietly, he gave the answer as he had heard it during the hours from midnight on.

"Icarus Montgolfier Wright."

He repeated it slowly so the questioner might remember the order and spelling down to the last incredible letter.

"Icarus Montgolfier Wright.

"Born: nine hundred years before Christ. Grammar school: Paris, 1783, High school, college: Kitty Hawk, 1903. Graduation from Earth to Moon: this day, God willing, August 1, 1971. Death and burial, with luck, on Mars, summer 1999 in the Year of Our Lord."

Then he let himself drift awake.

Moments later, crossing the desert tarmac, he heard someone shouting again and again and again.

And if no one was there or if someone was there behind him, he could not tell. And whether it was one voice or many, young or old, near or very far away, rising or falling, whispering or shouting to him all three of his brave new names, he could not tell, either. He did not turn to see.

For the wind was slowly rising and he let it take hold and blow him all the rest of the way across the desert to the rocket which stood waiting there.

DEATH AND THE MAIDEN

FAR OUT IN THE COUNTRY beyond the woods, beyond the world, really, lived Old Mam, and she had lived there for ninety years with the door locked tight, not opening for anyone, be it wind, rain, sparrow tapping or little boy with a pailful of crayfish rapping. If you scratched at her shutters, she called through:

"Go away, Death!"

"I'm not Death!" you might say.

But she'd cry back, "Death, I know you, you come today in the shape of a girl. But I see the bones behind the freckles!"

Or someone else might knock.

"I see you, Death!" would cry Old Mam. "In the shape of a scissors-grinder! But the door is triple-locked and double-barred. I got flypaper on the cracks, tape on the keyholes, dust mops up the chimney, cobwebs in the shutters, and the electricity cut off so you can't slide in with the juice! No telephones so you can call me to my doom at three in the dark morning. And I got my ears stuffed with cotton so I can't hear your reply to what I say now. So, Death, get away!"

That's how it had been through the town's history. People in that world beyond the wood spoke of her and sometimes boys doubting the tale would heave chunks against the roof slates just to hear Old Mam wail, "Go on, good-bye, you in black with the white, white face!"

And the tale was that Old Mam, with such tactics, would live forever. After all, Death couldn't get in, could he? All the old germs in her house must have long since given up and gone to sleep. All the new germs running through the land with new names every week or ten days, if you believed the papers, couldn't get in past the bouquets of rock moss, rue, black tobacco and castor bean at every door.

"She'll bury us all," said the town 'way off where the train ran by.

"I'll bury them all," said Old Mam, alone and playing solitaire with Braille-marked cards, in the dark.

And that's how it was.

Years passed without another visitor, be it boy, girl, tramp or traveling man, knocking at her door. Twice a year a grocery clerk from the world beyond, seventy himself, left packages that might have been birdseed, could have been milk-bone biscuit, but were almost certainly stamped into bright steel cans with yellow lions and red devils inked on the bright wrappers, and trod off over the choppy sea of lumber on the front porch. The food might stay there for a week, baked by the sun, frozen by the moon; a proper time of antisepsis. Then, one morning, it was gone.

Old Mam's career was waiting. She did it well, with her eyes closed and her hands clasped and the hairs inside her ears trembling, listening, always ready.

So she was not surprised when, on the seventh day of August in her ninety-first year, a young man with a sunburned face walked through the wood and stood before her house.

He wore a suit like that snow which slides whispering in white linen off a winter roof to lay itself in folds on the sleeping earth. He had no car; he had walked a long way, but looked fresh and clean. He carried no cane to lean on and wore no hat to keep off the stunning blows of the sun. He did not perspire. Most important of all, he carried only one thing with him, an eight-ounce bottle with a bright-green liquid inside. Gazing deeply into this green color, he sensed he was in front of Old Mam's house, and looked up.

He didn't touch her door. He walked slowly around her house and let her feel him making the circle.

Then, with his X-ray eyes, he let her feel his steady gaze.

"Oh!" cried Old Mam, waking with a crumb of graham cracker still in her mouth. "It's you! I know who you came as this time!"

"Who?"

"A young man with a face like a pink summer melon. But you got no shadow! Why's that? Why?"

"People are afraid of shadows. So I left mine back beyond the wood."

"So I see, without looking."

"Oh," said the young man with admiration. "You have Powers."

"Great Powers, to keep you out and *me* in!"

The young man's lips barely moved. "I won't even bother to wrestle you." But she heard. "You'd lose, you'd lose!"

"And I like to win. So—I'll just leave this bottle on your front stoop."

He heard her heart beating fast through the walls of the house.

"Wait! What's in it? Anything left on my property, I got a right to know!"

"Well," said the young man.

"Go on!"

"In this bottle," he said, "is the first night and the first day you turned eighteen."

"What, what, what!"

"You heard me."

"The night I turned eighteen . . . the day?"

"That's it."

"In a bottle?"

He held it high and it was curved and shaped not unlike a young woman. It took the light of the world and flashed back warmth and green fire like the coals burning in a tiger's eyes. It looked now serene, now suddenly shifted and turbulent in his hands.

"I don't believe it!" cried Old Mam.

"I'll leave it and go," said the young man. "When I'm gone, try a teaspoon of the green thoughts in this bottle. Then you'll know."

"It's poison!"

"No."

"You promise, mother's honor?"

"I have no mother."

"What do you swear on?"

"Myself."

"It'll kill me, that's what you want!"

"It will raise you from the dead."

"I'm not dead!"

The young man smiled at the house.

"Aren't you?" he said.

"Wait! Let me ask myself: Are you dead? *Are* you? Or *nearly*, all these years?"

"The day and the night you turned eighteen," said the young man. "Think it over."

"It's so long ago!"

Something stirred like a mouse by a coffin-sized window.

"This will bring it back."

He let the sun wash through the elixir that glowed like the crushed sap of a thousand green blades of summer grass. It looked hot and still as a green sun, it looked wild and blowing as the sea.

"This was a good day in a good year of your life."

"A good year," she murmured, hidden away.

"A vintage year. Then there was savor to your life. One swig and you'd know the taste! Why not try it, eh? Eh?"

He held the bottle higher and farther out and it was suddenly a telescope which, peered through from either end, brought to focus a time in a year long gone. A green-and-yellow time much like this noon in which the young man offered up the past like a burning glass between his serene fingers. He tilted the bright flask, and a butterfly of white-hot illumination winged up and down the window shutters, playing them like gray piano keys, soundlessly. With hypnotic ease the burning wings frittered through the shutter slots to catch a lip, a nose, an eye, poised there. The eye snatched itself away, then, curious, relit itself from the beam of light. Now, having caught what he wanted to catch, the young man held the butterfly reflection steady, save for the breathing of its fiery wings, so that the green fire of that far-distant day poured through the shutters of not only ancient house but ancient woman. He heard her breathe out her muffled startlement, her repressed delight.

"No, no, you can't fool me!" She sounded like someone deep under water, trying not to drown in a lazy tide. "Coming back dressed in that flesh, you! Putting on that mask I can't quite see! Talking with that voice I remember from some other year. Whose voice? I don't care! My ouija board here on my lap spells who you really are and what you sell!"

"I sell just this twenty-four hours from young life."

"You sell something else!"

"No, I can't sell what I *am*."

"If I come out you'd grab and shove me six feet under. I've had you fooled, put off, for years. Now you whine back with new plans, none of which will work!"

"If you came out the door, I'd only kiss your hand, young lady."

"Don't call me what I'm not!"

"I call you what you could be an hour from now."

"An hour from now . . ." she whispered, to herself.

"How long since you been walked through this wood?"

"Some other war, or some peace," she said. "I can't see. The water's muddy."

"Young lady," he said, "it's a fine summer day. There's a tapestry of golden bees, now this design, now that, in the green church aisle of trees here. There's honey in a hollow oak flowing like a river of fire. Kick off your shoes, you can crush wild mint, wading deep. Wildflowers like clouds of yellow butterflies lie in the valley. The air under these trees is like deep well water cool and clear you drink with your nose. A summer day, young as young ever was."

"But I'm old, old as ever was."

"Not if you listen! Here's my out-and-out bargain, deal, sale—a transaction betwixt you, me and the August weather."

"What kind of deal, what do I get for my investment?"

"Twenty-four long sweet summer hours, starting now. When we've run through these woods and picked the berries and eaten the honey, we'll go on to town and buy you the finest spider-web-thin white summer dress and lift you on the train."

"The train!"

"The train to the city, an hour away, where we'll have dinner and dance all night. I'll buy you four shoes, you'll need them, wearing out one pair."

"My bones—I can't move."

"You'll run rather than walk, dance rather than run. We'll watch the stars wheel over the sky and bring the sun up, flaming. We'll string footprints along the lake shore at dawn. We'll eat the biggest breakfast in mankind's history and lie on the sand like two chicken pies warming at noon. Then, late in the day, a five-pound box of bonbons on our laps, we'll laugh back on the train, covered with the conductor's ticket-punch confetti, blue, green, orange, like we were married, and walk through town seeing nobody, no one, and wander back through the sweet dusk-smelling wood into your house . . ."

Silence.

"It's already over," murmured her voice. "And it hasn't begun."

Then: "Why are you doing this? What's in it for you?!"

The young man smiled tenderly. "Why, girl, I want to sleep with you."

She gasped. "I never slept with no one in my life!"

"You're a . . . maiden lady?"

"And proud *of* it!"

The young man sighed, shaking his head. "So it's true—you are, you really are, a maiden."

He heard nothing from the house, so listened.

Softly, as if a secret faucet had been turned somewhere with difficulty, and drop by drop an ancient system were being used for the first time in half a century, the old woman began to cry.

"Old Mam, why do you cry?"

"I don't know," she wailed.

Her weeping faded at last and he heard her rock in her chair, making a cradle rhythm to soothe herself.

"Old Mam," he whispered.

"Don't call me that!"

"All right," he said. "Clarinda."

"How did you know my name? No one knows!"

"Clarinda, why did you hide in that house, long ago?"

"I don't remember. Yes, I do. I was afraid."

"Afraid?"

"Strange. Half my years afraid of life. The other half, afraid of death. Always some kind of afraid. You! Tell the truth, now! When my twenty-four hours are up, after we walk by the lake and take the train back and come through the woods to my house, you want to . . ."

He made her say it.

". . . *sleep* with me?" she whispered.

"For ten thousand million years," he said.

"Oh." Her voice was muted. "That's a long time."

He nodded.

"A long time," she repeated. "What kind of bargain is that, young man? You give me twenty-four hours of being eighteen again and I give you ten thousand million years of my precious time."

"Don't forget, my time, too," he said. "I'll never go away."

"You'll lie with me?"

"I will."

"Oh, young man, young man. Your voice. So familiar."

"Look."

He saw the keyhole unplugged and her eye peer out at him. He smiled at the sunflowers in the field and the sunflower in the sky.

"I'm blind, half blind," she cried. "But can that be Willy Winchester 'way out there?"

He said nothing.

"But, Willy, you're just twenty-one by the look of you, not a day different than you were seventy years back!"

He set the bottle by the front door and walked back out to stand in the weeds.

"Can—" She faltered. "Can you make me look like yourself?"

He nodded.

"Oh, Willy, Willy, is that really you?"

She waited, staring across the summer air to where he stood relaxed and happy and young, the sun flashing off his hair and cheeks.

A minute passed.

"Well?" he said.

"Wait!" she cried. "Let me think!"

And there in the house he could feel her letting her memories pour through her mind as sand pours through an hourglass, heaping itself at last into nothing but dust and ashes. He could hear the emptiness of those memories burning the sides of her mind as they fell down and down and made a higher and yet higher mound of sand.

All that desert, he thought, and not one oasis.

She trembled at his thought.

"Well," he said again.

And at last she answered.

"Strange," she murmured. "Now, all of a sudden, twenty-four hours, one day, traded for ten million billion years, sounds fair and good and right."

"It is, Clarinda," he said. "Oh, yes, it is."

The bolts slid back, the locks rattled, the door cracked. Her hand jerked out, seized the bottle and flicked back in.

A minute passed.

Then, as if a gun had been fired off, footsteps pelted through the halls.

The back door slammed open. Upstairs, windows flew wide, as shutters fell crumbling to the grass. Downstairs, a moment later, the same. Shutters exploded to kindling as she thrust them out. The windows exhaled dust.

Then at last, from the front door, flung wide, the empty bottle sailed and smashed against a rock.

She was on the porch, quick as a bird. The sunlight struck full upon her. She stood as someone on a stage, in a single revealing motion, come from the dark. Then, down the steps, she threw her hand to catch his.

A small boy passing on the road below stopped, stared and, walking backward, moved out of sight, his eyes still wide.

"Why did he stare at me?" she said. "Am I beautiful?"

"Very beautiful."

"I need a mirror!"

"No, no, you don't."

"Will everyone in town see me beautiful? It's not just me thinking so, is it, or you pretending?"

"Beauty is what you *are*."

"Then I'm beautiful, for that's how I feel. Will everyone dance me tonight, will men fight for turns?"

"They will, one and all."

Down the path, in the sound of bees and stirring leaves, she stopped suddenly and looked into his face so like the summer sun.

"Oh, Willy, Willy, when it's all over and we come back here, will you be kind to me?"

He gazed deep into her eyes and touched her cheek with his fingers.

"Yes," he said gently. "I will be kind."

"I believe you," she said. "Oh, Willy, I believe."

And they ran down the path out of sight, leaving dust on the air and leaving the front door of the house wide and the shutters open and the windows up so the light of the sun could flash in with the birds come to build nests, raise families, and so petals of lovely summer flowers could blow like bridal showers through the long halls in a carpet and into the rooms and over the empty-but-waiting bed. And summer, with the breeze, changed the air in all the great spaces of the house so it smelled like the Beginning or the first hour after the Beginning, when the world was new and nothing would ever change and no one would ever grow old.

Somewhere rabbits ran thumping like quick hearts in the forest.

Far off, a train hooted, rushing faster, faster, faster, toward the town.

ZERO HOUR

Oh, it was to be so jolly! What a game! Such excitement they hadn't known in years. The children catapulted this way and that across the green lawns, shouting at each other, holding hands, flying in circles, climbing trees, laughing. Overhead the rockets flew, and beetle cars whispered by on the streets, but the children played on. Such fun, such tremulous joy, such tumbling and hearty screaming.

Mink ran into the house, all dirt and sweat. For her seven years she was loud and strong and definite. Her mother, Mrs. Morris, hardly saw her as she yanked out drawers and rattled pans and tools into a large sack.

"Heavens, Mink, what's going on?"

"The most exciting game ever!" gasped Mink, pink-faced.

"Stop and get your breath," said the mother.

"No, I'm all right," gasped Mink. "Okay I take these things, Mom?"

"But don't dent them," said Mrs. Morris.

"Thank you, thank you!" cried Mink, and boom! she was gone, like a rocket.

Mrs. Morris surveyed the fleeing tot. "What's the name of the game?"

"Invasion!" said Mink. The door slammed.

In every yard on the street children brought out knives and forks and pokers and old stovepipes and can openers.

It was an interesting fact that this fury and bustle occurred only among the younger children. The older ones, those ten years and more, disdained the affair and marched scornfully off on hikes or played a more dignified version of hide-and-seek on their own.

Meanwhile, parents came and went in chromium beetles. Repairmen came to repair the vacuum elevators in houses, to fix fluttering television sets or hammer upon stubborn food-delivery tubes. The adult civilization passed and repassed the busy youngsters, jealous of the fierce energy of the wild tots, tolerantly amused at their flourishings, longing to join in themselves.

"This and this and *this*," said Mink, instructing the others with their assorted spoons and wrenches. "Do that, and bring *that* over here. No! *Here*, ninny! Right. Now, get back while I fix this." Tongue in teeth, face wrinkled in thought. "Like that. See?"

"Yayyyy!" shouted the kids.

Twelve-year-old Joseph Connors ran up.

"Go away," said Mink straight at him.

"I wanna play," said Joseph.

"Can't!" said Mink.

"Why not?"

"You'd just make fun of us."

"Honest. I wouldn't."

"No. We know you. Go away or we'll kick you."

Another twelve-year-old boy whirred by on little motor skates. "Hey, Joe! Come on! Let them sissies play!"

Joseph showed reluctance and a certain wistfulness. "I want to play," he said.

"You're old," said Mink firmly.

"Not *that* old," said Joe sensibly.

"You'd only laugh and spoil the Invasion."

The boy on the motor skates made a rude lip noise. "Come on, Joe! Them and their fairies! Nuts!"

Joseph walked off slowly. He kept looking back, all down the block.

Mink was already busy again. She made a kind of apparatus with her gathered equipment. She had appointed another little girl with a pad and pencil to take down notes in painful slow scribbles. Their voices rose and fell in the warm sunlight.

All around them the city hummed. The streets were lined with good green and peaceful trees. Only the wind made a conflict across the city, across the country, across the continent. In a thousand other cities there were trees and children and avenues, businessmen in their quiet offices taping their voices or watching televisors. Rockets hovered like darning needles in the blue sky. There was the universal, quiet conceit and easiness of men accustomed to peace, quite certain there would never be trouble again. Arm in arm, men all over Earth were a united front. The perfect weapons were held in equal trust by all nations. A situation of incredibly beautiful balance had been brought about. There were no traitors among men. No unhappy ones, no disgruntled ones; therefore the world was based upon a stable ground. Sunlight illumined half the world and the trees drowsed in a tide of warm air.

Mink's mother, from her upstairs window, gazed down.

The children. She looked upon them and shook her head. Well, they'd eat well, sleep well, and be in school on Monday. Bless their vigorous little bodies. She listened.

Mink talked earnestly to someone near the rose bush—though there was no one there.

These odd children. And the little girl, what was her name? Anna? Anna took notes on a pad. First, Mink asked the rosebush a question, then called the answer to Anna.

"Triangle," said Mink.

"What's a tri," said Anna with difficulty, "angle?"

"Never mind," said Mink.

"How you spell it?" asked Anna.

"T-r-i—" spelled Mink slowly, then snapped, "Oh, spell it yourself!" She went on to other words. "Beam," she said.

"I haven't got tri," said Anna, "angle down yet!"

"Well, hurry, hurry!" cried Mink.

Mink's mother leaned out the upstairs window. "A-n-g-l-e," she spelled down at Anna.

"Oh, thanks, Mrs. Morris," said Anna.

"Certainly," said Mink's mother and withdrew, laughing, to dust the hall with an electro-duster magnet.

The voices wavered on the shimmery air. "Beam," said Anna. Fading.

"Four-nine-seven-A-and-B-and-X," said Mink, far away, seriously. "And a fork and a string and a—hex-hex-agony—hexagonal!"

At lunch Mink gulped milk at one toss and was at the door. Her mother slapped the table.

"You sit right back down," commanded Mrs. Morris. "Hot soup in a minute." She poked a red button on the kitchen butler, and ten seconds later something landed with a bump in the rubber receiver. Mrs. Morris opened it, took out a can with a pair of aluminum holders, unsealed it with a flick, and poured hot soup into a bowl.

During all this Mink fidgeted. "Hurry, Mom! This is a matter of life and death! Aw—"

"I was the same way at your age. Always life and death. I know."

Mink banged away at the soup.

"Slow down," said Mom.

"Can't," said Mink. "Drill's waiting for me."

"Who's Drill? What a peculiar name," said Mom.

"You don't know him," said Mink.

"A new boy in the neighborhood?" asked Mom.

"He's new all right," said Mink. She started on her second bowl.

"Which one is Drill?" asked Mom.

"He's around," said Mink evasively. "You'll make fun. Everybody pokes fun. Gee, darn."

"Is Drill shy?"

"Yes. No. In a way. Gosh, Mom, I got to run if we want to have the Invasion!"

"Who's invading what?"

"Martians invading Earth. Well, not exactly Martians. They're—I don't know. From up." She pointed with her spoon.

"And *inside*," said Mom, touching Mink's feverish brow.

Mink rebelled. "You're laughing! You'll kill Drill and *everybody*."

"I didn't mean to," said Mom. "Drill's a Martian?"

"No. He's—well—maybe from Jupiter or Saturn or Venus. Anyway, he's had a hard time."

"I imagine." Mrs. Morris hid her mouth behind her hand.

"They couldn't figure a way to attack Earth."

"We're impregnable," said Mom in mock seriousness.

"That's the word Drill used! Impreg—That was the word, Mom."

"My, my, Drill's a brilliant little boy. Two-bit words."

"They couldn't figure a way to attack. Mom. Drill says—he says in order to make a good fight you got to have a new way of surprising people. That way you win. And he says also you got to have help from your enemy."

"A fifth column," said Mom.

"Yeah. That's what Drill said. And they couldn't figure a way to surprise Earth or get help."

"No wonder. We're pretty darn strong," Mom laughed, cleaning up. Mink sat there, staring at the table, seeing what she was talking about.

"Until, one day," whispered Mink melodramatically, "they thought of children!"

"*Well!*" said Mrs. Morris brightly.

"And they thought of how grownups are so busy they never look under rosebushes or on lawns!"

"Only for snails and fungus."

"And then there's something about dim-dims."

"Dim-dims?"

"Dimens-shuns."

"Dimensions?"

"Four of 'em! And there's something about kids under nine and imagination. It's real funny to hear Drill talk."

Mrs. Morris was tired. "Well, it must be funny. You're keeping Drill waiting now. It's getting late in the day and, if you want to have your Invasion before your supper bath, you'd better jump."

"Do I have to take a bath?" growled Mink.

"You do. Why is it children hate water? No matter what age you live in children hate water behind the ears!"

"Drill says I won't have to take baths," said Mink.

"Oh, he does, does he?"

"He told all the kids that. No more baths. And we can stay up till ten o'clock and go to two televisor shows on Saturday 'stead of one!"

"Well, Mr. Drill better mind his p's and q's. I'll call up his mother and—"

Mink went to the door. "We're having trouble with guys like Pete Britz and Dale Jerrick. They're growing up. They make fun. They're worse than parents. They just won't believe in Drill. They're so snooty, 'cause they're growing up. You'd think they'd know better. They were little only a coupla years ago. I hate them worst. We'll kill them *first*."

"Your father and I last?"

"Drill says you're dangerous. Know why? 'Cause you don't believe in Martians! They're going to let *us* run the world. Well, not just us, but the kids over in the next block too. I might be queen." She opened the door.

"Mom?"

"Yes?"

"What's lodge-ick?"

"Logic? Why, dear, logic is knowing what things are true and not true."

"He *mentioned* that," said Mink. "And what's im-pres-sion-able?" It took her a minute to say it.

"Why, it means—" Her mother looked at the floor, laughing gently. "It means—to be a child, dear."

"Thanks for lunch!" Mink ran out, then stuck her head back in. "Mom, I'll be sure you won't be hurt much, really!"

"Well, thanks," said Mom.

Slam went the door.

At four o'clock the audio-visor buzzed. Mrs. Morris flipped the tab. "Hello, Helen!" she said in welcome.

"Hello, Mary. How are things in New York?"

"Fine. How are things in Scranton? You look tired."

"So do you. The children. Underfoot," said Helen.

Mrs. Morris sighed. "My Mink too. The super-Invasion."

Helen laughed. "Are your kids playing that game too?"

"Lord, yes. Tomorrow it'll be geometrical jacks and motorized hop-scotch. Were we this bad when we were kids in '48?"

"Worse. Japs and Nazis. Don't know how my parents put up with me. Tomboy."

"Parents learn to shut their ears."

A silence.

"What's wrong, Mary?" asked Helen.

Mrs. Morris's eyes were half closed; her tongue slid slowly, thought-fully, over her lower lip. "Eh?" She jerked. "Oh, nothing. Just thought about *that*. Shutting ears and such. Never mind. Where were we?"

"My boy Tim's got a crush on some guy named—*Drill*, I think it was."

"Must be a new password. Mink likes him too."

"Didn't know it had got as far as New York. Word of mouth, I imagine. Looks like a scrap drive. I talked to Josephine and she said her kids—that's in Boston—are wild on this new game. It's sweeping the country."

At this moment Mink trotted into the kitchen to gulp a glass of water. Mrs. Morris turned. "How're things going?"

"Almost finished," said Mink.

"Swell," said Mrs. Morris. "What's *that*?"

"A yo-yo," said Mink. "Watch."

She flung the yo-yo down its string. Reaching the end it—It vanished.

"See?" said Mink. "Ope!" Dibbling her finger, she made the yo-yo reap-pear and zip up the string.

"Do that again," said her mother.

"Can't. Zero hour's five o'clock! By." Mink exited, zipping her yo-yo.

On the audio-visor, Helen laughed. "Tim brought one of those yo-yos in this morning, but when I got curious he said he wouldn't show it to me, and when I tried to work it, finally, it wouldn't work."

"You're not *impressionable*," said Mrs. Morris.

"What?"

"Never mind. Something I thought of. Can I help you, Helen?"

"I wanted to get that black-and-white cake recipe—"

＊ The hour drowsed by. The day waned. The sun lowered in the peaceful blue sky. Shadows lengthened on the green lawns. The laughter and excitement continued. One little girl ran away, crying. Mrs. Morris came out the front door.

"Mink, was that Peggy Ann crying?"

Mink was bent over in the yard, near the rosebush. "Yeah. She's a scarebaby. We won't let her play, now. She's getting too old to play. I guess she grew up all of a sudden."

"Is that why she cried? Nonsense. Give me a civil answer, young lady, or inside you come!"

Mink whirled in consternation, mixed with irritation. "I can't quit now. It's almost time. I'll be good. I'm sorry."

"Did you hit Peggy Ann?"

"No, honest. You ask her. It was something—well, she's just a scaredy pants."

The ring of children drew in around Mink where she scowled at her work with spoons and a kind of square-shaped arrangement of hammers and pipes. "There and there," murmured Mink.

"What's wrong?" said Mrs. Morris.

"Drill's stuck. Halfway. If we could only get him all the way through, it'd be easier. Then all the others could come through after him."

"Can I help?"

"No'm, thanks. I'll fix it."

"All right. I'll call you for your bath in half an hour. I'm tired of watching you."

She went in and sat in the electric relaxing chair, sipping a little beer from a half-empty glass. The chair massaged her back. Children, children. Children and love and hate, side by side. Sometimes children loved you, hated you—all in half a second. Strange children, did they ever forget or forgive the whippings and the harsh, strict words of command? She wondered. How can you ever forget or forgive those over and above you, those tall and silly dictators?

Time passed. A curious, waiting silence came upon the street, deepening.

Five o'clock. A clock sang softly somewhere in the house in a quiet, musical voice: "Five o'clock—five o'clock. Time's a-wasting. Five o'clock," and purred away into silence.

Zero hour.

Mrs. Morris chuckled in her throat. Zero hour.

A beetle car hummed into the driveway. Mr. Morris. Mrs. Morris smiled. Mr. Morris got out of the beetle, locked it, and called hello to Mink at her work. Mink ignored him. He laughed and stood for a moment watching the children. Then he walked up the front steps.

"Hello, darling."

"Hello, Henry."

She strained forward on the edge of the chair, listening. The children were silent. Too silent.

He emptied his pipe, refilled it. "Swell day. Makes you glad to be alive."

Buzz.

"What's that?" asked Henry.

"I don't know." She got up suddenly, her eyes widening. She was going to say something. She stopped it. Ridiculous. Her nerves jumped. "Those children haven't anything dangerous out there, have they?" she said.

"Nothing but pipes and hammers. Why?"

"Nothing electrical?"

"Heck, no," said Henry. "I looked."

She walked to the kitchen. The buzzing continued. "Just the same, you'd better go tell them to quit. It's after five. Tell them—" Her eyes widened and narrowed. "Tell them to put off their Invasion until tomorrow." She laughed, nervously.

The buzzing grew louder.

"What are they up to? I'd better go look, all right."

The explosion!

The house shook with dull sound. There were other explosions in other yards on other streets.

Involuntarily, Mrs. Morris screamed. "Up this way!" she cried senselessly, knowing no sense, no reason. Perhaps she saw something from the corners of her eyes; perhaps she smelled a new odor or heard a new noise. There was no time to argue with Henry to convince him. Let him think her insane. Yes, insane! Shrieking, she ran upstairs. He ran after her to see what she was up to. "In the attic!" she screamed. "That's where it is!" It was only a poor excuse to get him in the attic in time. Oh, God—in time!

Another explosion outside. The children screamed with delight, as if at a great fireworks display.

"It's not in the attic!" cried Henry. "It's outside!"

"No, no!" Wheezing, gasping, she fumbled at the attic door. "I'll show you. Hurry! I'll show you!"

They tumbled into the attic. She slammed the door, locked it, took the key, threw it into a far, cluttered corner. She was babbling wild stuff now. It came out of her. All the subconscious suspicion and fear that had gathered secretly all afternoon and fermented like a wine in her. All the little revelations and knowledges and sense that had bothered her all day and which she had logically and carefully and sensibly rejected and censored. Now it exploded in her and shook her to bits.

"There, there," she said, sobbing against the door. "We're safe until tonight. Maybe we can sneak out. Maybe we can escape!"

Henry blew up too, but for another reason. "Are you crazy? Why'd you throw that key away? Damn it, honey!"

"Yes, yes, I'm crazy, if it helps, but stay here with me!"

"I don't know how in hell I *can* get out!"

"Quiet. They'll hear us. Oh, God, they'll find us soon enough—"

Below them, Mink's voice. The husband stopped. There was a great universal humming and sizzling, a screaming and giggling. Downstairs the audio-televisor buzzed and buzzed insistently, alarmingly, violently. *Is that Helen calling?* thought Mrs. Morris. *And is she calling about what I think she's calling about?*

Footsteps came into the house. Heavy footsteps.

"Who's coming in my house?" demanded Henry angrily. "Who's tramping around down there?"

Heavy feet. Twenty, thirty, forty, fifty of them. Fifty persons crowding into the house. The humming. The giggling of the children. "This way!" cried Mink, below.

"Who's downstairs?" roared Henry. "Who's there!"

"Hush. Oh, nonononononono!" said his wife weakly, holding him. "Please, be quiet. They might go away."

"Mom?" called Mink. "Dad?" A pause. "Where are you?"

Heavy footsteps, heavy, heavy, *very heavy* footsteps, came up the stairs. Mink leading them.

"Mom?" A hesitation. "Dad?" A waiting, a silence.

Humming. Footsteps toward the attic. Mink's first.

They trembled together in silence in the attic, Mr. and Mrs. Morris. For some reason the electric humming, the queer cold light suddenly visible under the door crack, the strange odor and the alien sound of eagerness in

Mink's voice finally got through to Henry Morris too. He stood, shivering, in the dark silence, his wife beside him.

"Mom! Dad!"

Footsteps. A little humming sound. The attic lock melted. The door opened. Mink peered inside, tall blue shadows behind her.

"Peekaboo," said Mink.

✳

THE TOYNBEE CONVECTOR

✳

✳

"Good! Great! Bravo for me!"

Roger Shumway flung himself into the seat, buckled himself in, revved the rotor and drifted his Dragonfly Super-6 helicopter up to blow away on the summer sky, heading south toward La Jolla.

"How lucky can you get?"

For he was on his way to an incredible meeting.

The time traveler, after a hundred years of silence, had agreed to be interviewed. He was, on this day, 130 years old. And this afternoon, at four o'clock sharp, Pacific time, was the anniversary of his one and only journey in time.

Lord, yes! One hundred years ago, Craig Bennett Stiles had waved, stepped into his *Immense Clock*, as he called it, and vanished from the present. He was and remained the only man in history to travel in time. And Shumway was the one and only reporter, after all these years, to be invited in for afternoon tea. And? The possible announcement of a second and final trip through time. The traveler had hinted at such a trip.

"Old man," said Shumway, "Mr. Craig Bennett Stiles—here I come!"

The Dragonfly, obedient to fevers, seized a wind and rode it down the coast.

 The old man was there waiting for him on the roof of the Time Lamasery at the rim of the hang gliders' cliff in La Jolla. The air swarmed with crimson, blue and lemon kites from which young men shouted, while young women called to them from the land's edge.

Stiles, for all his 130 years, was not old. His face, blinking up at the helicopter, was the bright face of one of those hang-gliding Apollo fools who veered off as the helicopter sank down.

Shumway hovered his craft for a long moment, savoring the delay.

Below him was a face that had dreamed architectures, known incredible loves, blueprinted mysteries of seconds, hours, days, then dived in to swim upstream through the centuries. A sunburst face, celebrating its own birthday.

For on a single night, one hundred years ago, Craig Bennett Stiles, freshly returned from time, had reported by Telstar around the world to billions of viewers and told them their future.

"We made it!" he said. "We did it! The future is ours. We rebuilt the cities, freshened the small towns, cleaned the lakes and rivers, washed the air, saved the dolphins, increased the whales, stopped the wars, tossed solar stations across space to light the world, colonized the moon, moved on to Mars, then Alpha Centauri. We cured cancer and stopped death. We did it— Oh Lord, much thanks—we did it. Oh, future's bright and beauteous spires, arise!"

He showed them pictures, he brought them samples, he gave them tapes and LP records, film and sound cassettes of his wondrous roundabout flight. The world went mad with joy. It ran to meet and make that future, fling up the cities of promise, save all and share with the beasts of land and sea.

The old man's welcoming shout came up the wind. Shumway shouted back and let the Dragonfly simmer down in its own summer weather.

Craig Bennett Stiles, 130 years old, strode forward briskly and, incredibly, helped the young reporter out of his craft, for Shumway was suddenly stunned and weak at this encounter.

"I can't believe I'm here," said Shumway.

"You are, and none too soon," laughed the time traveler. "Any day now, I may just fall apart and blow away. Lunch is waiting. Hike!"

A parade of one, Stiles marched off under the fluttering rotor shadows that made him seem a flickering newsreel of a future that had somehow passed.

Shumway, like a small dog after a great army, followed.

"What do you want to know?" asked the old man as they crossed the roof, double time.

"First," gasped Shumway, keeping up, "why have you broken silence after a hundred years? Second, why to *me*? Third, what's the big announcement you're going to make this afternoon at four o'clock, the very hour when your younger self is due to arrive from the past—when, for a brief moment, you will appear in two places, the paradox: the person you were, the man you are, fused in one glorious hour for us to celebrate?"

The old man laughed. "How you *do* go on!"

"Sorry." Shumway blushed. "I wrote that last night. Well. Those are the questions."

"You shall have your answers." The old man shook his elbow gently. "All in good—time."

"You must excuse my excitement," said Shumway. "After all, you *are* a mystery. You were famous, world-acclaimed. You went, saw the future, came back, told us, then went into seclusion. Oh, sure; for a few weeks, you traveled the world in ticker-tape parades, showed yourself on TV, wrote one book, gifted us with one magnificent two-hour television film, then shut yourself away here. Yes, the time machine is on exhibit below, and crowds are allowed in each day at noon to see and touch. But you yourself have refused fame—"

"Not so." The old man led him along the roof. Below in the gardens, other helicopters were arriving now, bringing TV equipment from around the world to photograph the miracle in the sky, that moment when the time machine from the past would appear, shimmer, then wander off to visit other cities before it vanished into the past. "I have been busy, as an architect, helping build that very future I saw when, as a young man, I arrived in our golden tomorrow!"

They stood for a moment watching the preparations below. Vast tables were being set up for food and drink. Dignitaries would be arriving soon from every country of the world to thank—for a final time, perhaps—this fabled, this almost mythic traveler of the years.

"Come along," said the old man. "Would you like to come sit in the time machine? No one else ever has, you know. Would you like to be the first?"

No answer was necessary. The old man could see that the young man's eyes were bright and wet.

"There, there," said the old man. "Oh, dear me; there, there."

✳ A glass elevator sank and took them below and let them out in a pure white basement at the center of which stood—

The incredible device.

"There." Stiles touched a button and the plastic shell that had for one hundred years encased the time machine slid aside. The old man nodded. "Go. Sit."

Shumway moved slowly toward the machine.

Stiles touched another button and the machine lit up like a cavern of spider webs. It breathed in years and whispered forth remembrance. Ghosts were in its crystal veins. A great god spider had woven its tapestries in a single night. It was haunted and it was alive. Unseen tides came and went in its machinery. Suns burned and moons hid their seasons in it. Here, an autumn blew away in tatters; there, winters arrived in snows that drifted in spring blossoms to fall on summer fields.

The young man sat in the center of it all, unable to speak, gripping the armrests of the padded chair.

"Don't be afraid," said the old man gently. "I won't send you on a journey."

"I wouldn't mind," said Shumway.

The old man studied his face. "No, I can see you wouldn't. You look like me one hundred years ago this day. Damn if you aren't my honorary son."

The young man shut his eyes at this, and the lids glistened as the ghosts in the machine sighed all about him and promised him tomorrows.

"Well, what do you think of my *Toynbee Convector*?" said the old man briskly, to break the spell.

He cut the power. The young man opened his eyes.

"The *Toynbee Convector*? What—"

"More mysteries, eh? The great Toynbee, that fine historian who said any group, any race, any world that did not run to seize the future and shape it was doomed to dust away in the grave, in the past."

"Did he say *that*?"

"Or some such. He did. So, what better name for my machine, eh? Toynbee, wherever you are, here's your future-seizing device!"

He grabbed the young man's elbow and steered him out of the machine.

"Enough of that. It's late. Almost time for the great arrival, eh? And the earth-shaking final announcement of that old time traveler Stiles! Jump!"

✳ Back on the roof, they looked down on the gardens, which were now swarming with the famous and the near famous from across the world. The nearby roads were jammed; the skies were full of helicopters and hovering biplanes. The hang gliders had long since given up and now stood along the cliff rim like a mob of bright pterodactyls, wings folded, heads up, staring at the clouds, waiting.

"All this," the old man murmured, "my God, for me."

The young man checked his watch.

"Ten minutes to four and counting. Almost time for the great arrival. Sorry; that's what I called it when I wrote you up a week ago for the *News*. That moment of arrival and departure, in the blink of an eye, when, by stepping across time, you changed the whole future of the world from night to day, dark to light. I've often wondered—"

"What?"

Shumway studied the sky. "When you went ahead in time, did no one see you arrive? Did anyone at all happen to look up, do you know, and see your device hover in the middle of the air, here and over Chicago a bit later, and then New York and Paris? No one?"

"Well," said the inventor of the *Toynbee Convector*, "I don't suppose anyone was expecting me! And if people saw, they surely did not know what in blazes they were looking at. I was careful, anyway, not to linger too long. I needed only time to photograph the rebuilt cities, the clean seas and rivers, the fresh, smog-free air, the unfortified nations, the saved and beloved whales. I moved quickly, photographed swiftly and ran back down the years home. Today, paradoxically, is different. Millions upon millions of mobs of eyes will be looking up with great expectations. They will glance, will they not, from the young fool burning in the sky to the old fool here, still glad for his triumph?"

"They will," said Shumway. "Oh, indeed, they will!"

A cork popped. Shumway turned from surveying the crowds on the nearby fields and the crowds of circling objects in the sky to see that Stiles had just opened a bottle of champagne.

"Our own private toast and our own private celebration."

They held their glasses up, waiting for the precise and proper moment to drink.

"Five minutes to four and counting. Why," said the young reporter, "did no one else ever travel in time?"

"I put a stop to it myself," said the old man, leaning over the roof, looking down at the crowds. "I realized how dangerous it was. I was reliable, of course, no danger. But, Lord, think of it—just anyone rolling about the bowling-alley time corridors ahead, knocking tenpins headlong, frightening natives, shocking citizens somewhere else, fiddling with Napoleon's life line behind or restoring Hitler's cousins ahead? No, no. And the government, of course, agreed—no, insisted—that we put the *Toynbee Convector* under sealed lock and key. Today, you were the first and last to fingerprint its machinery. The guard has been heavy and constant, for tens of thousands of days, to prevent the machine's being stolen. What time do you have?"

Shumway glanced at his watch and took in his breath.

"One minute and counting down—"

He counted, the old man counted. They raised their champagne glasses.

"Nine, eight, seven—"

The crowds below were immensely silent. The sky whispered with expectation. The TV cameras swung up to scan and search.

"Six, five—"

They clinked their glasses.

"Four, three, two—"

They drank.

"One!"

They drank their champagne with a laugh. They looked to the sky. The golden air above the La Jolla coastline waited. The moment for the great arrival was here.

"Now!" cried the young reporter, like a magician giving orders.

"Now," said Stiles, gravely quiet.

Nothing.

Five seconds passed.

The sky stood empty.

Ten seconds passed.

The heavens waited.

Twenty seconds passed.

Nothing.

At last, Shumway turned to stare and wonder at the old man by his side.

Stiles looked at him, shrugged and said:

"I lied."

"You what!?" cried Shumway.

The crowds below shifted uneasily.

"I lied," said the old man simply.

"No!"

"Oh, but yes," said the time traveler. "I never went anywhere. I stayed but made it seem I went. There is no time machine—only something that *looks* like one."

"But why?" cried the young man, bewildered, holding on to the rail at the edge of the roof. "Why?"

"I see that you have a tape-recording button on your lapel. Turn it on. Yes. There. I want everyone to hear this. Now."

The old man finished his champagne and then said:

"Because I was born and raised in a time, in the sixties, seventies and eighties, when people had stopped believing in themselves. I saw that disbelief, the reason that no longer gave itself reasons to survive, and was moved, depressed and then angered by it.

"Everywhere, I saw and heard doubt. Everywhere, I learned destruction. Everywhere was professional despair, intellectual ennui, political cynicism. And what wasn't ennui and cynicism was rampant skepticism and incipient nihilism."

The old man stopped, having remembered something. He bent and from under a table brought forth a special bottle of red Burgundy with the label 1984 on it. This, as he talked, he began to open, gently plumbing the ancient cork.

"You name it, we had it. The economy was a snail. The world was a cesspool. Economics remained an insoluble mystery. Melancholy was the attitude. The impossibility of change was the vogue. End of the world was the slogan.

"Nothing was worth doing. Go to bed at night full of bad news at eleven, wake up in the morn to worse news at seven. Trudge through the day underwater. Drown at night in a tide of plagues and pestilence. Ah!"

For the cork had softly popped. The now-harmless 1984 vintage was ready for airing. The time traveler sniffed it and nodded.

"Not only the four horsemen of the Apocalypse rode the horizon to fling themselves on our cities but a fifth horseman, worse than all the rest, rode with them: Despair, wrapped in dark shrouds of defeat, crying only repetitions of past disasters, present failures, future cowardices.

"Bombarded by dark chaff and no bright seed, what sort of harvest was there for man in the latter part of the incredible twentieth century?

"Forgotten was the moon, forgotten the red landscapes of Mars, the great eye of Jupiter, the stunning rings of Saturn. We refused to be comforted. We wept at the grave of our child, and the child was *us*."

"Was that how it was," asked Shumway quietly, "one hundred years ago?"

"Yes." The time traveler held up the wine bottle as if it contained proof. He poured some into a glass, eyed it, inhaled, and went on. "You have seen the newsreels and read the books of that time. You know it all.

"Oh, of course, there were a few bright moments. When Salk delivered the world's children to life. Or the night when *Eagle* landed and that one great step for mankind trod the moon. But in the minds and out of the mouths of many, the fifth horseman was darkly cheered on. With high hopes, it sometimes seemed, of his winning. So all would be gloomily satisfied that their predictions of doom were right from day one. So the self-fulfilling prophecies were declared; we dug our graves and prepared to lie down in them."

"And you couldn't allow that?" asked the young reporter.

"You know I couldn't."

"And so you built the *Toynbee Convector*—"

"Not all at once. It took years to brood on it."

The old man paused to swirl the dark wine, gaze at it and sip, eyes closed.

"Meanwhile, I drowned, I despaired, wept silently late nights thinking, What can I do to save us from ourselves? How to save my friends, my city, my state, my country, the entire *world* from this obsession with doom? Well, it was in my library late one night that my hand, searching along shelves, touched at last on an old and beloved book by H. G. Wells. His time device called, ghostlike, down the years. I *heard*! I understood. I truly listened. Then I blueprinted. I built. I traveled, or so it *seemed*. The rest, as you know, is history."

The old time traveler drank his wine, opened his eyes.

"Good God," the young reporter whispered, shaking his head. "Oh, dear God. Oh, the wonder, the wonder—"

There was an immense ferment in the lower gardens now and in the fields beyond and on the roads and in the air. Millions were still waiting. Where was the great arrival?

"Well, now," said the old man, filling another glass with wine for the young reporter. "Aren't I something? I made the machines, built miniature cities, lakes, ponds, seas. Erected vast architectures against crystal-water skies, talked to dolphins, played with whales, faked tapes, mythologized films. Oh, it took years, years of sweating work and secret preparation before I announced my departure, left and came back with good news!"

They drank the rest of the vintage wine. There was a hum of voices. All of the people below were looking up at the roof.

The time traveler waved at them and turned.

"Quickly, now. It's up to you from here on. You have the tape, my voice on it, just freshly made. Here are three more tapes, with fuller data. Here's a film-cassette history of my whole inspired fraudulence. Here's a final manuscript. Take, take it all, hand it on. I nominate you as son to explain the father. Quickly!"

Hustled into the elevator once more, Shumway felt the world fall away beneath. He didn't know whether to laugh or cry, so gave, at last, a great hoot.

The old man, surprised, hooted with him, as they stepped out below and advanced upon the *Toynbee Convector*.

"You see the point, don't you, son? Life has *always* been lying to ourselves! As boys, young men, old men. As girls, maidens, women, to gently lie and prove the lie true. To weave dreams and put brains and ideas and flesh and the truly real beneath the dreams. Everything, finally, is a promise. What seems a lie is a ramshackle need, wishing to be born. Here. Thus and so."

He pressed the button that raised the plastic shield, pressed another that started the time machine humming, then shuffled quickly in to thrust himself into the *Convector's* seat.

"Throw the final switch, young man!"

"But—"

"You're thinking," here the old man laughed, "if the time machine is a fraud, it won't work, what's the use of throwing a switch, yes? Throw it, anyway. *This* time, it *will* work!"

Shumway turned, found the control switch, grabbed hold, then looked at Craig Bennett Stiles.

"I don't understand. Where are you *going*?"

"Why, to be one with the ages, of course. To exist now, only in the deep past."

"How can that *be*?"

"Believe me, this time it will happen. Good-bye, dear, fine, nice young man."

"Good-bye."

"Now. Tell me my name."

"What?"

"Speak my name and throw the switch."

"Time traveler?"

"Yes! *Now!*"

The young man yanked the switch. The machine hummed, roared, blazed with power.

"Oh," said the old man, shutting his eyes. His mouth smiled gently. "Yes."

His head fell forward on his chest.

Shumway yelled, banged the switch off and leaped forward to tear at the straps binding the old man in his device.

In the midst of so doing, he stopped, felt the time traveler's wrist, put his fingers under the neck to test the pulse there and groaned. He began to weep.

The old man had, indeed, gone back in time, and its name was death. He was traveling in the past now, forever.

Shumway stepped back and turned the machine on again. If the old man were to travel, let the machine—symbolically, anyway—go with him. It made a sympathetic humming. The fire of it, the bright sun fire, burned in all of its spider grids and armatures and lighted the cheeks and the vast brow of the ancient traveler, whose head seemed to nod with the vibrations and whose smile, as he traveled into darkness, was the smile of a child much satisfied.

The reporter stood for a long moment more, wiping his cheeks with the backs of his hands. Then, leaving the machine on, he turned, crossed the room, pressed the button for the glass elevator and, while he was waiting, took the time traveler's tapes and cassettes from his jacket pockets and, one by one, shoved them into the incinerator trash flue set in the wall.

The elevator doors opened, he stepped in, the doors shut. The elevator hummed now, like yet another time device, taking him up into a stunned world, a waiting world, lifting him up into a bright continent, a future land, a wondrous and surviving planet . . .

That one man with one lie had created.

FOREVER AND THE EARTH

AFTER SEVENTY YEARS OF WRITING SHORT STORIES that never sold, Mr. Henry William Field arose one night at eleven-thirty and burned ten million words. He carried the manuscripts downstairs through his dark old mansion and threw them into the furnace.

"That's that," he said, and thinking about his lost art and his misspent life, he put himself to bed, among his rich antiques. "My mistake was in ever trying to picture this wild world of A.D. 2257. The rockets, the atom wonders, the travels to planets and double suns. Nobody can do it. Everyone's tried. All of our modern authors have failed."

Space was too big for them, and rockets too swift, and atomic science too instantaneous, he thought. But at least the other writers, while failing, had been published, while he, in his idle wealth, had used the years of his life for nothing.

After an hour of feeling this way, he fumbled through the night rooms to his library and switched on a green hurricane lamp. At random, from a collection untouched in fifty years, he selected a book. It was a book three centuries yellow and three centuries brittle, but he settled into it and read hungrily until dawn. . . .

At nine the next morning, Henry William Field staggered from his library, called his servants, televised lawyers, scientists, litterateurs.

"Come at once!" he cried.

By noon, a dozen people had stepped into the study where Henry William Field sat, very disreputable and hysterical with an odd, feeding joy, unshaven and feverish. He clutched a thick book in his brittle arms and laughed if anyone even said good morning.

"Here you see a book," he said at last, holding it out, "written by a giant, a man born in Asheville, North Carolina, in the year 1900. Long gone to dust, he published four huge novels. He was a whirlwind. He lifted up mountains and collected winds. He left a trunk of penciled manuscripts behind when he lay in bed at Johns Hopkins Hospital in Baltimore in the year 1938, on September fifteenth, and died of pneumonia, an ancient and awful disease."

They looked at the book.

Look Homeward, Angel.

He drew forth three more. *Of Time and the River. The Web and the Rock. You Can't Go Home Again.*

"By Thomas Wolfe," said the old man. "Three centuries cold in the North Carolina earth."

"You mean you've called us simply to see four books by a dead man?" his friends protested.

"More than that! I've called you because I feel Tom Wolfe's the man, the necessary man, to write of space, of time, huge things like nebulae and galactic war, meteors and planets, all the dark things he loved and put on paper were like this. He was born out of his time. He needed really big things to play with and never found them on Earth. He should have been born this afternoon instead of one hundred thousand mornings ago."

"I'm afraid you're a bit late," said Professor Bolton.

"I don't intend to be late!" snapped the old man. "I will not be frustrated by reality. You, professor, have experimented with time travel. I expect you to finish your time machine as soon as possible. Here's a check, a blank check, fill it in. If you need more money, ask for it. You've done some traveling already, haven't you?"

"A few years, yes, but nothing like centuries—"

"We'll *make* it centuries! You others"—he swept them with a fierce and shining glance—"will work with Bolton. I *must* have Thomas Wolfe."

"What!" They fell back before him.

"Yes," he said. "That's the plan. Wolfe is to be brought to me. We will collaborate in the task of describing the flight from Earth to Mars, as only he could describe it!"

They left him in his library with his books, turning the dry pages, nodding to himself. "Yes. Oh, dear Lord yes, Tom's the boy, Tom is the *very* boy for this."

✳ The months passed slowly. Days showed a maddening reluctance to leave the calendar, and weeks lingered on until Mr. Henry William Field began to scream silently.

At the end of four months, Mr. Field awoke one midnight. The phone was ringing. He put his hand out in the darkness.

"Yes?"

"This is Professor Bolton calling."

"Yes, Bolton?"

"I'll be leaving in an hour," said the voice.

"Leaving? Leaving where? Are you quitting? You can't do that!"

"Please, Mr. Field, leaving means *leaving*."

"You mean, you're actually going?"

"Within the hour."

"To 1938? To September fifteenth?"

"Yes!"

"You're sure you've the date fixed correctly? You'll arrive before he dies? Be sure of it! Good Lord, you'd better get there a good hour before his death, don't you think?"

"*Two* hours. On the way back, we'll mark time in Bermuda, borrow ten days of free floating continuum, inject him, tan him, swim him, vitaminize him, make him well."

"I'm so excited I can't hold the phone. Good luck, Bolton. Bring him through safely!"

"Thank you, sir. Good-bye."

The phone clicked.

❋ Mr. Henry William Field lay through the ticking night. He thought of Tom Wolfe as a lost brother to be lifted intact from under a cold, chiseled stone, to be restored to blood and fire and speaking. He trembled each time he thought of Bolton whirling on the time wind back to other calendars and other days, bearing medicines to change flesh and save souls.

Tom, he thought, faintly, in the half-awake warmth of an old man calling after his favorite and long-gone child, Tom, where are you tonight, Tom? Come along now, we'll help you through, you've got to come, there's need for you. I couldn't do it, Tom, none of us here can. So the next best thing to doing it myself, Tom, is helping you to do it. You can play with rockets like jackstraws, Tom, and you can have the stars, like a handful of crystals. Anything your heart asks, it's here. You'd like the fire and the travel, Tom, it was made for you. Oh, we've a pale lot of writers today, I've read them all, Tom, and they're not like you. I've waded in libraries of their stuff and they've never touched space, Tom; we need *you* for that! Give an old man his wish then, for God knows I've waited all my life for myself or some other to write the really great book about the stars, and I've waited in vain. So, wherever you are tonight, Tom Wolfe, make yourself tall. It's that book you were going to write. It's that good book the critics said was in you when you stopped breathing. Here's your chance, will you do it, Tom? Will you listen and come through to us, will you do that tonight, and be here in the morning when I wake? Will you, Tom?

His eyelids closed down over the fever and the demand. His tongue stopped quivering in his sleeping mouth.

The clock struck four.

✳ Awakening to the white coolness of morning, he felt the excitement rising and welling in himself. He did not wish to blink, for fear that the thing which awaited him somewhere in the house might run off and slam a door, gone forever. His hands reached up to clutch his thin chest.

Far away . . . footsteps . . .

A series of doors opened and shut. Two men entered the bedroom.

Field could hear them breathe. Their footsteps took on identities. The first steps were those of a spider, small and precise: Bolton. The second steps were those of a big man, a large man, a heavy man.

"Tom?" cried the old man. He did not open his eyes.

"Yes," said a voice, at last.

Tom Wolfe burst the seams of Field's imagination, as a huge child bursts the lining of a too-small coat.

"Tom Wolfe, let me look at you!" If Field said it once he said it a dozen times as he fumbled from bed, shaking violently. "Put up the blinds, for God's sake, I want to see this! Tom Wolfe, is that you?"

Tom Wolfe looked down from his tall thick body, with big hands out to balance himself in a world that was strange. He looked at the old man and the room and his mouth was trembling.

"You're just as they said you were, Tom!"

Thomas Wolfe began to laugh and the laughing was huge, for he must have thought himself insane or in a nightmare, and he came to the old man and touched him and he looked at Professor Bolton and felt of himself, his arms and legs, he coughed experimentally and touched his own brow. "My fever's gone," he said. "I'm not sick anymore."

"Of course not, Tom."

"What a night," said Tom Wolfe. "It hasn't been easy. I thought I was sicker than any man ever was. I felt myself floating and I thought, This is fever. I felt myself traveling, and thought, I'm dying fast. A man came to me. I thought, This is the Lord's messenger. He took my hands. I smelled electricity. I flew up and over, and I saw a brass city. I thought, I've arrived. This is the city of heaven, there is the Gate! I'm numb from head to toe, like someone left in the snow to freeze. I've got to laugh and do things or I might think myself insane. You're not God, are you? You don't look like Him."

The old man laughed. "No, no, Tom, not God, but playing at it. I'm Field." He laughed again. "Lord, listen to me. I said it as if you should know who Field is. Field, the financier, Tom, bow low, kiss my ring finger. I'm Henry Field. I like your work, I brought you here. Come along."

The old man drew him to an immense crystal window.

"Do you see those lights in the sky, Tom?"

"Yes, sir."

"Those fireworks?"

"Yes."

"They're not what you think, son. It's not July Fourth, Tom. Not in the usual way. Every day's Independence Day now. Man has declared his Freedom from Earth. Gravitation without representation has been overthrown. The Revolt has long since been successful. That green Roman Candle's going to Mars. That red fire, that's the Venus rocket. And the others, you see the yellow and the blue? Rockets, all of them!"

Thomas Wolfe gazed up like an immense child caught amid the colorized glories of a July evening when the set-pieces are awhirl with phosphorous and glitter and barking explosion.

"What year is this?"

"The year of the rocket. Look here." And the old man touched some flowers that bloomed at his touch. The blossoms were like blue and white fire. They burned and sparkled their cold, long petals. The blooms were two feet wide, and they were the color of an autumn moon. "Moon-flowers," said the old man. "From the other side of the Moon." He brushed them and they dripped away into a silver rain, a shower of white sparks on the air. "The year of the rocket. That's a title for you, Tom. That's why we brought you here, we've need of you. You're the only man could handle the sun without being burned to a ridiculous cinder. We want you to juggle the sun, Tom, and the stars, and whatever else you see on your trip to Mars."

"Mars?" Thomas Wolfe turned to seize the old man's arm, bending down to him, searching his face in unbelief.

"Tonight. You leave at six o'clock."

The old man held a fluttering pink ticket on the air, waiting for Tom to think to take it.

＊ It was five in the afternoon. "Of course, of course I appreciate what you've done," cried Thomas Wolfe.

"Sit down, Tom. Stop walking around."

"Let me finish, Mr. Field, let me get through with this, I've got to say it."

"We've been arguing for hours," pleaded Mr. Field, exhaustedly.

They had talked from breakfast until lunch until tea, they had wandered through a dozen rooms and ten dozen arguments, they had perspired and grown cold and perspired again.

"It all comes down to this," said Thomas Wolfe, at last. "I can't stay here, Mr. Field. I've got to go back. This isn't my time. You've no right to interfere—"

"But, I—"

"I was deep in my work, my best yet to come, and now you run me off three centuries. Mr. Field, I want you to call Mr. Bolton back. I want you to have him put me in his machine, whatever it is, and return me to 1938, my rightful place and year. That's all I ask of you."

"But, don't you *want* to see Mars?"

"With all my heart. But I know it isn't for me. It would throw my writing off. I'd have a huge handful of experience that I couldn't fit into my other writing when I went home."

"You don't understand, Tom, you don't understand at all."

"I understand that you're selfish."

"Selfish? Yes," said the old man. "For myself, and for others, very selfish."

"I want to go home."

"Listen to me, Tom."

"Call Mr. Bolton."

"Tom, I don't want to have to tell you this. I thought I wouldn't have to, that it wouldn't be necessary. Now, you leave me only this alternative." The old man's right hand fetched hold of a curtained wall, swept back the drapes, revealing a large white screen, and dialed a number, a series of numbers. The screen flickered into vivid color, the lights of the room darkened, darkened, and a graveyard took line before their eyes.

"What are you doing?" demanded Wolfe, striding forward, staring at the screen.

"I don't like this at all," said the old man. "Look there."

The graveyard lay in midafternoon light, the light of summer. From the screen drifted the smell of summer earth, granite, and the odor of a nearby creek. From the trees, a bird called. Red and yellow flowers nodded among the stones, and the screen moved, the sky rotated, the old man twisted a dial for emphasis, and in the center of the screen, growing large, coming closer, yet larger, and now filling their senses, was a dark granite mass; and Thomas Wolfe, looking up in the dim room, ran his eyes over the chiseled words, once, twice, three times, gasped, and read again, for there was his name:

THOMAS WOLFE.

And the date of his birth and the date of his death, and the flowers and green ferns smelling sweetly on the air of the cold room.

"Turn it off," he said.

"I'm sorry, Tom."

"Turn it off, turn it off! I don't believe it."

"It's there."

The screen went black and now the entire room was a midnight vault, a tomb, with the last faint odor of flowers.

"I didn't wake up again," said Thomas Wolfe.

"No. You died that September of 1938. So, you see. O God, the ironies, it's like the title of your book. Tom, you *can't* go home again."

"I never finished my book."

"It was edited for you, by others who went over it, carefully."

"I didn't finish my work, I didn't finish my work."

"Don't take it so badly, Tom."

"How else can I take it?"

The old man didn't turn on the lights. He didn't want to see Tom there. "Sit down, boy." No reply. "Tom?" No answer. "Sit down, son; will you have something to drink?" For answer there was only a sigh and a kind of brutal mourning.

"Good Lord," said Tom, "it's not fair. I had so much left to do, it's not fair." He began to weep quietly.

"Don't do that," said the old man. "Listen. Listen to me. You're still alive, aren't you? Here? Now? You still *feel*, don't *you*?"

Thomas Wolfe waited for a minute and then he said, "Yes."

"All right, then." The old man pressed forward on the dark air. "I've brought you here, I've given you another chance, Tom. An extra month or so. Do you think *I* haven't grieved for you? When I read your books and saw your gravestone there, three centuries worn by rains and wind, boy, don't you imagine how it killed me to think of your talent gone away? Well, it did! It killed me, Tom. And I spent my money to find a way to you. You've got a respite, not long, not long at all. Professor Bolton says that, with luck, he can hold the channels open through time for eight weeks. He can keep you here that long, and only that long. In that interval, Tom, you must write the book you've wanted to write—no, not the book you were working on for them, son, no, for they're dead and gone and it can't be changed. No, this time it's a book for us, Tom, for us the living, that's the book we want. A book you can leave with us, for you, a book bigger and better in every way than anything you ever wrote; say you'll *do* it, Tom, say you'll forget about that stone and that hospital for eight weeks and start to work for us, will you, Tom, will you?"

The lights came slowly on. Tom Wolfe stood tall at the window, looking out, his face huge and tired and pale. He watched the rockets on the sky of early evening. "I imagine I don't realize what you've done for me," he said. "You've given me a little more time, and time is the thing I love most and need, the thing I always hated and fought against, and the only way I can show my appreciation is by doing as you say." He hesitated. "And when I'm finished, then what?"

"Back to your hospital in 1938, Tom."

"Must I?"

"We can't change time. We borrowed you for five minutes. We'll return you to your hospital cot five minutes after you left it. That way, we upset nothing. It's all been written. You can't hurt us in the future by living here now with us, but, if you refused to go back, you could hurt the past, and resultantly, the future, make it into some sort of chaos."

"Eight weeks," said Thomas Wolfe.

"Eight weeks."

"And the Mars rocket leaves in an hour?"

"Yes."

"I'll need pencils and paper."

"Here they are."

"I'd better go get ready. Good-bye, Mr. Field."

"Good luck, Tom."

Six o'clock. The sun setting. The sky turning to wine. The big house quiet. The old man shivering in the heat until Professor Bolton entered. "Bolton, how is he getting on, how was he at the port; tell me?"

Bolton smiled. "What a monster he is, so big they had to make a special uniform for him! You should've seen him, walking around, lifting up every-thing, sniffing like a great hound, talking, his eyes looking at everyone, excited as a ten-year-old!"

"God bless him, oh, God bless him! Bolton, can you keep him here as long as you say?"

Bolton frowned. "He doesn't belong here, you know. If our power should falter, he'd be snapped back to his own time, like a puppet on a rub-ber band. We'll try and keep him, I assure you."

"You've got to, you understand, you can't let him go back until he's fin-ished with his book. You've—"

"Look," said Bolton. He pointed to the sky. On it was a silver rocket.

"Is that him?" asked the old man.

"That's Tom Wolfe," replied Bolton. "Going to Mars."

"Give 'em hell, Tom, give 'em hell!" shouted the old man, lifting both fists. They watched the rocket fire into space.

＊ By midnight, the story was coming through.

Henry William Field sat in his library. On his desk was a machine that hummed. It repeated words that were being written out beyond the Moon. It scrawled them in black pencil, in facsimile of Tom Wolfe's fevered hand a million miles away. The old man waited for a pile of them to collect and then he seized them and read them aloud to the room where Bolton and the servants stood listening. He read the words about space and time and travel, about a large man and a large journey and how it was in the long midnight and coldness of space, and how a man could be hungry enough to take all of it and ask for more. He read the words that were full of fire and thunder and mystery.

Space was like October, wrote Thomas Wolfe. He said things about its darkness and its loneliness and man so small in it. The eternal and timeless October, was one of the things he said. And then he told of the rocket itself, the smell and the feel of the metal of the rocket, and the sense of destiny and wild exultancy to at last leave Earth behind, all problems and all sad-nesses, and go seeking a bigger problem and a bigger sadness. Oh, it was fine writing, and it said what had to be said about space and man and his small rockets out there alone.

The old man read until he was hoarse, and then Bolton read, and then the others, far into the night, when the machine stopped transcribing words and they knew that Tom Wolfe was in bed, then, on the rocket, flying to Mars, probably not asleep, no, he wouldn't sleep for hours yet, no, lying awake, like a boy the night before a circus, not believing the big jeweled black tent is up and the circus is on, with ten billion blazing performers on the high wires and the invisible trapezes of space.

"There," breathed the old man, gentling aside the last pages of the first chapter. "What do you think of that, Bolton?"

"It's good."

"Good hell!" shouted Field. "It's wonderful! Read it again, sit down, read it again, damn you!"

It kept coming through, one day following another, for ten hours at a time. The stack of yellow papers on the floor, scribbled on, grew immense in a week, unbelievable in two weeks, absolutely impossible in a month.

"Listen to this!" cried the old man, and read.

"And this!" he said.

"And this chapter here, and this little novel here, it just came through, Bolton, titled *The Space War*, a complete novel on how it feels to fight a space war. Tom's been talking to people, soldiers, officers, men, veterans of space. He's got it all here. And here's a chapter called 'The Long Midnight,' and here's one on the Negro colonization of Mars, and here's a character sketch of a Martian, absolutely priceless!"

Bolton cleared his throat. "Mr. Field?"

"Yes, yes, don't bother me."

"I've some bad news, sir."

Field jerked his gray head up. "What? The time element?"

"You'd better tell Wolfe to hurry his work. The connection may break sometime this week," said Bolton, softly.

"I'll give you anything, anything if you keep it going!"

"It's not money, Mr. Field. It's just plain physics right now. I'll do everything I can. But you'd better warn him."

The old man shriveled in his chair and was small. "But you can't take him away from me now, not when he's doing so well. You should see the outline he sent through an hour ago, the stories, the sketches. Here, here's one on spatial tides, another on meteors. Here's a short novel begun, called *Thistledown and Fire*—"

"I'm sorry."

"If we lose him now, can we get him again?"

"I'd be afraid to tamper too much."

The old man was frozen. "Only one thing to do then. Arrange to have

Wolfe type his work, if possible, or dictate it, to save time; rather than have him use pencil and paper, he's got to use a machine of some sort. See to it!"

The machine ticked away by the hour into the night and into the dawn and through the day. The old man slept only in faint dozes, blinking awake when the machine stuttered to life, and all of space and travel and existence came to him through the mind of another:

"... *the great starred meadows of space* ..."

The machine jumped.

"Keep at it, Tom, show them!" The old man waited.

The phone rang.

It was Bolton.

"We can't keep it up, Mr. Field. The continuum device will absolute out within the hour."

"Do something!"

"I can't."

The teletype chattered. In a cold fascination, in a horror, the old man watched the black lines form.

"... *the Martian cities, immense and unbelievable, as numerous as stones thrown from some great mountain in a rushing and incredible avalanche, resting at last in shining mounds* ..."

"Tom!" cried the old man.

"Now," said Bolton, on the phone.

The teletype hesitated, typed a word, and fell silent.

"Tom!" screamed the old man.

He shook the teletype.

"It's no use," said the telephone voice. "He's gone. I'm shutting off the time machine."

"No! Leave it on!"

"But—"

"You heard me—leave it! We're not sure he's gone."

"He is. It's no use, we're wasting energy."

"Waste it, then!"

He slammed the phone down.

He turned to the teletype, to the unfinished sentence.

"Come on, Tom, they can't get rid of you that way, you won't let them, will you, boy, come on. Tom, show them, you're big, you're bigger than time or space or their damned machines, you're strong and you've a will like iron, Tom, show them, don't let them send you back!"

The teletype snapped one key.

The old man bleated. "Tom! You *are* there, aren't you? Can you still write? Write, Tom, keep it coming, as long as you keep it rolling, Tom, they can't send you back!"

The, typed the machine.

"More, Tom, more!"

Odors of, clacked the machine.

"Yes?"

Mars, typed the machine, and paused. A minute's silence. The machine spaced, skipped a paragraph, and began:

The odors of Mars, the cinnamons and cold spice winds, the winds of cloudy dust and winds of powerful bone and ancient pollen—

"Tom, you're still alive!"

For answer the machine, in the next ten hours, slammed out six chapters of *Flight Before Fury* in a series of fevered explosions.

✳ "Today makes six weeks, Bolton, six whole weeks, Tom gone, on Mars, through the Asteroids. Look here, the manuscripts. Ten thousand words a day, he's driving himself, I don't know when he sleeps, or if he eats, I don't care, he doesn't either, he only wants to get it done, because he knows the time is short."

"I can't understand it," said Bolton. "The power failed because our relays wore out. It took us three days to manufacture and replace the particular channel relays necessary to keep the Time Element steady, and yet Wolfe hung on. There's a personal factor here, Lord knows what, we didn't take into account. Wolfe lives here, in this time, when he *is* here, and can't be snapped back, after all. Time isn't as flexible as we imagined. We used the wrong simile. It's not like a rubber band. More like osmosis; the penetration of membranes by liquids, from Past to Present, but we've got to send him back, can't keep him here, there'd be a void there, a derangement. The one thing that really keeps him here now is himself, his drive, his desire, his work. After it's over he'll go back as naturally as pouring water from a glass."

"I don't care about reasons, all I know is Tom is finishing it. He has the old fire and description, and something else, something more, a searching of values that supersede time and space. He's done a study of a woman left behind on Earth while the damn rocket heroes leap into space that's beautiful, objective, and subtle; he calls it 'Day of the Rocket,' and it is nothing more than an afternoon of a typical suburban housewife who lives as her ancestral mothers lived, in a house, raising her children, her life not much different from a cavewoman's, in the midst of the splendor of science and the trumpetings of space projectiles; a true and steady and subtle study of her wishes and frustrations. Here's another manuscript, called 'The Indians,' in which he refers to the Martians as Cherokees and Iroquois and Blackfoots, the Indian nations of space, destroyed and driven back. Have a drink, Bolton, have a drink!"

✳ Tom Wolfe returned to Earth at the end of eight weeks.

He arrived in fire as he had left in fire, and his huge steps were burned across space, and in the library of Henry William Field's house were towers of yellow paper, with lines of black scribble and type on them, and these were to be separated out into the six sections of a masterwork that, through endurance, and a knowing that the sands were dwindling from the glass, had mushroomed day after day.

Tom Wolfe came back to Earth and stood in the library of Henry William Field's house and looked at the massive outpourings of his heart and his hand and when the old man said, "Do you want to read it, Tom?" he shook his great head and replied, putting back his thick mane of dark hair with his big pale hand, "No. I don't dare start on it. If I did, I'd want to take it home with me. And I can't do that, can I?"

"No, Tom, you can't."

"No matter *how* much I wanted to?"

"No, that's the way it is. You never wrote another novel in that year, Tom. What was written here must stay here, what was written there must stay there. There's no touching it."

"I see." Tom sank down into a chair with a great sigh. "I'm tired. I'm mightily tired. It's been hard, but it's been good. What day is it?"

"This is the fifty-sixth day."

"The *last* day?"

The old man nodded and they were both silent awhile.

"Back to 1938 in the stone cemetery," said Tom Wolfe, eyes shut. "I don't like that. I wish I didn't know about that, it's a horrible thing to know." His voice faded and he put his big hands over his face and held them tightly there.

The door opened. Bolton let himself in and stood behind Tom Wolfe's chair, a small vial in his hand.

"What's that?" asked the old man.

"An extinct virus. Pneumonia. Very ancient and very evil," said Bolton. "When Mr. Wolfe came through, I had to cure him of his illness, of course, which was immensely easy with the techniques we know today, in order to put him in working condition for his job, Mr. Field. I kept this pneumonia culture. Now that he's going back, he'll have to be reinoculated with the disease."

"Otherwise?"

Tom Wolfe looked up.

"Otherwise, he'd get well, in 1938."

Tom Wolfe arose from his chair. "You mean, get well, walk around, back there, be well, and cheat the mortician?"

"That's what I mean."

Tom Wolfe stared at the vial and one of his hands twitched. "What if I destroyed the virus and refused to let you inoculate me?"

"You can't do that!"

"But—supposing?"

"You'd ruin things."

"What things?"

"The pattern, life, the way things are and were, the things that can't be changed. You can disrupt it. There's only one sure thing, you're to die, and I'm to see to it."

Wolfe looked at the door. "I could run off."

"We control the machine. You wouldn't get out of the house. I'd have you back here, by force, and inoculated. I anticipated some such trouble when the time came; there are five men waiting down below. One shout from me—you see, it's useless. There, that's better. Here now."

Wolfe had moved back and now had turned to look at the old man and the window and this huge house. "I'm afraid I must apologize. I don't want to die. So very much I don't want to die."

The old man came to him and took his hand. "Think of it this way: you've had two more months than anyone could expect from life, and you've turned out another book, a last book, a fine book, think of that."

"I want to thank you for this," said Thomas Wolfe, gravely. "I want to thank both of you. I'm ready." He rolled up his sleeve. "The inoculation."

And while Bolton bent to his task, with his free hand Thomas Wolfe penciled two black lines across the top of the first manuscript and went on talking:

"There's a passage from one of my old books," he said, scowling to remember it. "*. . . of wandering forever and the Earth . . . Who owns the Earth? Did we want the Earth? That we should wander on it? Did we need the Earth that we were never still upon it? Whoever needs the Earth shall have the Earth; he shall be upon it, he shall rest within a little place, he shall dwell in one small room forever . . .*"

Wolfe was finished with the remembering.

"Here's my last book," he said, and on the empty yellow paper facing the manuscript he blocked out vigorous huge black letters with pressures of the pencil:

FOREVER AND THE EARTH, by Thomas Wolfe.

He picked up a ream of it and held it tightly in his hands, against his chest, for a moment. "I wish I could take it back with me. It's like parting with my son." He gave it a slap and put it aside and immediately thereafter gave his quick hand into that of his employer, and strode across the room, Bolton after him, until he reached the door where he stood framed in the late-afternoon light, huge and magnificent. "Good-bye, good-bye!" he cried.

The door slammed. Tom Wolfe was gone.

✳ They found him wandering in the hospital corridor.

"Mr. Wolfe!"

"What?"

"Mr. Wolfe, you gave us a scare, we thought you were gone!"

"Gone?"

"Where did you go?"

"Where? Where?" He let himself be led through the midnight corridors. "Where? Oh, if I *told* you where, you'd never believe."

"Here's your bed, you shouldn't have left it."

Deep into the white death bed, which smelled of pale, clean mortality awaiting him, a mortality which had the hospital odor in it; the bed which, as he touched it, folded him into fumes and white starched coldness.

"Mars, Mars," whispered the huge man, late at night. "My best, my very best, my really fine book, yet to be written, yet to be printed, in another year, three centuries away . . ."

"You're tired."

"Do you really think so?" murmured Thomas Wolfe. "Was it a dream? Perhaps. A good dream."

His breathing faltered. Thomas Wolfe was dead.

✳ In the passing years, flowers are found on Tom Wolfe's grave. And this is not unusual, for many people travel to linger there. But these flowers appear each night. They seem to drop from the sky. They are the color of an autumn moon, their blossoms are immense, and they burn and sparkle their cold, long petals in a blue and white fire. And when the dawn wind blows they drip away into a silver rain, a shower of white sparks on the air. Tom Wolfe has been dead many, many years, but these flowers never cease. . . .

THE HANDLER

MR. BENEDICT CAME OUT OF HIS LITTLE HOUSE. He stood on the porch, painfully shy of the sun and inferior to people. A little dog trotted by with clever eyes; so clever that Mr. Benedict could not meet its gaze. A small child peered through the wrought-iron gate around the graveyard, near the church, and Mr. Benedict winced at the pale, penetrant curiosity of the child.

"You're the funeral man," said the child.

Cringing within himself, Mr. Benedict did not speak.

"You own the church?" asked the child, finally.

"Yes," said Mr. Benedict.

"And the funeral place?"

"Yes," said Mr. Benedict bewilderedly.

"And the yards and the stones and the graves?" wondered the child.

"Yes," said Benedict, with some show of pride. And it was true. An amazing thing it was. A stroke of business luck really, that had kept him busy and humming nights over long years. First he had landed the church and the churchyard, with a few green-mossed tombs, when the Baptist people moved uptown. Then he had built himself a fine little mortuary, in Gothic style, of course, and covered it with ivy, and then added a small house for himself, way in back. It was very convenient to die for Mr. Benedict. He handled you in and out of buildings with a minimum of confusion and a maximum of synthetic benediction. No need of a funeral procession! declared his large ads in the morning paper. Out of the church and into the earth, slick as a whistle. Nothing but the finest preservatives used!

The child continued to stare at him and he felt like a candle blown out in the wind. He was so inferior. Anything that lived or moved made him feel apologetic and melancholy. He was continually agreeing with people, never daring to argue or shout or say no. Whoever you might be, if Mr. Benedict met you on the street he would look up your nostrils or perceive your ears or examine your hairline with his little shy, wild eyes and never look you straight in your eye, and he would hold your hand between his cold ones as if your hand was a precious gift, as he said to you:

"You are definitely, irrevocably, believably correct."

But, always, when you talked to him, you felt he never heard a word you said.

Now, he stood on his porch and said, "You are a sweet little child," to the little staring child, in fear that the child might not like him.

Mr. Benedict walked down the steps and out the gate, without once looking at his little mortuary building. He saved that pleasure for later. It was very important that things took the right precedence. It wouldn't pay to think with joy of the bodies awaiting his talents in the mortuary building. No, it was better to follow his usual day-after-day routine. He would let the conflict began.

He knew just where to go to get himself enraged. Half of the day he spent traveling from place to place in the little town, letting the superiority of the living neighbors overwhelm him, letting his own inferiority dissolve him, bathe him in perspiration, tie his heart and brain into trembling knots.

He spoke with Mr. Rodgers, the druggist, idle, senseless morning talk. And he saved and put away all the little slurs and intonations and insults that Mr. Rodgers sent his way. Mr. Rodgers always had some terrible thing to say about a man in the funeral profession. "Ha, ha," laughed Mr. Benedict at the latest joke upon himself, and he wanted to cry with miserable violence. "There you are, you cold one," said Mr. Rodgers on this particular morning. "Cold one," said Mr. Benedict, "ha, ha!"

Outside the drugstore, Mr. Benedict met up with Mr. Stuyvesant, the contractor. Mr. Stuyvesant looked at his watch to estimate just how much time he dared waste on Benedict before trumping up some appointment. "Oh, hello, Benedict," shouted Stuyvesant. "How's business? I bet you're going at it tooth and nail. Did you get it? I said, I bet you're going at it tooth and—"

"Yes, yes," chuckled Mr. Benedict vaguely. "And how is your business, Mr. Stuyvesant?" "Say, how do your hands get so cold, Benny, old man? That's a cold shake you got there. You just get done embalming a frigid woman! Hey, that's not bad. You heard what I said?" roared Mr. Stuyvesant, pounding him on the back. "Good, good!" cried Mr. Benedict, with a flesh-less smile. "Good day."

On it went, person after person. Mr. Benedict, pummeled on from one to the next, was the lake into which all refuse was thrown. People began with little pebbles and then when Mr. Benedict did not ripple or protest, they heaved a stone, a brick, a boulder. There was no bottom to Mr. Bene-dict, no splash and no settling. The lake did not answer.

As the day passed he became more helpless and enraged with them, and he walked from building to building and had more little meetings and con-versations and hated himself with a very real, masochistic pleasure. But the thing that kept him going most of all was the thought of the night pleasures to come. So he inflicted himself again and again with these stu-pid, pompous bullies and bowed to them and held his hands like little bis-cuits before his stomach, and asked no more than to be sneered at.

"There you are, meat-chopper," said Mr. Flinger, the delicatessen man. "How are all your corned beeves and pickled brains?"

Things worked to a crescendo of inferiority. With a final kettle-drumming of insult and terrible self-effacement, Mr. Benedict, seeking wildly the correct time from his wrist-watch, turned and ran back through the town. He was at his peak, he was all ready now, ready to work, ready to do what must be done, and enjoy himself. The awful part of the day was over, the good part was now to begin!

He ran eagerly up the steps to his mortuary.

The room waited like a fall of snow. There were white hummocks and pale delineations of things recumbent under sheets in the dimness.

The door burst open.

Mr. Benedict, framed in a flow of light stood in the door, head back, one hand upraised in dramatic salute, the other hand upon the door-knob in unnatural rigidity.

He was the puppet-master come home.

✳ He stood a long minute in the very center of his theater. In his head applause, perhaps, thundered. He did not move, but lowered his head in abject appreciation of this kind, applauding audience.

He carefully removed his coat, hung it up, got himself into a fresh white smock, buttoned the cuffs with professional crispness, then washed his hands together as he looked around at his very good friends.

It had been a fine week; there were any number of family relics lying under the sheets, and as Mr. Benedict stood before them he felt himself grow and grow and tower and stretch over them.

"Like Alice!" he cried to himself in surprise. "Taller, taller. Curiouser and curiouser!" He flexed his hands straight out and up.

He had never gotten over his initial incredulity when in the room with the dead. He was both delighted and bewildered to discover that here he was master of peoples, here he might do what he wished with men, and they must, by necessity, be polite and cooperative with him. They could not run away. And now, as on other days, he felt himself released and resilient, growing, growing like Alice. "Oh, so tall, oh, so tall, so very tall . . . until my head . . . bumps . . . the ceiling."

He walked about among the sheeted people. He felt the same way he did when coming from a picture show late at night, very strong, very alert, very certain of himself. He felt that everyone was watching him as he left a picture show, and that he was very handsome and very correct and brave and all the things that the picture hero was, his voice oh, so resonant, persuasive and he had the right lilt to his left eyebrow and the right tap with his cane. And sometimes this movie-induced hypnosis lasted all the way home and persisted into sleep. Those were the only two times in his living he felt miraculous and fine, at the picture show, or here—in his own little theater of the cold.

He walked along the sleeping rows, noting each name on its white card.

"Mrs. Walters, Mr. Smith. Miss Brown. Mr. Andrews. Ah, good afternoon, one and all!"

"How are you today, Mrs. Shellmund?" he wanted to know, lifting a sheet as if looking for a child under a bed. "You're looking splendid, dear lady."

Mrs. Shellmund had never spoken to him in her life, she'd always gone by like a large, white statue with roller skates hidden under her skirts, which gave her an elegant, gliding, imperturbable rush.

"My dear Mrs. Shellmund," he said, pulling up a chair and regarding her through a magnifying glass. "Do you realize, my lady, that you have a sebaceous condition of the pores? You were quite waxen in life. Pore trouble. Oil and grease and pimples. A rich, rich diet, Mrs. Shellmund, there was your trouble. Too many frosties and spongie cakes and cream candies.

You always prided yourself on your brain, Mrs. Shellmund, and thought I was like a dime under your toe, or a penny, really. But you kept that wonderful, priceless brain of yours afloat in parfaits and fizzes and limeades and sodas and were so very superior to me that now, Mrs. Shellmund, here is what shall happen. . . ."

He did a neat operation on her. Cutting the scalp in a circle, he lifted it off then lifted out the brain. Then he prepared a cake-confectioner's little sugar-bellows and squirted her empty head full of little whipped cream and crystal ribbons, stars and frollops, in pink, white and green, and on top he printed in a fine pink scroll, "SWEET DREAMS," and put the skull back on and sewed it in place and hid the marks with wax and powder. "So there!" he said, finished.

He walked on to the next table.

"Good afternoon, Mr. Wren. Good afternoon. And how is the master of the racial hatreds today, Mr. Wren? Pure, white, laundered Mr. Wren. Clean as snow, white as linen, Mr. Wren, you are. The man who hated Jews and Negroes. Minorities, Mr. Wren, minorities." He pulled back the sheet. Mr. Wren stared up with glassy, cold eyes. "Mr. Wren, look upon a member of a minority. Myself. The minority of inferiors, those who speak not above a whisper, those afraid of talking aloud, those frightened little nonentities, mice. Do you know what I am going to do with you, Mr. Wren? First, let us draw your blood from you, intolerant friend." The blood was drawn off. "Now—the injection of, you might say, embalming fluid."

Mr. Wren, snow-white, linen-pure, lay with the fluid going in him.

Mr. Benedict laughed.

Mr. Wren turned black; black as dirt, black as night.

The embalming fluid was—ink.

"And hello to you, Edmund Worth!" What a handsome body Worth had! Powerful, with muscles pinned from huge bone to huge bone, and a chest like a boulder. Women had grown speechless when he walked by, men had stared with envy and hoped they might borrow that body some night and ride home in it to the wife and give her a nice surprise. But Worth's body had always been his own, and he had applied it to those tasks and pleasures which made him a conversational topic among all peoples who enjoyed sin.

"And now, here you are," said Mr. Benedict, looking down at the fine body with pleasure. For a moment he was lost in memory of his own body in his own past.

He had once tried strangling himself with one of those apparati you nail in a doorway and chuck under your jawbone and pull yourself up on, hoping to add an inch to his ridiculously short frame. To counteract his deadly pale skin he had lain in the sun, but he boiled and his skin fell off in pink leaflets, leaving only more pink, moist, sensitive skin. And what could he do about the eyes from which his mind peered?—those close-set, glassy little eyes and the tiny wounded mouth. You can repaint houses, burn trash, move from the slum, shoot your mother, buy new clothes, get a car, make money, change all those outer environmentals for something new. But what's the brain to do when caught like cheese in the throat of a mouse? His own environment thus betrayed him; his own skin, body, color, voice gave him no chance to extend out into that vast, bright world where people tickled ladies' chins and kissed their mouths and shook hands with friends and traded aromatic cigars.

Thinking in this fashion, Mr. Benedict stood over the magnificent body of Edmund Worth.

He severed Worth's head, put it in a coffin on a small, satin pillow, facing up, then he placed one hundred and ninety pounds of bricks in the coffin and arranged some pillows inside a black coat and a white shirt and tie to look like the upper body, and covered the whole with a blanket of blue velvet, up to the chin. It was a fine illusion.

The body itself he placed in a refrigerating vault.

"When I die, I shall leave specific orders, Mr. Worth, that my head be severed and buried, joined to your body. By that time I will have acquired an assistant willing to perform such a rascally act, for money. If one cannot have a body worthy of love in life, one can at least gain such a body in death. Thank you."

He slammed the lid on Edmund Worth.

Since it was a growing and popular habit in the town for people to be buried with the coffin lids closed over them during the service, this gave Mr. Benedict great opportunities to vent his repressions on his hapless guests. Some he locked in their boxes upside down, some face down, or making obscene gestures. He had the most utterly wondrous fun with a group of old maiden ladies who were mashed in an auto on their way to an afternoon tea. They were famous gossips, always with heads together over some choice bit. What the onlookers at the triple funeral did not know (all three casket lids were shut) was that, as in life, all three were crowded into one casket, heads together in eternal, cold, petrified gossip. The other two caskets were filled with pebbles and shells and ravels of gingham. It was a nice service. Everybody cried. "Those three inseparables, at last separated." Everybody sobbed.

"Yes," said Mr. Benedict, having to hide his face in his grief.

Not lacking for a sense of justice, Mr. Benedict buried one rich man stark naked. A poor man he buried wound in gold cloth, with five-dollar gold pieces for buttons and twenty-dollar coins on each eyelid. A lawyer he did not bury at all, but burned him in the incinerator—his coffin contained nothing but a pole-cat, trapped in the woods one Sunday.

An old maid, at her service one afternoon, was the victim of a terrible device. Under the silken comforter, parts of an old man had been buried with her. There she lay, insulted by cold organs, being made cold love to by hidden hands, hidden and planted other things. The shock showed on her face, somewhat.

So Mr. Benedict moved from body to body in his mortuary that afternoon, talking to all the sheeted figures, telling them his every secret. The final body for the day was the body of one Merriwell Blythe, an ancient man afflicted with spells and comas. Mr. Blythe had been brought in for dead several times, but each time had revived in time to prevent premature burial.

Mr. Benedict pulled back the sheet from Mr. Blythe's face.

Mr. Merriwell Blythe fluttered his eyes.

"Ah!" and Mr. Benedict let fall the sheet.

"You!" screamed the voice under the sheet.

Mr. Benedict fell against the slab, suddenly shaken and sick.

"Get me up from here!" cried the voice of Mr. Merriwell Blythe.

"You're alive!" said Mr. Benedict, jerking aside the sheet.

"Oh, the things I've heard, the things I've listened to the last hour!" wailed the old man on the slab, rolling his eyes about in his head in white orbits. "Lying here; not able to move, and hearing you talk the things you talk! Oh, you dark, dark thing, you awful thing, you fiend, you monster, get me up from here. I'll tell the mayor and the council and everyone; oh you dark, dark thing! You defiler and sadist, you perverted scoundrel, you terrible man, wait'll I tell, I tell on you!" shrieked the old man, frothing. "Get me up from here!" "No!" said Mr. Benedict, falling to his knees. "Oh, you terrible man!" sobbed Mr. Merriwell Blythe. "To think this has gone on in our town all these years and we never knew the things you did to people! Oh, you monstrous monster!" "No," whispered Mr. Benedict, trying to get up, falling down, palsied and in terror. "The things you said," accused the old man in dry contempt. "The things you do!" "Sorry," whispered Mr. Benedict.

The old man tried to rise. "Don't!" said Mr. Benedict, and held onto him. "Let go of me!" said the old man. "No," said Mr. Benedict. He reached for a hypodermic and stabbed the old man in the arm with it. "You!" cried the old man, wildly, to all the sheeted figures. "Help me!" He squinted blindly at the window, at the churchyard below with the leaning stones. "You, out there, too, under the stones, help! Listen!" The old man fell back, whistling and frothing. He knew he was dying. "All, listen," he babbled. "He's done this to me, and you, and you, all of you, he's done too much too long. Don't take it! Don't, don't let him do anymore to anyone!" The old man licked away the stuff from his lips, growing weaker. "Do something to him!"

Mr. Benedict stood there, shocked, and said, "They can't do anything to me. They can't. I say they can't."

"Out of your graves!" wheezed the old man. "Help me! Tonight, or tomorrow, or soon, but jump up and fix him, oh, this horrible man!" And he wept many tears.

"How foolish," said Mr. Benedict numbly. "You're dying and foolish." Mr. Benedict could not move his lips. His eyes were wide. "Go on and die now, quickly."

"Everybody up!" shouted the old man. "Everybody out! Help!"

"Please don't talk anymore," said Mr. Benedict. "I really don't like to listen."

The room was suddenly very dark. It was night. It was getting late. The old man raved on and on, getting weaker. Finally, smiling, he said, "They've taken a lot from you, horrible man. Tonight, they'll do something."

The old man died.

People say there was an explosion that night in the graveyard. Or rather a series of explosions, a smell of strange things, a movement, a violence, a raving. There was much light and lightning, and a kind of rain, and the church bells hammered and slung about in the belfry, and stones toppled, and things swore oaths, and things flew through the air, and there was a chasing and a screaming, and many shadows and all the lights in the mortuary blazing on, and things moving inside and outside in swift jerks and shamblings, windows broke, doors were torn from hinges, leaves from trees, iron gates clattered, and in the end there was a picture of Mr. Benedict running about, vanishing, the lights out, suddenly, and a tortured scream that could only be from Mr. Benedict himself.

After that—nothing. Quiet.

The town people entered the mortuary the next morning. They searched the mortuary building and the church, and then they went out into the graveyard.

And they found nothing but blood, a vast quantity of blood, sprinkled and thrown and spread everywhere you could possibly look, as if the heavens had bled profusely in the night.

But not a sign of Mr. Benedict.

"Where could he be?" everybody wondered.

"How should *we* know?" everybody replied, confounded.

And then they had the answer.

Walking through the graveyard they stood in deep tree shadows where the stones, row on row, were old and time-erased and leaning. No birds sang in the trees. The sunlight which finally managed to pierce the thick leaves, was like a light-bulb illumination, weak, frail, unbelievable, theatrical, thin.

They stopped by one tombstone. "Here, now!" they exclaimed.

Others paused and bent over the grayish, moss-flecked stone, and cried out.

Freshly scratched, as if by feebly, frantic, hasty fingers (in fact, as if scratched by fingernails the writing was *that* new) was the name:

"MR. BENEDICT"

"Look over here!" someone else cried. Everybody turned. "This one, this stone, and this one, and *this* one, too!" cried the villager, pointing to five other gravestones.

Everybody hurried around, looking and recoiling.

Upon each and every stone, scratched by fingernail scratchings, the same message appeared:

"MR. BENEDICT"

The town people were stunned.

"But that's impossible," objected one of them, faintly. "He *couldn't* be buried under *all* these gravestones!"

They stood there for one long moment. Instinctively they all looked at one another nervously in the silence and the tree darkness. They all waited for an answer. With fumbling, senseless lips, one of them replied, simply:

"*Couldn't he?*"

GETTING THROUGH
SUNDAY SOMEHOW

It was Sunday noon and the fog touching at the hotel windows when the mist did not and rain rinsing the fog and then leaving off to let the mist return and coffee after lunch was prolonging itself into tea with the promise of high tea ahead and beyond that the Buttery pub opening belowstairs, or the Second Coming and the only sound was porcelain cups against porcelain teeth and the whisper of silk or the creak of shoes until at last a swinging door leading from the small library–writing room squealed softly open and an old man, holding on to the air should he fall, shuffled out, stopped, looked around at everyone, slowly, and said in a calm drear voice:

"Getting through Sunday somehow?"

Then he turned, shuffled back through, and let the door creak whisper shut.

Sunday in Dublin.

The words are Doom itself.

Sunday in Dublin.

Drop such words and they never strike bottom. They just fall through emptiness toward five in the gray afternoon.

Sunday in Dublin. How to get through it somehow.

Sound the funeral bells. Yank the covers up over your ears. Hear the hiss of the black-feathered wreath as it rustles, hung on your silent door. Listen to those empty streets below your hotel room waiting to gulp you if you venture forth before noon. Feel the mist sliding its wet flannel tongue under the window ledges, licking hotel roofs, its great bulk dripping of ennui.

Sunday, I thought. Dublin. The pubs shut tight until late afternoon. The cinemas sold out two or three weeks in advance. Nothing to do but perhaps go stare at the uriny lions at the Phoenix Park Zoo, at the vultures looking as though they'd fallen, covered with glue, into the ragpickers' bin. Wander by the River Liffey, see the fog-colored waters. Wander in the alleys, see the Liffey-colored skies.

No, I thought wildly, go back to bed, wake me at sunset, feed me high tea, tuck me in again, good night, all!

But I staggered out, a hero, and in a faint panic at noon considered the day outside from the corners of my eyes. There it lay, a deserted corridor of hours, colored like the upper side of my tongue on a dim morn. Even God must be bored with days like this in northern lands. I could not resist thinking of Sicily, where any Sunday is a fete in regalia, a celebratory fireworks parade as springtime flocks of chickens and humans strut and pringle the warm pancake-batter alleys, waving their combs, their hands, their feet, tilting their sun-blazed eyes, while music in free gifts leaps or is thrown from each never-shut window.

But Dublin! Dublin! Ah, you great dead brute of a city! I thought, peering from the hotel lobby window at the rained-on, sooted-over corpse. Here are two coins for your eyes!

Then I opened the door and stepped out into all of that criminal Sunday which awaited only me.

✳ I shut another door in The Four Provinces. I stood in the deep silence of this Sabbath pub. I moved noiselessly to whisper for the best drink and stood a long while nursing my soul. Nearby, an old man was similarly engaged in finding the pattern of his life in the depths of his glass. Ten minutes must have passed when, very slowly, the old man raised his head to stare deep beyond the fly specks on the mirror, beyond me, beyond himself.

"What have I done," he mourned, "for a single mortal soul this day? Nothing! And that's why I feel so terrible destroyed."

I waited.

"The older I get," said the man, "the less I do for people. The less I do, the more I feel a prisoner at the bar. Smash and grab, that's me!"

"Well—" I said.

"No!" cried the old man. "It's an awesome responsibility when the world runs to hand you things. For an instance: sunsets. Everything pink and gold, looking like those melons they ship up from Spain. That's a gift, ain't it?"

"It is."

"Well, who do you thank for sunsets? And don't drag the Lord in the bar, now! Any remarks to Him are too quiet. I mean someone to grab and slap their back and say thanks for the fine early light this morn, boyo, or much obliged for the look of them damn wee flowers by the road this day, and the grass laying about in the wind. Those are gifts too, who'll deny it?"

"Not me," I said.

"Have you ever waked middle of the night and felt summer coming on for the first time, through the window, after the long cold? Did you shake your wife and tell her your gratitude? No, you lay there, a clod, chortling to yourself alone, you and the new weather! Do you see the pattern I'm at, now?"

"Clearly," I said.

"Then ain't you horribly guilty yourself? Don't the burden make you hunchback? All the lovely things you got from life, and no penny down? Ain't they hid in your dark flesh somewhere, lighting up your soul, them fine summers and easy falls, or maybe just the clean taste of stout here, all gifts, and you feeling the fool to go thank any mortal man for your fortune. What befalls chaps like us, I ask, who coin up all their gratitude for a life-time and spend none of it, misers that we be? One day, don't we crack down the beam and show the dry rot?"

"I never thought—"

"Think, man!" he cried. "You're American, ain't you, and young? Got the same natural gifts as me? But for lack of humbly thanking someone somewhere somehow, you're getting round in the shoulder and short in the breath. Act, man, before you're the walking dead!"

With this he lapsed quietly into the final half of his reverie, with the Guinness lapping a soft lace mustache slowly along his upper lip.

I stepped from the pub into the Sunday weather.

I stood looking at the gray-stone streets and the gray-stone clouds, watching the frozen people trudge by exhaling gray funeral plumes from their wintry mouths.

Days like this, I thought, all the things you never did catch up with you, unravel your laces, itch your beard. God help any man who hasn't paid his debts this day.

Drearily, I turned like a weathercock in a slow wind. I stood very still. I listened.

For it seemed the wind had shifted and now blew from the west country and brought with it a prickling and tingling: the strum of a harp.

"Well," I whispered.

As if a cork had been pulled, all the heavy gray sea waters vanished roaring down a hole in my shoe; I felt my sadness go.

And around the corner I went.

And there sat a little woman, not half as big as her harp, her hands held out in the shivering strings like a child feeling a fine clear rain.

The harp threads flurried; the sounds dissolved like shudders of disturbed water nudging a shore. "Danny Boy" leaped out of the harp. "Wearin' of the Green" sprang after, full-clothed. Then "Limerick Is My Town, Sean Liam Is My Name" and "The Loudest Wake That Ever Was." The harp sound was the kind of thing you feel when champagne, poured in a full big glass, prickles your eyelids, sprays soft on your brow.

Spanish oranges bloomed in my cheeks. My breath fifed my nostrils. My feet minced, hidden, a secret dancing in my motionless shoes.

The harp played "Yankee Doodle."

And then I turned sad again.

For look, I thought, she doesn't see her harp. She doesn't hear her music!

True. Her hands, all alone, jumped and frolicked on the air, picked and pringled the strings, two ancient spiders busy at webs quickly built, then, torn by wind, rebuilt. She let her fingers play abandoned, to themselves, while her face turned this way and that, as if she lived in a nearby house and need only glance out on occasion to see her hands had come to no harm.

"Ah . . ." My soul sighed in me.

Here's your chance! I almost shouted. Good God, of course!

But I held to myself and let her reap out the last full falling sheaves of "Yankee Doodle."

Then, heartbeat in throat, I said:

"You play beautifully."

Thirty pounds melted from my body.

The woman nodded and began "Summer on the Shore," her fingers weaving mantillas from mere breath.

"You play very beautifully indeed," I said.

Another twenty pounds fell from my limbs.

"When you play forty years," she said, "you don't notice."

"You play well enough to be in a theater."

"Be off with you!" Two sparrows pecked in the shuttling loom. "Why should I think of orchestras and bands?"

"It's indoors work," I said.

"My father," she said, while her hands went away and returned, "made this harp, played it fine, taught me how. God's sake, he said, keep out from under roofs!"

The old woman blinked, remembering. "Play out back, in front, around the sides of theaters, Da said, but don't play in where the music gets snuffed. Might as well harp in a coffin!"

"Doesn't this rain hurt your instrument?"

"It's inside places hurt harps with heat and steam, Da said. Keep it out, let it breathe, take on fine tones and timbres from the air. Besides, Da said, when people buy tickets, each thinks it's in him to yell if you don't play up, down, sideways, for him alone. Shy off from that, Da said; they'll call you handsome one year, brute the next. Get where they'll pass on by; if they like your song—hurrah! Those that don't will run from your life. That way, girl, you'll meet just those who lean from natural bent in your direction. Why closet yourself with demon fiends when you can live in the streets' fresh wind with abiding angels? But I do go on. Ah, now, why?"

She peered at me for the first time, like someone come from a dark room, squinting.

"Who are you?" she asked. "You set my tongue loose! What're you up to?"

"Up to no good until a minute ago when I came around this corner," I said. "Ready to knock over Nelson's pillar. Ready to pick a theater queue and brawl along it, half weeping and half blasphemous . . ."

"I don't see you doing it." Her hands wove out another yard of song. "What changed your mind?"

"You," I said.

I might have fired a cannon in her face.

"Me?" she said.

"You picked the day up off the stones, gave it a whack, set it running with a yell again."

"I did that?"

For the first time, I heard a few notes missing from the tune.

"Or, if you like, those hands of yours that go about their work without your knowing."

"The clothes must be washed, so you wash them."

I felt the iron weights gather in my limbs.

"Don't!" I said. "Why should we, coming by, be happy with this thing, and not you?"

She cocked her head; her hands moved slower still.

"And why should you bother with the likes of *me*?"

I stood before her, and could I tell what the man told me in the lulling quiet of The Four Provinces. Could I mention the hill of beauty that had risen to fill my soul through a lifetime, and myself with a toy sand-shovel doling it back to the world in dribs and drabs? Should I list all my debts to people on stages and silver screens who made me laugh or cry or just come alive, but no one in the dark theater to turn to and dare shout, "If you ever need help, I'm your friend!" Should I recall for her the man on a bus ten years before who chuckled so easy and light from the last seat that the sound of him melted everyone else to laughing warm and rollicking off out the doors, but with no one brave enough to pause and touch the man's arm and say, "Oh, man, you've favored us this night; Lord bless you!" Could I tell how she was just one part of a great account long owed and due? No, none of this could I tell.

"Imagine something."

"I'm ready," she said.

"Imagine you're an American writer, looking for material, far from home, wife, children, friends, in a cheerless hotel, on a bad gray day with naught but broken glass, chewed tobacco, and sooty snow in your soul. Imagine you're walking in the damned cold streets and turn a corner, and there's this little woman with a golden harp and everything she plays is another season—autumn, spring, summer—coming, going in a free-for-all. And the ice melts, the fog lifts, the wind burns with June, and ten years shuck off your life. Imagine, if you please."

She stopped her tune.

She was shocked at the sudden silence.

"You *are* daft," she said.

"Imagine you're me," I said. "Going back to my hotel now. And on my way I'd like to hear anything, anything at all. Play. And when you play, walk off around the corner and listen."

She put her hands to the strings and paused, working her mouth. I waited. At last she sighed, she moaned. Then suddenly she cried:

"Go on!"

"What . . . ?"

"You've made me all thumbs! Look! You've spoilt it!"

"I just wanted to thank—"

"Me behind!" she cried. "What a clod, what a brute! Mind your business! Do your work! Let be, man! Ah, these poor fingers, ruint, ruint!"

She stared at them and at me with a terrible glaring fixity.

"Get!" she shouted.

I ran around the corner in despair.

There! I thought, you've done it! By thanks destroyed, that's her story. Fool, why didn't you keep your mouth shut?

I sank, I leaned, against a building. A minute must have ticked by.

Please, woman, I thought, come on. Play. Not for me. Play for yourself. Forget what I said! *Please.*

I heard a few faint, tentative harp whispers.

Another pause.

Then, when the wind blew again, it brought the sound of her very slow playing.

The song itself was an old one, and I knew the words. I said them to myself.

> *Tread lightly to the music,*
> *Nor bruise the tender grass,*
> *Life passes in the weather*
> *As the sand storms down the glass.*

Yes, I thought, go on.

> *Drift easy in the shadows,*
> *Bask lazy in the sun,*
> *Give thanks for thirsts and quenches,*
> *For dines and wines and wenches.*
> *Give thought to life soon over,*
> *Tread softly on the clover,*
> *So bruise not any lover.*

> *So exit from the living,*
> *Salute and make thanksgiving,*
> *Then sleep when all is done,*
> *That sleep so dearly won.*

Why, I thought, how wise the old woman is,
Tread lightly to the music.

And I'd almost squashed her with praise.

So bruise not any lover.

And she was covered with bruises from my kind thoughtlessness.

But now, with a song that taught more than I could say, she was soothing herself.

I waited until she was well into the third chorus before I walked by again, tipping my hat.

But her eyes were shut and she was listening to what her hands were up to, moving in the strings like the fresh hands of a very young girl who has first known rain and washes her palms in its clear waterfalls.

She had gone through caring not at all, and then caring too much, and was now busy caring just the right way.

The corners of her mouth were pinned up, gently.

A close call, I thought. Very close.

I left them like two friends met in the street, the harp and herself.

I ran for the hotel to thank her the only way I knew how: to do my own work and do it well.

But on the way I stopped at The Four Provinces.

The music was still being treaded lightly and the clover was still being treaded softly, and no lover at all was being bruised as I let the pub door hush and looked all around for the man whose hand I most wanted to shake.

THE PUMPERNICKEL

MR. AND MRS. WELLES WALKED AWAY from the movie theater late at night and went into the quiet little store, a combination restaurant and delicatessen. They settled in a booth, and Mrs. Welles said, "Baked ham on pumpernickel." Mr. Welles glanced toward the counter, and there lay a loaf of pumpernickel.

"Why," he murmured, "pumpernickel . . . Druce's Lake . . ."

The night, the late hour, the empty restaurant—by now the pattern was familiar. Anything could set him off on a tide of reminiscence. The scent of autumn leaves, or midnight winds blowing, could stir him from himself, and memories would pour around him. Now in the unreal hour after the theater, in this lonely store, he saw a loaf of pumpernickel bread and, as on a thousand other nights, he found himself moved into the past.

"Druce's Lake," he said again.

"What?" His wife glanced up.

"Something I'd almost forgotten," said Mr. Welles. "In 1910, when I was twenty, I nailed a loaf of pumpernickel to the top of my bureau mirror. . . ."

In the hard, shiny crust of the bread, the boys at Druce's Lake had cut their names: *Tom, Nick, Bill, Alec, Paul, Jack.* The finest picnic in history! Their faces tanned as they rattled down the dusty roads. Those were the days when roads were *really* dusty; a fine brown talcum floured up after your car. And the lake was always twice as good to reach as it would be later in life when you arrived immaculate, clean, and unrumpled.

"That was the last time the old gang got together," Mr. Welles said.

After that, college, work, and marriage separated you. Suddenly you found yourself with some other group. And you never felt as comfortable or as much at ease again in all your life.

"I wonder," said Mr. Welles. "I like to think maybe we all *knew*, somehow, that this picnic might be the last we'd have. You first get that empty feeling the day after high-school graduation. Then, when a little time passes and no one vanishes immediately, you relax. But after a year you realize the old world is changing. And you want to do some one last thing before you lose one another. While you're all still friends, home from college for the summer, this side of marriage, you've got to have something like a last ride and a swim in the cool lake."

Mr. Welles remembered that rare summer morning, he and Tom lying under his father's Ford, reaching up their hands to adjust this or that, talking about machines and women and the future. While they worked, the day got warm. At last Tom said, "Why don't we drive out to Druce's Lake?"

As simple as that.

Yet, forty years later, you remember every detail of picking up the other fellows, everyone yelling under the green trees.

"Hey!" Alec beating everyone's head with the pumpernickel and laughing. "This is for extra sandwiches, later."

Nick had made the sandwiches that were already in the hamper—the garlic kind they would eat less of as the years passed and the girls moved in.

Then, squeezing three in the front, three in the rear, with their arms across one another's shoulders, they drove through the boiling, dusty countryside, with a cake of ice in a tin washtub to cool the beer they'd buy.

What was the special quality of that day that it should focus like a stereoscopic image, fresh and clear, forty years later? Perhaps each of them had had an experience like his own. A few days before the picnic, he had found a photograph of his father twenty-five years younger, standing with a group of friends at college. The photograph had disturbed him, made him aware as he had not been before of the passing of time, the swift flow of the years away from youth. A picture taken of him as he was now would, in twenty-five years, look as strange to his own children as his father's picture did to him—unbelievably young, a stranger out of a strange, never-returning time.

Was that how the final picnic had come about—with each of them knowing that in a few short years they would be crossing streets to avoid one another, or, if they met, saying, "We've got to have lunch sometime!" but never doing it? Whatever the reason, Mr. Welles could still hear the splashes as they'd plunged off the pier under a yellow sun. And then the beer and sandwiches underneath the shady trees.

We never ate that pumpernickel, Mr. Welles thought. Funny, if we'd been a bit hungrier, we'd have cut it up, and I wouldn't have been reminded of it by that loaf there on the counter.

Lying under the trees in a golden peace that came from beer and sun and male companionship, they promised that in ten years they would meet at the courthouse on New Year's Day, 1920, to see what they had done with their lives. Talking their rough easy talk, they carved their names in the pumpernickel.

"Driving home," Mr. Welles said, "we sang 'Moonlight Bay.'"

He remembered motoring along in the hot, dry night with their swimsuits damp on the jolting floorboards. It was a ride of many detours taken just for the hell of it, which was the best reason in the world.

"Good night." "So long." "Good night."

Then Welles was driving alone, at midnight, home to bed.

He nailed the pumpernickel to his bureau the next day.

"I almost cried when, two years later, my mother threw it in the incinerator while I was off at college."

"What happened in 1920?" asked his wife. "On New Year's Day?"

"Oh," said Mr. Welles. "I was walking by the courthouse, by accident, at noon. It was snowing. I heard the clock strike. Lord, I thought, we were supposed to meet here today! I waited five minutes. Not right in front of the courthouse, no. I waited across the street." He paused. "Nobody showed up."

He got up from the table and paid the bill. "And I'll take that loaf of unsliced pumpernickel there," he said.

When he and his wife were walking home, he said, "I've got a crazy idea. I often wondered what happened to everyone."

"Nick's still in town with his café."

"But what about the others?" Mr. Welles's face was getting pink and he was smiling and waving his hands. "They moved away. I think Tom's in Cincinnati." He looked quickly at his wife. "Just for the heck of it, I'll send him this pumpernickel!"

"Oh, but—"

"Sure!" He laughed, walking faster, slapping the bread with the palm of his hand. "Have him carve his name on it and mail it on to the others if he knows their addresses. And finally back to me, with all their names on it!"

"But," she said, taking his arm, "it'll only make you unhappy. You've done things like this so many times before and . . ."

He wasn't listening. Why do I never get these ideas by day? he thought. Why do I always get them after the sun goes down?

In the morning, first thing, he thought, I'll mail this pumpernickel off, by God, to Tom and the others. And when it comes back I'll have the loaf just as it was when it got thrown out and burned! Why not?

"Let's see," he said, as his wife opened the screen door and let him walk into the stuffy-smelling house to be greeted by silence and warm emptiness. "Let's see. We also sang 'Row Row Row Your Boat,' didn't we?"

✳ In the morning, he came down the hall stairs and paused a moment in the strong full sunlight, his face shaved, his teeth freshly brushed. Sunlight brightened every room. He looked in at the breakfast table.

His wife was busy there. Slowly, calmly, she was slicing the pumpernickel.

He sat down at the table in the warm sunlight, and reached for the newspaper.

She picked up a slice of the newly cut bread, and kissed him on the cheek. He patted her arm.

"One or two slices of toast, dear?" she asked gently.

"Two, I think," he replied.

LAST RITES

Harrison Cooper was not that old, only thirty-nine, touching at the warm rim of forty rather than the cold rim of thirty, which makes a great difference in temperature and attitude. He was a genius verging on the brilliant, unmarried, unengaged, with no children that he could honestly claim, so having nothing much else to do, woke one morning in the summer of 1999, weeping.

"Why!?"

Out of bed, he faced his mirror to watch the tears, examine his sadness, trace the woe. Like a child, curious after emotion, he charted his own map, found no capital city of despair, but only a vast and empty expanse of sorrow, and went to shave.

Which didn't help, for Harrison Cooper had stumbled on some secret supply of melancholy that, even as he shaved, spilled in rivulets down his soaped cheeks.

"Great God," he cried. "I'm at a funeral, but *who's* dead?!"

He ate his breakfast toast somewhat soggier than usual and plunged off to his laboratory to see if gazing at his Time Traveler would solve the mystery of eyes that shed rain while the rest of him stood fair.

Time Traveler? Ah, yes.

For Harrison Cooper had spent the better part of his third decade wiring circuitries of impossible pasts and as yet untouchable futures. Most men philosophize in their as-beautiful-as-women cars. Harrison Cooper chose to dream and knock together from pure air and electric thunderclaps what he called his Möbius Machine.

He had told his friends, with wine-colored nonchalance, that he was taking a future strip and a past strip, giving them a now half twist, so they looped on a single plane. Like those figure-eight ribbons, cut and pasted by that dear mathematician A. F. Möbius in the nineteenth century.

"Ah, yes, Möbius," friends murmured.

What they really meant was, "Ah, *no*. Good night."

Harrison Cooper was not a mad scientist, but he was irretrievably boring. Knowing this, he had retreated to finish the Möbius Machine. Now, this strange morning, with cold rain streaming from his eyes, he stood staring at the damned contraption, bewildered that he was not dancing about with Creation's joy.

He was interrupted by the ringing of the laboratory doorbell and opened the door to find one of those rare people, a real Western Union delivery boy on a real bike. He signed for the telegram and was about to shut the door when he saw the lad staring fixedly at the Möbius Machine.

"What," exclaimed the boy, eyes wide, "is *that*?"

Harrison Cooper stood aside and let the boy wander in a great circle around his Machine, his eyes dancing up, over, and around the immense circling figure eight of shining copper, brass, and silver.

"Sure!" cried the boy at last, beaming. "A *Time* Machine!"

"Bull's-eye!"

"When do you leave?" said the boy. "Where will you go to meet which person where? Alexander? Caesar? Napoleon! Hitler?!"

"No, no!"

The boy exploded his list. "Lincoln—"

"More *like* it."

"General Grant! Roosevelt! Benjamin Franklin?"

"Franklin, yes!"

"Aren't you *lucky*?"

"Am I?" Stunned, Harrison Cooper found himself nodding. "Yes, by God, and suddenly—"

Suddenly he knew why he had wept at dawn.

He grabbed the young lad's hand. "Much thanks. You're a catalyst—"

"Cat—?"

"A Rorschach test—making me draw my *own* list—now gently, swiftly—out! No offense."

The door slammed. He ran for his library phone, punched numbers, waited, scanning the thousand books on the shelves.

"Yes, yes," he murmured, his eyes flicking over the gorgeous sun-bright titles. "Some of you. Two, three, maybe four. Hello! Sam? Samuel! Can you get here in five minutes, make it three? Dire emergency. Come!"

He slammed the phone, swiveled to reach out and touch.

"Shakespeare," he murmured. "Willy-William, will it be—you?"

✳ The laboratory door opened and Sam/Samuel stuck his head in and froze.

For there, seated in the midst of his great Möbius figure eight, leather jacket and boots shined, picnic lunch packed, was Harrison Cooper, arms flexed, elbows out, fingers alert to the computer controls.

"Where's your Lindbergh cap and goggles?" asked Samuel.

Harrison Cooper dug them out, put them on, smirking.

"Raise the *Titanic*, then sink it!" Samuel strode to the lovely machine to confront its rather outré occupant. "Well, Cooper, *what*?" he cried.

"I woke this morning in tears."

"Sure. I read the phone book aloud last night. That *did* it!"

"No. You read me *these*!"

Cooper handed the books over.

"Sure! We gabbed till three, drunk as owls on English Lit!"

"To give me tears for *answers*!"

"To what?"

"To their loss. To the fact that they died unknown, unrecognized; to the grim fact that some were only truly recognized, republished, raved over from 1920 on!"

"Cut the cackle and move the buns," said Samuel. "Did you call to ser-monize or ask advice?"

Harrison Cooper leaped from his machine and elbowed Samuel into the library.

"You must map my trip for me!"

"Trip? Trip!"

"I go a-journeying, far-traveling, the Grand Literary Tour. A Salvation Army of one!"

"To save lives?"

"No, souls! What good is life if the soul's dead? *Sit*! Tell me all the authors we raved on by night to weep me at dawn. Here's brandy. Drink! Remember?"

"I *do*!"

"List them, then! The New England Melancholic first. Sad, recluse from land, should have drowned at sea, a lost soul of sixty! Now, what *other* sad geniuses did we maunder over—"

"God!" Samuel cried. "You're going to tour *them*? Oh, Harrison, Harry, I love you!"

"Shut up! Remember how you write jokes? Laugh and think *backward*! So let us cry and leap up our tear ducts to the source. Weep for Whales to find minnows!"

"Last night I think I quoted—"

"Yes?"

"And then we spoke—"

"Go on—"

"Well."

Samuel gulped his brandy. Fire burned his eyes.

"Write *this* down!"

They wrote and ran.

✳ "What will you do when you get there, Librarian Doctor?"

Harrison Cooper, seated back in the shadow of the great hovering Möbius ribbon, laughed and nodded. "Yes! Harrison Cooper, L.M.D. Literary Meadow Doctor. Curer of fine old lions off their feed, in dire need of tender love, small applause, the wine of words, all in my heart, all on my tongue. Say 'Ah!' So long. Good-bye!"

"God bless!"

He slammed a lever, whirled a knob, and the machine, in a spiral of metal, a whisk of butterfly ribbon, very simply—vanished.

A moment later, the Möbius Machine gave a twist of its atoms and—returned.

"Voilà!" cried Harrison Cooper, pink-faced and wild-eyed. "It's *done!*"

"So soon?" exclaimed his friend Samuel.

"A minute here, but hours there!"

"Did you succeed?"

"Look! Proof positive."

For tears dripped off his chin.

"What happened? What?!"

"This, and this . . . and . . . *this!*"

✳ A gyroscope spun, a celebratory ribbon spiraled endlessly on itself, and the ghost of a massive window curtain haunted the air, exhaled, and then ceased.

As if fallen from a delivery-chute, the books arrived almost before the footfalls and then the half-seen feet and then the fog-wrapped legs and body and at last the head of a man who, as the ribbon spiraled itself back into emptiness, crouched over the volumes as if warming himself at a hearth.

He touched the books and listened to the air in the dim hallway where dinnertime voices drifted up from below and a door stood wide near his elbow, from which the faint scent of illness came and went, arrived and departed, with the stilted breathing of some patient within the room. Plates and silverware sounded from the world of evening and quiet good health downstairs. The hall and the sickroom were for a time deserted. In a moment, someone might ascend with a tray for the half-sleeping man in the intemperate room.

Harrison Cooper rose with stealth, checking the stairwell, and then, carrying a sweet burden of books, moved into the room, where candles lit both sides of a bed on which the dying man lay supine, arms straight at his sides, head weighting the pillow, eyes grimaced shut, mouth set as if daring the ceiling, mortality itself, to sink and extinguish him.

At the first touch of the books, now on one side, now on the other, of his bed, the old man's eyelids fluttered, his dry lips cracked; the air whistled from his nostrils:

"Who's there?" he whispered. "What time is it?"

"Whenever I find myself growing grim about the mouth, whenever it is a damp, drizzly November in my soul, then I account it high time to get to sea as soon as I can," replied the traveler at the foot of the bed, quietly.

"What, what?" the old man in the bed whispered swiftly.

"It is a way I have of driving off the spleen and regulating the circulation," quoted the visitor, who now moved to place a book under each of the dying man's hands where his tremoring fingers could scratch, pull away, then touch, Braille-like, again.

One by one, the stranger held up book after book, to show the covers, then a page, and yet another title page where printed dates of this novel surfed up, adrift, but to stay forever on some far future shore.

The sick man's eyes lingered over the covers, the titles, the dates, and then fixed to his visitor's bright face. He exhaled, stunned. "My God, you have the look of a traveler. From *where*?"

"Do the years show?" Harrison Cooper leaned forward. "Well, then—I bring you an Annunciation."

"Such things come to pass only with virgins," whispered the old man. "No virgin lies here buried under his unread books."

"I come to unbury you. I bring tidings from a far place."

The sick man's eyes moved to the books beneath his trembling hands.

"Mine?" he whispered.

The traveler nodded solemnly, but began to smile when the color in the old man's face grew warmer and the expression in his eyes and on his mouth was suddenly eager.

"*Is there hope, then?*"

"There is!"

"I believe you." The old man took a breath and then wondered, "Why?"

"Because," said the stranger at the foot of the bed, "I love you."

"I do not *know* you, sir!"

"But I know you fore and aft, port to starboard, main-topgallants to gunnels, every day in your long life to here!"

"Oh, the sweet sound!" cried the old man. "Every word that you say, every light from your eyes, is foundation-of-the-world true! How can it be?" Tears winked from the old man's lids. "Why?"

"Because I *am* the truth," said the traveler. "I have come a long way to find and say: you are not lost. Your great Beast has only drowned some little while. In another year, lost ahead, great and glorious, plain and simple men will gather at your grave and shout: he breaches, he rises, he breaches, he rises! and the white shape will surface to the light, the great terror lift into the storm and thunderous St. Elmo's fire and you with him, each bound to each, and no way to tell where he stops and you start or where you stop and he goes off around the world lifting a fleet of libraries in his and your wake through nameless seas of sub-sub-librarians and readers mobbing the docks to chart your far journeyings, alert for your lost cries at three of a wild morn."

"Christ's wounds!" said the man in his winding-sheet bedclothes. "To the point, man, the *point*! Do you speak truth!?"

"I give you my hand on it, and pledge my soul and my heart's blood." The visitor moved to do just this, and the two men's fists fused as one. "Take these gifts to the grave. Count these pages like a rosary in your last hours. Tell no one where they came from. Scoffers would knock the ritual beads from your fingers. So tell this rosary in the dark before dawn, and the rosary is this: you will live forever. You are immortal."

"No more of this, no more! Be still."

"I can not. Hear me. Where you have passed a fire path will burn, miraculous in the Bengal Bay, the Indian Seas, Hope's Cape, and around the Horn, past perdition's landfall, as far as living eyes can see."

He gripped the old man's fist ever more tightly.

"I swear. In the years ahead, a million millions will crowd your grave to sleep you well and warm your bones. Do you hear?"

"Great God, you are a proper priest to sound my Last Rites. And will I enjoy my own funeral? I will."

His hands, freed, clung to the books at each side, as the ardent visitor raised yet other books and intoned the dates:

"Nineteen twenty-two . . . 1930 . . . 1935 . . . 1940 . . . 1955 . . . 1970. Can you read and know what it means?"

He held the last volume close to the old man's face. The fiery eyes moved. The old mouth creaked.

"Nineteen ninety?"

"Yours. One hundred years from tonight."

"Dear God!"

"I must go, but I *would* hear. Chapter One. Speak."

The old man's eyes slid and burned. He licked his lips, traced the words, and at last whispered, beginning to weep:

" 'Call me Ishmael.' "

✳ There was snow and more snow and more snow after that. In the dissolving whiteness, the silver ribbon twirled in a massive whisper to let forth in an exhalation of Time the journeying librarian and his bookbag. As if slicing white bread rinsed by snow, the ribbon, as the traveler ghosted himself to flesh, sifted him through the hospital wall into a room as white as December. There, abandoned, lay a man as pale as the snow and the wind. Almost young, he slept with his mustaches oiled to his lip by fever. He seemed not to know nor care that a messenger had invaded the air near his bed. His eyes did not stir, nor did his mouth increase the passage of breath. His hands at his sides did not open to receive. He seemed already lost in a tomb and only his unexpected visitor's voice caused his eyes to roll behind their shut lids.

"Are you forgotten?" a voice asked.

"Unborn," the pale man replied.

"Never remembered?"

"Only. Only in. France."

"Wrote nothing at all?"

"Not worthy."

"Feel the weight of what I place on your bed. No, don't look. *Feel.*"

"Tombstones."

"With names, yes, but not tombstones. Not marble but paper. Dates, yes, but the day after tomorrow and tomorrow and ten thousand after that. And your name on each."

"It will not be."

"*Is.* Let me speak the names. Listen. Masque?"

"Red Death."

"The Fall of—"

"Usher!"

"Pit?"

"Pendulum!"

"Tell-tale?"

"Heart! *My* heart. Heart!"

"Repeat: for the love of God, Montresor."

"Silly."

"Repeat: Montresor, for the love of God."

"For the love of God, Montresor!"

"Do you see this label?"

"I see!"

"Read the date."

"Nineteen ninety-four. No such date."

"Again, and the name of the wine."

"Nineteen ninety-four. Amontillado. And my name!"

"Yes! Now shake your head. Make the fool's-cap bells ring. Here's mortar for the last brick. Quickly. I'm here to bury you alive with books. When death comes, how will you greet him? With a shout and—?"

"*Requiescat in pace?*"

"Say it again."

"*Requiescat in pace!*"

The Time Wind roared, the room emptied. Nurses ran in, summoned by laughter, and tried to seize the books that weighed down his joy.

"What's he *saying?*" someone cried.

✳ In Paris, an hour, a day, a year, a minute later, there was a run of St. Elmo's fire along a church steeple, a blue glow in a dark alley, a soft tread at a street corner, a turnabout of wind like an invisible carousel, and then footfalls up a stair to a door which opened on a bedroom where a window looked out upon cafes filled with people and far music, and in a bed by the window, a tall s pale face immobile, until he heard alien breath in his room.

w of a man stood over him and now leaned down so that the window revealed a face and a mouth as it inhaled and then gle word that the mouth said was:

THE WATCHFUL POKER CHIP
OF H. MATISSE

WHEN FIRST WE MEET GEORGE GARVEY he is nothing at all. Later he'll wear a white poker chip monocle, with a blue eye painted on it by Matisse himself. Later, a golden bird cage might trill within George Garvey's false leg, and his good left hand might possibly be fashioned of shimmering copper and jade.

But at the beginning—gaze upon a terrifyingly ordinary man.

"Financial section, dear?"

The newspapers rattle in his evening apartment.

"Weatherman says 'rain tomorrow.'"

The tiny black hairs in his nostrils breathe in, breathe out, softly, softly, hour after hour.

"Time for bed."

By his look, quite obviously born of several 1907 wax window dummies. And with the trick, much admired by magicians, of sitting in a green velour chair and—vanishing! Turn your head and you forgot his face. Vanilla pudding.

Yet the merest accident made him the nucleus for the wildest avant-garde literary movement in history!

Garvey and his wife had lived enormously alone for twenty years. She was a lovely carnation, but the hazard of meeting *him* pretty well kept visitors off. Neither husband nor wife suspected Garvey's talent for mummifying people instantaneously. Both claimed they were satisfied sitting alone nights after a brisk day at the office. Both worked at anonymous jobs. And sometimes even they could not recall the name of the colorless company which used them like white paint on white paint.

Enter the avant-garde! Enter The Cellar Septet!

These odd souls had flourished in Parisian basements listening to
rather sluggish variety of jazz, preserved a highly volatile relationsh

months or more, and, returning to the United States on the point of clam-
orous disintegration, stumbled into Mr. George Garvey.

"My God!" cried Alexander Pape, erstwhile potentate of the clique. "I
met the most astounding bore. You simply must see him! At Bill Timmins'
apartment house last night, a note said he'd return in an hour. In the hall
this Garvey chap asked if I'd like to wait in his apartment. There we sat,
Garvey, his wife, myself! Incredible! He's a monstrous Ennui, produced by
our materialistic society. He knows a billion ways to paralyze you! Absolutely
rococo with the talent to induce stupor, deep slumber, or stoppage of the
heart. What a case study. Let's *all* go visit!"

They swarmed like vultures! Life flowed to Garvey's door, life sat in his
parlor. The Cellar Septet perched on his fringed sofa, eyeing their prey.

Garvey fidgeted.

"Anyone wants to smoke—" He smiled faintly. "Why—go right
ahead—*smoke*."

Silence.

The instructions were: "Mum's the word. Put him on the spot. That's
the only way to see what a colossal *norm* he is. American culture at absolute
zero!"

After three minutes of unblinking quiet, Mr. Garvey leaned forward.
"Eh," he said, "what's *your* business. Mr. . . . ?"

"Crabtree. The poet."

Garvey mused over this.

"How's," he said, "business?"

Not a sound.

Here lay a typical Garvey silence. Here sat the largest manufacturer and
deliverer of silences in the world; name one, he could provide it packaged
and tied with throat-clearings and whispers. Embarrassed, pained, calm,
serene, indifferent, blessed, golden, or nervous silences; Garvey was *in*
there.

Well, The Cellar Septet simply wallowed in this particular evening's
silence. Later, in their cold-water flat, over a bottle of "adequate little red
          were experiencing a phase which led them to contact *real* real-
          this silence to bits and worried it.

          how he fingered his collar! Ho!"

          though, I must admit he's almost 'cool.' Mention Muggsy
          Beiderbecke. Notice his expression. *Very* cool. I wish I could
          so unemotional."

✳ Ready for bed, George Garvey, reflecting upon this extraordinary evening, realized that when situations got out of hand, when strange books or music were discussed, he panicked, he froze.

This hadn't seemed to cause undue concern among his rather oblique guests. In fact, on the way out, they had shaken his hand vigorously, thanked him for a splendid time!

"What a really expert A-number-1 bore!" cried Alexander Pape, across town.

"Perhaps he's secretly laughing at us," said Smith, the minor poet, who never agreed with Pape if he was awake.

"Let's fetch Minnie and Tom; they'd love Garvey. A rare night. We'll talk of it for months!"

"Did you notice?" asked Smith, the minor poet, eyes closed smugly. "When you turn the taps in their bathroom?" He paused dramatically. "Hot water."

Everyone stared irritably at Smith.

They hadn't thought to try.

✳ The clique, an incredible yeast, soon burst doors and windows, growing.

"You haven't met the Garveys? My God! lie back down in your coffin! Garvey must rehearse. No one's that boorish without Stanislavsky!" Here the speaker, Alexander Pape, who depressed the entire group because he did perfect imitations, now aped Garvey's slow, self-conscious delivery:

"'Ulysses? Wasn't that the book about the Greek, the ship, and the one-eyed monster! Beg pardon?'" A pause. "'Oh.'" Another pause. "'I see.'" A sitting back. "'Ulysses was written by James Joyce? Odd. I could swear I remember, years ago, in school . . .'"

In spite of everyone hating Alexander Pape for his brilliant imitations, they roared as he went on:

"'Tennessee Williams? Is he the man who wrote that hillbilly "Waltz?"'"

"Quick! What's Garvey's home address?" everyone cried.

✳ "My," observed Mr. Garvey to his wife, "life is fun these days."

"It's you," replied his wife. "Notice, they hang on your every word."

"Their attention is rapt," said Mr. Garvey, "to the point of hysteria. The least thing I say absolutely explodes them. Odd. My jokes at the office always met a stony wall. Tonight, for instance, I wasn't trying to be funny at all. I suppose it's an unconscious little stream of wit that flows quietly under everything I do or say. Nice to know I have it in reserve. Ah, there's the bell. Here we go!"

"He's especially rare if you get him out of bed at four A.M.," said Alexander Pape. "The combination of exhaustion and *fin de siècle* morality is a regular salad!"

Everyone was pretty miffed at Pape for being first to think of seeing Garvey at dawn. Nevertheless, interest ran high after midnight in late October.

Mr. Garvey's subconscious told him in utmost secrecy that he was the opener of a theatrical season, his success dependent upon the staying power of the ennui he inspired in others. Enjoying himself, he nevertheless guessed why these lemmings thronged to his private sea. Underneath, Garvey was a surprisingly brilliant man, but his unimaginative parents had crushed him in the Terribly Strange Bed of their environment. From there he had been thrown to a larger lemon-squeezer: his Office, his Factory, his Wife. The result: a man whose potentialities were a time bomb in his own parlor. The Garveys' repressed subconscious half recognized that the avant-gardists had never met anyone like him, or rather had met millions like him but had never considered studying one before.

So here he was, the first of autumn's celebrities. Next month it might be some abstractionist from Allentown who worked on a twelve-foot ladder shooting house-paint, in two colors only, blue and cloud-gray, from cake-decorators and insecticide-sprayers on canvas covered with layers of mucilage and coffee grounds, who simply needed appreciation to grow! or a Chicago tin-cutter of mobiles, aged fifteen, already ancient with knowledge. Mr. Garvey's shrewd subconscious grew even more suspicious when he made the terrible mistake of reading the avant-garde's favorite magazine, *Nucleus.*

"This article on Dante, now," said Garvey, "Fascinating. Especially where it discusses the spatial metaphors conveyed in the foothills of the *Antipurgatorio* and the *Paradiso Terrestre* on top of the Mountain. The bit about Cantos XV–XVIII, the so-called 'doctrinal cantos' is brilliant!"

How did the Cellar Septet react?

Stunned, all of them!

There was a noticeable chill.

They departed in short order when instead of being a delightfully mass-minded, keep-up-with-the-Joneses, machine-dominated chap leading a wishy-washy life of quiet desperation, Garvey enraged them with opinions on *Does Existentialism Still Exist?* or *Is Krafft-Ebing?* They didn't want opinions on alchemy and symbolism given in a piccolo voice, Garvey's subconscious warned him. They only wanted Garvey's good old-fashioned plain white bread and churned country butter, to be chewed on later at a dim bar, exclaiming how priceless! Garvey retreated.

✳ Next night he was his old precious self. Dale Carnegie? Splendid religious leader! Hart Schaffner & Marx? Better than Bond Street! Member of the After-Shave Club? That was Garvey! Latest Book-of-the-Month? Here on the table! Had they ever tried Elinor Glyn?

The Cellar Septet was horrified, delighted. They let themselves be bludgeoned into watching Milton Berle. Garvey laughed at everything Berle said. It was arranged for neighbors to tape-record various daytime soap operas which Garvey replayed evenings with religious awe, while the Cellar Septet analyzed his face and his complete devotion to *Ma Perkins* and *John's Other Wife.*

Oh, Garvey was getting sly. His inner self observed: You're on top. Stay there! Please your public! Tomorrow, play the Two Black Crows records! Mind your step! Bonnie Baker, now . . . that's it! They'll shudder, incredulous that you really like her singing. What about Guy Lombardo? That's the ticket!

The mob-mind, said his subconscious. You're symbolic of the crowd. They came to study the dreadful vulgarity of this imaginary Mass Man they pretend to hate. But they're fascinated with the snake-pit.

Guessing his thought, his wife objected. "They *like* you."

"In a frightening sort of way," he said. "I've lain awake figuring why they should come see me! Always hated and bored myself. Stupid, tattletale-gray man. Not an original thought in my mind. All I know now is: I love company. I've always wanted to be gregarious, never had the chance. It's been a ball these last months! But their interest is dying. I want company forever! What shall I do?"

His subconscious provided shopping lists.

Beer. It's unimaginative.

Pretzels. Delightfully "passé."

Stop by Mother's. Pick up Maxfield Parrish painting, the flyspecked, sunburned one. Lecture on same tonight.

✳ By December Mr. Garvey was really frightened.

The Cellar Septet was now quite accustomed to Milton Berle and Guy

Lombardo. In fact, they had rationalized themselves into a position where they acclaimed Berle as really too *rare* for the American public, and Lombardo was twenty years ahead of his time; the nastiest people liked him for the commonest reasons.

Garvey's empire trembled.

Suddenly he was just another person, no longer diverting the tastes of friends, but frantically pursuing them as they seized at Nora Bayes, the 1917 Knickerbocker Quartette, Al Jolson singing "Where Did Robinson Crusoe Go With Friday on Saturday Night," and Shep Fields and his Rippling Rhythm. Maxfield Parrish's rediscovery left Mr. Garvey in the north pasture. Overnight, everyone agreed, "Beer's intellectual. What a shame so many *idiots* drink it."

In short, his friends vanished. Alexander Pape, it was rumored, for a lark, was even considering hot water for his cold-water flat. This ugly canard was quashed, but not before Alexander Pape suffered a comedown among the *cognoscenti*.

Garvey sweated to anticipate the shifting taste! He increased the free food output, foresaw the swing back to the Roaring Twenties by wearing hairy knickers and displaying his wife in a tube dress and boyish bob long before anyone else.

But, the vultures came, ate, and ran. Now that this frightful Giant, TV, strode the world, they were busily re-embracing radio. Bootlegged 1935 transcriptions of *Vic* and *Sade* and *Pepper Young's Family* were fought over at intellectual galas.

At long last, Garvey was forced to turn to a series of miraculous tours de force, conceived and carried out by his panic-stricken inner-self.

The first accident was a slammed car door.

Mr. Garvey's little fingertip was neatly cut off!

In the resultant chaos, hopping about, Garvey stepped on, then kicked the fingertip into a street drain. By the time they fished it out, no doctor would bother sewing it back on.

A happy accident! Next day, strolling by an oriental shop, Garvey spied a beautiful *objet d'art*. His peppy old subconscious, considering his steadily declining box office and his poor audience-rating among the avant-garde, forced him into the shop and dragged out his wallet.

"Have you seen Garvey lately!" screamed Alexander Pape on the phone. "My God, go see!"

"What's *that*?"

Everyone stared.

"Mandarin's finger-guard." Garvey waved his hand casually. "Oriental antique. Mandarins used them to protect the five-inch nails they culti- vated." He drank his beer, the gold-thimbled little finger cocked. "Everyone hates cripples, the sight of things missing. It was sad losing my finger. But I'm happier with this gold thing-amajig."

"It's a much nicer finger now that any of us can *ever* have." His wife dished them all a little green salad. "And George has the *right* to use it."

Garvey was shocked and charmed as his dwindling popularity returned. Ah, art! Ah, life! The pendulum swinging back and forth, from complex to simple, again to complex. From romantic to realistic, back to romantic. The clever man could sense intellectual perihelions, and prepare for the violent new orbits. Garvey's subconscious brilliance sat up, began to eat a bit, and some days dared to walk about, trying its unused limbs. It caught fire!

"How unimaginative the world is," his long-neglected other self said, using his tongue. "If somehow my leg were severed accidentally I wouldn't wear a wooden leg, no! I'd have a gold leg crusted with precious stones made, and part of the leg would be a golden cage in which a bluebird would sing as I walked or sat talking to friends. And if my arm were cut off I'd have a new arm made of copper and jade, all hollow inside, a section for dry ice in it. And five other compartments, one for each finger. Drink, anyone? I'd cry. Sherry? Brandy? Dubonnet? Then I'd twist each finger calmly over the glasses. From five fingers, five cool streams, five liqueurs or wines. I'd tap the golden faucets shut. 'Bottoms up!' I'd cry.

"But, most of all, one almost wishes that one's eye would offend one. Pluck it out, the Bible says. It *was* the Bible, wasn't it? If that happened to me, I'd use no grisly glass eyes, by God. None of those black, pirate's patches. Know what I'd do? I'd mail a poker chip to your friend in France, *what's* his name? *Matisse!* I'd say, 'Enclosed find poker chip, and personal check. Please paint on this chip one beautiful blue human eye. Yrs., sincerely. G. Garvey!'"

✳ Well, Garvey had always abhorred his body, found his eyes pale, weak, lacking character. So he was not surprised a month later (when his Gallup ran low again) to see his right eye water, fester, and then pull a complete blank!

Garvey was absolutely bombed!

But—equally—secretly pleased.

With the Cellar Septet smiling like a jury of gargoyles at his elbow, he airmailed the poker chip to France with a check for fifty dollars.

The check returned, uncashed, a week later.

In the next mail came the poker chip.

H. Matisse had painted a rare, beautiful blue eye on it, delicately lashed and browed. H. Matisse had tucked this chip in a green-plush jeweler's box, quite obviously as delighted as was Garvey with the entire enterprise.

Harper's Bazaar published a picture of Garvey, wearing the Matisse poker-chip eye, and yet another of Matisse, himself, painting the monocle after considerable experimentation with three dozen chips!

H. Matisse had had the uncommon good sense to summon a photographer to Leica the affair for posterity. He was quoted. "After I had thrown away twenty-seven eyes, I finally got the very one I wanted. It flies posthaste to Monsieur Garvey!"

Reproduced in six colors, the eye rested balefully in its green-plush box. Duplicates were struck off for sales by the Museum of Modern Art. The Friends of the Cellar Septet played poker, using red chips with blue eyes, white chips with red eyes, and blue chips with white eyes.

But there was only *one* man in New York who wore the original Matisse monocle and that was Mr. Garvey.

"I'm *still* a nerve-racking bore," he told his wife, "but now they'll never know what a dreadful ox I am underneath the monocle and the Mandarin's finger. And if their interest should happen to dwindle again, one can always arrange to lose an arm or leg. No doubt of it. I've thrown up a wondrous facade; no one will ever find the ancient boor again."

And as his wife put it only the other afternoon: "I hardly think of him as the old George Garvey anymore. He's changed his name. Giulio, he wants to be called. Sometimes, at night, I look over at him and call, 'George,' but there's no answer. There he is, that mandarin's thimble on his little finger, the white and blue Matisse Poker-Chip monocle in his eye. I wake up and look at him often. And do you know? Sometimes that incredible Matisse Poker Chip seems to give out with a *monstrous* wink."

ALL ON A SUMMER'S NIGHT

"You're getting too big for this!" Grandpa gave Doug a toss toward the blazing chandelier. The boarders sat laughing, with knives and forks at hand. Then Doug, ten years old, was caught and popped in his chair and Grandma tapped his bowl with a steaming spoonful of soup. The crackers crunched like snow when he bit them. The cracker salt glittered like tiny diamonds. And there, at the far end of the table, with her gray eyes always down to watch her hand stir her coffee with a spoon or break her ginger-bread and lay on the butter, was Miss Leonora Welkes, with whom men never sat on backyard swings or walked through the town ravine on sum-mer nights. There was Miss Leonora whose eyes watched out the window as summer couples drifted by on the darkening sidewalks night after night, and Douglas felt his heart squeeze tight.

"Evening, Miss Leonora," he called.

"Evening, Douglas." She looked up past the steaming mounds of food, and the boarders turned their heads a moment before bowing again to their rituals.

Oh, Miss Welkes, he thought, Miss Welkes! And he wanted to stab every man at the table with a silver fork for not blinking their eyes at Miss Welkes when she asked for the butter. They always handed her things to their right, while still conversing with people on their left. The chandelier drew more attention than Miss Welkes. Isn't it pretty? they said. Look at it sparkle! They cried.

But they did not know Miss Welkes as he knew her. There were as many facets to her as any chandelier, and if you went about it right she could be set laughing, and it was like stirring the Chinese hanging crystals in the wind on the summer night porch, all tinkling and melody. No, Miss Welkes was cobweb and dust to them, and Douglas almost died in his chair, fasten-ing his eyes upon her all through the soup and salad.

Now the three young ladies came laughing down the stairs, late, like a troupe of orioles. They always came last to the table, as if they were actresses making entrance through the frayed blue-velvet portieres. They would hold each other by the shoulders, looking into each other's faces, telling themselves if their cheeks were pink enough or their hair ringed up tight, or their eyelashes dyed with spit-and-color enough; then they would pause, straighten their hems, and enter to something like applause from the male boarders.

"Evening, Tom, Jim, Bill. Evening, John, Peter!"

The five would tongue their food over into their cheeks, leap up, and draw out chairs for the young belles, everyone laughed until the chandelier cried with pain.

"Look what I got!"

"Look what *I* got!"

"Look at mine!"

The three ladies held up gifts which they had saved to open at table. It was the Fourth of July, and on any day of the year that was in any way special they pulled the ribbons off gifts and cried, Oh, you shouldn't have done it! They even got gifts on Memorial Day, that was how it was. Lincoln's Birthday, Washington's, Jefferson's, Columbus Day, Friday the Thirteenth. It was quite a joke. Once they got gifts on a day that wasn't any kind of day at all, with notes printed on them saying: JUST BECAUSE IT'S MONDAY! They talked about that particular incident for six months after.

Now there was a crisp rattling as they cut the ribbons with their fingernails which flashed red, and far away at the end of the tunnel of people sat Miss Leonora Welkes, still inching at her food, but slowing down until at last her fork came to rest and she watched the gifts exposed to the crystalline light.

"Perfume! With Old Glory on the box!"

"Bath powder, in the shape of a pinwheel!"

"Candy, done up in ten-inch salutes!"

Everyone said how nice it was.

Miss Leonora Welkes said, "Oh, how nice that is."

A moment later, Miss Welkes said, "I'm all done. It was a fine meal."

"Don't you want any dessert?" asked Grandma.

"I'm choke-full." And Miss Welkes, smiling, glided from the room.

"Smell!" cried one young lady, waving the opened perfume under the men's noses.

"Ah!" said everyone.

✳ Douglas hit the screen door like a bullet to a target, and before it slammed he had taken sixty-eight steps across the cool green lawn in his bare feet. Money jingled in his pocket, the remains of his firecracker savings; and quite a remains, too. Now he thudded his bare feet on the warm summer twilight cement, across the street to press his nose on Mrs. Singer's store window, to see the devils laid in red round rows, the torpedoes in sawdust, the ten-inch salutes that could toss your head in the trees like a football, the nine inchers that could bang a can to the sun, and the fire balloons, so rare and beautiful, like withered red, white and blue butterflies, their delicate silk wings folded, ready to be lit and gassed with warm air later and sent up into the summer night among the stars. There were so many things to pack your pockets with, and yet as he stood there, counting the money, ten, twenty, forty, a dollar and seventy cents, precariously saved during a long year of mowing lawns and clipping hedges, he turned and looked back at Grandma's house, at the highest room of all, up in the little green cupola, where the window was shut in the hottest weather, and the shades half drawn. Miss Welkes' room.

In half an hour the kids would come like a summer shower, their feet raining on the pavement, their hands full of explosions, little adhesive turbans on their burned thumbs, smelling of brimstone and punk, to run him off in fairy circles where they waved the magical sparklers, tracing their names and their destinies in luminous firefly paths on the sultry evening air, making great white symbols that lingered in phosphorous after-image even if you looked down from your night bed at three in the morning, remembering what a day and what an evening it had been. In half an hour he would be fat with treasure, breast pockets bulging with torpedoes, his money gone. But—now. He looked back and forth between the high room in Grandma's house, and this store window full of dynamite wonders.

How many nights in winter had he gone down to the stone public library and seen Miss Welkes there with the stamp pad at her elbow and the purple ink rubber stamper in her hand, and the great book sections behind her?

"Good evening, Douglas."

"Evening, Miss Welkes."

"Can I help you meet some new friends, tonight?"

"Yes'm."

"I know a man named Longfellow," she said. Or, "I know a man named Whittier."

And that was it. It wasn't so much Miss Welkes herself, it was the people she knew. On autumn nights when, for no reason, the library might be empty for hours on end, she would say, "Let me bring out Mr. Whittier." And she went back among the warm stacks of books, and returned to sit under the green glass shade, opening the book to meet the season, while Douglas sat on a stool looking up as her lips moved and, half of the time, she didn't even glance at the words but could look away or close her eyes while she recited the poem about the pumpkin:

> Oh—*fruit loved of childhood—the old days recalling,*
> *When wood grapes were purpling and brown nuts were falling!*
> *When wild ugly faces we carved in its skin,*
> *Glaring out through the dark with a candle within!*

And Douglas would walk home, tall and enchanted.

Or on silver winter evenings when he and the wind blew wide the library door and dust stirred on the farthest counters and magazines turned their pages unaided in the vast empty rooms, then what more particularly apt than a good friend of Miss Welkes? Mr. Robert Frost, what a name for winter! His poem about stopping by the woods on a winter evening to watch the woods fill up with snow. . . . .

And in the summer, only last night, Mr. Whittier again, on a hot night in July that kept the people at home lying on their porches, the library like a great bread oven; there, under the green grass lamp:

> Blessings on thee, little man,
>   Barefoot boy with cheeks of tan . . .
> Every morn shall lead thee through,
>   Fresh baptisms of the dew!

And Miss Welkes' face there, an oval, with her cobweb graying hair and her plainness, would be enchanted, color risen to her cheeks, and wetness to her lips, and the light from the reflection on the book pages shining her eyes and coloring her hair to a brightness!

In winter, he trudged home through icelands of magic, in summer through bakery winds of sorcery; the seasons given substance by the readings of Miss Welkes who knew so many people and introduced them, in due time to Douglas. Mr. Poe and Mr. Sandburg and Miss Amy Lowell and Mr. Shakespeare. ·

The screen door opened under his hand.

"Mrs. Singer," he said, "have you got any perfume?"

* The gift lay at the top of the stairs, tilted against her door. Supper had been early, over at six o'clock. There was the warm lull now before the extravagant evening. Downstairs, you could hear the tinkling of plates lifted to their kitchen wall racks. Douglas, at the furthest bend of the stairs, half hid in the attic door shadows, waited for Miss Welkes to twist her brass doorknob, waited to see the gift drop at her feet, unsigned, anonymous, sparkling with tape and gold stars.

At last, the door opened. The gift fell.

Miss Welkes looked down at it as if she was standing on the edge of a cliff she had never guessed was there before. She looked in all directions, slowly, and bent to pick it up. She didn't open it, but stood in the doorway, holding the gift in her hands, for a long time. He heard her move inside and set the gift on a table. But there was no rattle of paper. She was looking at the gift, the wrapping, the tape, the stars, and not touching it.

"Oh, Miss Welkes, Miss Welkes!" he wanted to cry.

Half an hour later, there she was, on the front porch, seated with her neat hands folded, and watching the door. It was the summer evening ritual, the people on the porches, in the swings, on the figured pillows, the women talking and sewing, the men smoking, the children in idle groupings on the steps. But this was early, the town porches still simmering from the day, the echoes only temporarily allayed, the civil war of Independence Afternoon muffled for an hour in the sounds of poured lemonade and scraped dishes. But here, the only person on the street porches, alone, was Miss Eleanora Welkes, her face pink instead of gray, flushed, her eyes watching the door, her body tensed forward. Douglas saw her from the tree where he hung in silent vigilance. He did not say hello, she did not see him there, and the hour passed into deeper twilight. Within the house the sounds of preparation grew intense and furious. Phones rang, feet ran up and down the avalanche of stairs, the three belles giggled, bath doors slammed, and then out and down the front steps went the three young ladies, one at a time, a man on her arm. Each time the door swung, Miss Welkes would lean forward, smiling wildly. And each time she sank back as the girls appeared in floaty green dresses and blew away like thistle down the darkening avenues, laughing up at the men.

That left only Mr. Britz and Mr. Jerrick, who lived upstairs across from

Miss Welkes. You could hear them whistling idly at their mirrors, and through the open windows you could see them finger their ties.

Miss Welkes leaned over the porch geraniums to peer up at their windows, her heart pumping in her face, it seemed, making it heart-shaped and colorful. She was looking for the man who had left the gift.

And then Douglas smelled the odor. He almost fell from the tree.

Miss Welkes had tapped her ears and neck with drops of perfume, many, many bright drops of *Summer Night Odor*, 97 cents a bottle! And she was sitting where the warm wind might blow this scent to whoever stepped out upon the porch. This would be her way of saying, I got your gift! *Well?*

"It was me, Miss Welkes!" screamed Douglas, silently, and hung in the tree, cold as ice.

"Good evening, Mr. Jerrick," said Miss Welkes, half rising.

"Evening." Mr. Jerrick sniffed in the doorway and looked at her. "Have a nice evening." He went whistling down the steps.

That left only Mr. Britz, with his straw hat cocked over one eye, humming.

"Here I am," said Miss Welkes, rising, certain that this must be the man, the last one in the house.

"There you are," said Mr. Britz, blinking. "Hey, you smell good. I never knew you used scent." He leered at her.

"Someone gave me a gift."

"Well, that's fine." And Mr. Britz did a little dance going down the porch steps, his cane jauntily flung over his shoulder. "See you later, Miss W." He marched off.

Miss Welkes sat, and Douglas hung in the cooling tree. The kitchen sounds were fading. In a moment, Grandma would come out, bringing her pillow and a bottle of mosquito oil. Grandpa would cut the end off a long stogie and puff it to kill his own particular insects, and the aunts and uncles would arrive for the Independence Evening Event at the Spaulding House, the Festival of Fire, the shooting stars, the Roman Candles so diligently held by Grandpa, looking like Julius Caesar gone to flesh, standing with great dignity on the dark summer lawn, directing the setting off of fountains of red fire, and pinwheels of sizzle and smoke, while everyone, as if to the order of some celestial doctor, opened their mouths and said Ah! their faces burned into quick colors by blue, red, yellow, white flashes of sky bomb among the cloudy stars. The house windows would jingle with concussion. And Miss Welkes would sit among the strange people, the scent of perfume evaporating during the evening hours, until it was gone, and only the sad, wet smell of punk and sulfur would remain.

✳ The children screamed by on the dim street now, calling for Douglas, but, hidden, he did not answer. He felt in his pocket for the remaining dollar and fifty cents. The children ran away into the night.

Douglas swung and dropped. He stood by the porch steps.

"Miss Welkes?"

She glanced up. "Yes?"

Now that the time had come he was afraid. Suppose she refused, suppose she was embarrassed and ran up to lock her door and never came out again?

"Tonight," he said, "there's a swell show at the Elite Theater. Harold Lloyd in WELCOME, DANGER. The show starts at eight o'clock, and afterward we'll have a chocolate sundae at the Midnight Drug Store, open until eleven forty-five. I'll go change clothes."

She looked down at him and didn't speak. Then she opened the door and went up the stairs.

"Miss Welkes!" he cried.

"It's all right," she said. "Run and put your shoes on!"

✳ It was seven thirty, the porch filling with people, when Douglas emerged, in his dark suit, with a blue tie, his hair wet with water, and his feet in the hot tight shoes.

"Why, Douglas!" the aunts and uncles and Grandma and Grandpa cried, "Aren't you staying for the fireworks?"

"No." And he looked at the fireworks laid out so beautifully crisp and smelling of powder, the pinwheels and sky bombs, and the Fire Balloons, three of them, folded like moths in their tissue wings, those balloons he loved most dearly of all, for they were like a summer night dream going up quietly, breathlessly on the still high air, away and away to far lands, glowing and breathing light as long as you could see them. Yes, the Fire Balloons, those especially would he miss, while seated in the Elite Theater tonight.

There was a whisper, the screen door stood wide, and there was Miss Welkes.

"Good evening, Mr. Spaulding," she said to Douglas.

"Good evening, Miss Welkes," he said.

She was dressed in a gray suit no one had seen ever before, neat and fresh, with her hair up under a summer straw hat, and standing there in the dim porch light she was like the carved goddess on the great marble library clock come to life.

"Shall we go, Mr. Spaulding?" and Douglas walked her down the steps.

"Have a good time!" said everyone.

"Douglas!" called Grandfather.

"Yes, sir?"

"Douglas," said Grandfather, after a pause, holding his cigar in his hand. "I'm saving one of the Fire Balloons. I'll be up when you come home. We'll light her together and send her up. How's that sound, eh?"

"Swell!" said Douglas.

"Good night, boy." Grandpa waved him quietly on.

"Good night, sir."

He took Miss Eleanora Welkes down the street, over the sidewalks of the summer evening, and they talked about Mr. Longfellow and Mr. Whittier and Mr. Poe all the way to the Elite Theater . . .

THE COLLECTED WORKS OF
RAY BRADBURY

NOVELS

FAREWELL SUMMER

ISBN 0-06-113154-7 (hardcover)

50 years in the making, this is the eagerly-anticipated sequel to the beloved *Dandelion Wine*.

DANDELION WINE

ISBN 0-380-97726-5 (hardcover)

A deeply personal, well-loved, fictional recollection of the sacred rituals of boyhood.

THE MARTIAN CHRONICLES

ISBN 0-380-97383-9 (hardcover)

The masterfully imagined chronicles of Earth's settlement of the fourth world from the sun.

SOMETHING WICKED THIS WAY COMES

ISBN 0-380-97727-3 (hardcover)
ISBN 0-380-72940-7 (mass market paperback)

A unique coming-of-age story that thrusts two young boys into the shadowy realm of a nightmare.

FROM THE DUST RETURNED

ISBN 0-380-78961-2 (mass market paperback)
ISBN 0-694-52628-2 (unabridged cassette)

Follow the story of the beloved Elliott family and their "abnormal" adopted son Timothy.

DEATH IS A LONELY BUSINESS

ISBN 0-380-78965-5 (trade paperback)

A stylish noir tale of murder and mayhem amidst the murky shadows of 1950s Venice, CA.

A GRAVEYARD FOR LUNATICS
Another Tale of Two Cities

ISBN 0-380-81200-2 (trade paperback)

A young scriptwriter spends a mysterious, magical Halloween in a Hollywood graveyard.

LET'S ALL KILL CONSTANCE

ISBN 0-06-056178-5 (mass market paperback)

An aging starlet runs in fear from something unnamed—and vanishes as suddenly as she appeared.

GREEN SHADOWS, WHITE WHALE
A Novel of Ray Bradbury's Adventures Making *Moby Dick* with John Huston in Ireland

ISBN 0-380-78966-3 (trade paperback)

Bradbury's tale of writing the screen adaptation of Melville's *Moby Dick*.

FAHRENHEIT 451

ISBN 0-694-52627-4 (unabridged CD)
ISBN 0-694-52626-6 (unabridged cassette)

An unabridged audio edition of one of Bradbury's greatest novels.

FOR YOUNGER READERS

AHMED AND THE OBLIVION MACHINES
A Fable

ISBN 0-380-97704-4 (hardcover)

An enchanting fable for children of all ages about an ancient god and a surprised boy.

STORY COLLECTIONS

BRADBURY STORIES
100 of His Most Celebrated Tales

ISBN 0-06-054242-X (hardcover)
ISBN 0-06-054488-0 (trade paperback)

100 treasures from a lifetime of words and ideas—tales that amaze, enthrall, and delight.

THE ILLUSTRATED MAN

ISBN 0-380-97384-7 (hardcover)

18 startling visions of humankind's destiny comprise this phantasmagoric slideshow.

THE OCTOBER COUNTRY

ISBN 0-380-97387-1 (hardcover)

A spellbinding journey to the "Undiscovered Country" of the legendary author's imagination.

THE CAT'S PAJAMAS
Stories

ISBN 0-06-077733-8 (trade paperback)

A walk through the six-decade career of this "latter-day O. Henry" (*Booklist*).

ONE MORE FOR THE ROAD

ISBN 0-06-103203-4 (mass market paperback)
ISBN 0-06-008117-1 (unabridged cassette)

A father's regrets, a lover's last embrace, a child's dreams of the future—all delivered with Bradbury's wit and style.

DRIVING BLIND

ISBN 0-380-78960-4 (mass market paperback)

Glorious grand tours through fantasy and time, full of thrills and unexpected turns.

QUICKER THAN THE EYE

ISBN 0-380-78959-0 (mass market paperback)

21 tales, from an aging couple's murder games to a family's trip through alternate futures.

A MEDICINE FOR MELANCHOLY AND OTHER STORIES

ISBN 0-380-73086-3 (trade paperback)

A collection of wonders, like a magical ice-cream suit and a child's game called "Invasion."

A SOUND OF THUNDER AND OTHER STORIES

ISBN 0-06-078569-1 (trade paperback)

A sterling collection of 32 of Bradbury's most famous, surprising, and outrageous tales.

I SING THE BODY ELECTRIC!
And Other Stories

ISBN 0-380-78962-0 (trade paperback)

28 classic Bradbury stories and one luscious poem—a cavalcade of delight and terror.

NON-FICTION

BRADBURY SPEAKS
Too Soon from the Cave, Too Far from the Stars

ISBN 0-06-058568-4 (hardcover)
ISBN 0-06-058569-2 (trade paperback)

A collection of essays offering commentary on Bradbury's—and America's—greatest influences.